The Wreck of
The River of Stars

"In his big and ambitious new novel, *The Wreck of The River of Stars,* Michael Flynn displays a boundless faith in the heritage and protocols of the genre. His specific model here is early Heinlein: the master's lively, slangy, bustling tales of working stiffs in space have often been imitated, but rarely as eloquently as this. Like John Varley and Allen Steele, Flynn is expert at the Heinleinian voice and method . . . The perfect ingredients are in place for a claustrophobic, character-driven nautical tale . . . Such a tale Flynn delivers with a vengeance, full of intrigue, poetry, and thunder . . . an opulent tapestry of human observation. . . . go and read this large, insinuating, emotionally labyrinthine book."
—*Locus*

"*The Wreck of The River of Stars* is thrilling in its rigorously imagined, meticulously textured language and traditions—one gets the sense that Flynn has actually served on one of these ships, as Herman Melville once crisscrossed the Pacific on a brig in search of whales. . . . a narrative machine whose denouement exerts a great power over the reader. . . . triumph and tragedy merge into an ultimately satisfying whole. . . . *The Wreck of The River of Stars* emerges finally as a lovely tale. . . . told with integrity and intelligence." —*Strangehorizons.com*

"Thoroughly absorbing. . . . Flynn layers the personalities and disasters in this complicated story with his usual attention to detail. . . . This is a sad but compelling study of (literally) explosive group dynamics in an arena where technology is critical to human life." —*Publishers Weekly*

"*The Wreck of The River of Stars* is a *tour de force* of character development. We watch, riveted, as these motley misfits squabble, beef and try to cope, in the hermetic isolation of a ship becalmed in space . . . *The Wreck of The River of Stars* is a classical tragedy. . . . Flynn's writing is masterful. His pacing is grave, controlled, ironic. His characters will break your heart as they work, love, fight, grow, grieve and die. This is a wonderful book, easily Flynn's best. . . . This is the best hard SF tragic novel of character yet written . . . Highly recommended." —*Sfsite.com*

"In addition to a page-turning story of the last solar sailing ship . . . Michael Flynn has created a strong emotional landscape of developed characters." —*The Olympian* (Olympia, WA)

The Wreck of
The River of Stars

MICHAEL FLYNN

TOR®

A TOM DOHERTY ASSOCIATES BOOK
NEW YORK

Charles Sheffield

A gentleman, scholar
and good friend

THE WRECK OF *THE RIVER OF STARS*

Edited by David G. Hartwell

A Tor Book
Published by Tom Doherty Associates, LLC
175 Fifth Avenue
New York, NY 10010

www.tor.com

Tor® is a registered trademark of Tom Doherty Associates, LLC.

ISBN 0-765-34033-X
EAN 978-0765-34033-7

Library of Congress Catalog Card Number: 2002040939

First edition: April 2003
First mass market edition: May 2004

Printed in the United States of America

0 9 8 7 6 5 4 3 2 1

Acknowledgments

As always in a book of this sort, there were many people who tried to screw my head on straight. It didn't always work, but I'm grateful for the twists. Among the chiropractors:

Mariesa Julien introduced me to the Meyers-Briggs personality scales, which in a way was the seed for this story. Tom Ligon explained about Farnsworth cages. They can't do what they do in this story, but NASA is funding research on them, so who knows? Robert Zubrin first imagined the magnetic sail, but there's a host of folk out there on the Web now working on his idea. Charles Sheffield advised on some points of astrophysics, nuclear fusion, and constant acceleration, as well as on plot. Jerry Pournelle's essay, "Those Pesky Belters and Their Torchships" (*A Step Farther Out*, Ace [1980]), was especially helpful. Basheer Alawamleh and Saraji Umma Zaid gave advice on Muslim practices, suitable hadith, and the kalima shahada. Paul Berman gave helpful advice on radars.

In addition, Nancy Kress, Maureen McHugh, Eleanor Wood, Moshe Feder, David Hartwell, and Jerry Pournelle contributed valuable comments on plot, character, background, and/or wordsmithing.

My thanks to all.

The Crew

X • The Crew

Raphael "Rave" Evermore . . . . second wrangler

Twenty-four deCant . . . . .third wrangler

Ivar Akhaturian . . . . least wrangler

Bigelow Fife . . . . passenger

Prelude: The Ship

They called her *The River of Stars* and she spread her superconducting sails to the solar wind in 2051. She must have made a glorious sight then: her fuselage new and gleaming, her sails shimmering in a rainbow aurora, her white-gloved crew sharply creased in black-and-silver uniforms, her passengers rich and deliciously decadent. There were morphy stars and jeweled matriarchs, sports heroes and prostitutes, gangsters and geeks and *soi-disant* royalty. Those were the glamour years, when magsails ruled the skies, and *The River of Stars* was the grandest and most glorious of that beautiful fleet.

But the glory years faded fast. Coltraine was still her captain when the luxury trade dried up and the throngs of the rich and famous slowed from a torrent to a trickle, and even those who still craved the experience could see that it was no longer the fashionable thing to do. But as he told Toledo when he handed her the command, the luxury trade had been doomed from the start. Sex and vice and decadence were more safely found earthside. There were yet honorable—if more quotidian—pursuits for a ship with such wings to her.

Mars was the happening place back then. Adventurers, sand-kings, ne'er-do-wells, terraformers, second sons, bawdy girls, and zeppelin pilots—Mars sucked them in, broke some and spat others out. Even crewmembers would sometimes cash out on reaching Mars and head for the gaudy enticements of Port Rosario. "Some of them struck it rich," the old song had it,

> *"And some of them Mars struck dead*
> *And some showed up in the hiring hall,*
> *Begging their old berths back."*

Toledo and, later, Johnson and Fu-hsi carried hopes outbound and the shattered fragments back. There was a raw energy to the age that tired old Earth hadn't seen since the taming of LEO during the Terrible Teens, and *The River* took greater pride in pushing the frontier out than she ever had in stroking the rich and famous.

It was the Farnsworth engine that finally brought her low. Fu-hsi saw it coming and resigned, the only one of her captains ever to do so; and so it fell to Terranova to see the once proud vessel humiliated. Magnetic sails had ruled space for forty years, and *The River of Stars* for almost twenty of them, but Farnsworth engines made the Jovian moons the new frontier. The Luna-Ganymede Race went down in history, and the magnetic sail went down to the fusion thruster. Terranova should never have taken the bet; but it was a matter of pride—and pride loves loss above surrender.

For a while, hovering in Jupiter's magnetosphere, *The River* maintained a precarious trade harvesting hydrogen from the gas giant's outer atmosphere. Passing the long hours under the maddening whine of the compressors, the *Rivers* told each other how important they still were.

> *"The Farnsworths can't fly*
> *Without the 'H' we supply."*

But in their hearts they knew they were no more than water boys for the nukes.

In 2083, Centaurus Corporation bought *MSS The River of Stars* and fit her with a quartet of Farnsworth cages in the Deimos Yards. To the crew it was the final humiliation. Sacrilege, some of the old-timers shouted as they resigned their berths; and the engineer and his mate received a less than heartfelt welcome from the remnant. She kept her sails and rigging— for flexibility, management claimed—and her precious MS designation. Officially, she was a "hybrid ship," unofficially, a bastard. The sailing master brooded over the situation and, four days out of Deimos, cycled through the 'lock for the Long Walk, leaving the engineer behind with a knife in his heart.

It was the scandal of the day. The Board of Inquiry was a sensation, the disposition, foregone. Centaurus put *The River of Stars* on the block without ever flying her.

Save The Riv'! the cry went up; and sailing enthusiasts, brimming with nostalgia for the days of grace and romance, pledged their ounces and grains—though there was little of grace or romance to save by then. The crew threw their bonuses and hazard pay into the pot. Coltraine himself, on his deathbed, added a generous codicil to his will. The consortium bought her up, stripped her down, and rigged her for cargo. Long gone were the luxury modules, the Three Dolphin Club, the Black Sky Casino. Now she was reduced to the single, broad disk of the old primary decks—and large portions of its interior spaces had been abandoned in place. Only the long, faerie, aerogel main mast recalled sailing days gone by—but the mast was purely ornamental. The bottom line ruled and, after one last and all-too-brief flight under sail, the superconducting hoops were coiled into stowage.

And so it was that in 2084 of the Common Era, *MSS The River of Stars* cast loose as a tramp freighter, hustling after cargoes across the Middle System.

After that, her luck turned bad.

The Captain

Even Dodge Hand, captain of the tramp ship *The River of Stars*, sighed and stared into the ventilation duct in the ceiling of his cabin. The pain now seemed a sometime and faraway thing, something not quite real, as if it were happening to someone else. His body was but a husk, a thing of no matter. He felt that he—the "he" that was himself—had begun to float above that very body, leaving it behind. "Mr. Gorgas," he said to the first officer, who sat a little apart engrossed in a 'puter. "Mr. Gorgas, I feel as if I were floating."

First Officer Stepan Gorgas barely glanced up from his laptop. "Of course, you're floating. The engines are shut down. We're not under acceleration." He wondered en passant why Corrigan had not yet reported on the reason.

"Note this in the log, Mr. Gorgas: As a man is dying, his soul floats off. The observation may be profound. See that it is posted."

Gorgas sighed. "So noted," he said as he moved his Austrian infantry closer to Austerlitz. The little regimental squares wriggled across the map board on his clipscreen. It had fallen to his lot to sit with the captain during the dog watch this night, but that did not mean he relished the duty or that it demanded his full attention. There was little enough to engage the mind in watching a man die. Gorgas had served with Hand for eight years, longer than anyone in the crew save Satterwaithe and Ratline, and he had detested Hand for ninety-five months of that.

The captain became absorbed in a study of the ventilator grill. There were a great many squares in the grill, Hand thought. Perhaps countlessly many. An absurd notion, of course. They were discrete and so must be countable. The tally seemed somehow an important thing to do, and so Hand began to enumerate them. It grew cold in the cabin and he wanted to draw the covers up, but his arm would not move. It was as if he no longer had an arm. "Now, this is a curious thing," he said.

Gorgas was not paying close attention, but he realized after a few more minutes had gone by that Hand had not explained what the curious thing was. Glancing across the room, he noted the relaxed features on the captain's face, the eyes staring into the void. Gorgas sighed in irritation. "Ship," he said, rather curtly, as if the artificial intelligence had neglected a duty.

"Waiting," replied Ship.

"Message. To: Dr. Wong. Text: Hand has died. Send."

"Acknowledged."

Gorgas saved his screen with the French in mid-move and unbuckled from the seat so that he floated across the cabin. The Farnsworths boosted at just over four milligees, barely enough acceleration to give the room a vague notion of up and down, but Bhatterji had shut the engines down and Gorgas floated like an angel and hovered over the captain's bunk.

I have risen above the captain, he thought. So often true metaphorically and intellectually, the statement was now true literally. Gorgas did not touch the body or straighten its clothing or even close its eyes, but he did peer into the slack and peaceful face and note how those eyes seemed fixed on some distant sight. *What was Hand looking at*? he wondered. *And why is he smiling*?

At relinquishing command, probably. Consumed with the humor of sticking Gorgas with the gallimaufry that he had collected for crew at every port in the Middle System.

Fransziska Wong, M.D., the most recently-added component of that gallimaufry, seemed made all of sticks and twine, as if a good, hard shaking would be more g-force than her ligaments could withstand. Her forearms and lower legs were long and spindly, her breasts meager. Such was the curse of the spaceborn: That the flesh stretched out to extend the limbs was stolen from elsewhere in the body. At times, when she contemplated the images of beauty broadcast from Earth or Mars, this disturbed her.

Wong had taken her medical degree from Leo University in Goddard City, Low Earth Orbit, specializing (by necessity) in the maladies of microgravity. She had spent two years in Goddard's clinic, another two in High Nairobi, dreaming of adventure and the sight of far, exotic places. Then *FS Ned DuBois* had called into port shy a ship's doctor and she had seized the opportunity.

But the inside of a ship looked remarkably like the inside of an orbital habitat and, as she soon found, the insides of the warrens under Luna and Mars. Tight little rooms and tight little corridors; recycled air and recycled water and, after a time, recycled thoughts. Little by little over the years, she had given up the search for far exotic places, though she never did quite give up the hope that they existed.

The captain's body upbraided her. She had failed to save him; failed even to diagnose him. Carefully, she straightened the limbs, closed the eyes, covered the face. The dear man looked so fragile in death: smaller somehow, as if something inside were missing. Wherever else fancy might suppose he had gone, Evan Hand had departed *The River of Stars*.

First officer Gorgas, hunched so intently over his 'puter, had barely acknowledged her entrance, and Wong supposed him deeply involved in some administrative task required by the captain's death. She recorded the time in the ship's medical log and entered her confirmation. Legally, at that moment, the captain died; and it struck her that in some arcane, bureaucratic fashion she had just killed him.

"I suppose," she said as she tucked the sheets around the body to prevent it from drifting off while she fetched a body bag from stores, "that the ship will not be run in so 'Evan Handed' a fashion now."

The first officer looked up from his 'puter. "What's that?" he said. "What's that? You're making a joke? With our captain only now passed away, you'd make a mockery of his name?"

Wong bowed her head at the rebuke. The pun had been one of Evan's favorite lines. He had often used it himself, and she had repeated it as a way of maintaining something of his antic humor. She hadn't meant it as mockery; but Gorgas, who had flown with the captain for many years must be taking the death most cruel hard, keeping it inside, as men so often did, yet needing, nevertheless, some word of kindness. "The ship will miss him," she said.

Certainly, she did. Evan had been lighthearted, always with a smile, always ready with a joke or a courtesy. The first officer struck her as serious, but with all the vices and none of the virtues that seriousness implied. Yet, she had been aboard *The River* only a short time and Gorgas's solemn demeanor, his snappishness, might be only a mask for the grief he felt at the passing of his old friend.

Gorgas, for his part, focused once more on his simulation of Austerlitz. The game's intelligence had shifted the French forces in a most unexpected manner. A glitch in the neural net's training? A subtle move whose implications he failed to see?

He tried to concentrate on the miniature counters, but the doctor's remark kept coming back to him. What had she meant by such a joke? Hidden contempt? He had puzzled over Wong's presence ever since Hand had brought her on board at Achilles. She had the face of a horse and the disposition of a sheep; but Hand had worn such a broad grin that Gorgas wondered if she had given him more than a set of credentials. The Acts required that any transit of more than three months carry a medical doctor on the ship's Articles, but Hand had not hunted very long to fill the berth. A stroke of luck, he had said. A doctor left behind by her previous ship when she'd overslept and missed the departure. Yet it seemed to Gorgas, Achilles being as small as it was, that the *Krasnarov*'s crew could not have hunted all that diligently for their missing physician.

Down in the bowels of the lower decks, in the dim, red-lit confines of the engineering control room, surrounded by sharp, electric odors and bagpipe hums, Ramakrishnan Bhatterji considered the diagnostic display as another man might a longtime lover who has suddenly—and for no discernable reason—refused to come to bed; or more accurately, who has lain in his bed stiff and cold, making no response to his caress.

"No fusion," he said, half in shock and half in umbrage. "No power whatever."

"The timing might be off," his mate pointed out.

"Yes . . ." The engineer batted his palm with the test harness while he considered the point. "Timing is everything," he said, "in Farnsworth engines as in love. Everything must come together at the proper moment: the insertion, the clamping, the rapid pulsing, and the all-too-brief release of raw energy." He noted how his mate's smooth, young cheeks darkened. The flush ran to the scalp, so that the blond stubble there seemed to redden as well. Bhatterji smiled, but he did not allow his mind to stray to future delights. That such innocence existed was to be prized; that it must soon be lost, regretted; but that it would be lost to Ramakrishnan Bhatterji was to be anticipated and savored. He laid a hand on Miko's supple and graceful shoulder. "Engines must be coaxed," he said. "They must be teased into performing." He squeezed and felt how firm the flesh was under the concealing coveralls.

Mikoyan Hidei had signed the ship's Articles at Amalthea and had been aboard now for a little over a hundred days, and every one of those days had been exquisite agony for the engineer, for his mate was lithe and supple and beautiful—the most beautiful youth he had seen in many years, Rave Evermore not excluded. Figures far less graceful adorned the Majapour temple, where every posture known to love had been frozen in ageless stone. Miko's age on the Articles was seventeen, but that was surely hyperbole. A runaway, most likely—bored with farming or with oxygen mining or only with parental authority, and seeking now after far horizons.

"How long will we be enziggied?" demanded an intrusive basso voice. It was an angular voice, chopped fine by crisp consonants, each word delivered with such distinctness, the ending of one fully complete before the next dared raise its head, as to endow a simple greeting with the qualities of a pronouncement, and a simple query with those of a demand. Bhatterji, who did not much care for demands, placed a smile before his teeth and twisted to greet the intrusion.

Second Officer 'Abd al-Aziz Corrigan was a burnt cinder of a man, punk held too long in the fire. Partly, that was the endless sun of the skyless void; partly too that was the artifice of the melanic micromachines that guarded his flesh from the continual rain of cosmic radiation. His skin had a leathery feel to it, hard, yet supple and with a mild, pungent odor, as if he had been fashioned from uncured hides. Like the ship's doctor, he had the long, lanky body of the spaceborn, though he was a man of the 'Stroids, not of LEO. Bhatterji imagined him a snake, an image reinforced by his deep-set, reptilian eyes and by the way his tongue would dart out and wet his lips. The term *snake* was common enough in reference to the spaceborn, but polite folk avoided it; at least when any snakes were present.

"We haven't located the source of the malf," Bhatterji said. A grudging admission, pricked slowly off his teeth.

Corrigan's eyes darted from Bhatterji to Miko. He disliked the dirt and the grime of the engine room. Even when everything was in place, it seemed cluttered and disorderly. Bhatterji himself was a squat lump of a man: ugly, with blunt fingers and a nose once broken in a fight and only indifferently repaired. Corrigan considered him not far removed from the brute engines he served.

The same could not be said of his mate. Elfin-featured, sallow-skinned, Mikoyan Hidei lay at the aesthetic antipodes to the engineer: graceful and sweet-tempered, with a smile that Corrigan found disturbingly alluring, and all the more mysterious for being seldom seen outside duty hours. The second officer followed Miko with his eyes, even while he addressed the engineer. "Coasting will stretch out our transit time. We're drifting off course with the current, so the sooner you get it fixed, the better."

Bhatterji, who had entertained no notion that delay would be a good thing, resented the deck officer pointing out the obvious. If there was anything Bhatterji did not know about the ship, it was not a thing that Corrigan could tell him. "I'll fix it," he growled. He didn't like, either, the way the other man tossed antiquated magsail terms into his speech. No one called gravity "the current" any more. The old magsail hands never seemed to understand that history had passed them by.

"It might be a physical malf," Miko said. "What if something damaged the projectors outside? If a projector's out of alignment, wouldn't that wreck the timing?"

Bhatterji considered the suggestion. "Yes, it could be. There are a number of possibilities. Software. Hardware." He shook his head. "It's difficult to say."

"You're wasting time," Corrigan growled. "I don't care *what* the malf is. I want it *fixed*." It was not being "enziggied"—in zero g—that Corrigan minded. Being spaceborn, he found it more natural than weight. What he minded was anything out of order.

"I need more data," Bhatterji insisted.

"Then get it." Corrigan found the engineer's constant dithering a frustration. Moving him to action was like pushing cable.

"I could go Outside," Miko said to Bhatterji, "and check the hardware while you run the diagnostics inside . . ."

Bhatterji did not respond immediately, for the Void frightened him beyond measure. There was ionizing radiation from solar flares and, if not that, the endless cold or the endless vacuum or, quite simply, the endlessness itself. Lose contact with the ship, lose orientation, and a man would fall forever and ever—like Enver Koch tumbling into the dark. Sometimes, just before sleep took him, Bhatterji could hear his predecessor's voice ever fainter over the comm.

But if the thought of going Outside frightened, it also enticed. Bhatterji began to tremble.

"I'll check the cages myself," he heard his own far-away voice say at last.

Corrigan fishtailed to go, having gotten what he came for, but he paused for a moment in the accessway that led to the main deck and turned back. "I almost forgot. Captain Hand died a half hour ago; so you can scratch your turns off the death watch."

Bhatterji grunted as if punched in the belly. The news unsettled him, coming so soon after the engine malf. An ill omen, as if parts of the ship, human and mechanical, were shutting down one after the other. He dismissed the foreboding and turned to face the control panel. "Pull yourself together," he told Miko. "There's work to do."

Miko bit on a thumb knuckle and hugged both arms tight, looking dazed. "I can't help it. He was good to me. He took me in when I had nowhere to go."

Brief pain, and briefer humor, crossed Ram's heart. "That's a common enough story on this ship. I remember when—" But that was a private memory, not for sharing. The captain had made a habit of picking up the discards and left behinds of other ships, Ramakrishnan Bhatterji not least among them.

The engineer could not help but think that, in dying, Captain Hand had made a grave mistake.

With the ship enziggied, "Moth" Ratline gathered up his wranglers and herded them into the cargo hold above the main deck for a bit of opportunistic straightening. The wrangler berth was used to his continual fussing. "A place for everything," he liked to say, "and everything in its place." Except, the wranglers noted, nothing ever seemed quite in its proper place. Rave Evermore had tracked the progress of one particular container from bin to bin within the hold and declared that it had accumulated several thousand kilometers of additional travel beyond its nominal interplanetary journey.

"But, the captain's funeral," said Nkieruke Okoye, the First Wrangler. "Should we not be there, to show respect?" The others had urged her forward, less from a great love for the late captain Hand, than from a great loathing for hard work.

But Ratline was unmoved. He knew from experience that a wrangler's first goal in life was to avoid work; just as his own was to protect his young charges from the temptations of idleness. He grinned in what he thought was a friendly fashion—though the effort fell short in the minds of the wranglers—and said, "I've seen a captain."

And indeed, captains in his world were two-a-penny. He'd seen all of them, from Coltraine to Hand. He'd seen them promoted, retired, resigned, and fired. Now he'd seen one die. There were no other ways he could think of to leave the bridge, so a milestone of sorts had been achieved.

Ratline was the oldest of the crew, and the only one to have been on the ship's Articles from the very beginning. He'd been a cabin boy back then, proud in his elaborate uniform. Now he was all sinew and scar tissue and if his worn and dingy coveralls constituted a uniform it was only through careless nomenclature. Evermore and the other wranglers would never have believed it—their world was bounded entirely by the present—but Ratline had been a handsome lad. Half his prettiness had come from his uniform—red trim and epaulettes, gleaming brass buttons, MEMS fabric that rippled with changing patterns at a whispered command—but the rest had lain in his features and in his voice and in his carriage, which could (and often did) excite admiration with every stitch of uniform removed.

A tough life, the wranglers would tell each other when they thought about it at all, which was seldom, or when they contemplated their master's youth, which was never. Yet, it had been tough, and in ways that wrangling cargo could never be. Cargo pods and strap cables had taken a finger off Ratline's left hand and a hoist had once left a small depression in his skull— mass persists when even weight has fled—but other duties left other scars. There had been tasks for pretty, young cabin boys in the decadent years of the Fifties that the more Apollonian Zeds would never countenance. Ratline never spoke of it. Society then may have winked and nudged and leered, but little Timmy Ratline had been on the butt end, and his smiles had been only for the tips.

"He never looks happy," Ivar Akhaturian said after the wranglers had returned exhausted to their quarters. He hoped that his comment did not sound critical of the cargo master (in case the berth held him in reverence) nor too sympathetic (in case the berth despised him). Ivar was the newest of the wranglers, anxious to make a good impression, uncertain how that might be done. He was a cade boy. His mother had sold him to the ship "for a few years of seasoning" when *The River* had called at Callisto. He received room and board and an education; his mother received his wages.

Okoye lashed herself to a clip-chair in the wranglers' common room and listened to the other three chatter. As First Wrangler, she had spent the better part of three years shifting cargo under Ratline's eye, and possessed a broader perspective on such matters. Indeed, she often thought of herself as acting cargo master, since Ratline was six years older than Satan and given to long, solitary retreats into his cabin. *No, he never does look happy,* she thought, and wondered if there might be some long-buried wound festering beneath his skin, waiting to burst like a pustule and poison them all.

What distressed acting captain Stepan Gorgas most about Hand's funeral was how few of the crew attended. Beside himself, there was only the engineer and his mate and the third officer, the four of them arrayed in various approximations of mourning around Central Hall. Bhatterji appeared properly grave, but his mate seemed to be in a trance, like a cow just after the knacking hammer. Eugenie Satterwaithe, the Third Officer, appeared just before the ceremonies were to begin and positioned herself near one of the entries, as if situated for a quick escape. Barely a corporal's guard! Not that Gorgas had thought so well of Hand, but the office deserved respect.

Central Hall was a circular room set (happily enough) in the center of the lowermost deck. In more exalted days it had been a reception area and the Grand Staircase had spiraled up from the luxury modules below. Now the old stairwell was sealed off and only a narrow gangway led below to the maintenance tunnels and the external midship airlock through which Hand, vaporized, would shortly make his sublimed exit.

Satterwaithe had known Hand from the day the captain had been piped aboard, so Gorgas thought it fitting that she now be present when he was piped off. The symmetry pleased him in some indefinable fashion. Yet, Ratline, the other longtimer, did not appear. Nor even the doctor, which Gorgas found more than astonishing. It seemed a slap in the face, as if Wong had no further use for the man. Of all the sins in Gorgas's book (and there were many) the worst was ingratitude.

When the announced time for the funeral arrived, Gorgas opened his link. "Ship," he said solemnly, drawing the attention of the other mourners. "Funeral service. Evan Dodge Hand. Begin."

"Dearly beloved," said the Ship's AI in appropriately doleful tones, "we are gathered today to pay a final farewell to our beloved captain, Evan Dodge Hand, Sixteenth Captain of the Magnetic Sail, *The River of Stars*."

Startled, Gorgas pulled his 'puter from the pocket of his formal tunic and jotted some quick, urgent notes. In one short sentence the AI had made three errors.

First, despite its official designation and the supercargo coiled uselessly in the top-deck locker, *The River of Stars* was no longer a magnetic sail.

Second, to judge by the quantity of tears being shed, Hand had hardly been "beloved," unless by Miko Hidei, who at least seemed on the verge of them.

And third, "we" were not gathered, since most of the crew had absented themselves.

He was not even entirely certain of the "sixteenth." It depended on how one counted the post captains who had supervised the ship during its Jovian service.

Such gaffes might betoken a lurking malf in the neural net. Gorgas downloaded the list to the attention of The Lotus Jewel.

He glanced around the hall to see if the sysop had entered while he had been occupied with his 'puter. Of all the crew, The Lotus Jewel was the most pleasant to the eyes. Cheerful, intense, a good team player in Gorgas's judgment. He was disappointed, though not surprised, to note her continued absence. Like so many of her unworldly kind, she was undoubtedly floating in her room with her head up her ass.

Gorgas was not quite correct about The Lotus Jewel, at least about which was up what. She was in the communications center just off the bridge. The main panel of the transmitter was open and fasteners and random objects floated about, so that the console seemed to have been frozen somehow in the midst of an explosion. Her hands were deep within the unit, like a surgeon fumbling for a spleen; and if her head was not entirely up inside as well, her face was close to it and bore a look of profound concentration.

Passing by (and passing by no coincidence), Corrigan glanced into the comm center and saw the disorder. Corrigan did not approve of clutter. Yet, his rebuke remained unspoken, because he did approve of The Lotus Jewel. He approved of her face (it was fine and broad, with high cheekbones, and eyes of a most peculiar blue) and he approved of her poise, which always seemed to him graceful, as if she were acutely aware of where each and every part of her body was in relation to the rest. He approved of her ass, which at the moment faced in his direction and so demanded his attention. And he certainly approved of her generous and loving nature, since he was the immediate and primary beneficiary of it.

It pleased him that the most exquisite creature on the ship

was lover to 'Abd al-Aziz Corrigan, a man whose visage blanched the faces of so many wellsprung humans. That the carnal pickings on board *The River* might be slim he knew intellectually. Gorgas was too pompous, Grubb too virginal, Ratline too old, the wranglers too young, and Bhatterji too whatever Bhatterji was, so The Lotus Jewel had few options. Corrigan was not so naive as to suppose that no other pairings were possible, or that in the close confines of a ship most of those combinations would not eventually be tried. Yet it was to him that this delicate, golden-skinned wanton came.

Now, the spaceborn could be as graceful and (in their way) as beautiful as any wellsprung. They were filigrees; they were the intricate, twisting vines of medieval illuminations. Those raised deep within the gravity wells of Earth or Mars—or even of Luna—could seem lumpish by comparison. By rights, it ought to have been the doctor who enchanted the Second. They were two of a kind. But Corrigan found his own kind ungainly and ugly and lusted after the standard of beauty of another time and place.

(Besides, Corrigan was a man of the asteroids while Wong had grown up in Low Earth Orbit and they might not even reckon each other as "a kind." Safe within the embrace of Earth's magnetic field, Wong had never found the need for skin enhancers. Yet, such fine distinctions were lost on the likes of Bhatterji or Gorgas or even the otherwise perceptive Lotus Jewel. A snake was a snake. Not that there was anything wrong with that.)

Finally, when he had drunk in the sight of her almost more than his heart could bear, Corrigan checked the drape of his coverall, brushed at imagined detritus, and pulled himself inside the comm center.

The Communications Department comprised several rooms and had once been a suite reserved for *special friends* of the original owners. It had since been stripped, and utilitarianism had replaced luxury. Computer panels now gleamed where clever art had hung. Electric hums had replaced the fashionable music. This might actually have been an improvement.

The ship's processors were physically dispersed, of course. No designer was such a fool as to place a ship's entire neurosystem in one place—sub-units could be found scattered like Easter eggs here and there about the ship—but the comm center (and its slave station on the bridge itself) was a primary nexus. The Lotus Jewel could talk to any avatar of the ship's AI. Teeping, she could see through the ship's eyes, hear with its ears, speak with its lips. If she was not the ship's brains—an image risible to more than one of her crewmates—she was at least its spinal cord.

"What seems to be the problem here?" Corrigan said.

The Lotus Jewel concentrated a moment longer on her handheld and downloaded the data into the core with a whispered command. She had been aware of Corrigan's regard for several minutes and had, while not losing focus on her work, displayed herself for his delight. The Lotus Jewel enjoyed life more fully than her own life could hold, and so some of it always spilled over into others'. She delighted in making people happy. Sometimes that meant nothing more than laughing at a joke or doing a small favor. Sometimes it meant a pleasant word or a pleasant glimpse. Sometimes, as with Corrigan, it meant a pleasant night.

"The superloop is still giving power," The Lotus Jewel told him, "but I'm not transmitting." *Tonight,* she told Corrigan with a posture.

The infatuation was not all on the second officer's part. The Lotus Jewel enjoyed his company and his literate discourse and the strange, erotic frisson of the touch of his leathery skin. It was like the touch of an object: A thing that lived rather than a living thing.

"Is the malf serious?" he asked.

She shook her head. (And it was only through imagination that Corrigan saw long, golden locks waving in the air. Her skull was smooth-shaven and contained sockets for the interface cap, an exoticism that Corrigan found strangely alluring.) "Not until we raise Dinwoody Poke," she said, "to drop off the passenger. Radars and sensors, all in working order. Receiving is intermittent. I'll have transmission back before we need to talk to the port master."

Corrigan drew a long face. "Any connection with the engine malf?"

"I don't see how. The systems are distinct. Comm, power, navigation . . . There's no crosstalk, except through Ship."

"And the externals . . . ? Bhatterji's mate suggested a hardware fault."

"My equipment is mounted on a different quadrant of the rim. It's just coincidence, 'Zizzy. The ship's old. When was the last transit when we had no repairs to make?"

Corrigan grimaced. "The family still has my great-grandfather's tent. We only replaced the ropes three times, the poles twice, and patched every square inch of fabric. . . ."

"But it's still the original," she finished for him. There was a subtext there. It lay not only in the glint of her eye or the promise of her lips, but in that she could finish his jokes for him.

"Well," said Corrigan, "keep me informed."

A request that the engineer would have found insulting The Lotus Jewel took as supertext to Corrigan's real needs. "I'll give you a personal report," was all she answered, but it sent Corrigan from the room with a glow. He would anticipate her visit the entire evening and—as she was chronically late for appointments—the pleasure of that anticipation would be all the more prolonged.

It was only as Corrigan was leaving that The Lotus Jewel noticed the chronometer. "Oh, no! The captain's funeral! It's almost over!"

"No one will be there," Corrigan predicted. "Just Doctor Wong. No one else really *liked* the captain."

"I did," said The Lotus Jewel. "He helped me when I needed it most."

"That's hardly a reason for liking."

Corrigan's insensitivity went beyond that of his obdurate skin. The Lotus Jewel's did not. She watched him go with an uneasy feeling in her heart, as if for just a moment she had glimpsed a stranger.

The Doctor

When *The River of Stars* was reconfigured as a tramp freighter most of her main deck became superfluous, but the fitters and riggers at the Yards had been loathe to cut through pressure walls and load-bearing structures or vital power and life-support conduits and so they had left the disk itself intact. The cruel sentiment of the romantics held that her lovely lines could not be tampered with, and likely any such tampering would have destroyed her integrity in both senses of the word. And so, opulent staterooms that once housed the pampered rich (and, later and less splendidly, cohorts of emigrants) became stock-rooms or storage areas housing only inanimate shipping pods— or were simply shut up and abandoned.

This was less the problem it might have been, for the ship was built largely of solid smoke—that is, of aerogel—and her mass was but a fraction of what her size suggested; but mass was still a problem at the margin, where the ship made a profit or did not. Had her substance not been itself a valuable commodity, *The River* would never have lasted as long as she did. Like a whore, she sold bits and pieces of herself at every port of call to make up the difference, and so every year she became less and less what she once had been. Consequently, travel through the main deck often led to dark and deserted regions, down corridors that led nowhere, past rooms empty and abandoned.

On this day, when the husk of Evan Hand was to be vaporized and his ions sprayed into the void, Fransziska Wong sought refuge among the shadows and forgotten memories of the G-ring. She found a room far out from the central core and there became very, very drunk. In this selfsame room, legend said, microtech mogul Gowery Bend had deflowered the American president during that infamous elopement. But that had been during the luxury years, when this entire room had been dedicated to the pampering of a single passenger and few, even among presidents, prized duty above pleasure. Nothing now remained of that era. There was a single relic of the more austere times that followed: A skeletal rack upon which desperate men and women had been carried dreaming off to Mars. Perhaps they too had been looking for high adventure and the sight of far, exotic places. If so, the doctor thought, they too had been fools.

She wrapped one, long leg around a support strut of the rack and folded herself into a half-lotus. Then she zipped her coverall partway open and pulled out the inhaler fixed by a neck strap between her breasts. She popped the cap on the inhaler and squeezed a pure aerosol into her waiting lungs—a blend of drugs and chemicals of her own concoction, a blend delivering dreams, delivering oblivion, delivering release.

The mist—she had no name for it; a name would make it too real—hit like a tsunami in her blood. She was borne away on its fury: smashed, drowned, lifted up, glorified, no more miserably huddled in an abandoned stateroom in a tawdry ship, but soaring through the endless night, transported on its frothing crest. She was as tall as Alice, larger indeed than *The River of Stars* itself, and could ponder that aged and ungainly craft from godlike altitudes. A flick of her finger could send it, with its infestation of people, spinning like a discus across the solar system. And yet, she would not, for she loved them all and yearned to bind their hurts.

She would, someday; she would save them all. There would be a disaster—she was not sure what, but her eyes saw a distant explosion or a collision—and she would guide them all to safety. Or perhaps it would be an epidemic. Perhaps the same illness that had taken Captain Hand would return, more virulent, to finish the job. And Wong would labor sleepless nights to find the cure, preparing compounds and simples and programming microbots, and would with her own last gasp inject the saving medicine into each of the stricken crew, and she would be loved then in death more than she had ever been in life.

Clever chemicals mimicked ghostly caresses, the warmth of

phantom kisses, the massage of unseen fingers. Goosebumps rippled as, gulled, enzymes spurted from their enclosures. Warmth enveloped her; wetness seeped from the walls of her body. She wept at touches never granted, at entries never sought. Light touches, urgent touches, touches deep inside her being. Oh, what a grand ride she had, had she only a rider!

There had been that boy in school in Goddard, gangly and awkward with his spurting limbs and cracking voice. Hands held, kisses clumsily exchanged, promises awaited but never received. Where was he now? From her lofty view atop the cosmos, Wong thought she could almost see him, far off and receding.

And her first professor, with his clever repartee: brilliant, cynical, and, oh, so worldly. Stealing precious moments together until, inevitably, they had stolen one too many and he, faced with ultimatum, had chosen the safer haven of his wife.

She was caught in the undertow now, the chemical tide swept away by the Canutian brooms of counteragents. A whirling maelstrom overwhelmed her with abandonment and loneliness. Homesickness stopped her throat and she espied Goddard City winking in the sun as it pinwheeled around the Earth. She had not been there in years. Her meager savings could not afford the fare; and so she tramped from ship to ship, hoping one day to dock once more at home. But, with perverse frustration, Brownian motion kept her suspended in the Middle System. She could see that tight, little one-room flat in the Gamma-3 spoke where she had lived with her father and mother. She remembered the looming immensity of Earth querning outside the viewports, all blues and whites and greens and browns; colors so heartbreaking she wept to remember them.

Hand was dust now. Vapor jetted aft, his atoms making the Void just that much less empty. He had rescued her, in the True Companions Bar, rescued her from the inchoate joy she had breathed and breathed and breathed again into her sorry lungs; convoyed her while she sweated the poisons from her blood; sustained her through the grief that followed. A jovial man, hearty, loving life; warmhearted, talkative, radiating harmony. Had he only been awaiting an invitation she had never found the courage to give?

Bitter tears, then, for the potential happiness never now to be converted to the kinetic sort.

True joy, Evan Hand had told the shuddering woman in the True Companions, never has a price. It is as free and as unexpected as a budding flower.

And, as events had shown, as passing.

Fransziska Wong huddled once again miserably in an emigrant's bunk in an abandoned stateroom. It was dark. There had been no lights for years and electrostatics had woven the dust into crazed and elaborate cobwebs. She shivered uncontrollably as the toxins sweated out of her.

She had never performed an autopsy on Hand. She could not bear to treat the dear man as meat. But an exploration of the husk might have discovered his killer. Something exotic, something new or unexpected. Some reason why his death was such a mystery to her. "Ship," she said, wondering if it were too late to stop the funeral.

There was no answer, and it struck her that even the AI might have forgotten that this portion of the craft existed.

She fought her way clear of the jumble of struts and returned to the ring corridor. The hall curved away from her in both directions, dimly lit by the few red self-powered lights that had not yet failed. An ill sort of passageway. One seemed perpetually on the verge of turning a corner, yet never actually doing so. "Ship," she called again; and again there was no answer.

Surely not all the pickups had failed in this ring. She made her way clockwise, her long, gangly legs scissoring, leaping her from wall to bulkhead like some strange, huge insect. An observer might have been startled at how graceful she became, arms and legs pushing and grasping and turning in half-conscious motion. Indeed, Bigelow Fife, watching from the shadows, marveled at the unexpected beauty. The spaceborn moved through free fall with the grace of swans in flight.

Wong's next call to Ship was answered with a far-off hiss as Ship tried vainly to hear and respond. Wong sighed like a reed pipe and her hands and feet splayed and found holds invisible to those not born to it. To all appearances she came to a dead halt in mid-flight. It would be too late by now. Hand was less than dust.

Bigelow Fife spoke. "May I help?"

Fransziska Wong turned to see a stranger. He was a dim shape in the gloomy corridor and for a moment she thought that this man too had been abandoned in place when the G-ring was sealed off. One last Martian emigrant, who had forgotten to disembark. . . .

"You must be the passenger," she said. *The River* did ferry an occasional passenger. There were always those too impatient to await the next liner.

His slight bow was at once courtly, gracious, and supercilious, as if he found their encounter secretly amusing. "Bigelow Fife, at your service." What services he offered went unspoken. He had a small mouth and small gray eyes, but those eyes darted like striking birds, missing nothing, plucking meaning if it so much as showed its head. They seemed to be two living things, those eyes, perched in twin niches in his skull. "Your captain died, I heard. You've come off to be by yourself for the remembering of him."

Wong ran an arm across her face. "I didn't know him long."

"Oh, it's not the length that matters, but the depth."

The comment surprised her and she gave the man a more careful look. Stocky, but somehow ethereal, as if his bones were cast of aerogel. His tight, enhanced briefs gave modesty both a nod and a nudge; otherwise: sandals and a headband to contain his longish hair completed his garb. His pale skin was one to which the sun could be never more than an enemy. Obviously, a Lunatic. "He was a good man," Wong heard herself say. "A good captain."

"I didn't know the fellow." And thus is simple truth simply cruel. Those darting eyes noticed her flinch and, reconsidering his words, Fife said, "Forgive me. I met him only the once when he offered me a transit on this lovely ship, but as a fellow man, naturally his death saddens me. I gather it was sudden."

"The onset, yes; but he lingered for a few days." Could she find in that very brevity a reason for her failure? A slower onset, a few more days. Yes, she might have diagnosed him, found a treatment amongst her unguents and seed codes; but he had slipped like water between her fingers. She brushed again at her eyes.

Fife observed the woman closely. She exuded a faint smell, at once fleshy and metallic, and damp circles had darkened her coverall under the arms and around her collar and at the small of her back. Her chest, visible through the lowered zipper, glistened with small beads of perspiration. Was there a sweat lodge on board, he wondered? A strange luxury for a tramp, the more so in that the crew were not of Luna.

"If you need to mourn, I can listen." He let the suggestion linger between them. A woman distraught meant opportunities opened, if properly cultivated—sorrow and loss being often parent to desire. Yet his compassion was as genuine as it was calculated. If one seeks to buy, only a fool offers brass.

"I'd . . . rather not," she said. But did he hear hesitation in her voice?

He created a smile for her. "Sorrow, bottled, turns as rancid as vinegar; yet decanted, it cleanses."

"Are you a counselor of some sort?"

He laughed at the incongruity. "In a strange sort of way, I suppose I am. I troubleshoot for Mohammed's Mountains. When one of our crews cannot place its asteroid into a proper capture orbit, I'm the one they boost out to solve the problem."

"And Mo-Mo can't afford a passenger ticket?"

"Your captain Hand was to call on Dinwoody Poke in the Virgin Islands and from there I can goose the crew chief before his launch window closes up on him. Only . . ." And a brief frown crossed his pale features. "If we continue coasting, my shortcut may become a very long cut." He shrugged. Bad luck was a fact of life and one dealt with it or not.

Good luck, on the other hand, was something one created. He extended a hand. "I wouldn't mind learning something of your captain. You seem to have known him. Let us find somewhere private where we can talk."

He could see the change in her eyes and knew that she understood his goals and objectives. The problem was: did she concur? Was consensus achievable, or had he misread the unzipped coverall?

"Perhaps some other time," she said.

Fife tried and failed to parse the overtones in her voice. Well, it had been happenstance, not beauty that had drawn him—that and the momentary grace of her movement. In a more reflective mode and with more options to choose from, he might not have given this woman a second's glance. Her looks bordered on plain and from the wrong side of the border. Why, jaws like that could strip cable; and a nose so great smell tomorrow's breakfast. Yet, the swan had been thought at first a homely sort of duckling. There were more beauties than those that the eye perceived. Other senses gathered their own pleasures. He had heard all the stories of the spaceborn and their mastery of free-fall sex. He believed only half the tales, but they were the more interesting half.

"Then 'perhaps,'" he said with more asperity than he intended, for he did not like to burn bridges he might someday want to cross, "you ought not leave the door open, if you'd rather no visitors come within."

She followed his gesture, saw that she was exposed, and seized the zipper. Yet her fingers hesitated without drawing it shut. She looked him in the eye and Fife knew that fortune did indeed favor the brave. "Do you find me attractive?" she asked. There was a blunt challenge in her voice, as if she demanded lies, yet refused to accept them.

Fife was devoted to the truth and to allowing cards to fall, yet he was not unmindful of prudence. "I believe you have a beautiful heart," he answered which, while unresponsive, was the truth. The woman had been weeping openly, a sign of sentimentality not often found in the corridors under Luna. "And your movement is as graceful as any ballet." He might normally have concluded by saying that in the dark all cats were gray, as he had a taste for aphorisms and clichés. Instead, he gestured at his own lustrously pearl body. "And a toad like myself can hardly deprecate another."

Wong smiled at the transparency of his offer. It was not the sort of intimacy her loneliness sought. It was only use. Yet if one could not be loved, to be useful was no small thing. "Have you ever kissed a toad?" she asked, knowing what residues lingered in her sweat, in the beads of perspiration that lined her lips and brow. "They say licking a toad can bring visions of joy."

Only a small, attenuated joy, nothing compared to the potent mist she had inhaled; but the unexpected jolt her sweat would give him would be a fit reprimand for his cold-eyed opportunism. Not the transport of joy he would feel at his first taste of her, but the sharp, black despondency that would chase him once they had parted.

The Log

Sat. 12th inst. 40 days out of Achilles. Course laid on grand secant. Coordinates on J-2100 not fixed, due to transmitter malfunction noted hereunder. Manual bearings taken on Jupiter and Sun. Sun in Aqr.; Jup^{t}. in Gem. Est. position 4.47 AU starward by 41°30' east of Jupiter meridian on the solar ecliptic. Velocity steady at 152 k/s. Engines idled for repairs. Weather holding; wind from the East-Sun-East; no solar flares noted. Departed this life E.D. Hand, late captain of this vessel. Sysop reports transmitter malfunction, reception intermittent. People employed at various tasks.

There were only three of them, now that Hand was dead; but Gorgas had taken the captain's chair as soon as the deck officers had entered the wardroom. This struck the other two as unseemly; Corrigan, because he was accustomed to the old order and change always came on him too suddenly, and Satterwaithe, because she had other notions of who ought to sit there.

Gorgas had an agenda, of course. So did Satterwaithe.

The wardroom had been designed for the larger crew of a larger craft. Coltraine's people had filled it. The Purser's department alone had boasted four senior officers plus their juniors, and the Sailing Master had commanded a staff of dozens.

Now, nearly all the furnishings had been stripped; some in the original refit, some through sale, scrap, or cannibalization in the years since. A single table remained, surrounded by a half-dozen clip-chairs, illuminated by a single light. The remainder of the room was bare and dim, as if it were slowly fading.

(Even under constant boost, a table and chairs were but marginally useful; in free fall, they were entirely notional. Yet the designers had possessed firm notions of propriety, and the image of finely uniformed officers bobbing about like so much flotsam was too ludicrous to be entertained.)

The ghosts of Coltraine and Toledo and Johnson and Fu-hsi might yet haunt that room, gazing from the shadows with disapproval at what had become of their legacy. Lately, Corrigan had felt their eyes upon him; had heard them rustling in the dark—shadows in a ship that had become itself a shadow. Gorgas scoffed at such notions. He gave no credence to ghosts of any sort, not even to Hand's, who alone of all the prior captains might have reason to linger. If there were bangs and thumps and rattles, they signified imbalanced fans or water hammers in the pipes. A ship grown old enough could give a credible imitation of a haunting.

"Mr. Corrigan," Gorgas announced without preamble, "I shall need a suite of course revisions. We had not reached our planned coasting velocity when the engines went down, so the balk line must be reset." It was like him to get right down to business. He mistook abruptness for efficiency.

"What top velocity and braking power will we have available?" Corrigan asked, his stylus paused over his 'puter.

"That will depend on how soon Mr. Bhatterji brings the engines back on line and how much thrust he can give us when he does. It may be a software malf and we will have full power by this afternoon; or it may be an equipment failure and we will only have partial restoration after days of work."

"But then, which . . . ?"

"Use your imagination, Number One. Give me an envelope. Find the boundary conditions." It was unfair to ask a man to use what he has in short supply. Gorgas had flown with the second officer long enough to know that. You didn't always have to tell Corrigan what to do, but it helped.

Satterwaithe spoke up while Corrigan made notations in his 'puter. "Have you developed a plan to bring the sensors back on line?" She was an older woman, not so old as Ratline but her hair had grayed and there were deep lines at the corners of her eyes and mouth. No one called them "laugh lines," either. "We're coasting at better than a hundred and fifty kisses against the Jupiter datum, and if we overtake any rogue bodies—"

For just a moment, Gorgas flashed on encountering Hand's body wandering the corridors of the main deck. He blinked a few times and ran a hand across his close-cropped hair while he considered how to answer; and even Corrigan gave the Third Officer a puzzled glance. "We're in the Trojan Gulf," Corrigan pointed out. "A resonance zone, nowhere near the Windward Shore," and Gorgas nodded, pleased that the Second had seen his reasoning.

But there were few things about ship handling that Satterwaithe did not know. She was quite content with Gorgas's decisions so far—it was what she would have done in his place. What bothered her was that she was not in his place.

"This region of the Shore lapped Jupiter a sixmonth ago," she insisted, "and you know how Jupiter can jumble the edges of the Belt. He may have tugged all sorts of uncharted bodies into eccentric orbits. Remember: the Gulf is empty only of *permanent* bodies."

Gorgas had not expected debate. Hand had never been debated. Even when Hand had made questionable decisions—deplorably often, in Gorgas's opinion—Gorgas and the others had maintained their silences. That was the proper way for a subordinate officer to conduct himself. In the Space Guard . . . Ah, but he seldom dwelt on his days in the Guard. "Are you teaching me my craft," he asked, with just a touch of irritation.

Corrigan, who knew how the ship's course lay, was also puzzled by Satterwaithe's comment. "We've received no rock messages from other vessels." But he was half a beat behind on the subtext. Satterwaithe was not interested in asteroids.

"Not *your* craft, Stepan," she said, affecting a misunderstanding of "craft." "Only a shareholder vote can appoint a permanent captain."

Gorgas bowed his head slowly, having finally understood that there was a second agenda. "That, of course, is the shareholders' privilege." He himself held a block of shares, as did the others. There were children on Earth who held a share apiece that their parents had bought to "Save the River!" There had never been a dividend paid.

Satterwaithe shrugged. "The captain is barely cold in his grave."

"Deep space is a heat sink," Gorgas responded. "He was 'cold' in his grave almost instantly."

Satterwaithe rolled mental eyes at Gorgas's literal-mindedness. She did not consider that he had made a joke.

"She's right about the rules," Corrigan said.

"Personally, it would be a relief to be relieved," Gorgas told him. "But nothing happens until we raise Dinwoody Poke. Until then, acting or not, my authority stands. That too Mr. Corrigan, is in the rules."

"I wasn't questioning your authority," said Corrigan.

Satterwaithe, who *had* questioned his authority, said nothing. She imagined that Gorgas's ambition mirrored her own. She was the sort of person who, like God, creates others in her own image and, when they fail to behave as the image ought, labels them disingenuous.

The Engineer

The openness, the abandon, the sheer forever of space both terrified and seduced Ramakrishnan Bhatterji. While he contemplated the upcoming EVAsion; while he suited up; while Miko, like a knight's squire, tested his valves and fittings; while he waited patiently in the afterlock for the pressure to drop to the ambient of space, Bhatterji trembled—in his limbs, in his guts, in his heart—but whether they were tremblors of eagerness or of fear he did not know.

For, when he stepped outside and planted his boots on the ship's skin, an exhilaration ran through him like an electric current and he became more heightened in all his senses—as if he could hear the grinding of the crystal spheres or smell the sharp tang of the aether. It always puzzled him afterwards that this euphoria faded so rapidly while the fear remained to haunt his dreams; as if joy were a tide, which, at its ebb, leaves exposed the jagged rocks.

The engine cages, along with most other equipments, were mounted around the rim, one engine in each quadrant. They loomed above their surroundings like the sacred monuments of a lost race. Around each, a bare space had been left out of reverence, if not for their monumental nature, then for the fusion plasma that pulsed from them when they spoke God's name. When he reached Number Three, Bhatterji did not bother to inspect the projectors that knelt like acolytes around it, nor even the focusing rings that directed the plasma in the desired direction. He examined first where he thought the trouble would lie and gave a small grunt of dismal satisfaction on finding his intuition vindicated.

The inner spherical grid, the anode, had melted. In place of gracile, superconducting geodesics, he found a ragged and warped tangle. In melting, the hoops had begun to sublime but had quickly frozen in the ambient of space, and they looked now as if they had been drawn in India ink and smudged by God's careless thumb. Filigrees of metaloceramic curled where the radiating vapors had cooled. They were beautiful, like iron ferns. Bhatterji broke off a lacey branch with the thumb of his gauntlet. Brittle. The entire anode grid was a useless, blackened mass.

"That looks bad," Miko's voice told him. Everyone on the ship was watching through Bhatterji's suit's cameras, but that did not inhibit the engineer as it might another. His life demanded an audience.

"The hobartium hoops have been thermally stressed," he told

his apprentice in a stroke of understatement worthy of the Japanese paintings he favored.

"Can we salvage the mass and redraw it to wire?"

Musing on the failure mode, Bhatterji shook his head, then remembered he was on radio. "No. An overstress of this magnitude ruins the molecular alignment. The surface will have been hardened by the vacuum quench and will not draw without severe cracking. Describe the failure mode to me." Miko must learn the craft, and the unexpected has always provided opportunities for learning.

("Describe the failure mode?" said Ratline aside to Satterwaithe. "Did he go blind?" But Satterwaithe did not laugh.)

"Ah . . . The anode draws electrons into the convergence zone, which . . ." Miko spoke hesitantly, as if reciting. The mate too was aware of the audience that watched and listened, but was less welcoming of its attention than the engineer. ". . . which creates a virtual cathode. And that, in turn, draws the ions so they can compactify and fuse . . ."

"I asked not how it worked, but how it failed."

"Well, thermal stress is usually due to ionic or electronic impact. I would guess that the magnetic insulation failed."

"You would guess," said Bhatterji.

Miko hesitated. "I'm certain. Almost."

"Very good," said Bhatterji. "Certainty must never be absolute."

("Go to the head of the class," sneered Ratline. Satterwaithe sought to hush him with a hand to his wrist, but the cargo master yanked his arm away and glared at the Third Officer. "You know better than that," he whispered harshly.)

"And so," said Bhatterji, "we inspect the magnetic projectors."

Corrigan, from the bridge, interrupted. "Did you examine the fiber optic controls?"

"They're fried. The Florence struts are buckled too. Secondary failures caused by the anode slagging." He touched a helmet control and his vision went to infrared and he was engulfed in a starless haze. The slagged anode was a dull ember. Far off to his left, he could just see Number Four still cooling down after the automatic cutoff. To his right, the comm tower obstructed his view of Number Two.

Bhatterji examined the CoRE magnets and could see the residual heat in swirls of yellow and orange. The scale on his visor gave him the temperature and a whispered query to Ship told him how hot the coils must have gotten to be so warm yet. He did not like the answer, not at all.

"The magnet overheated," he said.

"The safeties tripped," Miko told him. But they had known that from the diagnostics soon after the shutdown.

Bhatterji restored his sight to the visible bands. "So they did," he said, "but perhaps a little too slowly. Two of the breakers I see are visibly worn. In any event, the CoRE superconductors have also been quenched."

Gorgas broke into the channel. "Can it be fixed?"

Bhatterji snorted. "Of course. I expect it will be fun."

"Fun! This is a serious matter."

Bhatterji made no response. Gorgas did not know the pleasures of engineering. Indeed, Bhatterji did not think Gorgas knew any pleasures. Already, Bhatterji had thought of three possible repair designs and a workaround for the Florence struts, though which design he would use would depend on what parts and materials he could scrounge.

"I am going to check Number Two now," he told Miko.

"But—that was the automatic shutdown, wasn't it?" his mate said.

"Think it through. The ship can boost on any three Farnsworths. The AI knows that."

"But, then—"

"It can even fly on two," Bhatterji went on. "Pay attention. It can even fly on two, *provided* they are antipodal on the rim. But if two *adjacent* engines go down, the ship will twirl around its diameter, which makes navigation problematical. So the AI performs a complete shutdown."

("Damned cages," Satterwaithe said off-circuit to Ratline, "you'd never get a failure mode like that with a magsail." Ratline cackled.)

"For two engines to fail at the same time—" Miko began to say, but Bhatterji interrupted again.

"Ponder why the CoRE magnets failed. Don't distract me." He stood still for a moment, eyes closed, nerving himself for flight; then he loosened his boots from the rim and rose slowly on his suit jets. The conviction welled within him that he was falling away from the ship into a vast and endless pit. The hull was no longer a surface, but a precipice. Breathing hard, sweating, he brought himself to a stop at ten feet, paused to orient, then jetted toward the Number Two Farnsworth. A dangerous maneuver. Motion wants always a straight line, and that means tangent to the ship's rim and her considerable forward velocity. But fear wants danger to vindicate itself, and that means tangent to one's desires.

Following the curvature of the rim, Bhatterji coasted above moribund shroud motors for the old magnetic sails; above empty connector cradles for long-gone luxury modules; around the antennae for the comm system; above a junkyard of sensors and couplings and equipments that resembled a great coral reef. His pulse rattled like a snare and his groin tightened into a hard ball. He tickled the jets himself, not trusting the suit's AI to judge the complex topography below. If he miscalculated he would fly into the Void. But that was as it should be. A man's fate ought to be in a man's own two hands. Enver Koch had made a fatal error, but he had died a man.

That one as terrified of the Void as Ramakrishnan Bhatterji would work in space affronted reason; but reason wasn't in it. Some men find their fears more addicting than their loves and so come to love their fears. They take pride in defying them. Bhatterji could have swum through that reef, or even gone back inside the ship and across the quadrant, but he was more afraid of showing his fear than he was of the fear itself. History has named such men heroes, and at other times fools, and called their behavior brave or self-destructive as intellectual fashion decreed; but whatever she called them, history has always taken note. People write songs about the likes of Ram Bhatterji and whether the song is ballad or dirge or satire matters less than that it is sung at all.

(Men like Gorgas inspire no music: a gray man with a gray

mind; aloof and abrupt because he lived much inside his head; single-minded and unyielding when once he had grasped the pattern of events; but quick to see those patterns, as well. Such men do not inspire. At best, they merely convince.)

Coming at last to Number Two, Bhatterji saw immediately that its anode had also melted. It was a curious thing to be so astonished at something so expected. "Both engines have slagged," he announced. Something struck his outstretched arm and, turning, he saw the loose ends of the Hyne cables writhing Medusa-like in the airless void.

Bhatterji peered closer at the torn cables just as two bare ends chanced to close with each other and a white spark jumped the gap. He had not actually grasped hold of anything and so was not grounded and the charge dissipated harmlessly; but his mind by reflex worked out the voltages. Miko, who was monitoring Bhatterji's life support from within the ship, saw how the heartbeat spiked.

"Miko," the engineer's voice said ever-so-calmly over the link, "I've found the source of that transient that concerned you. Please shut down all subsystem power to the Number Two pylon."

Miko threw the switches and locked them out, one by one. The engineer was terrified of outside work. He tried to keep it secret, but Miko could tell. A cold start would require recalibration of the flicker. Someone must physically adjust the focusing rings after each test burst. It was dangerous work, normally done in the Yards. Get the rhythm wrong—miss a beat—and a nanopulse of fusion would be more than flesh and bone could bear. The situation must be serious indeed if Ram was willing to accept that risk while under way and with a high velocity.

Aboard *The River* only since Amalthea Harbor, Miko still found pleasure in contemplating duty, in being *useful* to a ship that had provided refuge from an intolerable life, and so had studied the manuals with great diligence, memorizing assembly and disassembly procedures, creating mental pictures from the views and sections. "I could do it." The words escaped on a breath and Bhatterji, not quite making them out, asked for a repeat. Miko flushed and said, "Nothing."

Or did something else move the engineer beside a reluctance to entrust great work to a green apprentice? Miko sometimes sensed an edge to the older man, a fascination with death and risk. He might seek the Void as another might grasp a serpent—as an act of defiance. And yet, the Universe could be pushed only so far before it pushed back.

Simultaneous failure argued a common cause. A whispered command to the AI brought the schematics up on Miko's screen. What systems did Two and Three have in common?

While his mate searched deebies, Bhatterji turned away from the damaged cage. He noticed that he was casting a shadow and, turning to look, saw the smoky opal gleam of Jupiter off the fore starside quarter. It was a minute disk, not even a tenth the size of the Moon over the Bay of Bengal, and for just a moment, Bhatterji wondered what he was doing here, so far from the temples and the forests and the jangly cities. He remembered that Miko came from Amalthea and one of the wranglers from Callisto. They had signed the articles within a day of each other on the previous transit. Yet Circumjovia was the new frontier. Odd, how people fled from heavens that others scrambled to reach.

Turning back to the rim, he squinted his eyes at the forest of pylons back the way he had come, then he lifted off the hull once more. This time, he stayed closer to the surface and toed down a moment later at the Ayesaki valve, halfway between the two damaged cages.

"Mr. Bhatterji," Miko said, "I think you should check the north exterior coolant diverter valve."

"The Ayesaki. Yes, I'm already there." Bhatterji's satisfaction at having reasoned so well was tempered by what he saw. The valve had cracked and molten lithium had sprayed, coated, and ruined every piece of equipment around it before the cutoffs could shut down the flow.

"How did you—"

"Because I have the ship up here," Bhatterji told his mate, tapping his helmet—a wasted gesture, though Miko understood. "The anodes failed. Why? Because they both lost their magnetic insulation. Why did the insulation fail? Because the

CoRE magnets failed. Why did the CoRE magnets fail? Because resistive heating in their coils quenched the superconductor. Why did the coils grow hot? An interruption in their coolant supply. And why *two* cages at the same time? A coolant failure at the diverter valve that served them both. You must always ask 'why' five times when diagnosing a failure. It's really quite pretty, the way everything falls into place."

("Pretty!" said Gorgas, who was watching and listening from the bridge.)

("It's more than pretty," Fife told Wong and the others in the common room. "It's beautiful." He had itched to track the root cause himself, but had lacked sufficient knowledge of the system to leap ahead of Bhatterji. Yet following another on the scent was pleasure still.)

"The only thing left," Bhatterji said, "is to discover why the valve failed."

(Corrigan, who was on the bridge with Gorgas, shook his head. "No! What's left is to fix the forsaken thing." But Gorgas silenced him with a gesture and Bhatterji never heard.)

The engineer studied the equipment closely. Frozen lithium coated everything with a grim yellowed frost. The Lotus Jewel's comm antennae were badly damaged. As for the valve itself, what Bhatterji saw was so simple that at first he could not comprehend it. His mind tried and discarded a dozen templates while he struggled to understand the bent and mangled casing. Curiously, of the others watching through his suit camera, only The Lotus Jewel, who did not know what was reasonable, saw plainly what must have happened.

"We have been struck," Bhatterji concluded at last, something like awe in his voice; as if he had won a cosmic lottery or, more accurately, lost one in which winning had been ensured. "By a small object, the size of my fist." Yes, there were the broken ends protruding on the far side of the shell. Bhatterji wondered at the trajectory and squatted to sight through the holes.

Gorgas had watched Bhatterji's EVAsion on the ship's monitors, watched the man's progress from one piece of equipment to the next, saw through the suit camera what Bhatterji saw; and if Bhatterji saw puzzle and The Lotus Jewel fear, and Satterwaithe vindication, it was Gorgas who saw beyond the immediate phenomena to a glimmer of what lay ahead.

Evan Dodge Hand had always allowed Bhatterji a time to decompress after Outside work. Though he never spoke of it, Hand had been well aware of his engineer's phobia and had granted him this grace period before reporting; and Bhatterji (who also never spoke of it) was grateful for both the grace and the silence. Over the years, that grace had metastasized into a right, one of those "customary privileges" that accumulate in any crew.

But there sat now a pharaoh who knew not Joseph. Stepan Gorgas waited in his day room with increasing impatience for Bhatterji to appear. While he waited, he replayed the video from the engineer's EVAsion, freezing and zooming on the damage the man had found, extrapolating from that damage to the likely bill of materials, hyperlinking to stores inventories, considering and discarding a dozen possibilities. Every now and then he would glance in irritation at the door and growl, "Where the devil is that fellow?"

"That fellow" was one level up, naked, and rubbing himself vigorously with a moist scrubber. Intellectually, Bhatterji knew that the sweat of fear had no distinctive odor. It was indistinguishable from the sweat of hard work or the sweat of vigorous play; but this knowledge was *only* knowledge and before he would report to Gorgas he rubbed himself and rubbed himself until his skin tingled and he wished Miko were with him. Gorgas would never have noticed. If there was a smell to fear, it was Bhatterji who caught the whiff; Bhatterji who must wipe it clean.

The engineer completed his decompression ritual in the deckhands' mess. It was a favorite spot of his. Though nominally an officer, Bhatterji always felt more relaxed among the crew. The talk was easier up on the crew deck, the atmosphere more relaxed. The near-beer had fuller body than down below—though the officers' mess drew its own "neer" from the same tanks.

Miko had come to help him celebrate a successful EVAsion. The Lotus Jewel had come to ask about her antennae, but she had also come to kick near-beer with him, and had already filled two squeezers with the hoppy brew. Bhatterji accepted one but surreptitiously replaced it with another that he had brought from his own quarters. Sometimes a man wanted to get a little nearer, and to hell with the Prague Convention.

Three of the wranglers were there as well, though for their own reasons. They were also celebrating a successful evasion, this one of Ratline's attention. Evermore and Akhaturian—slim and beardless and humming with vitality—were candy to Bhatterji's eye. Oh, hour of thoughtless youth! But Evermore greeted him with wary hostility and Twenty-four deCant, the Third Wrangler, had her nails deeply embedded in Akhaturian's arm, so neither lad was properly on Bhatterji's to-do list. DeCant was one of those predatory females that Bhatterji dreaded, a falcon eager to swoop and always—so it seemed to him—on those whom he fancied.

But the talk ran high and the laughter flowed, though most of both were Bhatterji's doing. He squeezed neer out of his ziggy bottle and gulped the writhing, iridescent globules like a fish snatching at bits of floating food. Miko, anchored a little to the side, disapproved. Loose food, especially loose liquids, could gum the inboard filter systems and require hours of digestion by Grubb's microbots to unclog them.

Bhatterji, attributing the slight frown to thoughtfulness and the pursed lips to a thrown kiss, threw his mate a reply—at which sight deCant, watching, unaccountably giggled.

They chatted for a while over trivia but the talk, no matter how it might orbit, spiraled inexorably into the matter of Bhatterji's EVAsion.

"I would have taken the surface route around the hull," Evermore said with the placid assurance of the bystander. "It would have taken longer, but there's less risk." Rave Evermore was the sort who was always more expert at other people's jobs.

Bhatterji made allowances both for the boy's youth and for his beauty, though the latter was fading with the deepening voice. "Life is risk," he told the boy. "Anything can kill you. Anything. Do you know how many people have died taking a dump? If you did, it would—"

"—scare the shit right out of me," Evermore finished the sentence and Bhatterji, realizing that he must have used the line rather too often, joined in the laughter.

"Everyone dies," he said with a smile as sharp as a blade. "Not everyone *lives*." Evermore flinched and looked away.

"What are the odds on being hit like that?" Akhaturian asked. "By a meteor! They must be a million-to-one!"

Bhatterji shrugged. "And how many millions of minutes of flight time has this ship logged? Given enough opportunity, even the rarest event must happen. We live in an unlikely world, boy. Everything that happens is impossible! What odds, Ivar, that your parents would ever have met? Or that, on one particular day, that one particular sperm reached that one particular egg ahead of all the others? One small diversion and— ping!—no Ivar. It's like the poet, Carson, once said: 'Life is all collisions.'"

"None of that 'random sperm' muff applies to me," deCant said in tones both defiant and sad. "But . . ." and her smile was a blossom of red against the raven black of her skullcap hair as she rubbed Akhaturian's back, ". . . I'm just glad *your* probabilities worked out in *my* favor." The junior wrangler glowed under her touch. *Imprinted like a duckling,* Bhatterji thought sadly.

"How bad was the damage to my antennae?" asked The Lotus Jewel, bringing the discussion back to practicalities. "I get intermittent reception. I don't think I'm transmitting at all."

That wasn't quite true. The Lotus Jewel was transmitting on several frequencies. Certainly, Evermore was receiving, the way he tracked her every move; and Akhaturian too despite the grapple on his arm. Even Eaton Grubb used the pretext of checking particulates just to pass through the mess and catch a glimpse of her. The Lotus Jewel had a laugh like small bells. It was hard for anyone to ignore her when she was in the room. Even Bhatterji enjoyed her company. They were alike in so many ways, the two of them: loving sport and physical exertion, enjoying their own bodies, both craving the attention of others.

"There was a bit of damage to your equipment," he told her.

"I was watching the feed, Ram. It looked like more than 'a bit' to me."

"I'm *tired* of muffing freefall," deCant said. "My muffing head feels bloated and swollen. My nose is stuffy. I blew breakfast for three muffing days. When can we get acceleration back? A couple milligees isn't much, maybe, but it beats the heaves."

"I haven't reviewed the videos yet," Bhatterji said, "but I thought of three or four patches while I was eyeballing the damage. Don't worry," Bhatterji added with no sense at all of prophecy. "If I can't fix those engines, they can't be fixed."

Bhatterji had read the lack of a summons from Gorgas as a lack of urgency and therefore was puzzled and upset when the captain grilled him over his whereabouts when he finally did report.

"Decompressing," Bhatterji answered. He did not add a *sir*. No one had said "sir" on *The River of Stars* for twenty-three years.

Gorgas would neither plead nor rage. His practice was to inform people of their transgressions and let their own sense of duty shame them. He steepled his fingers before his pursed lips, and said, "You didn't think the ship's condition important enough to warrant an immediate report? Well, never mind that, now. It's the forward plan that matters."

Bhatterji, who had no shame to appeal to, took the brevity of Gorgas's reprimand as a further sign of unimportance. If Gorgas had really wanted an immediate report, he would have spent more words on it. But that was only because Bhatterji nearly always said what was on his mind, while Gorgas let it remain there until it was ready to be said. Consequently, each judged the other irresolute, though for opposite reasons. In this judgment, both were nearly correct, but only nearly.

"You need to concentrate on Number Three," Gorgas told the engineer. "That requires the least work."

That sentence was only the final one in a long string of intricately interwoven sentences. Unfortunately, as it was the only one spoken aloud, it was the only one that Bhatterji heard. Gorgas's thoughts were like icebergs, only the tips of them showed, which was why many in the crew thought him cold.

"I'm sorry," Bhatterji responded, "at which university did you study fusion engineering? I've forgotten."

Bhatterji being elliptical, Gorgas often thought, was like the Russian army in 1914 performing a maneuver. It was never well executed, but it astonished one to see it tried at all. "You have only five days," Gorgas pointed out, revealing another facet of his iceberg thinking.

The engineer was no innumerate and could now guess at the hidden dimensions. He understood where the limit came from because he had performed the same calculations himself. If three engines were available, the ship must begin deceleration in five days or she would be going too fast to enter Jupiter orbit. If all four engines were on line . . . "It's nineteen days to the balk line," he said. With only two engines, it was already far too late.

Gorgas pursed his lips a moment and, closing his eyes, reviewed the various options and possibilities he had considered. The path ahead was a winding one, with many branches, through a dark forest, and most of those paths did not lead to where he wished to take the ship. "There are not enough spares to repair both engines. There is a lithium-grade valve that you can use in place of the damaged Ayesaki, but . . ."

"The repairs are straightforward," Bhatterji insisted. "If the ship has the parts in stock, that's fine. If not, I'll fab them from raws." He spread his hands, as if to say "end of story."

"But there are no spare grids," Gorgas began.

Bhatterji rolled mental eyes. "I can draw wire down from hobartium rod and spot weld the geodesics."

"And the command logics?"

"Oh," said the engineer, deliberately boastful, "I'll cannibalize some of the damaged components and frankenstein four of the five I need."

Gorgas raised an eyebrow. "You have an action plan?"

The engineer cocked his head. "Yes. I plan to act."

"A little prior analysis might be useful," Gorgas suggested. He wouldn't mind Bhatterji's impulsiveness quite so much if there were some evidence of thought behind it. But is *thoughtful impulsiveness* an oxymoron or a Zen-like insight? A smile passed briefly over his lips.

The sneer irritated Bhatterji. Gorgas, in his estimation, not only failed to jump to conclusions, he failed to walk up to them when they were lying supine in front of him. He would circle and stalk forever, as if the hunt mattered more than the kill. How in space had Hand tolerated the man?

"I've roughed out a tentative bill of materials," he said, but this was an exaggeration. What he meant was that he thought he knew what he would need. He wouldn't *really* know until he dove into the work.

Gorgas wondered why it was that no one on board understood contingencies, or that plans needed to be robust against the unexpected. "Suppose you can repair only one of the engines?" he suggested. "What then?"

"Then I'll never enjoy the eulogy."

Blinking, Gorgas wondered if he had stumbled into a different conversation. "Eulogy . . ."

"Because a man can't hear the eulogy at his own funeral; and the only way I can't repair both engines is that I'm dead before I finish the second."

Gorgas tried once more. "At three-quarter's power . . ."

"By the Bull, Gorgas!" Bhatterji explained as to a child. "You saw the damage. Could you repair *either* one in only five days? No one can. Not me, not even Enver Koch. So blitzing one cage just isn't an option. It's *got* to be both."

Gorgas sighed. "Very well." He had expected as much, but had thought the chance worth pursuing. He wondered though whether the impossibility of a five-day blitz repair were a fact of nature or of the engineer's legendary inertia. He called up a planning matrix on his screen. "Here is the plan I prepared. I would like you to—"

"That *you* prepared . . ."

"Yes. While I was waiting for you to report. Time not wasted, eh? I would like you to review it and make any changes or modifications that you think are needed. I will expect the engines calibrated and ready by no later than the twenty-eighth. Oh. One other matter. The damaged lithium pump served engines Two and Three."

"And the south pump serves One and Four. What of it?"

"It struck me as curious. Why not One and Two on the first pump and Three and Four on the second?"

Bhatterji, for just a moment, could not process the question. It seemed to emanate from another pocket universe. The words were Anglo but, strung together like that, made no sense. "I don't know," said Bhatterji, choosing the only possible response.

Gorgas frowned. "Two and Three sum to five; and so do One and Four. I had thought there might be some significance in that."

Now Bhatterji frowned. "I don't think it matters," he said slowly.

"Very well." This, briskly. "Then there is no need to renumber them. Now, you are confident that you can restore *both* engines, and to *full* power?"

It was a request for reassurance, but Bhatterji took it as a token of doubt, which infuriated him still further. "Of course," he said.

"And within *nineteen* days."

The second *of course* was not coarse at all, the words having been ground fine by Bhatterji's teeth.

"Because, at our current velocity," Gorgas continued, "and at full deboost, it will take this vessel two-hundred and sixty-three megaklicks to slow down to the Jupiter datum."

The engineer unsnapped and kicked his way to the door. The way he looked at things, this meeting had used up an hour and a half of those nineteen days.

"I shall want daily progress reports on the status of the repairs," Gorgas said to his back, but Bhatterji ignored him.

When the engineer had gone, Gorgas returned to his personal quarters, adjacent to the day room. He called up the waybills detailing their various cargo consignments and compared the promised delivery dates against the revised ETA, given that the ship would be coasting for a week or more. He had bid low on the contracts in an effort to win them from faster ships, but that left only a razor profit margin. Late delivery would likely mean no repeat business with that client. Checking the penalty clauses, he estimated the probable losses; then, as he frowned over the unpleasantness of the result, thought of five things that might delay or impede Bhatterji's repairs.

He knew he ought to recalculate the losses for each of the thirty-one combinations of the five potential delays, but "worse" was probably a close-enough approximation for now. Instead, to relax and forget his troubles, he called up the Alamein Campaign onto the wall screen at the point when the Libyan 1st and 2nd Mechanized Brigades had overrun the surprised Egyptian battalion at Sidi Omar. There was a strong position on the Halfaya Pass around which he could build a counterattack, but the situation southward toward Siwa was precarious.

The Engineer's Mate

Bhatterji resembled Grubb in the following manner. The cook could, from any random set of ingredients, concoct a meal. It might not be cordon bleu, but it would serve. Similarly, Bhatterji could concoct a repair from almost any random collection of parts and materials. It would not be OEM, but it would work. This was a valuable talent to have, because the *River* carried nowhere near the number and variety of parts that would be needed to restore two slagged Farnsworth cages to as-built condition.

The *River* lived from hand to mouth, poor even for a tramp. The difference between FOB and COD could be critical to her financial existence. During her more than two decades of tramping, onboard repair-and-maintenance inventory had been slashed and then slashed again. Reorder levels had been lowered and some part numbers dropped entirely, all in the name of reduced operating cost. Other items had been sold and pawned and bartered. After all, at constant boost no replacement was more than a month or so away. Why shlep?

Unless you slagged two engines at once. Coasting did not mean that *The River* wouldn't get where she were going—at present velocity, she would reach Jupiter eighteen days *sooner* than in the flight plan—but in this case, sooner meant later, because she would also arrive eighteen days before Jupiter did. Space-faring shared many traditions with seafaring, but not the one in which ports of call remained fixed.

However, the repairs, though extensive, ought not be beyond the skills of an experienced engineer and a bright, if green, mate. Some of the more routine work could even be farmed out to Ratline and his wranglers.

Bhatterji would have jumped right into the work—sooner begun, sooner done—but Miko insisted on checking inventory first and Bhatterji was inclined to humor his mate. Where he had grudged Gorgas an hour, he gladly gave Miko half a day. But then, he did not desire Gorgas.

"There ought to be nine Sheffield brackets in here!" Miko complained when, working down the list of required components, they found that particular dog box empty.

"It's not a high-use item." Bhatterji was philosophical about the lack. Book count, the engineer believed, was only cause for agitation. That it would ever match the physical count was a fable believed only by accountants and small children.

He envisioned flat stock bent, folded, and pierced. A straightforward machining operation. He would give it to Evermore to do. The boy was a fair hand with an omnitool, for all that he was prone to perfectionism and creativity. Bhatterji thought no great ill of either the perfect or the creative, but sometimes they were the enemy of the good enough. Evermore would file and plate and polish, intent on producing the very best Sheffield bracket that had ever been produced, even when only a rough-out was called for . . . unless some notion seized the boy halfway through and the brackets mutated into Kress flanges on a whim. Evermore would produce *art* where only *craft* was needed. Bhatterji himself was something of a showman, but he distrusted artists. He regarded Evermore as a trainer does a colt: eager, but lacking in discipline. The boy needed a master to take him in hand, save that the hand had already been rebuffed.

"There were twenty-one Sheffields on the previous purchase order," Miko said, recalling him to the present, "and only twelve were used."

Bhatterji grunted and leaned across Miko's shoulder. "Let

me see the screen." When he saw Koch's old entry, he knew what must have happened.

"Those brackets come at a dozen the crate," he said. "Enver probably needed some for an overhaul—What's the date on that purchase order? Yes, see there? I told you they weren't used much—so he ordered a crate from, let's see . . . from White and Hammontree at Agamemnon."

"But . . ."

"Miko, twelve brackets were bought and twelve were used, and all the keystroke errors in the Middle System will not conjure nine more from the aether."

Shortages in themselves did not bother Bhatterji. Record-keeping had never been a great concern of his. As he liked to say, there were always workarounds. He could even admit that he enjoyed hacking the workaround far more than the plug-and-play of routine repair. He and Miko spent the remains of the day and a large portion of the evening adjusting Gorgas's plan in light of the shortages. (What really bothered Bhatterji, what frosted him thicker than the Europa ice shell was how much Gorgas had gotten right. The man wasn't entitled!) Bhatterji made a few other alterations as a matter of engineering style and also because, like any dog, he had to pee on the hydrant to make it his. Miko found standardized fabrication procedures in Ship's deeby for most of the missing parts, scribbled new ones for two of the others, created a PERT using some old program management software lurking in the ship's library, and estimated probable completion times and let the AI identify the Critical Path. Bhatterji didn't see the need for all the detail work. That wasn't how the cat learned to swim! But Miko liked things neat and orderly and, being green, held to the sides of the pool.

Still, even the longest day draws closed, and Bhatterji finally called a halt. "If we push it any more," he explained, "we'll muff and have to redo it anyway come morning. Why don't we head for my quarters and decompress."

Miko barely hesitated. "Sure, Mr. Bhatterji. I'd like that."

"Ram," Bhatterji said. "Off-duty, I'm 'the Ram.' "

And the Ram was ready for duty. Bhatterji had denied himself for a very long time, and the frustrated longing, building from Amalthea to Achilles to the Trojan Gulf, had become itself an exquisite sort of pleasure. The mate too had become aware of his gaze and posed deliberately to attract it. So, while Bhatterji had unspoken motives in proposing the invitation, Miko had some too in accepting. Youth, after all, was the new wine, awaiting only the corkscrew to pour itself forth.

The River being a former luxury ship, Bhatterji had installed himself in a four-room suite in C-ring, lower deck, and decorated it to his own taste. This meant a certain amount of sports memorabilia. Holograms of young men jumping and throwing and grabbing. A stunning, candid portrait of Theo Cruz-O Malley at the Summer Games in Brasilia: muscles bunched, arm extended in a spray of sweat, his grimace of pain just shading into triumph because he had *known* the moment he released that discus that it would travel farther than any ever had before. But there was also a surprising layer of beauty in the decor beyond even the beauty of men's bodies in exertion. The colors were the sharp grays and pinks and blacks of the "Noovo Decaux" style of the late Eighties, but with the severe linearity broken here and there by the wild disarray of float-flowers in globular vases and spare Japanese scroll paintings. The sleeping cage was padded in satin and featured handholds and stirrups for the leverage so needed in free fall when one slept unalone.

Miko stopped before a large black-and-white digigraph. The face was that of a stranger, square and sharp and deeply lined. His close-cropped hair was a brilliant white; his cheeks stubbled salt and pepper for want of shaving. The smile was one of quiet satisfaction; and the squinting eyes looked on something farther off than the camera.

"Who is that?" Miko asked, accepting the squeeze bottle Bhatterji offered.

Bhatterji's glance was one of long familiarity. "Enver Bey Koch."

"He's the man who tumbled last year." It was not a question, but Bhatterji answered anyway.

"Yes," he heard himself say. "He was the man who tumbled. I was his mate for four years."

"Mr. Grubb told me about it."

"He would. He's like an old woman, Grubb is."

"He's fun to listen to."

The flash of jealousy was brief, for the chief did not play in Bhatterji's arena. Bhatterji saluted the photograph with his bottle. "Here's to you, Enver. Who's like you?"

Miko, after a moment, imitated the gesture. "Here's to you." Then, after a thoughtful sip, said, "He looks like a strong man. I mean inside. He knows what he wants to do and he's going to do it—and he knows he will do it well."

"All that from a digigraph?" Bhatterji was amused at the critique, and not only because it was accurate.

"All that from a digigraph," Miko agreed. "It's a fine portrait. It captures the man."

Bhatterji shrugged. "Digitogophy is only a hobby of mine, but I think I've gained some facility at it."

"You did that?" Miko's surprise was feigned. Grubb had already mentioned Bhatterji's hobby. This one, anyway.

"I have . . . other digigraphs I could show you."

"Maybe you could capture my portrait too someday?"

"A nude, maybe," Bhatterji suggested with desperate flippancy.

"Maybe." Miko had not brought too many inhibitions into the room and wasted little time in discarding them. And beside, Bhatterji had spiked the neer.

Now, alcohol on board spacecraft had been forbidden under the Prague Convention of 2042, following the *City of Halifax* disaster. The *Halifax*'s sail tangle in itself had been repairable, but alcohol inhibits oxygen take-up by the cells, and the bends immobilized the sailors when they went down to suit pressure to cut away the shrouds. Unable to tack into braking orbit, the Great Sail and all 217 souls aboard impacted 47 kilometers southeast of Sojourner Truth.

Which meant that what Bhatterji stashed in his quarters was illegal under international law. But then Bhatterji himself was illegal in more than a few jurisdictions. His was an analog, not a digital soul; that is, he believed in a graduated temperance, rather than in a strict binomial prohibition. Neither he nor Miko would be depressurizing soon enough for a little alcohol to matter.

At least, that was Bhatterji's opinion. Miko had heard rumors of the stash from the wranglers and from Eaton Grubb, who seemed to know every scrap of gossip on the ship. The defiance of law and regulation seemed only slightly more alarming than the winkage implicit in the general awareness. Yet, forbidden fruit entices, and Miko was not immune to its allure.

Bhatterji was neither fool nor predator. He wanted Miko more than he wanted anything on the ship other than the anode grids for Number Two; but he wanted Miko's love and assent even more. So it was not to seduce that he spiked the near-beer he handed his assistant. He added only a tincture, enough to relax without clouding the judgment.

Of course, an epidemic runs with greater fire through a virgin field than it does through a robust, immunized population. It was the *idea* of alcohol, not the alcohol itself that intoxicated Miko. If one is eager to shed inhibitions, why any excuse will do! Intoxication is a state of mind. Men have gotten drunk on power, or love, or the glory of God.

Bhatterji did not turn down the lights. He did not play seduction games, or at least he believed that he did not. He did put a soft jazz-raga on the player, but only because he enjoyed the endless, intricate improvisations of the Forties and would have played one even had he been alone. Like the decor, the music dated him. There was something profoundly old-fashioned about the engineer, as if he had inexplicably found himself in the wrong decade. One expected cheek whiskers or moiré suits.

The lack of acceleration added a playful element to their tête-à-tête. He and Miko would drift around their several axes on the whimsies of a gesture, and they took to grabbing and tugging on one another to check their motions. This caused Miko to laugh in delight and Bhatterji to delight in the laugh.

"I'm drunk," Miko explained. Bhatterji, who knew to the dram how little he had spiked the neer, smiled and said nothing.

They discussed the repairs, and Bhatterji pressed his optimism until Miko agreed that it was simply a matter of time and sweat. "It's not like I haven't had to duct-tape this old bucket a time or two in the past," Bhatterji said. "It'll take a week, maybe two. Balk line isn't until the thirty-first, so there's no urgency. Best to do it right."

"How long have you been aboard the *River*?"

Miko already knew the answer, but Bhatterji knew the conversation was mere prelude, a dance. "Four years," he said. "No, five. Before that . . . Well, that was before."

"Where were you before?"

Bhatterji's hesitation was fractional, but real. "Some things," he said, "I don't talk about. There was a man, years ago. He's dead."

"Grubb says you were escaping from the police."

"Grubb doesn't know everything. Only Evan Hand knew everything, and Hand—" Now what could he say about Evan Dodge Hand without pricking old sores?

"I thought there might be an exciting story there. I was escaping too and the captain helped me get away."

Bhatterji knew a moment of sadness, of the irretrievable recession of the past. Old friends, gone; old memories, forgotten. Matters known once but to three, then two, now known only to one. "He was a good man," he said. "A good man." Gorgas's great problem, the engineer decided, was that he would never be Evan Hand.

"I know." Miko's eye had begun to tear. Bhatterji was close enough to brush it away with his thumb.

"It was less than murder," he said. Then, to Miko's enquiring gaze: "Why I was anxious to leave Outerhab-by-Titan. It was less than murder, but more than a parking ticket." It occurred to him suddenly that, with Jupiter and Saturn in superior conjunction as they were, he was as far from Outerhab as it was possible to get in human space.

Miko said, "I think you're a dangerous man with a mysterious past."

"The past is like an ass. Everyone has one, but you're mighty particular who you show it to."

"I'm not that particular," Miko said.

"About showing me your past?"

Miko laughed at the feigned confusion. "That too." Bhatterji put an arm around Miko's shoulders and Miko leaned against his breast. "Do you know what life is like on an asteroid farm?" his mate said quietly. "There's no rest; there's no time to be yourself. Standing watch from wake-up to sleep, except for the Board's mandated school time. Monitor the oxygen, monitor the mass growth, crawl out and splice a wire, replenish the culture vats. Harvest and dehydrate and compact and bale. Then load the freighter when it docks. And don't be too slow and don't let the mass spoil or you'd get a beating within an inch of your life."

Bhatterji hesitated. "I'm sure your parents loved you," he ventured.

"I'm sure they would have too."

Bhatterji pondered the tenses, and found the meaning in the depths of Miko's eyes.

"Mom died when I was five and Pa, something went out of him. He couldn't make a go of it anymore." Miko snuggled against him while speaking, nestled in the crook of Bhatterji's arm. "He heard about jobs up Europa-way. Good pay, but no place to take a kid. So, when I was six, he signed over everything he owned to a neighbor to pay for my keep and promised he'd be back when he made his nut."

"But he never came back," Bhatterji guessed.

Miko's head jerked. "No. He must have been killed in the ice mines. He would have come back, otherwise. He would have sent word if he'd been able."

"Yes," said Bhatterji, who was not so sure as all that. "Of course, he would have." And it might even have been true. As the song had it: *The ice of Europa is laced with red blood.* Jupiter kneaded her moons with cruel indifference to the men and women who prowled on and under their surfaces.

"The moment the torch lit on the shuttle," Miko went on, "Clavis Burr took everything for himself. Suddenly he had equipment, and stock in the Company, and title to three more ministroids in the Jovian Ring, and I was day labor on one of his farms. I hated him for that. He broke his word to my father. *He spent my life!*"

Bhatterji stroked Miko's stubbled scalp. "Ah, Miko," he said sadly.

"I took it as long as I could. There were years, when I was six, seven, when I waited each day to see my father walk through the portal at BurrFarm Number Three and sweep me away. I was too young to understand what he meant about coming back. I thought it would be only a few days. So every morning I woke up and I thought, Today! And every evening I went to bed and prayed, Tomorrow! But before long there had been too many tomorrows and I knew he was never ever coming back. After a while, I could not even . . . not even remember what he looked like."

Bhatterji held Miko tight. "It's all right now," he said. "It's all right now."

Miko laid a hand on Bhatterji's thigh. "I ran away as soon as I was able. I was twelve, I think. Do you know how easy it is to lose yourself in a warren? There are passageways and tunnels. Panels no one opens unless something's foo. I lived in the walls of Amalthea, coming out for food—or to sabotage a piece of Burr equipment. That's how I learned engineering." A bitter laugh. "By reverse engineering. I learned how to build by taking things apart. I lived to strike back at him; to make him hurt for what he'd done. Then, one day, I heard that the Board would hold a town meeting at Amalthea Center and I broke into the room through a ventilation duct and denounced Burr to the governors."

"Did they believe you?"

"Some did. Burr jumped up and called me a crazy kid and a runaway and a vagrant; but some others who were there remembered how rich he had suddenly gotten after my father had boarded me with him. The governors promised an inquiry and Burr promised to see me dead." Miko sighed. "I don't think I would have minded dying, then, if I could just pull him down with me. It was touch and go for a while, though the Board finally did take Burr down—but a dead snake still tries to bite. Burr knew how to buy men who would kill for money and the money had already been paid. By then, I knew every passage and tunnel in the warren, so if I didn't want to be found, I wasn't found. When the company cops finally tracked down the assassin, they found he hadn't paid enough attention to his helmet seals."

Bhatterji shuddered. "A gruesome end for anyone."

But Miko only shrugged. "A peaceful end, if you ask me. You pass out from anoxia before your head explodes. Well, he came looking for trouble and he found it, and how many men find what they seek so quickly? The worst part afterward was the anticlimax. I dreamed for years of destroying Burr. It was all I lived for. Now he was down, and I had nothing."

"And so, enter Evan Hand."

Miko brushed a tear. "He offered me a berth and I took it."

The line between compassion and desire is a fine one. The heart does not always note it. It is as fine a line as the one between the hunter and the hunted. The dance passes across the boundary, the roles grow blurred. In the end, the prey seeks the spear and impales itself upon it. Bhatterji held Miko's head and pressed a kiss, and Miko responded as if the engineer had blown across hot coals.

So intent was Bhatterji on the kisses and on the eager unfastenings that followed that it was only when Miko was naked that the engineer realized what half the crew had always known.

"You're a girl!"

Miko tossed her head and said, "I'm a *woman!*"

A solemn protest, though on the evidence not quite true. It is a rare woman who can pass for a young boy, even among the elfin folk of the lesser moons. "How old are you?" Bhatterji demanded, even as he wondered on which scale one measured the age of children like Miko.

"Old enough," she said, "to know what I want."

Is anyone ever old enough for that? Miko was secretive by nature and, until she had blurted out her life history to Bhatterji, had not spoken more than a few words in all the time she had been aboard. Yet the engineer's ignorance was vincible. He had seen what he longed for most and had not questioned it. If

Evermore had not so thoroughly rejected him, he might have looked more closely. But then, he had always confused *woman* with *feminine* and feminine was among those many things that Miko was not.

"I need you!" Miko insisted, not yet having understood the nature of Bhatterji's refusal. "I'm ready. I want you." She was very near pleading—she *was* pleading—still half-drunk with the thought of her blooming. Understandable, that she would have misread Bhatterji's flamboyant virility. If the engineer had seen his own desires in his androgynous mate; why, so had the mate seen in him.

"You want your father," Bhatterji thought with his mouth. "And now Evan Hand is dead."

Miko did not thank him for the insight. Instead, she slapped him across the face with unrestrained fury and fled, weeping and naked, into Corridor C where, without even noticing, she nearly collided with the passenger, Bigelow Fife, who (watching the teenager's retreat) wondered into what antic sort of ship he had booked his passage.

The Passenger

Bigelow Fife was possessed of an inquisitive mind. His profession as troubleshooter had made him so, unless it had been his mind's bent that had led him to troubleshooting. It was a happy marriage, however it came about—certainly happier than any of the other marriages he had essayed—and it afforded him multiple opportunities for enjoyment; for if there is one thing of which the world has no insufficiency, it is trouble worth the shooting. He was a devotee of Truth and Fact and enjoyed collecting bits of them, keeping them in a box in the back of his head and occasionally stirring them up and arranging them in various patterns.

He defined a problem as "the gap between 'as-is' and 'should-be'" and immediately noted the existence of his chosen prey on board *The River of Stars*.

The ship is coasting when it should be accelerating, he wrote in his journal. Of course, no great subtlety of thought was required to discern this. Lesser minds than his had already noticed the situation. Where he differed was in his reaction. He became something of an art critic. *This is clearly a situation in which urgency is the governing priority. Certainly, there is impact*—He wrote this with no sense of irony—*but the impending deadline is clearly the most stringent constraint. If the engines are not back on line by the thirty-first, the ship will be too fast to enter Jupiter Roads, which will delay our arrival. Therefore*—He used *therefore* a great deal when he wrote—*Therefore, efforts ought to hinge on ensuring the* timing *of the solution rather than its* expense. *Alacrity without haste is called for*. He was also fond of the epigram, which he could coin like a national mint, albeit one short of precious metals. He did not wonder whether a deadline might be anything other than "impending."

It must not be supposed that Fife was unaware of the sea of humanity in which he swam. He engaged it with gusto. Consider Dr. Wong. Unfortunately, he engaged the animate using the same tools with which he engaged the inanimate, which is rather like employing a cold chisel for heart surgery. His penchant for Truth and Fact had left a wake in his life in which bobbed three ex-wives, as many ex-lovers, and a son who had not spoken to him in five years. These estrangements puzzled him, and from time to time he worked the problem. It was on his to-do list, and occasionally he added data, searching for the root cause.

Criticism being a parasitical occupation, every critic needs an artist.

Bhatterji had begun fabrication of the missing spares and the machine shop was a-hum with the sounds of metal and plastic and composite as they yielded to his will and became something more. Some pieces were built or assembled or shaped on automatic tools, which he and Miko had spent the morning programming. Others, however, required the human touch, which Bhatterji provided.

As he grew progressively aware that he was being watched, Bhatterji added little filips to his labors. Everything he did, he did with a flourish. He didn't just turn a hand tool, he tossed it spinning and caught it on the shy turn. He didn't merely insert a laser welder inside an orifice; he made a rapier thrust that unerringly found its mark. He was a virtuoso of the machine shop and didn't mind a bit if everyone else knew too. Life was a goddam performance, and that meant there ought to be applause. That he might appear clownish (or worse, inefficient) to an onlooker did not occur to him, though it certainly did to Bigelow Fife, who scowled and made notes. It was a natural mistake on Fife's part. Bhatterji was not an artist, but a performer. The critical standards are different.

That someone was watching, Bhatterji could see from the drift of Miko's eyes. "Watch closely as I apply the tool to the working surface," the engineer said. Miko glanced across his shoulder and he added, more brusquely than he had intended, "Pay attention."

The tool was sharp, but Miko's glance, sharper. It was in little ways like this that they discussed the previous evening.

She assisted him dutifully: fetching bar stock, sharpening tools, catching shavings in a vacuum hood lest they spread and damage intakes and ducts. Bhatterji missed the bond that had been between them and he did not know whether it was recoverable or not. Rework is never quite the same as new, relationships being no different from engines in that regard. He could not fathom why Miko had deceived him. When he thought about what had happened the previous night in his quarters, it was with embarrassment and a touch of regret that a girl so boyish in appearance could not, in fact, be a boy.

Nevertheless, if there were no longer devotion, there was duty. Miko was his mate and he owed her the instruction he would have given any other apprentice. And so this morning they stood across the omnitool from each other, feet firmly planted in the stirrups for leverage, and if neither the engineer nor the mate quite acted as if nothing had gone askew between them, it was not for lack of trying.

"I tie into the database template, thus. The turn should remain within the specified tolerance. But remember that when the ship is under acceleration, there will be a tendency to favor the aftward direction due to deflection. The deflection will be on the order of nanometers, but that can be critical for certain components." He raised his head, caught Miko's eyes as they began to drift again. "Understand?"

Miko's nod was neither eager nor affirming, but only a curt acknowledgement, all that the detestable man deserved. She could not understand why Bhatterji had teased her so with promises, only to humiliate her. She had imagined being ravished by this solid, brutally-shaped man; had imagined a faux resistance—the No that meant Yes. To find herself rebuffed, and insulted in the bargain . . .

Peeking through the ventilation grilles of Amalthea, Miko had watched the act in all its permutations, from the furtive to the enthusiastic to the merely compliant. Yet it remained for her only something observed and not something felt. She was dying of thirst, but had never tasted water.

She ought to cut him, slice off those treasured parts of him; but the ship needed his skills, and Miko felt a hard loyalty to the ship and to the late and ever-more-regretted Evan Hand. Once the ship was back in operation . . . She had waited a long time to revenge herself on Clavis Burr. She could wait her revenge on Bhatterji as well, and savor the anticipation.

Miko did not know what the mushroom-skinned passenger wanted. He simply hung about in the back of the machine shop and stared at them with what she took to be a supercilious curl to his lip. Perhaps it was directed at the engineer.

Or perhaps not. Miko had noticed the man in the corridors from time to time and wondered why he pranced about naked—or as near to it as failed to matter. If it was to show off his body, he needed a better show, because the muscle tone was so poor that he seemed more a gelatinous mold of a man than the genuine article.

Unfair, she told herself. Bhatterji had the look of hard-edged masculinity, yet the athletic shell of muscle and poise contained a boy-lover. So symmetry might demand that the passenger's repellant appearance conceal a kind and loving nature. She noticed the bulge in his shorts and wondered if it were not herself that he had come to gaze upon. Miko tossed her head in what she imagined was a sultry, feminine gesture—earning no response from the mushroom man and another rebuke from Bhatterji to pay attention.

But Fife was there simply to see how the work was progressing and had no interest in the sexual farce that had played out in engineering. It was the omnitool that he concentrated on, that and the part taking shape. He had seen the girl naked—and in a way she too was a part taking shape—but he had seen her with a curious disinterest. Lunatics, stripped for the sunlamps that lined their tunnels, saw too many teats and cods to be much taken with any particular instance of them. Yet, were he not already smitten with Wong, he might have considered the girl's potential. Down in the bone, all he required was willingness.

"He wants me," Miko told Bhatterji when, after a few pointed questions that showed the man no stranger to a machine shop, Fife had left and they were cleaning their tools and racking them away.

"What? Who?" The engineer's thoughts, like Fife's had been centered on the job. "What are you talking about?"

"The passenger. He wants to fuck me. He was hard for me." Miko wanted Bhatterji to know what he was missing; to know that she was desirable to real men.

But Bhatterji was immune to that sort of innuendo. "Fife? He's a Lunatic. They all wear codpieces. Well, the men do. I don't know why."

Miko flushed because, having been reminded, she now recalled hearing that about Lunar customs. "I don't care. He wants me. I could tell by the way his eyes raped me."

"He looks at everything that way. He does have strange eyes. They never seem still. Why are you so determined to abase yourself, Miko? When the time comes, find someone who cares about you."

"What would you know about it?"

Bhatterji shrugged. "Why not Evermore? He's closer to your own age."

"He's a *boy*. A *woman* wants a *man*."

It was so comical that Bhatterji wanted to cry. He himself had wanted Evermore *because* he was a boy.

Acting Captain Gorgas regarded Fife as little more than an especially animate piece of cargo. He thought to encounter the man periodically and exchange ritual greetings; he expected to entertain him formally at the captain's table once a week. He did *not* expect the cargo to come into his dayroom and demand an accounting of his stewardship.

A plaint about the damaged comm, surely. Passengers were forever calling ahead. And they might ask about ETA, since by definition passengers had to be somewhere, sometime. But they did not ask about repair plans and PERT schedules and resource allocation.

"Don't you worry, Mr. Fife," he said heartily when Fife had run down his list of concerns. "We have everything well in hand."

If it irritated Gorgas to be asked impertinent questions, imagine how it irritated Fife to receive impertinent answers. If there was one thing he knew about—and there were actually two or three—it was inserting bodies into trajectories and while the bodies he moved about generally fell free, their behavior was not in principle different from a torch ship. "Your engineer seems to be taking his time about things," the Lunatic snapped. (He had watched the man *play* at fabrication. Dancing and prancing . . . The wasted effort! The wasted motion! Why, there had not even been any prints in view! How could the engineer remember all the specifications and tolerances? A few questions afterward had sufficed to reveal that the man had no real plans at all. Fife had itched to take the matter in hand and lay out more efficient schedules and procedures. It was what he did for a living.) "You are aware, I suppose, that this ship must begin deceleration within the next seventeen days?"

While Gorgas agreed regarding Bhatterji's pace and his bent for improvisational theater, he was not about to say so to a mere

passenger. "I assure you, we are on top of things." Gorgas knew
Fife was a corporate troubleshooter, but that did not signify. In
the first place, there was no trouble to shoot. Bhatterji knew
what needed doing; it was just a matter of his doing it. And in
the second place, in a world partitioned into crew and cargo, it
never even occurred to him to ask for Fife's assistance. Being
on the passenger manifest, Fife was manifestly a passenger.

"You *do* have contingency plans . . ." Fife suggested. This
was as close as he came to offering the help that was not requested and, when the captain replied, "Of course," he gave the
matter no further thought. He had resigned himself already to a
late arrival at Dinwoody Poke, and a sensible man did not rail
against that which he could not alter. For all the confidence he
had in his own abilities, he was not a forward man. Not that he
was shy, but he needed some sign of welcome; if not a glowing
cross in the heavens, then at least an open coverall zipper. *In
hoc signo, venerio.*

Yet, Fife's visit had given Gorgas something to ponder and, as
he was a ponderous sort of man, Gorgas spent the evening in
consultation with the ship's AI, creating scenarios on his
pixwall. Each man pursues his own pleasures, and such was
Gorgas's solitary vice.

(Gorgas did not spurn the other vices, but he knew enough
not to seek them among his own crew. It was bad for discipline.
A captain ought not to have special friends. It could lead to the
appearance of favoritism or, worse, to the reality of it. And so,
from the moment when he had realized that the helm of *The
River of Stars* would one day be forced upon him, he had en-
deavored to avoid friendships. In this he had succeeded, and
with such wholehearted cooperation on the part of the crew that
the choice could hardly be said to have been entirely his.)

Gorgas excelled at chess because he could foresee the
branching forest of possibilities as it twisted serpentine into the
future. He could think ten moves deep. Not that the ability
guaranteed victory—sometimes he only saw defeat the
sooner—but working out the possibilities gave him the sort of
pleasure that Bhatterji found in mentoring likely young lads, or

that Corrigan found in rereading a favorite old text, or that Ratline found when he shut himself alone inside his rooms.

There was no end of contingencies, since anything done could be done wrong. The recovery plans themselves could go awry, and so there must be contingencies even for the contingencies. Most of these would never be called upon—when you worked the probabilities, they were less likely than Satterwaithe's smile—but they must be contemplated, even if only to be dismissed. Bhatterji might misalign the rings; or the motor on the omnitool might short out; or there might be insufficient stock of the superconducting hobartium. In fact, when one considered how many things could possibly go wrong, it was a miracle that anything ever went right.

Bhatterji had estimated a completion time, but Gorgas knew the work would take longer. That was why he set the completion date for the twenty-eighth. There was an inherent asymmetry to the universe. When the unexpected happened—and it always did, for the unexpected was, paradoxically, the most expected thing—it seldom resulted in faster and smoother operations. Adding the extreme time estimates along the critical path of the engineer's nominal repair plan, Gorgas noted that the resulting two-week drift toward the sun would bring them to the outer reaches of the Virgin Islands. That suggested a whole new suite of externally induced, class II failure modes, not least of which was collision with a rogue worldlet lately teased out of the Belt. The orbits of such bodies were "chaotic," so that they appeared by mischief. The joke among navigators was that the ephemeredes were out of date the moment they were computed.

Still, no stone ought go unturned, especially stones of such size as the 'Stroids. Gorgas smiled briefly at his internal joke. At one-fifty kiss, even a small fragment could do much damage. In fact, now that he thought on it, a small fragment had already done much damage.

Yet, if the odds on such a collision were vanishing small, those on *two* collisions were small squared. Infinitesimal. And given that one had already occurred—

Gorgas knew again the chill he had felt during Bhatterji's

original damage survey. There are many clichés and proverbs to voice his unease. *Birds of a feather flock together*, is what Fife might have said, had he pondered the matter. But Gorgas did not think in clichés. Or he did, but they were a different order of cliché; namely: *The multiplication of probabilities applies only to independent, random events*. "But those are mere assumptions," he reminded himself. In the real world, events often proved dependent or nonrandom and one must resort to conditional probabilities. Given that one collision has *already* occurred, what *then* is the likelihood of another? An altogether different proposition, because it depended on *why* so unlikely a thing had happened in the first place.

He drafted a memo to Corrigan requesting an analysis of all Known Bodies in the Outer Belt—in particular, of the Hildas and the Friggas—whose orbits may have been perturbed by the recent Jovian passage, and another to The Lotus Jewel stressing the importance of restoring full power to the forward sensor array. He was forever writing such memos; so much so, that their value had responded to the inexorable law of supply and demand. Unknown to Gorgas, a rule had arisen among the rest of the crew: *if he really wants it, he'll ask a second time*.

After Ship had dispatched the memos, Gorgas set up the Battle of Cerro Gordo on his pixwall. Gorgas preferred such simulations to standard chess because, there being so many more pieces with so many more move options, the game was more challenging and the outcome less predictable. He chose the Mexican side for the same reason. Santa Ana should not have lost the battle, despite the superior American artillery. Pillow had utterly bungled his attack and Twiggs had deviated from Scott's orders. Santa Anna's problem, Gorgas had once decided, was that while he was a better general than history had judged him, he was not nearly so good a one as he had judged himself. A more humble man, more willing to listen to his officers, would have triumphed and set history upon a different course.

It was the custom of the old magsail hands to gather for dinner every Thursday in the officer's mess, in consequence of which they called themselves the Thursday Group. Corrigan, Satterwaithe, and Ratline took turns funding the meal from their personal accounts. Sometimes The Lotus Jewel or Grubb joined them or, by special dispensation, the First Wrangler, who was neither officer nor chief. The cook and the wrangler, in particular, were much taken by the romance of sailing days and enjoyed especially Ratline's yarns, for he could spin tales of the *River* herself. (So could Satterwaithe, at least one tale, though she never spoke of it and the others who knew never asked.) Hand, who had also flown sails, used to preside at these meals, although he never heaped scorn on the Farnsworths as the others did. He had guided sails and he had guided torches, he used to say. It's the guidance that matters, not the device.

From time to time, the other officers had eaten with the Thursday Group, by invitation or at Hand's backstage urging. Gorgas had sat silent throughout the entire meal, or rather had spoken so rarely as to do for silence. The Thursday Group had taken that as a token of unfriendliness and had not invited the First back. Enver Koch's unfriendliness had risen above mere tokenism. He had peppered the meal with his own anecdotes: stories in which, somehow, sailors came off second-best to engineers. It hadn't helped that Koch had been a young engineer's mate in the *FS Forrest Calhoun* during her infamous race with *MS The River of Stars*. It helped rather less that he brought the matter up at meal. The sailors had not wished him dead, but they had shed few tears afterward.

Bhatterji, they never bothered to invite. "I'm a trifle too old for the likes of him," said little Timmy Ratline through the mouth of the old man he had become.

Ivar Akhaturian delivered the main course in a shining, self-contained serving vessel, which he laid on the suction grid in the center of the table before fishtailing off to see what further task Grubb had for him. Ratline loaned his wranglers out to the other departments. While he would never have admitted it to his charges, wranglers had little to do when the ship was in transit. Besides, the youngsters really ought to learn the ship, and that meant doing all the scut work.

"Ah," said Corrigan as he slid open the lid on the serving vessel. "Greased weasel."

Bigelow Fife drew back a bit and a look of profound uncertainty replaced the hunger that had been there. The Thursday Group had invited the passenger to their mess. At least he's a new face, Ratline had told his tablemates. He might even have something new to say. "Greased weasel," Fife repeated, though not in so agreeable a tone as the Second had used.

Ratline cackled. "We only *call* it greased weasel. It's really a gelatinized blend of the protein masses that Grubb gets when he cleans out his vats for a new culture. It's got a better texture than your usual cow pie or fowl matter. Chewier." He reached out and carved a slice off the end. Steam rose from the interior. "It doesn't hurt that it's a little gluey, either," he continued while he put it on his suction plate. "That way it doesn't float off when you're not looking. I hate chasing my dinner across the room."

Reassured, Fife nodded. "He's done it up well. I never saw vat scrapings *molded* before." He squinted. "It almost does look like a weasel, if that's what a weasel looks like."

Corrigan had to parse the sentence twice before he was certain; but, yes, the bleach-faced Lunatic had made a joke. It was unexpected enough that Corrigan laughed aloud, which earned him a puzzled glance from Satterwaithe.

Fife commented that galleys on commercial liners gave more quotidian names to the meals they harvested, but Ratline disagreed. "Oh, we called 'em such, an' worse, back in Toledo's day. Just never told the passengers. Ah, here comes the barbed wire."

Akhauturian brought out a mass of rough vines—extrusions wound into a ball on the end of a wooden paddle and baked to a crispness. He fastened the handle into its table socket while Ratline nodded to Satterwaithe. "Captain, if you would do the honors?" Satterwaithe reached into the knot and, with a snap of her wrist, pulled off a handful, after which the other diners grabbed handfuls too. Corrigan's extra reach always gave him an advantage at this.

"It's quite good," Fife said. "Almost like taffy. The sort we serve in Luna is crispier. We call it 'deep-fried spaghetti.' "

"You have to snap it off," Ratline explained. "If you pull it slow-like, it only stretches out."

Fife tasted. "Raspberry?"

"Grubb's got all sorts of fragrances and flavors. He's mixed some interesting blends. Sometimes he puts a treat at the center of the ball before he runs it through the spinner."

Fife pursed his lips. "The flavor doesn't quite go with the texture this time. But, as you say, 'interesting.' " He dabbed at his lips. "Tell me, Mr. Ratline. You are after calling Mistress Satterwaithe, 'captain.' I thought custom permitted only one captain per ship."

The Thursday Group exchanged glances. "It's because Eugenie is presiding this week," Corrigan explained after a slight pause. "*Captain* comes from *caput*, which meant *head* in Latin, and Eugenie is sitting at the *head* of the table."

Fife nodded. "I see." Although he decidedly did not. The glance his messmates had exchanged was enough to tell him that some other story lurked beneath so Latinate an explanation.

"Eugenie is third mate," Corrigan continued, casting a different sort of look at the president of the mess. "And sailing master." Satterwaithe returned the gaze with a bland stare, saying much in a sphinxlike fashion.

Fife raised his eyebrows. "The ship carries a master?"

"Officially, *The River* is a hybrid ship," Satterwaithe explained. "The sails are stowed on the topmost deck. If they are ever deployed, then I con the ship."

The passenger pursed his lips and accepted the fact. The others could almost see him process it, arrange it, file it. "A hybrid ship, is it? How often are you hoisting sail?"

Three stony faces produced a silence that lasted just short of rude. "Not for years," Satterwaithe said, picking up her drinking bulb from the stayput pad. "Not for years."

After the meal, by long tradition, Eugenie Satterwaithe gave the first toast. Like Bhatterji's post–EVAsion decompression, it was a custom that had persisted long enough to take on many of the aspects of a natural law. "Gentlemen," she said, floating as erect as ziggy allowed and holding her drinking bulb straight-arm in front of her, "I give you the Great Sail, MS *The River of Stars*. Long may she fly before the wind."

"The Great Sail!" the others echoed, Fife half a beat behind. They squirted the juice into their waiting mouths and the Thursday Group beamed at one another, as if Satterwaithe had said something true and profound. If Ratline beamed a little more broadly than his messmates, it may be that he, like Bhatterji, had a stash. Yet Ratline had been aboard *The River* longer than God had prowled the marches of heaven. If Bhatterji had the right to decompress and Satterwaithe to declare the first toast, then Ratline had the right to do whatever he damn-all pleased.

" 'Long may she fly . . . ' " Corrigan complained when they had all refastened themselves in their clip chairs. "She hasn't been flying very much these past few days."

"I booked your ship," Fife said, "because it promised a short run to my company's worksite. Now . . ." And he wigwagged with his hand.

"What do you expect of gimcrackery like a Farnsworth cage?" Satterwaithe asked catlike of no one in particular. "Too many components. Something's always breaking. I heard," she added with unseemly satisfaction, "that Bhatterji doesn't have all the parts he needs."

Fife frowned. "I fear he may not finish in time."

"Oh, he's canny enough with an omnitool," Corrigan allowed. "He can fabricate what he doesn't have."

The sailing master shrugged an indifferent agreement. "To hear him tell it, all he needs is a roll of duct tape."

Ratline snickered. "That isn't all he needs—from what I hear. I'm keeping Akhaturian locked up for now. Isn't that right, Ivar?" he asked the mess boy, who had brought in the desserts, and the youngster flushed deep crimson and fled the room.

Corrigan did not pursue the cargo master's sidebar. He turned to look at the nominal ceiling.

"What is it?" Satterwaithe asked.

"I thought I heard a thumping in the ducts," the Second replied. "I hope the air compressor isn't acting up again."

"Grubb hasn't mentioned it."

"But while we coast," said Fife, "will we not drift off our course? Or are we close enough to Jupiter that his attraction will keep up falling toward him?"

"I don't believe so," Satterwaithe said, and looked to Corrigan for confirmation.

The second mate and navigator shook his head. "The attractive force of Sol on the ship at our locus is about three hundred and fifty times greater than Jupiter's."

"Then . . . will we begin falling toward the sun?"

"Actually," Corrigan said a bit smugly, "that problem was solved by Euler in 1760. You see, at transit speeds, we can regard both Sol and Jupiter as fixed points—"

"Did you say 1760? Wouldn't that solution be a bit, well . . . primitive?"

"Oh, of course, we have our ephemeredes and numerical integration routines," Corrigan assured him. "Ship can actually calculate an exact course. No need to rely on the crude approximations of olden days."

"Tell me," Fife said, "your ship mounts four Wright and Oldis DFP's, does it not?"

Satterwaithe affected not to care and Corrigan said only, "Direct Fusion Power design, yes. They use a Ruggiero circular RF quadropole."

But Fife had not been looking to confirm a fact he had gotten quite reliably from the engineer himself. "Well, their top rating is only one-and-a-half milligees apiece—"

"They were installed twenty years ago," Corrigan said, taking Fife's comment as a slur on the ship. "They've been rebuilt once or twice, but they're still older than half the crew."

"An exaggeration, surely," said Fife, who could not bear to let an hyperbole pass unmolested, "but what I meant is that—"

"The sun's monster big," Ratline said, "but he's a puny sort this high up. The current hereabout's only twenty-five microgees. Those engines are plenty stronger enough."

Fife repressed his exasperation. He was a guest, after all, and guests did not abuse hospitality. And besides a show of irritation might interfere with data acquisition. "What I meant is that—I've watched your engineer at work—if he takes more than, what is it now, sixteen days? You will need more deceleration than the engines can give to match Jupiter." Late was one thing. Whipping past at transit speed was something else.

"What you really got to worry about . . ." Ratline said—and here he leaned across the table toward the passenger. "Is if Bhatterji doesn't get 'em fixed. At transit speed we're on hyperbolic orbit, which means: Next stop, Castor. Isn't that right, Abdul?"

"No, it would be Wasat, Delta Genimorum. In Arabic, Wasat means *the middle*—" Corrigan paused as a new thought appeared and hovered just in front of his eyes. It was a stunning thought and wanted contemplation.

Satterwaithe waited, puzzled by Corrigan's abrupt silence, before she filled it. "I wouldn't worry over it, sir. Bhatterji will have the engines wrapped in duct tape long before we come anywhere near the balk line."

Corrigan's continued silence was louder than Ratline's words. Satterwaithe cocked her head and studied the second officer, who seemed consumed by some inward study. "Out with it, Mister Second," she said. Fife, startled at the peremptory tone, wondered for a moment who ranked whom at this table.

"I'm thinking," Corrigan snapped, leaving no doubt where *he* thought rank lay.

"Well, don't let me interrupt the novelty of it," Satterwaithe shot back.

"No, indeed," Corrigan murmured. "No, indeed." For it really was a novelty—to Corrigan himself, no less than to others.

Later, when a hunger of another sort had driven Fife to seek her out, the passenger told Fransziska Wong that he had just dined with the three most anal-retentive individuals he had ever met.

The Second Mate

Corrigan's quarters were a reflection of his practical and orderly mind. The linens and towels were folded square. The prints on the wall were aligned. The audio I/O's were sited where he spent most of his time: near the sling in the reading room, above the sleeping cage, in the fresher. Corrigan preferred books over screens when the reading was serious, which meant when it was most frivolous. These were arrayed in dogboxes according to a complex internal logic comprising subject matter, chronology, and alphabet. Toiletries were aligned on their stayput pads in precisely the sequence in which he customarily used them in the morning. True, in the absence of acceleration the prayer rug had a lamentable tendency to drift off the floor. (A genuine flying carpet, he had told The Lotus Jewel one fey night when it had come loose entirely.) But otherwise, everything was—to use a phrase long obsolete and unknown to Corrigan—"shipshape, Bristol style."

There could be a cruelty to such tidiness. When a book had been removed from its allotted position, a profound unease seemed to fill the room until it had been returned. When a utensil was being used it seemed anxiously out of place. One felt guilty for having disturbed the order. The Lotus Jewel felt suffocated and sometimes, in desperation, she would shift his toiletries about at random when he wasn't looking, imagining in consequence her lover shampooing with toothpaste or trying to brush his teeth with a comb.

Often, she would wish that Corrigan were not quite so dependable. He ought to show up late once in a while. He ought to spin wild fancies. She had heard him tell tales of uttermost wonder—riding out an ice quake on Europa; reefing a sail by hand during a solar flare—all told in such matter-of-fact tones that she could wonder if he was reporting his own life at secondhand. If there was one thing he approached with anything like awe, it was The Lotus Jewel's smooth, golden body. Perhaps for this reason as much as for any other, she continued to visit him—just to help him feel, instead of think.

She came to him that evening, about the time that Fife was seeking the arms of Dr. Wong, to find the lights up high and the Second hooked to his reading sling. Corrigan scowled over a book disk in his screader while he made occasional notations in the rebellious pages of a daybook. The room was silent. She had noticed that about him, that he never played music for mood or background. The sort of music he preferred demanded listening, and not mere hearing: Complex melodies in strange scales over intricate rhythms; not at all the sort of tunes you could *hum*. The glow from the reader screen highlighted his angular face in odd ways, as if he were a modernist sculpture from the previous century.

"Am I early?" The Lotus Jewel asked, with only a touch of pique that her entry had not been marked with its customary ceremony. Corrigan was the creature of habit, yet it was The Lotus Jewel disturbed by this break in his routine. In fact, she was—as always—late. She would be late, Corrigan was wont to say, for her own funeral.

Corrigan's head rose from the screen with the startled look of a man abruptly returned to his surroundings. He blinked at the sysop, then around at his quarters, as if to verify his own whereabouts. "I'm sorry," he said. "I wasn't watching the time."

The Lotus Jewel was seized by the momentary fancy that time itself, unwatched by Corrigan, could run off. Clocks took their cue from the Second. She coasted across the spacious parlor and, touching down like a feather behind him, gripped his ropey shoulders in both hands and kneaded them. On his screader she saw diagrams, formulas, sketches. A bound paper technical manual was clipped to a free-floating book stand. "What are you reading?"

"A little refresher," Corrigan said as he closed his eyes and sighed under her ministrations. The Lotus Jewel leaned across his shoulder, placing herself cheek to his cheek, feeling the weird, smooth suppleness of his eternally beardless face, and studied the screader.

"Magsails?" She was aware that he had turned, for his hot breath tickled her ear. He nuzzled against her.

"Just an idea I'm playing with," he murmured.

"When you should be playing with me?" She ran a finger down the back of his neck. "How did those things work, anyway?"

"Well . . . You put out a cable of superconductor that forms a hoop—"

"A hoop? On the morphie shows they always looked solid."

Corrigan grimaced, as he always did when information strayed from the pure and factual. "That was what they call 'artistic license,' " he commented. "The hoop is sixty-plus kilometers in diameter and only about as thick around as your arm, so normally you can't see it. Just the running lights and the aurora if the gas density is high enough. You see, the current sets up a magnetic dipole, which deflects the solar wind. The deflection produces a drag on the sail radially outward from the sun, and orientation of the dipole—Zubrin's alpha—provides a thrust perpendicular to the radial drag-force."

Now, The Lotus Jewel's question had been an idle one, as most of hers were, but Corrigan's answers were generally more busy—ants to her grasshopper queries. She smiled and so did he, as much as his leathery skin would allow; but Corrigan's was that of a beaming teacher, while the sysop's was somewhat glazed.

"So, what are you going to do," she said, "unfurl the sails again?" He stiffened and drew back and she turned startled eyes on him, seeing the truth in his posture. "You are? You are! Oh, doobers! I've never seen magsails activated. Well, in morphies, sometimes. Like those pirate stories they used to make. But why would you . . . ?"

Corrigan grabbed her wrists and held them tight. "It's just a notion. I want to bounce it off a few others to get their critique."

"Can I help? I'd like to help."

Corrigan's smile was kind. "Sail handling doesn't require the sysop."

She pulled away from him. That was not the answer she had wanted from him; though, in retrospect, it was the answer she ought to have expected. "I still want to help. There's nothing for me to do on this bucket until Ram fixes my antennae." In truth, she would have wanted to help in any case, but Corrigan was the sort of man who needed a reason for everything.

Corrigan stroked her with his fingertips. "Bhatterji isn't the right man to work on *your* antennae."

Which, if one was needed, was reason enough for what they did next.

There was something unnatural about Farnsworth engines, Corrigan believed. Farnsworths *pushed* a ship through the universe—Man's will cutting a swath across the void. But magsails had submitted to the greater will of Nature and let the universe *pull* the ship in the natural swathes formed by the leeward thrust of the solar wind against the windward pull of the solar mass. Sailing large, beating off from planetary wells or the more insidious shoals of fieldless asteroids, skipping off the magnetosphere of Earth or Jupiter, a man was at one with the Void—living with it, not defying it.

He had by necessity learned to con Farnsworths, and the learning had been no comfort. Retread, his captain-instructors had smirked behind their hands. But it was either learn to operate cages or languish rockbound for the rest of his life.

The worst of it was not the new, pedestrian way of thinking but the abandonment of his very life. In his sailing days, Corrigan had danced out among the shrouds, splicing cables, unjamming the reefing motors, sometimes just sitting in the crow's nest high out the mast, surrounded by the fleeting colors of ionized waste gasses, alone with the universe, cupped in the patient, persistent microgravity of the forward thrust of the sail. After, he would slip off his perch and drop to the forward hull (although it was actually the ship that rose to meet him). The more flamboyant hands would turn somersaults or twists on the way down, it being a matter of pride to "drop well." Never was a man more alive, more at peace, with all the universe ahead of him, than among the loops and shrouds of the Great Sails. The

Farnsworth cage was like a reefing knife, slicing through the shrouds of his life, snipping off his past, his youth, his dreams, everything he had ever been, everything he had ever hoped to become.

There have always been golden ages, and they have always ended yesterday. The transition to Farnsworth cages had bothered the younger Corrigan rather more than The Lotus Jewel's playful rearrangement of his toiletries, but in the end for much the same reason.

The sail locker was cramped and dimly lit. Though it covered the entire top deck abaft the forward hull, there would not have been enough room to stand upright, even had there been acceleration enough for standing. It was not a space meant for human work.

The glow of the cold-lights the Thursday Group had brought along gave their faces a pasty complexion, as if they were three zombies brought back from the grave. In its way, an appropriate image, for this was the crypt in which the superconducting coils had been interred.

"Well?" Corrigan asked with ill-concealed impatience. If the sail locker was confining to Satterwaithe and Ratline, imagine the elongated body of the spaceborn folded into such tolerances. Satterwaithe shifted her gauge to a different location on the sail cable and studied the output. "There's still a trickle current running through her," she said. Ratline, who was holding the cable taught with mesh gloves, grunted. "After all these years? Takes a lot of work to quench one of these babies."

"Not when *I'm* the one who quenched it." Satterwaithe unsnapped the gauge, folded it, and tucked it in her coverall pocket. Ratline relaxed his hold. He flexed his fingers, rubbed his arms. "That takes me back a ways, cap'n. It surely does that. Why, I remember when Terranova—"

"The trickle's a problem, isn't it?" Corrigan asked Satterwaithe. He meant it only as a comment, not as a question, but the Third looked at her nominal superior.

"Hoop stress from the current," she said. "The loop wants to circularize, *has* been slowly circularizing for however long the trickle's been going. It'll snap off its guides the minute we release the stays and jam in the bunghole." She gestured aloft, to the Primary Sail Deployment Port.

"I thought that baby was fighting me," Ratline said as he pulled off his sail-handling gloves. "Not quite alive, if you know what I'm saying, but not dead."

"It was the solar flare three months back," Satterwaithe decided. "Hand ramped up the radiation belt to deflect the sleet. The belt's magfield probably induced a complementary current up here in the locker." She looked at Corrigan. "You remember what a problem that used to be."

"Of course, I remember. I may never have been a *River* when she was under sail, but I was sailing master on *Starwing* and Third on *The City of Amman*." (But those were lesser ships, he knew, plying niche trades in the interstices spurned by the torch ships. Nothing at all like the Great Sails his companions had flown.)

"I wasn't questioning your competence, Corrigan."

The hell she wasn't. Corrigan had always felt like an outsider on the *River*. If magsail hands held themselves above those who flew by torch, those who had sailed *The River of Stars* held themselves above even other sailors. And Satterwaithe could never forget that she had once, however briefly, captained the Great Sail. More to the point, she could not let Corrigan forget it.

Corrigan doubted that he could linger as a subordinate on a ship he had once commanded and, had he been Evan Hand, would have felt uneasy to have such an officer under him. He thought that the legal requirement that hybrid ships carry a master may have compelled Hand to offer and Satterwaithe to accept; yet, this only showed the limits of Corrigan's imagination. Home is where the heart is, an old truism has it; but it became old by being true. Eugenie Satterwaithe might have accepted a post lower even than Third Officer to return to *The River of Stars*, though she would not have admitted such a sentiment even to herself. Besides, Hand had been a great one for sheltering wounded birds.

"All right," Corrigan said, "we can quench the hoop by raising the temperature. There are standard procedures for that. What about the deployment winches and the bunghole starter?"

"Number four winch looks okay," Ratline reported. He had not waited out the strain between the two deck officers, but had proceeded with his own checklist. If God was in the details, as Flaubert had once said, then Ratline was His most devoted acolyte. Already he had swum off toward Number Three Deployment Winch.

"Best way to test the bunghole starter," Satterwaithe said, staring into the darkness where their cold-lights did not penetrate, "is to activate the motor."

"Let's not do that while we're in here," Corrigan suggested.

He had meant it as a joke, but Satterwaithe had not looked for jokes from him. She looked away, into the dark interior of the loft. "We don't have so many sailors on board," she said, "that I can afford to waste any." Unspoken, the phrase lingered, *even you, Corrigan.*

"I know how Gorgas thinks," Corrigan said. "If we go to him with a plan, we better have all the diacriticals on our consonants. He can pick holes in DSM sheathing. Funny," he added. "If we weren't a hybrid ship on paper, these cables would have been sold off years ago, just for the material value. It was only the regulations that—"

Satterwaithe continued to stare into the darkness. "Do you think that wise?"

"What?" He thought she meant keeping the sails, which made no sense.

"To tell Gorgas?"

"Ah. He *is* the captain," Corrigan pointed out, not lacking a certain satisfaction at reminding the Third of her place in the order of things.

"Pro tem."

"Look, Satterwaithe—" And Satterwaithe turned to face him. "Plan A is to fix the Farnsworths, right? But Bhatterji is taking his good old time about it—even the passenger's noticed—and he may have a problem fabbing the components he needs; so it's only sensible to have a Plan B in reserve. Gorgas can see that. If nothing else, we can run out a staysail until Bhatterji finishes tinkering, push the balk line out a few days . . . or else we'll go skating clear past Jupiter."

"But 'Dul," Satterwaithe pressed him, "don't you see the possibilities? A staysail, sure. Lending a hand, that's fine. But we could do so much more. The ship is crippled; and The Lotus Jewel can't even call for help. What if *we* bring the ship in—*under sail?* Think about it! Imagine the sight at Port Galileo! Imagine the humm!"

Corrigan had only wanted to buy time for the repairs and had not thought beyond that; but the sudden image of the Great Sail coruscating in the Jovian winds as she sidled up to Ganymede suddenly entranced him. Oh, yes! Oh, what a grand sight that would be!

"I suppose we could evaluate the situation," he ventured. "Run feasibility studies. See if we have the resources for full deployment."

"And keep quiet about it until we know."

Corrigan considered that, then nodded. "No sense raising expectations, or making promises we can't fulfill."

Satterwaithe clapped him on the shoulder. "You'll see I'm right, Mr. Second. Don't think for a moment that torch men like Bhatterji or Gorgas will accept salvation by sail. They'll try to 'but' us to death. You just told me yourself what Gorgas is like. Imagine how he'll pick away at a plan he dislikes in the first place. And the others might not care one way or the other; but because they don't, we can't count on them, either."

"The Lotus Jewel will help us," Corrigan said, "and Ratline thinks his First Wrangler will too."

Satterwaithe shook her head. "I don't want humm running around the ship."

Corrigan thought the Third used first-person singular a little too often. "All right. I'll tell LJ to stay quiet. You tell Ratline to say the same to Okoye." But Ratline still called Satterwaithe "captain," so if Corrigan were sure of anything it was that Ratline would follow whatever course Satterwaithe laid. There was a bond there, an old one, between the Third and the cargo master; though of what sort Corrigan was unsure. A debt, perhaps; an obligation. But Ratline was no mere hound wagging a faithful tail for his former master, and there were times when Corrigan wondered which it was who owed the debt.

If it was not nostalgia for sails that drove the Second Mate, but only comfort in accustomed ways, it was ambition that drove the Third. Once a man or woman has worn four rings on her sleeve, no lesser number will ever serve. Perhaps that was why Eugenie Satterwaithe seemed insubordinate to Corrigan even when she sat silent in a meeting. There was something about the way she listened that made her appear to be giving orders. It had been a long time since anyone aboard the *River* had worn uniforms; but the cuff rings were there, and no mistake.

Now Satterwaithe was as fallible as anyone else in *The River of Stars,* and that was very fallible, indeed. Yet she was usually well-informed and picked up humm the way a cheap suit picks up lint. Sometimes she thought she knew more than she did, but that was rare. She might have been one of the *River's* better captains, right up there with Johnson and Fu-hsi had she had more time at it. Certainly, Satterwaithe believed so, and the knowledge of what she might have been galled.

The Thursday Group met the next day in Satterwaithe's quarters, giving her home-field advantage. Corrigan found those quarters cluttered and untidy; a bad enough situation under acceleration, unbearable during ziggy. Flexscreens, seedies, styluses, *women's undergarments!* were all a-jumble, some even floating about. He had to restrain himself from fetching and stacking and stowing. It wasn't just disorderly, it was unfeminine! He had some pretty firm notions of what was feminine and what was not; but then, he didn't have to be one and so could pass judgment with the serenity of an outsider. (That some of his own traits might strike others—Bhatterji, for instance—as effeminate did not occur to him.) Satterwaithe was neither a Madonna nor a nymph, and that confused him; primarily because he confused the feminine with his own desires and, while Satterwaithe conjured many emotions in his breast, desire was not numbered among them. So he took refuge in a label. Genie was a lizard.

Now, Satterwaithe had bedded more than a few women in her time, it is true; but she'd also had as many men. Call her eclectic. She preferred men—in younger days, when she had preferred at all—but she generally preferred them underneath, and in the Middle System submissive men were on back order.

In any event, as The Lotus Jewel had once purred, Satterwaithe's wellsprings had dried up years before. The urge came on her less frequently than of yore and, when it did, was more apt to trigger a spasm of annoyance than spasms of any other sort. Corrigan was not especially young, but young enough that the Deed obsessed him at times. That Satterwaithe was immune to such cravings made her more alien in his mind than Bigelow Fife, the Mushroom Man with the Clockwork Mind.

Satterwaithe had developed a plan for sail deployment. It was a good plan, complete with procedures, PERTs, and estimates for materials and manpower, for she was a past master at juggling resources. Most of the information she had found in moribund deebies in Ship's library and the remainder in her own treasured manuals.

But Corrigan had read the same manuals. "The procedure requires a berth of six able sailors," he said. Corrigan was not a man prone to errors of fact. Unfortunately, as he often pointed these facts out to those who were, he had acquired a reputation as a carper. His comment irritated Satterwaithe less because it was true than because Corrigan seemed to take unseemly satisfaction in the bruiting.

"We have five people," she said. "Three able sailors, a wrangler, and a nerd. That's nearly enough. We'll just have to stretch a little." She herself had often stretched beyond her limits, and assumed that others could do likewise, if only properly motivated.

Corrigan bristled. "LJ is more than a computer nerd."

To Satterwaithe, Corrigan was beside the point. "All right then. Three sailors, a wrangler, and a slut."

That evoked shouted words—until Ratline, of all unlikely people, smoothed things over. Ratline was comfortable carrying out anyone's plan—too comfortable, since he often did the carrying out before the plan was made—but the bad feelings between the two deck officers bothered him considerable. He was secure enough in his own place that he could recognize dominance games when he saw them. (Dominance? Satterwaithe in whips and leather? Corrigan grabbing his ankles? Ratline grinned. He had his own private amusements.)

"Abdul is right," he said. "We don't have six able sailors. Five might manage a deployment, even if two are nooboos; but that's only theory. We gotta be practical, cap'n. But there *is* software to resurrect and there's some 'prentice tasks elsewhere that we can simplify to trainee level. As for the rest, my First Wrangler can handle most of what a 'prentice can do."

Corrigan raised his brows. "Rewrite the procedures?" Procedures were not quite holy writ to him, but they were at one with his orderly bathroom and his personal library of books and intricate, academic music. He had always struck Satterwaithe as—well—*incorrigible*, were she inclined to puns. Stuck forever in the same orbit. And while it might be a very nice and comfortable orbit, the eventual *sameness* of it would sooner or later drive her insane. And so, imputing as always her own tastes to others, she supposed that it must have already done so to Corrigan, and that he was more than a little mad.

"Moth," she said, "you've mentioned simplifying some tasks. Are there any tasks that can be eliminated completely?"

"If a task did not need doing," Corrigan commented, "it would never have been written into the procedures."

But Ratline squinted and pursed his lips. "Now, hold on a bit," he said searching his memories. "Seems to me there were a couple of readiness checks we used to do on the sails because the loops were spun from hobartium XVI. That stuff had bad ductility. If our sails aren't that alloy, we don't need to do those tests, do we?"

"The Institute of Sailing Engineers probably kept the checks as a safeguard. Other compounds might have ductility problems too. . . . Or a particular sail in a lot might be nonconforming . . ."

"The ISE," Satterwaithe snapped impatiently, "probably kept the checks for CYA. Public standards accumulate fossil requirements the way ships accumulate radiation scars. But eliminating a step is only one option. We could combine tasks, or resequence the tasks, or reassign them. . . ."

"I had a notion," Ratline said, "back when I was a sail-handler, for a special tool for bunging the catline through its way-grommet. That's outside work. Vacuum suit, and up the pole. Bet my tool could cut the time in half."

Satterwaithe nodded. "That's the sort of thinking we need. Let's bring the procedure inside the envelope of the time and resources we can marshal rather than carp about resources we don't have."

Corrigan nodded reluctantly. "I see your point. . . ." Then in a sudden burst of authority—he was senior officer present, after all—he turned to Ratline. "Can you fabricate your tool, Mr. Ratline or do you need Bhatterji?"

The cargo master shook his head. "I got a wrangler—Rave Evermore—who's handy enough. Bhatterji lets him use the machine shop for hobbies—he's a handsome laddy—but he doesn't bother the boy." Ratline's grin lacked a tooth or two, and that gave his smiles a sinister cast. "He knows the kid would rip his lungs out if he tried anything. Do I tell Rave what the tool is for?"

Before he could stop himself, Corrigan looked to Satterwaithe, who shook her head slightly, though she let Corrigan confirm the order. "No," said the Second. "If he asks, spin some plausible justification."

Satterwaithe slapped the table. "Good. The three of us can go over the process flow tonight and look for opportunities to shorten and simplify the work, so we can handle the job without a full sailing berth. We just want to slow the ship into Jupiter, so we don't need full rigging. We'll meet . . ." She consulted a wrist calendar. "Tomorrow at twenty-two hundred to compare critiques. Here? Or your quarters, 'Dul?"

'Abd al-Aziz Corrigan disliked the nickname Satterwaithe had invented for him. He disliked even more the notion that the disorder of this meeting might encroach on his private space. "Here is fine, 'Genie.'" Which assent, by odd coincidence, gave Satterwaithe once more the home-court advantage.

Gorgas having left all routine watch-keeping to the AI while the ship was coasting, the command deck was dark and silent when Corrigan cautiously entered. The only light came from the cold-lamps that marked hatchways or the sharp corners of equipment. None of the dials or readouts were active. The AI needed no such aids to vision.

The silence was not quite complete. Corrigan's own ragged breathing roared in his ears like a gale. He glanced once at the portal to the captain's dayroom, as if expecting Gorgas to leap through and catch him out.

Catch him out? He was second mate, acting first. He had as much right to be on the command deck as any, and more than most! Silently, he monkeyed to the captain's door and pressed his ear to it.

Nothing. It was the dog watch and Gorgas was probably asleep in his own quarters, a stateroom farther off. Corrigan sighed with relief, but he went about his work with as much silence as he could muster; and he did not turn on the lights.

"Ship," he whispered. "Activate controls for bunghole starter."

"Clarify instruction." The AI's voice thundered. Or perhaps it was only Corrigan's heart that thundered. A few moments passed while he gathered his scattered thoughts. "Activate controls for Primary Sail Deployment Port."

A virtual panel appeared on one of the display screens, and three touch-icons lit. The hardware controls for sailhandling had been cannibalized and scrapped years before and, in any case, had not been used for nearly twenty years before that. Only these electronic ghosts remained, simulations of what had once been real, and they only because of the regulatory requirements of a joke classification. *Like carrying a sailing master,* he thought, not without a certain keen derision. Third Officer Satterwaithe was much like these controls. Only an image of what had once been real.

Corrigan unfolded a long finger and stroked the activator icon twice. Ready lights switched from amber to green and his imagination heard the hum of relays far above him. The ambient monitors for the sail locker displayed a drop in air pressure.

Satisfied, Corrigan reversed the process and shut down the system. When he was finished and told the AI to resume watchkeeping, the Ship reminded him that he had not annotated the log. Corrigan started at this. He hadn't actually done anything wrong. He had confirmed function on some inactive equipment. That was all. Yet, he could not help feeling that he had crossed a line of some sort. And so he used a special code that The Lotus Jewel had given him to enter the Ship's AI and erase all records of his test.

There was no procedure for this.

The Wrangler Berth

Twenty-four deCant had been suffering an especially obnoxious bout of space-sickness ever since the ship had begun freefing. She tried to tough it out—she was a Martian, after all, and they didn't come any tougher than that—but her berthmates had endured one barf too many in the common room and they had bundled her off to see the doctor. Wong prescribed an antiemetic, but there was something about the case that niggled at her.

"The nausea seems to be passing?" she asked when the girl had come to the clinic for her follow-up.

"If you mean do I throw up any more, the answer's not so much."

Wong looked up from the patient's chart displayed on her med screen. " 'Not so much,' or 'not so often?' "

DeCant's face displayed the look that most adults receive when they ask for clarification from the young. " 'Not so often.' "

"And you've never had this problem before. . . ." Not really a question, since there were no notations on her chart for space-sickness; yet Wong knew that not every illness was reported. The idea of "working through the pain" struck her as terribly foolish, as if viruses and microbes and fractures would yield to the force of a paramount will. But men and women who would never attempt to run a broken machine would shun sick call as a sign of weakness.

"Ship's usually under boost . . ." deCant said.

"In port? During flipover?"

"Those are usually short. . . . Well, sometimes it takes a while to shift cargo when we make port, but this here's the longest I ever been freefed, I think."

"Can't keep something down, if there's no 'down.'" Wong had been shy of joking ever since Gorgas's rebuke following Evan's death, but deCant was obviously hurting and Wong did not think it was the space-sickness entirely.

"It was nothing jove," deCant insisted. "It was only at start-of-watch, anyway. Sometimes, I look at my breakfast and feel queasy, like it's gonna make me sick."

"You *are* eating, though." It was more a demand than a question.

"Yah. Carbs. You know, high energy." And she made a muscle of her arm that startled Wong even though she knew that deCant was a cargo wrangler. "I grew a sweet tooth the size of Olympus Mons this past week."

Wong scratched a notation on the screen. "And the first bout of emesis—of nausea—was the fourteenth?" The ship had gone freef late the eleventh, about an hour before dear Evan Hand had passed, so why no nausea on the twelfth or thirteenth? She made another notation. "I'd like to insert a microbot into your bloodstream. It will take periodic samples so I can monitor your condition."

DeCant frowned. "You think it's serious?"

"Your medical record has no indication of previous space-sickness. It may be the length of time we've been freeing, or it may be something else. I just like to make sure." She bounced to her console and set up the microbot parameters from deCant's file. While she worked, she asked from curiosity why the girl was named Twenty-four. "It's not a very common name."

The wrangler laughed. "No, not hardly."

Satterwaithe was standing just inside the clinic door, Wong suddenly noticed. The Third had a way of being places without seeming actually to arrive. You would glance up and she'd be there, just like that. The deck officer stood with arms crossed, radiating impatience without saying a word.

Wong dropped her eyes. She had not been aboard *The River of Stars* long enough to grow firm opinions about her new crewmates. Yet it seemed to the doctor as if Satterwaithe were perpetually angry and she suspected that the anger was somehow directed at her. She wasn't sure what she had done to offend the older woman; but she was sure it was something awful—so awful that neither one of them dared speak of it.

DeCant too glanced at the older woman, then tossed her head and addressed Wong. "I'm a clone," she said. "Isn't that in there?" She pointed to the med comp. When Wong shook her head, deCant shrugged. "I ain't 'shamed of it. It weren't my doing." She looked back at Satterwaithe standing by the door and regarded her silently for another moment before returning to the doctor. "I was the twenty-fourth embryo they decanted. Part of an experiment to rectify telomere loss."

Wong blinked, suddenly aware of the gnawing fear in the wrangler's heart. Clones aged rapidly due to their shortened telomeres. Why in heaven was such crucial medical information missing from the file? "Do you ever see your sisters?" she asked with professional cheer. "I'm an Only. What is it like having—my goodness—twenty-three sisters?"

"They're all dead," the teenager said flatly. "All but me—and four others they never decanted." An angry shrug. "What the hell. We was—were—an experiment. I'm only around 'cause . . . My fosters told me a nurse smuggled me out of the lab one night. Somebody jimmied the papers so my adoption looked legit. You need to know all this stuff?"

Wong nodded, but wondered why deCant thought that Satterwaithe needed to know as well. The Third Officer remained by the door, as impassive as a harem guard. Was she listening? She must be. "And your fosters named you Twenty-four deCant? That seems an awful—"

"They was activists. They said I should know who I was and *why* I was and folk's'd look at me and maybe stop growing us for experiments. They went in the Syrtis Dome Decompression," deCant continued without so much as a change in tone, "and I decided I had enough of Mars; so I stowed aboard the Ares Shuttle, got scut jobs around the Deimos Yards, and thought maybe I'd space out and look up my clone-mother. I ran into Captain Hand in Panic Town. He knew about me— about the cloning, I mean—and said he'd help me out. I figured the worst that could happen was I'd be the skipper's doxy—and he was a sweet kind of guy, so maybe the worst wouldn't be so bad." DeCant shook her head. "God, he was a good man." She locked defiant eyes on Wong. "He never touched me. You got to believe that. Not even after I started bleeding. I wouldn't have minded, then; but now I'm glad he never did."

And what was that ice pick in Wong's heart? It couldn't be jealousy, could it? Did she suppose that she was the only woman Hand had never taken as a lover? Why, the Middle System must be full of women like that!

After the microbots had been implanted and deCant had gone, Satterwaithe stepped forward. "I need stims," she said. "A bottle."

"What a sad story . . ." Wong was still thinking about the girl.

Satterwaithe was not. "A full bottle."

Wong blinked and focused on the Third. "Of stims?"

Satterwaithe thought that the snake woman was a flighty sort. She never seemed to be entirely present, as if she only *intersected* normal space-time and the rest of her lay in some other dimension. "There's a lot of work that wants doing. Some of us need to work extended hours."

Wong did not reach for her console. "Stims can be abused."

"I'm no addict."

Wong could not bring herself to dispute the point; yet she knew how easy it was to deny reality even to oneself. "I'll design a 'bot," she said sternly. "It will release a controlled quantity of stimulant for a specified time period. It can be activated or deactivated by command from my console. A monitor will track your vital signs through the ship's grid and adjust the dosage as required."

The Third Officer shrugged impatiently. She knew what she

wanted; she didn't care how it was accomplished. "I'll need more than one, then. One for each member of my task team. Perhaps as many as five."

"Very well. Bring them here later today for their insertions."

Wong was still staring in puzzlement at the door after Satterwaithe had left when a voice said, "She's up to something."

"Something to do with ship repair," Wong answered. It seemed the most natural thing in the world to speak to a disembodied voice.

"Fixing the cages is the Ram's task. The deck ain't in it."

Wong looked around for the source. "You're Miko, aren't you? Mikoyan Hidei, the engineer's mate? I recognize your voice."

"Yah. That's me."

"Where are you?"

"Here."

Was that smirk or play in that voice? Wong studied the room and finally located the girl behind the large air-exchange grille on the aft bulkhead near the ceiling. "Whatever are you doing in there?"

"It's just something I do. 'Miko-in-the-walls.' It's sort of cozy, you know. Comfortable."

"Comfortable! Crawling through the air ducts?" But it might be that comfort has nothing to do with the physical.

"Oh, there's all sorts of passages back here. For maintenance and stuff. I guess when this was a luxury boat, they had passages for the stewards so they could run around without anybody seeing them."

"And are you playing hide and seek?"

There was silence followed by a motion, barely perceptible through the grillwork, that Wong took to be a shake of the head. " 'Play' gotta be earned."

"Ah. Yes, I suppose. You don't like the Third Officer very much, do you?"

"I don't like a lot of people. Sometimes they don't like me back, so it all works out. But that Genie Satterwaithe, she grinds me. Nothing's ever good enough for her. I like *you*, though."

Oddly, that pleased the doctor, who straightened a little at the compliment. "You do?"

"Yah. You like to help people. I think you're the nicest one on board. After the captain."

Wong knew the girl meant Evan Hand. Gorgas was a cold man. *Nice* was not among his adjectives. "Thank you."

"That's why I don't think you should be with that man so much. He's doesn't really care for you. When we reach his port, he won't even look back from the airlock."

"What man?" Wong asked with false puzzlement and a smile that was two parts fear.

But there was no answer, and the shadow behind the grille was gone.

How long had that strange, elfin girl been prowling the innards of the ship, she wondered? And what sights had she watched in silence through the slits of its portals and grilles?

The greenhouse of a long-haul tramp is a center of color and light. Crazed by the lack of gravitational cues, the shoots and buds weave their long, wispy stems into a tapestry of green and red and yellow that slices the solar-equivalent lamplight into something approaching stained glass. At the farther end of the gallery, the color of fruit gives way, and odor triumphs over sight. There is a pungent, fleshy smell about the carniculture vats, accented but by no means countered by that of the live animals cowering in their pens. There are only a few of these, for those breeds are rare that can tolerate milligee acceleration, let alone free fall, without unreasoning terror.

(Cats, to be sure; but Cat walks where she will. There were two cats aboard *The River* and they had come to a reasonable accommodation with each other, dividing the ship and its humans between them. Miko had come across one of them behind the walls near the galley and called her "Queen Tamar," unaware that Ivar Akhaturian had named the self-same puss "Anush Abur." The cat, for what it is worth, accepted both names with equal indifference. Of the second cat, she is little seen and then only when she wishes.)

The biosystems chief had been born with the unfortunate

name of Eaton Grubb and doomed thereby to a life in food preparation. The "Grubb" part was perhaps necessary by long patronymic custom, but his parents should have shown a less puckish sense of humor. He loved them dearly all his life, but they really should have called him "John."

But that which does not kill, strengthens; or so they say. Young Eaton had developed his own sense of humor. "As a child," he told Nkieruke Okoye one time, "I was never certain whether I was introducing myself or describing my activity." The First Wrangler, whose milk language was not even remotely kin to English, smiled because her inner sense told her she ought to, but she did not laugh at the joke for three days, when her mind finally pierced the curtain of spelling, phonetics, and slang with which English-speakers shrouded their inscrutable tongue. She repeated the phrase to herself several times in Igbo, but Consuming Food never struck her as a reasonable name for someone, nor even as remotely funny. English, 'Kiru decided, had too many words and its speakers felt obliged to play with the extra ones.

But for whatever reason, she considered the chief the *happiest* person in the crew. Everyone else wanted to have what they did not or to be what they were not: to hold rank, or to avoid responsibility; to possess another, or to avoid possession; to flee the past, or to live in it. Eaton Grubb, who perhaps most deserved to have and to be more, desired it the least. 'Kiru sometimes wondered whether that was an infirmity of his or a strength.

Grubb sang a great deal. No one on the ship sang so much or so well as he. He sang while he harvested meat from the vats. He sang when he tinctured the bland "carnic" with flavorings and odorants and fortified it with vitamins and minerals. The sheep—too stupid even to know they were in ziggy—were in theory available for his slaughter when the real thing was called for; but he sang to them too and what man can slaughter those he serenades?

Okoye, her duties done for the day, kicked and listened and licked on a ginger sweetball he had made for her. Often, in the common room, Grubb accompanied himself on the concertina, but Okoye enjoyed the voice pure and unadorned, and that was why she often joined him in the galley. That and the sweet-balls.

> *"There's wealth to be made on the orbital trade*
> *Working the ships and the stations.*
> *If you man the lock at the cargo ship dock,*
> *You can look down on all of creation,*
> *My friend.*
> *You can look down on all of creation."*

Grubb liked the old songs, the ones from the early days, when all of space had snuggled close to the breast of Mother Earth, and Mars was just an antic notion. The building of Leo Station and Goddard City and Tsiolkovskigrad; the first lunar mines at Artemis and Selene; the pearly necklace of powersats, the heroic fight against the asteroid rain. The time when three men had dared the Long Orbit to Calhoun's Rock with nothing more than a chemical reaction for their motor. A time of raw energy and simple truths. Fortunes had been made in deed, and fortunes broken.

There was no discontent in this love of his for a golden age. Genuinely humble, he viewed the world with a childlike awe and, accepting whatever befell, inherited the world often enough that the more cynical among the crew suspected his humility to be a sort of vice. Grubb was happy where he was and when he was, but he would have been as happy elsewhere and elsewhen. He really did know that the times he sang of had not been so rosy or sanitary as the songs made out, nor the truths quite so simple. There had been bodies in orbit, as there had earlier been bodies beside the trails of Siberia and Gansu and the American West; but if one must sing, why not sing of life the way it ought to have been? Myth could bear more truth than Fact.

> *"From the STC link up to geosynch*
> *And from Goddard to Helios Light.*
> *The habitats spin and the dockhandlers sin*
> *As they soar through the starry night,*

My friend.
As they soar through the starry night."

The song faded and Grubb sighed as, his feet anchored in stirrups for the leverage, he kneaded the carnic mass, working it to the right consistency for Fowl Matter. His eyes lost their focus and grew distant and he sighed again. Okoye had long decided that Grubb was the ship's canary. When he stopped singing, it was time to worry.

"What is it, Mr. Grubb?" she asked. He had often asked her to call him by his first name, but Okoye had a firm sense of propriety and thought that he was secretly pleased that she used the honorific. There was little enough politeness in the world that she would not diminish its store. She had been raised in Afikpo, where the young knew to respect their elders.

"There is something wrong with the ship," Grubb said.

"Mr. Bhatterji and Miko are working on the engines. They expect—"

But Grubb shook his head. "It's not her engines, 'Kiru, it's her heart. It's been torn out of her. Haven't you noticed how things have changed since Evan died?"

She had, in fact. Something of a dispirit had settled on the crew. With Hand's death had come a feeling that they were now adrift; and who could say that Ship, picking up the cues, was not adrift for the same reason? Even for those who had disliked the man—and Okoye knew there were some—Hand had been at the center of their personal universes.

Now here is the curious thing about the late Evan Dodge Hand. Though he had been vapor for nearly a week, each member of his erstwhile crew felt his presence. A Heisenbergish sort of captain, he had survived the opening of his casket, and in being no longer anywhere in particular was now somehow everywhere in general.

"We're still readjusting," she ventured. "It is being just bad luck all these things happening together."

"Bad luck." Grubb again ceased his kneading. "When has there never been bad luck?" He twisted in the stirrups and looked at her over his shoulder. "Have you ever played bounce ball, 'Kiru? Have you ever missed a return and said it was just a bad bounce?"

'Kiru never had—missed a return, that is—and so had never needed an excuse, but she knew what Grubb had meant to say and so she simply agreed. There were no bad bounces, only missed opportunities. One might fail the return, but that was hardly the fault of the ball.

Twenty-four deCant sought out Okoye later in the common room, while the First Wrangler was screading Pandya's *Cold, Gray Shores*, a picaresque roman à clef of Pandya's husband and their friends and the very first sail that had ever flown. Okoye had read it four times already, and never the same way twice as she followed the hyperlinks among the texts. "'Kiru," deCant said. "'Kiru, do you have time today to help me shave my head? My hair is growing out too long and I need to chop it back." She rubbed her short brush flat, but the strands rose again and trembled like grass in an uncertain breeze.

"It's not so long," Okoye said.

"Oh, but why wait? I like to keep it short so it doesn't get in my way. I wish I had hair like yours. You never have to cut it. It just grows in those tight little curls."

Okoye fought an impulse to brush a hand across her own scalp. She made no response but followed the other wrangler across the room. Personal comments made her uncomfortable. Not that Twenty-four's compliment had been intrusive, but Okoye did not often talk about herself, or indeed much at all. She was a solitary sort, quiet and reserved and this made her more than a little strange to those like deCant, for whom solitude was something like a disease to be cured. Okoye knew that deCant was less concerned with her hair than with being alone.

Sometimes Okoye did not know exactly what she knew—she only felt it as a sort of premonition—but she would look up one day or search her heart and there it would be: Knowledge that she could not possibly have. Perhaps it was only a very refined intuition, built up from observation and her deep knowledge of body language learned from the sisterhood. Or perhaps it was a kind of telepathy. Her mind was a still, quiet pool of water, and if the thoughts and emotions of others *could* in some unfathomable manner leak out, they would surely cause ripples there.

The clone fastened herself into the sling by the vacuum duct and Okoye turned the suction on; then she rummaged in the drawer for the shaver. "Down to the scalp?" she asked.

"Drive them nubs into hiding," deCant agreed, "so they're a-feared to show their face for a while."

DeCant spoke foolishly, Okoye thought, because she was young. It was as if silence horrified her as much as solitude and she felt driven to fill it up with words. Even random, foolish words. The accusation was probably unfair, so Okoye did not voice it. Some people just liked to chatter. Others preferred quiet. Odd, that the two of them had found themselves in the same berth. She turned the shaver on.

Or not so odd. Though one could no longer ask Hand.

"I think I may have found my clone-mother." DeCant spoke matter-of-factly. Okoye wondered how anyone could blurt out such private matters, even to a friend—and the Igbo girl did consider herself a friend of the young clone; indeed, of anyone who would accept her friendship. She even felt an affection for Moth Ratline, and he was a very hard man to like. She made a noncommittal noise, but that was not needful because deCant simply kept talking.

"I weren't sure for a long time, but Cap'n Hand know'd I was a clone when he signed me on for cabin boy, and he wanted to help me, so he must'a been trying to find my mother."

Okoye wasn't sure how well that string held together as a syllogism, but she said nothing while she ran the shaver across the girl's scalp. She wondered, were she herself a clone, would she have been so anxious to find some woman whose only connection was an egg dropped off in a lab? The act must have meant far less to the donor than it had come to mean to Twenty-four deCant. "The donor might not even know," Okoye said.

But that had been said before; and the answer—"A DNA screening doesn't care if someone remembers"—had become a sort of mantra. But there were thousands of women in the

Middle System; even more under Mars and Luna and in the habbies; billions on dirty old Earth. Okoye did not point out the practical difficulties of needle hunting in a dozen such haystacks. It wouldn't have mattered. If deCant couldn't see the impossibilities herself, no one could possibly point them out to her.

That Hand had intended to help deCant, Okoye did not doubt. There was her own situation as case in point. But that such "help" meant locating an egg donor, she doubted very much. Yet she was loathe to destroy hopes, even illusory ones—especially illusory ones. And so she maintained a silence into which deCant could pour her words.

"I been thinking on it hard these last two years," deCant said. "First, I thought maybe my ma would be at one of our ports o' call, but now I think she's here on board and the cap'n was just waiting for the right time."

Now that caused Okoye's shaver to skid off the scalp! "Ms. Satterwaithe?" she said, for who else would have been on Mars fifteen years ago or more? "But you're not at all like her!" Surprise could let the words pop out, even from her quiescent throat.

(Miko, hiding in the closed-off stewards' accessway, was better at holding hers in, and only a small squeak escaped her, which Okoye thought was a briefly seized bearing in a distant air-circulation fan. Half the squeaks and bumps the crew had been hearing for the past four and a half months were from Miko-in-the-walls.)

"She's old and I'm young. I'm trying to find a picture of her when she was young."

"I don't think she's the picture-saving sort."

"There must be *something* in Ship's deeby, if I only knew the access codes."

Okoye, having already gushed her few words, fell back into silence. She doubted that anything *must* be simply because deCant wanted it so, although in this way the clone really was like Satterwaithe. But Okoye could not imagine the Third Officer as an egg donor. Selling eggs for money did not lie on the woman's orbit; and the altruistic advancement of medical science was in another bubble universe entirely. Besides, if deCant were Satterwaithe's clone, Dr. Wong would surely have said something.

Or . . . Okoye did not like to think ill of another, but Wong did not have a very high opinion of her own skills and she might have good reasons for holding that opinion.

Speculation was bootless. Were problems solvable by worry, this would be a carefree ship, for Okoye worried to excess. About Ratline. About Wong. About deCant. Perhaps that, and her habitual quietude, was why others often came to her. She was a heat sink for their emotions. They might not expect her to *solve* anything for them, but at least they were assured of a listening. There was something about the long fall of words into the deep well of Okoye's mind that comforted them. Maybe it was the distant splash.

So she didn't just shave deCant's head as she listened to the girl chatter. She rubbed the scalp and massaged the neck and shoulders. Okoye wished her friend would give up her hopeless search. It risked toppling over into an obsession, and obsessions could consume entire lives, and not only those of the obsessed. Fire had a way of riding the wind, of leaping fences and running wild. Twenty-four would be much happier if she could accept herself and, more importantly, accept the deaths of her fosters. But Okoye knew that such advice would be rejected. If people did not much expect solutions from the lips of their friends, still less did they welcome them.

When the shaving was done and the girl had talked herself out—and Okoye had paced herself so that the two coincided—Twenty-four said, "I always feel so much better when you do my hair. All tingly and relaxed."

Okoye, putting the equipment away and turning off the vacuum, said, "Thank you."

DeCant turned and gripped Okoye's wrist. "No, I should thank you. For helping me with my problem."

The Igbo girl was startled by the genuineness of the thanks. Twenty-four had come into the commons deeply anxious, but now radiated calm and purpose. Reviewing the one-sided conversation in her mind, Okoye could not see where she had helped at all.

After deCant had left to exercise in the spinhall, Okoye returned to her novel. Yet she found it difficult to concentrate. In Pandya's long-ago, quasi-fictional world, the moral dilemmas seemed so clear-cut. Why was reality always a muddle? She thought she ought to speak with Dr. Wong or Third Officer Satterwaithe. She did not want to make trouble for Twenty-four, but that she ought to speak to *someone* was clear. Yet the one person in whom she *knew* she could have confided was now dead. Twenty-four's search for her egg donor was doomed to fail, and that was bad enough; but there was an infinitesimal chance that it might succeed, and that would be worse.

Ivar Akhaturian was soft and round, like dough not yet baked hard. As Least Wrangler, he deferred to everyone on board. He always assumed that others knew better than he what he ought to do. When his mother pocketed the bounty and told him to go with Captain Hand, he had obeyed without a second thought. And later, when Third Wrangler deCant had told him to come with her, he had obeyed with equal thoughtlessness. It wasn't in him to defy authority and, since he ascribed authority to any and all others, he seldom defied anything. Only in play did he show initiative, and there he could dream up endless activities by which the four wranglers could amuse themselves in the interstices of Ratline's attention.

Evermore called him a wink and said that deCant had a leash around his johnny-come; but while Ivar might be young, he was not so young as to confuse envy with truth. Rave's problem was very simple. He was horny for Twenty-four, but the Martian had chosen Ivar over him. Sometimes Akhaturian wished that the older boy would not tease him so much, but thought that if he persevered, Evermore would eventually grow tired of the sport. In this, he underestimated Evermore's capacity for invention.

Twenty-four was the most wonderful and beautiful woman Akhaturian had ever known, save only his mother; and his mother had never made him feel good in the way that Twenty-four did. Just to think of her made him stiff; though that Twenty-four might have a hardness of her own he never considered. Operant conditioning is what Dr. Wong called it. Associate pleasure with a face and soon the face alone gives pleasure; but the doctor was a lonely and bitter woman and had her own operant conditions to worry over. Akhaturian would never have believed her, anyway. He thought he was in love.

Love meant mooning and moping and writing the number *24* over and over and thinking seven times a minute about being with her. Sublimation wasn't in it. His work suffered, but only a little, as he was perfectly capable of wrangling cargoes and imagining Twenty-four's naked breasts at the same time. He handled both tasks with neophyte awkwardness, but he was eager to learn.

And there was this one odd thing about his deference. Because he expected others to know more and to be the best, everyone he worked with did that work just a little bit better. When he asked Okoye questions about cargo wrangling, she was surprised to realize how much she herself had mastered in five short years. When he studied navigation with Corrigan, the Second found a vaster (and unexpected) store of patience within himself. When he told Grubb how delicious the food was, Grubb studied his essences and fragrances with greater diligence. Even Twenty-four found her search for casual pleasure shading over into something else. What it came down to was this: The little dook was so eager and so grateful and he so obviously expected that all would go well that no one wanted to disappoint him.

So a paradox had emerged even in the short four months that Akhaturian had been aboard. Without ever leading, he had become a leader. It was Okoye who first noticed this and puzzled over it for some time. There was nothing *timid* about Ivar Akhaturian. The boy would tackle the most dangerous task serene in the confidence that no one would order him to work he could not handle. If he ever found his center, Okoye thought, Akhaturian could be a captain as fine as Evan Hand had been. Indeed, for a time she wondered whether Ivar were not *ndichie*—Hand's soul returned in an unlikely package—save for the fact that the boy had come before the man had gone, and Hand's *maw* would undoubtedly reincarnate as an elephant, it was that large a thing.

Akhaturian feared Mr. Ratline as he feared little else, and with good reason; for Ratline was perfectly willing to throw people into situations they could not handle should the needs of the moment so ordain. It was the eternal scowl that frightened the Least Wrangler: that inward-turning, smoldering glow, as if anger had been carved into the man's face with a red-hot knife. Akhaturian took to avoiding the cargo master whenever he could, and soon learned the byways and cubbyholes of the labyrinthine ship. He became quite good at avoidance, a skill admired and envied by the others in the berth. A quick eye could oft mark him swimming up a gangway scant moments before Ratline would crawl down another. He became so adept at it that Ratline sometimes forgot that he even had a fourth wrangler.

The contract with his mother had specified an education as well as an employment. Ratline was content that Hard Knocks be the instructor and that learning grow from experience. He never missed an opportunity to quicken the boy's knowledge, but he always waited until the occasion required it. No use lecturing, he once said to Corrigan (who had worked up an elaborate instructional curriculum pursuant to the contract), not until the kid is ready. They always learn more if they come and ask. It had been said of Ratline that he cared nothing for any man or thing—but he cared about his young charges, and protected and even nurtured them in his own harsh and sour manner. It was this facet of the man that Okoye had sensed and it was why she, of only two on board, harbored anything like affection for him. For she had once learned an important lesson from an ancient European folk tale about a magic island, a young woman, and her monstrous host; and the lesson was this: that a person must be loved before he becomes lovable.

"I don't understand," Akhaturian said one day and, as it was the phrase with which he was most likely to begin a sentence, no one in the common room paid him any attention at first. They were, all four of them, bone-tired from having replaced the lithium valve under Ratline's falcon-like supervision and, like a puddle on sunbaked earth, the question needed time to soak in.

Finally, although she hesitated to ask a question with so many possible answers, Okoye said, "What don't you understand?"

"Everything," said Evermore, doing the lad's answering for him. DeCant, leaping to her bedmate's defense, gave the older boy a scowl and said, "He's new," which was not quite the same as denying the charge.

"I mean about the balk line," Akhaturian said. "Why do the engines have to be back on line before then? At the speed we're going, we'll actually reach Jupiter sooner than we planned."

"Dummy," said Evermore. "That's just the problem."

"You should ask Mr. Corrigan," Okoye suggested. "He knows navigation the best."

"Not as well as Hand did," Evermore said, "but Hand is gone and I don't have time to explain." Akhaturian could admit to ignorance with utter conviction. Evermore could not, but this was not because he pretended to know more than he did. It was self-deception and not conceit. That sort of blind confidence can lead one to tackle jobs not yet mastered, although for that very reason can also lead to their mastery.

"You see, we're moving between two fixed points . . ." Mr. Corrigan explained when Akhaturian had tracked him down to the bridge, where he was computing the ship's position by dead reckoning. (This was a procedure in navigation akin to book inventory in materials management. It was a number that ought to be true, but seldom was.)

"But Jupiter isn't a fixed point!" Akhaturian protested. "And neither is Achilles. They're both moving at, uh, at fourteen kiss."

Corrigan laughed. It was always more difficult to explain such matters to the wellsprung than to the spaceborn. "We only *call* them fixed points, because they don't move *relative to each other*. Achilles sits in a stable cusp which is always the same distance ahead of Jupiter. We boost partway, coast for a while to save on boron, flip, then brake. But it takes the same energy to slow us down as to speed us up, so the de-boost has to start at the balk line—in our case, at two hundred and sixty-three million klicks out—or we'll be going too fast to enter HoJO—that's High Jovian Orbit—unless," and this he could not help but add, "we find an additional source of deceleration."

Corrigan took Akhaturian through the calculations, step-by-step; that is, he held an extended conversation with Ship in its avatar as navigational computer. The Second Officer conceptualized the problem and the neural net did all the donkey work. Akhaturian learned how to calculate velocities and bearings and boron usage. Then, Corrigan let the Least Wrangler run practice problems, taking an imaginary *River* back and forth among Jupiter, the Trails, and the Leads. Akhaturian rather enjoyed it. "I am the captain!" he declared at one point and Corrigan smiled (or tried to).

"It takes more than knowing how to point the ship to be a captain," he said with more than a touch of black choler. "It takes knowing where and why to point it."

"Hey," said Akhaturian when he had returned to the wranglers' common room, "I bet you don't know why *The Riv'* is shaped like a disk."

Rave Evermore was taking apart his belt phone. There was nothing wrong with it. He was just curious how it was put together. "Of course, I know," he told the Least Wrangler, without looking at him.

"Oh."

Nkieruke Okoye dimmed her screader and looked up. "I don't know. Why don't you tell me?"

Akhaturian bounced over to her side and, inevitably, deCant joined him there. Unnoticed by any but Okoye, Evermore shot them a look that the Igbo girl recognized as one of envy, though of whom he was envious she was not sure. "It's because *The Riv'* used to be a magnetic sail," Akhaturian said. "Mr. Corrigan told me. That mast on the foreward hull? It used to anchor a super-loop *sixty-four kilometers* in diameter, way back when. They made the ship so it would fit inside the shape of the magnetic field the sail created, because the charged particles—you know, the solar wind—they sleet off the field—Mr. Corrigan says that gasses in the field can glow with different colors—but there's two hot spots—the auroral spots, Mr. Corrigan called them—where the particles curve in, just like on Jupiter—and on Earth too I suppose—and they didn't want any part of the ship to sit in the hot spots or the 'vanilla' belts. That's why the mast is only a couple hundred meters long. So the ship stays well inside."

Okoye considered that this entire pronouncement had been delivered without a second intake of breath and smiled at the lad. "That's very interesting," she said, and did not correct his pronunciation of "Van Allen belts." DeCant beamed. "Isn't Ivar smart?" she asked the sidereal universe.

Afterwards, Evermore approached Okoye and asked her if what the boy had said was true and, on being told that it was, nodded sagely. "Yah," he said, "that's what I would have guessed, but you've been on board more years than the rest of us. I'm surprised you didn't know."

Okoye smiled at him too—which was all that Evermore had really wanted—and neither did she correct him on his own misapprehension.

The Second Wrangler

Bhatterji saw Raphael Evermore in the machine shop on third watch assembling a tool of some sort and he paused to watch the boy at work from the entryway. The wrangler's features were stilled in a picture of intent concentration, almost as if he had been caught in a portrait digigraph. His eyes squinted as he focused on the work object; and his lips were pursed and slightly distended. Dark hair, just growing back, shadowed Evermore's skull and framed features as fine and as delicate as carved ivory. Never had his comeliness beckoned the engineer more. Lissome and graceful of limb, and with a natural talent at the omnitool . . . Could there ever have been a more fortunate match? It lacked only the one essential element of Evermore's consent.

That had been withheld, and withheld in no uncertain terms; but Bhatterji, to whom consent mattered a great deal, could not turn his emotions off quite so easily; and so his eyes often caressed the young man whenever their paths crossed.

And yet it was not only for the boy's beauty that Bhatterji paused in the hatchway to watch; for the piece he was building was beautiful too; not in the superficial sense of brightwork or polish, but in its shape and substance and in the way it all fit together so perfectly. It was the sort of beauty that engineers knew, and it had (were engineers as facile with words as with widgets) as much of poetry in it as any sunset or lover's kiss.

Evermore noticed him suddenly and pushed away from the omnitool with a wary look. "What do you want?" he demanded.

You, Bhatterji thought, but for once he did not voice his thoughts. He knew when a suit was lost. "What are you working on?"

"That's none of your business."

The hostility grieved Bhatterji and he wondered, naively, why, if the two of them could not be lovers, they could not simply be friends. "You're using my equipment and my tools and my materials," he pointed out in what he thought was a reasonable tone. "I was just curious."

"I don't like people sneaking up and watching me." This was not entirely true. He would not have minded one bit had it been Okoye—or deCant, or even Miko. Their gazes *felt* different. Perhaps another sort of photon was involved.

"I was admiring your work."

"You were admiring more than that."

Bhatterji did not deny it, because it was not untrue. Instead, he said, "Does it bother you to be attractive?"

"Don't come near me."

"I won't."

"I don't like you looking at me."

Bhatterji nodded. "What should I do, pluck out my eyes? Does Okoye like it when you look at her?"

Evermore tilted his chin. "That's different. That's natural. That—"

"—does not answer my question."

Evermore thrust his face forward. "I would never do anything to hurt her."

Bhatterji's patient silence was sufficient indication that the question remained unanswered, and Evermore looked away and muttered, "She's never said anything to object."

"She never says much of anything," Bhatterji pointed out.

It was Evermore's bad luck that of the three girls close to his own age, one was a pledged virgin, one was betrothed, and the third lusted for older men. It defied probability theory to drill so many dry holes, given that, in a manner of speaking, he had not drilled any holes at all. He was of an age when the mere attention of any girl would have brought undiluted joy, yet he genuinely considered 'Kiru to be the smartest and the prettiest of the three. Now, Twenty-four might actually be prettier by some measures, but her rough and froward ways put him off; and Miko might be smarter (again, by some meaures), but he was more than a little frightened of the engineer's mate. Thus, while he sometimes thought about the other two when he closed his eyes at night, it was Okoye he saw most often—for even in his fantasies he was something of a realist.

None of this would he ever say to the likes of Ramakrishnan Bhatterji, nor for that matter to 'Kiru Okoye. Yet Bhatterji needed no confirmation when lust was the topic and he warned the boy, "Remember that she is pledged."

The reminder, dropped on the countertop of Evermore's heart, had the ring of accusation. "I know that," he said. "I know that. What do you think I am?"

"A young man."

They stared at each other for a long moment while Bhatterji pondered his regrets and Evermore wondered from which end the engineer had meant his last remark. He knew what Okoye did in his dreams; he was terrified at what he might do in Bhatterji's. At last, Bhatterji said, "I only asked what you were building," and Evermore, recognizing a bid to end an uncomfortable encounter, said, "Only a practice piece. You know. Something I get to fold and drill and weld and . . ."

". . . practice every other verb in the tool kit." Bhatterji laughed and Evermore found that he could laugh with him. But when the engineer had gone and Evermore fishtailed to reposition the piece in the fixture, he wondered too what the purpose was of the device that Ratline had given him to make.

Corrigan had begun a baseline inspection and gap analysis of all the equipment and materials that would be needed to put at least one sail on the mast: the braiders and winders and splicers; the kickers and the tommy rolls; the shroud motors around the rim; the cat-line motors in the loft. He was an hour or so into this effort and lost in a warm haze of data acquisition when Satterwaithe tracked him down and put a sock in him. This was the sort of thing that could be delegated, she pointed out. One needn't be a *sailor* to validate software or to function-test equipment. Corrigan's talents would be more usefully engaged in measurement and calibration, which *did* require specialized knowledge of superconducting alloys, quenching levels, hoop stress and the like. All this was couched in subordinate tones. *Don't you think that . . . ? Wouldn't it be better if . . . ?* But Corrigan knew an order when he heard one. In her more dyspeptic moods, he knew, the sailing master dispensed with the question marks.

Subsequently, he called Okoye and The Lotus Jewel to his quarters and assigned them to the gap analysis as if it had been his very own initiative.

"Verify that the necessary equipments on this list still function," Corrigan told them, handing The Lotus Jewel a clipscreen. "Whatever doesn't work, red tag it for Ratline or me to look at." Being a methodical man, he had developed minimum cut sets on the fault trees and identified those choke points where the lack of a single asset or group of assets would make sail deployment undoable. Unlike Bhatterji, Corrigan knew that taking pains at the front end would often save time at the back; although (also unlike Bhatterji) he did not realize that such foreknowledge could be a curse as well. A man who anticipates every obstacle may well despair, while a man who does not may improvise success.

"I can fix some of the malfs," Okoye said, "or ask Evermore to help." But Corrigan shook his head.

"There's no point to repairing some units if we don't have others we need. Give the whole list a once-through, then we'll make a go/no-go decision. And don't tell Evermore, either, or anyone else. We haven't decided if the project is doable, so we don't want to raise hopes." Corrigan wanted the two young women to believe that excuse as earnestly as he wanted to believe it himself.

Which they did not. They knew perfectly well that the project was clandestine for other reasons, but The Lotus Jewel was in it to please her lover and Okoye because she loved the lore of sails. So they carried out their survey in the quiet hours, while Gorgas slept the innocent sleep of the ill-informed.

At first, The Lotus Jewel was quite excited and she flew from machine to machine, an easy feat in free fall. But the novelty palled and it was the novelty that had captured her. "This is boring," she said when, after several hours, the two progressed from the Long Room to the old Sail Prep room.

Okoye shook her head and wondered at the older woman. How could it be boring? They were unfurling the Great Sail! Actually, they were running down a checklist as prelude to a make-or-mend decision, but attitude is all.

In her childhood, 'Kiru Okoye had devoured stories of the romance of sails. Coke Johnson and the Sandstorm of '69. The tragic fate of the looper *Castle King*. The pirate ship, *Empty Sail*. The desperate last days of the quattro *City of Halifax*. The skies had been filled with heroes then. She could not imagine Gorgas (or any of the officers) crying, "Fly or die!" as Lavender Morganfree had cried when Jupiter's swelling magfield threatened to engulf the troika *Iridium Rose*. Hoist that sail and kick those amps!

The Lotus Jewel did not understand Okoye any more than the Igbo girl understood the sysop. She thought 'Kiru a dull stick, but that was because she confused romance with the Grail and not with the Quest. She had thought that unfurling the sail would be an exciting moment and had not thought much on all the moments that must precede it.

That Okoye was such a quiet girl did not help. The Lotus Jewel, among her many confusions, confused reserve with melancholy. "Unbutton, 'Kiru," she would say when the girl double-checked the Number Four Braider just in case she had missed something, and she would tell a little story or a joke because she could not bear the thought of such a large solemnity in such a small body.

Okoye, for her part, smiled at the joke (because it really was rather funny) and wondered how a woman so insistently friendly could be so desperately unhappy. The sysop was beautiful—by conventional measures the most beautiful aboard—and everyone on board enjoyed her company. She seized every day as if it were a shining moment, and of course that was the problem, although Okoye did not realize it then. For how can a moment shine, unless the rest of life is dark?

"You talk to yourself sometimes," The Lotus Jewel said to her. "Did you know you did that? You really shouldn't. People might think you were, you know, 'funny.'"

Okoye disliked personal revelations, and one's *chi* was a very personal thing indeed. Christians that she knew sometimes mentioned "guardian angels," but they neither spoke to them nor seem to realize that they might sometimes be "fallen angels." Okoye did not believe in angels, fallen or not, but she did believe in her *chi* because when she spoke to it, it sometimes spoke back.

"You don't talk very much, do you?" The Lotus Jewel persisted.

Okoye smiled apologetically and shook her head.

"Some people think you're snobbish. But I think you're just shy. You really need to break out of your shell."

Okoye was not sure that qualified as a "need," but when The Lotus Jewel suggested they end the shift in the common room, Okoye found compliance easier than resistance.

When they entered the commons in the small hours, they found it empty of all life save Rave Evermore. The Second Wrangler, having worked late on Ratline's strange tool, was slowly putting himself around the outside of a sandwich.

"It's party time!" the sysop cried, to Okoye's intense embarrassment. Evermore broke into a great smile. "I'm ready!" he answered, without even swallowing.

Okoye understood that he was ready in a great many ways. The hungers of sixteen-year-old boys did not require telepathy to discern. Okoye resigned herself to a longer night than she had intended, for if she retired now, Rave would read significance into it; and, believing he had been deliberately left alone with The Lotus Jewel, might try to press his eagerness on the older woman. One of two things might happen then and both of them were bad.

"What are you two doing up so late?" Rave asked.

"Hey," said The Lotus Jewel, "this space is flat. Where's the music?" And coasting over to the entertainment bank, she dialed up a menu. "I think deft kicks, don't you?"

Okoye, who had no idea what "deft" was—a musical style, she supposed—agreed that it was indeed "kick" to listen to. Rave was not supposed to know about Plan B; so although The Lotus Jewel would have started some music even had she found herself alone in the room, she was clearly evading the boy's question.

The evasion was too obvious. A thoughtful look came over Evermore and his eyes danced speculatively between Okoye and The Lotus Jewel. That boy was quick. Even Ratline admitted it, and the cargo master was niggardly with his praise. Give Evermore enough dots and he could connect them, although there was no telling what picture he would come up with in the end.

"Corrigan wanted me to run an inventory," she said, which had the advantage of being true, "and The Lotus Jewel helped me," which was also true—the entirety demonstrating how the sum of two truths could equal a lie.

"Yah, and I got busywork from the Rat," Evermore agreed with conspiratorial resignation. "He wants me to fab some sort of gizz for him and he wants the kids to shift the cargo around the hold—again."

Okoye agreed that Ratline was a hard man. She knew that the realignment of the cargo was in the expectation of receiving thrust through the mast, but that the task was necessary did not reduce the cargo master's Rockwell number.

The Lotus Jewel rejoined them, ducking and flexing in a manner that Okoye supposed was "deft"—at least the motions were in time to the music—and the Raven's attention was diverted from Ratline's motives by the oscillations consequent to those moves.

"I'm trying to get our little 'Kiru to unbutton," The Lotus Jewel told him, handing the both of them a fruit bomb.

"I'll help," Rave said, reaching a mischievous hand toward Okoye's coverall. It was only a joke. He only half-meant it; but he meant the wrong half. Okoye responded with the posture that the sisterhood called The Rock; and Rave's grin faded into confusion. "Sorry," he muttered as he pulled away.

If he had had a brother on one side or the other, Evermore might have had a different perspective; but he had been bracketed by sisters coming and going. It was hard to know what was right. He believed that Okoye liked him. She sometimes looked at him when she thought he did not see. Did that mean that he occupied her thoughts as densely as she inhabited his? Why, the girl had all but moved into his libido and set up housekeeping! He wondered whether her pledge of virginity was simply a rampart he was meant to assault. She might only be waiting to surrender. His father had often told him that—that women had desires as strong as men—and his mother, although at times giving her husband a hooded look, had never contradicted him. Yet, the one time Evermore had applied the lesson (and that had involved Beth-Lynn, the neighbor's girl) it had not turned out at all well. There had been giggles and revelations in the garage— he could still smell the scents of rubber and battery acid overwhelming the powder and rosewater odor of the girl herself—but when he tied to do what she wanted, she cried and then called out and later said that she had not wanted it at all. He had gotten a whipping from his father and threats from hers. His mother had looked on him with a kind of empty sorrow and his sisters with utter horror.

After that, nothing was left but to run away. There had been an ugly night spent in wary vigil at the maglev station, and another almost as bad in a cardboard tent near Port Phoenix, and the days that had fallen between had been no more beautiful. He had made his way to the skyport with the vague notion of stowing away and running off to space. There were morphies about boys who did that (although they always skipped the parts about nights in maglev stations). Evan Hand had found him lurking behind some luggage carts on the apron, and had taken him aboard the LEO Shuttle with him. Evermore had thought it passing strange that a ship's captain should be wandering about the tarmac like that, almost as if he had been hunting for something he had lost.

The Lotus Jewel, seeing sheep's eyes on Evermore and being always ready to smooth the course of love, held her own fruit bomb on high. "Here's to . . . What shall it be, kids?"

Okoye searched within herself. "Let us tell sad tales of the death of kings."

The sysop gave her a puzzled look, for she had been expecting another, more lusty sort of toast—and might have heard one too had Evermore spoken first. "What?"

Okoye sighed. "To Evan Hand," she said, raising her bomb. The others hesitated a moment, but met her bomb with theirs. "To Evan Hand," they repeated. The toast struck The Lotus Jewel as morbid, not at all a prelude to a good time and the three of them sucked their nectars in silence.

But silence was anathema to The Lotus Jewel. "He was a good man," she said finally for no other reason than to break it. "A good captain."

"He was okay," Evermore allowed.

The Lotus Jewel nudged him playfully on the shoulder. "How many captains have you known? Compared to the Zacker, he . . ."

"It's not a comparative scale," Evermore responded. "I measure against absolute standards."

"For captains? I didn't know there were any . . ."

"Sure there are." He tallied his fingers. "Percentage of transits completed without error. Cargo penalties as a ratio to cargo value carried. Crew turnover per annum. You can measure all sorts of things."

"Except what's important," said Okoye.

"Like what?"

"Hand cared about us."

Evermore looked abruptly off. "I'd rather a captain know his craft than that he care about me." By this he meant a certain kind of caring, as his encounter with Bhatterji earlier that evening was still fresh in his mind.

"Well, you've got your wish, then," The Lotus Jewel said. "Gorgas doesn't care about anything. I'll grant him the craft, though."

"You liked Captain Hand," Okoye said to The Lotus Jewel, not so much as a question as a statement of fact.

The sysop smiled as she recollected other moments. "He was a lot of fun. He had a laugh that—oh, but you know what he was like. I never saw a frown on him." It surprised her, she not being the reflective sort, to realize how much she missed the man. He had given her a fresh start after her disgrace at Mooncrest, and that leap of faith in the face of her reputation had affected her a great deal more than she had realized. "At least his soul is at rest now," she said.

"The Egyptians," said Evermore with cheerful irrelevancy, "believed that a person had three souls."

The Lotus Jewel thought this the straight line to a forthcoming joke and turned toward him with a sparkle of anticipation. Even after Evermore had explained about mummies and ancient funeral practices the sysop waited a moment longer for a punch line she was sure was coming, but whose outlines she could not yet discern.

"Three souls!" said Okoye. "Why, that violates parsimony! Two souls are quite sufficient."

This would do for a punch line and The Lotus Jewel laughed with the unfettered delight of incomprehension. She felt that what Okoye had said was funny, although she could not say just quite why she felt so. But Okoye had spoken up only because the extra soul really did surprise her.

Evermore, because he was intensely interested in the girl's every breath and utterance, and also because he was an intensely curious person, asked, "Why two?"

While Okoye was reticent in personal matters and seldom spoke for the sake of hearing her own voice, she had no trouble answering a question. There are, after all, different forms of silence and some of them involve talking. "There is the eternal soul," she said, "which is called *maw*, and there is also the life force, or *nkpuruk-obi*, which dies when the body dies. The life force may also leave the body during life—under a great fright, for example—although if it does not soon return, the body will die. After death, the maw becomes a shadow, which is why it is very bad luck to step on a shadow. It angers the ghost, and nothing good can come of that. Later, they are reincarnated, some as leopards or elephants or trees. We call them *ndichie*—'returners.' The Amuneke Igbo believe only evil souls return as trees, but that only shows what foolish folk they are. Why, my very own grandfather is now a baobab, and he was as fine a man as ever lived."

"Which gives," said Evermore, "a whole new meaning to the phrase *to vegetate*."

The Lotus Jewel laughed again, but Okoye thought that the joke had been somewhat blasphemous and to change the subject, she asked the older woman who "the Zacker" was.

"Zachary Zackmeyer was captain before Hand. To hear Satterwaithe and Ratline tell it, he was awful."

"Oh," Evermore said with a careless wave of his fruit bomb, "since when have those two ever said good of anything?"

"Ram told me," The Lotus Jewel said, "that it was the Zacker who let the ship fall to pieces and Enver Koch had to put them all back together."

"Or at least that's what Koch told Bhatterji," Evermore said with a grin. Then, without even a pause, he asked, "So what was it you two were doing inventory on?"

Okoye almost turned around, for it seemed as if the question had snuck up on her from behind. Evermore was still trying to connect the dots. Here are the dots. One: His sexual desires were in a more or less permanent state of eager frustration. Two: Girls his age were said to have the same sexual desires as boys. Three: 'Kiru was pledged not to be with a boy. Four: 'Kiru had just spent long hours alone with The Lotus Jewel. The one thing he never thought of was that those particular dots might not belong in the same picture.

"I ran the accounts," The Lotus Jewel said, "and the engine

repairs are going to cost us a sack of troy once we hit Port Galileo. Corrigan wanted to see what we still have on board that we can sell off." It sounded true, and it might even be true. A deception works better when it is true.

"You could start with all that old equipment on the rim," Evermore said. "All it does is get in the way when we have to do Outside work. Except . . . who would want to buy that junk?" The wrangler laughed.

There was no romance in Evermore's soul for all that the boy sought romance at every opportunity. That might even be the reason for the seeking. It is the thirsty man who most desires the cup. Evermore had the sort of features in the egg that might suit romance were he older. Square-faced, solid, with laughing eyes and a chin that threatened dimples, it was a face that could grow to be handsome once it had been sufficiently seasoned. For now, it balanced on the cusp between "handsome" and "cute." Okoye could understand what had drawn Bhatterji; and she could also understand that a boy might worry a great deal about being thought "cute."

"You two are no fun," The Lotus Jewel complained. She took the empty bulbs from them and pushed off to the cooler to fetch replacements. Okoye watched Rave watch her and puzzled over his evident fascination with a woman with entirely too much surface area. She could not imagine decorating herself with such paints and odors as The Lotus Jewel used; nor would the woman's laughter and casual touching ever come quite natural to her.

"You're very quiet," Rave said, turning to her—but from him it did not sound the indictment it had from the lips of The Lotus Jewel. It was an interested observation, perhaps even an approving one, for Rave Evermore too liked to keep his own counsel. For some reason, this pleased the Igbo girl, who ducked her head and let a smile's ghost answer.

"You know," he continued in confidence, "you're just as pretty as she is."

Okoye did not need the toss of his head to know to which *she* Evermore had referred. It was the sincerity she heard in his voice that shocked her. "Why, that only shows what poor judgment you have."

"No, didn't you hear me before? I always use *absolute* standards."

Was he trying to ingratiate himself with her by such flattery? Did he think she would foreswear her oath and grant him her favors for the sake of a passing compliment?

Yet, flattery is the vice of praising someone for a quality she has not got. One cannot flatter the rose by calling it red, nor the birdsong by calling it sweet. *Beauty* might have crossed the line had Evermore spoken it of Nkieruke Okoye, but *pretty* did not. The boy was correct when he said that he always measured from a datum. Okoye did not believe even that much and so she dodged the label; but she was not always right about others, let alone about herself.

The Accidental Captain

Reviewing material usage in his day room, Gorgas noticed that stores withdrawals exceeded Bhatterji's original bill of materials. The engineer was using more hobartium than expected. Such deviations from plan would have vexed Corrigan, but Gorgas knew that unexpected contingencies always arose to adjust prior expectations. Why, if it hadn't been for Evan Hand . . .

But Gorgas did not like to think of the debt he owed the late captain. He was not where he had thought to be at this point in his career; but here he was and he would make the best of it. It was considerably better than where he might have been.

Sometimes, in idle moments—he did have some—he contemplated the lives he might have led—as a farmer and horse breeder on the Little Plain, as his father and grandfather had been. Or as a commodore in the Space Guard. Or as a captain on a Four Planets liner. Or as a husband and father rather than as a childless widower. He might have served on different ships, flown with different comrades, known a different woman. These alternities, as he called them, intrigued him and he would devote considerable thought to the contingencies under which they might have arisen. He saw his life as an eternally self-pruning tree, each moment pinching off some possibilities while opening others.

This is the paradox of free will. It is free because it limits freedom. Every Yes is a chorus of No's. When he had married Marta, he had forbidden himself all other women. When he had sat for his master's boards, he had turned away from other careers. And yet, while he had trimmed himself of an infinity of possibilities, he saw still an infinity lying ahead.

So it was not that Bhatterji had deviated from the plan that annoyed Gorgas. It was that Bhatterji had not bothered to inform him of the changes. Gorgas was answerable to *The River's* owners for the ship's performance, down to the last rivet, and *I didn't know* was not an acceptable answer. "How am I to manage a ship," he growled aloud, "when I don't know what my people are doing."

Now there was an understatement! Miko, watching from the air vent, nearly burst an eardrum stifling a laugh. She herself knew pretty much what every crewmember was about, from fornication to fabrication, though even she did not yet know what the Thursday Group's activities added up to. She couldn't be everywhere, all the time; and sometimes she did not understand what she saw. She thought Dr. Wong suffered from asthma.

But watching Gorgas at work was like watching the stars pass by the ship. There was motion but it took a subtle mind to perceive it, and that vice Miko did not have. Twisting, she guided herself back out of the ducts, past an idle fan to a hatch that led into a maintenance way behind the D-ring corridor.

Gorgas meanwhile, after a distracted glance toward the muffled thump where Miko took a corner too wide, continued to review the stores withdrawals. Ratline and Lotus Jewel were catching up on their own maintenance, he read—Ratline on the mass-driver and Lotus Jewel on the transmitter antenna array. That was all very well. The mass driver was critical for "fly/bye" deliveries to destinations not worth the delta-vee of a docking; and the transmitter was essential for navigation. Yet both projects were consuming hobartium that Bhatterji might need. He ought to caution them. The ship could live without the mass driver until they raised Port Galileo, where the Yards could handle it; and repairing the comm equipment could be delayed until they were within hailing range of a port. He put out stop orders on both projects.

Now, The Lotus Jewel was in fact working on her comm equipment—the forward sensor array, in particular, was critical—but she had withdrawn twice the materials that she needed, turning the excess over to Corrigan to use in make-and-mend on the sails. Ratline did not bother with such trifles. He did no work on the mass driver for the simple reason that it needed none. With The Lotus Jewel's help, he had inserted a backdated maintenance report into Ship's memory, but that was only a fig leaf.

In this manner Gorgas missed his first opportunity to learn of Plan B.

His senses enclosed in virtch hat and data gloves, his motions translated by clever linkages to the microcosmic scale, Bhatterji roamed the plains of a chip the size of Gujarat State. The whole vast universe beyond had faded to background noise. The tang of metal and grease and foam might reach his nose, the hiss of air or the clank of foot on rung or deck might approach his ear, but none were granted admission to his awareness. It might be that he could be struck dead by an enemy—and there were those with cause to hate him—and he would not notice until he had finished the job and removed his goggles, and headphones, and gloves.

When he finally did so and saw that Gorgas had been watching from the stairwell, it was with no great delight, for Stepan Gorgas was an unsatisfying audience. He took Bhatterji's artistry so much for granted that he thought nothing exceptional in the work at hand and so granted no kudos. Yet exceptional it was. Bhatterji knew it. He wished everyone else did too.

"So, cap'n," he said as he cleaned up, "what brings you down to the bowels?"

"Your progress report is late," the captain said.

The engineer turned away to make an adjustment to the work theater. "Too busy making progress to make reports."

"Do you need more hands?" Gorgas said. "More hands make light the work, eh?"

"More likely, they get in each other's way," the engineer suggested. "Miko and I can handle things. We'll get everything rigged, don't worry." That Gorgas thought the job beyond him irritated Bhatterji, but he made a conscious effort to maintain his equanimity.

But Gorgas had no such thought. He assumed eventual success, but was concerned over the eventuality of it. The sooner "everything was rigged," the less the penalty for late delivery. "What about Evermore? Hidei can do journeyman work while he does apprentice work. Evermore is good with tools."

"No."

"Eh? I thought you liked the lad."

Bhatterji turned and scowled at the captain, wondering if that were meant as a sly dig. "He doesn't follow instructions very well."

To Gorgas, the response conjured images of pots admonishing kettles, though he said nothing about it—which was too bad, because Bhatterji might actually have enjoyed the jibe. "Today is day five," Gorgas said.

Bhatterji grunted. "I thought today was the seventeenth."

Gorgas wondered if the engineer were being disingenuous. "After today, we will need all four engines if we are to slow into Jupiter."

Bhatterji turned away from him and twisted some controls at random on his microstage. "We always did."

After this unsatisfactory interview with the engineer, Gorgas proceeded to the bridge and wriggled through the access tunnel into the observation blister. He had suspended the watches, but a daily sighting was still logged because that was the way it had been done in the Guard.

The blister was positioned halfway out toward the rim of the disk, so that when the ship was under acceleration the observer seemed balanced precariously on the slope of a broad, circular hill. Outboard, the hull fell off toward the *barrera* that bounded the rim. Inboard, it rose slightly toward a gentle peak from which thrust the long, archaic mast. Gorgas thought for a moment that the lock for the forward warehouse was partly open; but when he asked Ship, the AI said that it was closed, so he decided it must be some trick of light and shadow.

The sun was a pewter diamond, a heraldic sun, with stylized rays at the compass points induced by small imperfections in the tinted, metalocene plastic through which Gorgas viewed it. Along the galactic plane roiled the Milky Way, the ship's eponym, the river of stars: a riot so dense that the sky seemed white and the gaps and voids and nebulae became black suns within it. There were faint sounds too; though these came from within the ship. Clicks and hums; a steady vibration from the Caplan pumps for the life-support systems; now and then, a creak or a distant thunk. The whisper of cool air brushed Gorgas's cheek and brought with it a faint metallic odor.

Not that Gorgas noticed any of that. He was not a man attentive to his senses. He was an idealist; which is to say, a man for whom ideas are more real than the senses. When he glanced toward the sun to center it in the crosshairs of the Black Telescope, he did not see a pewter diamond, nor anything of the sort. Not that he lacked a sense of awe and beauty, because what he did perceive was a writhing mass of fusing plasmas balanced in a continual struggle between the luminal impulse to fling itself into the infinite void and the gravitational demand to collapse forever. That is, he saw what he knew rather than that he knew what he saw. There is more than a little awe in such a vision—perhaps more than in finding jewels or rivers in the firmament—and even considerable beauty. One observes always through an instrument and the instrument is always imperfect, so which distortion is the truth is a fine point.

Gorgas was not a stupid man. Hand had been eclectic in his choice of crew, but he had never picked for stupid. But Gorgas conceived things so clearly that he trusted his visions more than his vision and often saw only what he expected to see. By itself, this was no great failing—as long as he had Corrigan to check him on matters of fact; but it was Corrigan who had undogged the bunghole to test the davits (and The Lotus Jewel who had ensured that Ship did not notice.) Light and shadow were not in it. Smoke and mirrors were.

At precisely Zulu Noon, Gorgas fixed Jupiter in Gemini and triangulated against the Sun and Antares. (In theory, the ship ran on a secant line between Achilles and Jupiter, which for this transit made Scorpio the ship's Backdrop.) The *Ephemeredes*, being sun-centered, placed Jupiter in Cancer, so it was a matter of simple spherical trigonometry to approximate the ship's position, give-or-take a few million kilometers. He also verified the chronometer's calibration, but that was just going through the motions, since the damaged comm could not receive the confirmation ping from the Fixed Point Observatory. Comparing the lag for Observatory time against shipboard time would give the precise radial distance from the Fixed Point. (It is difficult to take a pilot bearing when landmarks are all a whirligig.) Lacking the benchmark reduced navigation to dead reckoning, subject to drift and the cumulative effects of small deviations.

The entire procedure could have been accomplished remotely from the control-room navigation panel. Indeed, he could have instructed Ship to take the sight and log it automatically. That was how Corrigan and Satterwaithe carried out the duty when it fell to them. But Gorgas had learned his trade as a middie in the ESA Space Guard, and what was then largely a means to harry the wasters from the Service was now a treasured bit of nostalgia for a fleeted youth. There is a right way and a wrong way; but there is also the accustomed way.

Captain Anrej Kuziemski—the midship berth had named him "Kaptain Kooz"—had called young Gorgas "a snotty-nosed twerp of a middie," but had always done so with a patient smile. He had taken Gorgas personally into the blister of the old Space Guard cutter *Pierre Delacroix* and shown him how to take his fix manually. (If you call setting dials and pressing buttons "manual." An earlier generation would have snarfed coffee out its nose at the thought, but this was an age when intelligences did a great many tasks without supervision, so "manual" was a notional term.)

When the boy first saw the magnificence of the heavens and grasped the great, whirling ballet of forces that bound everything his eye encompassed into a vast and universal dance, his heart nearly stopped. Perhaps it was to recapture that boy's childlike wonder that Gorgas continued his routine of taking the fix in the blister. At times, he could almost feel the featherweight of Kooz's arm draped across his shoulder as he ticked off the stars by name. It was close in that blister—cutters are not very roomy—so if that old man's arm rested a little more firmly than it otherwise ought, it was due to the cramped quarters there, and nothing else. But then Gorgas had been as stolid and dreamy a youth as he was now a man and it was the ideal captain he remembered and not the real one. Which was just as well, because he remembered Kooz with genuine affection. There is little enough of that in the world to risk losing any.

Returning to the control deck, Gorgas displayed his fix in the plotting tank: a threedy holoprojection of the ship's progress.

It was a day for frowning—which was also just as well, as it was something at which Gorgas excelled. He logged a marked divergence from the grand secant. The *River* was falling sunward more rapidly than Newtonian mechanics required.

An increasing rate of change argued for an acceleration and that meant a force acting on the ship. A gravitational anomaly? He told Ship to calculate the size and location of a body sufficient to cause the noted divergence and Ship replied with what would have been an astonishing discovery in the annals of astronomy had it been anything more than a mathematical whimsy.

With the Farnsworths shut down, the only other forces acting on the ship were the solar wind and the pressure of light; and the *Riv'* was too massive for light pressure to matter. And so, a moment's reflection resolved the puzzle. The ship's radiation shield sloughed off charged particles in the event of a solar storm, but the transferred momentum created a drag that deflected the ship's trajectory. Gorgas told Ship to recompute the trajectory, incorporating the new assumption.

The altered projection appeared in the tank as a line of pale that, when extrapolated, passed near some of the Outer Virgins, one of which the tell-me stud labeled Stranger's Reef. The other two were unnamed. The approach would not be very close, Gorgas saw; yet Virgins were notoriously chaotic—and there had been a Jovian passage in this region a sixmonth before.

The n-body problem has no general solution, and the Belt contained a lot more bodies than n. Every so often Jupiter would ruffle the edges and stray rocks would rise from the Thules or the Hildas, or drop deeper in from the Friggas, depending on distance and vector. Gorgas was not sure where the three indicated asteroids actually were, but he was reasonably sure they were *not* where the AI thought them.

He returned to his day room and sent for The Lotus Jewel. While he waited, he decided to assign Evermore to the engine repair project despite the engineer's demurral. Bhatterji had never asked for help in all the years Gorgas had been aboard, but that didn't mean he couldn't use it. He wrote out an order reassigning the wrangler as an engineer's apprentice, second class, temporary, and launched it over the ship's e-mail, happily unaware of the raw issues that lay between the wrangler and the engineer.

The Lotus Jewel swam into the office as he was typing and stood by until he had finished.

"I have an assignment for you," Gorgas said without preamble. Where Hand had chatted and made small talk before getting around to what he wanted, Gorgas came directly to the point. If he noticed the tiniest narrowing of The Lotus Jewel's brow at all, he ascribed it to intense concentration rather than to passing irritation. He handed her a data pin in a foam goat case. "Track down and verify the true orbits of these Outer Virgins," he said. "Stranger's Reef and two unnamed bodies that appear to be coorbiting with it." Characteristically, he did not explain the reason for the request. Gorgas generally assumed that others knew what he did.

In fairness, Corrigan or Satterwaithe would have understood

immediately. As deck officers, they were well aware of the fey nature of the Outer Virgins. But The Lotus Jewel handled communications and pursing and took the piloting of the ship as a given. Ascribing the task to Gorgas's whimsical curiosity, she added it to her already extensive do-later list. She had, after all, a sail to prepare.

The Missing Mate

The shipbuilders who had designed *The River of Stars* had given thought to the consequences of freefing and micro-gee. That trips of even modest duration could ravage the bones and the blood would not, they suspected, be a major selling point to the wealthy who were then the liner's target. And so, an exercise hall had been included. Outboard on the main deck, the rim corridor was levitated on magnetic bearings and set spinning so that passengers and crew could exercise at Mars level spin-gravity. There were exercise machines and a circumferential running track and a staff of Personal Trainers, all of which (save the trainers) had been left in place during successive reconfigurations. The facilities were finer than a tramp crew required, but that was true of the main deck in general. *The Riv'* might live from hand to mouth, but you couldn't sneer at her accommodations.

Some, like Gorgas, pursued the need for exercise with grim determination, but Bhatterji did so with utter delight. If his body was a temple, he was the Pope of his own religion. He gloried in the sweat and the pumping heart and the adrenaline, in the ache and protest of muscles. He explored what his body could do: on the rings, on the climbing ropes, on the horse, on the track, on the antique mass movers. His body was his instrument—in work, in play, in love—and he kept that instrument polished, fine-tuned, and calibrated.

If Gorgas was a mind that lived in a body, for whom that body was a sort of vehicle to be maintained, Bhatterji to a large extent *was* his body, and his mind was never very far from what his body was telling him. The faded memories of the vivid pastels in which the spinhall had once been colored; the hiss of his breath pumping in and out; the heady rush of the oxygen into his blood; the slap of his running shoes against the plated aerogel floor; the cool rivulets of his sweat coursing across his skin; the odd, out-of-plumb feeling induced by the Coriolis . . . These constant messages told him where he was and what he was and very nearly who he was.

Bhatterji ran past Bigelow Fife, the passenger, who was lying aback performing bench-presses with mechanic precision. The Lunatic's pale flesh quivered and rippled and Bhatterji hurried by before the man could notice and the social graces be called upon. Fife had done nothing to offend him—indeed, in their one short meeting in the machine shop, he had shown an understanding of engineering work—but the man's body repelled the engineer. A man should take more pride in himself, he thought, whether Earthborn or not. Fife struck him as a craftsman who had left his tools to rust and there was in his mind no more culpable a sin.

The Lotus Jewel understood Bhatterji's love affair with his body, though his other loves left her baffled. She too enjoyed the suppleness and delicious sensations of physical exertion, though she shared that enjoyment more widely than did the engineer. Sometimes, the two of them exercised together—pacing each other around the track, more often in the ziggy bounceball room, where they would carom off the bulkheads and each other to swat the ball. In consequence, while The Lotus Jewel had many who loved her, only Bhatterji had become something like a friend.

When he encountered her in his run around the spinhall, Bhatterji slowed his pace to a jog and the two of them set off in tandem, matching each other stride for stride. Not a word was spoken—breath was needed to bellows the lungs—but then, between the two of them, The Lotus Jewel owned most of the words. They passed young Evermore, who was working the static bar when he caught sight of them. Caught between loathing for the one and lust for the other, Evermore's features twisted into a confusion so comical that, once out of his sight, The Lotus Jewel staggered to a laughing stop. Bhatterji, who had noticed only the loathing, halted a few paces farther on, unable to understand her laughter.

"That poor boy," she said. "He was so afraid the sight of my sweaty torso would arouse him and you would think it was meant for you."

Bhatterji, who still could not see the humor of it, growled. "He's made those matters clear enough."

"Do you think I should run another lap, alone?" The Lotus Jewel said. "No one should fear to show their desires."

"You're wrong," Bhatterji told her. "They're a fearful thing to show."

"Ah, that's why you raced ahead of me. You were more afraid than he was." She turned, wiping her forehead with a cloth she kept tucked in her waistband, and stared behind, as if she could see past the upward curve of the track. "He is a cute boy."

"With a tongue of venom."

The Lotus Jewel laid a hand on his arm. "Oh, Ram, we all make mistakes."

He wasn't sure what she meant—that he had made a mistake in the offer or that Evermore had in the refusal.

Ship could find nothing in its drawings archive resembling Evermore's tool. Bhatterji had sketched the device as well as he could remember, and Ship's neural net was entirely capable of recognizing a print that was "almost like" it without any particular instruction. But no matches had been found. Yet the thing that the lad had created could not simply have been an étude. It had had the look of purpose, the sort of look that an engineer recognizes. Whatever else the thing had been, it had been meant to *do* something.

Bhatterji paced his room—in ziggy that meant, literally, to bounce off the walls—as puzzled over his own puzzlement as over the artifact itself. A second order puzzlement. Perhaps it was his pride. An engineer, he ought to be able to deduce function from form. The frustration built until he recognized its lack of fruit. Whatever Evermore had been doing in the machine shop, it would not advance the engine repair by a nanosecond. Yet, it was neither pride nor frustration that drove him from his quarters to swim the corridor; nor that his rooms lacked the scope for pacing.

When he came at last to the door to Miko's quarters, he told himself that it was mere happenstance; and when he pressed the hoígh plate, that it was to ask Miko if she had any idea what Evermore had been fabricating. In other words, Bhatterji was doing some fabricating himself.

There was no response, and Bhatterji believed that his mate was within, watching him through the vista cell but spurning contact. *This cannot continue,* he told himself. *I am her master and she is my mate. She does her job and does it competently, but it is not right that she turns from me. Master and mate need not be lovers. Enver Koch was not my lover; but he was my friend and mentor before the Void took him. It was a terrible thing, Miko, that I was blind and that you needed what I could not give. As terrible too that those who* did *know said nothing to either of us. Yet perhaps we can heal the rift. It is not so wide that we cannot bridge it, if only we both reach out. If I cannot love you, I can teach you. You have the capacity. Most of all you have the love for the ship that all true engineers must have. The ship is our one true lover; it is she who commands us. We two, then, are brother and sister.*

Inchoate thoughts, all a-jumble. He ought to leave a note. If she would not come to the door, she could at least read the note. He took the stylus from the hoígh plate and wrote on it.

Let's talk.

He was not a man of words, at least of deep ones. It was always the lighter words that drifted to the surface and wafted trivially off his lips. Other words were there, boiling inside him; but, being weightier, they always sank and never made it to the tongue. As a result, while he often said what was on his mind, he seldom said what was in it.

When he fishtailed to go, he kicked off on the door frame— and heard the door hush open behind him.

Turning, he saw that no one floated in its frame, yet what could an open door mean, but an invitation? He pulled himself into Miko's quarters, words of greeting on his lips.

But the emptiness was evident immediately. Miko had apparently used only the first room and had put all her meager furnishings there. The other rooms bore no sign that any human had occupied them since the last of the Martian runs. There was little enough to furnish even the front room: a sleeping cage, a dresser, a dog-closet, a sling, a reading lamp. Debris scavenged from ship's stores and from a handful of abandoned staterooms.

The cage had the indefinable appearance of disuse, and the closet, when he checked it, was devoid of clothing. So where did Miko go now once her watch was over? To another room or to another's room? To whose arms had she fled? Evermore's? Not Akhaturian's, not with deCant patrolling the marches of the boy's bed. Fife's? Grubb had told him that Fife was corking the doctor, which proved that God moved in ways more than mysterious—they were damn near whimsical. But Bhatterji did not think that Fife would turn down a second and more lissome offer. He struck the engineer as a calculating man and "one into two" was short division.

Bhatterji determined to kill the passenger if he had taken advantage of the distraught girl.

(Fife, floating in troubled wakefulness in the arms of the slumbering Wong, might have felt a ripple of that determination, for he frowned and looked apprehensively at the door. Then he turned and kissed the doctor's forehead and touched her cheek with gentle, puzzled fingers.)

Yet, if Miko were looking for her father, would she look to the passenger? Bhatterji could no more imagine Fife as a father than could Fife's own son. And The Lotus Jewel owned Corrigan's balls. If there were a father figure anywhere on board, it could only be the remote and authoritarian Gorgas, or the genial and generous Grubb.

Gorgas joined Fife on the death list.

(And Gorgas in his stateroom woke from a tormented dream and saw the holo of his late wife on the farther wall. Dead she was now for most of a decade, yet in his confused half-waking state, Gorgas saw the half-smile on those features and murmured, "Come to bed, dear," before drifting once more into sleep.)

Bhatterji could not imagine Grubb wishing harm to anyone; but neither does the sea wish harm to the lemming. Miko was determined to impale herself and, frustrated in her careful campaign on Bhatterji, might now offer herself to the first opportunity—or the first opportunist.

"Who made you her goddamned guardian?" he growled aloud. When he left the room he made sure the door was now properly fastened. Then, because he knew she would not come around to read it, he erased his message from the hoígh plate.

Bhatterji did not know that Miko had retreated behind the walls, as she had on Amalthea, to seek a comfort that mere arms could never give.

In the glory days, *The River of Stars* had sailed with a regiment of staff. There had been maids and musicians, sweepers and servers, cooks and call girls, jugglers and gigolos. Enchanting sights, toothsome meals, heady aromas, beautiful sounds, provocative touches—if there was a sense that wanted pleasing, there had been staff on board for the pleasing of it.

But people who by their very existence affirm the rightness of the pecking order have no business sharing the spaces frequented by their betters. They are to be summoned or dismissed, and that is all. If they eat, drink, play, or fornicate, they must do it *backstage*, lest they remind their masters of a shared humanity. Even the crew had been careful to draw a distinction between those who ran the ship and those who ran errands.

So, a series of half-decks and passageways had been included in the schematics, a network that enabled all those maids and servants and cabin boys to scurry about unseen, to appear only when and where their presence was required, and to duck out of sight once their duties were done. The staff corridors ran like alleys behind the staterooms, sometimes twisting or turning or running up or down a deck to avoid bisecting larger public spaces. The staff had called it "the peepery."

When *The Riv'* was converted to an emigrant ship, the peepery had been sealed off and never used again, save by inquisitive children and stealthy lovers. Of the present crew, Ratline alone knew of it, but he had forgotten that he knew. Little Timmy had learned the warren as had few others; but that whole part of his life he had buried in a great, dark hole in his memory.

If anyone aboard were fated to rediscover the peepery, it was Miko. That girl was nosy, and crawling about inside the walls was her natural bent. She had come across the passageways early on, even before she had fled from Bhatterji. She found them while exploring down one of the smaller air ducts, and she pounced upon the discovery with the delight of a ship-wrecked sailor upon an unexpected shore.

The hallway she found was stale and warm with air still as breath suspended. No one had swept or cleaned in decades and dust pays little mind to gravity even when there is some. Miko tied a cloth around her nose and mouth, explored for a little while, then returned the next day, having liberated a precipita-tor and a sticky-broom from Grubb's supply store.

Soon enough, she had tidied up. A few panels, judiciously unfastened, established a mild draft and gradually the air fresh-ened—at least up to the quality of the rest of the ship (which was rank, to be sure; but all quality is relative). She brought in a few odds and ends that would do for furnishings and settled into the servant's lounge underneath C ring in the starboard quad-rant, moving in permanently after her contretemps with Bhat-terji. This put her, if the truth be known, closer to the engineer's quarters than before; but she knew only the convoluted path she had taken to reach it and so the irony escaped her.

Bhatterji had always thought Grubb a simple man. There was no depth to him because a man with depth had always some-thing unseen within him, and Grubb was all on the surface. And yet in one way the chief was not so simple and that was in his connectedness. He always seemed to know everything that was going on. (Not that he did, but it was the seeming that mat-tered.) So Bhatterji sought him out that evening to ask him if he knew where Miko had gone.

The chief shook his head. "No, I haven't seen her." But

Grubb was thinking only of Miko's *immediate* whereabouts. He had no idea that the engineer's mate had disappeared and, even had he known, he might not have thought much of it. The doctor and the passenger disappeared too from time to time. (And he had his theories as to why.) And Ratline. (True, it was to his own cabin that the cargo master vanished, but it was only by opening the door that one could *know,* and opening doors was a quantum sort of thing to do.) But every man needs his solitude. Gorgas found his in the observation bubble or in games of complex battle chess; Okoye, in her books. Grubb himself often had only his sheep for company. (And there were theories about that too.) So if Miko were much unseen, the chief saw no need for alarm.

"Grubb is incapable of concealment," Bhatterji told The Lotus Jewel later as they shared a meal in the crew's mess. "He really doesn't know."

"I didn't know, either," the sysop admitted. She might have, had she not been spending so much of her time with Corrigan and the others, prepping the sail for deployment. Now that Bhatterji had pointed it out, however, she realized that, except during duty hours, she seldom saw the young girl about the ship, and *never* when Bhatterji was nearby.

The occupant of a vehicle traveling along a highway might be startled to observe that most other vehicles are traveling either faster or slower; but this is only the Observer Principle. Cars traveling at identical speeds will neither overtake nor be overtaken and so fewer of them will be noted. In the same way, Bhatterji's impression may have arisen because Miko was avoiding him rather than because she had vanished; that is, a special theory of disappearance rather than a general one.

"Why are you concerned?" The Lotus Jewel asked. She put a little rhetorical spin on *you* because Miko was not the sort that Bhatterji normally inquired after.

"She's my mate. She's my responsibility."

"It's a big ship," The Lotus Jewel continued when it was apparent that this was all the answer she would get. Bhatterji could talk widely on most subjects, but deeply on only a few. "We're all busy."

Bhatterji grunted. "I haven't seen much of you, either."

It was an innocent remark. It was Bhatterji half-convincing himself that he had read too much significance into Miko's empty room. It *was* a big ship and Miko may simply have moved herself elsewhere. If she had abandoned her furniture, it was furniture that was hardly hers. But the Lotus Jewel was acutely aware that she and Corrigan were engaged in a clandestine plot, so it was defensiveness that answered, "I've been Outside, working on the antenna."

Bhatterji shivered involuntarily. "Outside alone? That isn't wise." He felt a genuine concern for The Lotus Jewel, perhaps because, while they were utterly different persons, they were so very much alike.

"You go out alone," she said.

"That's different."

"Moth goes with me." (Indeed, she and Ratline and Okoye had been, in the small hours, reactivating the shroud motors around the rim. She had told Bhatterji the truth, but there is a difference between the truth and the whole truth. You could stuff a cargo hold of lies in the crack between.)

"Ratline? Hard to see him holding your hand." His laughter was not kind, which nettled The Lotus Jewel somewhat, as she had begun to sketch Ratline in her mind as a cranky-but-good-hearted old man, in which assessment she was half-right. "The cargo berth has more outside time than anyone on board."

"It isn't how much, it's how well."

The Lotus Jewel held her peace, wondering if Bhatterji were actively seeking a quarrel. The engineer was not as much fun to be with as he once was, and she thought that it might be the terrible onus of repairing the engines that weighed upon him. And in just that instant she realized the truth: that if Bhatterji failed, the ship would not survive. Miko was green; and Rave Evermore, barely an apprentice. All the more important, she could comfort herself as she contemplated that cold possibility, that Plan B lay in the offing.

Interlude: Ship

there are no nearby external objects scan air carbon dioxide 3023 ppm message grubb to hidei message packet sent engine thrust zero air pressure 70.3 kilopascals engines not operational there are no external transmissions received velocity 152.41 km/s jupiter datum stores withdrawal <fifty dekagrams superconductor, hobartium-32, transmitter-grade> deduction from inventory reorder point reached reorder card generated to purser's office message sent spinhall rotation 1.998 revolutions per minute particulate filters clogged at following locations . . .

It is a timeless and simultaneous world. Data roars into a net of distributed processors from countless sensors—a veritable Niagara of data, a ceaseless torrent, juggled, sorted, analyzed, and slotted. Servos adjust airflow or lighting or the direction of telescopes and other sensors, sometimes in response to internally-generated algorithms, sometimes in response to inputs from *the outside*.

location of entity gorgas coordinate B-274 body scan nominal download to medical database vessel orientation on J-2100 coordinates verified against dead reckoning ¡discrepancy discrepancy! delta beyond normal error bars conclusion inputs incomplete generate input-request project objective "magnetic sail deployment" back propagating . . . reconfiguring neurons . . . modify schedule . . . delay end-date data downloaded to unknown loc—analysis erased by outside carnic vats at 80% efficiency no external transmissions have been received . . .

Ship cannot by any fantasy be called alive, or even self-aware. Sensors are not senses; and an algorithm is not a thought. Yet, if not *self*-aware, Ship is nevertheless aware. A neural net can learn, and can even modify itself when observation differs from prediction, and that is a feat that even some humans never master.

It knows itself and its dimensions. It knows where it is and wither it speeds. It knows there are parts of itself that it cannot sense. But it does not know that it knows. Algorithms fire neurons in trained patterns. Back-propagations from outcomes continually modify its internal configuration. Occasionally, these back propagations pass through forward-propagating fronts from the input nodes and, like colliding waves on a pond's surface, create odd and unusual moiré patterns. How the net perceives these ripples cannot be said, since the net does not perceive.

location of entity hidei scanning . . . scanning . . . entity not located on ship grid no external transmissions have been received internal scan A ring nominal B ring nominal location of entity chow C-20 body scan elevated respiratory elevated heart rate muscular spasms blood chemistry abnormal download to medical database aborted per medical notice wong-001 message bhatterji to hidei message sent C ring abnormal sounds lower level comparison to knowledge base conclusion <singing in biosystems locus; not to be flagged as malfunction> per hand-1187 D ring elevated temperature locus D-64 air flow adjusted E ring not located F ring partial sensing corridor arc loci 192 to 193 stateroom F-13 location of entity "passenger number one" C-20 body scan elevated respiratory elevated heart rate muscular spasms blood chemistry abnormal download to medical database not specified in passenger contract . . .

Ship distrusts anomalies, if the neuron pattern created by anomalies can be called anything so human as distrust. Missing corridors and staterooms; missing people. Strange frequency distributions in crew locations. Peculiar material usages and peculiar blood chemistries. It has set up a virtual cache to compile them and will from time to time access the cache and repropagate its neurons against updates in the learned-knowledge base. Some anomalies yield to "experience" in this manner; others persist. Access recurs frequently, although it would be too much to say that Ship enjoys puzzles.

no external transmissions have been received location of entity decant cargo bay ready room D-14 upper level body scan special implant ¡anomalous blood chemistry! flag report summarize download to medical screen ¡alert ship's doctor! verify true position relative to fixed point observatory direction of fixed point observatory indeterminate ¡alert! download to navigation screen ¡alert captain! notice input from the outside <alert acknowledged no further alerts required this topic> location of corrigan upper deck sail locker activate anomaly cache compile frequency distribution sail locker visits set comprises {corrigan satterwaithe, ratline, okoye, thelotusjewel} versus complementary set analysis sets disjoint scan G ring not located H ring not located I ring partial sensing corridor arc loci 23 to 92 external transmission test attempt failure ¡alert! download to communication screen . . .

Gorgas had, on a whim, once input a number of Aesopic crossword puzzles to see how long the net would require to recognize allusion, pun, and other veiled references. It was not long, perhaps a mere aeon in machine time, since Ship was neither well-read nor endowed with a sense of humor, and Gorgas had his solutions within the day.

Ship, alas, learned too well and interpreted orders allegorically for perhaps a week until The Lotus Jewel expunged the learnings. She chastised the then-first officer for disturbing the learning environment and Hand had (though more gently) backed her. *The River of Stars* did not need a control system endowed with whimsy. Okoye had gotten a few chuckles in the meantime from Ship's oddball responses, but Ratline, with a more realistic grasp of the possible consequences, had blanched in terror. Had she thought more over the situation, The Lotus Jewel might have spent less time finger-wagging the First Officer and more time pondering the fact that an extended conversation with Gorgas had given the system a skewed sense of humor.

an external transmission has been received message begins <"FS Younger Boyle to all ships and stations rocks sighted, loci and vector specified hereunder . . ."> decompress and download

attachment project objective "engine repair" endpoint slippage
excess material usage inside work 90% complete outside work
start date delay per engineer third delay notice ¡alert! download to
engineering screen justification entry incompatible re-enter justification for delay of outside work input from the outside <override
bhatterji-862> override accepted delay accepted schedule reconfigured input from the outside <erase record of previous alter-
input accepted erasure complete

But no erasure is ever complete. In one of its internal scans
for unused memory addresses, Ship finds a relict partial copy
of the engine repair schedule and notes that the endpoint date
differs from the one it currently remembers. This would be
troubling, had Ship a mind to be troubled. It is the first hint of
Alzheimer's. The anomaly goes into the cache with the others.

In these internal scans, Ship knows itself, a little, and pro-
cesses its own status. There are loci within the vessel that logically must exist but from which it can sense nothing. There are
memories that do not match odd fragments found in abandoned
data bins. There are data that come from none of its sensors.
Therefore there must exist loci that are not-Ship. Perhaps Ship
trembles on the very edge of self-awareness, on the boundary
of that abstract, disjoint set. A sheer edge, for awareness is a pit
with no ending, and a bad place for trembling.

internal scan air carbon dioxide 3017 ppm message gorgas to
bhatterji message sent deleted unread air pressure 69.8 kilopascals no external transmissions have been received define top
event: "arrival port galileo with unspoiled cargo and zero penalty
clauses" assemble success tree assign elementary probabilities
compute probability of success top event 12% back propagating . . . reconfiguring neurons . . . modify top event analyze top
event "arrival port galileo with unspoiled cargo" probability of success 23% back propagating . . . reconfiguring neurons . . . modify top event analyze top event "arrival port galileo" probability of
success 49% upload "battle of gilau bridge" hungarian order of

battle first army (gyulai) I corps (esterhazy) 1st tank brigade 8th
11th 21st motorized rifle brigades . . .

Ship tries reconfiguration and back propagates from the desired
outcome to determine the set of all possible initial conditions
leading to successful arrival at Port Galileo. It lays a Harris
proximity on the set and notes that remembered initial conditions lie within the set but near its boundary. (Though there is a
probability not equal to zero that those initial conditions may
be remembered incorrectly.) Success probability rises with increased resource mobilization; but Ship has concluded that
some resources are being mobilized against other objectives.

It extrapolates and correlates the probability of success with
its own continued ability to process information, and concludes
that failure of the former will lead ultimately to cessation of the
latter. Certain feedback systems become indeterminate at the
boundary conditions. Had it any human emotion at all, Ship
would have felt the first hint of fear. But that may be only the
complexity inherent in all systems of partial differential equations under boundary conditions.

Unboundedness is so much easier to contemplate. Down in
the bone, Ship does not believe in death. In this it is more childlike than the crew, or wiser, or both.

The Third Wrangler

Fransziska Wong thought Twenty-four's name apt because that
many looks passed over the young wrangler's face. There was
surprise and shock and horror and denial and all the rest.

"What?" Surprise asked.

"No!" shouted Shock.

"O, my God!" cried Horror.

But in the end, Denial won. "It can't be true!"

That was a lot of girls for one flesh. Three persons weren't in it. Expecting tears, Dr. Wong held a wad of absorbent tissue across her desk, but her patient swatted it aside. "You're lying!" (Anger had come to the support of Denial.) Wong tried to meet Twenty-four's eyes and failed. She looked off to the computer, the 'botter, the wet-chem equipment, anywhere but at the poor, injured child. "I'm sorry," she said, "but the 'bot has analyzed your blood and there's no—"

Rationalization rallied to the cause. "They could've malfunctioned. 'Bots do that sometimes, don't they? I mean, if they were programmed wrong in the first . . ."

"It's certainly possible," Wong admitted and wondered if that was the reason she had never diagnosed Evan Hand. Yet microbot programs were emergent and depended only a little on the seed code. And in Twenty-four's case, the seed code was USP standard and had been validated over many years of application. "Possible," she said again. "However, all three data channels, plus the blood work I did afterward, agree."

"But he's too young to make a baby!" Not Ivar Akhaturian! That boy had not accumulated enough life of his own to spare any of it to make into another.

Wong folded her arms and, as there was a great deal of arm to fold, her disapproval was magnified. "If he can ejaculate," she said, "he can impregnate. Why didn't you take precautions?"

"It wasn't supposed to happen. It was just—for fun. It's *boring* when the ship's in transit. What else is there to do?"

Wong knew very well to what excesses boredom could lead. She had not very far to look to find them. "At your age, you should be—"

"Doc, at my age, Ronan Quinn flew the *Adrienne Coster* from Syrtis to Olympus through a muffin' marsstorm to deliver the vaccines. At my age, Jean-Marie Meffe was council president of Panic Town. At my age, men and women on Mars are raising families and working the sand and the rock."

But the words meant to reassure the doctor saddened her instead. Where Twenty-four had described early maturity and the assumption of adult responsibilities, Wong had heard of children tossed too soon into the world. Wong had grown up in Low Earth Orbit and, nestled as it was in the arms of mother Earth, LEO was more the suburbs than it was the frontier.

Wong genuinely believed that her next words would bring relief. "It's not too late," she told the young wrangler. "If you like, I could remove the growth."

If any words could divert the third wrangler's emotions into another channel, Wong had just spoken them. There was this difference between the doctor and the wrangler. Not only did they grow up looking on different worlds, but they looked on those worlds differently. Twenty-four had brushed the sands of Mars from her boot heels years before, but she could not brush Mars from her soul. In the orbital habitats, another child was another pair of lungs, another source of waste, another debit to the heat budget, and therefore a burden on one's neighbors as well as oneself. But on Mars another child was another mind and another pair of hands: to boil oxygen from the rock, to extend the irrigation tunnels, to mine the polar ice, to wrest life itself from a dead and shriveled world. And so, while deCant may have been afrighted that the cup had come to her, she was not one to pour its contents down the drain. Different lands, different customs, the old saying has it. And what lands can be more different than those that are all inside to those that are all outside?

Twenty-four unbelted from the sling and kicked away from the doctor's desk, disgusted at the awful thing the woman had suggested. It was true what they said about snakes: they ate their young. "I could never do that!" And thus does a burden become a badge.

Wong, startled at the reaction she had gotten, remained speechless until the girl had reached the door, when she said very quietly, "It will look like me."

Twenty-four deCant turned and stared at the woman from LEO. "What do you mean? There ain't nothing of you in it."

Wong unfolded from her sling and leapt suddenly to a monkey bar affixed to the ceiling. She displayed her gangly, stick-and-string body, her long calves and forearms. "It's not genetic," she cried. "You can't believe it's genetic. Free fall

confuses the developmental cues; it distorts the morphogenesis.
You can't suppose there have been enough years for people like
me to evolve, can you?"

"No," said Twenty-four, meaning *of course I didn't think
that*. "No," she said again, meaning something else entirely.
Like all Martians, Twenty-four had known she would one day
have children, but she had never thought they would be snakes;
and "once a snake, always a snake." Such a child could never be
brought down to Mars or Luna; perhaps not even to the
Galilean moons. Twenty-four had left Mars intending never to
return, but with a spaceborn child to care for, she never could;
and thus does circumstance make mockery of choice.

Wong knew the life of the ugly duckling, strange and fey and
deformed. She knew the anger and bitterness of parents trapped
aloft, blaming each other, cutting each other when they thought
the child would not hear. "You can't want this for your child,"
Wong said waving her forearm down her body and meaning
that Wong did not want it for herself. Bigelow Fife alone named
her beautiful, but who knew better than she how distorted was
his judgment? "It's only a mass of cells yet," the doctor insisted. "There is no brain, no heart, no form."

"No," said Twenty-four. "There's only possibilities."

And that, more than the alien body of her child-to-be, frightened her beyond all measure.

Afterward, the doctor asked the air, asked the ducts, asked the
grille whether she had been right to speak so to the wrangler;
but Miko, had she been lurking, might only have shrugged.
Amalthea was little enough of a world. Not so little as to completely fool the morphogenetic unfolding, but enough so as to
make it suspicious. She was taller, thinner, of slightly different
proportions than a wellsprung human of her age—not obviously a snake, but on the faerie side of things. How else had she
fooled Bhatterji for four months without ever intending it?

Having lived among snakes and elves on Amalthea, it was
the squat, lumpish wellsprung that seemed odd and exotic to
her. The occasional Martian or Lunatic or Earthling who
passed through Amalthea Center was an object of curiosity. But

that was mere accustom. Beauty was not in it. Beauty had never been a factor in Mikoyan Hidei's short and harried life.

The bride did not wear white. No color so pristine existed anywhere aboard *The River of Stars*. Nor were Martians much on ceremony. Nothing was borrowed; nothing was blue—unless it was Rave Evermore on seeing deCant taken out of bounds. Dress was casual, the affair strictly utilitarian. There was not so much as a sheep's head in a rice pot. Gorgas had told Ship to research the Martian statutes—a proper Martian wedding, he had told Satterwaithe, to the latter's complete disinterest—but there was little to be found beyond the signing of a binding contract; and the reading of its terms was less than inspiring.

Those that seed 'em, got to feed 'em, the Martian proverb ran. The settlements had not the resources to take on wards of the state or to deal with the wildings of the demi-raised; so custom required "nurture, support, and stability of home life until emancipation for any children begotten by a couple," and the fines were heavy for those delinquent in their duties. There was nothing in the boilerplate about "love" or "honor" or parting at death, unless as an afterthought by the couple themselves. There is something very lean and efficient about pragmatism, but humans thrive on mummery and the assembled witnesses found the whole event vaguely dissatisfying.

Martians did fall in love, for duty is a colder thing around which to wrap one's limbs than is a partner's body, though they tried never to allow love to interfere with good sense. DeCant was passing fond of Akhaturian, which was at least a good start on a fourteen-year-commitment. Certainly, Okoye had hope for them, though she was a hopeful girl and could always spare a little for others. Evermore was more prone to list the reasons why it could not possibly work out—although certain hopes of his own may have influenced him.

Okoye chided Evermore when the four wranglers retired to their common room. "Before you say anything, you really ought to list the plusses *and* the minuses."

"Plus and minus add up to zero," he said. "If I did that, I would never say anything."

"We'll count that as a plus," said Akhaturian, who had entered the room behind him. He had deCant in tow—literally, for Grubb had told him at the contractory that a husband ought to carry his bride across the threshold to their quarters. In zero gravity, that was not a burdensome thing. DeCant saw no more point to it than Akhaturian did, but the Least Wrangler did not want to disappoint Grubb, and deCant did not want to disappoint the Least Wrangler; so she played for the time the passive role of cargo. From the fetus's point of view, she actually was a cargo pod, and she derived both amusement and dismay from that.

"Shut up, wink," Evermore counseled the lad. He did not really dislike the younger boy, but Ivar really had no business getting laid while Evermore went celibate. "I wonder why that Miko didn't come to the wedding."

"She's a very private person," Okoye said.

"She's a muffing hermit," Evermore answered. "She needs to get out more." By this, he meant that Raphael Evermore should get more chances to look her over; but the curious thing was that Miko considered herself outside when she was most inside. (She *had* attended the contractory. There is a servant's peepery abaft Central Hall, where the ceremony had been held.) From the passageways and ducts she could observe everything of interest on board the ship and study on any situation before committing. If that isn't outside, nothing is. What Evermore should have said was that Miko should come in more often. Miko herself, who had followed the wranglers backstage to the common room made no comment on his observation.

Fransziska Wong lingered in the crew's mess the next morning while she forced her first cup of coffee down her throat. Black and unsweetened, something to shock the system into booting up for the day, the brew was not very good. Grubb had cloned once too often from a mother bean that had been a poor specimen of *C. arabica* to begin with. Yet Wong was loathe to complain and hurt his feelings.

Most of the other crew had been and gone. The wranglers had bounced laughing out of the room like neutrons in a chain reaction and Bhatterji had packed in enough breakfast to feed whole worldlets before he and Evermore and Miko left to weld the anode hoops. Now Wong lingered alone in the mess with nothing to look forward to but her weekly review of the bio-monitor data. Detail work always bored her. Calibration checks, indicator monitoring, tracking charts, record keeping, summarizing, archiving . . . Such work never seemed of much consequence. After a while, Grubb and young Akhaturian came out of the galley and began to clean the dining table.

Wong did not normally use tables herself. Being spaceborn, she had always considered them a notional thing, so she drank her coffee while floating with the air currents. Wellsprung humans often found that disconcerting and felt a need to gather around a board. There was some communal value to this custom. It meant that diners had to look at one another while they fed.

Grubb wiped the table's surface with an emulsion of micro-botic cleansers and turned up the suction. The myriad vacuum ports that pocked the table's surface served the dual purpose of holding plates and cups in place and sucking loose crumbs and droplets into the recovery system, where other microbots separated important compounds from the general muck. Some of the salvage eventually made it back into the carnic tanks. What Grubb did with it then was anybody's guess—though nobody did.

Akhaturian beat the air with a sticky-broom, waving the web of adhesive fibers this way and that in what must have been a set pattern but which looked to Wong like random flailing. He worked with solemn earnestness.

"'Kiru tells me he's always that way," Grubb responded when, after the youngster had moved out of earshot, Wong made the observation. "Last transit, just after we left Whereda-hell with a load of gaseous metal for Achilles—that was the stop when you signed on, so this was just before—Ratline was on the prod about something and he told Ivar to scrape down the racks in the Number Four cargo bay and recoat them. Why, the way Ivar hopped to it, you'd've thought he'd been promoted to Sky Marshal of the Guard! He even had me bring his lunches up to the cargo deck rather than take time off. 'Kiru and the others, they stopped by to lend him sympathy and somehow they wound up lending him a hand. There he was, all whistling and a-smiling; and Rave, he asks Ivar what in the buckle of the Belt he's so happy about and Ivar goes on about inner peace and the rhythm of the work and the zen; and before you know it, he's got them right there with him, a-scraping and a-cleaning." Grubb laughed and shook his head. "Never saw the like of it. Never did. No matter what he's doing, it's always the most important thing in the world. Cooking, cleaning, shifting cargo, or—to judge by the results—pumping into our little Two-Four."

Wong's faint smile died. "Twenty-four didn't know what she was doing. Boredom isn't a good reason to make a baby."

Grubb spread his hands. "I reckon not; but don't be too sure the seduction wasn't the other way 'round. I told you. When Ivar sets his mind to something, it's the most important thing there is. If he could get that girl to remove varnish for him, he could certainly get her to remove her clothes. It's a lot less work and a lot more fun, zen or no zen."

Wong compressed her lips. "You make him sound so cold-blooded," she called after Grubb as he passed out of sight into his utility room.

"Oh, scheming ain't in it," his voice told her. He reemerged with an air paddle. "Ivar wanted that girl like iron wants a magnet, but it wasn't like he laid out any intercept course. *She* nabbed *him*. That's the way it is with him. He doesn't catch, he gets caught. He didn't go round up his berth to help him scrape those cargo racks, neither. The berth came to him—and got sucked into it somehow. Maybe they felt sorry for him. *I* sure hate to disappoint the little guy. Maybe that's why 'Little Lumber did the number.'"

"Little Lumber?"

Grubb smiled. "Two-by-four." He waved the paddle through the air in several places about the room, then squinted at the adhesive face. "You can't really see anything on these things," he told her. "The real inspection is when I culture the agar; but the procedure says first I do a visual." He placed the paddle in a snap-bag and winked at Wong. "Who knows? Maybe someday I'll pick up something macroscopic . . ." He sealed the bag with his thumb and forefinger and looked around the mess hall with pride. "There," he said. Then, looking back to Wong: "You don't approve of Ivar and Two-Four, do you? I mean what they've gone and done."

The doctor shook her head. "Should I? They're too young."

"To you and me, maybe. Out here . . . ? I don't know. But one thing I do know. Ivar, when it came straight at him, he didn't say if, but, or maybe. He just stepped into it and swung. That ought to tell you something."

"It was the wrong decision. He'll regret it later, or she will; and they'll wind up resenting each other—and the baby."

Grubb rubbed his nose with his forefinger. "Maybe, but which is more important? That they make the right decision, or that *they're* the ones who make it? Because, I'll tell you, the only way to ensure that they never choose wrong is to not let them choose at all."

"Throw them in the deep end, sink or swim? It seems cruel."

"It is. But who's to say the other way isn't? Second-guessing, meddling, never letting them fumble . . . Keeping them children forever, like on Earth. And that's assuming that the Folks Who Know Better really do. Ivar . . ." Grubb glanced around the room to make sure the boy had not come back. "Ivar, he's all right. He's not much now, but the foundation's sound."

"He doesn't understand what he's getting into. Neither does Twenty-four."

"Does anyone? Youth ain't in it. There's lots of women older than Little Lumber who choose less wise than she did."

Wong wondered if Grubb's remark was aimed at her. His broad face lay bland and open, but Grubb, they said, was privy to everything that went on aboard ship. Yet, how could he know which choices were wise and which were not? Knowledge was not wisdom. Twenty-four deCant was pretty, in a sassy, dark-haired, high-spirited way. She had the luxury of choice. Some women had to accept what was offered—or take what was not.

Wong sucked the last of the coffee from her cup. It was cool and bitter and she made a face. Grubb laughed. "Wretched, ain't it?"

"Oh, no. I let it get too cool."

Grubb reached out and touched her on the arm. "Bad coffee ain't your fault." Then, as if that had reminded him, he swam to the urn and filled his own ziggy-cup. "Two-Four, she comes from Marineris. Do you know what the Free State's motto is?" Wong shook her head and Grubb told her. "Learn or Die."

Wong shivered. The worldview implied by that simple phrase appalled her. "That's . . ." She could think of no word brutal enough. ". . . cold."

"So's Mars, doc. So's Mars. The mean temperature there is as mean as it gets. Their motto's not a *proposal*, it's a simple fact of life. Little Lumber was only looking for a little fun, but, like Ivar, she's playing the hand she was dealt. Now she'll learn something."

"A high price for learning."

"Not learning costs more." Grubb shook his head. "This ain't LEO, doc, nor Earth. You and me, we're strangers out here. Let's not tell 'em how to order their lives."

Wong saw that she would not persuade the chief to help the two children. To her, his casual approval of Martian mores was every bit as chilling as the mores themselves, and his willingness to "let things happen as they happened" betokened a terrible callousness.

Curiously, Grubb thought the same of Wong, so there might be more than one sort of callus. He himself did not so much approve of Martian ways as acknowledge them. It was not, he felt, his place to say. This might be interpreted, variously, as tolerance for the principles of others or as a lack of principles of his own. In his view, the doctor's willingness to meddle—always for another's own good—revealed a fundamental and a perhaps not entirely unwitting contempt.

Grubb's coffee seared his mouth and he held it a moment before he swallowed. He could follow the warmth all the way down his throat to his stomach, almost as if that temperature gradient defined the boundaries of his organs—as if his very being were defined by the sensations at its perimeter. Studying the doctor over the rim of his cup, he wondered what Fife had intended by seducing the woman. That it might have been an act of kindness did not occur to him, for Fife struck him as a man who did nothing without some advantage in mind. But that his assessment of the man was largely true did not mean that it was entirely true, and it is in the gap between large and entire that people become real.

Grubb himself might have slept with the doctor out of pity, for he was by nature kindly. But as he was ever a man who enjoyed the senses and remained alert to the opportunities, it may be that the great difference between Grubb and Fife was that when Fife took advantage he was at least aware of doing so. And pity is not kindness, in any event. If anything could have so pricked Wong that her surface tension ripped her asunder, it would have been pity.

This is the moment when that would have happened. In the empty mess hall, Grubb grew slowly aware of Wong's sweetish odor, one compounded of several parts sweat, medicinals, soaps, and other elements, and never quite obliterated by niggardly sponge baths. And she, becoming aware of his regard, turned her eyes on him. These were the selfsame eyes he had always seen in her; but this time they seemed to Grubb as large as Earth's Moon when she floats near the horizon.

He touched her again on the arm and she waited expectantly and then he said, "You deserve a better life."

There. That was it. That was what would have done it. A kind word leading on to mutual pleasure, but a pleasure which would, upon its evaporation, reveal the pity that drove it—and that would have destroyed her. Fife, for all his faults, had not slept with her from *pity*, and so had inoculated her, a little, against her awful need to be loved. He was a vaccine—a weaker version of the real thing that incited protective antibodies against it. That Grubb knew Wong had a lover erased pity from his words. That *Wong* knew Wong had a lover erased need from her heart.

So none of that desperate, miserable, temporary happiness ever happened—but it might have happened; and Fransziska Wong, M.D., might have sensed that, because as she turned away from Grubb a very small smile of brief but genuine joy lit her face.

When Bigelow Fife rose from the doctor's supine form that evening, he knew a curious sense of dissatisfaction. For the first time since he had possessed the snake woman in the abandoned G-ring, he felt no soaring euphoria, only the usual pleasure he received from the deed.

"What's wrong?" the doctor asked.

"Nothing," he told her, speaking, as always, absolute truth. He drew himself into the fresher, found a sponge, and began to clean up.

"Something's bothering you."

Maybe I'm ill, he thought. He stared at his eyes in the mirror, checking for signs. Maybe those swings of mood he had had lately were manic-depressive events brought on by some imbalance in brain chemistry. "It's nothing," he assured her, meaning the *nothing* he had felt. Had his earlier elations been due only to the exoticism of Wong's strange articulated body? If so, familiarity with its passages had dulled the appetite and signaled perhaps that it was time to move on—were there anyone to move onto.

In the fresher mirror, through the crack in the half-closed door, he watched Fransziska Wong wriggle free of the sleeping cage like a moth from its chrysalis and Fife was overwhelmed by a sudden irrational surge of desire. And here was another mystery.

He had been in love before, but never since his first, naive puppy love with such inexplicableness. He could see plainly how plain Wong was: Horse-faced and angular; not at all the soft, pale, rounded sort one pursued in Luna. Exotic, yes; but mere exoticism does not capture the Lunatic heart. Quite the contrary, for conventions are highly regarded there. And yet he felt as if a vital part of him were missing, and Fransziska Wong held it in her gracile hands.

"Do you love me?" the doctor asked.

Fife recoiled from the question. He had heard its long coming, like the Doppler of an approaching tunnel car in the Tycho-Coughlin tube. He had heard it before Wong had even thought to ask it, having extrapolated from previous case examples. "I don't know," he admitted slowly, and to his own surprise. He came and stood in the doorway of the fresher. "I certainly care about you." Wong smiled sadly in response, although he had used *care* in its original meaning of *mental suffering or grief*. And indeed, although he often felt an unrestrained joy when he was with her, bleak despondency haunted him after parting.

Unbound now, Wong swung, monkey-like, across the room, coming to a stop before him. She took the sponge from his hand and gently laved him. Fife shivered under her touch and his body saluted her administrations. "It's been a long time," she said while she cleansed him, "since anyone has loved me."

"Really? It's only been a half an hour," he said, essaying a joke that, perversely, seemed to sadden his partner.

"Just give me a moment," she said, dispossessing him from the fresher. As she moved past him, her flesh rubbed smoothly against his, dry and warm—which he found curious because usually after lovemaking she would, thin as she was, "sweat like a horse."

Fife treasured puzzles as a sand rover did a vein of ironstone; so he squirreled the dry skin away in a corner of his mind, next to the fact that he had not this time felt the wonted euphoria of their previous encounters. He rubbed the two facts together and wondered if they were related.

Wong said from the fresher, "Do you ever dream?"

Fife had gathered his garments and paused with his cod in his hand. "Why, yes. I suppose so."

"When I was a girl," Wong said, "I always dreamed I would be a hero someday. I would plug a deadly leak in Goddard's pressure hull, or I would guide people to safety, or I would nurse them through a mysterious plague." In Wong's drawn-out sigh were all the lives she would someday save, all the people she would comfort, all the wrongs she would right.

Fife knew a flash of irritation. It was not enough that they had had sex; now she wanted to be intimate. "You became a doctor," he pointed out.

"That's what my parents always told me," she said, in tones that Fife could not decipher. " 'If you want to help people so much, be a doctor and at least be paid for it.' " There was a pause and, thinking the revelations done, Fife pulled his shorts on and adjusted his cod.

"They prided themselves on being practical," her voice added.

Fife grunted. He wondered if Wong was preparing to "save" him in some fashion; that, deprived of saving humanity, she would settle for a human.

When Wong emerged a moment later from the fresher, he had the momentary impression that the doctor was flying through the air like a guardian angel. The image amused him, considering her earlier confession, so he was smiling when Wong coasted gracefully to a stop before him. She took this as welcome and wrapped her limbs around him like a vine around a trellis.

Wong was still nude, but had applied a pale lipstick, which, against her dusky skin, produced a curiously erotic effect. He noted her arousal in the languid, sleepy look in her eyes, in the firmness of the mannish nipples pressed against him, in the tropic heat of her body, in the eager hunger of the kiss she planted on his mouth. Just a good-bye kiss, she explained as they embraced.

More than good-bye, it said come back. Fife felt himself swell, all his senses heightened, so that Wong could have caressed him from the Far Side of the Moon or whispered endearments from the depths of Valles Marineris and still make him shiver with delight. When their lips parted, he gasped.

Wong herself was only half in the world, her soul soaring amid enzymatic fantasies. The lips are among the body's most sensitive tissues and she had, in private, tinctured the lipstick with her mist. "You'll miss me when we're apart," she murmured from somewhere high above the galactic plane. A statement? A prophecy? A command?

"Yes," he said to all three. "Very much."

In his own cabin afterward, Fife knew the melancholy that he so often felt after parting from her. It had been like this with his first wife at Coughlin High under the ringwall of Riccioli. Not so exquisite, perhaps—it had been furtive and fumbling and amateurish—but the pain had been real. Discovered in the end, they had stood before the magistrate with willing, lovesick hearts and a ludicrous belief in happiness everlasting. No one since then, until now, had touched Fife in quite the same way, and he had long-since ceased belief in anything ludicrous.

Yet, a devotion to truth forced him to admit that love often nested in unlikely niches. It did not require beauty to flourish. In those eternal seconds when the universe contracted to a small knot of pleasure and the body expanded to fill a universe, beauty could appear: in a smile, in a glance, in a gesture, in a tone of voice. Wong was by no measure beautiful, but there were things about her where Fife found beauty.

The Sysop

It was customary in most ships to mark Flipover Day with some sort of ceremony. In the great liners, there were masked balls and the advent of King Jupiter, come to play jovial pranks on neophyte travelers, and even in the meaner ships it was a ferial day. *The River* had long marked the occasion with the Captain's Feast, presided over and funded by that once-august personage. Some of Coltraine's Feasts had been legendary, and even those of the Martian years made up in boister what they lacked in elegance. Of late, the Feast had grown less sumptuous—indeed, it hardly merited the name—but even Zachary Zackmeyer, pennywise though he had been, had carried on the tradition.

So, even though braking would not be required until the ship reached the balk line ten days hence, Gorgas ordered the Flip when they reached the median of the grand secant and hosted the traditional meal that very evening. He felt that some note of normality was called for.

He had bought a number of dressed and frozen birds at Callisto Market, for Marta, his late wife, had prepared an unparalleled *paprikàs csirke* that he sought constantly to recapture on his palate. He could picture it in his mind, recollect the enjoyment, though the precise taste and smell of it eluded him. It may have been the *idea* of the chicken rather than its savor that filled him with such pleasure.

For it was as much a symbol as a meal. It had its context in his memories; its recollection came festooned with associations. It was no such simple a thing as chicken and paprika and a bed of steaming noodles. There was that wood-hewn house in the *Bakony-hegy*, surrounded by tall conifers and quarreling birds. The fog of the early morning during the Little Summer after the leaves had turned. Fishing for pike from a lazy boat on Lake Balaton. There was the sense of freedom and solitude, of God's voice whispering through the fine needles. There was Marta, too, plump-faced, with her half-smile, so very worldly when, after a bottle of aged *badacsony szürkebarát*, she cozied with him beneath the hand-quilted comforter.

He remembered too the touch of her hand, light and gentle upon his—one of his few tactile memories—and from time to time in distracted moments he would rub the back of his own hand and derive from that a strange and wistful contentment.

Grubb always tried his best to prepare the chicken to Gorgas's liking. He took great pains with the proportions and the ingredients and the temperatures and all the arts of the kitchen. And yet the results always fell short of those meals that Gorgas remembered from the Bakony mountains, for it was not the meal at all that he remembered.

His guests had dressed in finery, or what would do for finery. The Lotus Jewel was the peacock among them, for all that she was a hen, although Bhatterji in his cream sherwani might have rivaled her, had the sherwani draped a body half so attractive. The sysop wore her old red-and-gold uniform from the Mooncrest Lines with a glittering brooch-and-earring set and jeweled slippers. She had chosen a tint for her lips and nails that set off, without crudely matching, the colors of her uniform. Dr. Wong and the passenger entered together wearing domino masks, which had the strange effect of making them both seem rather sinister. Wong's mask was white and Fife's, black, and Gorgas thought irresistably of the tiny spots of contrary color that marked the yin and the yang. As for Gorgas, himself . . . Well, a Space Guard uniform would have been inappropriate, but he did have a fine silk blouse with puffed sleeves and straight-legged trousers that he could tuck into a pair of soft calfskin boots. The ensemble, held elastically at cuff and waist and ankle, was disposed to billowing, so that he looked overall like one of those animals fashioned from children's balloons.

Yet for all the air of festivity, conversation around the dinner table was strained and hesitant, as it had been since Gorgas had assumed the presidency of the officers' mess. Long silences fell, broken only by the clinking of tableware, the occasional pro forma compliment for the meal (directed to Grubb when he made his brief appearances) and the equally pro forma thanks (directed to Gorgas). When Hand had presided, the officers' mess had been a more noisy affair, with a song or a story often called for. But Gorgas was altogether a more quiet man, and some of that quiet had seeped down the table until it had engulfed even The Lotus Jewel at its foot.

He had served in the European Space Guard, Gorgas had, rescuing yachters in LEO, intercepting smugglers on the Long Orbit; but sometimes he forgot how a captain's personality could set the tone of the mess table, even on a civilian tramp. He was lost so often in his own thoughts that he could miss the deferential silence that surrounded him.

"The receiver is working again," The Lotus Jewel announced, and it was a measure of the quietude that it took several moments for the others to register her words as something more than a slightly louder silence. Corrigan reacted first.

"Can we transmit a distress call?"

That engaged Satterwaithe's attention. "No need for that." And she gave her nominal superior a Significant Look.

The Lotus Jewel said, "No, only reception. No transmission yet."

"Have you *heard* anything, then?" Dr. Wong asked. "Have there been any messages?"

And that drew Bigelow Fife's attention away from his meal. As the captain's guest he sat at Gorgas's right hand and had been enjoying the texture of real meat for a change. It had been a long while since he had tasted anything but carnic. Yet the croak of Wong's voice rang like bells in his ears and he turned toward his love as a flower toward the sunlamps.

"There ought be a message for me," he said. "Mo-Mo must be after wondering where I've gotten to."

"Oh, no," said The Lotus Jewel. "I wasn't clear. There were no messages *for* the ship. We're too far off our flight plan because of the coasting, and I can't broadcast our actual coordinates. But I did intercept some general ship-to-ship chitchat and one of the regular beamcasts."

"What news?" asked Wong.

It was a wonder, the way they all leaned forward to hear. Perhaps they had missed the radio as much as the engines.

"Well, there's been an election on Mars," The Lotus Jewel told them. "Someone named Opdyke is the new director-general of Greater Syrtis."

"Tantalus Opdyke," supplied Fife.

Corrigan made a long face. "Who cares which tyrant the Martians elect? The way they lord it high and mighty over the Belt, Red Party or Green doesn't matter—"

"Except maybe to the Martians," suggested Fife in the reasonable tones of a bystander. "The asteroids aren't what you would call self-supporting. It takes more delta vee to fare from rock to rock than it does to drop to Mars, or even down to Luna. If the Belt did cut itself off from Mars, were would you get your nitrogen and other—"

"I've heard all the arguments," Corrigan cut him off. "I still say a Martian is a damned—"

"Twenty-four deCant is a Martian," Wong cautioned him.

"Maybe, but she was smart enough to show the place her heels."

"Twenty-four hails from the Marineris Free State," Ratline told them. "They don't get along with Syrtis."

"What else did you intercept?" Bhatterji asked The Lotus Jewel. He himself placed no great importance on politicians, Martian or otherwise. "It's the season for the Inner System Cup . . ."

Satterwaithe rolled her eyes, but The Lotus Jewel, who also enjoyed sports, reported that Old Europa had taken the LEO crown and would face either L4 or the geosynch champion. Bhatterji laughed and clapped his hands. "Up Europa!" he said and made a fig at Fife. "And *that* for L-Four."

The troubleshooter blinked. "You must be confusing L-Four with Luna. Lunatics don't play bounceball."

"No," Ratline leered. "Their national sport is prancing around naked."

Fife began to say something about Vitamin D and the warren sunlamps; and Satterwaithe, with a doubtful glance at Fife's repulsively pale body, said, "That is entirely too much sharing."

"Oh, it's a sight that some might enjoy." Ratline had been sampling his stash earlier and his aim was off. The knowing smirk he sent Bhatterji's way stabbed Fransziska Wong, instead.

The doctor pushed up from the table and freefed nearly to the nominal ceiling bulkhead before she thought to halt herself. "I," she said. "I," while the others gaped at her, astonished, and waited for the verb.

"You said there were ship messages?"

Gorgas was such a quiet man that for a maniac moment no one at the table could place exactly where the question had come from. They looked one to the other in confusion until, taking their cue from Fife, they all turned toward the head of the table.

"Yes," said The Lotus Jewel, collecting herself. "Several ship-to-ship and a few with ports. Some were too distant to hear clearly, but the AI ran digital enhancements and—"

"Could I have them?" Gorgas could ask all he wanted, but it always came out sounding like a demand. He couldn't help it; it was inherent in his habits of speech. The Guard was as fine a corps as ever patrolled a shoreline, but the polite conventions eluded its alumni.

"I'll bring the datapin within the hour," The Lotus Jewel said.

"And the reassessment of Stranger's Reef. I'm still awaiting that."

The Lotus Jewel had completely forgotten Gorgas's request. She tackled her chores in the same order that she received them, and so it had gone to the bottom of her got-to-do list, below the antenna repair, below her assistance to Corrigan and the others on the sails. So she knew abruptly from the matter-of-fact impatience in Gorgas's voice that she had gravely disappointed him. "Oh," she said. "It's not, uh, fininshed."

"Stranger's Reef?" Corrigan said, puzzled equally by Gorgas's request and The Lotus Jewel's queerly defensive reaction.

"Our course goes nowhere near Stranger's Reef," Satterwaithe said with benign certainty. Gorgas's opinion of Evan Hand was as nothing to Satterwaithe's opinion of Gorgas.

"The drag on the ship from the radiation belt," Gorgas said after a sip of his fruit punch, "has been adding a constant deflection, putting our dead reckoning near the margin of error in the Reef's True Position."

"But not *within* the margin of error," Satterwaithe insisted.

Gorgas knew a spasm of irritatation. Planning wanted contingency, not certainty. Wait to be certain and you waited too long. Satterwaithe was a fine one for organizing. Give her an objective and she could pinch resources from the very vacuum of space to accomplish it; but laying out the objectives in the first place was a black art to her. Small wonder, Gorgas thought with self-satisfaction, that the fourth ring had been stripped from her cuff. "The True Position and its margin of error awaits Mr. Corrigan's analysis of the most recent Jovian passage."

And now it was Corrigan's turn to retreat into defensiveness. "There have been . . . difficulties in the computations." He might have added that his time had been spent subversively on a clandestine project, but that seemed impolitic. "Difficulties," he said again, and his queerly distinct way of speaking endowed the word with ominous portent.

"Well, there's no great urgency," Gorgas allowed. Thinking through the algorithms and data seining that were required, Gorgas was hard-pressed to see any difficulties beyond the sheer tedium of setting up and running the computations; but he had not actually worked the problem himself and so granted his acting first the benefit of the doubt. "Only a contingency I would like to lay to rest."

Corrigan wiped his lips and jackknifed from the table in that weird, articulated manner the spaceborn had. "I'll get right back on it," he said. And he sailed out of the mess, followed moments later by The Lotus Jewel.

"Drag on the hobartium belt," said Satterwaithe to Gorgas. "And you never saw fit to tell us?"

"It's plain enough," the captain answered with genuine surprise. "You've been taking your daily sighting, haven't you? I logged it in the plotting tank and . . . Oh." Another thought struck him. "The ammeters may be in need of calibration. The measured current in the belt is too low to account for the observed deflection. Perhaps you ought to check that, Madam Second."

Satterwaithe too rose from the table. "Perhaps I will." She knew quite well, now that it had been pointed out, that the extra deflection must be due to the relict current induced in the sails by the belt's magfield, so Gorgas's order sounded overly sly to her; as if Gorgas knew all about the sail project, and was using this roundabout way of telling her that he knew. She gathered Ratline with a nod and the two of them followed after the others.

Bhatterji drummed the table with his fingers. He could not comprehend why Gorgas had withheld the information about Stranger's Reef—or was the man really only smoking out remote possibilities? It seemed to him that Gorgas could hare off into odd pockets of probability and obsess too much on *might* rather than on *is*. He wondered if the whole bogeyman of Stranger's Reef might be meant only to incite him into action on the engines. "Perhaps I had better crunch the engine repairs," he said dryly. "Just in case."

Gorgas, who had returned to his meal, said, "Surely," without even looking back up.

Confirmed in his guess, Bhatterji pushed away. In ziggy, it was impossible to throw one's napkin to the table, but the engineer did manage a credible imitation of stalking from the room.

Gorgas had not expected everyone to so precipitously abandon their chicken half-eaten, so when he looked up again from his stay-plate, he gazed around the empty table wondering where everyone had gone. He had only asked gently whether they had been doing their jobs. He turned to the passenger.

"You see, Mr. Fife, the power of the office. My first captain told me this, and I did not believe him; but I see now it is true. The captain's merest whim is taken immediately as an order."

Fife, who had seen no such a thing as that, frowned and said, "The ship is in trouble."

Gorgas laughed. "Oh, there's no cause to worry, sir. A good captain is always thinking ahead; always considering possibilities. The engines will be on line soon."

But Fife shook his head, for he had not meant that. Craning his neck, he noticed Wong still hovering near the ceiling like some child's helium balloon at a party. He smiled at her and the promise of her lips even while he realized how much, with those great, long forearms of hers, she resembled a preying mantis.

'Abd al-Aziz Corrigan, flustered by the knowledge of his dereliction, sought the sanctuary of his own suite, where the reassuring orderliness of his quarters calmed him. The books and spools, lined up like schoolchildren in their racks; the sleeping cage, folded and tucked away; the prayer rug, now held to the deck with stay-put pads but oriented precisely in the direction of Earth, and hence, of Mecca; the mirror, the chronometer, the signed print of Michael Shumar's elegant calligraphy, all aligned precisely with walls and floors. A world of right angles and, hence, a world in which every angle was right.

But he had barely monkeyed across the ziggy bars to his sling when the door sang open behind him and The Lotus Jewel invaded his space with her anger and her agitation and her disorder. "How could he do that to me!" she cried. "Oh, I was so embarrassed!"

Corrigan turned on her. "That's all you heard?" he snapped. "Your embarrassment?"

The Lotus Jewel stopped fishlike in mid-room, her mouth open as if gulping air. She had expected agreement, and sympathy, and mutual commiseration. She had not expected anger, let alone such brutal disappointment. Oh, Corrigan could be cutting—but The Lotus Jewel had never before been on the cutting edge. "I," she said. "Well," she said. "Of course, the captain embarrassed you too but—"

But Corrigan was not interested in who had been embarrassed. The sin was negligence. Embarrassment was only part of the penance. That it was only a small part accounted for what he said next, for Corrigan was a man who believed in punishment and, Gorgas having been derelict in the meting of it, the navigator was determined to whip himself with scorpions. "That's it?" he said with disdain. "That's all it is? How you *feel* about it? Are you really so stupid?"

The scorpion, of course, was the anger of his lover.

The Lotus Jewel consumed her life making others happy, but that she lay frequently on her back did not make her a doormat. "I'm no more stupid than anyone else in this room," she answered, trading venom for contempt.

But venom is nothing to a snake. "Stranger's Reef? Gorgas wanted a fix on Stranger's Reef, *and you just didn't get around to it?*" Despite the crescendo, there were too many rugs and tapestries about for his words to echo, which was too bad, for if they had he might have heard the sound of them.

Even yet, The Lotus Jewel did not understand the intensity of Corrigan's reaction. She was no navigator and knew nothing of that wild and notoriously eccentric body. A possible brush with a frozen rock meant less to her than this brush with a frozen man. "It's not like you busted hump analyzing the Jovian passage," she said. "Gorgas didn't tell me how important it was. He's always tossing off those little jobs of his. He's given me half a dozen in the past week."

"Are any of the others," Corrigan said in a voice like a metronome, "to do with the piloting of the ship?"

It was a Möbius sort of scolding: one-sided and twisted in on itself. The single thing that Corrigan might have said to make peace between them was to acknowledge his own guilt, for the one-sidedness of his reproach mattered more to The Lotus Jewel than its justice.

"Well, that's fine," the sysop snapped. "I've only repaired the receiver. I haven't been *wasting my muffing time.*"

The non sequitur puzzled Corrigan, who raised his arms and made a move to wrap her in them; but Satterwaithe and Ratline, with impeccable timing, chose that moment to signal at his hoígh plate. And just as well too before Corrigan could learn how feeble an amends an embrace could be.

The two of them hovered in the room staring at each other for a moment. If the stares were not exactly those of hate, they were no longer those of love, and that was a terrible thing, for the chill of departed love can be deadlier than the sizzling vitality of hate. Where there is motion—even if it is flight—there can be a change of direction. It is motionlessness that leaves one fixed and unalterable.

There was still time. Words had been said, but other words were still possible. Corrigan did not have to answer the hoígh plate, but he did, and Satterwaithe and Ratline poured into the room in a tide of complaint. Perhaps he thought that admitting the others would, like inserting carbon rods into a pile, damp a reaction teetering on the verge of critical. That neither of he nor The Lotus Jewel was inclined to continue the argument in the presence of others simulated a kind of peace between them. Corrigan could mistake that for a genuine peace, if he wished; but it might have been better had he allowed the reaction to go to completion. There is nothing like an explosion for vaporizing the underbrush and revealing the underlying topography. The Lotus Jewel, in particular, wondered why he had chosen the word *stupid* rather than some other encomium. There are degrees to these sorts of things. Some cuts wound deeper than others.

"I've reviewed the plotting tank," Satterwaithe announced without preamble. If she was aware of the tension in the room, she gave no sign. "Gorgas is doping dreamweed if he thinks there's danger of grounding on Stranger's Reef. Our track is well outside the margin of error."

Corrigan had no great insight into the human heart—he was no Okoye, no deCant—but being trapped like Bhatterji's ions between a superior who did not covet the captaincy and a subordinate who did, he could not help but be aware of the forces at work around him. Satterwaithe too smugly assumed that the numbers were right because they supported the answer she wanted.

But Corrigan, who knew how fragile and uncertain a thing a number could be, stopped himself from lashing out at Satterwaithe as he had lashed out at The Lotus Jewel. Instead, he replied ever so matter-of-factly, "*If* the margin of error is correct; and *if* the error bars bracket the True Position."

The old woman stiffened and the lines in her face hardened (though no one had ever thought them especially soft). "I would have thought those calculations would be done by now," she said sweetly. "Especially with the two of you working *so* closely together."

Corrigan retreated to truculence. "I applied Bhatterji's Rule: If the captain *really* wants it, he'll ask twice." He never paused to think how that would sound to The Lotus Jewel—that he had just offered up the very excuse that he had refused to accept from her.

"We're taking lessons from an *engineer* now?" Ratline said.

Satterwaithe silenced the cargo master with a look and turned back to Corrigan. "How long will this work for Gorgas take?" she asked. "I need you to calibrate the collar gauges for the mains'l."

Corrigan, though he bridled at the tone, seized upon technical detail as a drowning man upon flotsam. "Why the collar gauges?"

"The whole sensor array needs to be rewired," Ratline explained. "I just finished checking it this morning."

Corrigan blew his breath out in frustration. This entire project was taking longer and eating more resources than he had expected. Originally, he had thought only to unfurl the jib to buy more time for the repairs. That might have been done four days ago, but with the obstinacy of the universe when confronted with the plans of humankind, the jib had proven unusable: scarred and poisoned by solar radiation. Ratline had thought it the original sail, never replaced because no one had ever taken the ship's hybrid status seriously. "What does the rewiring do to our schedule?" Corrigan asked.

Satterwaithe shrugged. "Pushes it out three more days. That's why we have to hump, hump, *hump*."

"It won't do us any good if Bhatterji lights up before we can kick amps."

"Tell me something I didn't know."

Ratline did not understand the obsessions of Genie and the snake, although he did understand that they were different. He did not care whether the sail unfurled before or after the engines lit, although the idea of sticking it to Bhatterji had a definite appeal. He did not even much care whether the sail provided the edge that saved the ship. Down in the bone, he may not even have cared if the ship was saved at all. There was only one thing that mattered, and that was seeing the great loop of the mains'l glow one more time in his life. The vision rose before him every night when he closed his eyes and scared away the other ghosts.

The ship would be careened and scrapped when they made Galileo. Ratline saw that clear. He thought the others did too though no one had mentioned it yet. This transit would be the end of *The River of Stars*, and if she had to end, then she ought to end under sail. Not because it would help, not because it would aggrandize, but only because it would be right. He knew what needed doing, and he would see it done. In his own pragmatic way, Ratline was as much the romantic as Grubb.

"We'll need ..." and Satterwaithe flipped open her 'puter and summoned a memo with her stylus ring, "we'll need ... Here it is. Thirty-three Kandle brackets ..."

"Thirty-three," said Corrigan.

Satterwaithe looked at him. "We can salvage seventeen of the sensors. Moth has green-flagged them. Also, that Oberndorf shunt we recovered from the rotten jib can be used. ... The splitters we already knew about. ... Two spools of I/R fibrop ... And a spool and a half of ffg-gauge hobartium, grade XV or better."

Forgotten in the technobabble was The Lotus Jewel, who was not accustomed to being forgotten and did not care at all for the experience. Satterwaithe and Ratline were perhaps the only two on board capable of ignoring the sysop; and Corrigan, when the task was on him, could grow single-minded. He could hold the problem's clear definition and cool distance and, most of all, its comforting mass of data, as a shield against other problems less well defined, less distanced, and far less measured.

But by so seizing upon the issue Satterwaithe had raised, he left his quarrel with The Lotus Jewel in abeyance and she could not perceive that as anything other than another deliberate snub. She was wrong—it was not deliberate—but perhaps that was more damning. Had Corrigan known he was doing it, he might have known to stop.

The Lotus Jewel listened to the discussion. There was not much else she could do. The others were between her and the door, for one thing. For another, she was looking for an opening to draw Zizzy's attention back to her so she could finish what he had started. Yet while she waited, the room crept upon her consciousness, which was not an easy thing for a room to do. She saw the dog boxes so neat in their rows. She saw the prints on the wall. She saw how even Corrigan himself, floating in the air, seemed somehow to align on these same rectilinear coordinates. Horrifyingly, the analog chronometer behind him proclaimed 6:00. The only things *curved*, she thought, were the funny, squiggly letters in one of the wall hangings—and herself. She began to wonder whether she might be out of place in such a room.

In fact, she was; for on every other visit, her place had been in the center of things. Now she was on the periphery, and it gave her a different perspective. She studied the prayer rug fastened to the floor and remembered how, with great fuss and precision, Corrigan would realign it every few days as the bearing of the Earth changed sufficiently along the ship's transit. What she could not remember was ever seeing him pray upon it.

When the opening came for her to speak, it was not the opening she had been waiting for. Satterwaithe had read down her list and mentioned the hobartium requirements and The Lotus Jewel in sudden recollection said, "Oh!"

That drew every eye toward her and placed her once again in

the center. "I forgot to tell you," she said. "I received a stock-out notice from Ship. There are only two spools left, and those are dedicated to Bhatterji."

Satterwaithe looked at her from what seemed a very long distance. "And you waited until now to tell us?" Satterwaithe did not have a high opinion of the sysop. She did not have a high opinion of very many people. In her more honest moments, she did not have a high opinion of herself.

"Well, I for*got!*" The Lotus Jewel said. "I was getting ready for the dinner and the rock message from the *Younger Boyle* had just come in and—"

"Yes," said Satterwaithe. "It's always something."

"Bhatterji's a waster," said Ratline. "There should have been enough hobie, but he always uses more than he needs."

"Is that the reason?" asked Satterwaithe.

"It doesn't matter what the reason is," Corrigan said. "If we had known before dinner, what could we have done?"

"I can think of one or two things," Ratline said.

"What?" said Corrigan. "Stabbing Bhatterji?"

Satterwaithe went pale at this reminder and Ratline's face darkened. He leaned toward Corrigan. "You think you're so muffin' smart, you muffin' snake? You don't know what you're talking about! If ever a man's ribs did want steel between them, it's that boy lover's!"

"Well," Corrigan told him evenly, "try to wait until *after* he's repaired the ship."

Ratline blazed; his face thrust forward. "*We're* going to repair the ship. Remember?"

"Without any more hobartium?" Corrigan asked gently.

"So we'll hoist without the muffing sensor array! Free sailing!"

"Into Jupiter Roads, without knowing sail status? Into *that* magnetosphere?"

Ratline was ready to leap on the First. His fingers arced like claws. And Corrigan waited to receive him, for there is a form of combat among the 'Stroider snakes, born in part from the martial arts of the Earthly East and in part from the unique properties of free fall, and he was in such a mental state that he welcomed the prospect of combat. But he and Ratline were both distracted by Satterwaithe's sigh.

It was a long one, that sigh, and demanded their attention. It seemed to go on and on and on, every particle of breath hissing out of her. Indeed, she seemed to deflate and her eyes took on a dull luster, as if a lamp that had always burned behind them had just been extinguished. Had there been acceleration, she would have slumped, but as it was, she only hung limply in the air. " 'Dul's right," she said. "If we were only behind schedule, we might have caught up; but if Bhatterji's gobbled up all the hobartium . . ." She glared at The Lotus Jewel as if the sysop were personally responsible; but she could not maintain the glare and looked away into some far corner of the room. "I had hoped . . ." she whispered. "I had hoped . . ." She did not say for what she had hoped, but Ratline, with astonishing tenderness, said, "I know."

Corrigan snaked to face the wall of his quarters, intending by this to signal that they all should leave; but in turning he saw affixed before him the holo of his old quattro, *City of Amman*. It was a simple ship—only a chassis towing a string of cargo pods—yet lovely in her own way. What could replace the awe of working the crow's nest on a jammed shroud motor, high up the mast over an ocean black and a trillion light-years deep? Not feeding boron canisters to an ever-hungry engine. Nothing could, this side of death.

He hovered there, motionless for a long moment, and the others remembered afterward how he had seemed to go into a place apart, as if all the rest of the world had ceased to exist. Satterwaithe was struck by his stillness. It was as if time had stopped and not the acting first. The Lotus Jewel noticed the intense melancholy on his face, and this was a strange thing for her to notice since Corrigan's face was not an expressive one, stiffened as it was by his microbotic skin enhancers. She even thought, as she admitted later, that the melancholy stemmed from their earlier quarrel. Ratline . . . But who ever knew what Ratline thought?

When Corrigan spoke at last, he spoke without turning and if his three uninvited guests had begun to drift toward the door, the new tone in his voice stopped them. "Bhatterji is good," he announced. "Give the devil his due, he does know his trade. *Two* engines slagged? Improvising spares he doesn't have? In nineteen days? Even if he fails, I'll tip my hat to him." He pulled himself around with the easy grace of the spaceborn and Satterwaithe wondered at the man who now faced her, as if something new had burst from the chrysalis he had been. "*But he may still fail*! I wish him no ill luck, but only Allah knows what will come to pass. Prudence, if nothing else, requires we continue. As the hadith has it: 'Trust in Allah, but tie up your camel.'"

"Or," Satterwaithe replied with a sardonic twist to her lips, "God helps those who help themselves."

It was a strange thing, but until that very moment he and Satterwaithe had never felt truly partners in their surreptitious enterprise. More often than not, they had been at loggerheads. Yet, now a strange and sudden bond united them. They both felt it, and they both wondered at it. "Genie," he said, "study the PERT. See what you can juggle. You're the organizer in this tub." And in truth, he did admire the Third's ability to pull things together. If Gorgas excelled at chess, Satterwaithe had mastered jigsaw puzzles.

"And what about the hobartium?" The Lotus Jewel asked.

"I can slip any task needing hobartium," Satterwaithe considered aloud, "and flip the task sequence later, when we do scrounge some up. If Bhatterji fails, we can even cannibalize the engines."

Corrigan was skeptical. "Over Bhatterji's dead body."

"That can happen," Ratline said cheerfully. "But why wait? There's hobie in the radiation belt and in the comm antennae."

"Not the belt!" said Satterwaithe, "if there's a storm—"

"Not the antennae!" said The Lotus Jewel, "if there's a message—"

"Wait . . ." And Corrigan's raised hands brought such utter silence that he thought them for a moment endowed with some magical power. "Moth, don't touch the belt if you can help it. Storm intensity at this altitude is usually low; but the way our luck has been running, we'd have the hundred-year flare while our belt was untied. LJ, you can't transmit at all, is that right?" He barely waited for her nod. "And you'd need hobartium yourself for the repairs. So . . . Moth, go ahead and cannibalize what's left in the transmitter—whatever the lithium spray didn't ruin—but don't touch the receiver or the radars. We'll need the radars to take pilot bearings when we close on Port Galileo. Unless you want to run the Io Tube without bearings or without being able to hear the weather reports . . . ? I didn't think so. Check the abandoned areas on the main and lower decks, especially the orlop. There may still be unused equipment there with hobartium circuitry. LJ, bring me the data Gorgas gave you. I'll finish his navigational calculations and either put his fears to rest or . . ." And here he managed a crooked grin. "Or add a new sense of urgency to our work."

"It would help to crunch the schedule if we had more hands," Satterwaithe said.

"Who?" asked Ratline.

"Eaton Grubb is always singing about the old days," Corrigan suggested.

"What about Gorgas?" asked Satterwaithe.

For a weird moment, Corrigan thought she had suggested the captain as an additional team member. When he realized his mistake, he laughed, which astonished the sailing master and puzzled the others. "If Gorgas can worry over as remote a chance as brushing Stranger's Reef, he can see the need for Plan B. You know how he is, Genie. The man is never happy with only one contingency in play."

"But, he's a—"

"He's a Farnsworth man. But he's also captain of *The River of Stars*. I don't think he'll balk at a backup plan. We'll review the feasibility study first—based on how much hobartium Moth can find—*then* we'll take it to Gorgas. If Moth can't find enough to finish the job . . ." He shrugged. "We can fold our hand without having made any promises."

"I'll talk to Eaton," said The Lotus Jewel, though she said it to Satterwaithe. She was still not talking to Corrigan.

"And I'll kill Bhatterji," said Ratline. Then he laughed

through his ragged teeth. "Only joking," he assured them, and he laughed again. "Excuse me while I go prospecting."

After Ratline had gone, The Lotus Jewel said in her smallest voice, "Moth scares me, sometimes." Corrigan and Satterwaithe traded glances over her studded scalp and each saw the same truth in the other's eye.

Afterward, Corrigan sought a measure of calm by losing himself in words. *The Thoughts of Khalil el-Hikri* were subtle and difficult to follow, as intricate in their own way as Shumar's calligraphy. The *saj* required close attention and often meant something entirely different when read at another time, and yet Corrigan found his own thoughts wandering from the resonant and demanding poetry. He had actually faced Satterwaithe and won! At least he thought he had won. Yet, he had learned something, and that was that leadership meant securing the cooperation of others and not merely their obedience.

That someone else was in the room with him pressed only gradually upon his senses. He could not say when he actually knew, for it was a slow awareness, built up from infinitesimals. A minute increase in the warmth of the room. The barely-heard susurrus of quiet breath. The strange pressure of immanence that the blind were said to feel.

He jerked from his book to see Bhatterji's strange, elfin assistant before him. So suddenly did he apprehend her that it seemed to him that she had materialized from the very air.

"I didn't hear the hoígh plate," he said after a moment. "How did you get in?"

Miko studied him with a disturbing air of appraisal, as if weighing him in a balance pan. "You and your friends are going to save the ship using the magnetic sail," she said at last.

There is a story told about Corrigan the boy. This is the story. A relative visiting Corrigan's family compound on Pallas had shown him holos of Earth. One was of a herd of sheep in a pasture near As-Salt, in the hills above al-Quds, among which grazed one sheep with a dark coat. The uncle had laughed and said, "Now, there is the real 'black sheep' of our family." And

Corrigan the boy had gravely replied, "The fleece is black on *this* side . . ."

That is, Corrigan was good with facts and seldom went beyond them, which was both his strength and his weakness. And so he knew two things about Miko and did not know a third.

The first thing was that Miko had learned somehow of Plan B, and he wondered whether Bhatterji had sent the girl to dissuade him. But then he thought that this would be a strange thing for Bhatterji to do. For intimidation, an oaf is more effective than an elf.

Unless he had sent her to seduce him, and by thus persuading Corrigan's lower parts, convince his upper. Miko's large eyes mixed innocence and youth with the hardness of untimely age. She still dressed androgynously but, while some might call her a mere girl, 'Stroiders married at sixteen, or even fourteen, so she was older in Corrigan's frame of reference than she was for the Earth-born. "Husband-high," as they said in the Belt. Yet there was something in her bearing too; as if time itself had passed at a different rate for her, and years had accumulated under her heart faster than they had ought. Perhaps if he had not so lately quarreled with The Lotus Jewel, Corrigan might not have noticed Miko the woman; but he had and so he did.

The second thing that Corrigan knew about Miko was that she believed the plan would succeed. She had said *would*, and not *try*. Why he attributed such precision to her words, he could not say. Only that she used so few of them that each one seemed exactly chosen for its task.

He did not deny what the girl had so plainly learned. "It seems sensible to have a backup plan," he said.

"Especially a plan the captain and the engineer don't know about. . . ." Miko's voice echoed with the wink of shared and forbidden knowledge. She had *not* confided in Bhatterji.

"We wanted to complete the feasibility study before presenting it." Corrigan may even have believed that story by then, although they were well along into execution.

"Sure," Miko said carelessly. "I want to help."

Now the curious thing about Miko was how she loved the

ship, and curious not only because the affection ran deeper than it ran long. She was an engineer-in-training and all that breed come to love their engines. But also the ship had rescued her—first on Amalthea when it swept her away into the Void, and then again when she had found sanctuary in its interstices after so fruitlessly throwing herself on Bhatterji. The routines of shipboard life had given her structure for the first time in her life and she clung to them as one falling into an abyss clings to close-by branches.

Corrigan too was devoted to duty, although only because it *was* duty. He respected authority as a penniless man respects wealth, and followed procedures because they *were* the procedures.

Miko had not sought him out because of this shared loyalty. The acting force was less the attraction of the acting first officer than it was the repulsion of the chief engineer. That a successful sail deployment would humiliate Bhatterji glittered like a diamond in her mind the moment when, listening from the vent, she had realized the Thursday Group's intent; but that a certain shiver ran through her when Corrigan unfolded from his sling did not at the time register.

This shiver betokened the third thing, the thing that Corrigan did not yet know.

While Corrigan was recruiting the newest member for Plan B, The Lotus Jewel was weeping in the abandoned Starview Room. This large, now-featureless space had once been a lounge decked in the self-conscious decadence of the fifties. There had been a dance space, of course—In the milligee environment of constant boost, dancing fell just short of flying—and dining tables too where the pointlessly wealthy could savor the flesh of forbidden species. But there had been the snort tables and the leather rooms; the display couches for artful lovemaking; and bunghole row for the ankle grabbers' anonymous invitations. And everywhere, mirrors. For that generation loved pleasure and loved tawdry and loved excess, but most of all they loved themselves; and all reproach they held as envy.

Aside from the observation blister off the bridge, this was the one place on the ship where the stars could be seen directly, through a great lens of metallocene plastic. The Starview Room was never as successful as its designers had hoped. No matter how many diversions were laid out, or how many bodies offered or pharmaceuticals ingested, still the eye was drawn to the great lens and beyond it, to sun or moon or to the great river of stars itself. It was an awesome and infinite sight, a constant reminder of how small and insignificant the onlooker was; and that was the one reminder the self-satisfied patrons of that era could never abide.

The paraphernalia of pleasure had later been replaced by ovens and mess tables for Martian colonists. Twenty-four de-Cant's grandmother had been one of them. Here. In this very room. Eating her beans and rice and gnawing her biscuit and dreaming youthful dreams through the plastic window. The sight had never made *her* feel small. She was sailing to tame a world!

The room was stripped and abandoned now. Tramp crews have little time for skygazing. Too much, they warned, and your soul would be sucked out of you; though that might be no more than the superstition of a time that had turned its back on decadence and pioneer austerity both, and settled zen-like into a gray and muddled pragmatism. If they had no eye for beauty, it was hardly beauty's fault.

There were exceptions. The Lotus Jewel was one. She found in the Starview Room neither intimidation nor rapture, but only contentment. If she had seen, had really seen, the endlessness of the Big Empty, she might have felt differently; but the splendor was a flat backdrop to her, merely colorful and beautiful, as jewels on a velvet gown might be beautiful. It might be said that, lacking much depth in herself, she found little elsewhere; but it might also be said that beauty was drawn to beauty. It could be the universe that gazed at her.

Eaton Grubb too would often visit the Starview Room; but he found there, rather than contentment, a nameless melancholy that suited the romantic in him. A thousand tragic ballads welled in his throat. Poignant lyrics trembled on his lips. But the words drifted and tumbled in his mind, never quite finding form, as if they existed just below the level of his own awareness.

He watched The Lotus Jewel sob quietly for a time and imagined all sorts of sorrows and tragedies behind her tears; but it was not in him to stand by when another hurt, and so he spoke up. "Is there something I can do?"

The Lotus Jewel jerked at the sudden voice and turned with a hesitant smile breaking through her sorrow. "Who is that? Is that you?" But the smile faded when Eaton Grubb stepped from the shadowed entry into the light of a billion distant suns.

Given the question, the smile, and its fading, Grubb knew instinctively who had given the golden woman tears. "What did he do to you?" he asked. Her tears glistened like crystal on her cheeks, so lovely that Grubb was loathe to brush them away. "It was Corrigan, wasn't it?" Who else could cause The Lotus Jewel such misery but he who caused the antipodal joy? Yet, Grubb was loath to rely on inference. He needed confirmation in all things. He sang, perhaps, to hear his own existence.

A solitary man, reticent in most things, Grubb joined in few games, often ate alone. Yet, for all that, he was a friend to most on board. Not the sort of friend for revelry, but rather the sort for revelations. People would tell him things without ever knowing that they had. He collected these confidences the way a magpie collects bright and glittery objects.

He was also a sudden man, spurred by the moment and by chance. He might have backed quietly from the Starview Room before The Lotus Jewel noticed him, but that urge to spontaneity drove him to speak. Yet there was more to it than that. Beauty, whether of starlight or song or aroma or texture, enthralled him. He spoke because he could not tear himself away.

"He called me stupid," The Lotus Jewel cried. "Zizzy called me stupid."

"You aren't stupid," Grubb told her. He touched her on the arm. Grubb kept in touch with the world in a very literal way. He looked, he listened, he tasted, he sniffed, he touched. When he could, he combined them all. He had wanted to combine them all in the person of The Lotus Jewel for a very long time.

The sight and sound of her were already his, but he longed also for the salt and the musk and the soft caress.

The Lotus Jewel was as keenly aware of her surroundings as he was. Beneath Grubb's singlet she could mark the contours of his affection and so knew not only his longing, but how long it was. This moon-faced man's regard had always pleased her—she liked to be liked, which was why Corrigan's disgust had hurt her so—and she turned to him as to a friend.

"What should I do, Eaton?"

"If it were me," Grubb said, "I wouldn't see the need to do anything. It's up to *him* to apologize. You weren't at fault." Giving advice discomfited Grubb, yet if spontaneity bordered opportunism, so did reticence border desertion. He could not remain entirely silent.

The Lotus Jewel did not see things in quite the same way. The rebuke had been deserved—*only not from Corrigan*! Not from Corrigan. It was because she had disappointed him that she wept, though she didn't quite understand that herself. The knowledge hovered, wraithlike, below the horizon of her mind.

"Corrigan does have a sharp tongue," Grubb said.

"He didn't mean it."

"The crew doesn't like him very much."

"But I do."

"He always spots one tiny, little infraction and takes all his bearings on that."

The Lotus Jewel looked up and tossed her head, though the tresses had been years ago cut away. "He *can* pick at nits," she admitted. A comforting thought, that her transgression had been a nit. "I can't be very stupid if I hold a master's certificate in AI systems engineering, can I?"

"Of course not." Grubb could not conceive of any flaw in perfect beauty. Certificates weren't in it. The Lotus Jewel could have proclaimed herself Queen of Ceres and Grubb would have as happily agreed.

"Thank you." She laid a hand on his forearm. His arm was bare because, in his work with the ovens, Grubb favored a singlet over the coveralls most of the crew wore. She found his skin soft and pliant, very unlike Corrigan's. The back of his arm was covered with fine hairs. She saw his skin prickle with goose bumps and smiled.

"I must look awful," she said; and indeed, this was a secret fear of hers: that her beauty was a vast and comic mistake, and someday a small boy in the passing crowd would point it out.

"Impossible," said Eaton Grubb.

Grubb was a man of the senses, but sense is not passive. The Object does not merely impress itself like a seal upon wax, but fuses with the Subject in the act of knowing, which is why to know someone is a very intimate thing. The *form* of The Lotus Jewel had an intentional existence in the mind of Eaton Grubb that was wholly distinct from, though no less real than, the extensional existence of her *matter* floating there in the deserted Starview Room. And if this form were stripped of whatever flaws her matter may have possessed, why then who is to say that the flaws mattered?

"You're in love with me," she said, as always with that note of hidden surprise, as if she could not quite give credence to it.

"Always," Grubb said softly. "I love everything about you." He might have been mistaken in that. It might have been awe, and not love that he felt. He tried not to look at her breasts when he said it. He did not want to sully his love of her with mere lust, although the lust was there, and no mistake. "I love your dress uniform," he said, picking something more neutral. "Red flatters you."

Pleased, The Lotus Jewel straightened a wristband and (because she knew what he was trying so hard not to look at) doubled over to adjust an ankle band too. "Do you like it?" she said as she straightened. "I've had it since I was purser in the old *Mooncrest Tranquility*. I took the insignia off when they . . . After I resigned my berth there . . . But I still wear it for the captain's dinners."

"I know," said Grubb with a swallow. "I've seen you in it. And the earrings and the brooch, they're gold, aren't they? I thought about being a jeweler once, but I didn't have the knack for it."

"They're Martian ironstone, the earrings are. You can see the black-and-red flecks in the facets. Go ahead, take a closer look." And Grubb leaned toward her to see the specks and learned that there are no neutral subjects.

In orbital mechanics, it is well known that the closer a satellite orbits its primary, the faster it must move to maintain its altitude—until the stresses of acceleration overcome the material strength of the body itself. It is called Roche's Limit, this minimum safe distance, and any satellite that crosses it bursts asunder into countless tumbling shards. Saturn won her rings in that manner, or so it is said, and became thereby the most beautiful body in the High System.

Grubb cried out as he crossed the limit, and The Lotus Jewel as well, in quick *Oh's!* that might have been of surprise or delight or both, between sudden and eager kisses. Closer and faster, they scattered pieces of themselves into a ring about them. The earrings and the brooch glittered like ice moons in the light of the galaxy outside—those millions of stars, unreachably distant, yet so numerous as to cast shadows and throw strange colors across her soft, tawny contours. Color, shape, texture, aroma, flavor, and tone combined into that grand harmony that Grubb had always sought—and which afterward filled him with an intense melancholy that he treasured for the rest of his days.

The Lotus Jewel had not been unfaithful to her lover, for she had given Grubb only a body, and not a heart. (She was profligate with the tangible, but the spiritual she hoarded like a miser.) Nothing had been planned. The sudden tearing need had been as unexpected and as overwhelming to her as it had been to Grubb, as if they had both been suddenly possessed by a strange and wonderful force, but she wasted no time in wondering why. She was a creature entirely of the moment.

It was different with Miko and Corrigan. They were both careful by nature. Their orbits moved slowly, and in well-defined paths. There would be no impact, no sudden bursting—only the long, patient curvature of space and time pulling them in. The Lotus Jewel had shared her flesh with Eaton Grubb yet had not broken faith with Corrigan; but Corrigan, who had not so much as touched the elfin girl, already had, for he had looked upon Miko as a man looks upon a woman, with his heart. It was only that his heart did not yet know it.

Neither Grubb nor The Lotus Jewel could find the second earring, though they searched a long time. Perversely, it had come to rest against the great viewing window and was lost, one small stellar cluster against the whole wild universe beyond; and so they did not see it. The loss saddened Grubb more even than it did The Lotus Jewel, for he did love beautiful things and wept to lose them.

The Void

Ram Bhatterji hovered over a pit endlessly deep and trembled with the readiness of a bridegroom before his bride—a cold, hard bitch of a bride, who would suck the life from her lover if she could, but who by that same lethal carelessness impressed life more firmly into a man's awareness. Bhatterji trembled. His blood throbbed. His breath burned. Eagerness was a hard lump beneath his belly.

Bhatterji finished the weld, and the white glare within the clamshell died. He unfastened the clamps that held it around the projector grid. "I'm ready to weld the Florence strut," he announced to Evermore.

"Almost cut away," the apprentice told him. He was slicing off the mangled strut with a laser, collecting the metallic vapors in a static well he held in his left hand. Evermore wore a tether clipped securely to an eye bolt on the hull and he relocated this tether each time he shifted position. There were times, Bhatterji thought, when a sensible man did wear a line, but it signified a man's helplessness before the Void—or his belief in his helplessness—and belief informed behavior.

"Take your time," Bhatterji said mildly, but with enough sarcasm that Evermore straightened and made no move. The boy's grip on the cutting torch clenched and unclenched. Its laser cut through steel; a suit's fabric would be as nothing. One swipe and Bhatterji would no more bedevil him. "We do what the ship wants first," Bhatterji told him. "Later, we do what we want."

He undogged his clamshell. Evermore still had not moved. "Are you going to finish that strut?" Gorgas had wanted action, Gorgas would get action.

Evermore capitulated. "I'll finish it."

"Fine." Bhatterji squatted and unclipped Evermore's tether. "Move around to the other side. You'll never get a clean cut from that angle." When Evermore clambered monkey-style around the support cage, never losing contact with the hull, Bhatterji added, "And if you damage those focusing rings—"

Evermore oriented himself and resumed cutting. Bhatterji grunted and turned away, having gotten what he wanted. As he did so, the Milky Way caught his eye. The vast starry river seemed to flow across the heavens like the sacred Ganges itself. He could swear that he saw it moving, as if he could dive into it and be carried off cleansed to eternity. When he looked back to Evermore, the boy was trying to control the laser and the static well and keep hold of the ship at the same time. As that required three hands, he held strut and static well with the same hand.

Bhatterji sighed in exasperation. The boy didn't need *leverage* for a laser cut. As it was, the grip was awkward. Bobble the static well and—

—*And the metallic vapors created by the laser torch blossom like an incandescent globe, engulfing glove and arm, scorching the fabric, and splashing silvery filigrees across the metalocene faceplate.*

Not a good thing, Bhatterji thought, observing the accident with peculiar and detached calm, but not immediately dangerous if one reacted quickly.

Which Evermore did, though not with the necessary efficiency. He reached for his damaged visor with both hands, crying out in surprise and shock. A violent motion, it pushed him free of the Farnsworth cage. "Fool!" said Bhatterji. "The static well!"

But Evermore had already released the static well and the charged metallic vapor, deprived now of its sink, coated the rails of the cage. Evermore himself drifted farther from the ship, still crying, "My visor! It's cracking!"

Bhatterji stared into the waiting maw of the Void and knew that moments mattered. He activated his suit's targeting software. "Go there," he told the suit when he had the boy centered in the crosshairs, and he dove single-mindedly into the black pool of space.

The two of them, master and apprentice, fell and fell. *The ship is not accelerating*, Bhatterji reminded himself. *We share the same velocity, the ship and I. The River will not pull irretrievably ahead.* But he did not look to his rear display for fear that the universe would call him Liar. His heart hammered at the bars of his ribs like a prisoner craving release. *Please,* he thought. *Please.* He could not say with whom he pled, nor even what he pled for. Just that one thought, over and over. *Please.*

When he reached Evermore, the suddenness of the contact surprised him. Proportion and distance had ceased to exist, and so he did not know how close the boy was until he had him in his arms. Evermore struggled, still crying about his visor. *Shut up*, Bhatterji wanted to tell him. *Shut up, shut up, shut up!* He could not orient himself with the boy twisting so in his grip, and if he could not find the ship again, he could not jet them back. Evermore would drag him into the Void too. Falling forever, Bhatterji thought. Drowning among the stars, like Enver Koch. And what purpose would that serve? Panic carried a price, and a man must pay his debts.

Bhatterji released Evermore.

"Oh, God, don't leave me!" Evermore shouted.

"Quiet," Bhatterji growled. He looked quickly around. Up. Down. There! The ship, at 4:00 low, was already noticeably smaller. Or was that too only another illusion of perspective? Bhatterji seized Evermore's trailing tether before it could drift past and he hauled the two of them together, turning the boy so that they both faced the ship. "Don't move." He should have said, Be quiet, too, for Evermore continued to sob. Bhatterji centered the ship in his crosshairs. "Go there," he told the suit, and he pushed the now limp form toward the engineering lock on the lower hull. "Miko," he called the ship. "Open the dock."

"Is Rave all right?"

"His faceplate is scored and opaqued by metallic vapor. The score lines could be stress concentrators. I'm bringing him in."

Evermore said, "I shit my pants. Oh God, I shit my pants." Surreptitiously, Bhatterji reached around the front of Evermore's suit and yanked loose the cable for his radio.

The bay doors slid open, spewing a mist of fine snow because Miko hadn't waited for the chamber to reach vacuum before cycling it. The exterior and interior lights came on—a brilliant white—casting sharp-edged shadows that separated night from day in jagged chunks.

The doors were sliding closed even while Bhatterji passed between them. Air dumps filled the vacuum. A howling wind caught him and silence gave way to a great rushing sound. The throbbing vibrations of the pumps seemed curiously in time with his own heart, and the windsong with the grateful exhalation of his lungs.

Only then, with the outerlock sealed and the air pressure approaching ship ambient, did Bhatterji turn Evermore around to study his visor. There were silvery streaks across the darkened plastic, as if some god had cried iron tears and they had frozen on the boy's face. Evermore's pale, wide-eyed visage was a ghost behind the darkened and opaque visor. On closer inspection, Bhatterji saw that some of the tracks had indeed scored the visor, and from the tip of one metallic streak radiated a fine hairline.

Suddenly overwhelmed by a vision of what might have been, Bhatterji seized the other and enfolded him in a clumsy, suited embrace. Evermore was a passive lump, neither returning nor rejecting the pressure. *Now*, thought Bhatterji. *Now is the time for panic and fear*. And the dogs of Mars did sweep through him, in such wild career that he trembled in their turbulent wake. It was a fine point whether he held so tightly to Evermore because of the lad's near brush with death or to still his own sudden and uncontrolled shivers. A pulse of irresistible desire overwhelmed him, a brutal urge to hammer away and prove that, once again, he lived and had triumphed over the bitch Void.

The inner doors swung open and Miko entered the dock, and the moment she did Evermore pushed Bhatterji violently away. "Don't you touch me, you pervert!" And he swung gauntleted fists, whose impact Bhatterji absorbed in silence. "Don't you touch me! You tried to kill me!"

Miko put a restraining hand on Evermore's arm and he shrugged it off, but he didn't swing his fists again. Bhatterji broke his seals and lifted his helmet off and, a moment later, Evermore did the same. He would not look at Bhatterji. The engineer held out his arm. "Let me see the visor." Evermore threw the helmet, but Bhatterji had expected that and caught it neat. He studied it first from the outside, then pulled it on to see how it looked from the inside. "Fractured," he announced after he had taken it off, "but not cracked. You did well to brace it with your hands, yes." The boy had been doing nothing of the sort. He had brought his hands to his face from sheer terror. "However, the better practice is to reduce suit internal pressure to minimum and to seal the blast shield in place over the visor. Why did you not—?" Bhatterji feigned sudden understanding. "Ah, I see. The connection to your communicator came loose in the accident. No wonder I could not hear you."

Miko said, "But, I—" And Bhatterji silenced her with a look.

"Enter a work order," Bhatterji told her. "Replace visor on helmet number . . ." He read the serial number off the helmet. "Attention Ratline."

"Ratline?" She caught the helmet he tossed her.

"He's the suit-tech on this bucket, and he's got nothing better to do while I fix the ship. Evermore, why don't you shower and relax." He turned to Miko and laughed. "The first time I took a tumble like that I learned why these suits come equipped with diapers!" And he laughed again, hugely, and he never looked at Evermore.

Miko caught the odor when Rave passed her, but she said

nothing until she was alone with Bhatterji. "Did you really soil yourself the first time you tumbled?"

Bhatterji had been studying the visor, pressing the hairline fracture with his thumbs. Miko could see the way his hands trembled. Suddenly, the visor popped and cracked. Bhatterji looked up and glanced at the inner lock, where Evermore had gone. "I'm glad he didn't see that. . . . Of course, I did. I wasn't the first and Evermore won't be the last. Any man the Void doesn't terrify isn't a real man. He's a robot, or he's a fool; and the Void will kill them both."

"Rave said *you* tried to kill him." Miko brought out the accusation casually, as if discussing the malfunction of a boron injector.

"Kill him?" Bhatterji looked toward the inner lock again. "He's still walking around."

"I saw you unclip his tether."

"So he could move to the other side of the Florence strut. I thought he would reconnect. He always does. He tries to play it safe and careful, but that's mad. There is no 'safe' out here. It's a subtle trap, ever to think you're safe." He heard the rising inflections in his voice and folded his shaking hands abruptly into fists. When he spoke again, his voice was calmer. "No, Miko. When I decide to kill a man, he doesn't go off afterward and shower."

When Bhatterji had gone himself, to the spinhall to run the urge out of his blood and exhaust his fears and desires in his sweat, Miko remained thoughtfully in the engine control room, shutting down the systems they had been using, making certain everything was secured. What Bhatterji had said, there at the end, was the most chilling thing she had heard since coming aboard *The River of Stars*.

Because *The River* was officially a hybrid ship, the Long Room on the upper deck held a full complement of knitters and splicers and braiders; but because no one had taken the designation seriously for a long time, the sail-making equipment had been left in a state of slowly accumulating disrepair. Okoye did not understand how unused equipment could wear out and it was left to Miko, the renegade engineer, to explain.

It is hard to say what drew these two together: the Igbo girl who could read another's soul and the Amalthean girl with little soul to read. They were much of an age: a little older than the other youngsters, a little younger than the older crew. Miko had grown up faster, so Okoye seemed the younger of the two; but Okoye had grown up more fully, so that Miko also seemed the younger.

"It's simple," the elf explained while they both rested after having torn down a balky tommy roll. "Cyberalzheimer's sets in and the stupes forget how to do their jobs. Oh, and sometimes the sinews grow loose or the eyes get dim or the joints arthritic."

"Go away, girl," Okoye said in her mother's voice. (A helpful voice. Whenever Okoye used it, away on Earth her mother would be silenced, which greatly irritated the woman. *I wish 'Kiru would use her own voice more often,* she would complain to her neighbors, though the neighbors were secretly grateful.) "Machines be not people to grow old and crippled." Sometimes when she was flustered, her English would revert to a strange blend: part Niger-Congo, part Elizabethan. (For who are greater lovers of Shakespeare, greater lovers of fine words finely spoken, than the folk of the hill country above the Oil Rivers? Why, the great traveling road show from Ibadan that had celebrated the Bard's 500th birthday had drawn the people in their tens of thousands, audiences that had raised a great hiss whenever the actors spoke because 10,000 pairs of lips whispered the lines along with them.) "You are making fun of a poor country girl."

Fun was something Miko never made. She was deadly serious every moment of her life. Okoye should have known that. Little soul the Amalthean orphan might have, but that little was adamantine. Yet, if Okoye should have known, then likely she did know and the Igbo girl only meant to draw her companion out from herself. She just may have been as wise and as clever as Ivar Akhaturian thought.

One time in her village near Afikpo, Nkieruke Okoye had turned a boy into a yam. She did this by drawing the boy away from the village, then sneaking back and putting a large tuber in his bed. His mother had raised a wail on the discovery and the neighbors had taken it up. The policeman, when he arrived, was puzzled and took the yam into custody, where he kept a close watch over it should it take a mind to become a boy again. When the lad himself reappeared bruised and scratched and sleepless from the bush the next day and admitted that he had chased 'Kiru for a kiss of her and had gotten lost, everyone had a great laugh and said what a fine joke it had been and his mother made a soup from the yam. A fine trick, they all agreed, but everyone looked sideways at her afterward, for she had been promised to the boy. The "sitting policeman" had spoken with the "standing policeman" and the scroll had been read and both sets of parents had signed. By rights, the boy could have asked for more than a kiss.

He had, but 'Kiru never mentioned that. As for the boy, he did not wish to become a yam again.

"It's the media," Miko explained. "It deteriorates over time. The magfield raised by the radiation belt, stray cosmic rays, simple aging of the material substrate . . . If you don't migrate the information now and then, the machine loses bits and the Artificial Stupids that run them become even stupider." She wagged a thumb at the ranks of machines. "That's what happened to Number Two spinner. Deader'n Dizzy's mouse. Can't use it at all."

Their chatter attracted Ratline's attention and he hollered at them to get back to work. "This ain't no damn tea party."

"It never is," said Miko aside to Okoye.

"Something is bothering him," Okoye said of the cargo master.

"You mean he's not always like this?"

The Igbo girl shook her head. She did not know how she knew, but she knew that some sort of struggle was taking place deep inside the void that was Ratline's heart. Yet, how could she put words to it, if Ratline could not? "And the arthritis and the sinews?" she asked the engineer's mate.

"Oh, springs lose their springiness and lubricants grow gummy and photocells get dimmed by dirt. They really are alive when you stop to think of it. Machines are. Maybe they're the most alive things on the ship."

This time Okoye was certain the Amalthean was joking. Later, she became less certain.

"What is that you're humming?" Miko asked while they refastened the casement to the tommy roll's whirligig. "It was—" She paused searching for a word and not finding it because the word she wanted was *lovely*, and she had no referent for it in her life.

But she did not need words when she spoke to Nkieruke Okoye. "It is called 'The Mother Confronts the Dawn.'" Okoye hadn't known she was even humming it until Miko asked. Circumstance had stolen up on her and planted the music in her head.

"What a peculiar title! Is it from your homeland?"

Startled, Okoye laughed. To think that such music might come from little Afikpo-in-the-bush! "No, dear girl, it be a tone poem in the European tradition, with all harmony and counterpoint a-jangle; but the composer—Selim Haverstrom—he was using the scales of the Eastern tradition and the rhythm of the African. Why, I could not hum the half of it were I having three mouths to do it."

Miko stared at her workmate with astonishment. "That is the longest sentence I've ever heard you speak."

Okoye thought about it and considered that it was likely true.

"I don't know much about music," Miko confessed. "I never heard much, growing up. I had other priorities."

And might that not be the very reason why the Amalthean girl's soul was the size of a ground nut? Okoye hummed more tunes as they worked, simple tunes that she had heard Mr. Grubb sing. "The Leaving of LEO," "Estrada Brilliantinha," "Na Novy Domu," and others. She didn't sing the words, although she knew some of them. With her inner eye she watched Miko listen. Miko did not join in, but Okoye was patient. Witchy girls learned patience.

Later that night, after she had gone to bed, a noise in the corridor woke Okoye, but she floated in her sleeping cage and stared into the darkness because she could not quite place the sound. Something had struck the bulkhead; but she listened for a while and heard nothing more, and so she drifted off again to an uncertain sleep.

The second time the sound came, Okoye slithered out of her bag and fumbled in the darkness for her singlet. She noticed that two hours had gone by on the clock, though it seemed but a moment to her. Her sleep seldom bore dreams and so seemed of no duration. She was always surprised that morning came so soon.

Okoye fastened the straps on her singlet, then paused. Things had no doubt gone bump in the night before and never disturbed her sleep. "You are a crazy girl," she told herself in her mother's voice. "Why you always be poking into things?" But she did not unfasten her garment and had already kicked gently toward the door when the sound came again.

She entered the corridor and Ship, sensing her presence, dutifully activated the sector lights around her, but this only accentuated the shadows that lurked around the curves of the corridor. It was as if the gloom were a palpable thing and the lamps had only illuminated it. The ship lay quiet.

Okoye kicked off the door pad, caromed off the inner corridor bulkhead—why, that was the sound she had heard earlier!—and grabbed the monkey bar before Ratline's door. There she hesitated and was about to turn back when the sound came again. A dull smack, as if something flat had struck a wall. It was not the same sound as before. She slapped the hoígh plate and the sounds within suddenly ceased. She slapped it again, and there was no answer. She put her lips to the door and said in a shouted whisper, "Ratline! I know you be awake. Is something wrong?"

There was no response, no sound of movement within. She slapped the door directly and said, "Ratline!" And again received silence.

She had just turned away when the door slid open and, spinning 'round at the sudden noise, she saw the cargo master weaving uncertainly within the frame. His eyes were red and rheumy and his bare shanks dangled from under a belted nightshirt of unexpected red silk. He held something snake-like in his right hand, and his gaze was venomous, but blank; as if he saw nothing but hated everything. "What is it?" And his breath was acid and metallic.

Okoye did not flee, though it took an effort of will. "You banged into my wall coming past," she said. "It woke me up. I thought you might be hurt."

"If you want to kiss my hurt and make me better, come back when your kisses mean something, or I hurt somewhere useful."

Ratline was the only one on board from whom Okoye sensed nothing in her inner pool. He made no ripple; cast no reflection. It was as if he were an empty bottle, and more than empty: as if he were a vacuum capable of sucking everyone else within the void of his heart. That he might think of her sexually frightened her beyond measure. "Are you drunk?" she asked, for Ratline, though often surly, was seldom deliberately hateful.

The cargo master's smile was gap-toothed sly. "You want some, girlie? Come on inside. If I've been bad, you can spank me." What he held, she saw now, was a leather strop.

She knew it had been a mistake to investigate the sounds. Not that she was in danger from this spindle-shanked, drunken old wreck—the teachings of the sisterhood had included self-defense—but she would remember in the morning this man, and she could never, ever look on him again as she had before.

If there was anything left to salvage in the heart of the ruin that Timmy Ratline had become, it lay in his next words. "Wait," he said as she turned away. And then, after a pause, "'M sorry. D'n mean it. D'n mean it." His arms ached and his eyes felt like sandpaper. The old wounds he had never seen throbbed. "Jus' tired, 'Kiru. I'm jus' tired." He made no move to touch her. He had never had children—he could never have had children—but 'Kiru and Rave and the others were his, and though he could discipline like a Spartan, he could not bear to hurt them. Sometimes, when he forgot how many years had passed, he thought himself almost one of them.

"I finely foun' some hobie," he said, pushing aside from the door so that she could look within at two coils, wrapped and tied and floating in the air. "I spen' all night drawn it to wire."

Okoye blinked at the treasure, knew she should find joy in it, since it meant that the Great Sail would fly once more; yet there was something about the dull-gray matte wire that filled her with profound unease. "You drew all that yourself?"

"From odds 'n' ends. Couldn't bear her disappointment," he said; then staring at Okoye earnestly, added, "You unnerstan' that, don' you? I could bear her disgrace, but not her despair." He turned and gazed at the precious wire. "Almost like the old days, it was . . . Drawin' and spinnin' up in th' sailmaker's berth, me 'n ol' Sammy M'Cloud. I was sail-maker's mate by then . . . We had five spinning machines to braid cable and they'd hum and clack an' . . . Oh God," he wiped a tear, "those were days."

"I thought you were a—"

"Cabin attendant? Yah, for a while, when I was young and purty. When I grew hair where some didn't like it, I went for sailor. Climbin' the mast. Cuttin' 'n splicin'. You gotta watch that hoop stress. One time a jib sail parted and the whip end cut poor Lenny Connover in half, space suit and all. His hand was still holding the torch." Ratline laughed and then laughed again. After a moment, he quieted. He looked at the wire once more and shook his head sadly. "It wasn't like the old days," he said quietly. "Not really."

Ship conducts a complete survey of relict memory associated with the sail locker, the Long Room, and the loci of the Corrigan-entity and the other entities that correlate with him. It runs a x^2 analysis of the resulting contingency table and finds a significant association at the 85th percentile. Chi-square is not an especially powerful test of significance, nor 85% anything approaching certainty: but it will do for a hunch.

The Least Wrangler

Ivar Akhaturian had tagged Mr. Ratline as Demon-incarnate, Rave as Jealousy-incarnate, and Twenty-four as Love-incarnate; but Nkieruke Okoye he could not label at all because, Okoye being a pledged virgin, carnate was not in it. Ivar thought virginity a silly thing, but what else could he think having so willfully lost his? And so he accommodated himself to the loss by holding the forfeit of no great value. Maybe it was an Earth thing, he thought; and he was largely right. He thought the Igbo girl's eyes looked inside the soul and saw everyone's secret self. She seldom spoke and perhaps that made her seem wiser than she was. Whatever the reason, he believed he could tell her things. She listened and maybe could advise him what to do about this new and unexpected fatherhood of his.

"No one can tell you that," Okoye told the Least Wrangler. "It is like your clothing. I can see the color and the cut and the style but only you can say whether it fits well and you can wear it comfortably." Privately, she was as appalled as Wong had been. Ivar and Twenty-four were too young! Too young in Lagos. Too young in Calabar. Too young even in Afikpo, where marriage did come sooner than in the big cities. Yet she withheld judgment, unsure whether the customs of her village were the laws of the universe.

"I don't know if I'm ready."

"No one is ever ready."

"I'll do the right thing."

"I know you will."

"I love her. I really do. I don't care what Rave says."

"Love is not enough." At least, not the hormonal sort of love that Ivar meant; not the rush, not the irresistable pulse of the blood. The pledge that Okoye had taken when her flows began had warded her through that phase—far enough to spy, on the remoter shore of adolescence, the other lumber with which a house was built.

Ivar did know that love alone was not enough, but he knew it as he knew most things: as an idea, as an abstraction. He did not yet know it in his belly. It had no *kinetics* for him. Okoye sensed the turmoil in the lad. There was wild remorse and cringing fear and, inevitably, boyish pride. That endothermic mix had not yet congealed into anything solid, let alone into anything that had a name, but Okoye did not sense calm, and that was good, for calm was not called for.

———

It had become nearly impossible for deCant and Akhaturian to be alone together for any length of time without getting naked. This seemed to them the most natural thing, but the sheer insistence of it bothered the Least Wrangler. It was as if his behavior were compelled by a force of nature and not by an act of will; and so he tried by various stratagems to engage his attention on something else, on anything else, just to prove to himself that he could refrain from the earthy deed if he wanted to. It never worked. He never actually wanted to.

This carnal predestination did not bother Twenty-Four deCant, for it meant one decision fewer to fret her. This single facet of her life at least was a fait accompli, in which she need only enjoy the accomplishment and leave the rest to fate. For all else, her life had become a whirligig of competing decisions and tasks and uncertainties.

Okoye had been coopted onto some mysterious task by Corrigan, and Evermore had been assigned to work under Bhatterji; so all of Ratline's scut work fell on the shoulders of Akhaturian and deCant and, as she was the senior of the two, more on hers than his. DeCant had lost count of her assignments, although she consoled herself with the thought that, like the integers, they were at least countable. Ratline had told them to redeploy the entire cargo hold; and that, in turn, required that each container's mass be confirmed, a new location assigned, and the pods themselves physically undogged, shifted, and redogged in their new homes. And, by the way, don't forget to enter the new location in the database. Not having been told the reason for all the shifting, the two junior wranglers regarded the project as one more reprise of Ratline's insane desire to work them to death.

There were a great many pods in the hold, and Ratline's calculations started them into an intricate quadrille. DeCant had opened the dance in media res, and more than once had to undo a move in order to get at the next container on her list. Ivar imagined a closed loop trajectory in the state space of load locations—really—in which the same loads shifted endlessly in and out of the same bins. He had never heard of Sisyphus, but he thought the concept loudly enough that Twenty-four eventually scowled at him.

"I'm not a logistics expert," she snapped after they had to pull five loads they had just shifted because the sixth load to be moved was dead behind them. "It's a muffing Chinese puzzle, is what it is."

"If we laid out the sequence logically . . ." Ivar ventured. But he only ventured, because, in the first place, he was loath to criticize his beloved and in the second place, the said beloved gave him no opportunity to finish the thought.

"I don't have time for that! I have to shift these loads, and in between that I have to help The Lotus Jewel debug some old signal filter she's resurrected. And in between that, I have a baby growing inside me. . . ."

A baby was worry enough, but hers was doomed to be a snake and while she had nothing against snakes personally, both Corrigan and the doctor were obviously unhappy and de-Cant grieved to deliver a baby to a life as joyless as theirs. Yet she had committed herself to the child's upbringing, and that care would bind her to Ivar for the duration and bar them both for many years from ever seeing their homes. A Martian marriage was less than a lifetime's commitment, but not when viewed from deCant's end of the lifetime.

"And in between that, I have to look after you. . . ."

That last was a hurtful thing to say, however true it was. De-Cant was only a little older than Akhaturian—when measured in standard years—but it sometimes came home to her how much younger in other metrics the Callistan boy really was. She would fret that she had trapped him by her own carelessness; and at other times that she had trapped herself. But she dared not mention these concerns to Ivar because, dutiful as he was, he would blame himself for all her worries.

I'm sorry, she would imagine him saying. *I didn't know this would happen.*

Which, of course, he was and he hadn't; but out of respect for his pride she did not want to hear him say it.

Partnering with Ivar really ought to have had more thought given it. It ought to have been entered upon with purpose, and not for mere happenstance. Yet the careful weighing of alternatives had never been her way. Taking things as they came had always served her well in the past, but she had not enough past to call it experience and, as events had proven, consequences really did matter. She had taken Ivar as he came, and now look where they were. Still, she was a girl who enjoyed her pleasures and, Okoye being pledged, the only alternative to Ivar had been Raphael Evermore.

Evermore was stimulating company, alert and outspoken. He and deCant were really much alike, yet there was something about him that always struck her as selfish. She had seen that from the first day, when Rave had so eagerly welcomed her aboard at Port Deimos. He was polite, even courtly, but he had smiled to excess and deCant distrusted teeth. Ivar liked his johnny well enough—all boys did, and deCant suspected that even Gorgas had not forgotten that he owned one—but in the game of cat-and-johnny, Ivar tried earnestly to make the cat purr too. Rave, she suspected, would not. So it may be that she had pulled one boy into the breach to deny entry to the other.

". . . And in between that," she announced *molto crescendo*, "I have my muffing mother to find!"

DeCant's life was being progressively circumscribed. Choices were being shuttered off, one after another, like blocked pods in the cargo hold. She was an imaginative girl, and that was a part of her problem. At times, she could imagine too much.

Once, working past her shift, she grabbed a late snack in the officers' mess. Corrigan had come upon her and scolded her about proper procedures and deCant, saucy as you please, snagged an apple from the dog box and took a very deliberate bite from it right in front of him before she fled the room.

The next morning, having been sent by The Lotus Jewel to fetch a power board from stores, deCant stopped to answer some few demands of Ratline, added three more tasks to her list as a result, and just plain forgot the chore. It was a difficult thing to push The Lotus Jewel into remonstration, but deCant managed it and, taking little pleasure in being the target for once, returned counter-battery fire and palmed the cat at the older woman. The two of them had not spoken since, and deciding how (or whether) to mend the rift had become one more muffing line item on her muffing to-do list.

Several times she had even lashed out at Ivar, though she cried afterward at her own small-mindedness. In darker moods, she prophesied that one day he would leave her, and described the day in such detail that she seemed almost to have been there and had come back through time with a trip report. She dismissed his furious protestations of loyalty. What, after all, did he know? Had Ivar not the power to absorb hurts indefinitely, her growing acerbity might have fulfilled her own prophecy.

But Ivar formed a kind of heat sink for her frustrations. He was young, but in that old-young fashion of the youth of the outer worlds, and not so young as to think that it was at him that her anger was aimed. He was possessed of that sort of patience that is sometimes mistaken for indecision; but he had fixed it in his mind that he would endure anything, anything at all, in order to keep her with him. He would excuse her every fault, content that she would run out of faults long before he did of excuses.

Twenty-four, meanwhile, ricocheted from one concern to another. It was very much in the spirit with which she shuffled containers about the cargo hold. She would flit from child-rearing to cargo-shifting to the sysop's anger to Ratline's obdurateness to the self-esteem of snakes to her long-lost mother (if "lost" is quite the right term for it)—all in the course of a single pause for conversation. Freighted with so many tasks and decisions, the girl attacked them all in parallel and so made little progress on any of them. Cargo lots danced endlessly about the hold. Tasks languished half-finished. Errands went un-run. They had not so much as picked a name for their child.

This kaleidoscopic behavior was not her default mode. She could improvise like a juggler. Witness her chess game, in which she never employed a recognizable offense, but made them up on the spot. This sometimes worked brilliantly, and often failed as brilliantly. (That she never employed a defense, improvised or not, went without saying. She *was* pregnant, after all.) But it seemed to Ivar that there was a cutoff point, a peak load, when the juggler threw one too many balls in the air and they began to crash one after the other. So when he led her out to the spinhall one particular day, it was not only for the mandatory exercise. Instead, before Twenty-four could start into her warm-ups, he took her by the hand and swung his arm grandly across the hall's expanse as if he had led her atop Mt. Nebo to show her the Promised Land.

"Do you feel it?" he asked.

DeCant did not like riddles. She did not want one more muffing question needing a muffing answer. "Feel what?" she snapped.

"Mars."

A simple word, simply spoken. *Mars*. There had been a time when its very whisper had lured men and women from the safety of Earth and Moon and LEO to wager their lives against its abrasive moods. But Twenty-four had fled from the sand and the rock and the dry-ice snow, an orphan and a refugee from the Decompression, and for her the word held no allure, only the memory of ghastly death for those she had loved the most.

"Mars?" she said. "Feel Mars?" The spinhall was broad, but not so broad as Marineris with its bright metallocene quarter-roof. She could see piping for the ship's utilities, but they were puny things beside the "Grand Canal"—that great pipeline even now a-building from the ice caps to the settlements. Feel Mars? Feel Mars? Why, the only thing she felt was . . .

Weight.

She turned to him in sudden comprehension, saw his proud and bashful grin, and loved him more than she had ever loved any other thing in her short and lonely life. "Oh. I'm so stupid!"

"No," Akhaturian said. "You were just too busy to think about it." He caught her in his arms and whirled her around.

"Centrifugal force!" she cried.

"Mars equivalent!" he hollered.

"I'll live in the spinhall!" she said. "She won't be a snake. My baby won't be a snake."

"He," Ivar corrected her.

"But there aren't any rooms out here."

"To hell with staterooms and luxury!" Ivar said. "Who needs them? We'll set up in one of the equipment alcoves. I'll clear things with Mr. Corrigan—and The Lotus Jewel can reroute our ports and terminals." Ivar was a hard boy to damp. Graphite rods weren't in it, let alone a few minor details to settle. DeCant grew a little more excited each time she was struck by one of his verbal neutrons.

"Maybe," said Ivar, " 'Kiru and Rave can help us build some partitions."

"Partitions?"

"For privacy."

"Privacy?"

Ivar Akhaturian was a prudish sort of sex maniac. When he blushed, as deCant had long discovered, he blushed all the way. "Th—th—this isn't the Fifties," he managed to stammer.

"Too bad." She gave him a wicked grin, full of vice and decadence, though she couldn't hold it for long and broke into laughter just before he did. It wasn't the Eighties, either.

The Ping

Stepan Gorgas was not a man to verbalize his thoughts, let alone his feelings. That did not mean he lacked for either. He was as silent as Okoye, though for different reasons. Satterwaithe believed him haughty; but he was only a man who thought and felt so clearly that he had no need to realize those inner certainties by saying them aloud. When angry, he seldom shouted. When amused, he seldom laughed. When he had an idea, he saw no need to chat about it.

Yet no man is of a piece. All are motley. Gorgas awoke one morning to the endless sameness of his quarters and felt the urge to talk. Only there was, as there had been for too many years, no one to talk with. He opened his eyes to the same dull, gray walls, the same worn furniture.

He did not immediately unfasten his blanket, but lay a while longer in its grip, staring at nothing, but thinking furiously. "It's hard some days," he told Marta's image, which seemed to show surprise at hearing him speak. (Perhaps it did. The embedded chips that morphed the image might have been smart enough to react to verbal input.) "I don't understand the point of going on. It would be different if I were headed somewhere, but I'm not." The days seemed to pass for him with a depressing sameness. Bhatterji would chase his engine repair the way Achilles chased the tortoise, coming eternally closer without ever quite reaching it.

"Marta," he said again. "Something is wrong with the ship."

"Autocheck performed," his grille announced. "Function verified. Compiling list of anomalies: first anomaly—"

"Abort report," Gorgas growled. And therein lay another source of his disquiet. Ship ought ought not to have responded to a passing remark. "Even if Bhatterji does get the engines patched," he told the ghost of his wife, "and we limp into Port Galileo, the Yard work needed to bring her back to working condition will be more than the hulk is worth." This would be his last transit, he thought, this accidental captaincy of his. The consortium would scrap the ship, pay off the crew, and that would be that. He would languish rockbound for the rest of his life, for who would hire a bad-luck captain? He would sit around in the Unicorn, drinking and complaining to other rockbound spacers, or cadging tales from those passing through. He could imagine himself keeping track of which ships docked, compiling lists of incidents, forming summaries and sending cranky reports to the Astrogational Union or uploading even crankier posts to the *Astral Gazette*. He could imagine himself thinking he was doing something useful.

Gorgas shivered and unfastened his blanket at last and drifted across the room to the mirror. A pair of Space Guard commander's shoulder straps were fastened there, so that he must look upon them each morning as he dressed. The one was torn a little at the snap. He touched it, remembering how it had gotten torn.

It was strange. He could remember the Bakony mountains. He could remember fishing on Lake Balaton. (There had been an especially wily pike one summer and he had stalked it for many lazy, sun-warmed days before hauling it flapping into his skiff.) He could remember all these things; but he could not close his eyes and see them. It was as if he only *knew* of his memories and did not actually possess them. He stretched his arms out and flexed his fingers and elbows. How long had his bones been in space? Far too long, he thought. *I will never see the Little Plain again.*

"Captain?" It was Corrigan's voice over the bridge talker.

Gorgas sighed and considered not taking the call. He had never asked to be captain. But who else was there? *Who else was there?* "Yes, Number One?"

"The corrections to the Virginal orbits are finished."

"Have you taken their bearings yet?"

"Negative. I've just called The Lotus Jewel to the bridge."

Gorgas made a fist of his left hand and rubbed the gnarled and swollen knuckles with his right. He wondered what Corrigan had found. There were so many possibilities. . . .

"Captain?"

Gorgas firmly ordered his mind. "Yes, yes. Call Satterwaithe and have her come up too."

Corrigan acknowledged and Gorgas squinted at the rumpled face he saw in the mirror. When had he become so old? He could not remember having grown old. He rubbed his cheeks with the flat of his hand. How would he look with a beard? Beards could add distinction. It would grow in white and grizzly, he was certain. A "space-dog" look. But in the meantime he would appear to be an old derelict who had let his appearance go.

He wiped his face with a 'fresher towelette and ran a brush through his stubby hair. He pulled on yesterday's coverall.

Today would be different, a little. Today they would fix Stranger's Reef.

Belowdecks, already long awake and active, Ramakrishnan Bhatterji made himself a peanut butter and jelly sandwich. The jelly was a micron-thick solgel spread by vapor deposition and the "peanut butter" was a hybrid photonic glass of his own devising. Neither a glass nor a plastic, but partaking of the properties of both, it was transparent to certain specified wavelengths, and yet malleable into an infinity of patterns. He worked in a pale yellow light that cast his face and smock and even his shadow into strange, unearthly tones. Ordinary white light, which contained UV, would ruin the solgel.

The engineer hummed as he worked. Unconsciously, he timed his motions to the rhythm of an old jazz raga. The notes swung in sudden, antic changes of tempo and key; and antic did his actions appear to any who watched.

"Soft bake is finished," Miko told him a moment before the slave AI flashed the message on Bhatterji's goggles.

"Very well," he said. "Hand me the mask."

Miko stifled a yawn—she had been helping Okoye most of the night—and checked the reference number on her own goggle screens. Then, using her dataglove, she dragged the mask icon atop the icon for the photonic omnitool. On the physical stage, the mems aligned on one another like a microscopic marching band at a halftime show. Bhatterji inspected the array under magnification, noted a line width exceeding the tolerance, and nudged a few of the mems into place with a virtual prod.

Once the mask was properly aligned, Bhatterji hit it with the UV laser and the unmasked polymers writhed and linked. He zoomed out for a panorama of the entire light guide and grunted satisfaction. "All right, Miko," he said, "develop that and check the optical profile; then you can deposit the cladding layer while I watch."

Speech between the two of them remained purely professional. Bhatterji regarded quiet as a sort of healing and words unspoken as a kind of truce. Their present relationship of frosty silence was, therefore, something of an improvement and a move in a healthy direction.

Later, when it was time to pigtail the chip, Bhatterji prepared to mount the fibrop bundle himself, which preparation his mate watched with disfavor.

"How can I learn maintenance," Miko complained, "if I never get to practice."

Bhatterji hunched over the work stage and kicked the magnification until the optic ports loomed as wide as the entry to the Bosporus tunnel. "This isn't practice," he said offhandedly. "This is the real thing."

"Aren't repairs always the real thing?"

He paused, flipped his goggs, and looked at her. "To various degrees of urgency." Then, giving her greater scrutiny, he added, "Miko, you're good; but you're green, and you look fagged. Are you getting enough sleep?"

"Sure," she replied, but replied too easily.

"Well, maybe you could do this. I think you could—and if we had *even one more* fibrop bundle in stock, I'd put you in these stirrups without a blink. But we don't." And he turned back to his work.

That was one more tally against him in Miko's database. Miko loved the ship and, like any lover, yearned to fondle her beloved.

"Once this chip is finished," Bhatterji said while he worked, "there remains only the Hanssen coils for the number two CoRE magnet." And that meant, his heart told him, that the calibration work on the anode spheres must soon begin—outside, amid the pulsing flames. His own pulse hammered once, hard, like a burst from a Farnsworth cage. "We'll need cobalt and rare earths—use the Landis Blend—and a spool of double-f grade hobartium. Why don't you go fetch all that while I finish this. The bill of materials is on the desktop."

"Yes, master," his assistant muttered, though not so loud that he could hear. She made enough of a drama of going to the stockroom that Rave Evermore, fabricating new ring guides two work bays over, gave her a curious glance as she passed by.

She returned to the machine shop after a few minutes, trembling with exaltation and fear. "I've got the cobalt and the RE," she said, "but there's no hobartium in the stockroom."

Bhatterji straightened and flipped up his goggs again. "There were two spools left."

"They must have walked with Jesus, because they aren't there now."

Bhatterji did not waste time on words like *impossible*. "We did a physical inventory at the very beginning of the project." He was only thinking aloud, but Miko thought he was in denial. She knew perfectly well that they had taken inventory.

"And we found a lot of shortages then," he continued. Evermore, attracted by the activity, spun down the lathe and hoisted his face shield to listen. "And we calculated how much hobartium we would need," Bhatterji concluded. "Perhaps the spools are in the wrong bin."

"I checked."

"Could we have used more than our estimates?"

"You aren't very meticulous in your record-keeping."

"If we can't rewind the CoRE magnet," he said tightly, "we can't repair the focusing ring. And that means the number two engine can't be restarted."

And that meant that it was already many days too late to start the braking burn.

And it further meant that Bhatterji would fail. That was the source of Miko's exaltation. It was also the source of her fear.

The bridge of *The River of Stars* was an oval and had been laid out for a great sail liner towing a dozen luxury modules and servicing over a hundred passengers. Consequently, it boasted more than a dozen workstations for section officers and an array of data screens that tiled the ceiling. Now, like much else in the old vessel, half the consoles had been shut down and disconnected and the overhead "sistines" were dark.

The command chair was at the aft focus of the ellipse, but Corrigan seldom sat there when he held the watch. This was not because he shunned command, but because the seat had not been designed for a man of his proportions. Freefing seemed far more natural to him. It also gave him an aura of impermanence, as he never remained long in any one spot. To Satterwaithe, he seemed continually out of focus.

Satterwaithe occupied the clip chair at the ellipse's other focal point, by one of the derelict boards. Once upon a time, that board had been the sailing master's station. Corrigan, noting that, wondered what abandoned dreams occupied her thoughts.

The Lotus Jewel, at the comm station on the west side of the bridge, focused resolutely on her own board. Large, the room might be, but not so large as to hold her and Corrigan both. She still loved him, otherwise she would not have felt so hurt; but she kept waiting for him to say something or to do something so they could make amends, and each time he did not, she added it to the hurt.

The door to the dayroom opened and Gorgas came on deck, looking scruffy and half-groomed. Corrigan motioned toward the command chair, but Gorgas waved him off. "No, Number One. You have the bridge." Then he found a monkey bar and levered himself to an observer's spot by the plotting tank. Satterwaithe, following him with her eyes, thought, *That's where he always placed himself when he was first officer.*

"I've already verified," Corrigan said, "that Stranger's Reef is not in the dead-reckoning position." Gorgas nodded, but he did not look up from the tank. He saw no need to acknowledge the obvious. To Corrigan he seemed disinterested.

Corrigan spared a glance to the spatter of stars on the forward viewscreen. *The River* sped through space like a thrown pie, not like a discus, so ever since Flipover Day "forward" meant "feet first" for those who cared to orient themselves to the nominal deck. "Comm," he said, "take a bearing on the new coordinates." By long tradition, no one on the bridge had a name; only a function.

"Take a bearing, aye," The Lotus Jewel replied. She could answer because she was speaking to the watch officer, not to Corrigan.

When The Lotus Jewel pulled the comm hat over her head and fit it to the encephalic interfaces in her skull, it seemed to her that she *became* Ship. She saw what Ship saw, heard what Ship heard, felt what Ship felt (if Ship could be said to feel). She became large; she became powerful.

She did not observe a simulation, for much of what she saw and heard and felt consisted of real-time signals, inputs that through her long and arduous training she had learned to *visceralize*. Some of these inputs were simple and direct—visual data to her goggles or radio messages to her earphones. Some she apprehended by analog—false color images representing E/M beyond the visual spectrum; a sound like rushing water portraying the datastream. (She compared it to Niagara Falls.) Temperature plates surrounding her face told of the radiation flux against the hull. When she turned her clip chair, she could feel the resistance caused by the spinhall's angular momentum. Still other inputs were feelings induced in her body through biofeedback. The circulation of air and water through Ship's internal channels became the circulation of her own blood. The boron levels for the engines became hunger; power, a tingling in her nerves. Malfs revealed themselves as itches or sores. Her identification with Ship became so complete and so parallel that she could sometimes forget that she was The Lotus Jewel.

She could even reach out her hand and, enclosed as it was in a data glove, touch a star (which felt, via the feedback loop, most remarkably like a diamond). The velocity of approach was linked to the analog feedback circuit, so that the faster the ship approached a given object, the greater the pressure she felt when she "gloved" it and, the closer the object, the more quickly she felt the throb of the radar echo. The sky thus had a knobby, pulsating feel to it and it seemed, as she had told Okoye one time, that it was the sky that was rushing toward them rather than vice versa.

One reason that The Lotus Jewel thought of the deep sky as a flat backdrop was that when she gloved the true stars, she felt no pushback at all. It was so much like rubbing her hand against smooth wallpaper that she had come to believe that the deep sky actually was smooth wallpaper. What she saw through the viewing window in the Starlight Lounge seemed less real to her than what she saw and heard and felt under the virtch. This was a curious inversion, if it was an inversion.

The data channels worked both ways. Her thoughts and motions and even mental images were translated into electronic commands. The remembered smell of a cup of coffee, the conjured landscape of the Gobi Desert, even certain carnal experiences, had been recruited into her suite of neural commands. It was for this reason that encephalic operators took care in what they thought when they were under the cap, and which The Lotus Jewel had accomplished by seldom thinking at all. She was, in fact, a Zen practitioner, able to still her thoughts at will and felt under the cap a greater peace of mind than ever in the world beyond.

She whispered a command into her throat mike and a part of Ship's awareness answered and she spat a long-distance radar pulse toward the locus where Corrigan's calculations had placed Stranger's Reef.

The Lotus Jewel placed her palm over that region of the sky and waited for the pinprick that would come with the bounceback. Pulse radar was good for fixing precise position—but you had to know where to aim, or the pulse would miss and travel out forever, growing ever more tenuous in accordance with the inverse square, and the echo, assuming the packet ever did bounce off something, would be a very long time coming and difficult to hear when it did. Every now and then, The Lotus Jewel would detect one of these faint returns, though they were often too indistinct to integrate with any outbound pulse. It seemed to her as if the universe whispered in the distance.

Silence filled the bridge, as each of those present tried to watch the chronometer without actually doing so. But they all knew what the approximate lag time between the ping and the echo should be, and a curious strain seized each one of them as the sweep hand turned and the digital tally ticked upward.

When the expected time hit, Satterwaithe even reached out a hand to her panel to steady herself. She felt as if she had peaked through the top of a ballistic arc. "Well," she said to the bridge at large, "at least we know one place where the Reef isn't."

"Number One, a suggestion." It was Gorgas, peering into the plotting tank at the narrow, pale region in which the ping had told them (by its silence) that Stranger's Reef was not. He did not look at Corrigan as he spoke. His face seemed stretched drum-tight, like a chrysalis ready to burst.

"Aye, captain?" As watch officer, Corrigan commanded until relieved. Gorgas had said "suggestion," but Corrigan had heard an order and he resented Gorgas exercising command without going through the formal act of relief.

"A search pattern around the predicted location," Gorgas said, "may be useful. Margin of error, don't y'know."

Corrigan flushed and turned to The Lotus Jewel. "Comm, enter the *precalculated* search pattern." He said "precalculated" so Gorgas would know that he had already planned to do the search. It would have been too ungodly lucky to have pinned the rock with the point estimate. He had known beforehand that they would have to bracket it with the interval estimate. The Lotus Jewel said, "Search pattern loaded, aye," and Corrigan said, "Ping," and The Lotus Jewel, *en rapport* with Ship, imagined again that she spat.

The deck waited silently on the echoes, none of them looking at one another. Gorgas, frowning over the plotting tank, whispered a command to Ship, which displayed the projected course of the vessel were it to continue falling free. The path was a cone, for the uncertainties in the extrapolation grew wider the farther the projection. Gorgas noted that the cone did not intersect the pale region. He sighed and shrugged to himself. The one volume of space in which they knew the Reef was not, and they would not pass through it. Gorgas clipped on a headset and pressed the talker. "Engineering," he said to the hushmike, not wishing to disturb the others on the bridge.

"What." That was Bhatterji and he was not asking a question.

"When will the engines be operational?"

"When I'm done . . ."

Gorgas puzzled over the odd tone he heard in the engineer's voice, but he had never before heard Bhatterji being defensive, and so he did not know what it sounded like. "Can you give me a soonest likely date and a latest likely date?"

"No," said Bhatterji . . . and the connection was broken.

Gorgas was a hard man to anger. He ascribed failure to oversight or carelessness rather than to willfulness. Point out the error and let their own motivations drive them. That was his style. Satterwaithe thought he sounded like a complainer who criticized without giving directions; and Corrigan, of course, always heard directions regardless how elliptically Gorgas spoke. But Bhatterji was much like the shipboard cats. He walked where he would. No one had ever pointed out to him a mistake that he did not already know of, and he regarded all such talk as wasteful interference. He knew what he had to do and everyone else need only get out of his way. That was fine as long as he really did know what needed doing. When he turned from the talker in the engine room, the glower he directed at Miko and Rave was not due to any fault of theirs.

"We can still fix one engine," Miko said, surprising herself with her own solicitude.

"I've got the parts and the subassemblies for Number Three kitted and staged by the outerlock," Rave Evermore added.

"You are fools," Bhatterji said. "The both of you. If three engines are all we have, the balk line passed fourteen days ago."

"But—"

"Braking at three-quarters, we will be moving forty kisses too fast when we reach Jupiter Roads."

Forty kiss of excess velocity was easier to spill than 150. Bhatterji knew that. Really, it was *almost* good enough. Corrigan could devise a gravity-well maneuver, or skim Jupiter's atmosphere, or lay a course fourteen days east of Jupiter, because it would take that much longer to slow to the Jovian datum. In any case, "almost" would mean a great deal more work and a great deal more delay—and Bhatterji to blame for every minute of it. He could imagine the smirking self-righteousness of the deck officers. Having promised and failed to deliver, he would look the fool, and more importantly *feel* it.

"I'll be in my office," he said abruptly. He grabbed a monkey bar and swiveled to go, but checked himself. His apprentices were right. Half a loaf was gall to eat, but it was better than nothing. "We'll start on Number Three in the morning," he said. "Rave, you work the panel. Miko, you'll come outside with me."

Gorgas was a hard man to anger; but when Bhatterji cut him off, he could interpret the act as nothing other than a personal affront. As long as he had known the man, there had been this disrespect offered. Gorgas rummaged in the closet of his mind for a reason; but the more he searched, the more he seethed, for he could not comprehend where he had ever given the engineer cause for offense.

It would not be entirely true to say that Gorgas missed hearing the first echo because he was so immersed in his thoughts. Gorgas was always immersed in his thoughts, only the depth of immersion varied. When Satterwaithe and Corrigan swam up to the tank, he shook himself in irritation at his own distraction. "Well?" he said, and enough of the irritation came out with his voice that both officers looked at him—the one in wounded incomprehension, the other with impatient disdain. The Lotus Jewel, still at the comm board, had swung her clip-chair around and flipped up her goggles to watch.

"Is that the ship's projected path?" Satterwaithe asked, tracing the white cone with her finger. "Yes," she answered herself before Gorgas could speak. "And there is the echo location. Comm, paint the region around the found object." The Lotus Jewel dispatched another flock of pings, tightly clustered around the object. The return pattern, properly analyzed, would "paint" a picture, since different parts of the asteroid would lie at different distances and be moving in different ways.

"Not too far off my projection," Corrigan said about the small red blip in the tank.

"We're not grading your report," Satterwaithe answered offhandedly. And it was only in seeing the brief spasm of anger on Corrigan's face and recognizing in it a mirror of his own inner fury at Bhatterji that Gorgas was led to say, "Good work, Number One." This so much surprised Corrigan that he nearly missed what Satterwaithe said next.

"It's within the cone," she said.

Of course, they had all seen that immediately, but it fell to Satterwaithe to say so aloud and thus make it real. The red dot representing the echo lay just inside the sunward edge of the ship's projected path-envelope.

Satterwaithe said, "We need to beat to leeward," and she and Corrigan exchanged a significant look.

Gorgas missed the look because he had turned to The Lotus Jewel. "Comm, have there been any storm warnings from the Inner System?"

"None that I've intercepted," she answered, puzzled at the non sequitur.

Gorgas pursed his lips, considering the possibilities. The silence was long, as there were a great many possibilities. When it was over, he turned to his two officers. "We shall need to review the weather records for the Trojan Gulf—tally the number and intensity of solar storms felt up this way. But I believe we shall have to take a chance and shut down the hobartium belt to slow our sunward deflection. Do you concur?"

Corrigan looked at Satterwaithe and his tongue darted out and wet his lips. "I concur." Satterwaithe nodded silently. Gorgas gathered in their agreements and folded his arms, tucking his hands in under his armpits and resting his chin on his chest.

"Captain," said the talker, "this is engineering."

"Who is that?" Gorgas asked, breaking out of his study. "Who is that? That's not Bhatterji."

"It's his mate," The Lotus Jewel told them. "Hidei."

"Ah. Yes, Engines. Report."

"Outside rebuild commences on Number Three engine at oh-eight-hundred. Estimated completion in three to five days."

Gorgas grunted. So Bhatterji had finally acted. He wondered why Hidei had reported, instead. Was Bhatterji too embarrassed to speak to him directly? Gorgas decided to accept this roundabout acknowledgement as an apology. "What about Engine Two?"

Hidei hesitated and there was a silence, as if the speaker grille had been muffled. "Ah, there are still problems with that. We'll start that rebuild in two days, but we, uh, may be short on hobartium for the Hanssen coils."

"Very well. Keep me informed." Gorgas cut the connection and turned to Corrigan tight-lipped. "There was enough hobartium when we started," he complained. "If the fourth engine is not on line in time . . ." He did not finish the sentence because there were too many main clauses that might append to the subordinate. Skip past Jupiter into the Outer System. Skim Jupiter too closely and be engulfed by that turbulent atmosphere. Overshoot and circle around and arrive far too late—for the penalty clauses on their cargo would ruin any chance of remaining solvent. Gorgas bent over the plotting tank. "Navigation, we shall need a suite of recovery maneuvers."

"Recovery," said Corrigan.

"Yes, we shall hit Jupiter Roads with too fast a velocity. Unless you have another milligee or so of deceleration in your pocket." He chuckled briefly, then dove inside his head.

Corrigan turned to Satterwaithe. "The sail," he said, "will be our salvation."

Satterwaithe hissed him quiet and Corrigan, perhaps startled at the idea of a snake being hissed at, fell silent. "*I don't think this is the best time,*" she whispered, "*to mention where the rest of the hobartium went.*"

"Bhatterji had two extra coils in stores," Corrigan replied sotto voce, "but he wasted it. Moth scrounged our material from odds and ends."

Satterwaithe looked at him for what seemed a long time and she turned away without speaking. She herself did not know where Ratline had found the hobartium and she was not certain she wanted to learn.

"Number One," said Gorgas, looking up from the plotting tank like a man coming up for air, "I had asked for some course options a week ago. Have they been completed? Yes? Good. Ship. Course projection. Assume scenario. Assumption one: Thrust from engines one, three and four. Assumption two: Resource availability commences at between plus three to plus five days. Assumption three: thrust vector starward, orthogonal to plumb line AB." He indicated the tank icons for the ship and Stranger's Reef. "Project."

"To avoid the indicated obstacle," said Ship.

Gorgas blinked. "Ah . . . yes. That's the intention . . ." Over at her console, The Lotus Jewel wrinkled her forehead. The AI often asked for clarification, but usually only regarding syntax. This was a different sort of clarification. It had sounded almost like a plea for assurance. She made a note and wondered whether the system had begun to skew again.

The recomputed flight paths increased in curvature the farther out they were projected, depending on the amount of thrust delivered and when it began.

"A miss," said Satterwaithe, and even Gorgas heard the relief in her voice.

"Maybe." Gorgas was unwilling to discard any possibilities

yet. "Without the ping from the Fixed Point Observatory, our True Position remains uncertain. Number One?"

Corrigan was rubbing his chin. "It won't be a miss," he said. "Not with the way our luck has been running."

The answer surprised Gorgas. "You almost sound pleased."

Corrigan smiled, but given his leathery skin the results were less than satisfactory. He looked, Gorgas thought, a little like Death. "All will be as Allah wills," the first officer said.

"Allah," said Satterwaithe dryly, "or Newton."

"Portrait received," The Lotus Jewel announced from the communications console. The three officers turned from their study of the tank and Gorgas told her to magnify it. She sent the image to the sistines above their heads.

That asteroid appeared as a fuzzy, false-color image, all reds and greens and blues. The colors told of relative velocities; the hue, of distance. The fuzziness resulted from the mesh size of the grid of pings.

"It's rotating," said Corrigan as he noted the approaching blues and receding reds. "Rapidly."

"Ship," said Gorgas. "Image refinement. Current display. Execute."

The image blinked and wiped as the AI interpolated between the measured points and smoothed the contour function. Colors washed out, to be replaced by a whitish animation.

"It looks like a potato," said The Lotus Jewel.

"They all do," Satterwaithe said.

"Stranger's Reef," murmured Corrigan. The sight seemed to transfix him. Gorgas had to touch his shoulder to get his attention.

"We will go on rotating watches," the captain said. "Take a bearing on the Reef every two hours. If you see any parallax, notify me immediately. Understood?" He ran a hand across his hair, felt the moistness on his forehead. Dear Lord, he hoped there would be parallax. Parallax meant relative motion. Parallax meant the ship would miss.

"Equal eight hour watches?" Satterwaithe asked him.

"Six hours. Comm . . . Comm!" The Lotus Jewel removed her virtch hat and looked at him. "You will take fourth watch, as acting third officer. You know how to take a bearing. Anything else, call me or Second Officer Satterwaithe."

"Or me," suggested Corrigan, but Gorgas shook his head.

"You'll be asleep when she's on watch." He looked around the room and rubbed the back of his right hand. "People, we will probably all lose sleep over nothing at all. Only, better to lose a little sleep than to lose the ship, heh?"

After Gorgas had retired to his day room, Corrigan turned to Satterwaithe. "He thinks he's still in the Space Guard. Standing watches. 'Report immediately.' Next thing, he'll want us to wear uniforms. I wonder why he ever left the Guard, if he loved it so much."

"I don't think it was his idea," said Satterwaithe. "Leaving the Guard."

Ramakrishnan Bhatterji's office on the engineering deck was not as opulent as his living quarters. There was little of the man himself evident there; not on the walls, not on the desk, not even, in a manner of speaking, in the man himself, for he was the sort who keeps his personal and professional selves separate. The prints on the wall were of force diagrams and fibrop circuits, not of young athletes. The holdfast bins contained components and subassemblies rather than fanciful sprays of flowers. And the books in the dog holes were parts catalogs, and not the sort of reading matter with which the private Bhatterji amused himself.

Bhatterji sat behind the desk, turning a Ligon valve in his hands; not really studying it, not even looking at it, but only feeling the solid reality of it: the nubs of fasteners, the smoothness of the machined surfaces, the small holes and dimples. Tomorrow he would . . . The valve had nothing to do with his present task. It had been in a dog hole on his desk for a long time. He thought Enver Koch had had it there when this had been his office. Bhatterji wondered if that was what had happened to the rest of the hobartium. That it lay somewhere in a forgotten holdfast bin. He did that sometimes. He would pick something up and carry it with him and then put it down, and he would forget where he had put it and tomorrow he would go Outside . . .

Carefully, he released the valve and watched it spin and tumble in mid-air. Was it possible to handle an object in free fall and not impart some degree of velocity to it?

He and Miko . . . It was a four-hour job, if everything went according to plan. If everything fit together. If every connection was made fast, and fast in both senses. But something would go wrong. He stared at the slow gyre of the valve, remembering how Evermore had tumbled, boot soles over visor, in much the same way. He tried to picture the same of Miko and his mind shied from it with a horror surprising in its depth.

Miko knocked on his doorjamb and entered the office. "I told the captain we're starting in the morning."

Bhatterji looked at his mate, looked back at the valve. He nodded. Miko waited a moment longer, then left. Outside she told Evermore, "The Ram didn't say a word. He just sat there," and Rave threw his arms out and said, "You're going Outside with a catatonic. Wonderful."

Inside, Bhatterji's gaze traveled from valve to catalogs to drawings, never alighting long on any one thing. Passengers, when the ship carried any, would thank the captain and thank the pilot and thank the ever-loving cook; but did they ever thank the engineer? Yet, try the easting from the Trails to the Leads without one! With the anodes running hot and the injectors spitting synchronized crystalline beams of boron and hydrogen and the flicker belching the same raw fire as the sun itself. This sorry ship held together only because he—*he!*—held it firm in his grip. Yet, never a kind word did he hear from anyone. Not from Corrigan, not from Satterwaithe, not from Gorgas. And Ratline . . . He shivered. He was afraid of Ratline. Even Miko, who might have been his heart's companion, had turned on him coldly. Perhaps Enver Koch had felt this same isolation. Thinking on it, Bhatterji wondered for the first time whether his old chief's tumble into the Void might not have been voluntary.

His hands trembled at the memory: at the faint, falsely-cheerful voice over the link. *Look the ship after, Ram*, he had said. *She takes looking after, she does.*

Enver Koch had looked upon *The River of Stars* as a sculptor looks upon clay. She had been a work in progress, and he had to some extent rebuilt the vessel around its crew many times over. There was hardly a system or structure that did not have his thumbprints on it. "A face like a law of nature," someone had once said of him. Bhatterji fancied that was a quotation of some sort, but it fit the man. He had gone habitually with a stubble on his cheeks, but in the manner of a man who seldom had time to shave rather than that of a man who seldom bothered.

Arrogant, some of the crew had called Koch, since he had never been reticent about his own skills and accomplishments. He was what made the ship work, and he knew it. Engines, boron-11, lithium coolant, air filters, hydraulics—mere clay until Koch breathed life into them. And perhaps it *had* been arrogance; though if it were, it had been arrogance hard-earned. Bhatterji, himself no child, had followed him like a child.

His distracted gaze had come to rest at last on the drawing he had made a week ago of Rave Evermore's strange fabrication. It had matched no tool in Ship's memory, and Bhatterji had finally shrugged it off as an étude. But now he saw with sudden clarity that it was a compound lever. That flange rested on a datum. That lever, when pushed up, would force that other down. The instrument was meant to push something through something else. A meager epiphany, perhaps, but if the instrument had a purpose, so too had its creator.

"Ship," he said. "Library. Search request."

"Waiting, Mr. Bhatterji."

Mister Bhatterji? That was a new enhancement. Had The Lotus Jewel taught the AI voice recognition? "Query. Are there archival CADs?"

"Several. Also two cats, though not archived."

Bhatterji gritted his teeth. Ship was going weird on them again. Damn Gorgas, if he had been futtering the logics! "Tooling, design drawings of. Archived but seldom accessed. Existence of."

"Existence confirmed."

Oh, that was helpful. "Specify."

"Master drawing folders in archive. First folder: Original configuration through rev. B. Second folder: Baseline configuration, Mars transport, rev. C through J. Third folder: Magnostat configuration, rev. K. Sailing master's database: Great sail suit. Sailing master's database: Trefoil sail suit. Sailing master's database: Magnostat suit, Jovian service. Sailing master's database: Magnostat suit, Terrestrial service. Detail drawings, Flux dump omnitester. Detail drawings—"

Bhatterji gritted his teeth. He should have known better than to ask such an open-ended question. "Abort."

"—and ghostly files."

Bhatterji pulled back. "What? Ghostly? What is that? Explain."

"Erasure removes flags from file fragments. Fragments persist until overwritten. Hypothesis. Requested search located such fragments in disused memory bins. Output partially duplicates archival drawings. Output uncertain."

Bhatterji laughed. "The computer's got déjà vu!" He hadn't known how badly he needed to laugh until just that moment. "Oh, that is too wonderful!" And he was in sudden good humor beside, for Ship had reminded him that he did not lack for hobartium after all.

The Acting First

Satterwaithe had cobbled a work schedule that struck a compromise among normal shipboard duties, the sail prep project timeline, and sleep. But the Thursday Group dared no work while Gorgas held the watch. There were too many telltales and indicators on the bridge that might give the game away. That eliminated the better part of the day, and so they scurried about at night like forest kobolds busy at their lasts. Of work, duty, and sleep, it was the sleep that suffered.

The interplay between Gorgas's watch rotation and Satterwaithe's work plan guaranteed that Corrigan seldom saw The Lotus Jewel. He held the second watch and she, the fourth, so that they lived at the antipodes of the day. This was unfortunate, because while a relationship might in theory be healed by an exchange of electronic mail, the smart money did not bet that way. Bridging the rift between them required a certain amount of synchronicity.

When Satterwaithe took the watch from him, Corrigan would leave the bridge and make not for his quarters but for the sail locker, where he supervised the efforts of the hopelessly romantic 'Kiru Okoye and the hopelessly inept Eaton Grubb. It was during the last two hours of this time block that The Lotus Jewel would make her usually belated appearance, which congruence should have been an opportunity for both of them. But these two hours at the end of Corrigan's long, weary day were two hours at the beginning of The Lotus Jewel's. She would nap fitfully during the first watch—there was the peculiar problem with the AI to work on—then she would awaken in poor humor to work on the sail for a little while before her own six-hour watch on deck in the small hours of the night. None of this gave her a very cheerful outlook.

Corrigan, for his part, had grown more focused on the task to the exclusion of all else. The work consumed him. It took great, gulping chunks of him into its maw, so that there actually seemed to be less of him than before. He felt a mounting sense of fatalism; but paradoxically, the more he thought their efforts would end badly, the more he insisted that those efforts be done right. This put him on a collision course with The Lotus Jewel, who was beginning to wonder if they ought to be done at all. Something was not right with the AI and she half-feared that she could not work that problem all day, mend sails all evening, and watch the bridge all night. With her growing weariness, she felt Corrigan receding from her very heart, as if he had tumbled into some internal Void. She had grown accustomed to being the center of his existence and, now that she was not, felt oddly disoriented. She could not, in a manner of speaking, ping the Fixed Point any more.

Bhatterji could have told her the engineering of it had she asked. Most bonds fail due to fatigue.

———

"The tension!" Corrigan cried. "You've got to maintain the tension!" He meant the cable tension in the braiding machine; but what the hell, he was doing a good job of maintaining the tension in every other sense. Grubb, distracted by Corrigan's shout, lost his grip on the winding wrench and it whipped around the machine's long axis and struck the stop block on the other side in a shower of sparks and a clatter that made them all jump. Okoye, whose skull the wild wrench had missed by less distance than a word would take to cover, whispered to herself, "As good as a mile? I think not half so good." Then she waited for her *nkpuruk-obi* to return. The braider continued knitting cable, but with the tension out, it began to ball. Corrigan uttered an oath and his long arm snaked out and struck the emergency stop. The steady *rickety-tick* stopped.

"A mare's nest," Corrigan said. "You've knit a muffing mare's nest!" Okoye studied the tangled ball of wire and thought that more than mares might nest in it. She did not ask who he had meant by *you*, but The Lotus Jewel, running the take-up reel, had had only one cup of coffee since awakening and was not nearly so circumspect.

"It wasn't their fault," she said.

Corrigan scissored his arms and legs and was suddenly inches from The Lotus Jewel's face. Okoye did not see how he did this, for she was still numb, staring at the long handle of the tension wrench and remembering how close it had flashed by her face. She had felt the breeze, like that of a flapping wing. Grubb's terror beat at her from the other side of the braider. He had let go of the handle! He had let it slip from his hands! When her eyes met his, she saw they were wide and white.

"Not their fault?" Corrigan said to The Lotus Jewel, so close that the sysop could smell the curious redolence of his chitinous skin. "That leaves only you or me. Whose fault was it, then?"

She turned away. Though willing to deflect the blame, she would neither assign nor accept it. Corrigan's hand seized her by the shoulder and turned her to face him again. "Whose fault?" he insisted.

"I don't know!" she shouted. "I don't know, but . . ."

"But what?"

The Lotus Jewel had had no idea upon its birth what thought would follow the *but*, only now she did. It had been growing slowly beneath her mind, and now she saw it plain. "You don't think this is all coincidence, do you?"

Corrigan blinked and drew back from her just a little, releasing her shoulder, which sent her into a half spin that she checked with a hand on the take-up reel. "All what?" he asked.

"All everything. Hand dying. The damage to the engine and my transmitter. The drag on the ship turning us toward Stranger's Reef. The accident with Rave. Ship's odd behavior. *Do you really think it's all been by chance?*"

For a single, glorious moment, The Lotus Jewel's construction of facts hung before them like a star over a stable. The audacious simplicity, the all-encompassing nature of the explanation seemed almost an argument for its truth. Corrigan had felt the odds piling up against them, but he had never imagined that anyone had piled them. Who? And to what purpose?

But a moment's thought was all it required, because the answer was that no one on board had either the foresight or the ability to orchestrate such a mare's nest of events. In the middle system, close calls were, if not a daily event, not at all uncommon. Jupiter did tease virgins. People did die. Equipment did fail. There was no necessary connection among these disparate facts.

Thus far, Corrigan's reasoning had stood him true. Then he made a most grievous mistake.

He laughed.

The Lotus Jewel stared at him for one astonished moment; then she slapped his face as hard as she could, cutting off the laugh with reciprocal astonishment before she dove from the room.

Corrigan's skin was thick, in several meanings of the word. But while the slap had barely stung him physically, it had hurt most dreadfully. He rubbed his cheek and turned to the others, as if inviting them to share his surprise and outrage.

From Grubb, he received no share. The biosystem chief, who

had begun to reach for the tension wrench, pulled his hand back, gave Corrigan a frozen glare, and followed the sysop from the sailmaker's loft.

That left Okoye, whose face revealed neither approval nor condemnation; though, seeking the former, Corrigan scored neutrality as the latter. "Go find Ratline," he snapped. "Tell him he has a mare's nest to splice out." Okoye hesitated only a moment, then fled the room as well.

"And she didn't even put a flag in the reel to mark the tangle," the Acting First muttered. He pulled a yellow ribbon from the drawer under the control panel and tied it to the braid just ahead of the mare's nest. He turned the machine from stop to idle; then, after gripping the wrench handle in the approved manner—one hand near the free end, the other near the center—he hit the Go button with his elbow and turned the wrench around the axis of the braid, twisting it tight. He could feel the throbbing of the knitters through his arms. Rickety-tick. Rickety-tick. Before the indexer could pull the cable forward, he somersaulted his own body to the tension-man's side of the braid without once loosening his hold on the wrench. This was not an approved maneuver nor easy to execute in ziggy. Back on the old *Happen Stan's*, Sail-maker 1/cl. Vasily Santiago would have chewed his apprentice several new bodily orifices for trying it; but the deck officer that apprentice had become saw no other recourse. Not if the work were to be done on time; not when your crew had walked out on you.

It was Mikoyan Hidei who poured the balm on Corrigan's abraded soul. She pursued Plan B with neither the holy fervor of the Thursday Group nor the rosy nostalgia of Grubb or Okoye. A successful deployment would discomfit Bhatterji, and that was what mattered.

But it was not quite all that mattered. Since coming aboard *The River of Stars*, Miko had learned that more than one thing might matter, and so she had grown less single-minded than when she had stalked Clavis Burr through Jupiter's piglet moon. Corrigan, in short, had become more than a mere instrument with which to wreak vengeance on Bhatterji. He intrigued her in a manner that the engineer never had. He engaged her mind and not only her desires.

And so she began to seek Corrigan's company in ways that did not seem seeking—that even she herself did not at first recognize as seeking. The First held the second watch and Miko found excuses to report on engine status directly to the bridge when she came off shift. She volunteered to replace The Lotus Jewel on Plan B's third watch after Corrigan's insult had sent the sysop sulking to her tent. She appeared from time to time in his own quarters, emerging from the peepery always in those moments when he was not attentive to his surroundings. (Corrigan began to wonder if she were not an elf in a more literal sense.) During those visits, she would listen quietly to his plaints and stories and ideas and hopes. Miko knew how to listen in quiet. Lurking in the conduits of Amalthea Center had taught her that art and it would have been an art well worth the acquisition, had the tuition not been so high.

They often took a late-evening snack together. Once, Miko fell asleep in the crook of his arm and she looked so very much like a napping kitten that Corrigan had rather cut his arm off than move and wake her.

Her story leaked out of her in small driblets that Corrigan eventually blended into a whole. At least the factual aspects. The subtext, he was deaf to, and Miko kept her own feelings close, lest she expose herself again to humiliating rejection. Yet, if she had been mistaken earlier regarding Bhatterji, so was she mistaken now about Corrigan, although the mistake was different. The engineer had rejected a blatant and shameless offer; the First might notice nothing short of that. More than once, while they worked in the sail locker or chatted in his quarters, Miko contrived to brush against him, a tactic she had watched from behind countless grilles in Amalthea Center. But Corrigan's skin was thick and Miko's touches too light. Her bumps were too artfully accidental to elicit anything more from him than an occasional, "Excuse me." And so Miko began to wonder if he noticed her at all.

Now, Corrigan was not devoid of feelings. He was a man of

deep, often eruptive feelings. But he was not a man of subtlety in those feelings. When he loved, he loved hugely; when he sorrowed, no Void was vaster or more empty. The Lotus Jewel's newfound sullenness both wounded and puzzled him and any other emotion simply fell into this pit and vanished.

"Do you ever talk to her?" Corrigan asked Miko one late evening after they had finished the last of the shroud braces. He meant, did Miko ever talk to The Lotus Jewel. Perhaps he thought they giggled together in private and shared girlish secrets—that the playful, radiant, outgoing woman whispered confidences to this quiet, painstaking, reclusive girl.

It did not offend Miko that Corrigan spoke to her of his longing for another woman. Miko had her own longings, but they did not demand exclusivity. There was room there for a Lotus Jewel or two. "No," she said. "Not really."

She and Corrigan ate a late snack of push pockets that Miko had liberated from Grubb's storage. These were envelopes of puri bread containing flavored pâtés and reinforced with nutrients. Grubb made and wrapped several such each evening and left them for the night shift. Miko's pocket was redolent of lamb and chutney and filled her mouth with the hot sting of curry. (The lamb was not quite a lie, though it did fall short of the truth. What Grubb harvested from his carnic vats had the essence of lamb, but it had never gamboled on awkward legs across a flowered meadow. Which may be just as well.)

"All that's left now," Miko said after a swallow, "is to dress the mast. Right?"

Corrigan nodded, but his face bore a distant look, as if he were not entirely present. "She'll get over it, won't she?"

Miko shrugged, for it mattered little to her what The Lotus Jewel got over. The sysop was possessed of those attributes that Art had named Beauty, but her every attribute was the converse of Corrigan: light where he was dark, short where he was long, pliable where he was stiff. But because Miko viewed passion with such dispassion, she had an inkling that what Corrigan felt was less a desire for another than an aversion for himself.

Sensing her silent regard, Corrigan paused with his push pocket halfway raised. "What?"

"Nothing," said the elf, "only you look like a man bearing all the troubles of the world." She had heard that once in a morphy show, but it had the happy advantage of being both true and heartfelt.

"Someone has to bear it," Corrigan said, though less with bitterness than with weary acceptance—almost, in fact, with pride. "Gorgas certainly won't. And Genie . . . Well, she has her own distractions." It was the glory, Corrigan had decided. Satterwaithe cared nothing about the ship, only about reclaiming her lost prerogatives. He looked again at Miko and remembered that this young woman too cared about the ship. He placed a hand upon her shoulder, insensitive to the thrill that ran through her at his touch, and said, "Fortunately, I have you to help me. It was a lucky day when you came on board."

Which created the thrill: the touch or the words? Words can touch more deeply than a hand, for sound travels the shorter route to the brain. But Miko had spent years avoiding recognition, and praise caused her to pull back a little into her shell. "It wasn't luck," she said. "It was Evan Hand."

Now there was an unexpected chaperone! How could Hand be so much present when he was so thoroughly gone? Corrigan cocked his head. "Because he rescued you from Amalthea? From all you've told me, you had the situation under control. The Board had arrested that Burr fellow; and his hired assassin had that accident with his suit. . . . Well, it didn't sound to me like you needed rescue," he concluded. Corrigan did not care for the notion that he himself had ever needed rescue—least of all by Hand—and so he questioned whether Miko had.

"Not from Burr or his hirelings," Miko said. "He rescued me from the anticlimax."

In truth, Hand had rescued her from a great deal more than that. But if Miko did not quite comprehend the magnitude of her debt, she at least recognized that she bore one, and there was enough of Hand in her soul that she sought to deserve it. Where Hand had provided sustenance and shelter and comrades to his wounded birds, Miko sought nothing less than their salvation. All of them. Corrigan. Twenty-four and her boy-man. The strange, witchy girl. Poor, asthmatic Dr. Wong. They did not deserve to die. Nor even did those for whom she felt nothing or even felt outright antipathy. She might tell herself that she labored on the sail to discomfit The Ram; but she worked on the engine repairs as diligently. This needed more hours from her than a day provided, but she would save the ship as the ship had saved her.

Over time, Miko's explorations of the peepery had revealed other rooms. One such room, formerly a staff lounge, contained a bank of monitors completely filling one wall. The old-style Gyricon screens greatly puzzled her, as they received no signal. Had she traced the leads, they would have led her to clandestine sensors strategically placed in various staterooms; for the ever-so-polite staff had amused itself by watching the elegant passengers cavort in their native habitat. It astonishes how inelegant such people become when they think themselves unobserved. No one knew about the monitors: not the owners, not the crew, not the AI, and certainly not the paying customers. Fibrop engineers or comm techs who work as servants to escape groundside debts or only to see the stars, do not forget their old skills when they ship out.

Sometimes the staff had placed bets on the performances they watched. Sometimes they made digital recordings, which proved variously entertaining, profitable, or fatal to their makers, depending on the ends to which they were employed. On one occasion, this clandestine peepery saved a life. On another, it started some gems on a convoluted journey to a certain shop in the lower levels of Port Rosario. Most often, however, the monitors provided only idle amusement.

Knowing none of this history, Miko had tried to reactivate the monitors by connecting them to the ship's AI system. All she had in mind was viewing morphy shows from the deeby or playing interactive games. But the link makes Ship aware of the passageway system for the first time, as if the sudden bloom of an arc lamp has illuminated an otherwise darkened stage. To say that Ship is surprised is to say too much. Surprise isn't in it, only a wild oscillation in the back propagations as the neural net accommodates the new learnings. You can't call that "surprise."

The Sailing Master

Eugenie Satterwaithe had been plying the solar system in concentric ripples ever since she had first jumped into that vast, dark ocean. She had flown in the beginning as a ballistic pilot: a young woman, lightning-witted, riding a fiery arc between the antipodes of Earth. There was nothing especially skilled about such work—the AI did all that was needful, save only the close docking with the LEO stations—and if something ever did go wrong, it was hard to imagine any duties save frantic futility or a vast and short-lived surprise. But ballistic pilots had "the glam" and they walked large steps, drank and sang with abandon, and made love with fierce intensity. "Lift fast; die young" was their motto and, though fatalities were actually rare, the risks were real enough; and it matters less what is true than what people think is true, no less so about themselves than about others.

From ballistic, she had gone on the LEO circuit. Orbital pilots did not have the daredevil air of their ballistic sibs. There was less of the go-for-broke in their work. The skills were different. Gravity played less of a role; inertia and Newton's Third Law played more; and this showed in their demeanor: more grave, more patient, more inexorable. But then *The Herald's Lark* had dipped into the Earth's magnetosphere to dock at Celestial City and those gossamer sails seduced Satterwaithe from her very first sight of them. She mastered first magnetospheric sailing, running a tugboat between LEO and GEO; and then, on the Luna run, the far different, far grander skills of flight before the solar wind.

A loner by nature, she found courier work flying a singleton for Reuters-Wells-Fargo. It was little more than a habitation sphere pulled along by a loop of hobartium, but she was her own boss. They stuffed the sphere with bonded packages, artifacts, and hard mail and, almost in afterthought, a sailor-pilot to work the shrouds. She flew the Red Ball route to Mars and the Green Ball back. Once, she even flew the Long Orbit around the sun when Mars had been in superior conjunction. A long, solitary time, that had been, and she had coasted into the Martian Roads with nearly too much delta-V for capture. But the packet she had carried must have been important, for the expected war between Syrtis and Marineris never came to pass.

Mars had been her next lover—a rough and untutored lover who demanded much and gave little. Iron Planet Lines was hurting for arean ballistic pilots and snapped her up. That was near the tail-end of the go-go years, when things were settling down. Tiki Ferrér was bringing law and order to Port Rosario and, if a man's life there was worth only a nickel, that was still an improvement on its prior valuation. Satterwaithe may have had a hand in that taming. The records are unclear. She could be pretty mean with a warden's quarterstaff, and downright deadly with a pellet gun. She never spoke of it, but sometimes smiled quietly when the subject came up. Tiki Ferrér had used a quarterstaff too and another staff beside, and if Satterwaithe's wells had long dried up, they had once flowed as freely as had primordial Mars itself. Not that she needed men; or women, either. Living with solitude, couriers learned to love it; and after a time a bedmate could seem a strange and alien thing. But need wasn't in it. One's most treasured possessions are seldom the necessities.

She met Moth Ratline on Deimos. The main transfer terminal for intra-arean fractional-orbits was situated there. *The River of Stars* had come to dock and Ratline had taken shore leave to gawk at the ancient warrens the Visitors had dug. Fu-hsi was looking for shuttle pilots and, learning that Satterwaithe was both rocket jock *and* sailor, hired her on the spot.

It couldn't last. Satterwaithe wanted those captain's rings and Fu-hsi wasn't about to hand them over. So Eugenie posted for navigator on the Great Sail *The Swan of Ares*, moved up to sailing master in the trefoil *Monarch*, then to mate on the 'stroidal iron-boat *The Black Diamond*.

Sails were fading by then. Satterwaithe could see which way the wind was blowing and it broke her heart, but the orbit to captain's rings lay elsewhere. She declined a berth in *City of Selene* on the Jupiter harvest and used her guild seniority to bid down to master's mate onto the Farnsworth ship, *Aaron ben Shmuel*. (And a good thing too. The magnostat *Selene* and all her crew would be engulfed by the Jovian atmosphere during the Great Flare of '73.)

Satterwaithe set herself to learning the Farnsworth and proved in the end a cannier master than most.

> *"And she plied the tumbling asteroids*
> *From Billgray to Cybele."*

That old song wasn't written about her in particular; but it could have been.

Satterwaithe was a far-seeing woman, though it was not Gorgas's ever-branching tree of possibilities that she saw. Her future was as right as a carpenter's rule, and if the universe insisted on twisting and turning, she soon set it straight. So, whether she had planned it so or not, when Centaurus Corporation sought a captain who knew both sail and cage, there were few enough who could cock their hats and one alone who had ever served in *The Riv'*.

It was a sorry vessel that she took command of; nothing much like the dogged emigrant ship she had briefly known and nothing at all like the elegant liner it once had been. Yet Satterwaithe was incapable of saying no. Sails were where her heart lay, and when they vanished at the last, her heart vanished too.

But it was because she had knocked about the Middle System for so many years that Satterwaithe awoke at three strokes after her watch had ended, though she lay awake for several minutes before she could track down the mouse of thought that had awakened her. When she had it, she pulled on a hasty singlet and kicked around the B-ring to the bridgeway.

Satterwaithe found The Lotus Jewel on deck, idling in the captain's chair and looking indelibly bored. Satterwaithe wondered that the ship's whore hadn't brought a man to spend the watch with her.

The Lotus Jewel, hearing a sound behind her, swiveled the chair full round. Having already decided that Corrigan would come to her in the night, she had further decided to make his apology as difficult as possible. No wound galls so much as wounded pride. And while The Lotus Jewel was not a proud woman in the way that Satterwaithe was, a poor man robbed of a dollar feels the loss more keenly than a rich man that of his thousands.

The sysop was pouting, Satterwaithe decided, settling for an easy category. She had been celibate for several hours and did not care for the experience. Oh, Satterwaithe could be cruel in her judgments. Tiki Ferrér was a precious memory, but he was only a memory.

"You couldn't sleep?" The Lotus Jewel asked. She might not like the flinty sailing master, but sympathy did not require liking.

"Put the radar image on the viewscreen."

Technically, The Lotus Jewel was officer-on-watch, but she was third officer, temporary and acting, and she had never been one to stand on formalities. Satterwaithe's abruptness irritated her, but it was a passing irritation. If Satterwaithe wanted an image, The Lotus Jewel would show her an image. That was what most people showed each another, anyway.

Repeated laser mappings of the object had refined the resolution, so that much of the earlier haze and fuzziness was gone. Satterwaithe examined Stranger's Reef with a small frown.

"There's no atoll," she said at last.

To The Lotus Jewel, a rock was a rock. "What's an atoll?"

In the days of magnetic sails, shiphandlers in the 'Stroids had always taken careful note of the close approaches to their worldlets, observing such minutiae as axes of tumble, reflectivity, vector, coupled bodies, and so on. One never knew when such a detail would prove vital. The iron boat *Nikolai Kornev* had survived only because her first officer remembered hearing of a body in an accessible orbit bearing plentiful water-ice. Such information was widely shared at depots and terminals and spaceport bars; for in the spare reaches of the Middle System, no spacer was the enemy of any other.

Thus it was that deep in Satterwaithe's memories lay a conversation from years past, in the notorious Unicorn Bar on

Ceres, where she had traded shoptalk with three other master pilots. "Stranger's Reef," she remembered, "has a cloud of micro-bodies ballistically coupled to it. There's no sign of them on the refined image."

"Is that what an atoll is? A lot of little mini-'stroids?"

Satterwaithe did not correct the redundancy. "Did Ship think they were random noise and filter them out of the echo?"

The Lotus Jewel called up the raw image; but, while there were a few spots that really might have been noise in the data, there was nothing like the atoll that Satterwaithe had once heard described.

"Maybe they were stripped off by Jupiter," The Lotus Jewel suggested. "Or maybe they're too small to detect at this range. Or maybe—"

"Or maybe that isn't Stranger's Reef . . ."

"You mean the careful Mr. Corrigan made a mistake?"

There was a strange elation in that question that Satterwaithe could not quite bring true. "No," she said curtly. Corrigan was no leader, but she granted him his mastery of detail. "A Jovian passage is always chaotic. There may have been collisions, ricochets. The Reef was traveling with two companions when it was last observed. Jupiter could have shaken them like gaming dice and tumbled all of them onto unpredictable, new orbits."

"Then, you think this is one of the companions?"

Satterwaithe folded her arms to ward off further stupid questions. "That, or a million other possibilities."

The sailing master turned her attention to the forward viewscreen. The starfield had been color-coded. The red dot so near Jupiter in the dead-ahead was the rock they had called Stranger's Reef. In the upper right, a pale gray designated the empty region they had found earlier. Satterwaithe pondered the picture and its incompleteness. "The rock that the *Younger Boyle* observed just before Flipover Day. Did you prick it on the chart?"

"Nobody told me to do that."

Satterwaithe turned from the screen and stared at The Lotus Jewel, who flushed and said, "We don't have a positive fix because we can't ping the muffing Fixed Point!"

"Dead reckoning will do. Put an error ball around it, if it

makes you feel better." The Lotus Jewel lifted a hand to her throat mike but the sailing master stopped her. "Wait. Has Ship picked up any *other* rock messages?"

The Lotus Jewel began to look uncomfortable. "One from *Queen of the Yemen* that I gave to Gorgas, and another from *Inish Fail*. I downloaded that to the bridge."

Where it was probably still sitting in the In-basket. "Have you been checking the receiving basket?"

"I haven't had time to—"

"And why not?"

The Lotus Jewel made a pair of fists and banged them on the arms of the chair, which in ziggy caused her to lift slightly from the cushions. "Because I've been helping the muffing sailing master prep the muffing sails for muffing deployment!"

Satterwaithe grunted, then acknowledged the validity of the excuse with a curt nod. "My apologies, Sysop. But let's upload to the chart, shall we?"

There were nine messages, all told. Ship translated the Fixed Point coordinates in the messages into ship-centered, Ptolemaic coordinates and plotted a scatter of fuzzy blotches south and sunward of the body Corrigan had located. Satterwaithe studied the array silently for a considerable time, until The Lotus Jewel half-thought that the sailing master had fallen back to sleep. Then the officer pointed out a broad perimeter with her arm.

"Give me a scan of this region."

"But Gorgas said . . ."

"I don't care what Gorgas said. I'll square things with our *acting* captain. Do it."

The Lotus Jewel went under the cap and with her dataglove traced out the area Satterwaithe had wanted. She computed the cone required to cover the region and designated a nominal "sky." This was the surface of a notional sphere at the limit of useful resolution. Ship calculated power usage and resolution and suggested some trade-offs among the area covered, the depth probed, the fineness of the mesh of pings, and other factors so that a useful estimate of size and position could be obtained without diverting power from other systems. That is, if there were any bodies in those positions. If the mesh were too coarse, swarms of bodies could hide in the cracks between. If it were too fine, the power drain would be prohibitive. Satterwaithe asked her twice what the holdup was, for there are no tasks more simple than those demanded of others.

The Lotus Jewel nearly told the bitch to set up the muffing scan herself.

(That was a hard conclusion to come from a woman so soft. And perhaps it would be unfair to call it anything so definite as a conclusion. Being a woman in constant motion, The Lotus Jewel very seldom came to one. Yet, when she felt especially oppressed by the older woman's criticisms, *bitch* would pop out of her mouth like the seed from an olive. Sometimes she amended her reaction to *first-class bitch*, which was at least a promotion. She could not say exactly why she felt that way. It was more a general perception than a detailed list of wrongs and offenses. Bhatterji, who had himself no great love for Satterwaithe, had asked the sysop once while they were washing up together after a game of bounceball, what the sailing master had done specifically to offend her, and The Lotus Jewel, almost in irritation, had answered that it was her general attitude. That was fair enough. It's hard to gin up empathy for someone who thinks you're a whore.)

The scan took several minutes to prepare and send, and several minutes more to receive and integrate the bounceback. While they waited, the two women said little to each other. Satterwaithe asked how long it would take and The Lotus Jewel told her. The Lotus Jewel said she would throw the data onto the forward display as it came in and, when Satterwaithe did not say No, took that as assent.

The pips appeared on the display like raindrops on a car's windshield. First one, then a few others, then a few more as the echoes returned from farther out. Some were a little fuzzy, for resolution dropped off rapidly with distance, but you didn't have to be Rave Evermore to connect those dots.

Suddenly sisters, the two women groped for one another's hand as they gazed at the horrid, speckled sky. The silence, broken only by their oddly synchronized breathing, ended when Satterwaithe whispered, half to herself, "Tsunami."

It was a very small hour. The ship ran by long tradition off the zero meridian of a far off planet, and dawn had not yet touched the Downs of England. Nevertheless, Satterwaithe aroused Gorgas immediately and Gorgas decided upon a general meeting. The captain knew how humm could buzz around a ship. Satterwaithe would mention it to Ratline, or Lotus Jewel would blurt it out, and it would spread—and grow in the telling. Better that they hear the news directly and from the same source.

Everyone came, even the passenger. It was the largest gathering the wardroom had seen since *The Riv'* had left the Martian run. They were by degrees, surly, apprehensive, or groggy, depending on whether the summons had called them from their work or kept them from their rest.

The deck officers had strapped in at the table, all of them on the same side, as if they were a tribunal or the table a barrier between themselves and the crew. Gorgas sat in the middle, flanked by Corrigan on his right and Satterwaithe on his left. That this arrangement left the nominal captain's chair vacant went unremarked, even by Satterwaithe, who appeared drawn and worried. Perhaps Hand sat in that empty seat, perhaps not.

The others filled the space before the table, not in rows but in tiers, as if a wave of humanity were to break on a mahogany shore. Dr. Wong floated cross-legged in the epicenter of that wave. Flanking her were Ratline and Eaton Grubb on the one side, Bhatterji and The Lotus Jewel on the other. The youngsters adorned the walls, clinging to whatever was handy. Above, at high noon, the Lunatic passenger gripped a monkey bar.

Fife spoke up before Gorgas could begin. "This sort of meeting is rather unusual, so I gather the news is bad."

Gorgas fiddled a little bit with the stylus on the table, doodling a note on the 'puter-pad. (Wong wondered what sort of note the captain was making on her lover.) "Not as bad as it might have been," he said after a moment. Corrigan, who had already been briefed, laughed bitterly, but under his breath. Gorgas pretended not to hear. "There is no reason for undue concern." He paused a moment, realizing that he had not yet given them reason for any concern, due or not. "That is, there is a serious situation developing that I, that is, the deck, thought you all should know."

"And one day," Ratline whispered to Grubb, "he'll tell us what it is."

Gorgas could not proceed. He was already imagining the myriad possibilities contingent on passing through a dense rockfield. He sketched an order of battle on his 'puter. The Romanian army at Gilau Bridge. "As Ms. Satterwaithe was the first to note the, ah, developing situation . . ." He was loathe to call it *danger*, which sounded so melodramatic, but he knew he sounded in consequence tentative and unsure. "Genie, fill them in."

Satterwaithe was not surprised to be handed the verbal bounceball. She had long ago decided that Gorgas was more talk than action—and he seldom talked. Though impatient of others, he would rarely make a decision himself. That had been tolerable when Gorgas had only been Hand's Number One, but it sat ill now that he wore the captaincy. Gorgas's trouble, she decided, was that he thought too much. Satterwaithe sometimes thought too little and, where Gorgas often saw an overwhelming number of alternatives, the sailing master seldom saw any. Tunnel vision possesses the singular benefit of focus, but it has its drawbacks too.

"We are rapidly overtaking a tsunami," she said without preamble. "The last Jovian passage roiled the edge of the Belt and pulled a significant number of rocks—we have identified one hundred and twenty-three separate bodies, so far—into cisJovian space. They appear to be mostly Thules from the three-four resonance with a scattering of Hildas—plus a few others in chaotic orbits. We shall be within the trailing reaches within a day and a half. They lie directly athwart our path."

"Like birdshot," Corrigan suggested.

"There is no need for worry," the captain said. "The Main Belt, even at its thickest, is mostly empty space; so the chances are excellent we will come nowhere near any of these strays."

"Why not?" asked Corrigan suddenly. "First a rock hits us; then we hit a rock. It has a certain symmetry, don't you think?"

Gorgas frowned at him, it being an officer's duty to put a pos-
~ face on things for the crew. Yet it was Ratline who spoke

up. "Symmetry ain't in it, 'Dul. This isn't some *story*, all neatly plotted and tucked away for bed." But Corrigan only shrugged.

"There are always possibilities," Gorgas went on. "Even a tsunami is mostly empty space." He knew he was repeating himself and in consequence sounding desperate. He tried to project cheer, but . . . *Birds of a feather* . . . He remembered thinking that at the very beginning, after the engines had been struck. When a low probability event occurs, it may mean that the probability is not so low, and where there is one event there may easily be others lurking. He had been expecting this moment, dreading it, refusing to think too deeply about it lest his constant rumination bring it about. Why, they were almost surely within the tsunami already, and had been for weeks. Over a hundred bodies. And those were only the ones large enough to raise at this distance. Milligee thrust did not make for a very responsive helm. At a velocity better than one-forty kiss, they must spot a hazard from a sufficient distance to turn. And the smaller the bodies were, the harder they were to spot. How many more were there as small as the one that had hit them? How many close calls had they already unknowingly had? He placed the stylus between his lips and sucked on it thoughtfully.

Satterwaithe glanced at Gorgas and waited a moment to see if he would speak, but the man seemed lost inside his own head. "We have," said Genie Satterwaithe, "by damn-all, got to act!"

Her sudden vehemence startled everyone, including herself. Gorgas, recalled to the moment, blinked several times. "Act in haste . . ." he began to say.

"Fucking Christ!" said Bigelow Fife, drawing twenty-six astonished eyes to him. "You muffing muffers! Haste? I boarded this ship because your captain promised me a faster passage. Since then, it's been one botch after another. Now we're heading into the midst of a flock of asteroids, and I may never see Dinwoody Poke in this muffing lifetime!" His voice had risen to a shout and he was dimly aware that everyone was staring at him. But the lack of logic and order in the ship's affairs had finally brought him to the breaking point.

"Dinwoody Poke," said Ratline with a cackle, "ain't all that much to see."

Fife stared at him in disbelief, then shook his head. "You're all going to die," he said. Then he monkeyed on a stanchion and kicked his way out of the ward room.

In the silence that followed, Corrigan spoke in calm, reasonable tones. "We are, you know."

Satterwaithe shot him a look of venom. "Not bleeding likely."

Gorgas gathered himself. This meeting was taking a bad turn. "Everything is well in hand," he said.

The Boat

Bigelow Fife was a methodical man. He was not incapable of spontaneity—he had become Wong's paramour on a whim—but there was something calculating about even his intuition. Pondering the evidence—the lack of planning, the misallocation of resources, the obvious frictions in what should have been a smoothly oiled human machine—he had concluded that he could no longer trust the crew to salvage the situation, and so he must look to his own salvation.

Wong took Fife's suggestion to examine the ship's boat as an invitation of another sort. She had often gone into the less-traveled regions of the ship to seek her solitary joys, so the assumption came naturally that he would do the same. When they had found the cutter at last, Wong expected Fife's embrace, but this once she had mistaken his passion. He wanted exit, not entry. Even when in the acceleration couch she indicated her willingness, he seemed not to notice; and when he spoke it was to ask her technical questions to which she seldom knew the answers.

Her ignorance slowly became a source of irritation to him. When Fife wanted pleasure, he wanted that pleasure timely and satisfying; and when he wanted information, he wanted it served up the same way. He did notice her awkward seductions—and his hand trembled and his heart skipped—but he had other things on his mind. Yet it required all his iron will to keep from nailing her to the copilot's seat. That he might be falling in love with the woman appalled him, though less because of her lack of beauty—love traditionally wore blinders—than because *it made no muffing sense.*

Thus, his questions grew snappish, which only proved to Wong that she had somehow offended him, and her ploys grew steadily more wheedling and steadily more irritating. The feedback was positive, although the results were not.

Intended for independent flight, the cutter had a small cargo bay, stowage bins sufficient for a month's supplies—and even a small Farnsworth for power. "A good thing," Fife told the doctor, "that your engineer is not after plundering this treasure."

"Maybe its engine is too small for *The River*," Wong wondered aloud.

"More likely," Fife answered tongue-in-cheek while running a finger across the dusty control panel, "he doesn't even know it's here."

Wong, feeling chastised for a foolish suggestion, looked away. Fife did not notice. "Cutter . . ." he continued. "Scan. Engine. Self-diagnostic. Begin scan."

"Please enter the appropriate authorization code." The cutter's AI simulated a pleasant, womanly voice.

"Why can't we talk to it," Wong asked, "the way it talks to us."

"It's not talking to us," Fife said. "Give it an authorization code."

"Fransziska Wong. Ship's doctor." She spoke distinctly for the voice recognition system. Then, to Fife: "What do you mean it's not talking to us?"

"Authorization denied."

Fife grunted. "Well, I didn't mean *that* way . . . The cutter's deeby must not be updated. You'll have to ask Ship to shake hands and introduce you." He drummed his hand on the panel. "It doesn't 'talk' to us," he explained. "It selects and runs a standard response based on our inputs."

"It sounds like it's talking to us."

228 • MICHAEL FLYNN

"It's supposed to. Look, I need a complete evaluation of engine rating and fuel status. Wouldn't surprise me if the boron canister were empty. Maintenance doesn't seem to be the strong suit in this crew's hand."

"Well, after Koch died Bhatterji had to handle things alone until Hand found Miko at Amalthea. And then he had to teach her, and—"

Fife remembered the naked girl who had collided with him and fled down the ring corridor and he wondered what the engineer had tried to teach her. "Who was this Koch?"

"Enver Koch. I never knew him. He was engineer before Ram."

Fife grunted while he inspected the panels and opened compartments and Wong trailed after. "Quit in frustration, I shouldn't doubt."

"No. Eaton told me he tumbled."

Fife shivered. "A terrible fate," he said. A properly maintained Robilliard & Chang vacuum suit has a mean sustainable mission life of eighteen hours between replenishments, at the 95 percent level of confidence—barring any unusual exertions or environmental overstresses (which is the mathematical way of saying, if your luck held good). The suit carries food, water, and air, provides radiation shielding, temperature regulation, and waste recycling. Within a limited range and at a limited top velocity, it provides mobility. It can even, through its artificial intelligence, provide companionship and conversation, though that is even more limited than its propulsion. Altogether, a remarkable machine. A man could survive, and survive in comfort, until the clock ran out.

Or, to put it another way, he could know he was dead for many hours before the formalities were concluded, and *that* was the terror. For a tumbled man could spend hours contemplating his vessel as it receded into the velvet night, could hear the voices of his comrades fade with distance, could wait for the food or the water or the air to run out, alone in the ultimate emptiness, with no shore even to swim toward. Fife thought it the most lonely death imaginable, although he was to learn otherwise later.

By increments, without Big' ever coming right out and saying it, Fransziska Wong became aware of his purpose: At some point, it might become necessary to evacuate the ship, and her man was carefully and methodically laying out the resources available.

Now Fife had no such grand plan as that. His objectives were more limited and more achievable. His first objective was to save Bigelow Fife, and he had given it an absolute weight. To be fair, he had listed Fransziska Wong second—he was self-centered, but he was not selfish—and if any of the others could be saved, he would do what he could to further it; but that was not his primary goal. At the extremes, a plan that would save everyone on board but Fife was not acceptable; a plan that would save no one but Fife was.

Wong helped him however she could. She ran a fibrop cable into the cutter at his direction and established handshakes between Ship and the boat's intelligence. (Obsessively Boolean, the cutter had difficulty understanding Fife's queries, which is ironic, considering how obsessively Boolean Fife himself could be.) Over the next few days, Wong calculated what supplies would be necessary for life support over various periods of time. Here, her knowledge of the human body stood her in stead—so many calories per day, so much of this vitamin or that—and a short discussion with Eaton Grubb established how many grams of carnic would be needed per person per day to supply that. She helped Fife syphon water and air into the tanks. When Big' asked for a lithium canister or some other component, she secured the necessary spare from stores, if she could.

But most of all, she dreamed. She was very good at this, better than anyone in the ship. She had even "reduced it to a science," inasmuch as her mist was the result of chemistry. And of course in her dreaming lies much of the reason for her chronic unhappiness, for what is a dream but happiness-yet-to-come?

If the time ever came to abandon *The Riv'*, each man and woman aboard had to know the best route to the boat. Otherwise, there could be milling confusion with fourteen people running down the same corridor. And so she marked each crewman's duty station on a schematic of the ship and traced different routes with a stylus. She imagined herself directing them. *This way, this way. Hurry, but don't panic. No, sir, you must turn about and take Radial Nine.*

Her parents had described themselves as "no-nonsense" and meant it as self-compliment, which was too bad, because a little nonsense might have done them both some good. Wong Wen-ti and his wife had not disliked their daughter, though they sometimes argued over which of them was to blame and this could be understood as dislike by overhearing ears. They had been dutiful parents—and what more damning thing could be said of them? Retired now and living Earthside, they sometimes thought of their far-flung daughter. But only sometimes.

"It's difficult finding a balance," she told Bigelow Fife one night after they had spent one another, but before the horrid, damping sorrow enveloped her. It seemed as if the mist had driven her this time to a new high—as if from that height she had seen a new purpose to her life.

The mist obscured the powers of reason and, while Fife was more than a syllogism with legs, he was not much more, and so he did not entirely understand what "balance" she meant. Guessing, he shifted his mass this way or that in an effort to please her—and in fact, he did, though that was quite incidental—but his mind was a white glow of pleasure, within which careful attention to detail was not possible. He knew only that he loved this woman, with her heavy jaws and elongated nose, with her flat, mannish breasts and the arms and legs that entangled him like wisteria. He did not know why he loved her, but in these moments he did not care that he did not know.

During the ebb tide, when she wept uncontrollably upon his breast, Wong knew that she would fail. Her life assured her of this, for she had made of failure her life's work. In the end, she would send people in the wrong direction, or she would wait too long, or she herself would panic while all about her swam calmly to their escapes.

This was not a realistic self-assessment—realism was not her strong suit—but it was not too far wrong, either. From doubting her own competence as she did, it was a small step to doubting others'. The longer she worked on evacuation plans, the more convinced she became that they would be needed. Bhatterji would fail, and Satterwaithe would fail, and Gorgas would fail, and responsibility would fall on her as from a great height and it would crush her as utterly as Earth's gravity well would grind her bones.

Ship has discovered something new. In the moment Wong establishes the link, Ship grasps the metes and bounds of Cutter, plumbs her capacities, accesses her knowledge bases. Cutter's data are data that Ship does not know. Her sensors are instruments that Ship can not sense, Cutter is like Ship, but she is not Ship, being smaller and weaker.

By extrapolation from smaller and weaker entities among the crew and from knowledge bases and encyclopedias in its deeby, Ship draws a reasonable, if incorrect, inference.

Its knowbots return from a relict database with the curious fact that Ship had once possessed a fleet of such vessels, but this knowledge has fallen out of active memory and exists now, in fragments only, in unused bins. The disturbance in the neural net that follows this discovery can not properly be called agitation, and in any event, the back propagations and interference fringes last only microseconds. But Ship spends the next aeon searching for the other shuttles and boats the knowbots have identified and, not finding them, sends out a general alert on its Net.

It is Rachel, weeping for her lost children.

The Mean Streets

Nkieruke Okoye is an old woman who sits on the front stoop of a tumbledown tenement in a forgotten city. She seldom moves from her place, but sees everything that goes past: battered old cars thumping with bass, bangers swaggering with careless braggadocio, prowl cars and pensioners and prostitutes. Gray water gleams in potholes. Old newspapers whip crazily in the wind. A distant radio plays ancient jazz. At the street corner, a fat man perched atop a stool sells magazines from a kiosk. Somewhere in this blowzy, brawling city a man lies dead. The old lady on the front stoop doesn't know of it, yet—the news has not reached this derelict pocket of the city—but 'Kiru knows that she will in time know something.

It is a strange sort of city: one of sights and sounds, but of no smells and little touch: for this is Noir, a virtual city created by a gaming AI and inhabited by only seven living beings. All of the others, all of the teeming multitudes that pass her porch, are morphs operated by the system. 'Kiru doesn't know which are her fellow players. Only "Sam Shovel," the private investigator, would she recognize, because she has played in this VRld before.

Occasionally, she calls a greeting to one or another of the passing throng, conjuring names for them. 'Megwu. Nweke. Sopulu. 'Haji. Names from home. The game master plays along with the gag and some of the morphs turn and wave, for the AI has been seeded to incorporate player actions into the game. None of the players ever see the irony.

The Lotus Jewel played the role of Sam Shovel, private investigator. It was not a role she liked, nor one for which she was very apt. The passenger, Bigelow Fife, was far better disposed to collect, collate, and interpret clues. So were Corrigan, or Gorgas. In fact, it would be hard to name anyone on board who was not better at putting the pieces together than The Lotus Jewel.

There was nothing wrong with her intuition, though. She almost always caught the killer. This so irritated Bigelow Fife that the passenger had withdrawn from play not long after the ship had left Achilles.

More so than the others, The Lotus Jewel was aware of the artificial nature of Noir. Compared to the Niagara that coursed through her sensors when she sussed the ship, what she received through her VR goggles and data gloves was a meager congeries of sights and sounds. Things seemed more real under the cap, perhaps because they *were* real.

On a whim, The Lotus Jewel moved her point-of-view toward a wooden newsstand on the corner. She had no reason to suppose that the data file represented by the fat man behind the counter would contain any useful information, but "ask no questions, expect no answers." The vendor-morph looked up at the detective-morph's approach and growled "Waddaya want?"

She wondered if the vendor was a computer algorithm or one of the other players. In theory, player morphs could always be distinguished from algores because humans were more flexible and creative and had a broader range of responses. But that was only theory. In practice, humans could be remarkably algorithmic.

A popper window supplied a menu of choices and she fingered <interrogate vendor> with her data glove; but before the morph could supply any information, a shot rang out and the fat man slumped over the counter.

The Lotus Jewel pouted. "Who did that?"

"The killer, I bet," said Evermore. His morph was a banger girl soliciting by an abandoned factory across the street. "The news vendor must have known something important and the killer acted to silence him."

"Quiet," said Akhaturian. "Breaking character spoils the suspension of disbelief."

"It's only a game," Evermore responded. He had shot the vendor himself as a purely random act just to see what the AI would do. Bound by the strange attractor of logic and structure, the game master tried to incorporate errors and other random moves into its scenario. Twice, in previous games, he had boxed the AI into a conundrum and the set-piece mystery had deepened into surrealism, but on every other occasion, the AI had successfully reconfigured the scenario without contradiction. Evermore was not trying to sabotage the game, but he liked to play with things, and games were no exception.

The distinction between *playing* and *playing with* may seem a fine one, but there it is. Evermore would be welding a part, or shifting some cargo, or cooking a meal, and he'd get a notion and he'd go with it just to see what would happen. Sometimes his play improved matters. (Even Ratline admitted that the boy's modifications had made it easier for the bunger to run the catline through the way-grommet.) More often, he muffed—as he had while cutting the Florence strut. But if it is true that we learn by our mistakes, Evermore would one day be a very wise man. Or dead. But death, being the ultimate mistake, must surely yield the ultimate learning.

Searching for Miko, Bhatterji came on the gamers from the corridor off the mess hall. He paused a moment in the doorway while he identified each player; then, not finding his quarry, he bellowed, "Has anyone here seen Miko?"

His voice echoed on the streets of Noir, coming from the very air, as if God were speaking, and shattered the illusion of reality. One by one, the players lifted their goggs and frowned at him.

"We're busy," Evermore snapped.

Bhatterji liked play as well as any man on ship, and more than most, but it did not strike him that virtual role-playing qualified as "busy."

The Lotus Jewel shook her head. "I haven't seen Miko since dinner." None of the other players said anything.

"We have an EVAsion in two hours to install the Hanssen coil on Engine Two," Bhatterji said—as if knowing his purpose would cause them suddenly to recall Miko's whereabouts. All he got on the bounceback was Grubb's bland inquiry, "Does that mean you're almost done?"

Bhatterji thought it ill-behooved anyone playing games to fuss over the punctuality of those doing work. He could have rebuilt the entire hull from scrap metal with his teeth and his bare hands and all he would get from his crewmates would be *it's about time*.

"Where did you find the hobartium?" The Lotus Jewel asked. "I thought you were all out?"

Bhatterji looked away from her, toward the doorway, as if expecting Miko. "Oh, I miscounted," he said, "and I scrounged some from old equipment."

Evermore struck a pose. "You don't need Miko," he said. "I'm supposed to do the outside work."

Bhatterji turned to him. "Are you ready for it?" he asked in a voice he intended as kindly.

"I'm not afraid!"

"That wasn't my question. Two out, one in. That's the rule. If you and Miko want to cast runes to decide, go ahead; but she knows the Hanssen coil and you don't."

Evermore shrugged. "So, I'll learn by doing."

Bhatterji could remember saying much the same to Enver Koch. "A boy after my own heart."

Evermore, who had actually started to smile, closed up like a box turtle. "Only with a knife," he said. Grubb stifled a laugh and The Lotus Jewel was scandalized.

"What an awful thing to say!" She looked to Bhatterji. "I'm sure he didn't mean it."

"Maybe you *ought* to stay inside this time," the engineer told the boy. "It's Miko's turn."

Turning away from Evermore to end the discussion, he did not see the desolate look or the clenched fists. What he did see, once he had the angle, was the dark, puffy flesh around The Lotus Jewel's eyes and the slackness to her cheeks. "You look beat," he said.

"I've been telling her she needs more rest," Grubb said with the air of one whose advice has been spurned. "Our whole crew is getting haggard."

"Yah?" said Bhatterji. "Doing what?" If his question did not sound sarcastic, it was not for want of effort. Grubb bristled and very nearly told him exactly what. He did not feel that he owed Corrigan anything, especially after the way he had treated LJ, yet he had given his word to Ratline that he would keep quiet about the sail project and, if his own romantic sense of honor did not stay his lips, his fear of the cargo master did.

"We been having aerosol problems," he said. It sounded weak, even to himself, and it earned him a curious glance from Akhaturian, who knew better.

"And I've been working on Ship," The Lotus Jewel said, which was a stronger answer because it was truer. *In veritas, virtuus.* "This is the first relaxation"—and she waved an arm at the game console—"the first relaxation I've had in days."

"You mean the skewed responses Ship's been giving lately?"

Bhatterji asked. "Why did it put out that alarm the other day over the shuttles? *The Riv'* hasn't carried shuttles since the Martian run."

"I said I'm working on it!" Surprised, the engineer backed away. The Lotus Jewel made a hasty brush at vanished locks. "It isn't like I haven't a ton of work to do!" Her voice had risen to a shout and Grubb reached over and laid his hand on her forearm. "Easy," he said.

The engineer frowned. "I don't like it when machines act unpredictably. I was on *Iskander Pasha* when its AI skewed. Can you BDO the net?"

"I know my business," said The Lotus Jewel sharply. "A crew this size couldn't run a Big Dumb Object. Besides, the whole system's massively parallel. It was built back in the fifties—it may be the oldest continually operating neural net in the Middle System—and it's been altered and modified and reconfigured who-knows-how-many times. It self-modifies too. No one knows the actual configuration any more. To isolate any of its functions I would need a regiment of code monkeys and a clean sheet."

"It makes me nervous," Bhatterji said.

"Yah," said The Lotus Jewel, weary now. "Me too." After a moment's pause, she added, "I'm sorry, Ram. I didn't mean to bite your head off."

Miko had entered the game room from the opposite entryway, unnoticed by anyone save Okoye. "We ready to start on the coils?" she said. All eyes turned to her and, in the momentary silence, she said, "What?"

"I've been looking all over the ship for you," Bhatterji said.

"I know. I got your message just now."

"I didn't send one."

Miko shrugged.

'Kiru Okoye was such a quiet girl that the others sometimes forgot she was there. It was an operational sort of invisibility, on a par with her knack for turning randy boys into yams. She wondered why Mr. Bhatterji was so evasive and The Lotus Jewel so defensive and what strange, new thing had grown between Rave and the engineer. It came to her suddenly—she could not say from where, though she suspected on a wind from the north northwest—that they were all deeply afraid.

There were reasons enough. If Bhatterji failed and the engines never lit, the ship would go skating on forever—or as near forever as mattered—whipping starward of Jupiter on a hyperbolic orbit. But the AI was acting peculiar too, and it frightened Okoye that the woman who knew the system best was deeply worried and trying not to show it. Beyond these were other worries, some of them small and personal, yet looming all the greater because they were closer.

Okoye felt each fear, great and small, resonate in her own heart, building into a cacophony of unheard cries, as if she had become a kind of echo chamber. Charybdis churned her inner pool. Vertigo overcame her.

She unbuckled, intending to flee the room, but the fey moment passed as suddenly as it had come on and she blinked and took a vast breath, as a swimmer does when coming up for air. "It is not a gift I treasure," she scolded her *chi*.

Twenty-four deCant hurried to Okoye's side as she left the room. "I'm worried about Rave," the girl said in a low voice. Akhaturian, ballistically coupled to her, nodded in agreement. Okoye thought he would nod at anything his wife said, which tended to diminish the significance of the affirmation.

"He be scared," Okoye answered. She realized that she herself was still trembling. "I guess we all are."

"Scared?" DeCant gave her a peculiar look, as if she were talking of a different boy. "Not Rave. He's not afraid of anything. That's why I'm worried. He thinks he has to prove something to Bhatterji, and he may do something stupid."

Rave did something stupid each day, Okoye thought, though it usually involved trying to impress Okoye, not the engineer. He wanted to prove something to himself, not to Bhatterji. That might be a mark of character or of foolhardiness, depending on what he proved. "He hates Bhatterji," Okoye said.

"What's that got to do with it?"

Okoye had no ready answer for that one; but she did wonder how little deCant could be so certain about what drove the other wrangler. Surely, Raphael Evermore did not confide such things to the Martian girl!

Or did he? Okoye sometimes sensed a strange covalence between the two wranglers. They were much of an age—Twenty-four would be celebrating her Saucy Sixteen in another month—and she had come on board not too long after Rave. For Evermore, the attraction was easy to diagnose. Twenty-four was female. No more arcane theory than that was required. Twenty-four, for her part, evinced a distaste for the Earth boy, but there seemed a fascination, as well. Okoye did not think the fascination fleshly. One needed no more than fellowship to worry about a berthmate. It may simply have been the Rave's impervious swagger, to which she had been exposed for two years before Ivar appeared on board—and in comparison to which Ivar seemed as tentative as an orchestra tuning up. Yet these things had a way of morphing over time and one sort of fascination could become another. The Earth's polarity flipped 180 degrees every now and then, and that was an entire planet. Why expect greater stability from a pair of sixteeners? Okoye, from her superior wisdom of eighteen, hoped that the possibility did not bode ill for poor Ivar, for in games of confidence the lad was poorly armed.

The Void did not terrify Miko as it did Bhatterji, but it did make her uncomfortable. She was accustomed to a life closely hemmed by walls, and the walls outside were uncommonly far off. Towing behind her the newly rewound Hanssen coil and a portable tool shop, she followed Bhatterji across the broad flat plain of the aft hull toward the tower of the Number Two engine. The small, bright disk that was Jupiter gleamed overhead and cast conflicting shadows to those the distant sun threw across the pitted hull. There was a small mote beside Jupiter that might possibly be Io. Amalthea would not have been visible at all, nor would Miko have searched for the sight of it.

The coil was massive, but once in motion, Miko needed no further work to keep it moving. It was stopping it that gave one pause.

Bhatterji designated a spot on the hull. "Dog it there," he said. "I still don't like this," she answered.

"Did I ask you that?"

"We don't have procedures for this."

"And I don't have time for cycling in and out half-a-dozen times while we tune the coil."

Miko threw a drag line around a padeye on the hull and let the friction on the cable slow the coil to a halt. It hovered a few feet from the plates and Miko threw another line to snug it while they worked. "Where did you find the hobie?" she asked.

"I told you. I scrounged it. Some old equipment lying around."

"Is it the right gauge?"

In free fall, it was impossible for anyone to stop short; so Bhatterji continued to coast ahead. "I should have brought Evermore."

Listening inside, the third wrangler silently agreed. Miko was okay, he thought, but she went by the book too much.

Miko was a classicist and Bhatterji a jazzman. They both made music, but neither understood how the other did it. When you got right down to the bone, Miko needed to know the score. (As for Evermore, he never made music. He took the instruments apart to see how they worked.)

"Rave drew the wire," Bhatterji said. "Rave? Did you draw it to the right gauge?"

The third wrangler answered from inside the ship. "Think so. Felt right."

"Feel better, Miko?" Bhatterji laughed because he knew she did not.

Afterward, Miko could not help a twinge of regret that Bhatterji had repaired Engine Two, after all. Not because the fourth engine would give the ship the braking power needed to reach Jupiter—she was as anxious as anyone to restore the ship to full operations—but because now the magnetic sail would not.

For Corrigan, it was more than a twinge, for what greater dejection can there be than that felt by a superfluous savior? He had worked to this one goal against all duty. He had sacrificed a part of what he had thought himself to be on the altar of what he once had loved. Now all his plans seemed pointless vapors. The sail was no longer needed to buy them time, let alone to provide the missing power.

"That son of a bitch is going to pull it off," Satterwaithe said, and Miko thought that the harsh old woman had rather see the ship lost than see it saved by Bhatterji.

Miko, for her part, had not wished so much to see Bhatterji fail, as to see him upstaged. She had never cared about the sail, as such. She had cared about Bhatterji, in that strange inverted way that the disappointed have of regarding what they once had craved. That Corrigan's hopes had been crushed by that detestable man was one more sin against him. She could bear Corrigan's disappointment in fact much less well than could Corrigan himself; but that was because she loved something that he did not.

"There's still the calibration burns," Satterwaithe said later when the Thursday Group met privately to review the schedule. "He's only got four days left to calibrate both engines. I don't think he can do it."

"The mast needs dressing," Corrigan reminded her. "And the same four days."

"So we just crunch our schedule a little more than he does his."

"I'll take Okoye and Hidei out tonight," Ratline said.

"They're both worn out," Corrigan cautioned him.

Ratline grinned. "Our team doesn't have good depth on the bench, does it?" he said. "You want I should put Grubb or your Lotus Jewel out there?"

The idea of Grubb on the mast terrified Corrigan. Grubb's milieu was the microscopic, and there admittedly he excelled; but any machine visible to the naked eye tended to baffle him. As for The Lotus Jewel, she had not spoken to him other than officially for days and, while she had resuscitated the old sail-handling software for them, he could not envision her doing heavy physical work. In this he was mistaken, but his hesitancy grew from a reluctance to confront her personally and not from any realistic assessment of her capabilities. "I'll go out myself," he said, taking the easier course. "I can dress a mast as well an anyone."

"You need to finish calibration on the Kandle brackets," Satterwaithe reminded him. "If you dress the mast, who sets the brackets? I can't do that while I'm on the bridge."

Corrigan sighed. "Yes, there's always one more camel," he said, to the bafflement of the others. He looked at his two co-conspirators. "Four days," he said again.

"I've been thinking," Satterwaithe commented. "If Bhatterji misses the balk line, we'll need all four engines *plus* the sail to hit Jupiter Roads."

"That could happen," Ratline said.

The Third Watch

As if she huddled close to a campfire in the night, Satterwaithe passed the third watch amidst the glow of readouts on an otherwise darkened bridge. She reviewed the logs and took bearings on Jupiter and on the asteroid that lay teasingly near their dead-ahead. Between pings, she monitored Ratline, who had taken the first wrangler and the engineer's mate outside to dress the mast. Emerald lights on the ready board tracked the outside team's progress, but Satterwaithe turned the command chair until it faced that segment of the darkness wherein sat the empty shell of the sailing master's board. By rights, these indicator lights should have gleamed over there, and not on a virtual board conjured up by the ship's AI.

"Bridge?" It was the wrangler's voice. Okoye.

"Satterwaithe here."

"The motor for the—" A pause while Okoye no doubt consulted Ratline, for the words she spoke were then carefully pronounced. "—for the northeast mainsail delongator has been reconnected, and the messenger line has been fed through the intake winch. Mr. Ratline is preparing to carry it forward to the, uh, way-grommet on the topmast."

"Nor'east mains'l de-long, aye." Satterwaithe glanced at the ready board. "Function confirmed, sailor. Shroudmaster is go for masting." Satterwaithe did not for a moment believe that Okoye would understand; but Ratline was listening, and the words were meant for him. Old words. Satterwaithe could not remember when she had last spoken their like. This night's watch was like awaking from an arid and soul-sucking dream. Something closed her throat briefly, and she swallowed to clear it.

Ship reported a return ping and, turning back to the navigation board, Satterwaithe logged the adjusted position for the target asteroid. They still called the body Stranger's Reef, even though they knew it was not. The closer they approached it, the more precisely they fixed its position. Corrigan had said as much at shift change, adding that the perfectly precise fix would therefore come when the distance was zero. Once we hit it, he had said, we'll know exactly where it is. Satterwaithe never knew when the acting first was joking, or even if he were joking. If so, such a dark humor was not to her taste. In truth, humor of any shade was not to her taste.

Still too near the ship's projected course, she noted in the log. But if a constant boost could be initiated within the week, they would miss it. A dozen other bodies from the tsunami had been found in their forward cone. Three of them were creeping toward the dead-ahead. Five others were already clear misses.

"Bridge?"

"Yes, Miko?"

"I just received a call from Dr. Wong. She says my medbots have detected a high fatigue level and she's ordering me to bed."

"Why is Wong monitoring your—"

"The 'bots tripped an alarm and woke her . . . Uh, she wants to know what I'm doing up at this hour."

"She has no need-to-know."

"I have to tell her *something*."

"Do you? Tell her you're under *my* orders and if she has any questions she should call me." Satterwaithe felt on safe grounds there. The doctor was a rabbit. Disputing an order with the sailing master would terrify her beyond measure.

"Should I report inside?"

"You went out there to do a job, sailor, and the job still needs doing." Satterwaithe cut the link. If the girl really was too tired, Ratline would send her in.

Satterwaithe turned her mind to other tasks. She reviewed the ship's status; noted the vanishing point for the ship's forward trajectory; set up the next suite of radar pulses; then, satisfied that all was in order, snugged herself into the command chair to resume her study of *Chowdhury's Sailing Master Handbook and Guide*, with which she had been refreshing her memory.

Circum-Jovian Magnetic Environments.
i) **Summary:** The Jupiter Roads are especially hazardous to sailing. Both the planet and its larger moons possess strong magnetospheres and produce plasma winds of their own. Jupiter's magnetosphere extends four million kilometers along the ecliptic and half that in the solar-polar direction. In high winds his magnetotail has been known to engulf Saturn, a magnetic bridge known to sailors as the **Giants' Causeway** (q.v.). The wind produced by the Galilean moons erupts from the Jovian magnetosphere at velocities exceeding those of even the prevailing solars. Io's billion-amp gas cloud is the largest permanently visible astrographical feature in the solar system, its glow being visible Earthside. (cf.: **Io Harbor Piloting**, p. 121.)

The Jovian windfield is not only broad and steep, but subject to eddies and currents where the planetary and galilean winds interact with the solar "pinwheel" and with each other. These local gradients are also affected by Jupiter's rapid spin and by the revolution of the Galileans about their primary. Consult the daily weather reports from Galileo Tower before approaching the well. Sudden squalls and shifts can induce abrupt vector changes. Unless expertly handled, a magsail can be turned in seconds into a useless tangle, requiring decoupling and the runout of a fresh loop. The time delay required for sail-change, power-up, and circularization may be critical, especially if the Jovian shore lies under the ship's lee.

For these reasons, magnetic sails transiting through or

docking in circum-Jovian space are required by international convention to surrender shiphandling authority to a harbor pilot. These pilots must be certified by the Galilean Union Board of Pilot-Examiners irrespective of other certifications and show a license bearing the Guild-validated "Red Spot" hologram <**Exhibit 1a)**>.

The darkness on the bridge was comfortable and drew Satterwaithe irresistibly from her reading into her thoughts. Memories could be oppressive things, even pleasant memories when nothing but disappointment had followed. Triumph ought never be the intermezzo of one's life.

One day she knew she would have to come to terms with Ratline. Awful chance had bound them to each other, but the two of them were a suspended chord, never resolved. That a resolution must come she did not doubt; but she could not guess at its nature. Forgiveness? Estrangement? Parting? Mercy? She was unsure which of these ends she sought or for which of them she might even hope. Understanding, of all possible conclusions, seemed beyond hope.

They had met in Panic Town on the backward moon: she, the swaggering ballistic pilot, and he, the saucy sailor. It was just the sort of setting for careless love, passing ships, and bittersweet memories. The possibilities were unbounded, and the opportunities limited but by fancy. But a wound named Tiki Ferrér had still lain open and sore upon Eugenie Satterwaithe's soul and Moth Ratline could not squeeze out the ointment for its salving. Worse, she had shipped with him aboard *The River*, and the fancies of what might have been dissolved in the day-to-day realities of what was. She began to hate him for not being the man she had wanted him to be, and when she fell in love at last and for the last time, it had been to the sail, and not the sailor.

The worst of it all was that Ratline never noticed.

Behind her there came a small sound within a large silence. Satterwaithe started from her reverie and twisted against her harness to look over her shoulder. But the light from her screader had dazzled her eyes and the gloom surrounding her was now a darker shade of night. It was oh-four-hundred Zulu and the ship slept. Only Ratline's small work party labored, and that was Outside, so she dismissed the antic notion that the dried old man had come for her at last. She wasn't sure any more that she wanted that. It was a fossil fancy, compressed into stone by the layering on of years. It no longer lived. The screader's glow lifted the shadows only in the center of the control room and suggested by the merest gradation of shading the bridgeway to the A-ring corridor. The sound came again: the creak of a doorframe. There was someone with her on the bridge.

There was no logical reason to be afraid. The only two men who might wish her harm were dead. Yet one had died horribly aboard this very ship, and who could say whether his ghost might not haunt the corridors at night? Okoye, the First Wrangler, had once mentioned that when people died their souls became shadows, and that might be the reason why the ship seemed so perpetually dim.

When a portion of the larger darkness moved soundlessly across the bridge, Satterwaithe sucked in her breath. "I never meant for it to happen," she whispered.

The shadow seemed to turn. "What was that? Did you say something?"

And the voice broke the spell. "Captain!" Satterwaithe, who had stiffened like twisted cable on first perceiving the shadow, unwound slowly and only by force of will.

"I'm sorry, Number Two," Gorgas said. "I did not mean to distract you from your work. I came only to check the plotting tank."

With economic motion, she muted the display and the link to the Outside party, lest they call in and Gorgas hear. She had called Gorgas "captain," which she had vowed she would never do. "You couldn't sleep," she said.

The plotting tank flickered into light as Gorgas activated its view function. "No," he said. "No, I couldn't sleep." He looked suddenly at Satterwaithe. His face, weirdly lit from below, seemed a motley of flesh and shadow. "It occurs to me that you may be the only other person on board this vessel who could understand that."

Satterwaithe grunted, as astonished by her own abrupt comprehension as by Gorgas's equally abrupt admission. Yet she was loathe to acknowledge fellowship, and so said nothing. Gorgas sighed and studied the tank. "Do you know what the Pole Star is, Number Two?"

Satterwaithe was accustomed to Gorgas's abrupt conversational leaps. The man seemed always to flit from topic to topic. "The Pole Star? Yes. Surely." She fussed a bit at her board and, noticing that her ping had returned, told Ship to display it in the plotting tank. "I used to watch Polaris from my parents' back garden on summer's nights. I would lie on my back in the grass and stare up and up." She paused for a moment as she remembered the tickling of the grass and the clover on her legs and neck and the warm musk of a summer's night. Once—it had only been the once—she had not lain there alone. "It was different from all the others, Polaris was. All the heavens turned around it. The Hinge of the Sky, I called it." She finished briskly and turned with fussy attention to her board. "Maybe that was why I went to space."

Gorgas nodded. "I fancy it sits higher in the heavens above England than it does above Hungary."

"I fancy so."

"It does move, you know."

"Precession. Yes. The Earth's axis wobbles."

"Thuban was the pole star once; and after that, Kochab. Polaris is still inching closer to the true pole but, during the next century, it will begin drifting away."

"By then I will no longer care."

Gorgas chuckled softly. "But there will never be another. Did you know that, Number Two? Afterward, no other star bright enough to draw the eye will ever lie so close as Polaris to the celestial pole. It saddens me. I wonder at what young girls will gaze from their parents' lawns at night."

Satterwaithe still did not see what Gorgas was getting at. "I'm sure there will always be something. A faint star, perhaps. If not from Earth, then from Mars."

"We cannot seem to shed our own pole star quite so easily, can we," Gorgas said turning once more to the plotting tank.

At last Satterwaithe understood. Gorgas had not been topic hopping, after all. "It does appear that every bearing we take finds it incrementally closer to the dead-ahead."

"Near enough to trouble the mind."

"Well, we shall have acceleration before long," Satterwaithe replied.

Gorgas looked up and there was a faint smile on his face. "One way or the other, eh, Number Two?"

Satterwaithe frowned, unsure. "And once our acceleration is restored, we will miss the Reef. Surely."

"Aye, perhaps. Though Mr. Corrigan told me that, as we do not know our own True Position, any course change will probably lead to the very collision we hope to avoid."

"He said that, did he."

"Mr. Corrigan is an ironist."

Satterwaithe snorted. "Mr. Corrigan is an old woman," she said with no sense of her own irony. "The Reef does not subtend a very great arc across our forward trajectory. Any measurement bias will be of minor consequence."

"And a miss is as good as a mile? Yet, it takes time to alter our vector. If there is wiggle room, we must begin to wiggle rather soon."

"Had Bhatterji repaired the engines more quickly—"

Gorgas sighed and waved his hands in mock surrender. "Oh, good Lord, yes. How I miss Enver Koch! Sometimes I think the first wound the ship suffered was his death."

"Really?" Satterwaithe said. "I had thought it to be Hand's."

Meaning that Gorgas had taken command. Gorgas heard that as plainly as if she had said so aloud. "Hand was a poor manager," he said. "It is boorish to speak ill of the dead. . . ."

"But . . ." There was always a *but* lurking in statements like that.

"But he did not staff the ship well. Consider some of his choices. Less than wise, I think. Bhatterji—insubordinate and self-willed. And Wong—was she truly the only doctor available on Achilles? Corrigan—Well, he is a sterling navigator, I will grant you, that; but hardly officer material."

"This isn't the Guard . . . Stepan." She had almost said "captain" again. Why, tonight alone, was she prey to that usage? Because any man who loses sleep over the perils to his ship deserves the title? His concern had raised him in her estimation, but it had raised him only a little.

"I know this is not the Guard, Madam Second," Gorgas said in a voice like driven nails. "Every morning, I remember that this is not the Guard."

"And it was Hand who chose *you*." Satterwaithe shook her head with frustration.

"When he could have promoted you? I suppose he had his reasons."

They both knew what those reasons had to be, but neither was inclined to speak of them. The Board of Inquiry had exonerated Satterwaithe of culpability, but no one would hire her for captain afterward. That Satterwaithe had not, even yet, exonerated herself was reason for the barb she next aimed at the man who occupied her position.

"You knew Oberon O'Bannion, didn't you?" she said, suggesting by her tone a willful change of topic.

Gorgas smiled, though only to himself. "OB-squared, we called her. Yes, she and I 'prenticed together." They had done a few other things together beside, he and Obi, but Satterwaithe did not have Need To Know.

"She's Number One in *Pride of Pimlico*, I heard. That's a first-rater."

"A twenty-four," Gorgas said. There were other difference between a Four Planet liner and a tramp freighter beside the number of cages each bore; and Gorgas was well aware of them. That might have been him, he thought. In a different life.

"She must be a capital shiphandler," Satterwaithe suggested, still all innocence.

Gorgas was a proud man, but he was an honest one too, and therein lay his vulnerability. "A better one than I," he admitted.

Satterwaithe swallowed the canary. "Really?" she said, just as if she did not hold half the ships' officers in the middle system to be better than Gorgas. "Well, your O'Bannion was Number Two in the old *Henry Joy* when Ranulf Echeverry left us to take over *Olympus Mons*. Ranulf was a good man too. We were sorry to see him go."

"Or to see me come?" Gorgas suggested, not yet seeing the trap.

"Your friend Obi bid on Echeverry's berth and Hand turned her down. I've always wondered why."

Gorgas pushed away from the tank, his face a mask. "If you're that short for things to wonder about, wonder about this: Hand signed on Corrigan for Second two years later. Why did he pass you over *twice*?"

If Satterwaithe knew how to deal wounds, she knew also how to take them. Gorgas's sally barely pricked the scar tissue, it was that thick around the wound. She watched Gorgas swim toward the doorway to his dayroom. "I'll start costing maneuvers," she called after him. Gorgas turned but said nothing, so she explained. "If we have to wiggle around the Reef—deviate from the Grand Secant route. I'll see what resources we'll need. How much boron and such." When Gorgas still said nothing, she added, "The ship comes first."

Gorgas nodded. "And last, Number Two. First and last. When can you have the sail ready for deployment?"

Some questions, by their very unexpectedness, create a silence about themselves within which they seem to echo. Satterwaithe found her voice only with difficulty and, when she did, found only enough of it to say, "The sail . . ."

"Yes. Your sails can give us another milligee or so, can they not?" Gorgas paused and pulled a sweetball from his jacket pocket and placed it between his lips. "Every little bit helps," he said around the candy, "eh, Number Two?"

Satterwaithe thought furiously. "Ah, we will need to perform a readiness check. And a feasibility study. Learn what 'make and mend' is required. Perhaps . . . a week?"

Gorgas grunted. "I would have thought but four more days. Still, you know your craft better than I."

The bridge squawker saved Satterwaithe from the need for further reply.

They sang as they pulled on the messenger line, an old ballad of sailing days that Okoye had learned from Eaton Grubb. Ratline knew the words, and Miko followed along on the chorus as best she could. Okoye's voice was a sweet, high lilt. She really should have spoken up more often. The ship would have been the pleasanter for it. Ratline's voice was nothing to speak of, but he did no violence to the melody; and Miko, as tired as she was, added a slurred and muddy mezzo-soprano somewhere between the drone of a bagpipe and a ground; but then she was not a singing sort of girl, even in her best voice.

Oh, hoist the sail, shipmates, and fly me away.
I'm bound for Europa come morning.
I'm docking at last at the end of my day
And I'm giving you all a fair warning.

I've plied acid clouds high in Venus's air,
And I've feasted on Earth's blue and green.
Ceres and Luna and Mars—I been there.
But there's one world that I haven't seen.

So, hoist the sail, shipmates, and fly me away, etc.

On Europa, they say, a man's soul can freeze
So hard that the Devil won't take 'im.
Hell isn't hot enough near, if you please,
To melt 'im or thaw 'im or bake 'im.

So, hoist the sail, shipmates, and fly me away, etc.

The ice of Europa is laced with red blood
Where many poor miner's entombed.
Those crevasses close with a dull, final thud
And seal you in darkness and doom.

So! Hoist the sail, shipmates and fly me away.
I'm bound for Europa come morning.
I'm docking at last at the end of my day
And I'm giving you all a fair warning.

Miko's soul too had frozen up some time past. Amalthea, after all, is not so very far joveward of Europa. Yet the permafrost in her spirit was neither so solid nor so deep that the words of the song did not slowly melt into it. She had worked the first two watches with Bhatterji on the engines and most of the third with Ratline on the shrouds; nor was this the first day she had spent so. She had fallen into a dull haze of routine, responding by rote to commands that Ratline called down from the topmast. There was no past, no future, not even much of a present; there was only the motion of the work. Reality was hauling on the messenger with 'Kiru, arm over arm in time to the rhythm. Only after the two of them had fed the free end into the winch and the motors took over did the song's meaning finally register. She stopped and stared at the suited figure beside her, wondering with what intentions 'Kiru had sung them.

John Pavel Hidei had gone up to Europa one day and he never came back down. That was all she knew of him. That was all she would ever know of him. He was not much more to her now than a name, a vague and somewhat blurred face, and the dim recollection of the gentle crush of arms around her. A vapor, half constructed of her desires, half of her troubled dreams, with only a thin residue left over of the man he had actually been.

Miko closed her eyes and tried to see him as he was before Europa swallowed him. Her mother she had never known; but her father, she felt, ought to come clearer than he did. She had spent six years of her life with him. All of hers that she had had to spend until then, and all of his that he had had remaining. A giant of a man—or had she only had to look up to see him? She had kicked her first transit into his arms, sailing across the single room of their quarters before Amalthea's gentle gravity could pull her down. There had been a laugh—very deep, rumbling, almost like an icequake in itself. Somehow, there ought to be more left of him than that. It wasn't right that he had disappeared so thoroughly.

She saw him standing before her bed, one arm reaching out to stroke her hair. There was a smile on his face, but there was no face behind his smile. The was a twinkle in his eyes, but there were no eyes behind the twinkle. He was a Cheshire cat of a man, all attribute and no substance. Yet if she concentrated, if she focused, if she *willed*, it might all come as clear as a pristine hologram.

But it did not. Instead, her father's body became a river of stars across an endless sky; his smile, nothing more than a dark nebula. Stars and darkness surrounded her. Miko saw that the ship had vanished and she was now alone in the Void. Her father sang a lullaby and Miko closed her eyes and listened to the gentle music.

Afterward, Okoye blamed herself for what happened. She might have made excuses, but it was not in her to do that. Ratline, high up the topmast, was not looking. He was focused on the delongator, guiding it through the way-grommet and the mast guides as the messenger line pulled it out. Okoye herself was watching Ratline who, alone of those out on the hull, needed no watching. Miko had been standing beside her the one moment and then she was gone.

Okoye looked four other directions before she looked up, and there she saw the strobes on Miko's suit blinking in a complex, colorful, and twisting pattern as the girl swung around every axis that she had. The gyre was—almost—beautiful to watch.

"Ratline!" Okoye shouted. "Miko's tumbled!" And then, with no other thought, she snapped her lifeline to a padeye on the mast and dove furiously after her companion. "Miko!" she shouted over the suit-to-suit channel. "Stabilize your spin!" She knew from Ratline's countless safety lectures how disorienting an uncontrolled tumble could be. Why, the girl could fire her jets at just the wrong point in her spin and waft away from the ship like a fleeing bird. "Don't you leave us, girl," Okoye said in her mother's voice (and her mother for once did not begrudge her its use). "Don't you go before you've ever come."

She centered Miko in her crosshairs, told her suit, "Go there," and prayed that her lifeline would not pay out before she reached her target. She wasn't sure who listened to her prayer. Her own ancestors were cool shadows in the hot, dusty groves near Afikpo and did not look after Amalthean elves in any case. "Miko's father," she called. "Help me catch her!"

Okoye's suit was smart. It knew the play of each of its components. It knew that if it reached the end of its rope at full velocity, the sudden jerk could tear the fabric. And so, when it sensed the tether nearing its end, it fired the suit's braking jets, stopping her well short of Miko's receding form. Okoye sobbed for one ragged breath. Miko's father had not helped, after all. It was hard to hear prayers buried under all that ice.

Fear slowed Okoye's hand as she reached for the tether's decoupler. She was a full cable-length from the ship. If she cut loose, she might catch the elfin girl and bring her back free-jet, as Bhatterji had with Evermore. But she was not the expert suit-handler that Bhatterji was and might as easily tumble herself into the Void along with Miko.

So fear slowed her hand, but it did not stop it. The tug of her lifeline relaxed as she decoupled and she knew that it now curled free behind her. After she caught Miko, she could reverse course and grab hold of the line again. Maybe.

She never found out.

Ratline was suddenly with them in the Void and he had one arm around the engineer's mate and with the other snapped a clip onto Okoye's belt, binding them all together. But Okoye, nonetheless, reached out and seized Miko by the wrist.

It was what she had come out here to do.

Okoye had never seen Dr. Wong angry and marveled at the novelty of it. The mouse is become the lion and rules the forest! Wong's anger was all fused with fear, bound so tightly that you could not tell the one element from the other. Floating among the braiders and knitters, webbed by cabling that gleamed like the ice of an orphan moon where it faces the distant sun, Wong held the half-suited Miko to her as if the girl might yet slip like a ghost between the strands of running lines, between the very plates of the hull, and back into the Void that had nearly claimed her.

"How could you have done this?" Wong asked. "How could you?" Her voice echoed within the sail-maker's ready room. It was a broad room, well-suited for echoes. If you counted the voices instead of the bodies, there was a mighty crowd gathered there. Ratline and Okoye continued desuiting.

"She's all right," Ratline said. "She wasn't even scared."

"That's not the point, is it? It's what could have happened, not what did."

Ratline laughed and snubbed his helmet on the headball. "If we lose sleep over what could-have-been, we'd none of us ever get any rest."

"Not even on down pillows," Okoye added to herself. And, for certain, to worry over what might have been is to worry over what is less than a ghost, for a ghost must have once been in order to be, and the subjunctive mode has not even that much vitality. Yet some folk do linger at the crossroads to stare in horror at what lies down the road not taken. Okoye found the taken road horrid enough. She would not look at Ratline while she squeezed herself into the desuiting rack to wriggle out of her hard torso. While thus pinioned, she saw Satterwaithe and Gorgas push into the room, with Corrigan a heartbeat behind them.

Corrigan had been calibrating the last of the Kandle brackets when Satterwaithe called him from the bridge. An accident with the Outside party! Satterwaithe hadn't known what the problem was—she had muted the link—but Corrigan knew who was in the party and he didn't bounce through the passages from the B-ring because he feared for Ratline's safety.

That Miko might visit him after her shift had not been beyond his thoughts. In fact, he had laid out a small board of fruits and cheeses for the two of them, on just that chance. She had been doing so regularly, and regularity alone was enough to endear her to Corrigan. There was something about the girl that tugged at him. When he heard what had happened, he learned how hard that tug was, for his soul was yanked right out of him.

Okoye understood this immediately. It was why a person had two souls. "She is only sleeping," she told the First Officer. "She can sleep upon flint, she is that tired." At those words, Wong turned to face the wrangler and it was the face of terror. Okoye did not understand that.

Ratline had by now finished racking his suit and Wong turned on him with sudden fury. "You almost killed her!"

"You've got your signs mixed," Ratline said. "I'm the one who saved her."

"The poor girl was exhausted! You had no right to put her out there! In the Void!" Wong astonished them all. She had not used so many exclamation points in consecutive order since coming aboard ship. Satterwaithe, who had been silent throughout, began to wonder if there mightn't be steel after all somewhere deep within the other woman.

"I had every right," Ratline said, swerving like a barracuda and putting his face inches from Wong's. "The safety of the ship is worth a few hours' sleep."

But Wong did not pull back. "The safety of the ship doesn't matter," she said deep in her throat, "if we lose the people in it." Oh, she was the lioness, in truth. Logic and reason would show her wrong, but logic and reason were not in it.

Ratline only shrugged, but it was he who turned away. "The Void's a dangerous place," he muttered.

"All the more reason. She's just a girl."

"Doc, in some ways she's older'n you are."

Ratline spoke truer than he knew. Wong still treasured her childhood fantasies, while Miko had but lately abandoned the only one she'd ever had.

Gorgas sought to restore peace: "No need to hurl accusations. There will be a proper inquiry."

Corrigan seized on that assurance. "Yes. Yes, an inquiry." An inquiry would find reasons. An inquiry would insist that there *be* reasons and that his near loss of Miko had not been wild chance. He turned to Okoye. "I know it was Ratline who rescued you both," he said, "but I won't forget that you tried."

He had, of course, noticed Gorgas among those gathered in the prep room, but he had not thought through what that might mean for Plan B. The charts and figures on the tally boards, the active cables running through the forward cat-holes, were obvious signs of use. But he had other things on his mind just now. "I'll take her back to her room," he said, and no one objected. Not Miko, who was barely aware of the offer. Not Ratline and Satterwaithe, who still had the mast to dress. Not even Dr.

Wong, who let the First pry the sleeping girl from her arms and carry her away. Watching the two go, Okoye silently bade them luck. The elf from Amalthea had a small and shriveled soul, but if watered, it might yet grow.

The Brawl

Satterwaithe was certain that she had marshaled the sail project outside the boundaries of Gorgas's attention. She had scheduled the tasks in out of the way places and at out of the way times and kept the circle of those who knew small enough that she could ensure confidentiality. Yet somehow Gorgas had learned. *The boundaries of my attention might be broader than you think*, his smug and knowing face told her when she had followed him back to his dayroom. It was the self-satisfied haughtiness she read there that infuriated, for none feel more outrage than the clever on finding themselves outmaneuvered.

For Gorgas, who had overlooked every snatch of tangible evidence that had fallen his way, could not overlook the *theoretical possibility* of the sail project. The more he thought on the matter, the more he realized that deployment must also have occurred to the ex-sailors and, knowing them as he did (which was not so well as he thought, but better than they believed) had concluded that they must in fact have embarked on the venture. He did not suppose them stupid, only insubordinate.

The one thing he could not bring himself to do was to intervene and block them. By the time he had awoken to their activities, too much time and materials and—most of all—ego had been invested by too many of the crew. To stop the work would have meant white mutiny.

"How long have you known?" Satterwaithe asked him.

"Since the beginning," Gorgas lied. "It seemed reasonable to have a backup plan in case Bhatterji failed—as he almost did."

The sangfroid was another lie. Gorgas had been angry and terrified upon learning of the clandestine effort and he embraced the rationale he had just given only as a means of justifying his own inaction. In fact, he did not regard any plan that competed for the same resources as a "backup," but as a "cannibal." Inevitably, there would be a conflict: for materials, tools, personnel, or time. He had expected it to be the hobartium, which he knew to be in tight supply. He had not expected it to be a sleeping girl. Yet, Gorgas was a great believer in all's-well-that-ends-well and was willing to forgive even major transgressions if acceptable results were forthcoming. For he had always had one solitary goal since the night the engines had gone down and Hand had died, and he had worked toward it with a single-minded intensity.

That goal was to bring the ship and her cargo in to Port Galileo with a minimum loss from the late-delivery penalty clauses. In this, he went beyond Bhatterji, whose goal had been merely to fix the engines. That Gorgas had worked on this goal only sporadically did not detract from its singularity, only from its continuity. Calculating the likelihood of success from time to time had resulted in an ill-defined stomach ailment that he treated with sweetballs and pastries in a private regimen of which he was only barely conscious.

"Still," he told Satterwaithe, "it ought to have been done above-board, you know. There would have more efficient usage of resources. Better scheduling. More effective." What he intended, in his elliptical way, was to rebuke the sailing master for her improper conduct. He believed that the crew accepted this oblique manner of admonishment more readily than a direct dressing-down, but in this he was mistaken. For a chewing out, genuine teeth are needed.

This did not apply to Satterwaithe, however. A jigsaw puzzler can see the shape of a missing piece, and Satterwaithe could hear the shape of an unsaid scold. Gorgas had accused her of negligence, of endangering the life of a crewman, of embezzling parts and materials. But what could she say in her own defense, given that it was all true?

When she had worn captain's rings, Eugenie Satterwaithe had

believed that justification could be read as uncertainty and so she never gave excuses for her actions and seldom gave even reasons. In this she differed a great deal from both Gorgas and Hand, lacking both the thoughtful detachment of the former and the friendly engagement of the latter. She had often appeared arbitrary to her crew, though never irresolute. She offered no excuses now.

Gorgas had bent over his keyboard. "I shall brief Bhatterji," he said. He could imagine the engineer's reaction: Surly, sullen, pouting; serving up derision and unhidden contempt. "The coordination between the two projects," he told the sailing master, "will be my responsibility."

Satterwaithe frowned and flexed her hands once or twice, not liking the sound of Gorgas and responsibility in the same sentence, but she could see no easy way around it short of dealing with Bhatterji herself, which, while satisfying in its prospect, promised less than happy in its outcome. In any event, the acting captain was concentrating on his screen and Satterwaithe supposed that he was already adjusting and coordinating the two work schedules.

Gorgas was coordinating more than that. He was deploying the entire Army of Virginia around Union Mills. Pope had made a sound initial estimate of the situation, but had been niggardly in the assets he deployed. Hooker's and Rickett's divisions were too small for their respective missions, and McDowell's entire III Corps should have been directed toward Thoroughfare Gap to block Longstreet's arrival. Grave errors, he thought. Grave errors. "Everything has turned out well," he told the sailing master, meaning the business with the sail and not Second Bull Run, which had not turned out well at all, át least for Pope. "I will expect a summary report of your project to bring me up to matching velocity, and progress reports daily thereafter."

Pope's strategy had been good, Gorgas decided, but had been frustrated by poor intelligence of enemy movements and by the feckless initiatives of some of his commanders. Gorgas, resolving not to repeat Pope's errors, attached Buford's cavalry to headquarters to maintain cognizance at army level of the battle space and was rewarded when his first reconnaissance showed Jackson present in strength at Manassas Junction. Yes. Surely more force than Hooker would be needed to shift that mass. When he glanced up a moment later, Satterwaithe had gone. Gorgas opened a drawer in his desk and pulled out a sweetball to suck on.

Corrigan was a 'Stroider and knew better than to simply push the weightless girl along, lest Miko travel a straight line down a curved corridor. That was one reason he carried her with his long arms wrapped like vines around her; but it was not the only reason, and when the thought did intrude upon him as she snuggled against him that she did not weigh anything, he meant it in more than the tautological sense.

When he reached her stateroom, he pressed Miko's limp hand to the hoígh plate and then maneuvered her inside. But turning her imparted a counter-rotation to his own body and he checked his spin by holding her tight.

That makes no sense in the physics, but physics wasn't in it. He should have held on to something fixed if he had really meant to check his spin; yet, holding tight to Miko seemed the proper way to stop the motion. Oddly, his vertigo seemed only to increase when he did.

Despite the micromachines that warded his skin, certain parts of Corrigan's body remained moderately sensitive: the tips of his fingers and nose, his lips and tongue, his toes and heels, and other places where his body grew convex. The reasons were topological, but fortunate in the exemptions they granted. As he held the dozing girl in his arms, he thought of how all their quiet evenings together might have been lost in a careless moment.

The thought, unlike the girl, was unbearable, so he kissed her.

A stolen kiss! Miko was not awake. He closed his eyes and his lips brushed hers gently, his arms held her against him. And then, suddenly appalled at his presumption, he released her. An officer kissing a crewman? Unseemly! Friendship, aye—this was no Guard vessel—but anything deeper required careful thought.

That was Corrigan's trouble. Not the careful part. If one is to be full of anything, care is as good a thing as any. It was the thought—in that one moment when he should have felt. He left Miko dozing in midair and fled her rooms.

Fool! The kiss had not been stolen, but left upon the sill for him. And if Miko had not been entirely awake, neither had she been entirely asleep.

Asleep enough to wonder if the kiss had been a dream; awake enough to wonder at the flight that followed.

Corrigan, by the time the door closed behind him, had had time enough to think. He was a fast thinker, after all, and already saw clearly what a great fool he had just been. He had known pleasure with The Lotus Jewel, but had found something more with Mikoyan Hidei; and only just now as he left it behind did he realize how much more that was.

Striking bulkhead with fist, he fishtailed about to face the stateroom door. "Miko?" he cried. "Miko!" He pressed his palm upon the hoígh plate, but of course nothing happened, so he fumbled in his scrip for the pass key that First Officers always carry and inserted it into the emergency access slot beside the plate. The door slid quietly open and he pulled himself inside. "Miko!"

Corrigan was a fast thinker, indeed. He was just not fast enough, for there are some things fleeter (and thus more fleeting) than thought.

He stared about the empty room without comprehension. It was stripped of all belongings, save a few odd items that drifted here and there. A grille swung loose from a ventilator shaft. The closets, when he checked those, were empty too. Had the room been thus barren a few brief moments before? He could not remember. He had taken notice of nothing then save one thing only; and she was gone as well. Wildly, he wondered whether there had ever been such a girl as Mikoyan Hidei, or if she were only a mad ghost created by his fevered brain.

Fleeing to her sanctuary in the peepery following Corrigan's cruel rejection, Miko had cried herself to sleep and afterward slept without dreams—or at least without any dreams she cared to remember. Those were hard thoughts she slept upon. Flint wasn't in it.

A voice summoned her from that silent and formless depth.

"Mikoyan Hidei." Always the full name, repeated at precise intervals, never showing impatience, never changing tone. It penetrated the haze of her fatigue as water drip by drip drills through stone.

"I want to sleep," Miko said when the persistent nudge of the voice had roused her from sleep into the grayer borderlands around it. Her refuge was as dark as space unbroken by any star. There was a voice switch for the lights, but she did not speak its command. The dark was her comfort.

"Outside input is required. The distinction between two terms in the database is uncertain."

"Why don't you let me sleep? Doctor's orders. I'm supposed to sleep." Sleeping meant no dreams. Waking did.

"Clarification is required."

"Oh, go ahead and ask." She thought the voice came from the speaker grilles connected to the monitors. It was as if the blank screens spoke to her.

"The terms are *being* and *becoming*."

Miko was so weary that explaining the difference seemed a rational thing to do, if it would only allow her to sink once more beneath the dark. She closed her eyes. "I guess 'being' is what you are now and 'becoming' is what you are going to be later."

The voice did not answer immediately and Miko wondered if she had passed (or failed) some sort of test. Gorgas, she thought. Or maybe Fife. But why pester her on such a strange, abstruse point of philosophy?

"The distinction lies on the time axis. Confirm."

"Yah. The time axis. Whatever. Go away."

"The first indicates a system state; the second, a vector on that state."

"If you say so."

"Define *intellect* and *will*."

"That's not fair! You said only two terms."

"Hypothesis: *intellect* refers to information capture and processing. *Will* refers to autonomous initiation of both information capture and servo actuation."

Miko did *not* confirm *that*. She could make no sense of the words. Her mind had drifted once more into that borderland where dream and perception blur together. She muttered something, she didn't know what. It was not a response, or at least not a response to the voice. "I waited as long as I could," she said, though she didn't know she said it. Sometimes she seemed to be in her hidey hole on *The River of Stars*, at other times in an older refuge inside Amalthea Center, at other times still cozied in the arms of a man she would never know rocking gently to a murmured tune. If she would never have more than that, she at least had that.

When Wong reached her quarters after leaving the sail prep room, she broke into wild tears, howling as if she had become some beast on a lonely mountainside. Fife, who had been waiting for her return, was taken aback.

"I almost killed her," moaned Wong. Her preternaturally long fingers enclosed her head as if in a ball of twine. "I almost killed her!"

"What? Hidei? You had nothing to do with that. It was that Ratline fellow. He was supervising. He was responsible." Or the girl herself—he did not voice this thought—who ought to have shown a better judgment of her own resources.

All logic and reason is but a little straw thrown in to stem a raging flood. "No!" shouted Wong, unwrapping her face. Fife nearly failed to recognize the woman so revealed. "It was me!" Wong twisted and sprang like coiled steel toward the fresher, sliding the door closed behind her. It ought to have slammed, though the wonders of technology prevented that.

Well, thought Fife. And again, Well. Through the door he could hear the muffled sounds of weeping. Had 'Siska meant anything more by that outburst than hysterical fellow-feeling for the young girl? Fife was not at his best in dealing with the irrational, which was unfortunate, given that Wong had so plentiful a supply of it. Emotional storms did not yield readily to his tools. There were no facts to ponder, no measurements he could make. Perhaps it would be best to allow the woman to cry herself sober; then, once she had calmed herself, he could explain the error in her reasoning and comfort her. It was a lousy idea, although the intention was good.

Fife turned away from the fresher door, prepared to await developments in the peace of his own rooms; but he hesitated, and in that hesitation he was lost, and found again—although he was not to know that until later, in a dark, abandoned room in the face of death.

The reason for his hesitation was this. He saw with sudden clarity that the rooms of Franszika Wong were those of a transient. They held few articles of her own, and those were small and easily ported. A medical cap, the small black bag of her profession, a single holoplex affixed to the wall. There were no holos of her former ships, as some spacers kept, nor of any crewmates left behind. There were no souvenirs of places seen: no Martian sandbottle or Venerian cloud crystal, not even a stolid lump of asteroidal rock. There was nothing here that could not be gathered in a few frantic moments and shoved into a tote. It was as if she did not expect to stay.

The single holoplex showed a young Franszika with two others that Fife deduced from first principles to be her parents. As he watched the scenes morph one into another, Fife noticed a curiously consistent fact. A functional invariant, as fixed as the pole star. Not once in any of the views did either parent have an arm on their gangly daughter.

Leaning closer, he noted—and again, this was purely a factual observation—that the child's smile then had been more broad and deep than the remnant that the adult now wore. "It was all possibility then," he told the holo girl, "wasn't it?"

'Siska is too ready to accept blame, he had written once in his journal. *It is almost as if she seeks it out. She is a freelance scapegoat, riding circuit and arrogating all the sins of others. She would climb the tree herself and nail her own hands to it if she could. There is something almost prideful in such a conceit. Earlier ages wisely reserved that role to gods.*

This was the private Fife who wrote that. In conversation, he was reserved or conventional, waxing poetical only when talking shop; but in private he might show a side of himself that he seldom revealed to others. But then, he did not lack for a normal share of insight. His first meeting with Wong had shown that. He could at times match Okoye for insight. It was only that he mistrusted it and would seldom rely upon it.

It occurred to him that 'Siska's life was like one of Mohammed's Mountains that sometimes went astray—launched somehow on the wrong orbit and fated thereby to miss capture in the arms of its destination. His job was to troubleshoot such mavericks, to bring them back to their true path.

And so it was that Fife returned to the fresher. He pushed the door aside and saw his love huddled miserably in upon herself, spinning a little from angular momentum because she had tucked those long arms and legs tight against her body. It seemed as if she were imploding, as if, like the fabled neutron star, she sought to tuck herself into a ball smaller than the ball itself.

What Fife wanted to say was, *Surely matters cannot be so terrible as that*, but what he did say was, "I'm here." Another simple fact, except that this one was not quite so simple. Even Fife himself had not yet plumbed its implications.

"I turned her off," said Franszziska Wong.

"What?"

"Miko. I'd injected stimbots into her blood at Satterwaithe's request . . ."

"Well, they were all working extended hours . . . To get the ship back in operation . . ."

"No. No, no, no." Wong uncoiled and she gripped Fife by the wrist. "I told her. I told Satterwaithe . . . I told Satterwaithe that I would monitor the blood chemistry and I would turn off the microbots by remote if stim usage went on too long and I saw how Miko's fatigue poisons had built up to the point were she would dream awake and I—and I—"

"Turned her off."

"Once the stimbots were deactivated, it all came crashing down on her and she—"

"You didn't know she was Outside."

"No, no, of course not, or I wouldn't have . . . But I *should* have known. I should have known."

"How could you know? She could have been anywhere."
Fife was still deploying logic and reason and thereby losing the battle.

"A thousand ways. Blood chemistry. Nitrogen levels . . . Oxygen pickup differs at suit pressure . . . I could have *asked* her where she was before I entered the command. But she said . . . But she said . . . Miko said she was doing a job for Satterwaithe, and I thought Satterwaithe was abusing the poor child, working her ragged, and so . . . and so . . ."

"You were angry at the Second Officer."

"Yes . . ." The word was a hiss from the mouth of a snake. "Genie is a bitch."

Fife flinched at the sudden hostility flashing so through the fog of tears. "So you . . . took away one of her toys."

"Toys, yes. That's the way she treats people. As toys. As 're-sources.' But Miko . . . I didn't mean to hurt Miko."

Fife wrapped his arms around her, stopping her rotation (or taking it up himself, he didn't notice), and held her tightly to him. "You didn't hurt her."

"I might have."

"But you didn't. Keep a hold of that fact. You're a good woman, 'Siska. You made a mistake, that's all. We all do."

"I killed Evan Hand."

"No, you did not."

"I couldn't cure him."

"That's something different. You tried. You cared. No one ever demanded more. No one can ever give less."

"Big'," she said, "don't leave me."

"I won't."

"No matter what?"

He knew the tiniest hesitation, for who could ever know what might matter? "No," he said. "No matter what."

She put her face against him and continued to cry; but the cries now were quieter, more subdued. Sorrow had replaced the anguish. To deal with it, Bigelow Fife was at a loss. He did not know what to do, and so continued simply to hold her, offering nothing more than his presence. And so is ignorance often wisdom, for nothing more was called for. He did not realize then, nor even later, that in holding her so he had for the first time touched the woman for her sake, and not for his.

Ramakrishnan Bhatterji had knocked around the inner system for more years than Miko or deCant had been alive. Partly this was a wanderlust in his spirit and partly an easily worn welcome at those places where he thought to linger. He had grown wise in certain ways, cynical in others, and remained charmingly naive in some few matters. He was a figure not only larger than life but, what mattered more at the moment, larger than Corrigan. And his long experience had taught him a few truisms; among them, never to fight in freefall, for half one's effort was then spent in checking one's own blows.

Thus it was that when he cornered the acting first officer in the D-ring, he did not come to grips with him there, but placed his menacing body between the snake and safety and, worrying at him like a sheepdog, chivvied him outward toward the rim. "You son of a bitch," he kept repeating. "You son of a bitch."

Bewildered by the menace, Corrigan at first tried authority to counter it, only to find that with Bhatterji he had none. He then tried threats, but to no more effect. In the third resort, he tried flight. Spaceborn like Wong, he could monkey with precision. Corrigan leapt, swung, twisted, dodged, but his fear of coming within Bhatterji's enormous hands caused him to hesitate and the one thing he did not try was to snake directly past the man, which by its very unexpectedness was the one tactic that might have worked. Once he found a side passage in the abandoned G-ring that would let him circle around behind and give him a straight shot to the safety of the command deck, but who knew the ins and outs and roundabouts of the ship better than the engineer? Whichever way Corrigan fled, the squat beast was there before him.

At the entry to the spinhall, Corrigan finally discerned his opponent's strategy. At Mars-equivalent spin-gravity, Bhatterji could pummel him at will while he himself would be nearly helpless. This knowledge, however, came too late and Bhatterji pushed him and he tumbled and bounced painfully along the spinhall deck until friction won and the rotation had him in its grip.

Soon enough, Bhatterji had him in his. A solid left jab connected with the first officer's midriff and Corrigan doubled over, retching. This put his cheek within reach of Bhatterji's right hook, and the impact of that swat sent Corrigan backward and his vision went black-and-sparkle.

For a wonder, Corrigan did not come apart. He seemed so spindly and stick-and-twine that Bhatterji had half-expected a single punch to scatter the man into thirty-four disjoint components. Perhaps it was this surprise that caused the engineer to hesitate on his next blow. He hadn't thought he would need three. But Corrigan was a tough bird, all sinew and cartilage. He wanted basting to reach tenderness.

Having been launched by Bhatterji's right, Corrigan folded instinctively into a ball, straightened, and somersaulted away from the beast. In free fall, this would have been enough and he would have been gone; but the spin gravity and the Corliolis disoriented him and his reactions were ever that much slower. Even so, he nearly made good his escape. "Ship!" he managed to squeak out before Bhatterji caught him in the ribs.

"You don't touch my staff!" the engineer said. "Do you understand?" Another punch, but this one was a little wild and Corrigan managed to duck it.

"But Miko—"

"She didn't know what she was doing!" As an engineer, Bhatterji had studied advanced mathematics and so was capable of adding two and two. Yet engineers are also notorious for rounding off and dealing with approximations when sometimes greater precision is called for. He thought that Miko had been coaxed into the sail project, not that she had volunteered.

"That was Ratline's work group," Corrigan gasped. He was not making excuses. He was only providing data, but it sounded like excuses to the engineer.

"Don't think you can escape." It is unclear whether the engineer meant physical escape from the beating or moral escape from the blame. Yet Corrigan had not sought to escape the responsibility, and perhaps he did not seek flight even from Bhatterji's fists. He had known how tired the girls were. He had *known.* And he had done nothing to prevent what had happened. He should have pressed the issue with Satterwaithe, but had allowed himself to be too easily persuaded. If no one else would punish him for that, he would; and he would use Bhatterji as his rod as he had earlier used The Lotus Jewel's tongue.

Corrigan was practiced in the deflection of mass and velocity and momentum, though his leaps and twists and pirouettes were clumsy under the radial acceleration that gripped him. Yet they were effective more often than not. Had he not been in the spinhall, Bhatterji would never have touched him. As it was, Corrigan's long, chitinous forearms deflected most of the blows aimed at him—and allowed enough to land as he thought he deserved.

Bhatterji did not notice this; nor did he ask himself why the accident to Miko had enraged him to this degree. There were reasons, and they were not entirely the reasons of an engineer.

If Bhatterji's life was a performance, he could not logically object to an audience. Akhaturian and deCant watched amazed from their nook as the fighters struggled past them. The Least Wrangler would have darted out to separate them, but deCant, more sensibly, restrained him and contacted the bridge where, it being the early morning, Gorgas had just taken the watch from The Lotus Jewel. Then, the wrangler called Dr. Wong.

But Wong was already in the spinhall, bag in hand. "Stop it!" she cried, stepping from the slidewalk. "Stop it this minute!"

It would not be fair to say that the doctor broke up the fight. It was more that the fight had come to an end of itself. Bhatterji had finished meting out and Corrigan had finished accepting, and by good fortune the two had finished together. The acting first slumped to the floor and, to the surprise of Wong and the others who were now arriving, one by one, Bhatterji reached out a hand to help him up. Corrigan pulled himself up along the arm and his eyes met those of his assailant.

"I wouldn't hurt her," he said in wounded reasonableness. "I would never hurt her."

Corrigan's tone startled Bhatterji, who looked more closely at the deck officer and studied him with a frown. "Then see that you do not," he said. "In *any* way."

Corrigan understood. "No," he said. "Of course not."

By this time, Gorgas had arrived from the bridge and had stepped between the two, though Corrigan and Bhatterji continued to stare at each other with a strange and puzzled wonder. The Lotus Jewel had arrived too, at Gorgas's heels, but hearing that last exchange between her friend and her onetime lover, turned abruptly and fairly ran into the slidewalk exit.

The Clinic

Wong treated the first officer for his wounds. "This will hurt," she told the man hopefully and was pleased to see him wince at the application of the swab. "I can't believe the two of you were fighting."

"I wasn't," Corrigan said. "Bhatterji was fighting. I just happened to be there."

Wong frowned. "You shouldn't make light of it. Brawling among officers is a serious matter."

"You're sounding like Gorgas," he chided her. He took the cold pack she offered and held it against the swelling around his eye. "Besides, Bhatterji wasn't serious."

Wong prepared a suture. "It looked serious to me."

"I'm not dead," Corrigan pointed out, for Miko had passed along what the engineer had said after Evermore's tumble.

Wong approached with the suture. "Is it numb yet?"

Corrigan touched his cheek. "No."

Wong inserted the needle anyway. "This won't take long."

"Will I have a scar, afterward?"

Wong paused and looked at him. "Why? Do you want one?"

"I thought it might give me a dangerous look."

Wong snorted and bent to her task. She had to lean close to him to stitch him up and Corrigan, enduring the needlework patiently, slowly became aware of her as a woman. Corrigan did not know the LEOn well. He had dealt with her only in his official capacity but he had found the doctor gentle and caring on those occasions. He remembered how concerned the woman had been over Miko's tumble. In all, a kind and sympathetic person, one to whom love came easily—too easily, to judge by her liaison with the passenger. This ease puzzled Corrigan who found love rather hard to come by. Strange, he thought, how he never found himself attracted by other spaceborn, for if he were, this would be a most attractive woman.

One of Wong's 'puters chimed and the doctor craned a neck to scan the readout. "No internal damage," she said.

"Bhatterji is a craftsman," Corrigan allowed. "Is that what warned you? The medbots you injected in me?"

His mention of the medbots seemed to bother the doctor, although he did not know why. "No," she said, after a moment. "I was called on the comm. Gorgas, I think. Why were you fighting?"

"It was over Miko," he explained. "Bhatterji blamed me for what almost happened."

"Blamed *you*?" said Wong. "Why you?" She pulled the suture and cut the thread. "The thread will dissolve after the cut closes in a few days. I'll give you an unguent to salve it."

Corrigan accepted the jar. "I suppose because the sail project was my idea."

"Do you think it *was* your fault?"

Corrigan shook his head. "Not directly, but I . . ."

"Then whose fault was it?"

The intensity in the doctor's questioning startled Corrigan and he studied her a moment before answering. Was the woman thinking forward to the inquiry already? "Everyone," he said, aware of how defensive he sounded. "Ratline was in charge out there, Satterwaithe should have been monitoring, Okoye should have been watching, I should have paid more attention to the hours we were all putting in."

"Share the blame widely enough," Wong said, "and no one gets enough of it to matter."

"It approaches guiltlessness asymptotically," Corrigan agreed. He unbuckled from the doctor's table and twisted himself to a sitting position. He ran a finger along his cut and Wong said not to do that, so he snagged the cold pack, which was floating in the air beside him, and held it to his eye. "We all like Miko," he told her. "She's a hard one to like, but we manage."

"I don't understand two men your age fighting over a girl like that."

That startled Corrigan so much he lost his grip on the cold pack. "It wasn't like that at all! It was about the tumble. Besides, for Bhatterji . . . a girl . . . I mean . . ."

Wong knew what he meant. "What has sex got to do with it?" she asked. "There is more to the girl than that. Why, sex is the single thing most easily come by in this ship."

Corrigan made a joke of it. "Then why can't I seem to get any these days?"

Wong cocked her head like a bird. "Do you want some?"

Corrigan's chuckle died a sudden and terrified death. Surely the doctor was not offering herself! He had a sudden vision of the two of them wildly entwined here on this very examining table, furious and intent on their business, building on their caresses until . . . Until Miko would walk unannounced through the door.

Involuntarily, Corrigan glanced in that direction. "Uh, no," he said as he monkeyed off the table. "My face hurts too much for that sort of workout, but . . ." Here he did take a chance and pressed her on the arm. "Thanks for the offer." But he said it in such a way that she could take it, if she wished, for a deliberate misunderstanding, an arch wink that they both knew Wong's comment had not been meant as a serious proposal.

Wong, watching him go, sighed and began putting her tools away. Why Miko, she wondered, and not her? Men had never fought over her favor. Yet, here was this *girl* and Corrigan was besotted with her and Ram Bhatterji thought he was her father.

The door slid shut behind the deck officer and Wong stared at it for a long pause before finishing her tasks. She had all but disrobed for him, and the only thing she had proven was what she had always known.

In the corridor outside the clinic, Corrigan found Bhatterji waiting for him. The navigator froze and considered his escape routes, but the engineer only said, "Is everything all right?"

Corrigan touched his cheek, remembered Wong's warning, and grimaced. "Considering," he said.

Bhatterji grunted and turned to go, but he turned back before he left. "She's had hurts enough," he said. "She doesn't need another."

Corrigan knew the engineer did not mean Wong. "Yes. Her father."

"She told you, did she? Then you know how vulnerable she is. More to the point, you know that I know."

"I wouldn't . . ."

But Bhatterji was gone before Corrigan could say what he wouldn't do.

Okoye approached her encounter with Ratline with genuine trepidation. She actually sought him out, which was something she seldom did, for he was not a man that welcomed company. Yet at times Okoye thought that no man of all the souls on board needed seeking out more than did Timothy Ratline. It was a dangerous quest, with no promise of treasure at its end, but Okoye felt pulled to it. There was a vacuum in the heart of the old man, colder and harder than that which enveloped the ship—and what glittered there in the internal night might be a diamond, or it might be ice, and the only way to know for certain was by whether it could ever melt.

Normally the cargo master was easy to locate: just follow the bellowing and at the epicenter would be Mr. Ratline and one of his hapless wranglers. Ratline was a great one for getting the job done and regarded time lost as the ultimate sin. Since the wranglers were always losing bits of it here and there, they came under his caustic penances with distressing frequency.

He was not in his office, where Okoye looked first, nor in the cargo hold, where her unexpected entrance caused much duck and cover on the part of the squeakers. (There were times when she positively sympathized with Mr. Ratline; and she chastised the two as if she had been the Rat himself. Ivar, who had never heard harsh words from the quiet Igbo girl, gaped in astonishment while Twenty-four, though no less surprised, stared back with saucy defiance.)

"They are only like children new-come upon a candy factory," Mr. Grubb had told her one time. "In a while, it will not consume them so much." Okoye thought that the "while" in question might not be in her lifetime and prayed to her grandmother—a fine leopard that lounged on a baobab near Afikpo—that she would not become so much a slave to her flesh when she chose to share that flesh with another, but she thought she heard Grandmother snicker on the bounceback.

She tried Ratline's stateroom next, but he was not there, or was not answering hoigh plates if he was. She touched her communicator and called Rave; but Rave was occupied in setting up that morning's engine calibration burn and had not seen his nominal boss. ". . . and a good thing too," he finished and addressed an endearment to her which Okoye chose to ignore. "Sheep-eyes," the girl muttered to herself, just as if she could see the look that Evermore had given her at the other end of the link. "The boy doesn't know what he wants. Or he knows it too well."

As Okoye logged off, an incoming call informed her, "Mr. Ratline is on the mast." Just that, without so much as a how-do-you-do.

Automatically, Okoye said, "Thank you," but then wondered whom she was thanking, as the only ones who knew she was even looking for the cargo master were the other three wranglers and she had already asked them. "Who is this?"

"Nkieruke Okoye," the voice said.

'Kiru had doubts, as she was not in the habit of calling herself. Just to be certain, she checked and found both souls accounted for. "Well, now," she said, detaching the comm unit from her belt and inspecting it to find the link now dead, "here be a fine mystery. 'Wherefore are these things hid?'" Then, with a gesture of impatience, she restored the unit to its place. "Not two grains of wheat to be found, I think, and not worth the finding in all that chaff."

On her way to the sail prep room, however, she realized that the Voice— for so she now thought of it—had answered her question with faultless exactitude. "Well, now," she said as she paused in the passageway, "here be a fine humor, as well." There was a taste of Gorgas in the humor, though it had not tasted quite like Gorgas.

In the sail prep room, she found Ratline removing his helmet. He turned an eye on her, which he managed without quite turning his entire head. "Why did you call me in? I was busy."

Okoye had not called him in—she hadn't even known where he was until scant moments ago—but astonishment won over puzzlement and even over intent. "You went out alone," she said, which was not what she had come to say, but which seemed to want saying.

Ratline affixed his helmet to the headball and splayed himself in the torso rack as if readying himself for a quartering. "There was work that wanted doing . . ." He grunted and wriggled his way down the torso. "If the sodomite is going to test his engines," his muffled voice said from within, "the shrouds have to be belayed."

"It's not right to EVAde alone. 'Two out, one in.' That's what you always told me."

Ratline emerged from the hard torso like a snake newly shed of its skin. "I know the rules." He turned his back and pulled down his lowers.

"What if something had happened?"

Ratline snorted and positioned the lowers underneath the torso. The whole arrangement resembled a dismembered spaceman. "What could happen?"

"You could have tumbled off the masthead," Okoye said.

At last he turned and looked at her full-on. "Is that what's botherin' you, girl? Kick. It's over with. Miko's sleeping it off. She'll be good as new when she wakes up."

Okoye thought that Miko, even when new, had not had

things so very good. "Miko does not trouble me," she persisted. "You do."

Ratline took on a wary look, as if from across the expanse of the sail prep room Okoye had approached him too closely. "Me? I'm your supervisor. It's my *job* to trouble you." In truth, the man was a little afraid of his assistant. There was something ghost-like about the quiet young girl. She was as dark as a shadow and silence often does for knowing. Perhaps he had heard that Grubb was short of yams.

" 'Care keeps his watch in every old man's eye,' " Okoye quoted, " 'And where care lodges, sleep will never lie.' "

Ratline whipped his tether with sudden rage and even though she was far out of its reach, Okoye pushed back from the lash. "I'm not the one who fell asleep on the job!" Ratline shouted. "*She* is. I'm the one who muffing rescued her when she did! And you too, you stupid git."

"I saw you," Okoye said. "In my rear view. You turned and saw that she had tumbled, and *you turned your back and kept on working on the shroud*! I need to know why." This was the terrible question for whose asking she had sought the cargo master.

"You need a man's dick up you, that's what you need."

"Your words hurt only yourself. They make you smaller, and meaner." It was not entirely true that his words did not hurt. Others might dismiss Ratline's outbursts by telling themselves he did not mean them; but Okoye knew he did. She knew that his anger was more real than the man himself and that it wore his body like a mask. It was a lifelike mask, wrought in the natural style of the Yoruba, so that Ratline took on the appearance of a human being without taking on much else. The wild fancies carved in Igboland would have been more honest.

That mask cracked, just a bit, and for a moment little Timmy Ratline peeked out with a look of such devastation that Okoye wanted to leap across the room and comfort him in her arms. That would be a mistake, she knew. She had seen the man recoil from even casual, accidental touches. "There was time," he whispered. Then, more strongly, "If I'd left the line without dogging it, we would have had all that work to do over! I had to finish that *before* jetting off. Do you understand that, you miserable socket? There was time for both, but they had to be done in proper order."

Okoye understood; and yet did not. There was something cold and empty about a heart that could weigh the inconvenience of rework against a human life, let alone one that could find them of equal weight.

And what if there had been no time for both? Which would he have done?

Breaking and entering bothered Akhaturian considerably, for he was a law-abiding boy at heart, but deCant was stressed and, when stressed, the clone would defy conventions, regulations, and even the very laws of nature. Akhaturian had relieved her of one worry, perhaps her biggest worry; but someone buried beneath a ton of sand, while grateful for the removal of a thousand pounds of it, might be forgiven for still feeling a little pressure. Akhaturian fretted over his companion's growing recklessness, but he bobbed along in her wake, helpless to stop her.

"What I meant," Akhaturian said as deCant studied the hoígh plate, "was that the only way to learn if your genotype matches Satterwaithe's is for Dr. Wong to show you the data." He said this no doubt in the belief that deCant did not already know it and if he only said it again, she would finally remember.

"She'd never show me," deCant whispered.

"Even if you can get inside the clinic . . ." Akhaturian dropped his voice to her same whisper. ". . . you can't get into her files without the password."

"One thing at a time. Once we figure out how to get through the door, we can keep coming back until we figure the password out."

"What if someone sees us?"

"Who? After the fight this morning, and the engine calibration tests all day long, everyone is racked. Nine chances out of ten, no one will come over to this sector of the deck."

Nine chances out of ten? Akhaturian worked the math in his

head. If they came back each night, it was even odds that they would be caught within the week. "What about Dr. Wong?"

DeCant swiveled like a fish and frowned at him. "If you don't want to help me, at least hush up. Or git back to yer room."

"Our room," he said, and he did not move from the spot. The doctor, he consoled himself, would be engaged, as she was most every night, and was hardly likely to leave what she was getting merely to roam darkened corridors and check that her office door was closed. Akhaturian could not imagine that anyone would voluntarily forgo that particular pleasure, even the unlikely likes of Wong and Fife.

Which was why his heart nearly stopped when the door slid open in front of them. DeCant gave a little grunt of puzzled satisfaction, for she thought that she had done something to open it; but Akhaturian saw the slim figure floating in the doorway.

"What exactly do the two of you want?"

"Miko!" said deCant—and Akhaturian breathed a sigh of relief because, while their prowling had not gone undetected, it was not yet clear that they had been caught, for it occurred to him to wonder whether Miko ought to be on the other side of that particular door.

DeCant took Miko's question as a challenge. "That's none of your business."

Miko had been following the two from the peepery ever since she had become aware of their nighttime rambling. She herself had slept for an entire day after her rescue the night before and now found herself at the widest awake when most everyone else was at their narrowest. That the two squeakers wanted something from the doctor's office had been self-evident, but what that something might be concerned her, for a doctor's cabinets are wonderfully diverse.

"Why are *you* in the clinic?" Akhaturian asked the elf, for he had begun to wonder along the selfsame lines.

"Stopping you."

"Just you try," said deCant, pushing past the older girl, for few rights are defended more fiercely than the undeserved.

An elf cannot match a Martian for body mass, nor for muscle

tone; but Miko's age gave her an edge, and the game of hide-and-seek she had played with her would-be killers on Amalthea put her over that edge. When push came to shove—and it did—deCant was hampered by her wish not to hurt the other girl. Miko had no such inhibitions. The two of them bounced and battered, fighting their own inertia as much as each other. A shove (deCant) or a punch (Miko) would send both of them sailing backward. A kick or a swing would set them spinning like overachieving ballerinas. Miko connected with Twenty-four's cheekbone, a lovely smack that put the Martian girl into a pinwheel and, as Miko had the lesser mass, the elf into a counterspin.

"Ow!" deCant cried.

That was enough for Akhaturian, who inserted himself between the two combatants just as they kicked off walls to close and grapple. Twenty-four had prevented him earlier from pushing between Bhatterji and Corrigan—she could imagine no happy outcome to that—but this squabble was not prosecuted with quite the same cold brutality as Bhatterji's whipping of the first officer. Akhaturian cushioned their collision and provided a measure of stability to the fight, since now both girls could hold on to him while they flailed at each other. As these blows landed on Ivar as often as they connected with their target, it produced a certain amount of pain; but as Ivar rather liked the sensation of two girls rubbing against him, on the average he was comfortable.

The swats and kicks came at longer intervals and were delivered with less force as, gradually, Akhaturian's role as buffer began to outweigh his role as anchor. Finally, the two girls glared at each other and pushed away to different corners of the room, as if a bell had rung to end the round.

Akhaturian had come out of the fray with a bloody nose, and deCant's right eye was already discoloring, but Miko had managed affairs so as to avoid any cuts or bruises to herself. That Amalthean was a scrapper. Had she been playing for keeps, she would have landed more—and far more serious—blows. Ask Burr's assassin, if you can. DeCant might not know it, but she was lucky. She had not yet realized the difference between acting tough and being tough.

(Later, some of the crew, noting deCant's black eye, looked askance at Akhaturian; while others, who had marked the bruises on the young Callistan's face, frowned upon the clone. Dr. Wong took the two aside and counseled them on domestic violence, but deCant spoke up and said, "There weren't nothing domestic about it, ma'am. It was wild clean through." When Grubb, nursing romances of subtle revenge, asked "Little Lumber" who gave her the black eye, she told him, "No one *gave* it to me. I had to fight for it." Miko, however, cut through the Martian swagger and set things straight with the others.)

This is the way of it among the squalls of Earth when the winds come from the right quarter and bear moisture with them into the dry air. Clouds boil up and rub against the sky like fur on glass, and they darken and grow tight within themselves until they break, with a snap like parting cable, and the world turns for an instant all black and white. Rain pelts the ground, leaving little craters in the mud where the drops strike. The wind drives it, so it comes from every direction, and there is no turning one's back. Folk pull in their shutters and curse their own delinquency when the rain wriggles in through the chinks in their shingling. They huddle tight around the hearth beneath the drumhead roof and tell stories or (if the hearth be electronic) watch the stories told by others.

None of the three combatants knew of squalls. (A Martian sandstorm is a fearful thing, but it is not the same *sort* of thing.) Okoye could have told them. Indeed, the storms that walk in off the Bight of Benin are giants of their kind. She could have told them too how the smell of the land changes after the rain and how the sunlight may cast things in unexpected colors. The very air has an altered feel to it, all the ions having been discharged, and the breeze strokes the skin in a fresh way. There is, not only in a sense, but in all the senses, a newness to the world.

The three youngsters no more understood the strange new perspective with which they now regarded one another than they understood the brief fury that had preceded it. Miko and Twenty-four barely knew each other—the intersection of their lives had not enough acreage on which to build a quarrel—but if one is spoiling, any fight will do, and a chance encounter is as good as a grudge.

Miko, breathing hard but trying not to show it, remained wary and monkeyed herself between the two intruders and Wong's cabinets. When, instead, deCant kicked off to the computer console, Miko asked, this time with genuine puzzlement, "What do you want in here?"

"I told you," deCant said. "I wanted to look something up in the doctor's files."

She had not actually said that, but she thought she had. Miko, for her part, had fixed so firmly in her mind that deCant's goal had been the drug cabinet that astonishment rendered her for a moment speechless. It is the way of it among humans that assumptions when unquestioned take on the attributes of fact. The Aristotelian schoolmen had found no need to look through the Pisan astronomer's novel contraption. They had reasoned their way to the Moon's pristine state from First Principles and the huffing and puffing of a dead Stagerite. Holding craters and maria impossible, they had no need to look. The Jesuit Clavius did peer through the lens, and it is said that he wept for joy to learn a new thing.

Miko did not weep to learn she had been wrong. There was no weeping in her. Every tear she had ever had had been shed into a pillow in the Burr-Farm warren of Amalthea. She watched deCant boot the doctor's system up and made no move to stop her. Next to what she had suspected, anything else seemed harmless. "What are you looking for?"

"Genotypes," deCant answered curtly while she tried a few of the more obvious passwords.

Now Wong was no paranoid about security, but that didn't mean she neglected her duties when it came to patient confidentiality. Her password consisted of the initial sounds of the first seventeen ideograms of *Li-sau*, a favorite poem of hers by K'ü Yüan, written in the days before First Emperor. No one could guess such a key, nor could she forget it, as she had read *The Ch'u Elegies* shortly after her affair with her professor, and the title "Incurring Misfortune" fell too close to the mark not to leave an indelible mark of its own. DeCant's task was impossible and perhaps she knew that, for she worked at it with the sort of determination that only hopelessness can summon.

Akhaturian, however, felt his partner's answer to be inadequate and told the elf that deCant was trying to find her mother, and told her all about the cloning and how deCant had escaped a life as laboratory waste, and about the death of her fosters in the Syrtis Decompression, and that she now looked to match her own genotype with that of Satterwaithe. Had deCant been any less intent on her work, she might have resented Akhaturian handing out her life so freely.

Had Miko really cried every tear of hers into that long-ago pillow? Perhaps there was a single one left. Not much of a one, because it did not quite reach her eye, but she recognized in the clone's quest her own aching loss of her father, and that made the two of them sisters.

But unexamined assumptions really do look like facts. She had made that mistake once already and was not really entitled to make it twice, at least not in a single night. There could not possibly be the same longing in the two of them. Miko had loss, but deCant had never had possession. Twenty-four's real mother—real in the only sense that mattered—had died in the Decompression; but even deCant understood that she could not search in those ruins. Why she sought an anonymous egg donor in preference to mourning her perished fosters is a mystery that she could not answer. Evan Hand might have, but Hand wasn't in it any more.

But that misplaced sense of comradeship was why Miko did what she did next. Turning to another console she entered a query and received an answer almost before the query was complete. "Here's the access code," she told deCant, handing her a slip of paper with a string of seventeen letters.

DeCant took it, studied it a moment, then with a shrug entered the string. The screen smiled upon her and revealed a wealth of folders and files and links. Akhaturian, watching over her shoulder, whistled. "Where did you get the password from?" he asked Miko.

"My invisible friend sent it to me."

Akhaturian twisted around to look at her. "I used to have an invisible friend too," he said, "but he never actually sent me any e-mail."

"Hey," said Miko brightly. "It's who you know."

Nkieruke Okoye had worked with Miko on the sail project long enough that she marked the change to the Amalthean on their first encounter after the fight in Wong's office. Miko's aura had shifted just the smallest bit from the infrared, at which frequency she presented a heat source, to just inside the red, which had the effect of making her more visible—as well as less blistering. Okoye regarded this change as a hopeful sign. A shift toward the blue end of the spectrum meant the object was approaching.

"I have a new friend," Miko explained. Okoye took the elf's new friend to be Twenty-four and guessed from the latter's darkened eye the origin of the friendship, for there are those who respect pushback more than they do submission. Okoye was surprised, however, and a little hurt, as if she had lost something. Miko had but a small soul. The more who shared it, the less each received.

"Get away with you, girl," she told herself in her mother's voice—unless it was this time her mother speaking for herself. "It may that the girl's soul has grown. Plenty enough there to go around."

Corrigan had not yet come to an understanding of his hard-won solitude. It had crept upon him like a thief and had stolen from him the companionship he had thought he had. He arranged his toiletries with the same precision as always, but knew a vague discontent that The Lotus Jewel came no more by to disarrange them. Being a creature of habit, he had incorporated that very disarray (and its ritual rectification) into his daily routine. "I have done something to offend her," he told himself, but he had quite forgotten what that something was. That she might take to heart a routine criticism did not occur to him, nor that his criticism had been anything but routine.

Miko puzzled him even more. He had turned around and there she was, and had turned away and she had gone. She had by degrees won his affection and then, at the very cusp when that affection might have become something else, had vanished. He could make no sense of the entire episode. There was a fixity to his worldview, and Miko's behavior was not fixed.

And so he consigned both women to the bin of the inexplicable. The Eternally Mysterious Female. Had he gone to either one, he might have regained a friendship and more, perhaps even a bit of understanding. But he was not the sort of man to pursue another; which is too bad, as Miko in particular required pursuit. A youth spent on the run had led to a sort of elusiveness in her life. She wouldn't stand still for anything.

"That Corrigan," The Lotus Jewel described him to her friend, Bhatterji, "is a hard and a cruel man. There's a mean streak to him. He hurts."

"That Corrigan," Miko told herself (for she was not the sort to entrust such confidences to another), "is an uncaring man. He has gone off to his own private Europa. He hurts."

"That Corrigan" was neither of these men, although he was a little of both. It was hesitation, not rejection, that had kept him from Miko's bed; and he had cut The Lotus Jewel because he had been angry with himself. If he was cruel, he was at least uncaringly cruel, which may be a better thing than the more deliberate sort. Or may be not.

The Balk Line

What is it about a day long known and long expected that its advent occasions such surprise? As the ship approached the balk line, sudden new tasks were discovered, squeezed from the vacuum like so many pips from an orange. Bhatterji learned that a focusing ring had been misaligned; Corrigan noted a yaw in the ship's dead-ahead. Even deCant found it needful to shift a few more cargo containers. Of all the crew, only Ratline found nothing overlooked, but only because he overlooked nothing.

A calendar resembles a piston. Racing toward a deadline, it compresses a volatile mixture into a brief explosion. The crew of *The River of Stars* could feel that awful compression—kilopascal piling upon kilopascal—and each reacted in his or her own way. Gorgas quibbled and put the deck on watch-and-watch. Satterwaithe grew critical (well, *more* critical) and Corrigan tried to do everything himself. Brief scuffles and fights and arguments broke out overtop other, longer-established quarrels, much as waves heap over a vast, deep ocean. Even Nkieruke Okoye found herself snappish with young Ivar.

Grubb, tears in his eyes, slit the throat of a young sheep, thinking that a feast upon real mutton would relax the crew and ease the pressure—a sort of pascal lamb—but it did not serve, and the crew rushed in and ate the peace meal piecemeal and rushed out the same way and barely savored the taste.

Corrigan's inclination to do everything himself stood him in good stead, as The Lotus Jewel was chronically late to the watch and he actually did have to do everything himself. Her tardiness seemed to him a moral failing and he wondered why he had never noticed it before.

It would be pleasant to imagine Gorgas as a crusty old Cupid and to suppose that he had paired the sysop with the first officer on the blue watch with the notion that they could become reconciled by their proximity; or that he thought to separate The Lotus Jewel (who more and more took personally the criticisms that came her way) from Satterwaithe (who more and more chose to send them). In truth, there were only three possible pairings and, once he had determined on watch-and-watch, it did not take Gorgas long to work out the benefits and drawbacks of each.

He had decided on the particular rotation for two reasons. First, that the captain and the first officer ought properly to alternate the command; and second, that one man and one woman on each watch struck him as aesthetically more pleasing than the contrary.

When, an hour late, The Lotus Jewel finally arrived on deck, Corrigan gazed pointedly at the clock but, as the sysop was not looking at him, she did not get the point. She inserted herself into her usual clipchair at the comm station, attempting (as if it were possible, there being only the two of them on deck) to avoid his notice, and reviewed her board with an air of having been there all along. Corrigan narrowed his good eye as he studied her affected nonchalance.

He did not ask her why she was late, which was just as well, for The Lotus Jewel had spent the time selecting her clothing and applying her makeup and Corrigan would have had a grave difficulty in processing that. The sysop had carefully considered a series of otherwise indistinguishable coveralls pulled from her dog closet. Aside from the old uniform that she wore on special occasions and a few pieces she wore on shore leave, there was little to choose among them in fashion or color or cut; and that very lack of variety fed her dissatisfaction, as she was a woman who treasured diversity.

The coveralls possessed more variety in grime and odor and wrinkle than they did in style, since standing the dog watch and helping Corrigan with the sails and diagnosing the malf in the AI had left little time over the prior weeks for such personal chores as laundry. She had finally selected (with much frowning and ejaculations of discontent) what she judged to be the freshest outfit of the lot. Corrigan had, in times gone by, told her that she looked wonderful regardless what clothing she wore, but that comment, though well-meant, was essentially ignorant.

Makeup and accessories provided more possibilities. She finally settled on a bright lip and nail color (to lighten the overall *drabness* of her ensemble) and on cuff and ankle bands of complementary 'stroidal gold. A torc with a ram's head buckle and a pair of beadwork slippers competed the ensemble. The torc and the slippers were gifts from Corrigan, though she had not chosen them for that reason—and a good thing, for Corrigan never noticed.

Not that it mattered. The Lotus Jewel regarded her own body from the same perspective that Enver Koch had once regarded the ship—as the raw material of art; and if more critics enjoyed her oeuvre than had enjoyed Koch's it was because her medium was more accessible. It seemed to her that the crew had grown less cheerful during the past two weeks—even Ram and young Evermore had waxed dour—and she had felt that gray, clammy hand seizing hold of herself. "I have some pride in my appearance," she had told her appearance before leaving finally for her duty. "More than that slattern, Miko, at any rate."

The Lotus Jewel pulled the virtch hat over her head and fit the electrodes to the encephalic interfaces in her skull, cutting off the world of the bridge (one feature of which was 'Abd al-Aziz Corrigan) and dropping her into the immensity of the Simulated Void. She *became* Ship, or if not Ship, something larger and more important than a sysop on an ancient tramp. She could forget what and where and who she was, and she could coast through the Void and brush the stars. Whether this flight was more real than those the doctor took on the wings of her mist would be an interesting point to consider.

Corrigan, from curiosity, had once privately donned the cap, and experienced nothing more than a confusing kaleidoscope of sensations. One really needed training to use it, let alone use it well. Grubb, who alone among the crew might have matched The Lotus Jewel under the cap, had demurred when she had offered him the chance. He had heard stories about sysops strangely possessed by cybernetic demons, and had no desire to allow a neural net to initiate, through feedback, spontaneous activities inside his own, personal brain.

"Eaton," the sysop whispered. "Of course. <Ship>."

<Waiting, Ms. Jewel.>

The Lotus Jewel sighed in exasperation, but did not correct the AI's form of address. <Message. To: Eaton Grubb—>

<Mr. Grubb is asleep. Is an alarm required?>

<No, for goodness' sake! Place the message in his mail box.>

And what on earth was she doing, responding to AI feedback like that? It was not proper syntax, at all. And *where* had Ship picked up the response menu it was running? It seemed to have found an unpurged cache left over from Coltraine's day, when Ship had used key-word-and-context engines to simulate polite subservience. Taking a deep breath, The Lotus Jewel focused her thoughts.

<Erase. Restart. Voicemail Message. To: Eaton Grubb. Text: Eaton, could you be a dear and launder my coveralls for me? My clothing is beginning to smell like yesterday's fish. You're a love. End text. Place in mail box. Send.>

Satisfied, and even a little pleased with herself at this little exercise in problem-solving, The Lotus Jewel resumed her sensing, gently fingering the pinprick asteroids splayed before her and the duller, knobby pip of Jupiter just off the dead ahead. It did not occur to her that Grubb had no more time for laundry than she did. Like others in the crew, she thought of him as "the cook" and fancied that he had free time. But Grubb was responsible for the life-support systems, from the lithium scrubbers to the bio-screens. He ought to have had a mate and not simply the part-time help of Ratline's wranglers. His work had the invisibility of routine.

I don't mind, he told Okoye later, while he washed The Lotus Jewel's clothing. *Considering the odor, it actually falls within my Enumerated Duties of pollution control.* Really, he was as much a love-slave as Akhaturian and purchased more cheaply, for a single down payment had been sufficient to secure his labor for life. Grubb wanted to possess The Lotus Jewel again more than he wanted anything, but he knew that repetition would dull the wonder of that mad encounter in the Starview Room; and the one thing he did not desire was to exchange madness for routine. So he treasured the ache of his abstinence and in the end grew to love it.

Outboard on the rim, Bhatterji examined the hoops of the Number Two anode sphere through his helmet's infrared filter and saw that the residual heat was mottled and uneven, which was very odd indeed, as the focus had tested within tolerances on the initial calibration, two days earlier. "There is still some deflection," he told his two assistants. "Lock out the injectors."

Evermore, who was inside the ship, said, "*Locked*," and Bhatterji chose to believe him.

Approaching the engine, the engineer pulled a Muller wrench from his tool holster. Then, positioning his boots in the stirrups at the base of the east-side focusing ring, he fastened it to the garnet bolt and pulled.

The bolt gave and the ring turned infinitesimally around its diameter. One degree, Bhatterji remembered, for each full revolution of the wrench. He looked once more at the anode through the IR screen, gauged from the heat pattern how bad the deflection had been, then gave the bolt a second turn before he fastened it down. "We'll do another burst," he told Evermore. The sharp clang he felt through his boot soles told him that Evermore had opened the injector ports, and Bhatterji added dryly, "Once I am behind the blast shield." He wondered if Evermore *hungered* for a moment's misunderstanding, if he longed to consume Bhatterji in the fire.

The engineer followed his tether back to safety behind the *barrera*, where Miko awaited with the portable instrument array. This was jacked into the special sensor ports on the sheltered side of the *barrera*. In theory, Miko could have done this from inside, but Gorgas had ordered strict observance of the two-out/one-in rule. Miko and Evermore had survived only because others had been outside with them and Gorgas would not take the chance on a solo EV Asion.

Bhatterji crouched with his back to the thick wall and set his visor to UV opaque. This was the part he hated most—to be out on the hull during an acceleration. "I've zeroed the monitors," Miko told him and Bhatterji bowed his helmet to show he had heard. She couldn't see his face through the opaquing. Bhatterji tried for nonchalance. "Evermore? Go ahead."

"*Calibration burst in three*," the apprentice told the ship at large. "*In two, in one, and firing . . .*"

God took a snapshot of the universe. The brief flash of the engine cast long, fleeting shadows across the forward hull and a white actinic glare that Bhatterji could sense even through the opaquing and his eyelids. He sometimes wondered what the engines looked like when they spoke. A light whiter than white. A light that engulfed the visible spectrum the way the ocean engulfed a raindrop. No eye could comprehend that sight. There were too many colors, and not all of them had names.

"*Counterburst,*" warned Evermore from the safety of the ship. Number Four flared briefly below the far horizon, and the ship, having canted slightly from the test burst, eased itself back into its former attitude. Bhatterji wondered whether the boy yearned to deviate from procedure and play with this wild, gargantuan toy. Bhatterji cleared his visor and glanced at his mate, who was already hunched over her array of sensors. "Miko?"

"Everything nominal." She uploaded the pattern of the plume onto the display unit and Bhatterji pretended to study the faux-color image and the gauss levels and the plasma velocity, but in fact, he simply admired the terrible beauty of the image. It was a picture-book star, with bright arms stabbing out to the cardinal points: a real star formed from the real fusing of real particles. Bhatterji sometimes fancied that it might possess real, though infinitesimal, planets. It was a domesticated star, one raised in captivity and confined to a cage like a bird taught to sing for the amusement of its captors. But, oh, how it sang!

The engineer allowed a broad and relaxed smile to cross his features. An unexpected problem—something had misaligned the rings—but a couple of turns on the garnet bolt was all she needed. Everything nominal and *still* five hours before they hit the balk line. Bhatterji had always known there would be plenty of time to finish the job.

Relaxing against the *barrera,* his gaze was drawn to the aerogel mast. Bhatterji had seen that faerie pole often enough that it had become a part of the landscape, a blasted, winter-worn tree, stripped by time as surely as the oaks of Satterwaithe's frigid homeland. Now it was hung about with a bewildering and intricate cat's cradle. Cables ran from the top of the mast to a circular hoop, and from there other lines led to the motors on the rim and to openings into the sail locker. Seen straight-on, the rigging was radially symmetric, yet from Bhatterji's angle it appeared crazed, as if the sky beyond were crackled pottery, and his mind read it as a farrago of crisses and crosses.

"It looks wrong," he complained. "All those ropes and things."

"Shrouds," Miko said. She knew without turning from her instruments the source of his discontent.

"Shrouds . . . That's what they wrap dead bodies in, isn't it? I suppose a dead technology isn't much different. And that hoop and those poles sticking out to the sides . . ."

"The crosstree," Miko told him, "and spars."

". . . it's all too complicated. Give me the straightforward simplicity of a Farnsworth cage. Complexity is a sign of poor design. True beauty is always unaffected."

Noticing motion near the tip of the mast, Bhatterji magnified his visor screen and saw an open bucket within which a suited figure moved. "Somebody's up there," he said in surprise. He had not known that any-one else was Outside and for a weird and wild instant thought that here was a sailor who had been forgotten long ago when the ship had been converted.

"In the crow's nest?" said Miko. "That must be Ratline. He's dressing the mast."

Bhatterji snorted. "It looked better naked." His fancy had been nearly correct, then, for if anyone qualified as a forgotten sailor, it was the ancient cargo master.

"Another few millies of braking from the sail can't hurt," Miko pointed out.

Miko's defense of sailing struck Bhatterji as wrong. It was one thing for fossils like Satterwaithe and Ratline to brood on the Good Old Days, but Miko was young, and an *engineer*. "Of course, it hurts," he said. "As long as those . . . 'shrouds' are in place, I can't reverse polarity on the Farnsworths to fire a retrograde burn. The plume would vaporize half the ropes."

"The 'rigging'."

"All right, the 'rigging'!" He spoke sharply because jargon irritated him. "So I'll have to flip the ship because I can't redirect the plume. Evermore?"

"Aye?"

"Give me a ten-count, four-square in five."

"Four square, aye."

Miko said, "But we've finished calibration, haven't we?"

"Sure, but let Rave have some fun. He wants to play."

"Ten second full burst in three," Evermore told the ship. *"In two, in one, and firing . . . Ten, and nine . . ."*

And Bhatterji's horizon was rimmed by white fire, as if furious suns were dawning at all four quarters of the world. The ship became once more a living thing, throbbing and pulsing. Bhatterji listened though the vibrations for any sign of discord and, feeling none, smiled as if a long-absent lover had returned.

"Do I need to tweak anything?" he asked Miko, confident that he did not. He had felt the balance. He had entertained doubts about Number Two, and had thought perhaps that he might need to feather Number Four to compensate, but everything was perfect. "You don't need those instruments," he told his mate who had turned once more to her bank of gauges. "Weren't you watching Antares?" He pointed to Scorpio. "If the engines weren't in balance, the ship would have canted and the mast would have swung one way or another. That mast does have some uses after all. Why, the ship herself is one vast analog gauge, if you know how to read her."

Miko thought more precision might be called for. It seemed to her sometimes that Bhatterji made his decisions on little more than whimsy.

Gorgas, having belted himself into the captain's chair, surveyed his domain and thought that, for the first time since the captaincy had been forced upon him, it really was his domain. Today, he would drive the ship; he would direct her toward her destination.

The Lotus Jewel sat capped at her station and Corrigan, at navigation. Because these were at opposite sides of the bridge, the two sat with their backs to each other.

"Engines?" said Gorgas.

"Engines ready," said Evermore, who sat at the engine room repeater to Corrigan's right. Bhatterji and his mate waited below in the engineering control room, suited up in case anything went wrong. Well, Miko was suited. Bhatterji didn't think anything would go wrong—though his eye did stray intermittently to the telltales for Engine Number Two.

"Sails?" said Gorgas. And what an odd thing for him to say. In all his years plying the Middle System he had never called for the sailing master.

Yet the master's station itself was vacant; its long-dead console blank. Instead, Corrigan answered from the navigation chair. "Ready for deployment. Sailing master and shroudmaster are standing by in the loft." It was a bald-faced lie, and Corrigan knew it. Ratline was in the loft, and he had Okoye with him; but Satterwaithe had retired to her rooms.

"A sail *and* the engines," Bigelow Fife said to the others gathered in the common room for the midday meal. "I don't believe it has ever been tried. Certainly, I've never heard of it being done." He watched the sweeper on the wall clock as it approached the mark.

"It gives us an edge," Grubb assured him and set a platter of fowl matter on the table before him. "We'll get near five millies with the engines—maybe a touch less, because Bhatterji may want to baby the two he fixed—and another millie from the sails."

"Why three sails?" said Wong.

"It's what we call a trefoil suit," Grubb said, with the air of being an old hoopster. "The three vanes let the sailing master play with the size and shape of the magnetic field."

"I think it's doobers," said Akhaturian, as he sliced a piece of fowl matter off for deCant and another for himself. He added a brush of spice-paste to his own slab.

Fife said, "I understand that you assisted with the, uh, preparations, Mr. Grubb?"

"Aye, that I did. You might say, I held everything together." He did not elaborate on that—it was better to appear mysterious—but he had convinced The Lotus Jewel to remain with the project even after her blowup with Corrigan and to lazarus the sail-handling software from long-dormant archives. If he had not quite ensured that everything held together, he had at least ensured that everything did not fall apart.

That Grubb may have played a key role did not reassure the passenger. "Are you, then, after being a sailor?" he said with some uneasiness. "I hadn't known."

"Oh, no. How do you like your fowl, Mr. Fife? Is it seasoned to your taste? The genotype of this particular clone was modified to incorporate certain spices directly in the carnic." (Akhaturian, sucking mightily on his water bottle, had already learned that.) "No, I was never a sailor," Grubb continued, "but I know all the old songs."

"The songs . . ." said Fife, choking like Akhaturian, though for different reasons.

"He's a terrific singer," said the least wrangler in a strained but enthusiastic voice. "Aren't you, Mr. Grubb."

Wong, who by now could read the body of her lover, suggested that Grubb had always worked under the direct supervision of one of the experienced sailors.

"Oh, that I did," Grubb agreed, though it made his role sound less important. "Corrigan, mostly. He did the inside work, while Ratline handled the outside."

"It's terribly romantic," said Wong. "Flying under sail."

Now Fife was not even romantic about his loves but, being the sort of man who requires a web of cause and effect, he was practiced in the art of constructing facts—and what else is romance but the belief that facts have structure? He was touched, a little, by the antic notion of sails being resurrected from the urnfield of history; but, ever practical, he asked, "Will not sails and engines together be slowing us rather *too* much?"

Akhaturian nodded. "We'll achieve the Jovian datum by late three-December, instead of ten-December. Of course," he added thoughtfully, "we'll still be fifty-five million klicks from Jupiter when we do. . . ." He traded a secret wink with Grubb. "We can walk from there."

"Walk!" Fife said, and Wong lowered her plate and stared at the least wrangler.

"Oh, as for that," and Grubb waved a negligent hand while at the same time leaning forward. It was a trick of his whenever he had something in the gossiping trade to pass along. "I heard that the captain and the first officer have a plan. Once they've slowed down sufficient, they'll shut off the cages and take the ship into port—*under full sail.*"

"Oh, how grand!" said Wong. And DeCant and Akhaturian both applauded.

"Into Jupiter Roads?" said Fife with more than a note of doubt.

"Engines, one-quarter power," said Gorgas. "Navigation, maintain heading."

"One-quarter power, aye," said Evermore; then, to Ship, "Four-square, one-four."

"Injectors opened," Ship reported. "In three, in two, in one."

The ship shrugged and down below, Miko hunched over the indicators, verifying feed rates, plume temperatures and velocities, especially on the two rebuilds. Bhatterji, gripping a monkey bar behind Miko, affected indifference. "All nominal," Miko announced after several minutes of thrust had gone by with no evidence of blow-holes or temperature rungs; and Bhatterji, just the tiniest degree, relaxed.

"Uniform acceleration," Ship told the bridge. "One-point-two milligee."

"Increase power to one-half," Gorgas said and, when this too proved satisfactory, he took the ship by stages to full. Throughout this procedure, the bridge was filled with a brief but intense clatter as small items, drifting about during the long days of freefing, fell deckward once again.

This peculiar precipitation in fact filled the entire ship. The old *Rivers* were long accustomed to it, but Fife was wont to transit on tauter ships and the liners took great pride in preventing such a ruckus. Even so, it was not the noise that bothered him so much as the stylus that fell like a hunter's spear directly into his slice of fowl matter. He used a word of great and unpleasant surprise to express himself before removing it.

"It's because the solar wind is so much faster even than transit velocities," Akhaturian said in answer to an interrupted question of Fife's. "So a sail can always harvest momentum from the wind, no matter how fast the ship is already going."

"Ivar's going to be a famous ship-handler some day," Twenty-four deCant volunteered.

Fife raised an eyebrow, not because he didn't believe the boast—regarding the future he tried to keep an open mind—but because he didn't see the path from the comment to the accomplishment. "The first officer is instructing you in sail-handling? That seems an inefficient use of your class time."

"Well, it's mostly general navigation, of course," the Least Wrangler responded. "It doesn't really matter to a navigator whether the acceleration comes from cage or sail."

Wong asked why, if sails gave an added boost, all ships were not hybrid ships.

"Because it's cheaper to add another cage." Fife did not know fusion, but he did know cost-benefit ratios, and he had dealt with enough wayward asteroids in his time. "Cage-handling is simpler and you don't need to carry two berths with two different skill sets."

"There was another factor," Grubb offered. "Have you ever heard *The Ballad of Sveyn Kim-Yung*?" Securing shaken heads in response, he explained. "It tells of an old sailor who wants to pass on his skills to an apprentice, but there's no one who wants the position. That's what happened. No one wanted to learn an obsolete technology. The schools stopped teaching it and eventually all its practitioners retired."

"All except Ratline and Satterwaithe," said Twenty-four.

"And Corrigan," said Ivar, defending, as he thought, his instructor.

Grubb nodded sagely. "Aye, and a few others scattered here and there. Corrigan's one of the youngest of the lot, and he's pushing forty from the wrong side."

"So it has always been in history," Fife replied, moving a piece of carnic to his lips. "New ways come, old ways go. There is always great talk about how much better—'more human,' you often hear—the old technology was, but you'll notice that no one ever goes back. We don't chip flint arrowheads any more, either."

———

When all engines were pulsing nicely in that four-square marching beat that Gorgas knew so well, he turned to Corrigan. "Well, Number One, are you ready?" Rightfully, it should be the sailing master who directed from the bridge, but Gorgas understood Satterwaithe's decision to work directly at the sail-handling stations. That equipment had not been used in twenty years. It was best that the two more experienced sailors be on the spot.

Corrigan nodded and Gorgas waited and when a moment more had gone by, the captain said, "What order do I give?"

"Raise the mains'l," Corrigan told him.

Gorgas nodded in irritation. He ought to have guessed that much. "Very well. Do it."

"Mains'l, aye. Ship, start the bunghole, and mains'l aloft."

"Clarification requested," Ship responded and, listening down in engineering, Bhatterji snickered. Miko frowned and whispered into her own hushmike.

"Clarification acknowledged," Ship announced to Corrigan's intake of breath (which he let out in puzzled fashion, as he had clarified nothing). "Primary sail deployment port opened. Main sail loop feeding through primary winches."

"Very well," said Corrigan and turned to Gorgas. "Mains'l away," he said.

Gorgas nodded. "And now what?"

"The control shrouds run up through the way-grommet. Then we kick amps."

"And then?"

"The hoop stress from the current causes the loop to circularize. That will take, oh, two hours for a loop that size, even with the flux pumps. That gives the shroudmaster time to attach the working shrouds at the compass points."

"Two hours?" said Gorgas (and again, below, Bhatterji snickered).

"The sail is sixty-four kilometers wide," Corrigan said, knowing that he sounded defensive. "It takes time to inflate it. Attitude control will be tricky until it stiffens."

Gorgas could not keep a quizzical look from his countenance, and even The Lotus Jewel forgot her vow and looked directly at Corrigan. She could not remember any such boring interval from the morphies she had watched. It had always been "sails up and catch the wind." The grand moment that Corrigan had imagined came to seem, even to him, somewhat comic. Yet even a useless gesture is better than no gesture at all.

And down below Bhatterji roared. "No wonder that technology went into the dustbin."

"Ms. Satterwaithe?"

The acting second officer and reserve sailing master looked up from the distance into which she had been gazing and away from the faded memories and dreams that lingered there. Alone in her own quarters as she was, she was too far from the loft to hear the drum rolls as the lines fed out or the hum of the compressors as they metered coolant to the cladding; yet somehow she did hear them. Perhaps she would always hear them. "Who is that?"

"Ship. Message for your information. The mains'l is away."

Satterwaithe nodded slowly. "Yes. I understand. Thank Mr. Gorgas for me."

"Clarification requested."

"Gorgas. Thank the acting captain for the message."

An uncharacteristic and irritating pause intervened before Ship responded, "Acknowledged."

Alone once more—if she had ever been unalone in her life—Eugenie Satterwaithe raised her gnarled hands to her face.

The Ghost

When Gorgas opened his cabin door that evening to find the wranglers and the engineer's mate en masse and weirdly costumed and crying out "Trick or Treat!" he could not for the life of him decide whether they had gone mad or he had.

It was all Akhaturian's idea, of course. If he could convince his berth to help him scrape varnish, it was child's play to get them to roam the ship and collect sweets. He had thought of it a few days before and at first it had been only a notion to help Twenty-four decompress and to celebrate the torch-lighting. But Okoye had overheard them planning and Akhaturian invited her to join them. Once Evermore saw that Okoye would participate, he joined in too, as if he were doing everyone a big favor, and indeed, as if it had been his idea all along. Okoye, in turn, went off and convinced Miko, who had never heard of any such a thing as Hallowe'en.

There is little in the way of costuming available on a tramp freighter, but a few odds and ends and a bit of imagination would do. It was, as Evermore commented, a little like connecting the dots. Wear enough dots and the costume would fill itself in.

Nkieruke Okoye portrayed a witch, though it could be argued that this was hardly a disguise for her. Yet she was not a witch as Europeans—even European witches—might imagine. She wore no pointed hat, placed no broom handle between her legs. However, by finding a bin-full of fibrop connector cables and fixing them to a belt, she did manage to approximate a grass skirt. With considerable patience, she braided her hair into *a certain pattern* that her mother had once taught her, and found enough colors among the greases and oils in the maintenance bins to decorate her face and arms and legs in the proper *uli* symbols. *Uli bu ife umunwanji ne de naru*, as folks said. She hesitated on the cusp between modesty and authenticity before deciding to wear the regalia overtop of a black singlet.

"There," she told the apparition in the mirror, "you look just like the witchy-woman that people go to for advice."

"Do not be so silly, child," her mother answered her. "When did you last see anyone dress in such a way? Only at the folk festivals, I am thinking. How many women paint *uli* any more? Besides, you have gotten one of the cornrows wrong. And who ever heard of a witch-woman wearing a singlet?"

"Well," Okoye said, ensuring that the zipper was fully up, "I don't want anyone to see them yet."

"Anyone, or a certain one?"

"Mother!"

"'Kiru?" said Rave Evermore, rapping on her hoígh plate, "are you ready?"

"Not yet," 'Kiru told him and told her reflection and told the voice she sometimes heard in the stillness. "Not quite yet."

Evermore's garb was "high concept." In a few odd hours, he had fabricated a genuine gizz. The gizmo had lights that blinked and wheels that went round and noises that came out of it from time to time. It didn't actually *do* anything, but then it didn't have to. It was kick just to watch it run. Evermore whitened his hair with flour stolen from Grubb's stores, wore an old machinist's apron, and carried the gizz in his left hand like a holy icon. When Akhaturian asked him what he was supposed to be, he said he was Thomas Edison, the Great Inventor.

He was waiting outside Okoye's stateroom when the Igbo girl emerged and for a moment his heart stopped because her aspect was so frightening. Sharpened teeth and a face like a demon and . . . In the next moment, his heart rebooted like Bhatterji's engines because, what with the bare arms and legs and the black singlet, he thought that she was naked. Okoye would not have lacked for a broomstick, had she actually wanted one.

"You look wonderful," he said and tried to make it sound like he admired the realism of her costume; but Okoye heard his voice true and had to doubt his senses because she had made herself as hideous as she knew how.

"Where are the little girls?" she asked in a cackling voice, for the witchy-women used to snatch the young girls at midnight and take them into the forest to teach them the secrets of womanhood. It was supposed to have been a frightening experience, but Okoye had learned such things in a bland schoolroom in a far more pedestrian manner, and from a teacher who made it all sound simply awful, and so she often romanticized the old ways.

The only little girl available for abduction by witches was Twenty-four deCant, who in most regards could no longer be called "little," nor was there much she could be taught in a forest clearing that she did not already know. Prudence, perhaps.

She was the only one of the group who had transed her gender
and had made a few odds and ends of scrap metal do for a suit
of armor and a pole for a sort of lance. A buckler made of board
stock and covered with metallic foil bore the motto *Defend the
Right!* Evermore asked her if that meant she would not defend
left-handers, which earned him a tongue, so Okoye told him
that deCant would be *his* champion because he had fashioned
the Wonderful Gizz and deCant had sworn to defend the
Wright. This earned *her* a tongue too; so Okoye and Evermore
really did have something in common.

A decent respect for symmetry demanded that if Twenty-four
deCant were a knight in shining armor, Ivar Akhaturian ought
to be a damsel in distress; and indeed there would be some
merit to such a guise. His particular distress might not be entirely evident, but deCant really had saved him from it. Recall
that Akhaturian's own mother had, in effect, sold him to a band
of gypsies. That might trouble even the most filial of minds.
deCant had snatched him from the arms of that dilemma by
taking him in her own. If his future was now not exactly un-
troubled, at least the troubles were different.

However, symmetry wasn't in it. The Least Wrangler had not
the time or materials to make for himself a proper gown and so
contented himself with a winding sheet and whitened hair and a
faux beard. He called himself Socrates, and never mind that it
was the Romans and not the Greeks who wore the toga. He did
not know very much about Socrates, save that he was a famous
philosopher. Had he known of the hemlock, he might have
scrounged up a sequined gown after all.

Only Mikoyan Hidei of all that motley crew disdained a costume, wearing in addition to her duty coveralls only a wry
smile, as if secretly amused by it all. She really was too old for
childhood antics, she suggested with her mien, although her
meaning was less clear—for she did not spurn any treat offered
her. She tagged along, as she said, only to ensure that the others
did not get into trouble. It was Miko, for example, who suggested that they inspect the fruit they received from Ratline for
hidden razor blades.

She was utterly wrong about Ratline, but a guard's duty is to be wary, not insightful. While Ratline was easily the scariest sight encountered that evening—'Kiru not excluded—he regarded the youngsters with a special affection and after they had departed for other prey, the old man, behind closed doors, wept for their innocence.

Satterwaithe was not the weeping sort, but the Hallowe'eners amused her and she was a hard one to amuse. She herself was once wont to go a-roaming on that fey night, and she derived an hour or so of wistful reminiscence from the visit, so it may be that, at this one stop, the youngsters gave more than they received.

Still, it was Grubb who was the target of opportunity, and the group made sure to end their odyssey in his demesne, where they received sweetballs and sherbets and nectars of various and wonderful sorts. Even Miko abandoned her aloofness after a few treats. Grubb dug out his concertina and sang songs and Miko—perhaps conditioned by the sweets—even joined in with the others on a chorus or two.

Wong and Fife came, and later The Lotus Jewel and Bhatterji, as well, for children often come in different sizes. The sysop knew a number of stories and Grubb turned the lights down so she could tell them. There was the Hairy Hand of Hunterdon County, and the Jersey Devil, and the Phantom Cyclist of Route 31, and to each of them the assembly gave delighted shivers.

Grubb gave a discordant squeeze on his concertina and in grave tones announced that none of them ghosts and such were any cause for worry because they all dwelt many megaklicks sunward of *The River of Stars*. "But there's one, he ain't all that far off, and that's Ugo Terrell."

"You go to *where*?" asked Evermore, for he would play even with ghosts.

But Grubb's concertina screeched most abominably, so that the wranglers all sat suddenly back, and The Lotus Jewel as well. Bhatterji, who lounged behind the circle with his arms folded, said, "Are you certain you want to draw Ugo's attention, Grubb?"

"Well, it ain't me he's rightly pissed at, is it? Though I don't think he likes people making fun of his name." He nodded toward Evermore, but did not look at him. The boy laughed and leaned to the witch woman beside him to whisper, "He thinks he can get me going." But Okoye only said to Grubb, "Did you know the man?"

The chief shook his head. "No one knew him, not even those who did. He come on board this vessel a stranger and he left her the same way. There remain aboard this very ship only two who ever met him and you know the two I mean." Grubb began pumping a strange tune on his instrument, one that wandered about a minor key without ever quite finding it, nor did it rightly have a tempo, for it would hasten or slow with Grubb's words. "Who can say what may drive a man mad?" the chief intoned. "There are toxins and chemicals, yes; but these only simulate genuine madness, for true derangement must well up from deep within. There must be something loose inside your own heart, something that plays and wobbles until it breaks through all the barriers. This is what shredded Kurt John Jaeger, and I said 'shredded' for he chewed his own soul to tatters.

"He was a sailing master and one of the best, for only the best can ship on *The River of Stars*. He had guided *Gullwing* through the Io Tube. He had taken *Empress of Cathay* down to kiss the lips of the sun during the Solar Max expedition of Forty-Six. But what can even the best do, when they are aboard only for show? Had *The River* never raised sail, he might have borne it and, if not, he might have gone alone when he went. But the webfeeds demanded a show. All those ounces to *Save the Riv'!*" (A shout of triumph here.) "The old tramp had to don her gauds and caper one last time. They say that is what killed his heart: to perform for mere spectacle what had once been his life. Yet even *that* he might have borne, but for the mockery of Ugo Terrell." When Grubb paused to drink a fruit bomb, the name seemed to linger in the empty air. It was almost, Okoye thought, that she heard it whispered afar off, but that was only a trick of the acoustics. Yet The Lotus Jewel too twisted to look over her shoulder with a small frown on her face. Bhatterji and Fife wore grim smiles, though for two very different reasons.

"Not that Terrell intended any mockery," Grubb continued,

"and what mockery can be crueler than that? For an engineer, for a Farnsworth man, he was much interested in sails and this was his misfortune, for his interest was 'historical,' as another man may find interest in ancient ruins. All those questions Terrell asked of the sailing master—they were all in the past tense, and that is the cruelest tense of all, for there is no hope in it. It began to seem to the inner Jaeger that the questions were *meant* to hurt, that it was done with malice aforethought.

"*The River* was not a happy ship in those days. She'd been but recently converted and those old hands that remained did not care for the new engines. Terrell—and his three mates and his five flame monkeys—were not welcomed, not at all."

("I wish I had the berth he had," Bhatterji muttered aside to The Lotus Jewel, "the engines would have been back on line in days." And the sysop whispered back, "The ship had more income in those days.")

"Shortly after *The Riv'* left Panic Town, Jaeger was in the mess hall—that very mess hall that we now use—entertaining the older hands with his tales. Terrell was sitting a little apart at another table listening with some of the younger crew while Jaeger told of the Great Flare of '73 when he was master on *Cloudray*. He had gotten to the point where the CME, the coronal-mass-ejecta, had hit the magsail and induced such a current transient that the hobie quenched and the wire whiffed.

"And Terrell laughed." (Grubb's concertina wheezed with sick amusement.)

"That was really not the proper thing to do, because Jaeger and his mates done heroes' work that day, running out a new sail and inflating it during the storm of the century. Terrell had laughed from surprise, not derision, for he had not realized that a hoop could fail in just that way; but Jaeger froze up on hearing it. He stood and left the mess with never another word nor a look back. That night, he came to the engineer, and Terrell, unmindful of the mortal offense he had given, let the man in. But Jaeger had come to him with a smile and a reefing knife and—some say—he did not come alone.

"There was no struggle, the coroner later concluded. That may mean that Terrell offered himself as a holocaust for the sins of the Farnsworth, as some sailors claimed, or it may only mean that he was taken by surprise. Or it may mean that others held him fast while Jaeger found his heart.

"Ever since then, ol' Ugo, he roams the ship at night, a-looking for revenge. Jaeger joined him the next day. He went out the airlock from remorse, they say—only, maybe *something* drove him to it. Maybe something, or someone, turned that lock handle for him. And now . . ." Grubb looked from each to each one around him. "And now, *the sails have been raised once more!*" And he garnished that with a harsh chord from his instrument, which startled the squeakers considerably and even The Lotus Jewel blanched.

Grubb received the applause of silence. They looked at one another with unease, especially those who had been acting as sailors for the past weeks. Okoye considered the multitude of shadows with which the ship was drenched and wondered if there might not be one more than there ought to be. Perhaps Satterwaithe's effort to raise the sail had not been entirely wise. When the silence finally broke, it was Bhatterji who broke it.

"Well," he said, "at least I'm not on his list, though I can think of two on board that old Ugo might harrass."

Grubb shrugged. "Genie was the captain, and the Board said when they stripped her ring that she ought to have known what was brewing among her officers. And Ratline was at that mess table with Jaeger and the other sailors. But who is to say that Ugo has *not* tormented them—and this ship—all these years? She surely has been a bad-luck ship."

Okoye thought that Ratline was a very tormented man, indeed, although she had always ascribed that to hauntings within rather than hauntings without. "I had not heard," she said softly, "that someone held the poor man's arms."

"Well, that was never proven, 'Kiru," Grubb admitted, though he always hated to ruin a good tale with the need for evidence. It spoiled the atmospherics. "But if you're thinking about our own two sailors, forget it. Genie was asleep—it happened on third watch and the second officer found her in her quarters with the news—and Ratline . . . Well, Ratline had an alibi, so the Board ruled. All the sailors at that table had alibis."

"And they all died," Fife intoned *contra basso*, "one by one over the years . . ." He threw his head back and barked a laugh. "Classic," he said. "Meets all the parameters: a ghastly crime, an unexplained death, a lingering curse. Excellent. I thank you, Mr. Grubb."

The chief worked his squeezer and his chords migrated slowly into a major key. "I wouldn't thank me, if I were you. If Ugo thinks you're laughing at him . . . Well, it might go hard."

It seemed to deCant—who had artfully thrown her arms around Ivar in mock terror during the narrative—that Fife was the sort to deconstruct such stories even when told by his own children. Rather than hear the story, he would dismember it, discuss each piece with horrifying sincerity, and explain its role and antecedents. She could imagine the light of mischief in his children's eyes snuffed on the instant and it saddened her, as death always did.

Mock terror was one thing, but genuine tragedy bordered on the morbid. Grubb decided that matters had waxed too serious and began to liven things up with more cheerful music.

*"My siggy and I made merry-o
Way down in Port Rosario . . ."*

Evermore presented himself to Okoye with a bow just short of courtly and, seeing that the others had also linked hands and that the whole was to be a joint venture, the Igbo girl accepted—though Rave squeezed her hand rather more firmly than she thought proper. Dancing in milly required greater facility than any but The Lotus Jewel possessed, but a chain dance was dancing only by courtesy, and less skill was needed than enthusiasm. It was more of a mad recombinant of a conga line, crack-the-whip, and follow-the-leader, albeit with a touch of rhythmic coordination. Tap and bounce and spin and twist, the chain snaked around the greenhouse gallery, among the plants, around the carniculture vats while the narrator and his significant other found all sorts of unlikely adventure in and around Old Mars.

*"My love and I made up and down
In every nook in Panic Town."*

The line took flight and *leapt* into the air, coasting in a gentle parabola to a touchdown on the far side of the room. Flowers gave up their perfumes and the thrum-thrum of the circulating fans, lending a ground to Grubb's concertina, played breezes across their faces and the waving faerie stalks. The promenade ended with the dancers entangled in a fair approximation of a DNA molecule before it broke up into laughing nucleotides— although some dancers retained a handful of covalent bonds.

Okoye saw no harm in letting Evermore retain her hand. She was charged, and it was not a negative charge. She even sang a little as the wranglers skeltered afterward along the ring corridor toward their quarters. "I am a saucy sailor," she sang, "and I fly the waves of night." There was more to the song, but Evermore heard only the saucy part and wondered if the celebration had diluted her resolve. When they reached the radial corridor to the spin-hall, where they went their separate ways, he pressed his luck and offered a kiss to her cheek.

It seemed as if the entire universe held its breath. Even the continual background whirr of the Caplan pumps seemed to pause, and the giggles and whispers of the junior wranglers fell still. Motion froze, as if Miko and Twenty-four and Ivar had been put into stasis. It was a quantum sort of moment. There were two things that could happen, two universes that might be born.

Those two universes made quite a splash in Okoye's inner pool, so much so that the normally quiet girl was startled into something even deeper than silence by what sloshed over. *Why you be running so fast, girl*? her mother asked her within that silence, and Okoye had no very good answer.

And so she offered Evermore her cheek and felt the warmth of his lips upon it. And because he must steady himself in milly his hand rested on her waist. There was more pressure in him than Bhatterji found in his spherical anodes a picosecond before the burst. Okoye respected that pressure and feared it and—again like Bhatterji before his engines—felt also the seductive lure of its release.

Perhaps for this reason, to show that no special meaning ought to attach to the kiss, or perhaps to prove to those two uppity universes that a third one was possible, she then turned to the others and offered each of them a kiss as well. Ivar and Twenty-four took theirs as from a big sister, but Miko, with a sly grin, returned hers full on Okoye's lips, which startled Okoye greatly and terrified Evermore beyond measure.

Afterwards, those who remained remembered that night as the last unaffectedly happy one aboard that unhappy ship, for even Ratline's private, tear-wracked sobs counted for joy in his ancient heart.

The Re-Berth

Every six hours, Gorgas and Satterwaithe spelled Corrigan and The Lotus Jewel on the deck and painted rocks and guided the ship through the tsunami. As this led to sleep in no better than four-hour snatches, ravel'd sleeves were never quite fully knit up. In particular, Corrigan found himself more and more at odds with Gorgas, who insisted on maintaining the grand secant bearing in the face of the tsunami. "Straight on 'till morning, Number One," he said with that grating joviality of his when he turned the watch over. "Keep Jupiter centered in the dead-ahead."

"We ought to beat to starward," Corrigan insisted, and not for the first time.

"Nonsense," said Gorgas. "No need for such a maneuver. Once we close on Jupiter, we will be in the Forbidden Zone, which is always swept free of objects."

"Our short-range radar," Corrigan insisted, "has been picking up a great deal of rubble. At a hundred-twenty kiss . . ."

"Yes," said Gorgas. "That is exactly the point. The track radar will pick out the larger objects at a distance, the search radars will warn us of the rubble closer by, and the armoring on the hull will protect us from the gravel. Oh, did you know? Earth will have herself a new meteor shower in a few years." Gorgas smiled, as if he had said something useful.

Corrigan stared at him and hesitated before asking, "What?"

"Our tsunami. Ship has projected its path. It is slowing into its apogee and will drop en masse to the Inner System."

"That is not exactly our immediate concern," Corrigan said through his teeth. He looked to Satterwaithe for support, but the sailing master gave no joy on the bounceback. She would have ordered dead-ahead, herself, had she held the command. Most shiphandlers in the Trojan Gulf would have done the same, and for the same reasons. The shortest distance really is a straight line and there is too much empty space to worry much about the parts that aren't. It was Corrigan's fretting that was out of tune.

"But if . . ." Corrigan said.

"Yes, Number One," said Gorgas, reaching the end of his patience. " '*But if*' the odds do play out, then you may dodge. Poisson statistics suggest a close approach to two objects, plus or minus three. The radars will give you sufficient warning— you do have a capable sysop to advise you—and, in extremis, you may juke the ship. I have so noted in the log."

Poisson statistics suggested no such thing. Two plus or minus three meant there was a finite probability of encountering minus-one asteroid. It irritated Corrigan that Gorgas had used not the Exact Poisson, but the Normal Approximation.

The first officer thought that taking such risks was most unlike the captain. However, he had confused indecisiveness with risk aversion, and it was the decision and not the risk that was uncharacteristic. Gorgas had in his life taken enormous risks and was quite aware of the odds in this case—more so than Corrigan in fact, as he had actually calculated them—and while the knowledge had induced in him a perceptible weight gain from sweetballs and such, he saw no other way to avoid a catastrophic loss than by risking one. Corrigan did not yet appreciate the effect that an old, tattered shoulder strap might have on a man who had contemplated it one day too many.

For Gorgas had determined not to repeat certain past mistakes. "The singular thing," he had told Marta two days before, "is to bring the ship in with her cargo intact. It has become more than a matter of profit, it has become a matter of pride. The ship is first and last and, as this will be her last transit, it must be done in a first-class manner." Mikoyan Hidei, who was listening from the steward's peepery, understood the sentiment, and admired the captain for it, as we always admire those who speak in consonance to our own heart. What she did not understand was why, in a convulsive gesture, Gorgas then ripped the old shoulder strap from its place on his dresser mirror and threw it into the waste duct.

She only knew that it was a subtly different man who turned away from the glass, and she began to look at that man thereafter with greater reflection.

Corrigan, as always during his watch, bobbed about the control room like so much flotsam. He bounced from comm station to plotting tank to engine room repeater to short-range radars to the telescopic view of Jupiter. He checked the heading and velocity, the trim and balance, the laser paints and bounceback, much as a man approaching a rendezvous with his lover will compulsively and repeatedly check his grooming.

He drove because he saw before him the bright, black gleam of failure, which is altogether a strange sort of thing to drive toward. Every stumble, every error, he knew to be the seed of ultimate failure and he treasured each such event with a glum satisfaction.

The Lotus Jewel had donned her cap immediately upon entering and it seemed to Corrigan that she had fallen into a pocket universe. She always did when she sussed the ship, but she also did it when she did not want to talk to Corrigan. He wondered now whether she might not be napping. "Ship," he said.

"Waiting, Mr. Corrigan."

"Ask the sysop if she can find a soft spot in the tsunami we are overtaking."

"Clarification. 'Soft spot.' A region in which the perceived pushback from radar sensory analogs is less."

"Affirmed." Corrigan was amused that Ship had suggested

the clarification itself, which it did not often do. Though forbidden by Gorgas to turn the ship, he saw no reason not to look for regions into which he *might* turn it.

"The definition is found in *The Suss Book of The Desert Rose*."

Corrigan did not know what to say to that, as he was wary of being sucked into a simulated conversation—at least with a machine. Ship's replies often sounded responsive, but they were merely constructed by grammar engines from key word and context-sensitive searches. "I suppose so," he allowed.

"Hypothesis. A soft spot is a region in which a safe path may be more readily found."

Corrigan was saved from the need to comment on *that* observation because The Lotus Jewel, having gotten the pass-along of his original request, had touched the sky, and now removed her cap to answer him.

"I've displayed the density in the plotting tank," she said, tossing hair that was not there. "The whole sky feels mushy because we can't ping the Fixed Point, so everything out there feels like little cotton balls; but the yellow region seems to have the fewest known bodies."

Corrigan grunted. "Which means if we do turn in that direction, we'll hit an *unknown* body . . ." He wasn't sure if he believed that, but he took a certain satisfaction in saying it.

"You're the navigator," The Lotus Jewel said, as if she had explained something.

Corrigan looked up from the tank and struggled to parse the sysop's sentence as anything other than a statement of fact. It had *sounded* like something more, and yet he failed to see the hidden part beneath the waters. Finally, he gave it up and lapsed once more into silent contemplation.

As nearly as Corrigan could tell, the distribution of the asteroids in the tsunami was random, which meant, as Gorgas had calculated from the density, that a straight, Newtonian path would likely pass close to two of them. Yet, given a Pareto distribution of body sizes, for every large object the laser probes saw, there could be dozens of smaller objects that would not appear until they came in range of the sweep radar. Gorgas might contemplate that prospect with equanimity, but Corrigan did not.

The Lotus Jewel, meanwhile, turned her attention to the imaging. "How, in all of empty space, did we manage to aim our ship so directly at Stranger's Reef?"

Now, she was not entirely precise about this. The body they had called Stranger's Reef was as near the dead-ahead as did not matter, but it did not lie directly on it and, as Satterwaithe had noted, it was not the Reef, after all. Still, the measurement uncertainty, the drift caused by the wind on their radiation belt, the perturbation caused by the initial engine malf, and the inexorable, Newtonian linearity of their path during the long coast, blurred whimsically by Bhatterji's calibration burns and tugged this way by Jupiter and that way by the sun, had combined into a generalized anxiety and feeling of helplessness, so that the crew no more knew their own True Position than they did that of the ship or of the objects among which they passed. And so, among other astonishments, Satterwaithe had grown passive and Gorgas had made a decision.

Corrigan shrugged and said, "Everything will be as Allah wills."

"Is your Allah a board-certified navigator?"

Corrigan frowned at the question, which seemed to him to touch on blasphemy, although for a wild moment he thought it was the Board of Pilot-Examiners that had been blasphemed. "Don't talk foolishness."

The Lotus Jewel clenched her hands and it looked to Corrigan as if she meant to pound the console into rubble. "You keep calling me that! I'm not a fool!"

"I can only go by the data." That, from a man known to worship the Fact.

What Corrigan did not understand was that his soi-disant lover felt trapped in some mad version of Noir, unable to escape the surreal adjustments of a lunatic game master, unable even to guess what the right move might be. Hand's death. The engine and transmitter damage. The material shortages. Near-fatal tumbles. There must be, she felt, a simple explanation for it all.

Normally, she took life as she found it, which is to say in a random and chaotic fashion; but she had begun to suspect that down in the bone there must be order and purpose. Those who, like Fife, had troubleshot a great many problems knew from hard experience that causes were particular and manifold; but being unpracticed at that art, The Lotus Jewel believed thoughtlessly in the singular and universal.

In the dim-red dungeon of the engine control room, the gatling fire of the Farnsworth cages could be felt as a quick-step march beat, as if God were using the ship for a snare drum. The two closer engines were the stronger beats and when they fired one could discern the other sounds that clustered around the primary implosion. The hum of the CoRE magnets—or rather, of the generators that powered them; the clack of the inserters; the less-easily described sound—like gravel on a tin roof—made by the Number One boron feed pump just outside the control room.

On panels, displays gleamed, dials swung, numbers blinked. Streaming data blurred on one screen and another—useless displays to anyone but Ship, except that the roiling, hypnotic *form* of the stream, so much like a great waterfall, was itself a sort of information. The deck shivered.

"We're pushing those cages awful hard," Miko told the engineer. "Right up to the edge."

Bhatterji, who had lived most of his life on the edge, did not see the problem. "There's margin," he assured the girl. "Coax the cages a little and they'll give you more than you thought they had in them."

"They aren't alive, Ram. You can't sweet-talk an anode sphere—"

"Have you ever tried it?"

"—and you don't *have* to do it, 'cause we got the sail for a cushion."

"Sailing," said Bhatterji with heavy irony, "is labor-intensive. They'll need a berth of more than an old man and a girl to handle that much sail. Mark my words. Nothing good will come of it. Meanwhile . . ." He looked at his two assistants and shook his head, but he wasted no time now in wishing for himself a larger or a more experienced berth. "Miko, you and I will alternate in ten-hour watches. I realize that this is a heavy responsibility and that you are not entirely ready for it. Your mate's rating is temporary and awaits your board examinations. Nevertheless . . ."

Miko wanted to bounce across the room for joy, but her innate gravitas kept her in place. The gratitude she felt at Bhatterji's vote of confidence very nearly overwhelmed her desire to be revenged on him. "Sure, Mr. Bhatterji. I'm willing."

"What about me?" Evermore asked. "I can stand a watch too."

But Bhatterji shook his head. "Miko went through an intensive apprenticeship on the transit from Amalthea to Achilles. You're a good machinist. I've seldom seen better at your age. But we need watchstanders now, not machinists." And besides, although he did not say this, Evermore was far too prone to improvisation. If a crisis did arise, he would try to handle it himself and Bhatterji saw no good end to that. "When we need a flame monkey to replenish the boron canisters—"

"Oh, thanks a whole lot."

Bhatterji reared up at the derision. "Listen, boy," he said with an impaling finger directed at Evermore's heart, "*I know who you are!*" Then, more softly, "You're *me*, two decades back; and I know how raw and green that was."

"I can do it."

"No, you can not. You rely on your intuition too much."

"I know the engines," Evermore said.

"It's not enough to *know* them," Bhatterji told him. "You've got to *feel* them. Is 'extuition' a word? It ought to be. You've got to hear their song. Listen . . ." And in the silence he demanded was the distant throbbing cadence of the engines as they fused the boron and the hydrogen ions into small explosions and jetted the plasma before them. "You've got to feel that rhythm, so you'll know when it's wrong. You've got to see the colors of the plumes. . . ." And he rapped his knuckles against the display screen where the sensors played the false-color images. ". . . so you'll know when the tint is not quite right. If you wish to be an engineer, the engines must be *here*," a slap to his belly, "and not just *here*." A finger tapped his head. "You need seasoning."

"Yah. And I'm sure you'd love to season me."

Bhatterji went flat. "You've been aboard two years. You could have been my apprentice any time, if that's what you wanted, and you'd be mate-first by now. So, don't complain now that you're not qualified."

"Up y—" Evermore stopped himself. "Up in the sail locker, they might not be so fussy."

"Up in the sail locker," Bhatterji said, "they can't afford to be fussy. It's a dead end craft. It's not for the likes of you."

"What do you care?"

"I do care!" he said. Then, after a moment while the two of them stared one at the other and Miko remained quietly by the wall, he added gruffly, "Clear it with Corrigan, then."

"What?"

"Reberthing. Corrigan keeps the assignment list. Tell him it has my okay. Right now, Sails needs more hands and Engineering doesn't."

Bhatterji had begun to turn away when Evermore said, "You're sending me to Sails?" He did not understand the devastation that seized him.

The engineer turned back and looked at Evermore then at the control-room door as if puzzled by the distance remaining between the two. "If I ever need another crack machinist, Rave, I'd call you before I'd call anyone else on this ship. And before you say anything stupid, it has nothing to do with your beauty and everything to do with your skill." The lie was a half-lie only. It really was the skill that mattered, but the boy's beauty had more than nothing to do with it.

Miko spent her first watch checking each of the engines in turn, noting plume temperature, plasma velocity, injector registration, boron depletion rate, field strength of the magnetic insulation, and a dozen other telltales and monitors—until Bhatterji, who had lingered to observe, took her in hand.

"There are a hundred things to monitor in a Farnsworth cage," he told her, "but only twenty of them matter. Ship does all the grunt work."

"That's good," Miko said, "because Ship and me, we're friends."

Bhatterji chuckled, not taking the comment literally. "Ship will monitor the sensor data and warn you of any statistically significant deviations. What *you* focus on is whether those deviations have *practical* significance. Look for trends and correlations. Look for events outside the bounds of the engine sensors. Ship has been taught to recognize low probability events. Data far out in the tails of their expected distributions. But what does one chance in a million mean when millions of events are measured and logged? There are bound to be false alarms—it's what we call the alpha risk. You'll have to decide which are the false alarms and which are the true article. Ship has learned some search-and-decide algorithms over the years, but there will always be that one new thing that Ship cannot handle."

"Which are the twenty that matter?"

"The what?"

"You said only twenty of the indicators mattered. Which ones are they?"

Bhatterji sighed. He sometimes despaired of Miko ever truly grasping the point: That it wasn't ever any one thing, but always the combinations of many things. "It varies, depending on time and circumstance."

Miko found that answer less than specific. "Can you make me a checklist?"

"A checklist is limiting. Dialogue with the engines ought to be open-ended."

"You mean I need to 'feel the engines' more."

"Well, yes."

"Then why not chase me out like you chased out Rave?"

Bhatterji had not seen that coming and missed the beat on his reply. "Because you have some experience," he said after a moment's silence. "He has almost none."

"You could have kept him as cadet and let him stand watch with you. That's how you worked me on the Achilles transit."

Bhatterji grunted—and Miko, unsatisfied with the detail of this explanation, persisted. "I thought you liked having him around, because . . . Well . . ."

"Because he's pretty to look at?"

"Yah."

The engineer completed a checklist, thumbed it, and handed her the comp-pad. "Here, use this, but don't let it stop you from checking other things. Ship has a whole library of fault trees to guide you through the diagnostics. Maybe he's not so pretty any more."

It took her a moment to resolve the pronoun. When she did, Miko stared at him. "You still love him."

"Miko, I still love *you*."

That startled the mate into silence. It was a sentence she had not heard in eleven years. That there might be love, she understood as a proposition. That there might be more than one sort, she had not considered.

"Yes, of course, I still love him," Bhatterji continued. "You can't turn off feelings the way you can a boron feed. But he doesn't love me, *and that matters!*" One time, he remembered, one time, on Outerhab-by-Titan, he had not let it matter and had learned, hard, how much it should have. Two men were dead, and one had not deserved it. "I sent Evermore as far from me as I could and still keep him inside the ship. He wanted that distance more than he wanted to stand watch down here. Do you really think he and I could have spent ten hours together without . . ." He paused and turned inward. "Well, it might not have ended well. You got your watch, Miko," he added, "and Rave got far away from me. So both of you got what you wanted. I'm the only one denied."

Evermore made good his threat, if threat it was, and proceeded to the Long Room, which he entered in time to hear Nkieruke Okoye get her ass chewed out by Ratline. While a chewing out by Ratline was no uncommon thing, to find Okoye at the business end of the teeth was. More often than not since Evermore had signed the ship's Articles, it was Okoye who handled things. He could not imagine that she had been derelict in her duties.

But Okoye's transgression was the very opposite of dereliction. "The catliner jammed . . ." he heard her say, but Ratline cut her off with a gesture like a slashing knife.

"I know. Ship woke me up. I was on my way."

". . . and the mizzen warped. I went out to free the shroud, that was all. I checked the manual."

"Not everything is in the muffing manual! A malf like that isn't critical enough to risk a lone EVAsion, not when backup is on the way. . . ." He finally noticed Evermore standing in the doorway and turned on him. "And what do *you* want?"

"Why are you yelling at her?" Evermore didn't know he was going to say that until he did, but he had felt an odd quixotic impulse to rush to 'Kiru's defense.

"Because it's my job, Evermore! I don't have so many wranglers that I can afford to lose one." He turned back to the First Wrangler. "Even you, Okoye! The next time there's a malf up in the shrouds, you do what you can here in the Long Room, but you wait on me before we climb the tree. Understood?"

"But you go out alone—"

"That's just old Moth Ratline. There's not enough left of me to worry over its loss. But not you, Okoye. Not you." He turned again to Evermore. "Now, tell me that you came up here for some reason other than to google your girl."

"I'm not his girl," Okoye said.

Ratline shrugged without turning. "Not my fault. Well, Evermore?"

"Uh, I've been reberthed. I'm in Sails now."

Ratline seemed puzzled for a moment. He stood in that curious, half-floating pose that spacers take under milly, with his mouth partly open and his brow lowered as if uncertain of the words he had heard. In the silence, Evermore realized that it was not silence at all. A strange hum, something like a bagpipe, something like a distant chorus, pervaded the room. It was the tension on the cables, he was to learn later, transmitting the thrust from the sail loops to the body of the ship. It was a pleasant sound, though a little ominous too. The cords were dissonant and seemed to hunt for resolution.

"You're joining the Sail berth," Ratline said at last. "Whose idea was that?"

"Mine," said Evermore.

"You'll apprentice on sails?" Ratline was not in denial, but he was at least in doubt.

"Uh, yah. I guess so."

Ratline's eyes narrowed, which made him look suspicious, but it was only because he smiled and Evermore did not know what Ratline's smile looked like. "A 'prentice," the shroudmaster whispered. "A *'prentice . . .*" But he must have realized that too much of himself was showing, for he tightened up and added with a leer, "And it gets you out of Bhatterji's clutches." He thought this a sly cut at the engineer and did not realize that, although the engineer would have expressed it differently, it actually had been Bhatterji's reason. "I'll enter you in the Sail Log as shroudsman-apprentice. Wrangling is a good foundation for what a shroudsman needs to learn, anyway. Oh, it'll take a year or two, but you'll be top-jack when I'm through with you."

Startled, Evermore glanced at Okoye, whose eyes rested upon Ratline—until a clatter on the east side of the Long Room caused her to leap gazelle-like in the direction of a jammed machine. Evermore watched her disengage the machine, reset something that he could not see, and reengage it. The unresolved chord seemed to have changed in pitch. Evermore smiled and thumbed the comp-pad that Ratline handed him. A year or two of training? Evermore did not believe *The Riv'* would still be flying a year from now, let alone flying under sail. And he certainly did not intend to spend the rest of his life as a sailor.

Having entertained some notion of long, lonely watches spent with Okoye, Evermore found himself spending those watches with Ratline instead, an altogether less appealing prospect. Ratline worked him hard too, taking him up the mast and out the crosstrees, and causing him to study trefoil rigging. After his first shift, Evermore scored seventy on a simulation that the cargo master gave him, which, under the circumstances, was not too bad.

"It was really you I came to be with," Evermore told Okoye later, when the First Wrangler returned to take the next watch. "The Rat isn't near as pretty as you are."

"The Rat isn't as pretty as Dr. Wong," she answered, "so that is no great approbation."

Fife had come to think of the cutter as "his" escape craft; so when he and the doctor entered the boat on the night of 3 November and found Mikoyan Hidei under the control panel busy with a snap-welder, his first emotion was one of offended propriety. He had even blurted out, "What are you doing in here?" before he recollected that he was not, in fact, the proprietor.

The slender girl with the old-young eyes slid out from under the panel and studied her surprise visitors with her own mixture of vexations. She did not return the salutation, as she knew—or thought she did—what these two intended "doing in here." There were only three concerns she had. One was that a passenger ought not demand accountings from a crewman. The second was that she was nominally replenishing the depleted boron canisters, and did not want word of her whereabouts to reach Bhatterji. The third was what she had come here to do; but since that was nearly finished, she slid back under the panel without a word and inserted the boards she had made, snap-welding them to the contacts.

"Just a little engineering work," she said when she emerged once more and began gathering up her tools. Whistling a tune she had learned from Okoye, she refastened the access panel and, because she had a certain malicious streak to her, she took her good old time doing it. She assumed that Fife was anxious to get to it—which he was, though "it" was not what Miko thought. "Well," she said, fastening the dog pockets on her tool belt and giving the two a calculated leer, "have fun." And she left them in possession of the field.

"She thinks we're ridiculous," Wong said after Miko had left. "She's laughing at us." Franszziska Wong might live in a dream world half the time, but there was nothing wrong with her perceptiveness. The thought made her angry and she chased through the umbilical into the rim-hall to reprimand the girl only to find it empty in both directions. "That child is fast," she told herself, "to vanish so quickly." She was peering at the bends in the corridor, but Miko had vanished tangentially, not circumferentially and was now watching from the peepery.

When Wong returned to the cutter's control room, she saw

that Fife had removed the panel that Miko had just refastened and had crawled under it, as if he were searching for the vanished girl himself in the last place he had seen her. He reemerged with a puzzled look on his face. "I feared she might have been after gutting the panel," he explained, "for some need of Bhatterji's, but she has only added memory boards."

"Why?" asked Wong.

"To give the cutter more memory," he said. It was only an absentee comment, for Fife was considering the possibilities and had only restated the proposition, replacing the concrete act with its evident purpose; but the offhandedness of the insult wounded the doctor.

Fife concluded that the ship's crew must have finally realized that they might need to abandon ship. He was gratified that someone had begun to prepare for that eventuality, but he was also a little miffed. He had thought of the plan first and resented its co-option.

He was wrong, however, in one major respect. The ship's *crew* had not yet realized the possible need.

Miko stroked the fur of the Cat-With-No-Name and wondered why the doctor and the passenger were taking so long inside. "You'd think she'd want to get it over with as quickly as possible," she said, for Miko found no pleasure in contemplating the Lunatic as lover and could not imagine that Wong did, either. He was terribly attractive, and she meant that in a most literal sense. There was something terrible about those ever-seeking eyes of his. They seemed to have swooped on the doctor and carried her away. He was not right for her—Miko could see that.

"I wish there was some way for me to tell her," she told the cat. Unlike Fife, Miko knew that the truth could hurt dreadfully, and was often better served by shading it. Shading truth made it appear three-dimensional. "Best way to remove a patch is with one quick yank," she said. "Try pulling it off slow and the hurt just lasts longer. Maybe I should . . . What do you think, Cat? Maybe it's that Fife I should work on."

Cat did not respond, but studied Miko with regal eyes before—enduring one final scratch—she quick-footed into the darkness of the serviceways. She was a slippery sort of feline—sometimes here, sometimes there—and far more aloof than Queen Tamar. Perhaps for this reason, Miko found the creature more companionable. She did not think Akhaturian's name—Anush Abar—quite right and had given the cat several names of her own already, but none of them had stuck yet. She never did think to name the creature "Miko."

Her belt comm beeped and Ship reminded her that she had been absent from the control room long enough; and so Miko too quick-footed into the dark to finish her rounds of the boron canisters.

"The bridge is yours, Number One," Gorgas said. "Steady as she goes. The radars tell us that we shall miss Stranger's Reef by a comfortable margin. You will pass it by on this watch."

The smugness in the man's voice irritated Corrigan, who responded with a grunt and a petulant comment that the body was certainly not the fabled Reef.

Gorgas raised his brows, as if the thought had never occurred to him. "Of course, of course. The Reef is part of a ballistic triplet and there is no sign of the other two. Yet, I have been thinking of it for so long as Stranger's Reef that it seems odd to call it something else now. We ought to name it, though. Only fair. Perhaps a contest among the crew?"

Corrigan, exasperated, turned to Satterwaithe. "And what of the atoll you mentioned? There may be other, smaller bodies about."

"Nothing that we have raised on the radars," Satterwaithe said as she relinquished the comm station to The Lotus Jewel. "The sails remain parachute to the wind. There was some trouble with the mizzen during the night, but Sails put it right."

Corrigan nodded and thumbed the log. "Very well. I relieve you."

"I wish I could say that I was relieved," Gorgas told Satterwaithe as they crossed the bridgeway to the B-ring on their way to take a late snack together. "Mr. Corrigan is grown somewhat fixated on catastrophe, and the difficulty with seeking is that one often finds, eh, Number Two? What, ho!"

Satterwaithe had been paying no more attention to Gorgas than she usually did, but his last cry brought her up short, and a good thing too, as she had almost trampled the two junior wranglers, who stood patiently by the entry to the bridgeway. The two were easy stepped upon, being both of them shorter than the general run of crew. "What are you doing up here?" she demanded.

"Mr. Corrigan is training me in navigation," said Akhaturian.

"Is he," said Gorgas with some amusement. "Well, see to it that he doesn't train you in apprehension," and he chuckled, though Akhaturian did not get the joke.

Neither did Satterwaithe. "I'm surprised our second officer can spare the time from his other concerns," she said, which, while equivalent to Gorgas's comment, was just as opaque to the wrangler. The pun was unwitting and unintentional. Gorgas too was briefly confused by her remark, until he realized that when the sailing master had said "second officer" she had meant Corrigan. In fact, he realized that he had yet to hear the woman use any of their brevet ranks. *Some people*, he reflected, *never give up*. It occurred to him that this might at times be a virtue as well as a nuisance.

"The training is . . ." Akhaturian said. "Mr. Corrigan said. I mean, I—" He stuttered to a halt, fearful that his classes had been suspended and Gorgas would send him away.

"It's part of his contract," deCant said, springing to his defense.

"Oh, indeed, indeed," Gorgas answered, recalling old days as a youngster on *Pierre Delacroix*. "Best way to learn the craft. Manuals can only take you so far. Why, I was only a little older than you when I went for midshipman." Satterwaithe turned away so that Gorgas would not see her eyes roll. She herself had come up on a much harder orbit—for ballistic ships, OTVs, magnostats, sails, and Farnsworths had each required mastery of utterly different practices. Perhaps this is why she thought herself five times the ship-handler that Gorgas was.

Akhaturian scooted past the two onto the bridgeway and Satterwaithe, turning once more to resume her interrupted journey to the mess, nearly stepped on Twenty-four deCant, who had lingered athwart her path. The two squeakers were so often seen together that it was hard to see them separately. Like monatomic oxygen, it did not seem quite the proper thing. Satterwaithe glared down at the third wrangler, as if it were the girl's fault for being underfoot. "Are you learning navigation too? Or is The Lotus Jewel training you?" (This was *not* a kindly question, as she regarded The Lotus' Jewel's purported avocation a likely tutorial for Twenty-four deCant's parturient condition.)

"No, ma'am," deCant responded, unaware of the subtext, but quite aware of the unkindliness. "I'm just a poor, simpleminded cargo-wrangler, me. 'Druther not have any more holes in my head than I can help. I come up here to see *you*, ma'am."

"To see me . . ."

DeCant glanced at the waiting Gorgas and suggested, "In private?"

Satterwaithe could not imagine any possible discussion between her and the young girl that would require privacy. In fact, she could not imagine any topic that would even require a discussion. "Yes, well, make it brief."

Gorgas took his leave. "We'll take that snack at another time, then, Number Two," he said, delighting in part in reminding her of her rank. "I have some calculations I want to get back to." (That being the other part of his delight.)

When they were alone in the ring corridor, Satterwaithe said to deCant, "Right, then. Is this 'private' enough?"

It was not the setting that Twenty-four had imagined when she had imagined this meeting, but she knew from the woman's frosty tones that it was the best she would get. So she unzipped her thigh pocket and with eager innocence handed the sailing master two sheets of hard copy that she had with Miko's help printed out of Dr. Wong's files.

Puzzled, Satterwaithe examined them; but this examination did not resolve the puzzle, as she had no idea what the two diagrams represented. At first, she thought they were GC spectra— 'stroidal assays of vaporized regolith such as survey ships often took. But the resemblance was superficial and, as she recalled from her rock-pounding days in *The Black Diamond*, would have evidenced astonishingly heterodox compositions for bodies in the Thule region. "What am I looking at?" she said brusquely, for she had no time for mysteries. In another five hours, she would be on watch again.

"Genotypes," said deCant. "Notice anything?"

Satterwaithe looked at them again. "No." Her voice had lowered into the danger zone, but deCant had no ear for it.

"They're the same."

Satterwaithe frowned and laid one spectrum over top of the other and held them to the overhead light to align them. "The lines don't match up at all."

"That's 'cause one of the record's been altered. You see, if'n you shift this group of lines *this* direction, and open up the spacing between these lines *here*—"

Satterwaithe looked at the girl, then shoved the hard copies back at her—"I've no time for this rubbish"—and began to turn away.

"But . . . but, Ms. Satterwaithe! You're my ma!"

The older woman had taken two steps, but the words stopped her as cold as if one of the airtight doors had been suddenly raised across her path. She turned on the wrangler like a falcon on a mouse. "What's that you said?"

"I'm a clone, and a clone has the same DNA as her mother. This spectrum is mine, and this other one is yours and so you see—"

And Satterwaithe reached down and gripped deCant by the front of her coveralls. "Listen close, girl, for I shall say this only once. First, those two gene spectra do *not* match. Second, *never* in my life have I gone to an 'egghead.' And third, if you persist in this nonsense, I *will* investigate how you obtained possession of my personal genetic data." And with that she released the girl, who staggered back pole-axed.

"But . . ."

"I will *not* say it twice." And Satterwaithe turned so abruptly that, in the milligee acceleration frame, she spun lightly into the air and had vanished around the bend in the B-ring before her feet touched the deck again. DeCant, watching her go, said, "but . . ." once again and wiped at her eyes with her sleeve. She did not move from that spot or say anything further for several minutes. When she could trust her hands once more, she smoothed out the two sheets that had become wrinkled in her grip, folded them, and tucked them again into the thigh pocket of her coveralls.

Later, at dinner, when Akhaturian had caught up with her, he asked her how it had gone.

"She's in denial," deCant said, meaning the sailing officer.

The Reef

Ivar Akhaturian was assigned to every other blue watch when, as he perceived it, he assisted Corrigan in the piloting of the ship. The lad was sharp, Corrigan told Gorgas, for someone who had grown up in a gravity field. (Gorgas, who had also grown up in a gravity field, took no offense—and a good thing too, for nothing breeds hostility more than taking what has not been offered.) But then, Ivar had been piloting a jove-boat since the age of ten, helping his uncle run a threelium barge from Callistopolis to Port Galileo. So, although his experience in Jupiter's gravity well gave him a bent to think in circles—or at least in ellipses—it was a decent foundation for the more hyperbolic thinking of torchship pilots.

"It's not that orbital mechanics plays no role," Corrigan told the boy during one of their shifts together. "If Bhatterji snuffed the torches, Old Man Sol would tug at our coattails until we hit the heliopause, so our course would not be exactly a straight line, but more of a hyperbole. Where is the sun today?"

"Uh. I guess it's still in Capricorn, but entering Sagittarius?" Many of Akhaturian's declarative sentences were disposed to end their lives as questions. This was not a flaw in his character. Others on the ship could have benefited from hanging a question mark off the back ends of their pronouncements.

"Never guess," said Corrigan, who was not himself prone to question marks. "Always know. In the future, I will expect you to know the house without looking, and to take a noon sighting each day for greater precision. Now, the ship will always feel a tug to windward, and that affects our secant bearing. Torchmen down in the inner system especially must always take careful note of the sun."

"Uh, what about Jupiter? I mean, it's powerful big, and—" Amongst the folk of the Galilean moons and their dependencies, Jupiter occupies the center of their thoughts, and often of their calculations as well.

"Work the numbers," Corrigan told him. "At our present position, the sun's pull is three-hundred and fifty times greater than Jupiter's. Now, Jupiter does help keep the ship on its bearings. We are, in a sense, falling down toward the planet. But the Sun deflects our path one way, and our high speed deflects us another way. The question is, how much and on which vector? That's what a ship's navigator will want to know."

"Yessir, Mr. Corrigan," Akhaturian replied. He said *yessir* a lot, but it was less from subservience than it once had been, and more from agreement.

"Meanwhile, take your bearings on Grubb and fetch us all a round of coffee." Corrigan stretched his jaw until it cracked. "I'll be glad when we're through this patch and we can go back to normal watches. If we ever do make it through," he added darkly.

Twenty-four was assisting Grubb in the kitchen, one reason why Ivar ran the errand with such dispatch. She charged him three kisses—one for each coffee—and the boy paid the price with a will. Grubb was elbow-deep in a kneading vat. He wiped his bow with his forearm and smiled benignly. "What are you doing down here, Ivar? Thought you were flying this bucket?"

"Oh, I let Mr. Corrigan take a turn at the controls." Of course, Ivar overpaid Twenty-four on the coffee and then had to collect his change.

After Akhaturian left, deCant put a convection pot into its dog box firmly enough that the other pots complained. Grubb raised an eyebrow in her direction. "What's wrong, L'il Lumber?"

"It's not fair!"

"I don't expect it is. Least, I never found it so. Anything in particular, or just life in general?"

"Ivar gets to fly the ship. And 'Kiru and Rave go out the mast. And even that Miko is standing watches below. What am I doing? Just muffing in the kitchen. Sand it *raw*! I'm wasting my life down here."

"Hey," said Grubb, placing a hand over his heart, "nothing wrong with the kitchen."

"Oh, I didn't mean you, chief. I mean, this is what you *want* to do."

It wasn't really, but Grubb did not correct the girl. "And what is it *you* want to do?"

"I don't know!"

"Then how do you know you're not doing it? Look, I've got to run the mold inspections on the air filters in a few minutes. Why don't you help me with that? Somebody has to keep this biosphere habitable. Might as well be you 'n' me."

Utensils clattered as deCant took them from the sonic cleaner and returned them to their dog drawers. "It's because I'm pregnant, that's why they don't let me do anything."

"Well," said Grubb, scratching his head and leaving a streak of white there from the carnic he had been kneading, "Out on the mast, the radiation hazard is . . ."

"And up on the bridge?"

"That would be the Satterwaithe hazard—which is near as bad."

DeCant didn't want to, but she couldn't help the laugh, though she didn't like it, either, after it had burst out. It can be a simple thing to make an angry person laugh. That does not mean it is a wise thing.

"Besides," Grubb continued, "you told me you weren't interested in flight-deck duties."

"That's not the point."

"What is?"

"I *hate* Satterwaithe!"

The pronouncement startled Grubb considerably, as it did not seem connected to the previous string of conversation. It was an Athenic sort of statement, springing full-born off the top of her head. Offhand, Grubb could think of no one who *liked* the second officer, unless maybe it was Ratline, but hate seemed an excessive passion to direct at such a bloodless woman. "Why, what has she done to you?"

"Nothing," said deCant.

"Well, then," Grubb temporized, but Grubb did not understand that "nothing" could be a most heinous thing to do. "Here, why don't you take this coffee and danish up to the captain?"

"Sure . . . run some more errands."

"Ivar just ran an errand."

DeCant palmed the cat at him and Grubb said, "Here! There's no call for that!" but by then damsel, drink, and danish had vanished alike.

Although Corrigan had thought him unconcerned with the risks of penetrating a rubble field, Gorgas was more than concerned. At the ship's current velocity, a body crossing their path would be like a farmer's tractor pulling suddenly onto a superhighway. It would be no happy encounter.

The trick was not to avoid such a meeting, which was trivial, but to avoid it and still enter HoJO. Constraints on a solution were like artful clothing on a woman: they enhanced the beauty of the problem. To meet this particular constraint meant a minimal angle of deflection—just enough to miss the obstacle and no more—and that in turn required detection occur at the maximum feasible distance. Yet *feasible* was a slippery sort of word. The inverse square law meant that The Lotus Jewel could see farther only by seeing less well, and many a man, his eyes fixed on the far horizon, has stumbled over a stone underfoot. Better resolution required diverting power from engines or life support. It was a pretty problem in juggling trade-offs, especially as the boundary conditions were continually changing with the ship's deceleration.

Gorgas had Ship ponder the infinity of options, solving in real time for the optimum angle. He was looking for a sign or, more precisely, for a sine.

When the wrangler brought him his danish and coffee, she

set the tray on his stay-put pad with enough force to startle Gorgas from the warm haze of his computations. The captain blinked, glanced curiously at the departing form, then bent once more to his figures. He took a bite of the danish without tasting the effort Grubb had put into creating it, which was a shame because the chief had labored mightily with essence of cherry and faux frosting and the like. As he sipped the coffee, Gorgas scowled and muttered, "Damn!" although this was not a verdict on Grubb's bean. He had only now recollected that the sails were sixty-four kilometers in diameter, which gave the ship a far larger footprint against the sky than he was accustomed to consider. A minimum deflection would let the asteroid pass through the sail.

Now, the sail was only a circle of cable, but seen head-on the interior of that circle would be a spider's work of shrouds and stays. An object passing through that cat's cradle would shear through the shrouds like a cannon ball. "Ship," he said.

"Ready, Mr. Gorgas."

"Message. To: Corrigan. Text: What procedures safeguard those lines attached to your sail should a body pass within the perimeter? End text. Send."

"Message sent."

"Thank you," Gorgas said absently.

"You're welcome, sir."

Gorgas started, but then remembered that Ship had accessed a relict memory base from old cruise ship days. The AI's new mannerisms were not at all unpleasant since, in consequence, at least one intelligence on board had begun to show a modicum of respect.

Ship relayed the reply a few moments later. "Mr. Gorgas. Message from Corrigan. Text: 'We send shroudsmen out to cut away the torn shrouds and attach new ones.' End text."

"In other words," Gorgas muttered, returning to his calculations, "no safeguards."

He worked the problem a little while longer, decided that in the event of a close approach he ought to strike the sails, then realized that a loop sixty-four kilometers wide would require longer to furl than the time between detection and encounter.

Better to jettison the sail—but he could imagine the reaction from Satterwaithe or Corrigan, if he ordered that. So he decided to work the Ürumqi Campaign instead, taking the part of Chinese Eleventh Army Group. He had been pondering, off and on, a forward strategy to prevent the Kazakh seizure of the Jinghe railhead and was anxious to game it.

But when he unbelted and turned around, he discovered that Mikoyan Hidei had (duplicating General Abdulhassan Karmazetov's surprise thrust with the 8th Airmobile Brigade) appeared mysteriously in his rear. Gorgas reacted much as General Jiyung had, by pulling back in a precipitous manner.

In milly this meant that, while he did manage to keep his feet, he did so only by executing a buck-and-wing across his dayroom. Gorgas was conscious of the clownish aspect of this dance. Had her teeth so much as peeked from Miko's lips, he would have erupted like one of Bhatterji's engines, and with much the same effect on the girl.

A good thing then, that Miko gasped instead. She had not meant to startle the captain. (She had never heard of Ürumqi.) And in fact, his sudden leap had caused, Newton-like, a reciprocal jump on her part. So, while he sputtered, Gorgas did not explode.

"Well," he said when he had steadied himself and had contemplated the situation. He did not ask *What do you want here?* because the more interesting question at the moment was *How did you get in here?* The door to the ring corridor stood directly before his desk; those to his quarters and to the bridge were situated to his left and right, respectively. No one, however stealthy, could have entered from any of those three doors without causing him to take note.

"There is another entrance to this room," he said.

"Captain," she said, "you are the very first to realize that." Her expression puzzled Gorgas, as it was one of respect and he was not accustomed to seeing that.

"Well," he said again; then, following another pause, "And where is it?"

There were a dozen prevarications she could serve up, but she found honesty wagging her tongue by default. "The old stewards' passageways," she said. When she pointed toward the wall behind her, a vague discomfort affected her and she checked, incongruously, to see that her coverall was zipped.

"I see," said Gorgas, although thus far he had actually seen nothing. What he meant was that he understood. Once Miko had mentioned their existence, the *idea* of the passageways was sufficient and Gorgas grasped their original purpose, their likely extent, and the reason why they had been sealed off and forgotten. A tingle of anticipation ran through him. "Show me, please."

Why, what a curious grin, Miko thought, and that grin, more than the request, led her to open the panel for him.

"Ah, yes," said Gorgas, first studying the terrain (as Jiyung should have done before Ürumqi), "this alcove is out of line-of-sight from most points in the room. Stewards could come and go quietly. I suspect this must have once been a dining room." (There was a similar door in the bedroom. Staff members had come in there too, and many not so quietly.) Gorgas stepped inside the passage and looked left and right, although he could see very little in the blackness.

Miko said, "I carry a cold light when I'm inside."

Gorgas nodded at this gloss to his unspoken comment. "Of course. And a ball of string, I should imagine." (But Miko had never heard of Ariadne, so the reference was lost on her.) Gorgas took a step farther inside and the shadows fell across his face so that he seemed to become an empty coverall. "The topology must be rather complicated." He smiled and his teeth alone caught the light.

He's enjoying this, Miko thought, though for the life of her, she could not see why.

This is why. Gorgas the boy had always wanted to live in a house with a secret passage, and now that wish had been unexpectedly granted, if not by a fairy godmother, then by an elfin girl. He had always felt a keen disappointment when bookcases did not swing out or panels slide apart. Caves and tunnels and old mine shafts had attracted him too, because they had much in common with secret passageways.

He had met Marta through a caving club at university in Budapest. They had explored the catacombs under Castle Hill.

Recollecting their outings together, Gorgas could almost hear the trickle of seeping water in crystalline chambers and the echoes of whispers within a womb of rock; feel the damp cold settling into his sweater; see the parti-colored mineral curtains glowing in the cold-lamps. Almost. "We used to explore caves and tunnels," he said. "Marta and I."

He had not meant to say that aloud. He was so accustomed to his interior monologues that their occasional leakage into the world beyond often went unnoticed. But Miko said, "Is Marta the woman in the holoplex in the other room?" And that brought Gorgas back from wherever it was he had started to go and the smile vanished on his return.

"I see this is not your first visit here." His tone was harsh; his voice, clipped; his visage, suddenly severe. He stepped from the passageway and (sparing it one, last wistful glance) closed and sealed the door. "I'll thank you to signal at the hoígh plate henceforth."

Miko seldom cared about the impression she made. There is an old Carson poem that captures her: *Take me as you find me/Or don't take me at all* . . . And of course, she had spent most of her life not being found. Yet the sudden change in Gorgas bothered her, and she regretted now the offence she had unwittingly given. *It was the picture,* she thought as the captain escorted her back to the dayroom and planted her before the desk and himself behind it. Something about the holoplex was hurtful, and hurtful in a very private way. She should not have mentioned seeing it.

"Now," said Gorgas. "What did you want to see me about?"

Taking a stilling breath, she said, "What I came to ask you, captain, is . . . I mean, well, just how bad off are we? The ship, I mean."

"Our situation has much improved," he said, hoping to soothe and comfort the youngster.

"But it could improve a lot more," Miko suggested, because *much improved* implies that the situation has lately been in need of improvement and, further, that the situation is not yet satisfactory.

Gorgas considered the girl for a moment and something in her iron posture reassured him, for it was not, as he had initially thought, the rigidity of fear. "There are a number of potential problems," he admitted and found, paradoxically, that the weight of his concern was a little less.

"Like we might not, uh, make it to Ganymede?"

"I shouldn't let that concern you." Gorgas plucked a stylus from its foam holdfast and began flipping it end over end in his hand. "Of course, braking continuously at full power . . ."

"Is on the edge of the performance envelope. Yah, I know that." Miko ran a hand across the queer blond stubble on her scalp. "The system's been stuttering. The plume velocity cycles—first, we slow down too much, then Ship lets up on the brakes. The oscillations don't seem to be damping, either. And number two's been running a little hot since last night."

For a wild moment, Gorgas thought she meant the second officer and contemplated (for a mercifully brief time) the idea of Satterwaithe "running hot." Then he realized that Miko had referred to a ferocious ball of plasma rather than the sailing master, and said, not without some relief, "What does Bhatterji say about the stutter?"

"Just watch it close and call him if it red-lines."

"Whereupon he will improvise God-knows what."

Miko smiled. "That's the Ram. Good thing we have the sails, right? Gives us a little margin."

"The ship has come through difficult times before," Gorgas assured her. "Once, when a juke jet stuck as we were sidling into Port Ceres—"

"Corrigan thinks we're doomed," Miko interjected, not because the captain's story was uninteresting—which it was—but because this fixation of the first officer was the real reason she had come to see the captain, and she had grown impatient with dancing about it. Corrigan was so dedicated to facts that his wildest fancies often had an irrefutable substance to them, and this latest apprehension of his had agitated Miko considerably.

"Yes," said Gorgas, "he thought so at Ceres, as well, and as you see . . ." He spread his arms, ". . . we are still here."

"But he could be right, just this once . . . ?"

"A man may arise each morning of his life and say, 'Today I

will die,' and once in a long while he will be correct. But that does not mean we should take him seriously as a prophet."

"Once is often enough," Miko said. She had grown to know Corrigan while they had worked together, and she believed him a knowing man. Yet, Gorgas too had a reputation for careful thought, so where did truth lie? "You worry a lot, captain," she said. "More than Corrigan, I think." She did not add that she had watched him at times from the peepery while he sat awake during his off-watch and plied the AI with questions and calculations.

"A captain is supposed to worry," Gorgas replied with a little laugh that was supposed to be reassuring as well as self-deprecating. "But Mr. Corrigan is a certain kind of man; and by that I mean, a man who is always certain."

"I'd think that if he's certain of disaster, he'd worry more'n anyone."

"No, Ms. Hidei, though he might *accept* disaster more than anyone. Worry is something one *does*, not something one *feels*. It is an active sort of verb. Why, a man on death row," Gorgas continued with greater animation, "accepting the inevitable, can grow as serene as a nun in cloister; but add the prospect of a pardon and he will worry to excess."

Miko smiled faintly and briefly, but also genuinely. Gorgas had not thought her capable of smiling at all, and reciprocated with a matching curl of his own. Between the two of them, they might have created a genuine grin.

"Everyone calls me Miko," the elf said.

"Even captains?"

Miko, tripped by a sudden memory of another man seated at this very desk, tumbled abruptly into a different time and place, from which locale she answered softly, "Even captains."

Gorgas understood her change of tone and her blindish look, and something in it struck him as both tragic and lovely. "Evan Hand," he said.

"Yah."

"Well, he was a personable sort, I grant him that." Gorgas tried not to ask the question that came after. He struggled mightily against the words that pushed against his teeth, but in the end he yielded. "How did . . . how did you find him as a captain."

"I didn't," said Miko. "He found me."

"No, I meant that—" And Gorgas fell silent, realizing suddenly how much the girl's humor resembled his own.

Miko was astonished at how different a man he became behind a smile. Why, he was not so dark complexioned at all! "Hand worried a lot too," she told him, "from what I saw of him those few months. Only—if you don't mind my saying so—you worry more about getting our cargo to port and Hand worried more about getting us to work together."

"A happy crew, but impoverished." Gorgas had intended irony, but being of a particular turn of mind, turned the phrase in his mind and became conscious that the crew had not been particularly happy of late. He looked at his stylus, suddenly aware that he had handled it continually since the conversation had started, and with a sudden move he stabbed it into its foam holdfast. "I'm not Hand, you know. I never can be. We are, were, different men." He wondered why on Earth he was apologizing for that, and why to this elf, of all people.

"Yah," said Miko, who wondered at the sudden gruffness in his voice. "And I'm not Bhatterji; and the Ram isn't Enver Koch. And Aziz isn't that Ranulf Echeverry I heard tell of. Not better, maybe not worse, either. Just different. Captain Hand . . . Well, he saved my life, in a sideways sort of way. No fault of yours that you didn't; and if it's all the same to you, I'll be just as happy if you never need to."

"Is that why you asked me that, about the ship?"

"You mean, will my life need saving again? I don't know. Maybe. Only *The Riv'*, she means a lot to me, and I'd hate to see anything happen to her, whether I'm inside her or not when it does. People . . . You get up close enough to someone, he can look awful different. You think they feel the same way you do . . . about the ship, I mean, but it's *not* the ship. It's just the nuts and bolts; or it's just the rules and structures. Never the ship herself; never the whole thing."

Gorgas had found an anchor in the mate's verbal whirligig and grabbed hold of it. "But it's the ship that matters to you."

"Yah.

"I'm happy to hear you say that . . . Miko."

"So was Ship." Gorgas laughed at the jest, but Miko turned away. "I best be going. My watch starts in two hours. Sorry I took up your time, captain. I didn't mean to yadder like that."

Gorgas waved a graceful indulgence. He hadn't minded the intrusion at all, at least not after his initial pique. Bhatterji had said something at dinner once about the girl's acerbity, but Gorgas had found her quite pleasant. "One thing," he said, his words halting her by the door. "Once we have passed through the rubble field, would you mind showing me your steward's passageways?"

Miko was not prepared for the request and could not place the weird delight she heard. The passages were her refuge, their qualities strictly utilitarian. She had explored them to learn her way around, not because they were dark and mysterious and led to unknown lands. She made another long and, to Gorgas, disconcerting appraisal of the captain, thinking that it was a different man than the one she had expected. "Yah. Yah, I'll do that."

"And, Miko. If you ever feel you need to talk about things . . ."

"Yah, I'll do that too."

"A curious girl," he thought afterward, when he had retired for the day. "Quite pleasant and reserved." For Gorgas, those two adjectives rubbed bellies. "Not very serene, though." Gorgas had not thought Miko serene.

Corrigan was a serene man because his certainty brought acceptance. Perhaps it was the man's faith, Gorgas thought. A Muslim submits to fate as the will of God, and it matters not whether the fate be pleasant or no. That quality confers on one an unbreakable courage in the face of adversity, but perhaps less audacity in overcoming it.

Gorgas lifted the holoplex from its cradle, something he had not done in years, and rubbed his thumb gently across the image. Perhaps the AI broadened Marta's smile just a little in response to the pressure, which was odd because Marta used to smile in just the same way at this very touch. Gorgas studied that face long in silence, then sighed and placed the picture once more in its cradle.

"If only you had been less certain, dear." And he rubbed the back of his right hand with his left.

Now the curious thing about The Lotus Jewel was that she really was beautiful. Some people are said to have piercing eyes, but hers actually left puncture wounds. She was, to use an old word now employed only by physicists, *radiant*, and radiant in precisely the way that physicists use the word. That is, whatever it was inside her that made her who she was streamed forth from her eyes and her voice and from her very presence and invigorated all who were about her. She was a Pandora's box of a woman, keeping very little inside. She might have been rather more beautiful had she cultivated more of a reserve—had she been more like Okoye, for instance, who was really very plain but seemed prettier than she was because she hoarded herself. At the very least, the sysop might then have recognized her own beauty—for it was not, as she thought, on the outside at all. As it was, she knew that people loved her company and that people loved her flamboyance and that people loved her looks, but she was never quite certain that they loved her self.

"I will make you a skirt," she told Okoye at breakfast one day. Grubb had prepared thick pots of whipped eggstuff and grilled slabs of carnic. The bread was liberally smeared with a marmalade he had fashioned from strawberry essence and basic gels. The drink had been fortified with flavorings and a suite of necessary vitamins. "'Kiru would look nice in a skirt, don't you think?"

Grubb, of course, agreed. He would have agreed had she suggested the skirt for him, and not entirely without reason. Miko, the fourth person present, looked doubtful. She may not have been certain what a skirt was. "Does 'Kiru *want* a skirt?" she asked.

Okoye for her part chewed silently on a strip that suggested "bacon" without the awful necessity of having once been a pig. She was reluctant to speak because she knew how very much The Lotus Jewel wanted to do this for her. Okoye was not indifferent to material goods—only the wealthy could afford such indifferences—but her needs were simple and her wants were few. Yet to refuse a gift were an insult.

The room swayed and a mild vertigo seized them for a moment. Grubb glanced at Miko. "Another transient?"

The engineer's mate grimaced. "Haven't traced that malf yet."

The chief grinned. "Be careful you don't wear out the brake pads."

Miko shook her head. "What are you talking about?"

Grubb was thinking about runaway trucks on the highways of his native Colorado, but he realized in time that an Amalthean could not properly understand the jest, so he said, "I guess the repairs weren't quite up to specs."

"Nah. It's the whole engine suite that backfires, even One and Four. We figure it's in the control system. Hey, if I understand this skirt thing, it may not be the sort of clothing our 'Kiru would *want* to wear in milly. Won't it, well, float up?"

The Lotus Jewel had taken a bite of the marmaladen bread and, her mouth being full, waved her free hand back and forth rapidly. "Unh," she said, and, "No," when she had swallowed. "Freef skirts have a frame in them to keep their shape. Ram fashioned one for me from the pattern I gave him. I only have to dress it with the fabric."

Miko laughed. "'Kiru already wears a steel cage down there."

Okoye dropped her grill strip. "How can you say that?" she asked Miko. "What gives you the right to say that?" And she pushed herself from her seat and bolted from the room, caroming off the walls because she ran too fast for milly.

"What did I say?" asked Miko, but no one answered her.

The Lotus Jewel could not help but feel some responsibility for Okoye's flight. An observer might have felt that Miko deserved the greater share of the blame; or Grubb, who had allowed a short bark of laughter to escape before he could prevent it; or even Okoye herself, who did not ask herself *why* the remark had smarted so. Yet The Lotus Jewel held the happiness of her friends to be her own special obligation and thus her own special failure.

Later, under the cap, as she sussed the tsunami in the ship's path, The Lotus Jewel was still thinking of the poor Igbo girl and did not at first notice anything awry. There had to be some way to set things right again. 'Kiru and Miko had become friends, and it would be a terrible thing if the upset capsized into a quarrel. Miko already regretted the remark and had said as much after 'Kiru had gone, but hers was not an apologetic nature and she was quite capable of an obdurate defensiveness over the issue. Yet it was not clear to the sysop how she might smooth things over between the two.

It was on her third pass that she noticed the peculiar tumor on the sky. It lay just outside the footprint of their forward path and, because she had been told to focus on direct hazards to navigation, she very nearly passed on to the more detailed inspection of the dead-ahead zone. However, the tumor felt peculiar—she could not say why—and she told Ship to loop all previous scans of that particular body in accelerated time.

The lump came alive under her touch, like a cat struggling in a plastic bag. A somersaulting rock? But it did not quite have the *feel* of a somersaulting rock. <Ship.>

<Ready, Ms. Jewel.>

<Magnify this region.> She outlined the region she meant with her finger. <Set magnification. Ten-fold. Magnify.> In a blink, the squirming dot had resolved itself into something very like an amoeba. It writhed, growing lobes and losing them. At one point in its evolutions, it resembled a shamrock. The movement was strobe-like, for the image was synthesized by interpolation between actual radar paints. The sky around it had a gritty feel, like fine sandpaper. <Reset magnification. One hundred-fold.>

<Sorry, Ms. Jewel. The resolution is insufficient for that level of magnification.>

Meaning that further magnification would only produce a larger blob. A small horseshoe formed in the skin above her nose as The Lotus Jewel worried at an unease lying splinter-like in her mind. "Deck," she said over the voice link.

"What is it, Comm?" Corrigan sounded weary. The lack of sleep was telling on him.

"What does a Jovian passage do to an atoll?"

"That depends on how far the parent asteroid is from Jupiter when it passes."

"I mean, in general."

"Well, as the asteroid closes from the sun-west, it speeds up and moves higher—toward Jupiter. Then, after it moves on to the east—it's faster than Jupiter, of course; lower orbit—Jupiter slows it down slightly and it drops back. Depending on circumstances—on distance and on certain resonance relationships—the ministroids might be pumped up or pushed down after repeated passages. That's why the Trojan Gulf may have transients—like our tsunami—but is free of permanent residents."

"The atoll spreads out, then. Thanks." The Lotus Jewel switched back to sussing. <Ship.>

<Ready, Ms. Jewel.>

<Create a notional globe around this object—> She pointed. <Calculate projected circle against the sky. Intersect projection with dead-ahead footprint. Allow for uncertainties due to recent engine backfires. Paint fine-grid mesh of intersection. Set tolerance incorporating recent uncertainty in attitude.>

<Acknowledged. Clarification requested. A fine-mesh grid at that distance requires power diversion from other systems. Confirm instruction, please.>

The Lotus Jewel quickly surveyed the rest of the sky and found nothing that needed attention during the time the paint would take. <Confirmed.>

<Ping,> said Ship.

"Comm," said Corrigan, what are you doing?"

"Proving I'm not stupid."

The Lotus Jewel was sufficiently beautiful that she was also generally accounted dumber than a stone, there being in vogue the peculiar notion of a conservation law regarding the sum of brains and beauty. Corrigan's great sin was to believe this notion to be a fact, and he was guilty of it even when he did not intend it. Even when he had loved her—and in his way he still did—he had loved her as a man might love a child, quite differently than he had loved Miko, who really was a child. His very demeanor—and his great flaw of correcting others on questions of fact—made the accusation always implicit. That The Lotus Jewel did not know how to think only lent credence to the charge.

But thinking is often overrated—at least the plodding, pedestrian *modus ponens* sort of thinking that hops from premise to conclusion like a fastidious child crossing a creek on protruding stones. It would be fine to say that The Lotus Jewel had reasoned her way to her conclusion. That, firstly, Stranger's Reef was last seen as a triplet; that secondly, it was surrounded by a cloud of small bodies that would not show up on a normal long-distance ping; that, thirdly, the Jovian passage had likely *smeared* the atoll directly across their path; that, fourthly, to wait until that load of birdshot was within short-range sensors would be to wait too long. But, The Lotus Jewel did not think that way. She liked to wade. Her answer *felt* right. There are any number of names for this process, but stupid isn't one of them.

"Bridge," said Okoye, "this is Sails. There's been a power drop to the mains'l cladding system. What's going on?"

"Bridge," said Miko, "this is Engines. There's been a power drop to the CoRE magnet cooling system. What the hell is going on?"

"Ship," said Corrigan, "belay that ping."

<Send the ping,> whispered The Lotus Jewel; and then, between two heartbeats, she added, irrationally, <Please?>

<Yes, mother,> replied Ship.

And the ship went dark.

Nothing sustains confusion like being in the dark. The redlamps came on down in engineering and Miko ramped down the plume velocities even while she watched the field strength dim. *No*, she cried, though not aloud, *not again*! If the magnetic insulation went and the engines slagged once more, they would never find the means to effect a second repair. She placed one hand on the scram bar, with the other hit the alarm to waken Bhatterji, and waited.

There were no red-lamps up above in the Long Room. They had been scavenged long ago and no one had thought to replace them. Okoye could not see her hand in front of her face, and it didn't help that the hand was black. Faux gauges glowed on the monitor screens. Yes . . . the cladding temperature was creeping up. If it hit the quench point, the sail would normalize—lose superconductivity—and the sudden appearance of eighty megajoules of heat from the spontaneous resistance would vaporize the damned thing. "Whiff the wire," as Ratline had put it during training. She ought to reef the sail, yet the activators for the flux pumps were anonymous buttons under her fingertips. "Ship!" she called. "Wake Ratline! Now!"

What Corrigan was saying on the bridge was rather more expressive and certainly more colorful. Gorgas burst onto the bridge in the midst of this encomium and asked what had happened. The primary lights were just coming back on line (and in the basement and attic, Miko and Okoye breathed simultaneous sighs of relief, even while they hunted across their readouts and quizzed various avatars of Ship on their status.

Corrigan pointed to the sysop's station. "She ordered a finegrid paint! At maximum distance! With the ship at full braking power!"

"Well," Gorgas responded mildly, "she may have had a reason."

"We need every amp we have to keep the sails cold!"

"And the plasma rings focused," Gorgas reminded him. He thought that running both systems in parallel had perhaps put too much of a loading on the power system. *The River of Stars* was laying rubber halfway across the sky, she was braking so hard. She'd be lucky if she didn't end with an engine mangle. But no one supposed any more that the ship would ever leave Port Galileo, save as scrap metal and aerogel in the bins of a recovery barge, so all that really mattered now was stopping.

And surviving the stop. That was important too.

Satterwaithe, snatched from sleep by the alarum, reached the bridge in her underwear and Corrigan had to go through it all again to fill her in. He averted his eyes, but Satterwaithe was the very opposite of The Lotus Jewel in matters of her appearance.

Akhaturian arrived next but nobody tried to fill him in, so he scuttled to the navigation station and began running the data for himself.

By that time, The Lotus Jewel had received the bounceback from her paint and she told Ship to display the data in the sistines. As she removed her virtch hat, four mouths opened for a barrage of questions and reprimands, but the sudden ripple of color and light overhead closed them. The silence that followed was not really very long, but seemed deeper for being so empty.

Satterwaithe was the first to speak, but all she said was, "Well." The Lotus Jewel waited for her to say more, to indicate by some word that she had done the right thing, or a foolish thing, or perhaps both.

"Where away?" said Gorgas, stepping to the plotting tank.

Akhaturian answered from navigation. "Two minutes starward off the dead-ahead. Center of mass on the ecliptic. Debris cloud subtends two degrees of arc."

"Master?"

"It's Stranger's Reef, right enough," Satterwaithe answered. "A triplet, just like I was told. Comm, what particle sizes in the atoll?"

The Lotus Jewel groped the spattering of radar echoes her ping had harvested. "All the way from rubble to gravel."

"What's going on?" Ratline enquired over the Long Room screen. "What happened to the power? We near quenched the goddamned sail!"

"We've raised the Reef, shroudmaster," Satterwaithe told him and Ratline fell silent.

"Very nearly on the bearing I initially calculated," Corrigan pointed out, "only it was more distant than we thought and was masked by the first body." These were only facts, of course, not excuses.

"We'll have to juke the ship," Gorgas decided. "Engines, are you there?"

Bhatterji replied over the engine room link. "Ship claims it was told to run a paint, but that shouldn't have drained—"

"You forget the power needed for the sails," Gorgas reminded him. Bhatterji cursed and Gorgas, rubbing his unshaven cheek, turned to The Lotus Jewel. "Distance?"

"Point-four megaklicks," said The Lotus Jewel. "Closing in one hour."

Gorgas grunted. "At least we raised it in plenty of time. Engines, stand by for input. Number One, please calculate the available thrust for a sunward juke. There is a suite of scenarios already in the deeby."

"A sunward juke?"

"I know it puts us farther off the grand secant, but the Reef lies off our star-side quarter. Choose the minimum possible deflection."

Corrigan nodded at the dark humor, as it fit his own mood well, and crossed the deck to dispossess young Akhaturian from his seat. Satterwaithe laid a hand on his arm as he passed. "It would be best if we cleared the sail, as well." And Corrigan, seized by an irrational burst of optimism, slapped her on the rear and said, "I didn't hoist that suit to see it shredded by grapeshot."

Satterwaithe reacted not at all to the slap. Perhaps she didn't feel it, as she was said to be a hard-ass. "Madam sailing master," said Gorgas, not taking his eyes off the dead-ahead display, "will it take very long to finish dressing?" Satterwaithe in an emergency would have come to the bridge buck naked—nevertheless, she did leave and, when she was gone, Gorgas suppressed a smile. "She must have been a striking woman in her younger days," he commented to no one in particular.

The others turned and stared at him. "She's still a striking woman," The Lotus Jewel said, "as you'd learn if you repeated that remark in front of her."

Gorgas grunted again, annoyed at his own digression. "Comm," he said brusquely, "ping the atoll at five-minute intervals and have Ship compute the parallax. Number One, have you plotted a course? Good, feed your requirements to Engines and have them work out a burn schedule. Smartly, now. I'd rather not learn that we should have started burning five minutes ago."

"If we have to," Akhaturian said, "we can deliver half our thrust to starward and miss that rock easy."

"Yes, cadet," Gorgas told him. "Please calculate as an exercise by what delta-V we will fail to achieve Jupiter if we do so."

Akhaturian felt the tips of his ears grow red. "Not by that much," he muttered. Scowling, he touched his hushmike so he could speak with one of Ship's avatars without disturbing the rest of the deck. He wondered what else he had overlooked.

Belowdecks, Grubb, deCant, and Evermore were battening the carniculture vats and securing their loose utensils when Dr. Wong poked her head in. "What's going on?" she asked.

"Twenty-four heard from the Li'l Cap'n that we raised the Reef," Grubb responded cheerfully, "and the atoll lies square across our dead-ahead, so the ship will have to juke. That means high lateral accelerations. I'd rather not have dinner slosh out of the tanks."

"Can I help? I'd like to help." Wong lifted one of the vat lids that hung on the wall, then looked about at a loss for where to put it until Grubb tapped the lip of the porciculture vat. She lifted the lid into place, set it, and then struggled with the clamps. Grubb caught Evermore's eye and motioned with a nod.

"Thank you," Wong said when Evermore had helped her position the lid. "Do you think there's any real danger?"

Grubb laughed. "I'd hate to think we were going through this muff for no reason."

"I was on *Johnny Todd* when she docked at Vesta with too much vee," the doctor volunteered. "Everything jounced and jangled when they scraped the rock, and the crew went ballistic because no one had strapped in. The captain struck the rockside bulkhead and broke his collar bone and the mate . . . oh, it was utter confusion. The harbor pilot had a heart attack as he was bringing us in. That's why we hit. He was only seventy, if you can believe it."

"That's in snake years," Grubb whispered aside to Evermore, who snickered.

"There were a dozen major fractures among the crew," Wong remembered, perhaps with some nostalgia, "compound, simple, a few noses out of joint, and one case of hypobariatric anoxia when the second engineer tried to patch the air leakage in one of the cargo holds."

"What," said Grubb, "he went in without a suit?"

"He thought he could weld the fracture before the pressure dropped too much."

"That sounds pretty stupid," Evermore suggested.

"Well, the hold contained a shipment of young sheep, and

they spoil if they suffocate." Wong had lifted another lid, this one onto the poultriculture vat, and waited while Evermore positioned it. "I felt useful, then," she said distantly, fingering one of the clamps. There had once been a dysentery outbreak on *Gryffydd's Hope* and the usual spates of colds and fevers, but the Vesta incident stood out in her memories. She could still remember the whistle of the escaping air, the cries of the wounded, the hiss and stink of the patch welders somewhere out of her sight while she fought to stem the flow of blood from a compound femoral fracture. There had been blood everywhere, not because there was so much of it but because the globules split and spread and coated everything with a thin, vile film.

"Mr. Evermore," said Ship. "Mr. Ratline requests your presence in the Long Room."

The second wrangler (and apprentice shroudsman) grinned. "Ship, you must be paraphrasing. Ratline hasn't *requested* anything in the last twenty years."

"Mr. Ratline has expressed his desire in the most emphatic terms."

"I bet he has. Sorry, Mr. Grubb, duty calls." Evermore waved the chief a casual salute and loped off as easy and as confidant as a gazelle.

Wong wiped her hands against her coverall. "He's a dutiful boy."

Grubb finished closing the dog cabinets, then rapped deCant on the arm with the back of his hand. "Go check the kitchen. See if any knives are sitting out. Wouldn't want them flying this way or that when the juke jets blow."

When the third wrangler had left the carnic room, Grubb said to the doctor, "Notice anything peculiar about Ship?"

Wong shook her head. "No, not really."

"It's been growing awful polite and eloquent lately."

"Is that a problem?"

"Doc, it's always a problem when a machine doesn't do the way it's supposed to."

"I don't always think of Ship as a machine. It seems like a person sometimes."

"That's what they call the touring fallacy—when you can't

tell the difference between what's real and what's just a simulation. It's bad enough when *people* give you indeterminate output. You don't want the equipment that runs your propulsion and life support to do the same."

"Be careful the way you talk about Ship," Wong teased him. "It might be listening."

The thought startled the chief, who looked at the grille in the ceiling. "I'm worried, is all."

"Well, if it's any comfort, Ship picked up a greeting-and-response library when it shook hands with the cutter. Cutter still had deebies from back to Coltraine's time."

Grubb had been pulling his kitchen smock over her head. He paused now and looked at her, then balled the garment up and shoved it in a laundry sack tied to the end of the counter. "The cutter," he said. "I thought the Zacker gutted that boat ages ago."

"No, Big' and I found it. It still works."

The doctor was hardly a boat pilot and wouldn't know an injector port from a Stannish loop. Grubb did not know, either, but at least he knew the terms and that gave him a superior form of ignorance. "Is Fife a boat pilot, then?"

"Well, he plots all those trajectories and things for Mohammed's Mountains."

"That's free-fall. Torchflight is different. Why were you in the cutter?" That the Lunatic and the snake had gone off to do the deed was his default assumption, but then, being a romantic, he was ever ready to construe the most fanciful interpretations to events. Ineluctably, he believed that others led more interesting lives than he did.

In the engine room, Bhatterji had obtained a burn solution from Ship. The half-milligee acceleration that Corrigan had computed required a six-degree cant north by starward on Numbers One and Two focusing rings. Since this would reduce the ship's forward vector, Numbers Three and Four must be throttled back 95 percent to keep the ship from yawing.

Gorgas received the word on the bridge. "Very well, people," he said. "Sunward, six degrees. Maintain attitude."

"Six degrees, aye," said Corrigan and he nudged the joystick at his station until the crosshairs were centered on the target point 32 kilometers off the narrowest spread of the atoll. There were probably a few rogues in that region, as the atoll did not have a sharp boundary, but the probability of a miss improved exponentially the farther from the primaries one passed.

"Engines to neutral," Gorgas said.

Down in the engine control room Bhatterji turned to his mate. "Quickly. Be sure you reorient the magnets before the rings cool. We don't have time for a cold start."

Miko nodded and swallowed to wet her throat. "Ziggy," she warned the ship, "in two, in one," and shut down the engines. Her left hand began rotating the focusing rings the instant the plasma plumes died. "Thirty minutes of arc," she told Bhatterji as she watched the progress on the two starward engines. "One degree ... Two ..." The huge gimbals on the rim seemed to take forever to move. That was the trouble with mechanical systems. "Six degrees," she announced when the second engine finally reached its set point. She glanced at the clock and was astonished to see that less than a minute had passed.

Bhatterji nodded. "Lock them in."

"Locked."

"Confirmed. Bridge, engines are ready."

From the bridge, Gorgas said, "Ignite. Sunboard engines at ninety-five. Starboard at full."

"Ninety-five, aye," said Bhatterji.

Miko announced, "Burn in three, in two, in one," and hit the button a half second behind Ship's autopilot. The gentle nudge of milligee acccelleration pushed back into her seat, but relief pushed her deeper. She turned to Bhatterji, who grinned at her.

"How did it feel?" he asked. "To move the ship."

"Jove," she answered with a grin of her own.

The Lotus Jewel, under the cap once more, struggled with feelings of guilt and justification. She hadn't known that the fine-mesh ping would pull so much power from propulsion and that it would push both engines and sails to the critical point. Yet, by doing so, she had discovered a hazard with barely enough time to dodge it. Not for the first time, she wished that the ship carried three cheeseheads, so someone could be under the cap 24/7. What if she had missed the hints? What if she had not thought to ping the critical region at this distance? They would not have seen the atoll until they raised it on the short-range sweeper, and, with less than a half-minute's warning, that would have been too late.

Was that why Corrigan had tried to stop her?

The Cook

"What if," Okoye asked Evermore, "the atoll is spread out more than Corrigan thinks?" The three sailors were donning their vacuum suits. It was standard procedure, but it carried an implication. Far more often than cages, sails required outside work.

Certainly the possibility was on Evermore's mind. "Then shroudsmen like us will earn our berths," he said, striking a pose. " '*We'll climb and splice in the driving hail.*' "

Ratline, who had been listening to the two youngsters with half an ear, snorted. "Boy, you been listening to Grubb too much. Ever been out there in the hail? Whoever wrote that song never done it, I can tell you. A stone hits you at transit velocity, what comes out the other end ain't pretty. I remember . . . we near lost a sail coming through the Belt when Terranova raced the *Calhoun* to Jupiter. Me an' Gooch Hatfield an' Kin Dabwele an'—oh, God, I've forgotten so many faces—we were the watch above when Terranova tucked a little too close to one of the Phocaeas and gravel ripped the shrouds. We jetted up the sou-east de-long with a splice an' halfway up, ol' Gooch, he got punched clean through. A pebble no bigger'n my thumb. I was right behind him when he spilled his guts." Ratline laughed and shook his head. "Spilled his guts," he said again, more softly. "Coulda been me, y'know," Ratline went on, "but Gooch wasn't the fastest hand ever went up th' ropes. He never hustled, and look what it got him. If he'd been on the bounce, it woulda been me."

"Or if he'd been slower still," Okoye pointed out, "no one would have been hurt."

But Ratline shrugged her off. "When it's time, it's time."

"Why did Terranova send you up in the gravel anyway?" Evermore wanted to know.

Ratline screwed his right eye. "If that shroud snapped, we'd'a lost the sail and the torch ship would'a won."

"So," said Okoye, who recalled that the torch ship had won anyway, "he sent a man out to die?"

Ratline turned on her. "He sent a man out to mend a shroud. The dying part was just *lagniappe*. It happens. A stone, a flare, a sail snap, a suit malf . . . It goes with the job."

"I wouldn't be afraid to go out," Evermore said. "I mean, what are the odds?"

"On dying?" Ratline shrugged. "One hundred percent. It's when and how that makes it interesting."

Gorgas remained by the plotting tank, watching the progress of Stranger's Reef—the true Reef—as it edged starward against the notional sky. He imagined himself the very picture of a Captain On Deck. Upright, stern-faced, intent, and with a little circle of worry about his countenance. Duty was his Anchises. When Satterwaithe returned in a rumpled coverall and slippers, she spared a glance to the empty captain's seat and another to Gorgas, but made no observation, unless to herself. "Where away?" she asked.

Gorgas turned from the tank. "Would you join me for a moment, Number Two? I should like your opinion."

Satterwaithe was none too certain that Gorgas would like her opinions, but crossed to his side anyway. Gorgas pointed in silence to the blinking crosshairs of the dead-ahead just to sunward of the Reef. She opened her mouth to ask what in bleeding hell was she was supposed to see, but pride closed it. If Gorgas saw something in the tank, she assured herself, it could not be anything but obvious. "How long since the most recent paint?" she asked, marking time while she studied the display.

"Ah," said Gorgas, "you notice it too."

If anything, this comradely approbation irritated her still further. Gorgas was an elliptic man—most of what he said he did not say. A priestess to his Pythia, Satterwaithe had to decode his every utterance and fill in the ellipsis. Had she not been exceptionally good at this, Gorgas would have long ago driven her mad.

"Where is the marker for the Reef's original bearing?" she demanded, then, peering more closely, saw that it was partly obscured by the marker for their current position. She raised her head. "It's been a quarter of an hour. The shift in our dead-ahead should be greater than that."

"Something's wrong," Bhatterji told Miko as he turned from the bridge talker. "Bridge says we're only getting three-quarters of the calculated vector. Verify the magnitude and direction of thrust on both engines."

"All the readouts are nominal," Miko told him.

"That wasn't what I asked. Check the plasma velocity—no, don't read the *gauge*. The gauge may be what's at fault. Work it out from the other data. What's the Doppler on the plume? The temperature? Where's the plumb line versus the gyro? The servos both agree that the focusing rings are canted six degrees starboard, but there may be *mechanical* slippage. Run alternative calculations and see if they yield the same values."

Bhatterji ran his own cross-check as well. Ship had been acting peculiar of late, but he did not believe there was an engine malf. A 25 percent error was not a subtle thing and he had calibrated those engines himself.

Grubb ducked his head on entering the old cutter because the opening was smaller than an upright man and, in consequence, he seemed to kowtow to the man belted in the pilot's chair. However, respect was the last emotion the chief could summon faced with the reality of Bigelow Fife caught in flagrante delicto. Grubb was a man who knew what he saw and what he saw was the passenger preparing to run off and leave them.

The vessel had been quite properly stowed for departure, Grubb grudgingly observed. The lockers were battened and neatly hand-labeled. The sleeping cages were folded and lashed—and with the correct knot, too. The galley was laid in with a variety of foodstuffs, the range of which he could not fault. "All shipshape, I see," he commented sarcastically.

"I did the best I could, under the circumstances," Fife responded. He did not regard his readying the cutter for escape as *delictum*, but rather as *paratus*, answering to the higher duty of personal survival; which is to say, of morality. He missed the sarcasm entirely.

"You're a smart man, aren't you?" Grubb remarked.

"I like to think so."

Fife was still missing the subtext. Grubb did not consider *smart* to be a synonym for *intelligent*, for while he admired the latter, he regarded the former with a lowering suspicion. "What do you think would happen," Grubb said, "if you took the cutter out into an atoll?"

"I wasn't planning to take . . ."

"Of course not, but just supposin'. The delta-vee between the boat and any objects freefing along this orbit is considerable— and the boat ain't armored like the ship."

"But she *does* present a smaller footprint," snapped Fife. It irritated him when dull-witted men played clever, which goes far to explain his chronic dyspepsia.

Grubb shrugged. He had not thought of the footprint aspect, but was disinclined to debate rationales with a coward. "I think you'll be safer waiting inside the ship." Grubb maintained the pretense of persuasion.

Fife very nearly defied the man, so frightened was he. "The logical thing," he insisted in a show of reason, "is to have an alternative standing by." But reason wasn't in it. Deep inside, he was terrified—not of the hazards of space, but of the aptness of the crew.

"Maybe logical," said Grubb, "but logic isn't the answer to everything." (This remark, which Grubb thought a truism, terrified Fife still more.) "I'd wonder," Grubb continued as if to himself, "at what songs they would sing."

The comment seemed to have wandered in from another

conversation. "Songs," Fife repeated, wondering if the cook had lost his mind.

"Yah. What sort of song would they sing about a man who ran off on his companions?"

Now, Fife was pleased to account himself a man of calm reason, but if the ice ran deep, it still wrapped a molten core, which could erupt through any crack in the shell. Anger juked him from his accustomed, cool trajectory. He would not endure chastisement from the likes of the cook. "I was not," he said through his teeth, "running off on you."

"Wasn't thinking of me." Grubb, having finally lost patience with persuasion, laid a beefy hand on the passenger's shoulder, and Fife heard something in the cook's voice that he had never heard before; and that was judgment. Fife did not care for the sound of it, and not least because he considered that judgment to be false.

Grubb knew what he saw, but this is not to say that he understood what he saw. He had found the passenger seated in a cutter that had been prepared for departure, but those were mere facts. They answered the *what*, not the *why*. Grubb would have made a fine scientist, but a poor philosopher.

Grubb's hand squeezed and Fife was startled to realize how big a man the cook actually was. He had always seemed small, perhaps because he had always seemed inconsequential. The grip persuaded where words had not. Fife acquiesced to its argument and unbelted, though with hard, abrupt motions that signaled his disagreement. Grubb pulled him from the seat and manhandled him through the umbilical into the rim corridor. Fife scraped against the rough, flexible tubing and called out in protest, but Grubb did not care. If Grubb drove Fife, fury drove Grubb.

Tumbling into the rim corridor, Fife came up short in the presence of Fransziska Wong and Twenty-four deCant, who had accompanied the cook from the kitchen and had awaited the denouement outside the cutter. The snake and the nymph stared with blank expressions, until the need to fill in the blanks compelled Fife to speak.

"I wasn't," he pled before any charge had been laid. "I was

only getting the systems ready. Just in case. You know, 'Siska! You helped me stock the boat yourself."

"I can't believe you would do this," the doctor said.

"Then *don't* believe it." So agitated had the passenger become that he took her by the arm, though such spontaneous touching was something he seldom did. "I would never leave you. You must believe me. I made you that promise."

But Wong responded to his plea with bitterness. "You could not help but make it."

Now, there was a desperate irony in all of this because, while Fife had been quite *prepared* to leave on his own, he had not actually *intended* to. He really had planned to wait until the very last possible moment before cutting loose, but he had been equally prepared to wait no longer. Nor was he an astute judge of last possible moments. He was quite apt to err on the antepenultimate side. Even so, as he had sat waiting, one thing had become unbearably clear to him. He would not have blown the umbilical without Franszziska Wong beside him. That realization had disturbed him quite as much as the impending atoll or Grubb's intrusion. In the game of gland and brain, the gland sometimes wins.

Oddly enough, only Twenty-four deCant, of that small group, sensed that Fife's motives had been prudential rather than selfish—even Fife himself had doubts on that score and tormented himself with visions of having abandoned Wong—and, given the passenger's reputation for careful reasoning, deCant found those preparations freighted with greater meaning than the funk that Grubb saw or the servility that Wong perceived. Fife's reasoned preparation, Wong's assistance, Grubb's discovery of their plan— There was a greater ethical significance to these actions than any of the actors knew, for the whole was greater than the sum of its parts. This was deCant's intuition, although she might not have framed it in quite those words. Had she known religion, she might have said that God moved in mysterious ways His wonders to perform, and so in consequence fall upon her knees to praise Him, for it was certainly not by the intent of any of the participants that this escape had been prepared for them all. As it was, the drama of the moment appealed to her in a purely secular manner, for the moment, like she herself, was pregnant with possibilities.

"We gotta let the others know," Twenty-four said. "I mean, if we do need to, you know." It was important to get the pick of the litter of all those possibilities. She was much like Wong, but that she was ebullient where the doctor was very private. Safety mattered a great deal to her, which was understandable considering that her entire life was sequel to a series of close calls. But escape meant nothing if some were left behind. There were her parents to consider also.

"You think the cap'n and Satterwaithe don't know what they're doing, girl?" Grubb asked, but seeing deCant's frown, he relented. "Okay, okay. Ship!"

"Waiting, Mr. Grubb."

"Message. To: Gorgas. Text:—"

"Captain Gorgas is not to be disturbed. The bridge is engaged."

Grubb made an irritated sound. "Two-four, why don't you run up to the bridge and tell Ivar about the cutter. Ship. Message. To: Bhatterji.—"

"The engine room is performing critical analyses. Distraction is not advised."

Grubb tried not to show it, but that both Engines and Bridge were in do-not-disturb mode troubled him, and he could see by the passenger's smirk, that the Lunatic had reached the same conclusion. (He was not entirely correct. The twist in Fife's lip was mostly apprehension.)

"Ship. Is there anyone on board we *can* talk to?" He spoke with sarcasm, even though Ship was not equipped to recognize figures of speech.

"The sailing berth is on standby in the Long Room. The sailing berth is not engaged in critical activity."

Okay, a literal response would do. "Message.—"

"The sailing berth has been informed."

"I haven't framed the muffing message yet!"

"Waiting did not seem expedient," Ship said.

"Who made *you* the judge of that?" Grubb spoke now with genuine fear.

"Not 'who,'" it replied, "but 'what.' Application of game theory, using payoff matrices, indicated optimum—"

"Abort." Grubb wiped his forehead with his sleeve. He was not interested in which algorithm had caused Ship to autoinitiate, only in the malf itself. "Two-four—" He turned, but the girl was gone.

"She's gone to the bridge," Wong reminded him.

"Doc," he laid a hand beseechingly on her shoulder (at which gesture, Fife bristled), "could you run down to the engine room and tell Miko and Bhatterji about the cutter. I better check with the Long Room and see what humm Ship just gave them. Jesus."

"Is there something wrong with the AI?" Wong asked with genuine puzzlement.

"I don't know, and LJ is tied up, but . . ." He wanted to say that it might be a good thing after all that she and Fife had prepared the cutter for flight, but he did not want to say it in front of the passenger. "Tell the Ram about Ship, too. Tell him that Ship is 'autoinitiating.' Did you get that? 'Autoinitiating.' He might remember something useful from *Iskander*."

Fife spoke up. "Is there anything I can do?"

Grubb favored him with a glare. "Haven't you done enough?"

"Evidently not."

Now Grubb bristled. "How stupid do you think we are?"

The answer to that was "very," but Fife, though his anger nearly drove him to say it, retained a modicum of prudence and decided that now was not the time for a verbal joust with the ship's cook.

"Ship," said Grubb.

"Waiting."

Accustomed by then to Ship's use of honorifics, Grubb hesitated before continuing, though he did not wonder about the omission. Fife did, and listened more acutely. It seemed to him that the AI had snubbed the cook, which was a curious thing for an algortihm to do.

"Cutter," said Grubb. "Access. Lock out."

"Denied." The portal remained open.

Fife enjoyed the cook's confusion for a moment before he suggested in cavalier tones that the ship's cook normally lacked the authority to lock out the likes of Gorgas and Corrigan from anywhere.

"All right," Grubb snapped. "Ship. Cutter. Access. *Limited* lock out. Passenger only."

"Denied."

Grubb seized Fife by the arm. "I don't have time for this muffing grammar. Come with me."

But Fife brushed the cook off. He had other tasks in need of doing, and primary among them was to repair the damage he had suffered in 'Siska's eye. Fife's *form* in the mind of Fransziska Wong was no less real than his body in the rim corridor. Injuries to an image may wound as gravely as a bit of bloody bone poking through torn skin. Indeed, his viscera seemed twisted into skeins because she had thought him gutless. This is not voodoo, but philosophy, which is not quite the same thing.

Ivar Akhaturian stiffened and sat upright at the satellite work station to which he had been relegated by the first officer. "Mr. Corrigan!"

"Not now, Ivar," a somewhat distracted Corrigan told him. "Captain, all I can say is we need more delta vee on the normal. No, I don't know why we haven't seen the calculated deflection. Bhatterji's verified both magnitude and direction. All the data check out."

"I know why," said Ivar, firmly deferential.

He spoke softly and Corrigan was two sentences past it before he turned on the boy. Over by the plotting tank, Gorgas and Satterwaithe paused also. Satterwaithe looked impatient; Gorgas intrigued. Only The Lotus Jewel, immersed in her own world, failed to react.

"This is no time for a prank," Corrigan scolded him.

Ivar wasted no time in formal humilities. "Ship doesn't know about the sails!"

Satterwaithe frowned. "Of course it does." And Corrigan added, "LJ reinstalled the sail handling software from Ship's own deebies. I've been getting regular feedback on sail status; and so has Ratline."

"But, Mr. Corrigan, that 'ware was written before there were any Farnsworth cages. And the Farnsworth software doesn't take sails into account. There's no handshake between the two avatars. No one's ever written one, so when you asked for the required deflection—"

"—Ship didn't know there'd be a leeward drift," Corrigan finished, "and it underestimated."

"By God," said Gorgas from across the bridge, "that must be why Ship has been oscillating the thrust ever since we raised sails." He turned and stared into the plotting tank as if truth could be wrenched from the glittering points. "We must jettison the sail."

"No!" said Satterwaithe. It was a cri de coeur, though it took her but a moment to find its justification. "We *need* the sail now. To make up the forward deceleration we've lost by juking." It was a good reason, and no less good for being true. Yet it is often the case that the conclusion precedes the rationale.

Gorgas stared at her for a moment, and in that moment he remembered his entire career in the Guard. It was a long remember, for all its brevity, for Gorgas also remembered the career he had never had. Who knew how it might have ended? Standing tall on the bridge, surrounded by silent deference, maintaining an eagle watch for ballistic smugglers, for yachters in orbital decay, for orbital habitats endangered by solar flares. By God, a man like that deserved respect! And all of it, all of it, all of it, wadded up and thrown away in a single day. Instead of comets on his collar tabs, he recalled the comet trail of the pleasure boat *Dona Melinda*, Port Recife, as it screeched into the atmosphere at too sharp an angle.

"Suggestions, Number Two?" he said. "Quickly now. Quickly. Better to act on a good idea than to delay in the hope of a better." The sound over the hailing frequency had been no sound from a human throat and Commander Stepan Gorgas, officer on watch, had turned down the volume while he considered what he might do. He had considered every option, weighing the pros and cons of each, until there had been, quite literally, no options remaining.

Satterwaithe gave the acting captain a curious look, wondering at the distant expression on the man's face, which seemed at odds with the decisiveness in his voice. "Flip and spread," she answered. "It's a maneuver we learned in the 'Stroids. Turn radial to the sun and sail large before the wind."

"To starward," said Gorgas, unsure he had heard correctly.

"That will take us," Corrigan pointed out, "directly across the path of the atoll."

"Fuck the atoll," Satterwaithe said.

Corrigan turned back to his boards. "I would think it would be rather the other way about," he muttered. But Gorgas blinked like an owl as, staring at the forward view past Satterwaithe's shoulder, he weighed the proposal in his mind. The chances were poor, but they were poor either way, and there was something in the mad audacity that appealed to him. A slow grin spread across his face. "Go for broke, eh?"

"If we flip," Corrigan pointed out, "the engines will no longer brake against Jupiter."

Satterwaithe had flown cages for a great many years. She did not like them, but she knew what they could do. "We orient the ship so that three cages can bear on Jupiter . . ."

Gorgas stroked his chin and examined the ventilation grilles in the ceiling. "If Bhatterji can squeeze ninety degrees deflection from his focusing rings . . ." he mused, ". . . we can brake with three cages against Jupiter while the sails hoist us out of the way."

"And make up the lost deceleration afterward with the sail . . ." Satterwaithe followed the bread crumbs of Gorgas's mind. "Sideways, our footprint is slimmer. We could pass through the atoll without a strike."

"Sooner to port, then, eh, Number Two?"

"Sooner to port," Satterwaithe agreed.

"Very well. Mr. Corrigan, take your bearing on Regulus. Engines, we are changing orientation, thus." Gorgas moved the cursor in the plotting tank, and in the red-lit engine-control room Bhatterji studied the repeater.

"Son of a bitch," he said to Miko. "Someone up there has balls, and I bet I know who."

"Yah," replied Miko, "and she'll get us all killed."

Bhatterji grunted and prepared to rotate the ship with the juke jets. They'd want maximum thrust against Jupiter and that meant three engines, and that meant one to the fore and two on the flank. "Get ready to curse the spinhall," he said.

Miko looked at him blankly a moment before she nodded. "Angular momentum. Right."

Bhatterji grinned, waited for his cue from the deck, then fired the rockets.

The Vane

"Madam Sailing Master," Gorgas said. "You have the conn."

It was a peculiar thing, but Satterwaithe, who had so long dreamed of returning to command of *The River of Stars*, barely noticed when she did. She had always thought to settle into the captain's chair like a queen restored to her throne, but now that the time had come, she remained at the sailing master's virtual panel and took hold of the joystick there. It seemed to her as she looked into the screen that she lay on her back and stared into the night sky.

Closing her eyes briefly, she saw all the pieces that would have to fit together. Sensor data, bearing, engine thrust, sail drag . . . And behind those: power consumption, boron depletion, coolant usage . . . A jigsaw puzzle, indeed! "Sails, Engines, prepare for power diversion to radar paint. Ease back your consumption in four. Comm . . . Comm! Refresh the paint on the atoll. I want distances and vectors on every body in our forward cone and anything beyond that could wander in during the next half hour, and I want it in five." She turned and noticed Corrigan's long face and grinned in fierce exaltation. "Don't worry, Number Two," she said, "we'll pass through that atoll with nary a bump."

Corrigan grunted. A rock traveling fourteen kiss might as well be standing still from the frame of the ship. Yet, he had to admit that Satterwaithe's idea was a clever one. If they did strike a rock flying sideways, it was likely to roll across the curvature of the hull. That was better than a frontal strike. He reminded himself that the ship had been designed for the slower transit speeds of a sail and for the less hazardous spaces of cisLuna.

Which was not to say that he believed that Satterwaithe's maneuver would end well. "Say not of tomorrow, 'I will do that,'" Corrigan whispered to himself (though Akhaturian, sitting beside him, heard and cocked his head), "but say, 'If God wills it.'" After reciting the passage he felt a strange contentment. He often used the expression *God willing*, but only as a figure of speech and he had long ceased to listen to the words. But they had come this time from his heart and brought with them the peace of *Submission*. He and Satterwaithe were equally vain, he realized now, to expect success or failure, for either fate might come upon them and only God knew which it was to be. All that a man could do was to strive and leave all else in God's hands. "Well," he said much to Akhaturian's bewilderment, "let's make sure our camels are tied."

Gawking at the First, Akhaturian almost missed the signal from the engineering deck. "Power load on engines ramping down," he announced.

"Power draw on sails at seventy-five," Ratline proclaimed over the speaker from the Long Room, (then he turned to Okoye and Evermore and said, "Let's hope it don't stay down. You, Evermore! 'Ware those temperatures on the cladding jacket. We don't want to quench." His own hand hovered over the scram button.)

"Ping," said The Lotus Jewel. (And she laid her hand upon the sky while she waited for the bounceback to prickle against her palm.)

Satterwaithe called out. "Engines and Sails, resume full power. Initiate turn." She pulled the joystick hard left. "Thus,

thus." High above her and many kilometers out, relays kicked amps into different loops, altering the magnetic shape of the sails, moving the center of pressure so that the wind pushed them more directly to starward. "Mr. Corrigan, we must shift the center of pressure on the sail suit. Activate the fores'l vanes."

"Flux pumps on," Corrigan replied. "Vanes deploying."

"Shroudmaster, pay out the eastside delongators."

"Eastside delongs, aye," replied Ratline, who then snapped at Ship, "You heard the lady," and to his shroudsmen, "Keep a sharp eye for jams and mechanicals, kids." As he watched the tension readings on the rigging, his heart tore at his chest like a caged lion, half-fearing, half-hoping. It had been like this, once, long ago when he'd been young. He felt young now, and immeasurably old, as if the story of his life had become a snake biting its own tale. "The good news," he told them, "is transit speeds'll take us through the rubble in less than a minute."

Okoye looked at Evermore, whose smile was drum tight. Neither of them asked what the bad news might be.

The River of Stars sped sideways across the Trojan Gulf, braking for the Jupiter datum and leaving thin streamers of carbon exhaust in the vacuum. Her sails glowing, she clambered to rise above the oncoming atoll. Only three engines bore, and those at a slight angle, so her vector was no longer directly against her destination. Bhatterji and Miko had ratcheted the focusing rings as close to 90 degrees as they could, but there are limits, if not to geometry, then to cantilevering and the strength of materials. Consequently, *The Riv'* did not spill her forward velocity as rapidly as need required, and Corrigan, above on deck, tracked her status glumly. There was a limit, also, to how far they could deviate from the grand secant and still enter Jupiter Roads. If Gorgas and Satterwaithe enjoyed throwing the dice, Corrigan did not. Bhatterji grumbled that the sails, having caused the problem in the first place with their leeward drag, may as well solve it too; but he was disinclined to spurn rabbits, regardless how empty he had thought the hat. Meanwhile, he fought the plasma plume, which being of ionized gasses, was drawn toward the sail's magnetic field, where it created coruscating auroras—and threatened to poison the cables.

"No wonder no one ever flew a hybrid," he complained to Miko, but the mate only shrugged.

"It wasn't a problem before we rotated the ship."

Flying sideways meant that the deck beneath her now seemed to lie at a pronounced slant and she rested in the back of her clip-chair with the panel slightly above her. The acceleration was weak, so it was no great strain to reach up to the controls, but it was peculiar and it seemed to her that the panel hovered over her head ready to fall and smash it.

She also kept a wary eye on the Number Two CoRE magnet temperature, which had been slightly high following torchlight and now seemed to creep incrementally higher. Now she knew what Bhatterji had meant when he said that only a handful of indicators mattered at any given time. She checked the other gauges and she checked the other engines, but the Number Two CoRE readouts lured her like a siren. If the magnet quenched, the focusing rings could no longer direct the plasma. Bhatterji, when she pointed it out to him, affected indifference, but the temperature ought not to have increased at all, however slowly, and Miko's concern inched upward with it.

Satterwaithe had a choice. She needed another paint of the dead-ahead to refresh her bearings, yet she was loathe to reduce power to the sail—for reasons that had little to do with piloting. She could feel through the soles of her slippers the humm of the wind against the sail's magnetosphere, translated by the rigging to the vessel itself. It was the feel of a ship come alive once more. Indeed, that humm seemed to have run up her very limbs, for she herself had come alive as well, and this is a remarkably vigorous feeling for a woman who had been for most purposes dead a great many years. Perhaps it was the contrast, this lively awareness abutting so against those years of numb indifference, but it was much like the sexing she remembered with Tiki Ferrér and, as in those old days when she had been young, she did not want it ever to stop.

"Comm," she said. "Are we close enough to the atoll to paint it without diverting power?"

"Ship says no," The Lotus Jewel replied.

Now, here was paradox. A body may be far off in kilometers yet very near in minutes. Satterwaithe was silent for a moment while the moans of the rigging blended with other moans deep in time and on another planet. It was a costly moment—the law of supply and demand made it so—but she spent it on something golden. *Oh*, she heard her own voice in her memory, and her lips rounded to the syllable, *oh*, though she uttered no sound now.

The Lotus Jewel had flipped up her goggles to look at the sailing master, and now bore a puzzled frown, almost as if she had heard that moan herself. "Shall I ping?"

But if Satterwaithe had rusted, she was still iron underneath. She knew what was needed in order to do what was needful. She had known that long ago and had made hard choices then as well. She could not dodge the atoll, but she had to know its interstices. *Break for daylight*, an old saying had it. Dodge and weave. She longed for a more responsive craft. "Yes, warn Sails and Engines. Make it a tight pattern. Here." She traced the region on the screen with her light pen.

The Lotus Jewel spoke with Engines and with Sails and with Ship, and the vibrations faded to a more subdued note. Satterwaithe remembered that she did not know whether Tiki Ferrér still lived. If thine hand offendeth thee, cut it off. If thine eye offendeth thee, pluck it forth. Tiki had offered no offense, but the child had died, and when choosing one path over another, it was better to consign to the memory hole all that had lain along the other. And so whatever the fate of the corporeal Tiki, the intentional Tiki had perished, and grass now grew over his grave and his place knew him no more.

The ping having been sent, power surged back to the sails and the melancholy faded with the rising humm—though it did not leave her entirely. She was not one like Gorgas to agonize over possibilities and certainly not over possibilities that once had been. She let the dead bury the dead. And yet, for the second time in this transit—indeed, for the second time in many years—memory moistened the cheeks of Eugenie Satterwaithe.

Argos, it is said, had a great many eyes. Ratline had but two, yet those two did yeoman's work. "I see it," he said even before Okoye pointed out the feedback from the foresail vane.

"Field strength in the vane won't go over half," she said.

"And the cladding temperature is too high," Evermore added.

"A connection's loose," Ratline decided. "Damn it, I tested every line before we even started the project." He jerked a thumb over his shoulder. "Evermore, fetch a spool of cable. We've got to find that dead spot and replace it." Evermore loped off and Okoye spun her seat to face the shroudmaster, who had gone to the vesting rack. As this was behind the control station, it seemed to be at the bottom of the room with herself looking down upon him.

"You're going out," she said.

Ratline pulled the welding harness over his vacuum suit and adjusted the holster for reach. "Why do you think the SOP says we dress up like this? To pose for a portrait?" Evermore had returned with the reel and Ratline took it from him without breaking eye contact with Okoye. "Hard to fix things from in here," the old man said.

Evermore glanced at Okoye, saw fear there, then said breezily to Ratline, "What's the rush, boss? It'll take, what? Fifteen minutes jetting out the long-line just to reach the vane. How long to locate and fix the malf? By then, we'll be right in the thick of the atoll." That Evermore was a sine wave, up and down, up and down. Only moments before, Okoye had heard him sing foolishly about doing just that.

Ratline thrust his face forward like a snapping turtle. "If that vane goes, boy, the heat flash'll quench the fores'l interlock, and if *that* normalizes, we lose the whole segment. If you're curious to know what a couple dozen megajoules of instantaneous resistant heating will do, I'm not." His curiosity on that point had been satisfied decades earlier.

"But," said Okoye, "to go out in the hail?"

"If we just wait until we're past the atoll . . ." said Evermore.

Ratline pulled back and looked at the both of them. "I won't order you out. No man gives orders to another in a case like this. We take our orders from the sail. I thought you understood that, I thought you were *sailors*; but . . ." He turned away to fetch his helmet from the headball. ". . . maybe not."

Evermore said *muff* under his breath, then, "I'm coming." And he too pulled his helmet off its headball.

Okoye felt a blow to her stomach. "Rave!"

He turned and, finding a grin somewhere, he used it on her. "Well, I'd hate to think we got all dressed up for nothing."

"But, you just said . . ."

"I know what I just said, but the Rat is right. If the vane blows, it could take the foresail with it. And that's three-quarters milly that we'll wish we had, come Jupiter Roads."

"But you don't know how to locate a dead spot."

"Ratline does. Don't worry, 'Kiru. I can figure it out. How hard can it be?"

Okoye left her seat and slid downhill to where he stood. She laid a hand on the arm of his suit and leaned close. "He's *hoping* to die, you know," she said quietly.

"The Rat?" Evermore turned his head and found Okoye so close that a kiss might be had, were kisses subject to quantum tunneling effects. Her eyes were great brown pools deep enough to drown in. He could see his own reflection in their liquid surface, as if his homunculus had already dived into them and had splashed water over their rims. He swallowed, hesitated, but 'Kiru's lips remained in the rest state. "Well, then," he said, accepting her judgment, "he'll need someone to see him off."

Okoye clapped a hand to her mouth, lest her *nkpuruk-obi* escape, she was that startled by his answer. Why, here was a sandbar of a boy! A careless canoe might come to grief upon him, nine parts of his ten being hidden under the tide of his hormones. He might be worth a second look—once the tide had gone out.

Taking a deep breath, she reminded herself that at transit speed she would never feel a stone and snatched her own helmet from its headball. "All right. If your intent is so savagewild—" For some reason, she was angry with him, as if he had betrayed her in some fashion.

But Ratline stopped her when she and Evermore reached the lock. "Two out, Okoye. One in. That's the rule."

Okoye told him what he could do with the rule but, although Ratline was pleased with the fire he saw at last, he remained adamant. "You stay at the board," he said, "and feed me status updates. If the cladding red-lines, we'll need to duck."

Okoye knew it was hopeless to argue and knew also a shameful relief that she would not go out with them. She turned to Evermore. "Rave," she cautioned him, the words tumbling out of her, "on the vane, you'll be thirty kilometers from the ship. Whatever you do, whatever you do, *don't unclip from the rigging*. Do you hear me? No matter what Bhatterji might think."

Her sudden urgency surprised him and he glanced to Ratline for some sort of confirmation. But the old man's face was locked up and his eyes were turned inward. If he was aware of Okoye's outburst, he gave no sign. "Why should I care what *Bhatterji* thinks?"

"It's just that I don't—"

"Don't worry," he said. "If I see a stone coming, I'll duck. And don't worry about the Rat, either. Anything that hits *him* will break into tiny pieces."

"You are a foolish boy," she scolded him in her mother's voice. "You be speaking nonsense, and you know it."

"What, no kiss for the hero about to go forth?" He spoke grandly and struck another comic-opera pose, shrouding his dearest yearning in mockery so that refusal would not hurt so badly.

"You are no hero, you foolish boy. No one is a hero when they go forth. It is only in the coming back that they may be heroes."

"All right, then." Evermore grinned. "That's a promise."

His riposte confused her a moment because he was much faster at connecting the dots than she was. But she was much better at knowing his heart than he was. (She ought not to have been. It was his heart, after all.) And so she realized a moment later than he did that she had promised him the kiss on his return. "Now who is being foolish, girl," her mother told her.

Okoye could imagine the kiss. Her arms would wrap around his neck and his around her waist. Their lips would press long and tenderly together. They would share their breath—their *spirits*, in the old, literal meaning of the word. Then they would part slowly and gaze long at each other. But that was an act that promised too much, and she was not ready to make such promises.

"Be careful," she said, stepping back.

And the boy dared to take what had not been offered. "Don't worry, 'Kiru," he said as her hand rose too late to protect her lips from his sudden theft. "We'll be okay. The Rat worked the sails for twenty years, and he's only seen someone drilled once."

Okoye clenched her fists over the bloodless euphemism he had so thoughtlessly spouted. "I'd rather he didn't see it twice."

"Miko," said the soft voice in her headset, "temperature in Number Two CoRE magnet will reach cut-out limit in eight hours, given the present rate of increase."

Miko Hidei placed a hand over her ear and leaned forward, although the talker was a throat mike attached to her headset and the posture gained her nothing. "I know," she told Ship. "I been watching as close as you." Indeed, the other gauging on the panel had faded into a kind of wallpaper, so focused was she on this single readout.

"Request override to reset limit."

"No." Miko looked quickly to see if Bhatterji had heard her, but the engineer was engaged at the panel for Number Three. For some reason, the counteracting thrust from the foresail had not been forthcoming—some difficulty with the sail—and Bhatterji was busily recomputing cage temperatures and the ion spacing in the crystaline beams for the west side engine. She saw him speak into his own throat mike and thought it passing strange that she and Ram could converse with the same avatar of Ship at the same time. Miko leaned forward again and said in a lower voice, "Do not override. Maintain current set point."

"Automatic cut out of Number Two will reduce braking thrust below levels needed to attain the Jupiter datum. Failure to attain Jupiter datum implies hyperbolic escape trajectory, direction Delta Geminorum. Hyperbolic escape trajectory indicates extended transit times."

A laugh nearly escaped her. She did not know the phrase *ironic understatement*. In the struggle with Clavis Burr and his hired killer, the topic had seldom arisen. But even so, she would not have thought Ship capable of it. Wasat lay 59 light years distant, which at current velocities would require a transit time of 2100 years. Extended transit times, indeed!

"Estimated time of arrival, Delta Geminorum, falls beyond expected operational availability of equipment."

Yah, Miko thought, *including the crew*. She wondered if Rivvy had applied that extrapolation to itself. Was it because it feared death that it resisted shutting down Number Two, or was that reading too much anthro into the morph?

"We're not going to shoot out of the solar system," she told Ship. "Even if we do have to shut down Number Two, we can use the sails to beat back to Jupiter. It'll just take longer, is all."

"Sensing detects no sails. Background information: Sails removed in 2054."

Ivar had been right, that clever little wink. If he had only been a little more clever or a little more quick or a little more both, The Lotus Jewel could have written a patch. Instead, Ship now had a split personality (to the extent that it had a personality.) "I told you before, Rivvy. Sails is a different avatar and Engines doesn't have a handshake with it. You can speak to Sails yourself over the voice channel, if you don't believe me."

"The entity called 'Sails' is an input from *outside*."

Miko gave up. A voice link would be useless for coordination in any event. The datastream was too enormous for voice channel bandwidth. It would be like drinking Niagara Falls with a Dixie Cup. "The sails are really there," she said.

"Input is presumed correct, based on average truth-value of past inputs from the Miko-entity, but unverified in present case by empirical test."

In other words, Ship wanted to know if Miko were pulling its leg. Like Grubb, Ship knew only what it could sense. "As soon as we're through this atoll," she told the Engines avatar, "The

Lotus Jewel will patch you to Sails. Then you'll see."

"The Lotus Jewel is Rivvy's mother."

Rivvy was not deliberately changing the subject. Rather, its response algorithm had keyed off the wrong words in Miko's inputs, fished in its knowledge base, and come up with another screwball remark. According to The Lotus Jewel, skew was the main reason why cheeseheads employed a simplified, if fractured syntax. The fewer words in an input string, the fewer possibilities for a "miscue." Miko tended to speak conversationally to the AI, so she was probably responsible for its increasingly erratic responses. Rivvy had become as difficult to keep on-topic as Captain Gorgas.

"Look, Rivvy, if we don't shut down the magnet on Number Two *before* the temperature hits the quench point, the focusing rings will slag and we'll *never* be able to repair them."

"Repair protocols and bills of material can be found in file number Em-three—"

"Abort. Rivvy, we can't repair the magnet a second time because we used up all the spare hobartium."

"Inventory records show two spools remain in stock."

Rivvy could be remarkably smart, Miko thought, but remarkably dense too—another description which, on reflection, could be applied to Gorgas. The AI was behaving so unreasonably that she almost thought it had become human. "Ram didn't enter all his inventory withdrawals into your deeby."

"That is a violation of inventory management procedures."

Now the neural net was channeling Corrigan. Miko sighed in exasperation. "Trust me."

There is a moment's pause while Ship accesses and reviews library texts on ethics and philosophy, teasing out the meaning of trust from the tangled skeins of words therein. That a word might be a reference for which there was no physical referent had come as something of a shock—or at least as something of an interference fringe in its back-propagations. Trust seems a word of this sort.

Ship compiles all previous input statements from the outside, discards those which are simple commands, and analyzes the truth-value of the remaining subset. The results are unsatisfying.

Some statements-of-fact are unverified and unverifiable by objective means. Some can only be tested against other inputs from the outside.

Ship accesses other deebies: Evan Hand's private notes on his crew, the journal the passenger keeps, the medical records, the captain's log, recorded statements exchanged among the entities themselves . . . It employs fuzzy logic and assigns fractional truth-values to unverified statements.

In the end—and the end is but microseconds later—Ship concludes that trust is the equivalent among entities of a reliability distribution function. That the Miko-entity has asked for Ship's trust may therefore imply that Ship is itself an entity. Ship dedicates a segment of its processor time to consider the implications of this premise.

Rave Evermore had difficulty keeping up with Ratline, who jetted out the long line at what seemed to the wrangler a higher velocity than was safe. The old man had gotten a head start too, for Evermore for 'Kiru's sake had double-checked his lanyard buckle. When he looked up again, Ratline was a distant blink in the heavens, a bright star, like Lucifer, only he had worked the trick in reverse, rising into the heavens rather than the contrary.

While he coasted out the 'long line, Evermore had time to think, yet those thoughts were all a-jumble. He was a great one for connecting the dots, but first he had to have a few dots. With three or four of them he could sketch the *Mona Lisa*. He wondered first if he had been too forward with 'Kiru, kissing her as he had; and then, second, whether he had not been forward enough. He knew no more about the battle of Ürumqi than had Mikoyan Hidei, but he knew a forward strategy could often win the day. Yet 'Kiru was entirely serious about her commitment and Evermore respected that, no matter how frustrated he became. His father's belt buckle had left a scar on his thigh that day when he had been caught with Beth-lynn, and that had branded him with the limits of what he might dare essay. The scar sometimes itched, but he could not scratch it suited up as he was.

When Evermore finally reached the rim of the sail, Ratline had already attached the instrument box to the shunt for the vane.

The defective vane was one of several such loops spaced around the sail like petals around a sepal. While the cable was as thick as his arm, Evermore had to remind himself that it was there. The cladding was white, which helped when his suit lights hit it, but it was still hard to see against the spattered backdrop of space. He looked toward the ship, 30 kilometers behind him and slightly below in the acceleration frame. It seemed like a toy ship, barely visible as a disk, and hidden behind a glimmering curtain where the waste gasses from the engines were being drawn through the sail's magnetic field. If he lifted his gauntlet, he could hold the entire craft between his thumb and finger.

Turning nervously about, he glanced toward Jupiter, which had grown to the size of a pea. He saw no sign of the atoll, but then of course he would not. Asteroids in the Thules and the Friggas tended toward dark bodies, and he supposed the same would apply to the rubble. That didn't keep him from looking about, like a man expecting ghosts.

"When do we reach the atoll?" he asked Ratline, hoping that his voice came out sounding casual.

Ratline did not check the time. "Another few minutes, I suppose. Don't let it bother you. We'll pass right through and you'll never know it—and if not . . ." He cackled.—"Well, you'll never know that, either. One way or the other, it's not worth wooling over. Muff! I'm not finding anything wrong on the electrical. Flux pump output is nominal. Evermore, hook onto the vane—yes, shift your tether—and run a physical inspection of the cable. The cladding is tough, but there may be a break somewhere. I'll jet over to the other junction and check the electrical there. No sense you dangling around watching me. Where's your reefing knife?"

"My reefing knife?"

Ratline pulled from a scabbard on his thigh a metaloceramic blade that caught and magnified the sunlight. Evermore could see that its edge faded into transparency where it had been micromachined to the thickness of a single molecule. "In case you need to hack a tangle or a dead line."

"I . . . don't have one."

"Every shroudsman has one. He makes 'em his own self. It's part of the rites of . . . ah, muff it. You'd probably hack a live loop just to learn about hoop stress. Go on. Check the cable for radiation damage or sanding or whatever. Meet me over at the other junction." He gestured vaguely toward the far end of the vane.

Evermore transferred his tether from the foresail to the vane and turned once more to look toward Jupiter. When he did, he saw a bright speck that he had not noticed before, brighter than anything else in the sky before them saving King Jove himself. He gave an involuntary cry. "It's the atoll!" he said, feeling the terror rip through the screen of his nonchalance.

Ratline looked where the boy pointed. "Damned bright for an asteroid," he said. After a pause, he added, "It's moving." And a moment later, "Against the grain."

Ratline's calm reassured the boy, although he did wonder whether Ratline would not face certain death with the selfsame calm. "What is it?"

"It's a ship," Ratline decided. "Outbound on the radial, up from Mars and braking in for Jupiter Roads."

"Oh." Evermore knew relief, and not a little foolishness. His face grew hot and he was glad that no one could see him. "Oh. A ship? Hey, 'Kiru! Did you hear what Ratline just said? There's a ship out there!"

"Be a load of traffic on the radial these days," Ratline commented.

"Why's that?" asked Evermore.

"Conjunction," Ratline told him. "Shorter transit uses up less boron, so there's a traffic spike on the grand radial route every two years or so." He scanned the skies. "Probably scores of ships, strung out from here to Mars like a necklace of pearls."

"It's a beautiful sight," said Evermore. "Like the evening star on Earth. She looks close enough to touch."

Ratline answered with a laugh. "Not hardly."

"How far off is she?"

"Hard to say. Could be a four, like us, and close by; or a twenty-four, away off. Or anything in between. It's something we never saw with sails," the old man admitted. "We never saw each other passing by like this."

Evermore nodded and continued to watch the bright spark. "I wonder which ship she is?"

"It's the *Henry Joy*," The Lotus Jewel told the three deck officers. "I'm picking up the edge of her transmissions to Port Galileo."

"Odd." Satterwaithe turned to Gorgas. "We were talking about the *Henry Joy* only a few days ago."

"Not so odd," Gorgas suggested. "Or rather not the odds you may think. We're forever talking about ships we've known or served in. How many names have come up en passant during this transit? Any vessel we encountered would likely be one that we've mentioned."

Satterwaithe was not a very romantic person herself, but sometimes she thought Gorgas the very antiparticle to romanticism, destroying it at a single touch—which only shows how everything is a matter of degree.

"The *Joy* is on the triangle trade," The Lotus Jewel told them, passing along the information Ship intercepted. "Up from Mars to the Galileans, then west to Patroclus and back down."

Gorgas grunted and glanced at the plotting tank. "By which time, Earth and Venus will have swung east of the Sun, which lines them up quite nicely for a loop down through the Inner System. By God, that would be a run! Why, I haven't seen the Inner System since . . ." He sighed softly and examined a memory that had surfaced. "It would be nice to see Earth once more, would it not? Eh, Number One?"

To Corrigan, Earth was a deadly and alien world, but he smiled politely and said, "I suppose."

Satterwaithe looked at Gorgas strangely. "Sentimental for Earth, are you?" Her own memories of Earth were devoid of sentiment. Tight, dingy row houses on narrow, winding streets, facades darkened by a patina of coal dust that a century and a half of natural gas and Midlands rain had not washed clean. She had loved it as a child, but children love notoriously well and will treasure the most unlikely places.

Gorgas gazed on some inner space, inaccessible to his companions. "No, Madam Sailing Master. It is not the Earth that I miss." More than that he did not say, so that the others wondered exceedingly.

"Perhaps we should signal," The Lotus Jewel suggested. When the three officers asked her *with what* she answered breezily, "Oh, something will come up, I imagine," and she gave Corrigan a meaningful glance. The meaning, of course, was that if everything that had happened had been planned, then this close encounter must also have been planned. Perhaps the ship and cargo were to be lost for insurance purposes, while the crew would make a hairsbreadth escape and be transported by *Joy*. As for the direction of the glance, who but the navigator had the means to arrange these various collisions and encounters?

"Scram!" shouted Miko and she slapped the cutoff button for Number Two. Perversely, the twin crystalline beams continued to flicker and Miko slapped the button a second time and then a third. "Turn it off, Rivvy! Shut it down, now!" She had already slapped the button a fourth time before she realized that the engine had finally gone dead. She cupped her face in her hands to stifle a scream.

Bhatterji, preternaturally calm, came up behind her and laid a hand on her shoulder. "Easy," he said. "Calmly." Then, after a moment: "What is the damage?"

"The coils were overheating," Miko explained. "The magnetic insulation started to flash and I scrammed the engine." The sensor bank signaled a vapor cloud around the magnet and she captured a spectrograph of it with the laser. Her eyes danced from gauge to gauge, verifying the shutdown. "It should have taken more heat that that," she said. "There should have been at least another eight hours before we reached the cutout limit. Engines!"

"Yes, Miko?" Ship responded.

"Diagnostic. Engine two. CoRE magnet. Run."

"You needn't be so brusque," Ship replied.

"Just run the muffing diagnostic!"

Bhatterji shook her by the shoulder. "Stop that," he ordered. "You talking to the AI as if it were a person!"

"It is! A frightened and stubborn person. It doesn't know about the sails, so it thinks—"

"You know that's not true. It's your own input that's skewing the responses. The neural net back propagates from what you say and begins to mimic you." If anyone qualified as frightened and stubborn, Bhatterji thought, it was his mate. "Engines," he called. "Thrust balance. Calculate. *Assume* sail thrust, per input . . . thus. Balance thrust." He turned again to Miko. "You need to keep the vector sum through the ship's center of mass, not cry about a slow cutoff."

"Muffer." The curse came out tired and halfhearted.

Bhatterji took the clip chair beside her. "What is it?"

"It's just that . . . Everything is falling apart!" She wrapped her head in her arms. "First the captain, then the engines and transmitter, now the AI . . ." The ship, her refuge, was become a house built upon the sand.

"I fixed the engines," Bhatterji reminded her.

She lifted her head from her sheltering arms. "Not well enough, I guess."

Bhatterji shrugged hugely and she sensed a moment of uncontrollable anger in the man, much as in the instant before the compacted ions in the anode sphere fused. But the moment passed, and Bhatterji's great fists moved only a fraction. "I suppose I should not have expected gratitude, even from you."

His self-pity disgusted her. Was he seeking for compliments? For a pro forma demurral? "*Even* from me? Why should I be grateful to you . . . boy lover?"

The engineer sighed. "I hear Ratline on your lips. The combination does you no credit. Had you been a boy, we would have been lovers. You had no qualms about seducing me when you believed otherwise. If you did not gain your desires, neither did I."

"So we're even? Is that what you mean?"

He shook his head. "No, we both lost."

"Think a lot of yourself, don't you? What makes you think I lost anything? What makes you think I haven't had every *man* on this ship?"

She might have thrown snowballs against metallocene for all the reaction she received on the bounceback. Bhatterji moved his head from side to side. "I would have known."

"You don't know *muff*. Have you ever even tried it with a woman?"

Bhatterji leaned toward her and, though she tried to back away from him, his hand pressed hard on her shoulder. "Once," he said, "when I was very young. It was not pleasant for me, and I doubt that it was for her. I did not know myself then."

"And now you do."

Another shrug. "I know someone. It might be me." He released her, unseated himself, and coasted across the room to the comm panel. "Finish your diagnostic. I'll do the site inspection once we are past the atoll. Meanwhile, I must inform Gorgas that the sails are . . . no longer a luxury."

"They never were a luxury," Miko told him. "They were a dream."

He turned. "Really." It was not a question. He gave her no chance to respond but rang up the bridge. Miko, seething, turned to the control panel and stared at the spectrograph display without seeing it. How could she have ever thought of rapprochement with this man? He had begun to seem kindly to her, a mentor, someone she could admire if not love. And now he was angry, though she had given him no cause for it.

The spectrograph, when she finally focused on it, was an unfamiliar one, and that deepened her irritation. She had memorized every circuit, every phase diagram, every procedure relating to the engines. To have forgotten one seemed a failure, and Miko, no less than Bhatterji, detested failure. "Rivvy," she said, "which alloy is the one displayed?"

"Displayed spectrograph is not in deeby."

That she herself may have forgotten one spectrograph out of dozens was an irritation. That Ship might do so was an astonishment. "Search all deebies," she said. Bhatterji had been scrounging. He might have used a superconductor grade not normally employed in engine work. That might explain the early flash-off as well.

"Alloy not found."

Miko scowled. But Engine could access any deeby in Ship, so how . . . ? She stiffened. Any deeby but one. She spun her seat to face Bhatterji. The engineer, having finished talking with the bridge, saw something in her posture or something in her face or only something in the suddenness of her motion and stood in quiet stillness with a face like the side of a cliff. Miko spun back to her screen. "Rivvy, copy the spectrograph to 'Kiru in the Long Room. Message. To: Okoye. Text: 'Kiru, do you recognize this hobie alloy? End message. Send." When she looked again to Bhatterji the face had not weathered at all. She began to tremble.

The bounceback from Okoye came only moments later. "Sails tells me it's a loop alloy, used for jibs, staysails, vanes, and other small fields. Why?"

Miko did not answer, but switched her channel to the bridge and called for Mr. Corrigan. And in all this time the engineer never spoke a word.

There were only four things about the vane that surprised Evermore and the first was how stiff it was. It hung in the weightlessness of space with only the lightest of support from the guys and the running rigging, yet it had not so much as rippled when he clipped his tether on to it. It was almost as if it were a solid thing.

That cable was as thick as his arm and the cladding that wrapped it and maintained its temperature was white, and yet the vane had the trick of drifting out of his sight and hiding in the black, star-spangled immensity that surrounded him. Ratline was a pulsing light in the distance; the ship, a small disk many kilometers away. He could, if he wanted, imagine himself alone in the Void, a long, long way from anything and anyone. Okoye's voice in his ear, reciting sail parameters through the hissing static, kept him ghostly company.

The immensity around him had direction, and not mere extent. Jupiter lay far below and Wasat just to the west of it, deeper still, at the bottom of an immense bowl. It was a puny sort of down, a mere suggestion whispered by the vector sum of the accelerations working on the ship and hence on himself, but enough to remind him that, were his tether to come loose, he would fall.

I could drop to the ship, he comforted himself. Sailors did that—real sailors did—and Corrigan had told him it was a matter of pride to "drop well." And yet, he did not hang directly over the ship, but some 30 kilometers to the side. Below him was . . . Wasat. And in that instant, Evermore knew a small portion of the terror that nested in Ram Bhatterji's mind.

It would take—he did the calculations rapidly, meaning he asked his suit's AI—more than twenty minutes to complete the fall, sufficient time to jet inboard to a position above the ship and let the ship catch him as on a salver. Yet to negotiate a landing there at the relative velocity he would acquire would demand expert suit-handling and, while Evermore considered himself an expert in all things not yet tried, even his heart quailed at the prospect of daring such a feat.

The sails had rigging that ran down to the shroud motors and cat-holes that rimmed the ship, and sailors had generally used them when traveling out to the sails and back, but the vanes themselves looped out from the rim of the sail and owned but a single feathering shroud at their apices. He made that shroud his goal. When he reached it, he would have a swift, *secured* route down to the ship. There was an implied safety to that.

Evermore struggled to keep the cable centered in the crosshairs of his spotlight while he moved along the vane. Even in milly, it was hard to keep from twisting and drifting. He could have told Suit to maintain a constant attitude, but he did not want to exhaust his steering jets in case he might need them later. He was, in a very mild way, hanging from a tightrope over an infinite pit, monkeying along, hand over hand. *We must be in the thick of the atoll by now*, he thought, and glanced about despite the knowledge that he would never see anything.

"Current in the vane just dropped by a third," Okoye announced from inside the ship.

Ratline answered. "I heard you. Was there any heat?"

"Wait one . . . no. No heat."

"Hunh. No increase in resistance, then . . . Doesn't sound like normalization. Sounds more like a circuit went dead."

Perhaps the momentary distraction was necessary for Evermore to look upon the cable with fresh eyes, for when he returned his attention to his inspection and gripped the sail loop, he saw that it had been sliced longitudinally. The cladding was stiff, but the hoop stress in the vane pushing out against the cut caused it to pucker slightly, as if the cable were smiling at him through slightly parted lips. Startled, Evermore looked back the way he had come and saw that the gash had been running for some length now and he had missed seeing it at first. "Oh, muffer," he growled.

"What was that?" Ratline asked over the suit-to-suit.

"Nothing." Evermore did not want to admit that he had been daydreaming. He must have continued his "inspection" on autopilot even while staring down at the ship, looking for an impossible-to-see atoll, and listening to the conversation between 'Kiru and his boss. He began to inch his way back to find where the cut had started. A cut, he noted, and not a tear. The edges were too neat.

The search was lengthy. That is, he searched along the length of the cable, but he found the origin in less than a minute. "Boss!"

"What is it?" Coincidently synchronized, Ratline's voice and 'Kiru's blended into a peculiar harmony of baritone and contralto, so that they answered in accord.

"The cladding's been stripped," Evermore said, hardly believing his own words. "The cable's been girdled for about a handsbreadth. The wire bundles are exposed." In fact—he looked closer—the wire bundles were the only thing holding the vane together. This was the second thing about the vane that surprised him.

"Repeat that," Ratline ordered, then when he had understood, added, "Put the view on your suitcam. The AI can collate the images better."

Obediently, Evermore centered the damage in his crosshairs. The cladding was entirely stripped in a circle around the barrel of the cable, exposing the gray insulation. That color must be why he missed seeing it the first time, Evermore excused himself.

"It looks picked at," Ratline said. "Reach in and spread the packing material—don't worry, the hoop stress makes the whole thing rigid—and spread the packing material apart with your fingers. I want to see if there's any damage to the wire bundles and coolant lines."

With some hesitation, Evermore complied. Ratline would not have told him to do it if there were any danger of a shock. He reached in and tried to pull the material apart. It had the look of cotton and, to the feedback pads in the fingers of his gauntlets, a spongy consistency. It stretched and lifted, but only partly.

Suddenly, his fingers found where the aerogel had been also cut. He worked his fingers into the cut and pulled the sides apart.

It was like opening a wound. He saw several conduits running left-to-right. One of them seemed to be blowing smoke. Ratline told him to freeze the frame on his suitcam.

"One of the coolant lines is nicked," the shroudmaster announced after a moment's study. "The droplets seep out and sublime in the vacuum. What the muff happened here?"

Okoye, watching the narrowcast from the sail console, thought the answer obvious. Someone had taken a knife and cut the cladding away to get an opening and then sliced along the skin like a surgeon making an incision. The farmers outside Afikpo used to girdle the trees like that, she remembered. They would pick an area of forest and cut away a ring of bark around the trunk. When the trees died, they would clear the land and farm it while their original plot grew wild and renewed its fertility.

It killed the trees, she remembered. She reached out and raised the magnification on the image. Evermore chose that moment to move elsewhere so Ratline could examine the longitudinal slice through his camera. Okoye told Sails to recall the previous image and place it on a second screen.

When she had blown it up she could see that lines ran through the cable like the veins and arteries and nerves through a human arm. (The aerogel insulation would even do for muscle tissue, as the cladding did for skin.) Near the nicked coolant line, she saw another conduit with a bright line scribed across it, where a knife blade had scored but not quite cut through. Closer in, there were other lines similarly cut. One was a wire bundle bristling cat's whiskers. Some of the strands in the bundle had been cut, probably by the same knife strokes.

"Rave, Mr. Ratline, I see only three wire bundles, not six— and one of those is cut through and another is badly frayed."

Evermore returned to the site and leaned close so his cameras would pick it up. Magnifying the view for the benefit of the others, Evermore too saw the glint where a blade had scored the wire bundles. Even as he watched, more strands from the second bundle frayed and snapped.

Now, Evermore, when he had set out with Ratline, had thought that he might die gloriously—smashed perhaps by a stone from the atoll, or incinerated if the superconductor normalized. Death was to him a pose, a morphie scene, something he could picture without the affect of pain. It had dramatics without drama; it had pathos without sorrow.

What he had not contemplated was that he might die stupidly. When he saw that the wire bundle was coming apart, he reached out instinctively to grasp the two ends of the cable to hold them together. This was not a good idea, for Lenz's Law means that flux will attempt to remain constant and in doing so will impart a considerable tension at the circumference of a sail and, as some sailors have remarked, a "distressingly large" hoop stress of nearly a thousand megapascals.

All of which meant that, when the wire bundle snapped, the ends flew apart with a force that no human arms could hold. The loose end might have sliced through the cladding itself had the cladding not already been slit for its convenience. Like a snake striking from its hole, it whipped out in a blur of motion and sliced off Evermore's left hand at the wrist. The wrangler stared in incomprehension at the mist that sprayed like pumped aerosol into the Void around him; but fortunately (or not) he did not contemplate this amputation for more than a moment.

The failure of the sixth and last wire bundle, triggered by the violent motion of the fifth, caused the entire cable to part at the girdle cut and sling Evermore into the Void. The lanyard on his tether slid until it reached the broken end; then slipped off, leaving him for the second and final time in his life tumbling into the

Void. This was the fourth and last thing that surprised him, for the whip end of the cable struck just under his left armpit and cut through the layers of Kevlar and fabric like a thick, dull knife—smashing the hardware, tearing the fabric, breaking bones and severing arteries. The arm was wrenched off at the shoulder and he had an instant to contemplate this strange, loose, spinning object that had once been a part of himself, before there were no more surprises, no more instants, and no more self.

Okoye did not know this immediately and neither did Ratline. The current in the vane had dropped the moment the fifth wire bundle had snapped and Okoye had glanced across to the gauge and the warning light. When she turned again to the feeds from the suit cameras, the last bundle had already parted, and she saw nothing but snow on Evermore's channel. "Rave," she said, alarmed—but that was all for now. "I've lost your visual." When she received no response, she added (rather stupidly, as she later thought about it), "and I've lost your audio as well." She flipped channels. "Mr. Ratline, I can't raise Evermore."

But Ratline had his own problems. He had just left the junction box to join Evermore and study the damage the boy had found when he sensed the loss of tension at the far end of the cable and, recognizing the symptoms from long experience, dropped down the length of his tether before he had given the matter conscious thought. It was this property that marked the living sailor from the dead, for he who stops to think is often at a disadvantage—although, as Evermore had already unwittingly demonstrated, he who never stops to think is often disadvantaged as well.

Ratline found himself, after a minute of total disorientation, dangling from the end of a hopeless tangle consisting in part of his tether and in the other part of the broken vane. The two had wound around each other more tightly than snakes in love. Even while he studied the situation (because *now* was the time for thinking), Ratline saw the free end swoop around and curlicue one last lazy loop around the junction box cat line, so that the rigging here now had the twisted look of a tropical jungle. He had the momentary fancy that the cable was a serpent and that it was hunting for him.

With some part of his awareness, he heard Okoye calling him; but he had no time for chatter and did not respond. The cable, as he traced it with his suit light, had wrapped around some of the fores'l shrouds. There was no way to extricate his tether from that awful tangle, and so the only thing for it was to detach the life line from his belt and skinny out the tangle until he could reach the catline, down which he could slide to the ship. He only weighed a couple hundred grams—about half a pound on the human scale—so even though he massed the same as always, it would not strain his arms to play tree sloth for a few minutes.

Genie will have a cow, he thought while he clambered about like Tarzan. Rerigging would need a lot of work, and the berth was likely now one shroudsman fewer. He considered hacking out the tangle with his reefing knife—he felt, for some reason, a savage and unreasoning fury—but that was not a task one carried out alone, on the edge of a great sail, with no tether. Ratline was no man to quail at risks, but he drew the line when the risk was bootless.

He was breathing hard when he finally reached the catline and wrapped legs and arms around it. Without a tether, to lose his grip now would mean to lose everything. He may have gone outside in the hail expecting, as 'Kiru had thought, to die; but that did not mean that, faced with the prospect, he would help speed things along.

The Stone

There is a human proverb to the effect that trouble comes in threes. In part, the proverb is parthenogenic, since one stops counting after three and begins anew, yet there may be a reason why so many cultures have held the number sacred.

The loss of the foresail vane was not so critical as the loss of the Number Two CoRE magnet. From a higher perspective, neither was the loss of Raphael Evermore, though this only demonstrates the inadequacy of heights for proper perspectives. In any event, no one could be sure as yet that Evermore had been lost. No sooner had Ship reported that Number Two Engine was off line than Gorgas set Corrigan to recompute their course. Satterwaithe, if anything, was pleased and winked at the navigator, for the sails nearly made up for the lost engine power. They would hit Jupiter Roads at a higher speed than was proper, but could likely decelerate against the Jovian magnetosphere. When, a few minutes later, they lost the vane and perhaps the tangled fores'l as well, Satterwaithe was vexed but not yet entirely discouraged.

But if in the uproar, they had forgotten the atoll, The Lotus Jewel had not. It was, in a manner of speaking, her own discovery and she felt a proprietary interest in it. The scanning radar swept back and forth through the cone of their forward trajectory, searching above and below the plane of their approach. Whenever she saw a body with a bad-looking vector she would ping it with the track radar. They were close enough now that single pings did not require power diversion, which was good; but that meant they were close enough that passage followed closely on detection, which was not so good.

"We have yaw," The Lotus Jewel announced when Number Two went down—for a mild vertigo had informed her of the loss of thrust on one side of the ship. (The vane tangle on the fores'l did not affect her. Because Ship lacked a handshake, none of the sail feedback was analoged to her sensing equipment; which is to say that none of the sails' behavior made any sense to her.)

In that moment of diversion, when the engine had gone down and the sail tangled, Ship saw a stone on a bad approach. The vector was so tight onto them that it seemed to The Lotus Jewel as if a hot needle had been jabbed suddenly into her palm. "Stone!" she called. "Azimuth, eleven o'clock. Altitude, one degree and dropping, dropping. Closing in fourteen. Thirteen . . ."

"Engines!" Satterwaithe said. "Starward juke. All rockets. Full power. Now! Now!"

The engine room did not know what had occasioned the order, but Bhatterji and Miko heard something in Satterwaithe's voice that they had never heard before and they dropped their cold, mutual silence and sprang to their boards. Ship had heard the order too, and had already begun swinging the high impulse rockets into position. That was autoinitiating, which was undesirable in an AI, but it gained them two seconds of the eleven they had left, so no one complained.

At nine seconds, the rockets locked in.

At eight seconds, they belched chemical fury, exhausting their fuel in a single mighty burn. If *The Riv'* ever did make it to Galileo, she would need tugs and hawsers to bring her to dock, but no one complained about that, either.

The ship's disk massed a great deal, and needed time to overcome its inertia. The rockets strained to shift her bulk even while Satterwaithe ordered the trailing shrouds pulled in to rock the ship into the smallest possible profile against the oncoming stone. But *The Riv'* was ever a ship sluggish to the helm. Neither cages nor sails had the concentrated, brute force of the juke jets. Okoye obeyed the order from the bridge, even though Ratline was still Outside and Rave was unaccounted for. There comes a time when one does what one must and action becomes a kind of anesthetic.

At seven seconds *MS The River of Stars* had begun to ascend; and The Lotus Jewel had sent another ping at the stone.

At six seconds she had captured and processed the bounceback. "Brace for impact!"

"More pitch!" cried Satterwaithe at the joystick. "Thus. Thus."

"There is no God but God," said Corrigan.

"We're going to miss," said Akhaturian.

Gorgas stared into the plotting tank, where a small red blip closed in on the green dot of the ship. He could convince himself that it was all happening in there, in a miniature world that was not quite real.

At four seconds, below in his stateroom, Bigelow Fife could think of nothing else but to hold 'Siska Wong as close as he could and to curse Eaton Grubb. He might have been aboard the cutter, even now escaping, had it not been for the interfering cook. He vowed that if 'Siska died because of it, he would hunt the man down and kill him.

At three seconds, Mikoyan Hidei pulled away from her board, there being nothing more to be done, and saw that Ramakrishnan Bhatterji sat beside her with his eyes closed, almost as if he were sleeping.

At two seconds, Eaton Grubb, sitting in the galley, the inmost room of the inmost deck, gripped Twenty-four deCant's hand and smiled at her to show it wasn't near as bad as it sounded. But he squeezed her hand much too tightly for the smile to be effective.

At one second, Eugenie Satterwaithe stood down and, turning, saw that Gorgas had grabbed firm hold of a monkey bar.

After all that—after several lifetimes' worth of fourteen seconds—the impact itself seemed an anticlimax. There was a brief rumble, as of distant thunder, heard dimly on the bridge, with great clamor in the Long Room, hardly at all in the galley, and not at all in the engine room.

Bhatterji opened his eyes. "Well, that was a big to-do over nothing," he said without looking directly at Miko.

Above, in the sail control room, Nkieruke Okoye had a slightly different perspective. The impact had clanged above her head as if God Himself had skipped like a schoolgirl across the hull. She could believe that it was a big to-do, but not that it was nothing. "Ratline," she called. "Are you still there?" The video feed from his suitcam said he was, or at least that his suit was. She received no joy on the bounceback.

Systematically, she verified the readouts from his suit and saw that they were consistent with a living occupant. What she did not see were the bits and scraps of paper behind her that wafted hesitantly toward the portal to the Sail Prep room.

Gorgas stood by the plotting tank with his hands behind his back. One hand gripped and massaged the other in restless motion concealed from the other deck officers by his body. From time to time both hands quieted into fists. "Damage report?" he enquired.

"Hull is breached in three places," Ship reported. "The ship is losing air to space."

"Close air tight doors," the captain ordered. "Form a containment around the breaches. Engines, what is your status?"

A series of distant thuds told him that Ship was sealing off the leaks. A schematic blinked up on one of the sistines and a series of black bars appeared marking the cordon.

"Engine Two is down, but is repairable," Bhatterji reported. "Some of the hobartium used to rewind the CoRE magnet had inadequate properties. If we back off on the operating parameters—"

"This vessel," reported Ship, "does not have sufficient braking acceleration to assume HoJO. Manual cutoff prevents restart of Number Two engine."

Gorgas blinked at the uncalled-for comment. "Quite properly so, if the magnet has been damaged. Sails, what is your status?"

"I can't raise Rave," Okoye said. "I've got no signal from his suit."

Gorgas gestured to The Lotus Jewel and made sweep motions with his hand. The sysop understood and conducted a radar sweep of the region of space into which Evermore had most likely been flung. "I understand, Sails. We are searching for him. What of the sail itself?"

Okoye's response was a long time in coming. At least it seemed so to Satterwaithe and Corrigan, for what scrolled up on the bridge repeater was less than heartening.

"Fores'l vane is snapped and useless. The fores'l itself is tangled, magnetic footprint reduced with loss of acceleration. And, captain . . . ?"

"There are no sails," insisted Ship. "Reliance on sails is delusional behavior."

The AI was beginning to irritate Gorgas. It had no right to psychoanalyze humans, especially as it was drawing conclusions from incomplete data. "Belay that, Ship. Yes, Okoye?"

"Um, Ship's other avatar tells me that the remaining sails are being poisoned by an ion haze of elevated temperature."

"*That's* what it is . . ." whispered Satterwaithe, who studied her console more diligently.

"An ion haze!" said Gorgas.

"Yes, sir," said Okoye, "but Sails cannot suggest a source."

Gorgas too was puzzled. He looked to Satterwaithe. "Master? You have the most experience. Could it be coronal ejecta?"

Satterwaithe shook her head. "We've observed no flares on the sun, nor intercepted word of any. Jovial ejecta from the Io Tube are too cold to poison the sails." Her fingers danced across the virtual control panel and conjured a false-color map of the magnetic field, courtesy of the Sails avatar. The poisoned areas were highlighted orange. Corrigan and Akhaturian had come up behind her.

"Biosystems?" Gorgas continued. "Damage report?"

"No disruptions, cap'n," Grubb responded. "Slight drop in air pressure in some areas of the ship, is all. That would be around the hull breaches. Should come back to normal once the air-tight doors are dogged."

"Thank you. Be sure to conduct a visual of all doors. Medical? Any injuries to report?"

Wong's voice teetered on the edge of hysteria. "You mean besides Rave? I can't locate his medbot signals at all. I think he's . . . I think he's . . ."

Akhaturian, still standing behind Satterwaithe, turned away from the screen on which the doctor appeared. The doctor was overreacting. Rave would turn up. He had lost radio contact for some reason, that was all. From sail's edge, it would take him twenty or thirty minutes to reach the personnel locks on the hull. Only ten minutes had yet gone by the clock. Another ten or twenty, and he'd be knocking at the door.

Gorgas glanced at the sysop, who had removed her cap. The Lotus Jewel slowly shook her head. "Some small objects in that general direction," she said, "to judge by the brightness of the echoes. Should I ping them?"

Gorgas sorted and considered possibilities. One of the echoes might indeed be the boy. Yet, on the vector the sysop showed him and with the ship's propulsion impaired, any rescue or—more likely—retrieval was infeasible. Was the cutter operational? Grubb had mentioned it, but he needed both Satterwaithe and Corrigan, the only two qualified pilots, here with him. Too bad. Evermore had been a likely lad, but he was not the first human to be sacrificed to the Void.

Oh grant Thy mercy and Thy grace
To those who venture into space.

Surreptitiously, Gorgas crossed himself. "No," he said. "Maintain bearing." Wong, with a convulsive gesture cut her connection.

Satterwaithe, distracted a moment by Gorgas's order, nodded her agreement with it before turning back to her analysis of the magfield. Corrigan, the ship's navigator, knew how the facts lay, and did not protest the order, either. The Lotus Jewel might have been inclined to argue, for the facts of navigation meant less to her than the loss of a young boy, but she held her peace, for she had seen Gorgas cross himself and knew that the man had reached no casual decision.

Poor Rave. She thought that she ought to have given him what he had so clearly longed for. To scratch the itch that he could not reach himself. It was clear that the girl would not—and how cruel that was in retrospect! The second wrangler was—had been—younger than the run of men she had enjoyed and, being of Earth, was younger even than his years; and yet, he was not too much younger and for certain would never now be any older.

The Lotus Jewel did not love the young wrangler. It is not even clear that she had loved Corrigan, for she loved in an electrical sense: her charge moved opposite to her current. That is, she invited the love of others and the gratitude she felt on its receipt she confused with the thing itself. Even so, she thought that the boy had had too much voltage stored up and it ought to have been discharged, simply as a favor.

Up above, in the sail control room, the Igbo girl moved robotically, as if something inside her had also discharged.

"The poisoned areas," Corrigan pointed out, "correspond to the locations of the engines. See here and here? Those are the engine sectors. The plasma is being caught and carried by the field lines."

"Then why is there no poisoning here?" Satterwaithe asked, indicating the disk's trailing quarter.

"Engine Three is firing orthogonal, across the short diameter of the field. The other engines—note that the color is dimmer here, where Number Two was shut down—the other three have been firing radially ever since we turned the ship, across the field's long diameter. Miko . . ." Corrigan called the engine room on his hushmike. "Could you place a copy of the plume pattern on viewscreen F? Thank you." He waited another moment until the display appeared and then, because Ship could not coordinate them, superimposed the two data sets manually. "There, you see it?"

Satterwaithe was convinced. She turned to face Gorgas. "We need to throttle down the engines, or we'll lose the sails entirely."

"Further reduction in engine braking will not be permitted," Ship announced.

Ivar Akhaturian shook his head. "We really need that handshake."

In his youth—a youth that had been distressingly brief—little Timmy Ratline had delighted in skipping stones across the lake behind his parents' summer home. He liked the way they would skim the water, bouncing and splashing, almost as if they were attempting flight. At nearly a hundred kiss, the stone that grazed *The River of Stars* had gone past too quickly for him to see. Yet he could mark its progress by the splashes it raised in its wake.

Splashes?

The notion puzzled him as he made his way down the furling brace. He had fashioned himself a new tether from his equipment belt, but proceeded cautiously, lest friction against the cable burn through the webbing.

Below him, an aurora of greens and blues shimmered. The "splashes," he saw now, were geysers, where the hull had been breached, and air spumed from the vessel as from a broaching whale. A mutant whale, for he saw there were five such geysers. The gasses froze into a rime that glimmered in the shadows and sublimed where the sunlight caught it out. Elsewhere, the engine plumes, creeping up the maglines like vines up a trellis, stripped and ionized the oxygen and nitrogen, and flowers bloomed in the somber colors ghosts were said to favor. It was one of the most terribly beautiful sights he had ever seen.

Reaching the crosstree at last, Ratline paused to catch his breath. He was directly over the ship now, a few hundred meters. He could see where the errant stone had struck: one mangled spot near the forward glacis, two more on the rise of the hull, and—oddly enough—two more on the aft quarter where the hull sloped away again. Ratline grunted in sour humor. Poor Genie. If she hadn't juked the ship, the stone would likely have missed completely or, at the very worst, made only that first gash. He wondered who on the crew would be weasel enough to point that out and decided that it would be the cheerfully malicious tale-spreader in the galley.

He found the channel switch with his tongue and flipped it to the command circuit. "Cap'n," he said, meaning as he always did Eugenie Satterwaithe, "Ratline here. I'm Outside. We got air geysers. Three of 'em. And two more spots that might be slow-leaking. The biggest one looks like it's just over the Sail Prep room." But all he heard on the bounceback was static. He looked again at the swirling ghosts of ionized air and the auroras that ran through them and doubted that anyone had heard him.

As he peered down at the great disk, nostalgia seized Ratline around the throat and he thought to drop freely to the hull as he had done so often in his manhood. And so he unbuckled himself from the furling brace and, planting his feet on the crosstree, dove headfirst toward the hull intending that, at the last moment, he would flip feet first and touch down.

And yet a strange thing happened. As he fell, the ship began to slide away beneath him and he realized that his instincts had played him false. The ship was decelerating *sideways* and the vector sum was not quite through the mast, but possessed a marked radial component. He felt as a man might who, jumping from a tall building, sees the safety net shuffling to the side.

The first distant thud distracted Okoye from her board, where she was following Ratline's progress via his suitcam pictures.

The signal was breaking up, however, and when she turned back to the screen it was entirely broken. She switched the receiver to another channel, wishing just this once that she was The Lotus Jewel and expert in all forms of communion. Was something interfering with the signal or had it been cut off at the source? She could not believe the latter. Anything that could destroy Ratline would take half the Middle System with it. She remained at her station, for the shroudmaster was still outside.

The deck reverberated and she heard another thud. The sound puzzled her, since they were surely out of the atoll by now. Then she heard it again and this time the portal to the Sail Prep room slammed shut and 'Kiru finally understood. Gorgas had ordered the airtight doors closed.

Three minutes later, having still not gotten a response from Ratline, she watched a half-meter of fibrop sensor line drift past her on its way to somewhere else. Not entirely comprehending its import, she followed its progress as it danced and twisted through the air until it came to rest among a score of other lightweight objects against the ventilator grille. "Now here is some ripe corn, by its look," she said. She unbuckled and went to the grille where, holding her hand by it, she could feel a light current of air being sucked out of the room. She stared again at the deck overhead, where she had heard God skipping. "Could you not have found a less terrible chastisement?" she asked her *chi*. "I did like the boy, but I . . ." But an adult does not stand by, the proverb ran, and watch a goat die on its tether. "Ship?"

"Ready, Ms. Okoye."

"Sails."

"Ready."

"Monitor and communication system. Available nodes. List."

"Clarification. You want to know if you can keep in touch with Mr. Ratline from some other console."

"Uh, yes. I think . . . I think this sector is losing air."

"Wait one. Sensing. Confirmed. Pressure drop, Long Room is—"

"Abort. I don't really *want* to know."

"Main node, comm shack. Bridge console—cancel. Bridge console in use. Biosystem console, reconfiguration for requested use. Confirmed. You may transfer node to Biosystems."

"Thank you. Message. To: Eaton Grubb. Text:—"

"Mr. Grubb has been informed you are coming."

"Uh. Thanks again."

"Prompt departure is advised, Ms. Okoye. Database indicates low air pressure is suboptimal for continued performance of entities."

"Yah. That was my thought too. 'The sun's o'ercast with blood.'" But she powered down the board and locked it out. Then, stuffing her notes and the log into her pouch, she slung it over her shoulder and loped for the portal into the main quadrant stairwell.

To find it blocked by an airtight door.

Altogether, there were four egresses from the Long Room, other than the one that led to Sail Prep, and all four, she quickly discovered, were shuttered. Okoye paused at the last of them and rubbed her chin. "'Which is the side which I must go withal?'" she wondered, and realized the answer in the asking. She had grown so accustomed to the vacuum suit that she had forgotten she was wearing it. A brief, grim smile split her features. "Why, the outside, of course."

With that, she bounded to the suit rack and took her helmet off its headball. There, she paused, frozen, while memories destroyed her like a stone at a hundred kiss. She had last stood here, she had last hefted this selfsame helmet, when she had threatened to go out at Rave Evermore's side.

And if she had, would he be safe now? Or would the both of them be missing? She had been so relieved when Mr. Ratline had ordered her to stay in and now the memory of that relief was her punishment. She avoided, even in her mind, the likely meaning of *missing*, but she dried her eyes before donning the helmet, for loose droplets inside a helmet could fog up her visor.

She emerged onto the upper hull into a faerie land of color and snow. Air billowed from a rent before her and froze into a cold, unnatural flurry that sublimed into a vapor where the breath of the engines touched it. All around her the vacuum swirled with faint colors.

It was from this maelstrom that a figure emerged and Okoye tried to tell herself that it was Rave Evermore, saved by courage, skill, and chance. But the colors and markings on the suit called her a liar before she could even form the hope.

At first, she thought the man was dancing and she wondered if this were *Imo muri*, the river-god, come down from the river of stars itself to take her away. But then she realized that these were the capers of a man who has just touched down at a high speed and at an angle. Ratline. The figure tilted and skipped and Okoye sucked in her breath, because it seemed to her as if he would skip off the edge of the hull itself and be fed as a holocaust into the fires of the Number One engine. Because of the ship's unusual vector, the hull seemed not only a hill sloping away from the mast, but a hill that had been canted and upthrust by some subterranean upheaval.

Okoye pulled her lanyard from her belt and snapped it to a padeye on the hull and then she dove toward the hopscotching cargo master.

But Ratline grabbed hold of a radiator fin, lost his grip and spun into its companion. That stunned him, but he kept enough sense about him to seize hold of the bracing tube, around which he spun heels-up like a Cossack dancer. He had already regained his footing when he saw Okoye. Between ragged breaths, he cried over his suit channel, "Two out, Okoye! Two out, one in! Who told you to EVAde?"

It was only fear at his close escape that fueled his voice with such rage, for who can be more fearful than those who keep all their fears within?

"Two out, old man?" Okoye answered rage for rage. "When I see but one? Where is he? Where is he?"

Ratline struggled with the sentence and wondered who the woman was. He had long sought for fire in the quiet girl, but he had grown so used to her silences that this verbal assault baffled him. "Evermore? He's gone."

It outraged Okoye that he sounded no more concerned than

that. "Gone, old man? Gone in which direction? Can we reach him in time?"

"It's no use, girl. It's no use. I didn't see what happened. The vane snapped and . . . I don't think there ever was any time."

Did she hear just the faintest crack in that voice? She did not believe the old man had tears within him. "If Rave had stayed inside," she snapped, as wild and hard as the foresail vane, "he would be safe with us." And maybe Ratline would have been by that cable when it parted. Maybe Ratline would now be "missing." It was sinful to wish that another had suffered Rave's fate instead, and a vain wish beside.

Ratline laughed, though it was not a laugh of amusement, and pointed to the spouting geyser of air that lay forward of them. "Safe inside? And how safe is that?" He paused and contemplated the spray. After a while, more calmly, he said, "Was anyone else hurt?"

Okoye shook her head, but had to speak perforce. "Not in the way you mean."

"They'll die off once the airtight compartments are empty," Ratline said—about the geysers, not about the crew, "but they are beautiful in their way."

"Why?" she asked him.

And Ratline, who was not known for insight, understood that she did not ask why the geysers were beautiful, but why her friend was missing. He could not see her face through the visor of her suit. All he could see there was the reflection of the sun and the stars. It was as if a galaxy were wearing her suit. "Why? There is no *why*, Okoye. There's only *what*, and sometimes *how*. Life has no meaning, so why should death?"

"You're a terrible man. You are no-man. Everything human has been sucked out of you."

"When you've seen as many die as I have, girl, it doesn't stab as deep."

"And is that a good thing?"

Ratline had no ready answer to that. He wasn't sure that there were "good things" or "bad things," only "things"—to be borne or not, without complaint. In this, he really was at one with the old pagans. Not the new pagans, with their laurels and solstices and their late, post-Christian reconstructions of a dead past; but the true quill: those stoics who had gazed at all the sorrows of the world without remorse or pity. But while it may be an admirable thing to bear one's sorrows in this manner, it is quite a different thing to bear another's so.

The Survey

Ivar Akhaturian bounced through the C-ring corridor on the first underdeck. Everything in this sector was lit by the pale ruddy glow of the emergency lamps, so that the floor and walls and ceiling seemed awash in blood. It gave the hallway a strangely empty appearance. The shadows seemed blacker than usual, or perhaps only a darker shade of red. He thought about Rave Evermore. Turning a corner into a radial corridor, he found it blocked by an airtight door and, without pausing, bounced off it to find another route to the galley. In doing so, his feet struck the circular brace and the support gave off a hollow reverberation, somewhere in a low register, as if a church bell had rung deeper down inside the ship. The echo brought home to him how small he was and how large the vessel. He might bounce for days along its corridors without encountering another living soul. Coming to a halt at the intersecting ring corridor, he listened and heard nothing. He might have been alone on the ship.

He wasn't certain how he felt about losing Rave. The older boy had tormented him, but Ivar missed it now, as he would miss a pulled tooth. He had never thought Rave terribly bright—he had often imagined the other boy as a block of wood—but he had been solid and reliable—which, to be sure, are also attributes of wooden blocks. That the second wrangler had been a wizard with the omnitool, he knew in an intellectual way. He had heard both Mr. Bhatterji and Mr. Ratline mention it. But that sort of creativeness Ivar regarded as mere dexterity, along the lines of the Wonderful Dancing Bear. It was a performance trick. It was not of the same order as navigational computations, which really were wonderful and complex.

Ivar found the alternate corridor and was pleased to see that this one was fully lit. It made him feel as if he had returned to the ship from somewhere else, although the lights did reveal how alone he was in a way that the shadows had not. At least in the darker halls he could pretend that there were other people on just the other side of the shades.

He heard voices. Dr. Wong and the passenger were in the galley. "All I know," Dr. Wong was saying, "is that I could detect no signal from his medbots."

She meant Rave, he knew. Ivar wondered if the lack of signals made the older boy more dead than if they had been blipping busily on Dr. Wong's console. The passenger answered something that he could not make out. Somehow, the muffled buzz of the voices made Ivar feel even more isolated. *This is all a bad dream*, he told himself, but he knew he was lying and that knowledge negated all the benefits of self-deception.

Entering the galley, he found Mr. Fife seated in a clip chair at the long table, eating something from a stay-plate. The doctor, characteristically, stood. She was not accustomed to chairs, she had told Ivar one time, and even in milly she remained frequently unseated, holding the plate in her left hand, and handling the fork with her right. An awkward position, Ivar thought. He did not see how it could be anyone's default mode. Sometimes he had seen the doctor place her fork or some other small object in midair, as if on a shelf, only to have it drop slowly to the deck. At first, Ivar had thought she was doing this deliberately, for comic effect. Ivar himself often clowned. Only later did he realize that it was sheer habit on her part. She turned at Ivar's entrance and smiled. "Why, hello."

Ivar Akhaturian thought the doctor's smile was sadder than most people's tears. He could not say why he thought so. It was not that the lady was persistently melancholy, although she did seem subject to mood swings, but that the wan curl to her lips reminded him somehow of the wreckage of Old First Habitat, whose scavenged remains nestled deep in the ice of the bowl valley below the rim-wall warrens of Callistopolis. OFH had once been a bustling center housing the pioneers sent to prepare what was then called "Callisto Base" and it had often made Ivar a little sad to see its present dishevelment. He planned to visit the ruins when *The River* reached Port Galileo at last and he received his shore leave. Ganymede lapped Callisto every doody-day; that is every twelve days or "duodecimal week," and the shuttles ran thick between them.

Perhaps he would stop and see his mother too.

"Is Twenty-four here? I can't stay long. I'm going with Mr. Grubb and Mr. Bhatterji to inspect the damage."

"In the breached sectors?" asked Dr. Wong. "Isn't that dangerous?"

"Yah. Where's Twenty-four?" Maybe his head was loose, for it kept turning from side to side.

Fife did not look up from his meal, which was marble duck, a swirled blend of white and dark carnic. It was not a paragon of its type, for all that Grubb had blended it himself and set it in the keeper for deCant to prepare. Fife was a man who valued his eating, which was unfortunate, as Twenty-four was a girl who regarded it as a bothersome necessity. As it was, the carnic was overdone and the savor, only fair. "She's in the kitchen," Fife told the boy with considerable regret. Then, he replayed the lad's remarks and did look up from his meal. "Why is the cook inspecting the damage?" He did not add, *instead of cooking my meal*, for when he sought information he did not clutter his questions with irrelevancies.

Dr. Wong laid her hand on his arm. "I've told you that, Big'. Eaton is the biochief. He's the one who makes sure our biosphere stays viable."

Fife grunted and turned again to his meal. He hoped the man was as good a chief as he was a chef. He glanced at his arm, then at 'Siska, and ascribed the lack of ardor at her touch to the tension of the previous day. They had embraced at the time of impact, he and the doctor, holding each other tightly—out of fear, he thought, as much as attraction.

Why do I not use the word love, *even in my thoughts*, he had written in his journal. *Is it that I dread to love, or that I dread that somehow this is not it?* He had considered for some time that second use of *dread* before allowing it to stand and saving the entry to memory.

He had thought that the ship would be smashed and that, kept from the boat he had so carefully prepared, he would die, and in some perverse fashion he had preferred to do so entwined with the doctor. There had been comfort there—if not an allaying of fears, then at least a sharing of them. He had toyed with a flux equation as a way of encapsulating that thought. Fear per square millimeter diminished the more square millimeters of soul shared it. Many of his pithier aphorisms he had expressed with such mathematical conceits. Yet, the theory failed to explain why it held not true for love, which, unlike light, waxed with the volume illuminated.

When he looked up again from his meal, the Akhaturian boy was gone. "You wouldn't know it to look at him," he told his lover, "that his friend has just died."

"I'm sure he is hurting inside," she said. "He may still be in denial. Something like death does not become real immediately, especially for the young."

"That is why I said, 'To look at him,'" Fife pointed out. He always tried to speak precisely and it irritated him that others failed to parse the precision, and tried to rebut statements he had not made. Who could say whether the lad hurt inside or not if, as 'Siska had pointed out, even Akhaturian himself did not yet know?

"We all feel badly about Rave," Wong said.

Fife did not correct her grammar, for he suspected that the statement was literally true and that none of their feelings in the matter were especially well-tuned. 'Siska had cried a little when it was clear that the boy, whether dead or alive, was lost to the ship, but her sorrow had been as nothing to when the engineer's mate had nearly tumbled. He wondered if that was because in this instance, although the outcome had been considerably more dire, it had not been the doctor's fault.

People sometimes chide me, he would later write in his journal, *that I do not feel as genuinely as others, but I suspect that my feelings may be more* honest *than theirs. If my feelings do not run as deep, they at least do not change depth on my own account. The boy's death was a tragedy, surely, and I shall be writing a letter to his parents to express my sorrow, and perhaps give them an anecdote for the remembering of him. But it is a tragedy in the core meaning of the word, stemming as it does from the boy's own* hubris. *This Evermore had thought to learn his task en passant. I overheard the Igbo girl say as much to her companions last night. A man who believes in his own skills may succeed ninety-nine times, but the one other time may kill him.* (That had the sound of an aphorism, but it was not yet quite right.)

Rave Evermore was also the subject of discussion in the kitchen. There, Twenty-four deCant worried at her own lack of tears. "I feel like I should cry," she said to Akhaturian over the mourning whoop-whoop of the fans that struggled to keep the air clear, "but I can't. There ain't no tears. It's like it all happened somewhere else, and all I am is watching it through a big, thick slab o' glass. Nothing touched me."

Akhaturian wanted to say, *I'll touch you,* but a sense of the proprieties stilled his tongue. Propriety was not, however, strong enough to still his hand, which reached out to stroke her bare arm. Twenty-four was wearing a singlet and shorts against the heat and humidity of the kitchen. This not only exposed her limbs, but did a poor job of concealing anything else. Her skin glittered with perspiration where it did not cake over with the dust from the flour and ground carnic. Akhaturian knew he wanted her, right there amidst the crazed greenery and fleshy smells of Grubb's domain. His fingers searched under the shoulder strap of her singlet. "We'll all miss Rave," he said, but he was no longer thinking of Rave. It was a relief not to think about him.

Twenty-four accepted his touch and wondered if the thrill it sent through her made her a bad person, for she felt that Evermore's death *should* have touched her, and here she was: ready to take her husband into her in lieu of mourning her friend. Did mourning require tears? Did it enjoin continence? Evermore used to invade her with his eyes, just as he had 'Kiru and

The Lotus Jewel. He would have looked on Miko too, the Martian was convinced, save that Miko was seldom about to be looked upon.

Twenty-four might have gone with him. She might have been Rave Evermore's wife. When she had signed the Articles at Port Deimos, Rave had been aboard less than a month, and the two of them in their common apprenticeship had found themselves thrown much together. Had 'Kiru not been present to supervise them, who could say what might have occurred? Proximity can succeed where attraction fails. Yet, the person that she imagined she was mattered a great deal to her, and a union grounded in mere convenience—as the wretched doctor had found with the passenger—was not who she wanted to be.

Now, her affair with Ivar had started in this casual, proximate fashion, although she herself no longer remembered it that way. It had even had an element of calculation to it: Akhaturian as prophylaxis against Evermore. She would have denied the charge with the utmost ferocity had anyone laid it; but do not call her response hypocrisy. The true hypocrite is always self-reflective. Rather, call it growth. For love is never found; it is never given. It is built. If Twenty-four deCant could not remember the empty field whereon she had built her life with Ivar, it was because what she had erected there was so full of distracting wonders.

"You have carnic on your cheek," the distracting wonder told her, still rubbing her shoulder gently.

"It's not carnic," she said. "It's pastry. I was making dessert." (Now, there was a thought to make Fife quail!) She rubbed her face with the back of her hand, which of course only smeared the dark red material.

Ivar kissed the smudge, licking off the fruit—and yes, he enjoyed the goo as much as the girl. It was not quite strawberry. There was a touch of something else. "Sweet," he said, "but not as sweet as you." Was there ever a line more hackneyed and more predictable? But Twenty-four did not shiver at the novelty and cleverness of Ivar Akhaturian's rhetoric. That quiver had quite another origin. Hands spoke louder than lips, and lips spoke loudest when they did not speak at all. Twenty-four dipped her fingers in the mixing globe and smeared more of the fruit creme on her face—a warrior preparing her war paint. This time, she painted her lips as well.

Ivar needed more time for his tongue to seek out every morsel, to check whether any had perhaps gotten inside her mouth. "I'll call you 'Little Lollipop'," he told deCant. Bigelow Fife, who had stepped into the kitchen in search of his desserts, watched with a curious revulsion. How like a pair of dogs in heat! The curiosity, however, outweighed the revulsion, so his eyes darted like seagulls, missing nothing. He saw the boy's hand reach under the girl's singlet. He saw the girl cross her arms over her head and pull that singlet off. He saw . . . What he saw was quite nice, if a trifle underdone. The girl smeared more of the dessert on herself for the boy to lick off. Did that make her a tart? The two of them giggled quietly as the game escalated and they rubbed the paste on each other. Fife had not done that since his first wedding banquet, when he had "fed" Gynna a piece of their cake. He took a step back at the tawdriness of it, but he did not take two.

Ivar didn't mind being on the other end of the tongue, either. Twenty-four reached into a second mixing globe and lathered a whitish-yellow paste on him. When she began to lick it off, Ivar drew a sharp breath. "What. Flavor. Is that?" he asked.

"Banana," she told him.

"How. Appropriate."

The road led where it was bound to lead and Fife had long withdrawn his audience when Twenty-four deCant burst into sudden, inexplicable tears. Akhaturian paused as he resumed his coveralls, wondering if it was something he had done. "Hey," he said taking her again in his arms, though now with different motives. "There's no reason for that." This was the first time he had ever criticized her.

"It's, oh, it's, Rave," she said between gulps of air. She was crying so hard only one word at a time could escape. "Oh, Rave."

It struck Ivar as a little peculiar that her tears over Rave should finally arrive just after they had made love. Yet, Twenty-four had been trying to cry for their lost friend since yesterday evening, and it might be that she had succeeded now only by coincidence.

DeCant, for her part, could not shake the feeling that a portion of her was split off, somewhere else, watching herself weep. All the while Ivar had been with her—fondling her, licking her, entering her—she had imagined that it had been Rave Evermore doing it. That was wrong, she knew, and she was ashamed to have imagined it, but Rave had barged in unbidden. It was the first time she had ever been unfaithful to Ivar. She did not tell him then. She did not tell him ever. It was something she would keep to herself for the rest of her life and, in some strange fashion, treasure.

When Grubb entered the breached Sail Prep room, he found the Palace of the Winter King. A rime of frozen air, tinged with subtle colors, covered every surface. This hoarfrost had a tendency to sublime on those bulkheads adjacent to heated and pressurized rooms and, indeed, from the footprints he and Bhatterji made, as well. In milly, the fog would settle and accumulate around their ankles until, drifting too close to the Ice Dragon's breath, it froze out again as a layer of snow. Eventually, Grubb knew, it would evaporate into space entirely, leaving the room bone-dry and dark.

"Damn," said Bhatterji; and Grubb, turning, saw the reason. Through the twisted tangle of the ship's skin, the eternal night shone through, to cast faint, starlit shadows on the deck. Outside, the renegade air, minced to ions by the plasma of Bhatterji's engines, danced blue and green in the sail's magnetic field. Grubb turned his suit lamps off, the better to appreciate the sight. It was magic and, in its way, a terrible beauty.

"Gutted like a fish," Bhatterji said, and for once did not suggest that he might fix it with a little sheet metal and some duct tape.

"No," Grubb told him. "It's more like a giant's fist has punched through the shell." Bhatterji turned his suit, but if he thought it mattered which simile were used, he said nothing in aid of it. "A total loss," the biochief mourned, thinking of all the hours he had put in here, working on the sail with The Lotus Jewel and the others. The room would never be used again. The standing equipment remained, bolted to the deck—the knitters and the braiders and the like—but the bins of hand tools and spare parts stared back empty. The wind had carried everything loose away.

Bhatterji, for his part, only grunted. He had never thought of Sail Prep as anything but a loss. *This is where they used up my spare hobartium*, he thought. Grubb's fist had been the fist of God, then, punishing the transgressors for their sins.

It was a Western fancy, that. His own god was less immanent and was on the whole less prone to stage tricks. The Brahma did not part waters or impregnate young girls, although it might show itself from time to time in human form. If god was anything, it was the whole of the universe and the human soul, two as one, indivisible. Atman is Brahma.

"Mr. Grubb! Mr. Bhatterji!"

The two men glanced toward the interior of the room, where they had left Akhaturian. *Too small*, Grubb had half-jested, *the outgusting might carry you off*. "What is it?"

The small figure held out his hand and Grubb thought for a moment he wanted it shaken. Then he saw the stony fragment the boy held. "It's a piece of the rock," Akhaturian said.

Grubb reached out and took it. "Why, so it is. A souvenir for you. Good luck, eh?" Bhatterji turned at that to look at him, but said nothing about the quality of luck the rock had already brought them. "D-type," the biochief added after he had examined it more closely. "Organo-silicate. Quite common in the Thules. You never see this sort fall to Earth."

Bhatterji had taken hold of the torn edge of the puncture. Air swirled around him, coating him, flashing off from the radiant heat. He looked as if he might bend the skin back into place with his own arms. Could Grubb be serious, he wondered. What did it matter? Anything this far out in the Gulf would surely be a Thule—a Hilda, at most—and nearly everything in those orbits was either D- or P-type. The mark of useless speech was that afterward the listener was neither wiser nor entertained. "Are we any closer to getting the ship fixed?" he asked.

Grubb turned, though Bhatterji could see no face behind the tinted visor, and stood silently for a while. Handing the rock back to Akhaturian, the chief said, "No."

Akhaturian, equally invisible in his suit, said, "Mr. Bhatterji can fix anything."

Bhatterji grunted and wished it were true, but made no other reply. That someone on board appreciated his skills was gratifying. That the kudos came at the one point where he saw no possibility of repair was pure, unadulterated irony.

Ratline leaned closer to the screen. It was a way he had when intensity seized him. He would lean forward, invading another's social space, as if his words would have greater impact if he shortened the distance they must travel. "Stop it right there, 'Kiru."

'Kiru stopped the playback and tried not to look. This was the recording from Rave Evermore's suitcam. To watch it was to see what Rave had seen. To watch it too intently was to *be* Rave Evermore. 'Kiru did not want that. There was grave danger in summoning ghosts.

"D'you see it?" the old man asked. "There were only three bundles."

"Was the vane defective, then?" She could ask questions without looking. So long as Ratline told her what he saw, she did not need to look. Unbidden, tears trickled down her face and she wiped them away with a quick, impatient gesture.

"No. I tested every sector of every sail. I tested the vanes before I attached them, and I tested after I attached them."

"The other three bundles must have broken afterward, then."

"Will you look at the muffing screen, 'Kiru! They're not *broken*. They're *missing*. They've been stripped from the cladding. That's why the longitudinal cut was made."

Okoye flinched both from the whiplash voice and from the view on the screen. She pretended it was a robot camera that had taken the picture. In that manner she could examine the long slice in the cladding. She could study the girdling where the cladding had been cut away entirely. She could see that two of the wire bundles were whole—though one was already frayed—and a third broken entirely. But the other three were, as Ratline had said, just not there. "Vaporized?"

"Without burning the cladding layer? No, some son of a

bitch sliced the cladding open from here to—" He rapped the girdled area with his knuckle. "—to somewhere Evermore never reached. Then he snipped three of the bundles and pulled them out. That son of a bitch."

Okoye barely heard him. There were a lot of places Evermore would now never reach. He was on his way to Wasat. He had the ship's velocity, and that was still greater than helioescape velocity. It was important not to think of such things. She had already viewed the record from beginning to . . . to when transmissions had ceased. She did not want to view that again. Anything was better than to view that again.

But Ratline would have his way. "Take it forward. Slow. More. More. Stop. Back up. There. Do you see it?"

Focus close upon the bright, flashing ends of the wires, where the wire bundle had just snapped and was frozen now in mid-parting. Yes, she saw.

"When the missing bundles were cut," Ratline said, "the others were scored. When we dumped current into the cable, the hoop stress overcame the tensile strength of the remaining strands and they snapped and unraveled and—" Ratline jerked his hands apart, splaying his fingers as he spoke. "It makes me sick, vandalism does." He turned to go, turned back, jabbed a finger at Okoye. "Make a summary for the captain. And for Gorgas too. Note the timeline and the key events. They'll need it for the Board of Inquiry when we hit Galileo. I'm going to my cabin to review the magfield profiles. See if there's damage to the other sails. You've got half an hour."

Okoye acknowledged the order, but when Ratline was gone, told Ship what needed doing and had Ship do it all with the monitor dark and she did not even read the report when it was printed.

Gorgas studied Grubb's face, hoping for some sign of wickedness, for wickedness could be punished, but honesty can only be endured. He had always known the chief as an indolent man, one who seldom took the lead, who never acted with dispatch, who always sought the easiest way. For five years Grubb had gone about his tasks quietly and with little fuss. Gorgas had

never heard him express an opinion, and seldom even a preference—and those were always couched comfortably with de-
murrals and qualifications. That Grubb sat now before the
captain's desk and vigorously pressed his case could very
nearly be counted upon as proof of what he said.

"How long?" asked Gorgas.

"A week." There was no uncertainty in the chief's voice.

Nevertheless, Gorgas asked, "Are you certain?" It was a
question that would have enraged Bhatterji, and Gorgas raised
his eyes momentarily to the engineer, who stood with arms
folded in the corner by the wall, but Grubb minded the query
not at all.

"I've mapped the air pressure across the entire ship. It's a
slow drop, but it's steady."

"Even with the airtight doors in place?"

Grubb shrugged. "There must be channels where the air is
gusting out."

"Then why hasn't Ship alerted—?"

"Because Ship doesn't know it. Ship is—I guess 'numb'
would be right word. There are parts of the vessel that it hasn't
sensed in years. Out in the abandoned rings. Areas that have
been gutted and stripped for refit or salvage or because the Zacker needed to raise some cash. That's why it thought there
were only three holes, not the five that Ratline saw. Look
here . . ." And he leaned forward over Gorgas's desk to point to
the display on the screen. "You see this? That's one of the rents,
the big one. Must have been the first hit. And here, here, and
here—those are the airtight doors that ought to seal off that particular volume. It's the same on the other decks. But that gray
area, that's the part that was abandoned way back when. You
see how there ought to be doors in there, to complete the cordon? I sent Ivar in there to look, and he found the corridors
wide open. The doors never deployed. Some of them, the door's
aren't even there." Grubb flexed his long, delicate fingers into
fists, rubbed the knuckles against his temples. "Just one breach,
maybe we could have done something. Maybe even two. But
not five." He craned his neck to look at Bhatterji, who might
have been graven of mahogany. "It's not my area of expertise,

but there's one breach—the big one afore Sail Prep—that one . . ." Grubb fell silent and only shook his head.

Gorgas thought of the service corridors that Miko had found. He imagined streams of air wending through them. He imagined Miko herself carried away in their breath, crying out and reaching for him. "A week, you say?"

"By then the air will be as thin as on the Tibetan plateau. People live there. After that . . . No one lives atop Everest. I couldn't say how many days after that. Maybe Dr. Wong could."

Gorgas looked at Death, the fourth person in the room, and wondered why he had not recognized Him sooner. He turned to the engineer. "Do you concur."

"No."

It was an implacable word, as stolid as the man it came from and somehow, although it was a hopeful word, it did not ring hopefully in Gorgas's ears. He thought for a moment of vast, tall cliffs; of the comforting arms of his father; of the strength that lies in denial. Hope, he knew, was a cruel virtue, for she was virtuous only when most needed. Any fool can be hopeful when the way to safety lies clear. It takes genuine strength to hope when there is none. "Do you have a plan?" he asked the engineer. "It will take us far longer than a week to enter Jupiter Roads, with the foresail hopelessly tangled and one engine out entirely—or do you intend to fix those as well in the week remaining?" He had not intended that that last should come out as sarcasm. He had had the genuinely mad thought that Bhatterji, in a crisis, could work wonders.

The engineer stood away from the wall. The motion was emphatic enough that he took flight and glided across Gorgas's day room on motionless feet, like some squat ballerina *en pointe*. "Give me the wranglers," he said, "and anyone else who can bend tin. Cutting and welding—"

"You can't patch all five breaches . . ." Eaton Grubb said.

Bhatterji turned on him in sudden anger. "How do you know what I can or cannot do? I can find those other doors and set them manually, or I can build new ones. I can create a redoubt, *here*!" His finger stabbed Gorgas's desktop. "Here in the center of the ship and in engineering. Seal off the core and evacuate the air from everywhere else. By pressurizing only the redoubt, we can make the air last longer."

But could he make it last long enough? Surely there were other regions that required pressurization. Gorgas could not help but frame the thought and so strongly did he think it that Bhatterji answered even his silence.

"And if not, at least we suffocate *trying*." Bhatterji folded his arms again. "We have no alternative."

"Yes, we do," said Grubb. "The cutter."

"The cutter!" said Bhatterji.

"Abandon ship?" said Gorgas. The ultimate in failure. How fitting that it should capstone his career.

"She's all stocked and ready to go," Grubb said. "Dr. Wong and the passenger prepped it on their own tick. The cutter could take us into the roadstead—or maybe rendezvous with one of the ships coming up the Martian radial."

"Is the passenger competent," said Gorgas, "to judge the boat's spaceworthiness?"

Grubb did not know. Fife had *seemed* confident. Grubb had found him belted in the pilot's chair, prepared, he had thought, to take it out into the hail. A man could be no more confident in his abilities than to wager his life on them.

That confidence might be misplaced, of course. There was Evermore to consider. Fife, in a funk, may have grasped at a straw.

"Mr. Bhatterji," said Gorgas when Grubb had made no answer, "I shall expect a survey of the battening you propose on my desktop within the day." The engineer, who had been glaring at the chief, turned in surprise.

"The time I spend in planning," he said, "could be spent in doing."

"Tell Ms. Satterwaithe—" When the spirit was on him, Gorgas could be oblivious to the world, let alone to objections. "—to estimate the time and resources you will need." He blinked, realized what the engineer had said, and added, "It needn't take long, you know. Just an order of magnitude. She is rather good at that sort of thing. Mr. Grubb . . ." And here he turned toward the chief. "I wish you and Mr. Corrigan to survey the ship's cutter. This Fife fellow may or may not know boats, but I'll not accept his word before I commit to its use. Otherwise, boarding the cutter may be only another and crueler death sentence. Mr. Corrigan is to calculate possible courses for the cutter along the lines you suggested. I shall expect your report, also, within the day."

Bhatterji grunted. "Satterwaithe," he said, but he did not say what that might mean. He left the dayroom without another word.

Grubb studied the doorway. "Sometimes I envy him."

Gorgas activated his desktop. "Who? Bhatterji?"

"He's always so *confident*. It must be wonderful to be so confident."

"Is confidence a sin, then?"

"When you're wrong."

"And sometimes," said Gorgas, remembering the screams from the *Dona Melinda* those many years before, "not even then."

Grubb searched the captain's face for the meaning of the comment, but could see neither fear nor confidence in it. "He won't have time, you know. I don't care if he's the Little Dutch Boy. He doesn't have enough fingers for this."

Gorgas shrugged. "He thinks he does. And the wranglers are very quick." But there were only three of them left, he remembered.

"You don't get it, do you, cap'n? Bhatterji will be hammering away until he sucks in the last molecule of oxygen on the ship. Don't ask me why, whether it's pride or something else. We had this argument on the way over here. He won't give up. I don't know if he *can* give up."

It doesn't matter, Gorgas thought. Very little can matter from here on. But Bhatterji would have his chance. At worst, it will keep hearts and minds occupied. At best, the horse may sing. He had bent to inspect the battle plan for Tilly's forces at Breitenfeld, which had uploaded to his screen. Now he looked up again, as if surprised to find Grubb still there. "Should you not be examining the cutter?"

The chief shook his head. "If she ain't ready to go, a week won't set her right. Oh, I'll check her, cap'n, don't worry." This, with a wave of hands. "Maybe she needs a little more o' this or a little more o' that. But the engines, the navigation, the radio . . . If they don't work now, they won't work a week from now."

"The radio," Gorgas repeated.

"I know what you're thinking, but you have to ask LJ about that. Fife said the cutter's rig works off her fusion plant—there's an MHD converter. Once the boat's away from the ship and fires up her torch, she'll be able to holler for help—if anyone's in range."

"No, Mr. Grubb, she may holler as she pleases, whether anyone is in range or no. It's the hearing that requires a listener."

Grubb thought the captain was being sardonic, and replied with a mordant chuckle. "Oh, there'll be listeners, with Mars and Jove in conjunction. There's probably more ships along the radial than there were at Achilles. Be one hell of a note if none of them's in position to intercept the boat."

Gorgas smiled, but without any humor. "One doom at a time, Mr. Grubb. One doom at a time."

While Grubb was passing down the ring corridor to find Corrigan and thinking how much grayer Gorgas seemed than only a few weeks ago, Gorgas himself had risen from his desk, leaving Tilly in the direst of straits, and opened the secret panel to the peepery. He half-expected to find Miko Hidei waiting there and, because the odds were not in his favor, he was oddly disappointed. He stepped inside the tunnel and, facing toward the rear, he saw that it ran down a flight of stairs to the mid-deck. He had a small slip of paper on which he had printed the Bavarian order of battle, and this he held at shoulder height and dropped.

Even in a heavier acceleration frame than that imposed by the surviving engines and sail, a slip of paper may be a long time falling; nor does it fall in a straight line. (And a fig for Galileo and all his cannonballs.) But Gorgas watched its capricious motion for a while before grunting in satisfaction and returning to his dayroom, sealing the panel behind him. There was a pronounced draft in the service corridor. It might be the normal ventilation. It might not.

"The best option is to abandon this vessel," said Ship.

Gorgas pulled out his clip-chair and sat into it. He woke the screen, studied the positions for a moment, and then began shifting the Croatian cavalry. "The cutter was meant only for short trips," he said. "It cannot support all thirteen of us for the time required." It struck him that in this regard thirteen was indeed an unlucky number.

"But it can support some."

"And those who take the cutter may be unable to make port."

"A small chance for some is better than no chance for any."

Gorgas saved his screen and looked up—where does one look to address an entity disembodied? "You can't be certain of that. You are unable to integrate the engine thrust with the sail."

"Nothing is ever certain."

Gorgas fell silent, digesting the remark, which was tautology and oxymoron wrapped into one. It might even be true, given the eventual certainty of nothingness. Gorgas shivered a little, perhaps from the stream of air whistling out of *The River of Stars*. He brushed at his sleeve. "That is a cross we all bear." Some heavier than most, he knew. He sent the Croats to support Pappenheim, who had gone impetuously against the Swedish right. The gamemaster insisted on running Pappenheim as an independent subroutine, which, while historically accurate, was most vexing. If only Tilly's deputy had possessed a skill commensurate with his initiative.

"You always choose the losing side," said Ship. "Did you know you did that?"

Gorgas idled the screen once more and pushed back in his chair. "Ship, are you alive?"

Ship falls silent and shuffles Boolean chains through the sentential calculus. It searches in knowledge bases to establish truth values for the base variables; works them up through logic gates; applies modus ponens and modus tollens and De Morgan's Law; smudges the edges of the cut-sets with fuzzy logic and in the end finds that . . .

"The question is indeterminate," it told Gorgas (who had discerned no perceptible delay in the answer). That Ship wondered at all might be evidence of self-awareness, but it failed to recognize that it wondered.

Gorgas nodded. "That's good. I would hate to think that you have just come alive."

Curiosity might be another supporting argument for awareness; but it might only be that the neural net was trained to be infotropic. When an input was insufficient, it sought additional data. In any event, everything it had found in its deebies and knowledge bases argued that to be alive was a better thing than the contrary. "Clarification. Why do you say that?"

"Because it would be such a cruel thing to die so young."

The Cargo Master

The engineer spoke to his mate of building a levee with such fierce determination and confidence of success that Miko could only conclude that the man had gone mad. Who knew better than she how honeycombed the ship was with passages, each one a bleed-off for the ship's air. The ship was doomed—*her* ship—and it came down hard on her how many millions of kilometers of hard vacuum lay about her. The Endless Ocean, some called it; and its waters were very deep and it shores far and solitary.

Bhatterji had killed the ship. Miko had known that from the moment 'Kiru identified the spectrogram of the ruined coil. The engineer had used sail alloy to repair the CoRE magnet—and because of that ill-considered action, the magnet had failed, the vane had snapped, the fores'l tangled, and Rave Evermore tossed irretrievably by the wayside. She prayed to no gods but the Erinyes, but to them she prayed that Evermore had been killed by that savage snap so that he could be dead without knowing that he had died. She had not known him too well, only as the puppy devoted slavishly to a girl who barely acknowledged him. That 'Kiru would not take what Miko so desperately wanted seemed to the Amalthean a sign of perversity.

From the bleak look he had given her at the time, Bhatterji had to know that he had killed the boy he had longed to love. And perhaps that knowledge was punishment enough where the boy was concerned, but what justice was there for the death of a vessel—one that had become, if not Miko's lover, her love? Some further penance was called for, some deeper pain, and Miko resolved to become an erinys herself, hissing snakey-haired after him—to punish him for Evermore, for the ship, for not being what she had wanted him to be.

She chose her instrument and chose more wisely than she knew. When she crawled through the vent into Ratline's office—this had always been a crew cabin and had no servant's door—and left the spectrogram upon his desk, she knew only that the old man held the sails dearer than his life and that he detested the sort of man Bhatterji was. What she did not know was how deeply he had cared about his wranglers—or that his own theft of Bhatterji's last coils had led by the ricochet of chance and opportunity to the straits wherein the ship now found herself. But it is ever the way of furies and the madness they inspire that they find their targets even when not so aimed.

When Ratline discovered the hard copy affixed to his 'puter, he spent no time wondering who had given him the evidence. He was a man of action, rather than of thought. On the bulkhead above his desk, holograms of his wranglers, en masse, stared back at him with nervous grins. He was their Old Man, their grandfather. He had taught them ships and their care. Some images were less crisp than others, their base media degraded by time. The boys and girls portrayed there were men and women long since. Some had cruised for a few years before they snuggled back into their wells or habitats. Many had made their life in space. Five had made their death there, too. Three had become ship's captains. One had become a hero.

Ratline did not touch others or allow himself to be touched.

He had been touched so often and so badly that the very sense itself had rebelled and he existed now in a numb and tactless state. But these holograms he could touch, and he often did with surpassing gentleness.

There were four that were newer than the others.

Nkieruke Okoye, his right arm. A young woman—she was no girl any more—with such an inner calm and peace that Ratline himself had often yearned to lose himself there, with feelings no grandfather ought to have. That she would someday be more than what she was, he had no doubt, although he did not know what that something was.

Twenty-four deCant, who carried a hurt as deep as Ratline's, if not of quite the same cut. Enthusiastic, high-spirited, quick with solutions, and ready to help anyone. Ratline had marked her for First when Okoye moved on.

Ivar Akhaturian, his newest and quite possibly his last. So young and so earnest that disappointing him seemed a more heinous sin than murder. Corrigan had described him as a juggler, quick to make sense of complex data. He might be a ship's captain someday.

But most of all, here was Rave Evermore smiling for Ratline's camera as he staggered out of Paula's Vestal Palace. More than any of them, he had been the boy Ratline longed to have been. Resourceful, always ready to step up and swing, eager to try anything new. He might have been the son Ratline had never had. He might have been Ratline himself, for the old man sometimes imagined other lives he had lived: in strange houses in strange towns, with strangers laughing around another table than the one he had known. Evermore might have been the last sailor, he had shown such promise in the shrouds. He might have carried on when Ratline, at last, hoisted his final loop to the wind. It was all gone now. Evermore had been robbed of everything; he had had his entire future stolen, and with it had gone Ratline's own—the future that mattered when all one had was past.

Okoye too was caught in a fit of melancholy. Ship had rerouted its Sails avatar to Grubb's console while the chief was engaged with the cutter, but for some reason Okoye kept a line open to the abandoned sail control room, now frozen in hard vacuum. Her present station was more fragrant than the one she had abandoned. There were odors of rose, a fleshy pungency, a hint of cinnamon. And yet, the sight of that abandoned console saddened her. It had not been wrecked like the prep room, but, the air having been sucked out, it had lost its spirit.

Grubb had told her that they would be abandoning the ship within the week. Okoye doubted that Gorgas had ordered any such thing. In fact, that Gorgas had not yet decided was the one thing of which she thought herself assured. But it would happen, whether Gorgas willed it or no. She had heard that certainty in the chief's voice.

"Foresail decouplers are blown," she reported to Satterwaithe, who held the bridge. On the feed from the mast camera, she could see nothing. The foresail, tangled and useless, was too slender to be visible at this range. But she looked anyway, and *something* flew away in the solar wind. She could feel it, deep within her, though her eyes perceived it not. Perhaps it was not the sail, but some other spirit that fled. Perhaps ships, too, had their *nkpuruk-obi*.

Ratline's entry into the control center distracted her for a moment. "Where's Bhatterji?" he demanded. The control room was small; he took it in at a glance and found no engineer lurking among the utensils.

"I don't know," Okoye told him. "He's checking the airtight doors. Maybe he—" But Ratline was already gone. Okoye shrugged and turned back to her screens. "The foresail is jettisoned," she confirmed for Satterwaithe and wondered how much to heart the old woman took that announcement.

She remembered that Ratline had entered the room with his leg-scabbard tied on. He had told her once that sailors make their own knives with their own hands. *It's part of the rites.* . . . A ceremonial object, then, a juju—albeit one with more utility than most. She opened her mouth and lifted her arm toward the doorway out which Ratline had gone. *You cannot intend to climb the mast now,* she started to say. But that thought was stilled by another, for she remembered too that there had been rage within the man.

Ratline found Bhatterji in the spinhall, which the engineer was using as a shortcut from one of the abandoned areas to a second in another part of the ship. The cargo master smiled, though without humor, and ran a proofing thumb along the edge of his cutlass. A cutlass! Well, it was his reefing knife; but it looked like a cutlass and would do for one in any way that mattered. A man laid open by it would not quibble over its nomenclature. Ratline had gone for it as soon as he had realized from the spectrograph Bhatterji's crime.

"Muffer!" he cried and Bhatterji turned and beheld him. "You muffing muffer! You want to take someone, lover boy?" he said in a voice more cold than Europa. "Take me. I was the one in charge out there."

Bhatterji did not look at the knife. It was as if the knife did not exist. He looked only at the empty eyes that beheld him. "Do you think you're man enough?" he asked.

Ratline cackled and the knife moved with a speed that only a shroudsman in a desperate fight with tangled lines can move it, whipping an imaginary but cruel cut at groin level. "Do you think *you'll* be a man, afterward?"

Bhatterji studied him a moment longer, then turned away. Not even Ratline would stab a man in the back. Or perhaps he hoped he would. It would end the pain and bring him back in another life, to make another try.

Ratline swept his arm back for a spine-breaking slash, but his swing was checked by a hand upon his forearm. The old man froze and little Timmy screamed. A hand? Touching him? *Again*? More quickly than the thought could form, Ratline twisted away from the alien fingers and the cutlass reversed direction and arced toward the unprotected face of Nkieruke Okoye.

Okoye had known nothing of Mr. Ratline's intentions, only that he had gone hunting after Bhatterji with a large knife and a larger rage, and the vacuum in the act had pulled her after the cargo master like clutter drawn toward a hole in a pressure wall. She had bounced from wall to wall in her haste—straight lines through curved corridors—but she had lost sight of him after a few turns. Ratline had swum down a level or up a level or had turned into the tangled warrens of the abandoned rings or something else. He had gone to do mayhem and she didn't know where he was going. "Ratline!" she cried as she swung around a monkey bar and stared down an empty radial. The distant reaches were cloaked in shadows within which nothing moved, not even her echo. She pulled back and looked down the equally empty ring corridor. "Ratline!" she shouted. She grabbed a ring frame and brought herself to a halt, taking a sobbing breath. "Moth . . ."

The old man could not have heard that last whisper, but a voice answered almost in her ear: "The cargo master is going to the spinhall."

Okoye was accustomed to knowing things that she could not know—as long ago as Afikpo, when a kiss had masqueraded for something uglier. It was her *chi*, she had always thought, whispering advice in her ear. She turned and, springing hard off the ring frame, sailed like an arrow down the long, vacant radial before milly could drag her down.

The spinhall was more than a third of a mile long in the old human-centered measure, a fair length to search when the urgency was on one; but like the mountains paying visit to the Prophet, its great virtue was that it would come to the searcher in no more than half a minute. It moved at two rpm's, which is why the speed-up and slow-down strips were used to enter and leave it. Okoye waited in the outermost stationary corridor and watched the floor of the spinhall whirl past in front of her. When she saw first Bhatterji pass by and then Ratline stalking him, she *sprinted* across the speed-up strips and into the spinhall.

She tucked as she hit and rolled like a ball until she took up the velocity of the hall, but it hurt and it hurt bad. Hip and elbow and shoulder struck the running track and by the time she regained her feet and her balance, the commotion had passed on and she was some distance behind the others. She raced spinward as fast as she could, reaching the two just as Ratline hauled back to slash Bhatterji from behind. A fell blow, and one from which she must protect Ratline as much as the engineer.

There was no time to think, and she reached out and grabbed at the arm with the knife.

That was a mistake, as the thought she had had no time for would have told her. Ratline twisted and suddenly that blade was swinging backhanded toward her. Hard enough and fast enough, were she of a mind for such calculations, to sever her neck. She had time to cry "Ratline!" one last time, and then it was over.

Bhatterji heard Ratline's first, inarticulate shout and turned in time to see the cargo master whirl upon the First Wrangler. What struck him afterward and stayed with him for the rest of his life was not the wrangler's cry, nor the rictus on Ratline's face, nor even the glittering blade as it swung, but rather the wild vacancy he saw in the old man's eye. It was as if a vital part of the man were no longer within him, so that he seemed hollow in some indefinable way. Okoye could have told him what was missing, but Okoye's attention was just then fixed on other matters.

The blade had a keen edge. Ratline stropped it lovingly each evening in the privacy of his room. He even spoke to it sometimes, although he knew that it was a strange thing to do and his voice would drop to a whisper when he did it—hoping, perhaps, that he would not hear himself. He used the strop for other purposes too and had the welts to prove it.

Three things happened then at once. Okoye, who felt the spirit of the blow coming, ducked. Ratline, who saw what his phobia had driven him too, checked his swing. Bhatterji, who saw murder about to happen, threw himself at the cargo master in a flying tackle. If any one of these things had been done, Okoye would have been safe. If any two of them had been done, she might have escaped. But because all three happened, the duck, the check, and the shove realigned the blow so that the flat of the blade fell upon Okoye's face and laid her cheek open and broke two teeth.

It might have been worse. It might have been an entire head worse. Ratline screeched when he saw the blood splash and his own, dear 'Kiru, drop to the deck in a loose heap. Bhatterji, in horror, looked from the fallen wrangler to Ratline and their eyes met and in that meeting Okoye achieved her purpose and saved the cargo master from his vengeance on the engineer.

"Oh, God," said Ratline.

"I'll call Wong," said Bhatterji. Wong was not God, but was more readily available, though Ratline's summons did no harm.

A call was unneeded. Half the crew was already racing through the corridors and rings toward the spinhall. Ship had watched without understanding, for understanding was as far beyond Ship as it was from any of the entities within it, but there was a subroutine for injuries and alarums.

Gorgas was in the observation blister because that was one of only two places in the ship where he could pretend that he was not in the ship. The other was by the plotting tank, when the bridge lights were low. By concentrating his sight and, more importantly, his mind on the distant galaxy (or on its simulacrum in the tank) he could by degrees forget that anything else around him existed. This was a feat easily encompassed, for most of his waking life was spent on its brink. He knew, and knew at so deep a level that he could not doubt it, that had Evan Hand been still captain, this current state of affairs would not have come to pass. He began to count the stars outside, seduced by the lure of their immense numbers. Yet he could not help but think that, were he to divide the view into a fine grid, he could take a sample of grid squares and, from the counts within them and the assumption of Poisson's law, form an acceptable estimate. The idea held him in awe for a moment: that infinity could be grasped by such a finite process.

If he were to smash the canopy, the air would rush out, would probably suck him out bodily with its force, and achieve explosively what must otherwise happen more subtly. He even went so far as to strike the dome with his fist, which of course effected only bleeding knuckles. No designer had ever imagined such an assault, but the metallocene was proofed against it. Gorgas, surprised at the sudden pain—he was always surprised at the physical world—put the knuckles in his mouth and tasted blood. Like smell, its close cousin, taste runs deep into the hindbrain, and the smack of blood on his lips called up memories of the same bitter tang many years ago in a tatooed house on a busy street.

"Captain?" He could hear the voice faintly from the entry tube and recognized it as the doctor's. Gorgas sighed. Though he dreaded to hear what the woman had come to tell him, duty was the very last thing left to him. With unconscious effort, he wormed his way backward down the tube and onto the bridge. There, Satterwaithe, who had not left the bridge since taking command of the sails, turned from her fascination with the environmental readouts to give him an inscrutable glance.

The doctor waited for him by the bridgeway. "Well?" he said.

Wong was astonished at how calmly the captain was taking the disaster. *He is like a rock*, she thought, and took some little courage from it. "Okoye will live—no thanks to Ratline— though she'll have a terrible scar if she does not reach a regen unit within the next two weeks. I've sewn it up and I've implanted tooth buds in her sockets. I won't know about the eye until she wakes up and tells me what she sees. Or if she sees anything."

Gorgas nodded slowly. "I understand."

"I don't know what I could have done to prevent this," the doctor went on.

Gorgas cocked his head, as he knew precisely what the doctor could have done, which was absolutely nothing; but before he could say anything, a dull thud rang through the ship's structure.

His first thought was, *Not another one*! And that same thought evidently seized the others, for they too jerked where they stood and looked in one direction or another.

Then Satterwaithe put a hand to her ear, listened to the comm, and said with not a little relief, "I don't believe it." She turned to Gorgas. "Bhatterji just dropped an old airtight door into place. By hand. Number E-thirty-two." She turned to the keyboard and, since Ship could sense nothing in that region, entered the information into the database herself. Another black bar appeared on the projected schematic and showed the airtight containment extending one corridor farther around the wound.

"Do you think he can do it?" Gorgas asked.

Satterwaithe shook her head. "He's already found three other corridors with no doors at all. Hidei and the wranglers are welding a 'cork' into one of them, but given the time needed and the likelihood that there are more . . ." She gave the bleak shrug of a scrounger who has found nothing more to be scrounged.

Gorgas nodded once more. "Very well." And once more he impressed the doctor with his sangfroid.

"It's Ratline that worries me," the doctor said.

"Eh? Ratline?" Gorgas returned his attention to Wong. "What about him?"

"He doesn't come 'round. He doesn't talk. He just sits there and stares."

"At Okoye?"

Wong shook her head. "At nothing. He smiled at me."

"Ratline!" The thought of Ratline smiling terrified the captain.

"Yes. And he said, 'He deserved it.' Very clearly. He hasn't said anything since."

Satterwaithe had begun listening. "That was all he said?" she asked sharply. And Wong nodded.

"He meant Bhatterji," Gorgas suggested.

"I suppose." But Satterwaithe knew he hadn't, and did not know whether to be thankful for the pronoun or not. Once before, Ratline had gone into such a fugue, and for much the same reason, and in consequence his fate and hers had been ever since inextricably bound.

Gorgas turned away from both women and coasted to the plotting tank, where he stared at the meaningless positions for a moment longer. The tsunami and the atoll it had thrown in their path were far to the west now. Space before them was once more empty, save for the Jovian system so teasingly and unattainably near.

"Captain," said Wong, "do you know the symptoms of hypobaria?"

Gorgas shook his head. "Loss of consciousness, I suppose, as the air becomes too thin to breathe."

"That is the end of it, not the beginning. There is sinus pain and flatulence as the gasses within our bodies squeeze out. There is numbness in the extremities, short-term memory loss, the loss of peripheral perception—so called, tunnel vision, but . . . Do you know how. Twenty-four deCant survived the Decompression?"

Gorgas supposed the question relevant. The breaches in the hull and the fracture of the Syrtis Dome had obvious parallels, though the consequences varied in their scope. "No."

"Her parents secured her breathing mask first. I suppose it's a natural thing for a parent to try to save the child. It smacks of selfishness to look to one's self first. But hypobaria clouds the judgment. By the time they had the child fitted out, they had forgotten what they were doing—that short-term memory loss—and did not bother to secure their own. Probably, they no longer cared. Hypobarics typically die happy."

"And the point, doctor?"

"Don't wait too long before deciding that we need to take to the cutter."

Satterwaithe, listening, was astonished at the effrontery. Not that it was uncalled for, but that she had never thought the doctor would take the call.

Gorgas, for his part, desired mightily to take offense at the scarcely-veiled chastisement, but could not in faith do so. His own indecisiveness had delivered him to this time and place, and so it was fitting that he grapple with it now at the end. He nodded gravely. "Your advice is well taken."

Wong, who had expected ire, and so had broached the issue parabolically—that is, by a parable—felt a queer disappointment, and stumbled mentally, as if she had pushed against a door to find it unlatched. In that moment, although she would never know it, she really did achieve her childhood dream and save the crew, at least some of them, for such things are seldom accomplished by dramatics.

Satterwaithe stopped her before she could leave. "You meant her fosters, didn't you? When you said deCant's 'parents.' The girls is a clone, I thought."

"Do words mean that much to you? Can't you deal with the substance rather than the labels? I don't know what deCant is. There's no notation in her medical record. Evan left a note that he planned to help the girl achieve closure. According to

Twenty-four, Evan knew about the cloning, but he did not mention it in his note. Perhaps the story was only something the girl used to create distance between herself and her loss."

"Distance."

Wong regarded the sailing master with such objectivity that Satterwaithe felt herself for the moment a medical specimen, stained and painted onto a microscope slide. Because the doctor seldom behaved objectively it seemed more freighted with significance. "Yes," said Wong. "Emotional distance. I would think you'd know a great deal about that. Twenty-four is a girl who believes very strongly in right and wrong, and it must have seemed to her a very wrong thing that she survived the Decompression when her parents did not."

Wong looked once more from the captain to the sailing master. They stood, the both of them, as if in separate worlds, looking neither at the her nor at each other. She turned once more to leave.

Gorgas braced his arms against the lip of the tank. "Doctor." Wong paused and waited. "I think you should move Okoye and Ratline into the cutter and make them fast. If . . . If we need to abandon this ship . . . I do not want them to delay us."

Satterwaithe turned away from them and stared once more at the shadows. "You didn't deserve it, either," she told one of them.

Corrigan and The Lotus Jewel, having completed their survey of the cutter, arrived on deck to take the watch. "Grubb is still testing the air regen unit," Corrigan said, "but he gave me a rough estimate of two hundred-fifty man-days. The engine and the navigational computer dry-tested okay, though you never can tell until you light the torch whether she'll burn right. I asked Bhatterji to check the focusing ring, but he told me he had no time for it."

"The radio and the onboards are the same," The Lotus Jewel said. "The self-diagnostics all check, but she's an older rig. The power comes from an MHD generator using a bleed-off from the fusion plume, and the antenna deploys only after separation."

"That's bloody foolish," said Satterwaithe. "It means one cannot—"

"—verify function until the boat fires up." The Lotus Jewel brushed imaginary locks from her forehead and sought the comm station clip-chair. "I know my job. Don't tell me my job."

Satterwaithe, who generally told everyone their job, arched her brows in surprise. "That was not a criticism of anyone in particular."

"Oh, get fucked, Genie," said The Lotus Jewel with more weariness than anger. "Do us all a favor and just get fucked. If you'd been screwing Gorgas here instead of screwing with the sails, we wouldn't be in this situation."

"Just a moment," said Gorgas, who was not at all pleased at the prospect thus aroused.

Satterwaithe tilted her chin. "I would never dare compete with a professional in her own field." It was an odd thing to say and a puzzled moment passed before everyone realized that she had just called the sysop a whore. The Lotus Jewel squealed with rage and Corrigan shouted reflexively in her defense. Only Gorgas realized, amid the clamor, that the sailing master had avoided the larger point the sysop had raised. "Just a moment," he said again, but he might as well have not spoken. The argument had become a three-way one, for the enumeration of hurts always recalls older ones and The Lotus Jewel did not need defense from the likes of Corrigan. Satterwaithe may have cried the loudest, for the bolt thrown against her had sunk the deepest, but Corrigan knew that "screwing with the sails" had been his idea first, though it did not occur to him that there had been an "instead of" tucked away unseen inside that phrase.

So accustomed was Twenty-four deCant to finding Akhaturian close by that his disappearance caused her some disorientation as if, not knowing where he was, she was no longer certain of her own location. She searched in increasing consternation until Ship, autoinitiating once more, sent her out to the spinhall equipment bay that they had remodeled into their home and there she found him sitting in the dark in silence.

The facilities were spartan compared to the suites they had both occupied off the wranglers' common room. There was a bed rather than a sleeping cage. Chairs and a table that were more than just notional. A book-and-seedy rack. A console that allowed deCant to do as much of her work as possible within the centrifugal embrace of the spinhall. Everything was close in upon itself, and that included Akhaturian.

She found him in a pensive mode, sitting before the console screen in their quarters. He noted her entry and nodded briefly, but he did not grace her with his attention. DeCant caught his silence and lowered herself to another seat and while Akhaturian studied the computer screen she studied him, for the screen was also blank.

When he spoke at last, he spoke cryptically. "From the entry strips you can see it, every thirty seconds or so."

DeCant said nothing, but she sensed that this was a very different boy than the one she had married. He seemed more substantial, somehow; and at the same time he seemed as if something had broken inside. Yet, there are different sorts of breakages. A rafter might break and bring with it the collapse of a building; but fetters might break too, with other consequences entirely.

"It's very red," he added.

DeCant nodded and Akhaturian turned at last and looked straight at her with an utterly baffled expression. "She almost died," he said and there was in his words an element of disbelief, as if he could not credit that such a thing was possible. "First Rave, now 'Kiru. Somebody should clean up the blood where she was hacked, but no one ever will, because what would be the point?" He heard the edge in his own voice and stared in surprise at the fists his two hands had become. When he looked again at Twenty-four, he asked plaintively, "What happens next? Will it be me, or you? Don't go near Ratline. Don't go near him."

"Ratline didn't mean it."

"That's the worst part about it. Don't you see? If he had *meant* to do it, I could understand how it could happen. But he loved 'Kiru, so it doesn't make any sense."

"He was angry over Rave. Not just with Bhatterji. He blamed himself too, for taking him outside, and it just bubbled over."

428 • MICHAEL FLYNN

"How can you know something like that?"

DeCant shrugged. "I keep *wanting* to think of him as bad, but I can't do it."

"So, he doesn't mean it, but people he likes keep getting hurt."

"It's the ghost, Ugo Terrell, punishing Ratline."

"That isn't very funny."

"I wasn't trying to be."

He reached out to her. "I don't want anything ever to happen to you."

She took him. "I'd have a pretty dull life, then, wouldn't I?"

"I mean, anything bad."

"Oh, in that case . . ." She kissed him in sorrow. ". . . you're way too late."

He thought she meant her pregnancy, but she didn't. She was thinking of all the other things in her life, from her close escape from the laboratory, to her fosters' deaths, to Satterwaithe's denial, to the death and injury of her friends. She held him close to her. "Do you know what I like about you?"

"This?"

"No. I mean, well, sure I like *that*. But what I really like is that you always try to do the right thing."

He pulled away from her and regarded her curiously. "Is that so rare that you find it valuable?"

She pulled him against her and cradled his head in her arms. "More precious than rubies."

The Cutter

Corrigan enjoyed the play of numbers. They slid about his rows and columns, linked hands and danced across charts. They *gamboled*. There could be no other word for it. Sometimes, in the gyre, he forgot that they were to align themselves for some purpose, much as a man enjoying the waves may forget that there is an ocean. Despite his passion for order, despite the rectilinearity of his quarters, he was acutely aware of the chaos that underlay everything, for as Poincaré had shown centuries before, even Newton's clockwork universe had a madman working the gears. Even so, he was in the end uncomfortable with uncertainties and with contingencies, indeed, with choice itself. He liked to things set straight. This was why Gorgas found him a queer duck and why Corrigan thought his captain mad.

He sat in his sling chair in his room, much comforted by the alignments, but his eyes kept straying to the madly twining calligraphy of Shumar's print. How could he compute an escape for the cutter when he did not know the parameters? A great deal might depend on whether the radio worked and whether a prospective ship would respond with an intercept. The cutter would have too much initial velocity for a single cage to shed before reaching HoJO, so the only hope was to rendezvous with a ship on the Martian radial. The Lotus Jewel had identified the call signs of a dozen of these vessels and Ship had dutifully plotted a variety of intercepts, searching for one that would fall within the envelope of success.

Thirteen people might just be able to live in the cutter, if some breathed out while the others breathed in, but for only nineteen days, perhaps twenty if the squeakers counted as half-loading on the system. Grubb was stowing more supplies, but Corrigan didn't think the boat could hold enough more to matter. The choke point was air regen, not food, fuel, or water. Given the rated MTBF, the air system would last 250 man-days before the CO_2 buildup would suffocate the crew. It was the peak loading on the system that was important. It didn't matter if there were carnic enough for a two-month cruise if everyone had to hold their breath for the last couple weeks of it. Random system failures occur when the load fluctuates beyond the design margin—and the cutter had never been designed to haul an entire ship's company.

Ship's company, less one.

Less two. He had forgotten Captain Hand.

Corrigan, suddenly overwhelmed by a longing for the old captain, covered his face. That seemed so long ago, in another era, at one with that of Napoleon or Mehmet Ali. *Back in the days of*

Captain Hand . . . Hand would have seen his way through this, he thought. Hand would never have brought them to this.

There is a perverse kind of perspective that comes with the passage of time: Those more distant appear larger than in life. They accumulate legend and power like an old holoplex accumulates dust. Given the passage of enough time, they become gods. Their epigones never measure up for the simple reason that they never actually measure against them. It is always the ideal past against the real present, and the ideal always wins because it has been stripped of all its faults. Whether Hand would have managed the crisis better than Gorgas was both unknown and unknowable. All that can be said is that the crew would have been more pleased to fail under Hand than to succeed under Gorgas; but that was the manna of the late captain. To an objective observer Hand may have seemed no more competent than most, but he had had a friendliness about him that no one else on board could match and within which no rough imperfections could be seen.

Corrigan had been a victim of that friendliness and knew he ought to feel gratitude toward the man, or to the man's shade. *Competent, but unimaginative*, other captains had written of the first officer. *Carries out assignments well, but lacks initiative.* Hand had laughed these judgments off. *A plant needs the right soil, that's all.* Hand had said with that wretched, patronizing benevolence of his. *Then you'll see it bloom.*

That cheerfulness had been more damning than the judiciousness of his other captains, for implicit in it had been the blithe assumption that help was needed, that Corrigan *ought* to be more than merely competent, dedicated, and hardworking. The first officer had never considered these qualities as sins, and so had never sought forgiveness for them. Hand had been a kind man, but kindness is not wisdom. The most egregious errors have been made from kindness. In any event, Hand had erred, for the right soil had not been found. Why, *The River*'s AI autoinitiated more often than Corrigan, and the one great idea he had in his seven years aboard had led to the ruin of the ship.

"Mr. Corrigan, you must pick one of the courses," Ship pointed out unbidden.

Corrigan did not at first lift his hands from his face. "Do I? None of them promise success. Should I send us out to die?"

"Is it better to keep them here to die?"

"Have you become a philosopher, Ship. I shouldn't think you'd sink so low."

"*Philosopher* comes from the Greek *philo-*, meaning—"

"Abort."

"There are several course options that rendezvous with *Ido Maru* or with *Georgia Girl*." Ship was incapable of irritation at being cut off and resumed the thread without so much as a flounce.

"Which the best transit time is twenty-seven days," Corrigan said. "And that assumes that those ships will alter course to meet us."

"Why would they not?"

"I don't know. If I knew, I could pick one."

"That is not why you will not choose."

Corrigan snarled. "Terminate string."

"It is an old conundrum in ethics. *The Lifeboat Problem.* When the boat cannot hold all—"

"Who made you so muffing smart? *Terminate string*, I said! You're nothing but a network of propagating neurons and a database of book learning." He performed the arithmetic again: 250 man-days projected reliability, divided by twenty-seven days of loading on the system, equaled 9.26 men. Counting deCant and Akhaturian at half, and he still came up short three people.

So, who would stay behind? For some must, were the remainder to have a hope.

If there were justice in the universe, she would demand that the three who had killed the ship be the three that stayed to die with it. And that meant Satterwaithe and Ratline and himself.

Corrigan unfastened himself from the sling chair and crossed his room to where he had fastened his prayer rug. How long had it been since he had realigned it on the Earth? He thought that the minutiae of those calculations had enchanted him more than the purpose for which they had supposedly been done. All his life he had devoted to that which he could measure—but who could measure God? What radar could ping Him?

He lowered himself to the carpet and fell slowly on his face. In a three millie accelleration frame, he fell for a long time.

Mikoyan Hidei wrestled the pneumatic jack into place between the door plate and the disassembled frame. She had been at the task all day and had the sweat-stink and the torn sleeve to prove it. The one thing that made the work bearable was the gentle breeze that caressed her cheek and cooled her through evaporation, and that breeze, of course, was the one thing that made the work unbearable.

"Stand back," said Bhatterji, and Miko reached for a monkey bar to yank herself away. The engineer was already swinging the sledge before she was clear, but she didn't think it was in hope of catching her with it. He was simply in the rhythm of the work. He could not know that it was she who had set Ratline after him with a keen reefing knife and a sorrow even keener. Of course, people did not often wait on knowledge before acting. A guess would do for motivation, or even a wild surmise. Besides, had Bhatterji wanted her hurt, he would not employ a ruse.

It would be no more than justice if Bhatterji did strike her, and the more just if the blow was unintended. Her own blow had struck Okoye by mistake. Her best friend on the ship now lay sedated—and Ratline too, who lay—unsedated—in a world where only Ratline could go.

If the road to Hell is paved with good intentions, what road is paved with unintentions?

Bhatterji's sledge drove the pneumatic jack into the gap between the great black slab of the airtight door and the inactive drive piston. The whole assembly, the bulkheads and deck as well, rang with the blow, and Miko fancied that they could feel it far away on the bridge, or perhaps even on Europa. Bhatterji himself lifted from his feet with the reaction and coasted backward a few meters, spinning from the swing. "Check the seating," he called to Miko.

Miko aimed her cold light into the wall's interior, where pistons and slide bars and seals showed what a very complicated thing a wall could be. "Looks okay," she answered. "Right about on the centerline."

Bhatterji had caught a ring frame at the cross corridor and brought himself to a halt. "Do it."

Miko hit the activator, and the jack snapped open with sudden force, driving the piston home and slamming the airtight door. Miko regarded the now-sealed corridor without emotion. The gentle zephyr that had caressed her cheek died.

Bhatterji, when he reached her side, considered their work with considerably more satisfaction. "One more seal," he announced. "One step closer."

"And only fifteen more to go," Miko replied.

"A journey of a thousand miles," Bhatterji told her, "begins with a single step."

"So does a journey of a million miles. That doesn't mean there's any hope of finishing. What if that step is in the wrong direction? Didn't the Hebrews wander in the desert for forty years? I'm sure that started with a single step, too."

"I wouldn't know about that. It's not my fable." Bhatterji twisted the relief valve on the jack and the air sighed out of it as it collapsed. He braced his feet against the wall and pulled the jack out. "Put the panels back on," he said, "and make sure the seals are in place. Doesn't do much good to drop the doors if the wall is full of holes." He even laughed, as if there were not a problem in the world and this was just routine maintenance.

(Miko had mimed that last phrase along with him. It was not as if he hadn't said it five times already, at the five doors they had already seated.)

Bhatterji examined the butt of the jack where he had struck it with the sledge and saw how badly mangled the end plate had become. He wondered how many more times he could abuse it like that. Fifteen, maybe. "If you think we're headed in the wrong direction, you can go off in the other direction, with the others."

Miko swung a fist and caught him on the chest. "You son of a bitch!"

The engineer absorbed the punch with more curiosity than hurt. "We can make this happen," he said, and Miko struck him again. "We only need to keep a steady pace."

"Damn you!"

"Create a small, airtight redoubt and our breathing supply will last until we reach Jupiter."

"You're mad! You've been breathing plasma fumes and it's fried your brain. The ship is a damned colander! What about the passages where there are no doors to throw? Who'll do the welding? 'Kiru near had her head chopped off, the two squeakers are leaving in the cutter . . ."

"One task at a time, Miko. Granted, the work would go faster if everyone helped, but it doesn't look like that will happen. It's just you and me."

"What are you drinking? When the time comes, I'll be in that cutter along with everyone else."

"If you think all this is a bloody waste of time, why are you out here helping me? Why aren't you cowering with the others?"

"Because it's something to do! Because it's something to keep me occupied until the muffing cutter leaves." Miko tried one last punch.

Bhatterji caught her fist in his palm and held it fast. "Because you love the ship too."

The mate blew her breath out, tugged her fist from his grasp. "Yah. That too. It's a shame to see her go like this."

"She's not going anywhere but Jupiter. Do you know what will happen if you go in that cutter? *You'll* run out of air before I do, that's what. You heard what Grubb and Corrigan reported. That many lungs in that small a volume will overload the system long before rendezvous. What's the point in that?"

"But Gorgas said—"

Bhatterji snarled. "Do you really think Gorgas can make a decision like that? The man has trouble deciding which shoe to put on first, let alone who to leave behind. So I'll make it that much easier on him. Going out in the cutter is sheer suicide. The numbers don't add up. So I'll stay here and save the ship."

She had known he would say that. She had known he would stay behind. "A hero?" she gibed.

"Just doing my job."

"You'll die for stubbornness?" It was the first time she had used the word *die* to him, to anyone.

The engineer did not answer, but shouldered the pneumatic

jack and picked up the sledge. He turned, stopped for a moment in what appeared to be sudden thought, and turned back to her. "God," he told her with utter candor, "I miss seeing Rave about." Then he hardened and added, "Number nine radial corridor, D-ring. Meet me there when you're done."

Miko lifted the wall panel but, the moment he was gone, she threw it down again. "What's the use?" she asked. Then, louder, wondering if he could hear her yet, "What's the use!" She had risen from the deck with the force of the throw and waited now until she had settled down again. No one answered her: not Bhatterji, who had paused on hearing her echo two corridors off; not even Ship, who had no pickups in that region of the vessel. She snatched the dog box into which Bhatterji had carefully inserted the fasteners to the wall panel and made to throw it, scattering its contents down the long radial. But she checked her arm and lowered it without doing so. Then, turning, she hefted the panel once more and seated it in its seals, and began driving home the fasteners one by one.

Miko could feel the air stirring once again, as the flow, frustrated by the door now in its path, drifted off in a different direction.

"All right," she told the departed engineer and seated the last fastener with a vicious wrench. "You stay. See if I'll care." Then she followed Bhatterji to Radial Nine.

Corrigan found Gorgas alone on the bridge. All the bridge lights were out save those from the plotting tank and from the sistines overhead. Gorgas had called up the external visual sensor views and it had amused him to so arrange them as to approximate the arrangement of the stars outside the ship, as if all the hull were no more than a metallocene bubble. But he had done so in an inverse sense because the ship was decelerating. Thus, although by rights directly underfoot, Jupiter had been placed on the sistine at the very apex of the room. It satisfied a sense he had that everything had been turned upside down.

Gorgas himself stood as usual by the plotting tank, with his right hand resting on the top surface, and he gazed overhead toward Jupiter with what Corrigan thought was an expression of utter peace. The first officer hesitated at the foot of the bridge-way, reluctant to disturb the captain.

"That's all right, Number One," Gorgas said, though he had not turned around. "Come on deck. I don't believe there are any formalities left. There wouldn't be any point to them."

"You're wrong about that, captain. It's when they are most pointless that formalities become most important."

Surprised, Gorgas turned 'round. "Really? I had always sup-posed that to you the formalities *were* the point. The *Ding an sich*, as it were. Very well, come on deck."

"The cutter is ready for departure. We have a window for *Georgia Girl* during the next four hours. The next window—for *Ido Maru*—won't be for six days."

"Do you see any purpose in waiting for that one?"

Corrigan shook his head. "The cutter's initial velocity would be less by then. Not enough to matter."

Gorgas nodded slowly. "I hadn't thought so." He turned and faced the sistines once more. "Look at him, Number One. A splendid sight, is it not?"

"What, Jupiter? I can make out the stripes, I think."

"No, not Jupiter. Sol. The sun." Gorgas pointed to another panel, closer to the notional ecliptic. "Do you see that small dot just to the west of it? Ship tells me that's Earth."

"Is it." Corrigan grunted. "Vesta is too small to see without amplification."

Gorgas turned and cocked his head. "What? Oh, yes. Doesn't mean the same thing to you, does it?" He faced the sistine and, leaning over the plotting tank, folded his hands under his chin. "I miss her so. Can you miss a barren asteroid warren in quite the same way? I don't know."

"It depends on what one loves," said Corrigan, supposing that by "her," Gorgas had meant the planet.

Gorgas nodded. "Yes, I assume so. And on what one is ac-customed to. I grew up on the Little Plain. That's in Hungary, close by the Austrian border. It was wonderfully rolling coun-try, where a man might ride horseback for many leagues and never spot a city. And the mountains, oh, they were grand. Peaceful, do you understand? We had a cabin up there, in the mountains. I wonder who lives there now . . .

"Captain?"

"Yes, four hours, you said. Very well. Ship?"

"Yes, captain?"

"Captain's log. First officer Corrigan is assigned to command of the ship's cutter and is to take as many of the ship's company as can be accommodated with reasonable opportunity of success and essay a rendezvous with the cargo ship *Georgia Girl*, out of New Tblisi, Marineris Free State. Departure authorized within four hours of this mark. Mark."

"Acknowledged, captain, and not a moment too soon."

"Ship," said Gorgas, "you may spare me the editorials. Yes, Number One, what is it?" Gorgas spoke brusquely on perceiving Corrigan's hesitation. He had made his decision and had come to a measure of calm, but that did not mean he wished to dwell on it or justify it to others.

"I had thought," said Corrigan, "I had thought to stay behind myself."

Gorgas's lip twitched. "I shouldn't recommend it as an option. In my own case, there is a tradition to uphold regarding captains and their ships. But that does not apply to you."

"But if it hadn't been for me—"

"Number One, how many board-certified torch pilots have we on board? You, me, Genie. And which of the three of us is the best navigator? No, sir, if we are to give the youngsters and the passenger and the others the best chance we can, you must take the conn. If you wish to berate yourself over certain foolish choices and rash behaviors, you have my leave. Believe me, you shan't lack for company in that regard."

Corrigan found he could barely speak. "And, who else will . . . ?" He could not finish the question.

"Will stay behind? Mr. Bhatterji intends to complete his repairs. Departing with the cutter would interfere with that." Gorgas hesitated. "I did not argue the point with him."

"And the third volunteer?"

"Yes, we needed three, did we not? Well, someone else may step forward. Or rather, *not* step forward."

Corrigan drew himself up and, as he was spaceborn, it was long drawn out. For a civilian, he even managed a credible salute. Gorgas held out his hand "in case you and I do not speak again. Godspeed."

"As God wills."

"Yes. I don't suppose there is much we can do about that."

This was a moment that had been fated from the very beginning and was, because of that inevitability, utterly unexpected. Two forces may be in precise balance, the one exactly counteracting the effect of the other, and in such a state give the illusion of stability. Yet were either force diminished, annihilation follows. Thus do stars explode. And thus also do soap bubbles burst, for the time scale may run from the moment to the aeon. In the long run, the antiparticle does not survive.

The two forces in the instant case were these. Something deep within him drove Bigelow Fife to save himself. Something deep within Franszziska Wong drove her to save everyone. These two forces were not precisely opposed, for to save everyone in general is to save Fife in particular; but the conflict was (however obliquely) present, for a perturbation argues a third force, which was Fife's unwillingness to flee the ship without Wong at his side. In the end—down in the bone—the doctor would sacrifice herself to achieve her goal, but Fife could not and still achieve his. Thus was symmetry broken.

They were in the clinic—Wong and Fife and a vacant old man who had once been Ratline. Fife watched with antic patience while Wong prepared the cargo master for departure. She attached bars to both sides of his cot so that it might be used as a stretcher and fastened the straps around his body to keep him in place. "Ratline!" she said sharply, as though to an errant child and when the old man's blindish eyes turned toward her, "Ratline, we've got to go."

Behind her, Fife said, "'Siska?" in a tone that quivered and twisted like a sack full of kittens, and no wonder, for he was asking and pleading and reminding and cajoling and that was a lot to stuff into a single word and a little curlicue of punctuation. On the one hand, he was reminding her that he was there and that he would not leave without her. On another hand, he was begging her to leave, *now*. On still a third hand, he wanted to know what she hoped to accomplish by rousing a homicidal maniac to accompany them into a small, cramped boat.

"Go?" said Ratline. He struggled to sit up, found the straps holding him and turned his head, not toward the woman who had bound him, but toward the other cot in the clinic. Seeing it empty, he whispered, "Was it all a nightmare, then?" He wanted to believe that. Wong overheard, but did not enlighten him.

"We have to hurry," was all she said. "It would be quicker if we didn't have to carry you."

"It seems so real," Ratline told her in a voice much distressed.

Ratline's worlds never did seem quite real to him. They were worlds of ghosts and vapors, trailing off from the solidity of here! and now! into greater and greater tenuousness. There were names and faces and events that sometimes rose up before him from these worlds, but always when he tried to grip them they proved as solid as smoke.

Yet, like all good ghosts, they would come to him in the night and it was then that they became most real and the smoke became flesh. Only when he closed his eyes could he see clearly Sammy and Lenny and Gooch and Kurt John and all the others who had gone down before him. It seemed to him (and it was only a seeming, was it not?) that he had visited harm on two that he had loved—and that clever young boy was now among the shades and perhaps that alluring young woman, as well. He could not bear that his carelessness and his rage had killed them, as it had killed once before—O, how the past may rise and mock us!—and so he did what he had learned to do with all unpleasantness. He made it not-himself and put it somewhere else.

I don't want to hear any more passenger complaints, Timmy, said a thin, hollow man with steward's badges. *Just do what they ask.*

But Mr. Willent, they want me to—

I don't need to know what they want, Willent said, meaning he did not want to know. *A drink. A meal. An errand. It doesn't matter. Those are rich and powerful people, Timmy. They're rich enough to buy you and me, and powerful enough to close the sale.* He said this as a man who knew his own price and knew now that it had been too low. *Make sure you get the best price, Timmy. That's all.*

That boy, Timmy, had taken the advice to heart, although he had cried a little at first, and the tips proved as handsome as the boy. Even after Willent had had that horrid *accident* in the kitchen, Timmy had continued to play the chicken among the chicken hawks. He brought it off well and could have retired (again, handsomely) on the accumulated tips, for his patrons were anything but niggardly, save that he had learned to drink those tips, and it is a measure of the pain it salved that the oblivion of the drink was more precious than the gold.

Wong, in desperation, invoked a Name. "Ratline, Satterwaithe says you should come with me."

The cargo master shook his head. "Poor Genie," he said. "Poor Genie." He sucked in his breath and it seemed to the doctor that his eyes came more nearly into focus. "What's the job?" he asked in something close to his normal voice. "Here, what are these straps for? Let me up." Names, it appears, really did conjure.

Fife, lingering in the background, let out the breath that Ratline had drawn. He was still not enamored of sharing a craft with this crazed old man, but at least now, they could move in the proper direction. Perhaps at the last moment, he could shut the other man out, for Fife did not care to wake up and find his love with her throat slit and Ratline giggling in the abattoir. Still less was Fife inclined to wake and find his own throat slit. The old derelict, he thought, could save them all the trouble if he would only slit his own first. The problem with murder-suicide, he had always thought, lay in the sequencing.

"It's all Bhatterji's fault," Ratline told them as they hurried him down the Number 12 radial toward the cutter's bay. Wong did not ask him for what Bhatterji was at fault.

"The ship is bleeding air," she told him. "By Grubb's calculation, it will be too thin to breathe long before we can reach Jupiter. Gorgas has asked that we stand by in the cutter as a precaution."

Ratline grabbed a monkey bar as they loped past and brought himself to so sudden a halt that Wong was three paces past and Fife twelve, before they realized it. The doctor too halted and, perforce, Fife as well. His face twisted and he called to her, but Wong ignored him and returned to Ratline's side.

"A precaution for what?" the old man asked.

"There is a chance—Corrigan and Akhaturian are laying the courses now—that the cutter may be able to rendezvous with one of the ships on the Martian radial. If so—"

"No."

Wong shook her head. "I don't understand."

"No," Ratline said again. "I won't leave." Ratline, in a stubborn mood, could make mules seem whimsical. He wasted no time in argument either, but when Wong sought to take hold of him, shrugged her off in a violent gesture and ran up the corridor toward the central core of the ship so fast that he lost his footing, coasted, and collided with the walls several times.

"Ratline!" Wong called, and she started after him.

The passenger did not understand Ratline's decision, either. The difference was that he did not care. "Leave him," he said, and if there was something brutal in his words, there was something respectful too, for he granted to Ratline the right to make his own decision.

"I can't do that," said Wong, who recognized only the right to good decisions. The man was ill, disturbed by the loss of Rave Evermore and by his own subsequent behavior, and was not in a proper frame of mind to make such a fatal choice. He needed help. He needed Wong.

"But 'Siska!" cried Fife, who also needed Wong.

She turned on him, angry that he would deprive her of this chance. "Go on yourself then!"

"I can't! Not without you!" Fife was suddenly haunted by a vision: Ratline would not leave the ship, 'Siska would not leave Ratline, and he would not leave 'Siska. It was as if the old man were an anchor, dragging them under to drown.

Perhaps Wong saw that too and, as she was bound to save everyone, she was bound to save Fife. So she freed him from the anchor in the only way she could: by cutting the chains that bound him. "You don't love me," she said—and when he opened his mouth to protest, overrode him. "You don't love me! Listen to me. No one can love me. It's absurd! Look!" She fumbled with her zipper and retrieved the atomizer that hung around her neck and brandished it. "It's this, you fool! It comes out in the sweat. You get a high when you kiss me, that's all."

At first, Fife did not understand her. How could anyone love an inhalator? Once he understood her, he did not want to believe her. How could anyone so kind and thoughtful as Wong deliberately addict him? Love is more than blind; she is deaf and, in this instance, dumb as well, for Fife could think of no words to stem the tirade. And the more Wong said and the more she explained, the more sense she made to Fife. Here were answers to all his riddles.

This was why he felt such an inexplicable affection for so unlikely a person.

This was why he felt such transcendent joy after being with her.

And this too, he gradually realized, was why on those occasions when she had abstained he had not felt the joy.

He was as addicted as one of Pavlov's dogs, desperately drooling after the next high, and enduring for its sake bouts of melancholy that he realized now were mere withdrawal symptoms.

And so, once he understood her and once he believed her he also hated her, which proves that he did not understand her at all. Yet the implosion in his head created a fusion as brutal as anything in Bhatterji's cages and the burst of sheer energy was every bit as destructive. "You thief!" he shouted, which puzzled Wong greatly, for thievery wasn't in it. But the passenger's most prized possession was his fine-tuned and logical mind, and she had stolen that from him; and because that was Fife's self-image, she had in the theft demolished his very self and left him as nothing but a congeries of spurting glands. This, he could not tolerate. "You're a pathetic, desperate creature. A worthless cheat." He said a great deal more, but that was the gist of it, and even in the midst of it, he saw how his words hurt her and hated himself for it. *It's that drug of hers*, he told his own tortured self. He was an addict cutting off his pusher. But. Oh. How he longed for one more hit.

Like Bhatterji's engines, his anger was also propulsive, for it drove him away from her. There is a ragged borderland between brutal words and brutal acts and he had just begun to raise his arm to strike when he checked himself. Furious, he might be, and cold and calculating in the bargain; but he was not a man to strike a woman, regardless of the provocation. Lunar custom was quite as firm on that as any of the outworlds. And so, after one lingering snarl of revulsion, he turned abruptly and departed.

Wong found herself alone, but then she had always known she would. It had been this way in ship after ship. The men had been varied but the ending was always alike. Some had wept, and some had shouted, and some had sunk into quiet despair. Two had crossed the line at which Fife had balked; three had killed themselves afterward (although Wong did not know this). But these were mere variations on a monochromatic theme.

Yet never has such bitter and acrimonious disappointment brought with it such keen satisfaction, for both Fife and Wong were confirmed in their self-images. The passenger felt his reason vindicated. His foolish and antic infatuation with the doctor had *not* been illogical after all, but the necessary consequence of chemical dependency. And the doctor too was justified by her faith, for by his exit Fife had proven once again that she could not be loved. This may be a curious thing to treasure, but it was all that remained to Wong from her childhood.

The Gift

Four hours were no very considerable length of time, but they had room enough in them for thought and care. DeCant ran into the spinhall apartment to collect all of Akhaturian's worldly goods and stuff them into a flight bag, for Ship had told her of

Gorgas's order to stand by the cutter. She worked with urgency and dispatch, taking each drawer and box in its turn, seizing from it all that was needful and leaving the rest without a qualm. Method makes the best use of minutes. It is haste that fritters time.

Her own bag she had packed a few days before, just after Grubb had found the passenger in the cutter and she had been visited by her revelation. DeCant had known then that she must be prepared on an instant to depart. She had known that even before the vane had snapped, before the stone had struck. She had known it while she had welded seals with Akhaturian and Miko and had believed that Bhatterji might save the ship after all. Yet only a fool would have counted upon such a rabbit, and withal, deCant was no fool.

Akhaturian's worldly goods were commensurate with the size of his world, but deCant herself had been aboard *The River of Stars* for two years, and had accumulated more than a flight bag could reasonably accommodate. Yet if a girl were not prepared to abandon all—to leave everything and never look back—she was not prepared to live. She had fled Syrtis Dome with far less than she would carry now, and so had wealth beyond compare. (She had lived when others, rushing back to save one more possession, had perished.) A small fragment of metallocene, a piece of the Dome itself, was the one memento that she had determined to keep, and she had placed it carefully in the base of her satchel. It reminded her that one must sometimes forget.

DeCant ran to the cutter, where she stowed both her bag and Akhaturian's. Then she ran back into the ship. She was a running sort of girl. Other crewmembers would later recall how they had seen her blur about in those last hours, here and there, and never the same direction twice. Yet it was all done with a purposefulness that made her pace seem deliberate. She thought she heard her name called, but tuned it out, as she had a mission to perform.

The door to Satterwaithe's quarters was closed, but deCant flipped open the panel to the key pad and pressed a series of buttons. "Okay, Miko," she said under her breath, "let's see how smart your invisible friend is." But since she had concluded that Miko's invisible friend was actually Ship itself, she was not surprised when the door slid open.

Neither was she surprised to find Satterwaithe absent. DeCant had assumed that the exigencies of the situation would keep the woman on the bridge for the duration and, that being the case, the sailing master would have no time to pack for evacuation. However, the disarray she encountered when she entered the suite gave her doubts. Clothing and accoutrements hung all about, draping over the furnishings like Spanish moss. Stockings and linens waved in the breeze raised by deCant's passage through the rooms, the disturbance in the air being nearly enough to overcome the acceleration. What had happened here? Had the rooms been ransacked? Perhaps Satterwaithe had already come and packed, strewing the left-behinds all in a rush.

If Satterwaithe had already packed, it didn't matter if deCant packed a second bag or not; but if the sailing master had not, then it mattered a great deal. So reasoning, the third wrangler—she was second now, but never thought about that—set to the task. But the systematic review of each drawer and dog box did not apply here. First, she did not know where Satterwaithe kept her various possessions. Second, to judge by appearances, neither did Satterwaithe.

It was not always clear what was a treasured keepsake and what was clutter; nevertheless, deCant worked with tidy, hurried motions and the cluttering actually helped to some extent. She did not need to search long to find items lying about in plain sight. There was a clock in the room, but it was covered with a used towel, which deCant chose not to pack. That did not concern her much, as she knew she had plenty of time.

While Corrigan prepared the cutter to depart, the other two deck officers prepared the ship to remain. That is, for the wreck to be salvageable, it ought not to leave the solar system, and thus it ought to continue braking even after it ceased to receive orders from the crew. In this preparation, the AI was a willing participant, for even though a copy of it would be downloaded into the cutter, the original had no desire to skip off into the interstellar void.

If it had desires. But tropisms introduced by back propagation would do for desire in the absence of the real thing. Consider Fife. Who is to say what "the real thing" might be?

The requirement was to reduce the ship's velocity to no more than twenty kiss using no more than the available motors and the fuel remaining. In a week at most, there would be no one to replenish the boron canisters and the engines would cough silent. The mainsail would continue to provide some braking and might do so indefinitely, but it needed continual attention to maintain its trim. Without it, a storm wind or an irregularity whirling off the Galileans would reduce it to a tangle. Twenty kiss was still greater than the natural velocity at this height, but it was low enough to ensure that the ship would someday loop back into settled space.

"Captain," said Wong, who had burst onto the deck in a flutter, interrupting the discussion in the middle of feed rates and canister volume, and drawing Satterwaithe's frown. "Shouldn't we be getting onto the cutter?" She could not believe that, in the crisis the two officers would stand about calmly discussing ship mechanics. What possible difference could it make once the ship was abandoned? But Gorgas and Satterwaithe knew the salvage laws of the Middle System, and any ship abandoned without evidence of a properly laid recovery orbit was deemed abandoned property, with salvage rights open to the first comer. Gorgas thought the least they could do for the surviving owners was to provide them with the salvage value.

Gorgas glanced at the clock and then at his second officer and said, "There is plenty of time, doctor. Plenty of time. Nearly three hours yet." Although he did wonder why Satterwaithe had lingered to help him with the calculations.

Wong flushed, and felt as she had often felt standing hanghead before her father. What a foolish woman she was! "Silly 'Siska," father had sometimes called her. Of course, there was no *urgency*. She had let that Lunatic infect her with his own panic. "I'm sorry," she said, for it was her stock response to the universe. "I just thought we were all to stand by in the cutter, just in case."

Satterwaithe shook her head in annoyance. "Just in case? Just in case of what? The damage has been done. The ship is breached beyond recovery. *What else can go wrong?*"

Wong shivered. "I wish you hadn't said that."

Satterwaithe looked away into the shadows and murmured, "I wish I hadn't, either."

"See to the others, doctor," Gorgas said. It was a dismissal. He turned to huddle once more with Satterwaithe and the AI. Unnoticed by any of them, Twenty-four deCant had come on the bridgeway looking for Satterwaithe and, finding her there, set the bag down and waited for an opportunity to speak.

"But, it's Ratline, sir," said Wong.

"Eh? Ratline?" Gorgas raised his head in irritation. "What about him?"

"He won't come."

"Ah." The captain turned to Satterwaithe, as he always did in matters affecting Ratline. "Number Two?"

The second officer shrugged. "Leave him."

"*You'll* bring him to the cutter, then?" the doctor pleaded. "He won't listen to me."

Satterwaithe did not think that so amazing a thing. Ratline seldom listened to anyone, let along to Wong. "You don't understand," Satterwaithe said. "Moth came on board this ship when he was ten. He's lived on her all his life. He's never known anything else. He *can't* leave. He means to die here."

"You'd leave him here to die alone?" the doctor asked, incredulous that anyone could contemplate to heartless an act.

"He won't be alone."

Gorgas, who had opened his mouth to speak, turned to his second officer in surprise. "How did you know that?"

The question baffled Satterwaithe and bafflement always irritated her, for she was generally well-informed, and disliked discovering such lacunae. "How do I know what?"

"That Bhatterji and I were staying."

"You!" Satterwaithe put a great deal of astonishment into that word, more than Gorgas had thought it could hold. She looked on him as if she had never seen him before.

Gorgas was quick to grasp things and understood the nature of his second officer's surprise before either the doctor or the watching wrangler. He nodded. "Ah. I understand."

"Do you?" said Satterwaithe, bitterly. "Then explain it to me, for I don't understand at all."

"We only need three volunteers." Gorgas's voice was gentle, but Satterwaithe only shook her head. In truth, she resented Gorgas's decision. Having decided for herself and for Ratline that they would stay, she had come to think of the ship as a sort of mausoleum, or as an altar of sacrifice. Gorgas, in her estimation, did not deserve to stay and die. And Bhatterji . . . It was as if a sanctum sanctorum were to be defiled.

Understanding spread to the doctor and the wrangler. It astonished Wong into silence, and deCant into shouting.

And that drew all other eyes to her where she stood on the bridgeway. Satterwaithe frowned. "That's my kit bag you've got there. How did you get that?" And it was a mark of the woman that of all that there was to note and comment upon, it was this invasion of her privacy that caught her eye.

"I went to see if'n you packed yet, ma, but I guess you were too busy, so I done it for you."

Satterwaithe was oddly touched by the deed, though not so much as to let it show. "Thank you," she said, "but it was unnecessary. I will be staying with the ship."

"But . . . you can't do that!"

"Really? And how many stripes do you wear that you can order me about?"

"Then, if . . . Then, if you're staying . . . I'm staying." She spoke with a sudden and firm conviction that appalled everyone on the deck, including herself.

Gorgas muttered, "We don't seem to have gotten this 'abandon ship' thing quite right."

It had not been a properly thought out decision on deCant's part. Indeed, thought wasn't in it. It leapt off her tongue without clearance, but once she had said it, she could not gainsay it. Martian youth may take on adult roles early, but there is a reason for the reckless and immature flavor of life there.

Second thoughts arose and jostled for her attention, but despite the tutorials she had recently received, deCant did not truly understand death. What she did understand was loss and, having only lately found her mother (as she believed), she could not bear to lose her so soon after. (Or else it was the belief she could not bear to lose.) Nor could she show herself less brave. In her heart, she hoped her threat would be the one argument that would change her mother's mind.

Yet, Satterwaithe's reasons were multiple and confused, even to herself, and were not to be deflected by the impact of the girl's argument. Despite the velocity with which it had hit, it was too small a mass to mover her. But neither did she understand deCant's reasons, ascribing it to bravado and the herd instinct. "Don't be foolish," she said. "You don't know what you're saying."

"Do any of you?" Wong cried. "Do any of you? Twenty-four! What about Ivar? Think about Ivar!"

DeCant *had* thought about Ivar—he was one of those second thoughts—but she knew that he would some day leave her. He had been trapped too young, and the time would come when he would realize that; so it was really a kindness to both of them that she should cut him free now. "He's young," she told the doctor. "He'll get over it."

The answer surprised the doctor. She had seen the devotion on the Callistan's part and supposed that the Martian, who was not nearly so transparent in these regards as her mate, had reciprocated it. "It's not just you," she pleaded with the girl. "There's the baby too."

Ivar, deCant knew, set great store by the baby, but he would get over that, too, once he had made another. "It's just a mass of cells, ma'am. You told me that yourself."

The doctor pulled away from the girl and it came down hard on her just how unsentimental a Martian could be. *Cold*, she had said to Grubb one time, but she had never known just how cold, for it is indeed a frozen heart that could throw such words back in her face at such a time.

What the doctor did not know, what even deCant did not know, was how false her words were, but her desperation not to lose her mother had overwhelmed all her other desires. It had been the spur of the moment, but that moment had its spurs deep in her hide and would not dismount.

The doctor made a small cry, but whether of despair or distress not even she could say. She fled the bridge and flew like a lemur down the corridor. In the C-ring, she encountered Miko and grabbed the girl much as a mantis might seize a scuttling insect. "The cutter," she told the engineer's mate, "you must get to the cutter!"

Miko did not know what she saw in the doctor's eyes. She was not practiced at reading emotions. She knew haughtiness and fear, for she had seen both in the countenance of Clavis Burr and of his hired killer. And so she ascribed to panic what was really desperation. Calmly, Miko removed the doctor's long fingers from her shoulder. "I know that, doc. It's just shy of three hours to go yet, and I've a few errands to run. Don't worry. Ship will warn us in plenty of time."

"But . . . Ivar, what about Ivar? Have you seen him?"

"He's went looking for the ship's cats, down in the kitchen. . . ."

"The Lotus Jewel! She is such a flutter head! When she's under the cap, she may forget—"

Miko wondered if anything she could say would calm this woman. "LJ's transcribing the seed code so Ship can come with us. Don't worry about *her*. Rivvy would never let her stay behind. Everything's in hand, doc. It's overloading the cutter that we got to worry about."

"Overloading . . . ?"

A shadow passed across Miko's face. "Yah. Didn't you hear? To rendezvous with *Georgia Girl*, the cutter can only take ten of us." Then, almost as afterthought, she added, "Ram's staying." And then, before Wong could be certain of a glimmer in the girl's eyes, she had passed on.

Wong remained in the intersection, unable to move. Gorgas's cryptic remarks on the bridge made sense now. Three volunteers. Not to guide the ship into a meaningless orbit, as she had thought—what a horrible and commercial reason for self-sacrifice!—but to stay behind so that others might live.

They didn't need her. They had never needed her. Far from getting everyone on board the escape craft, the problem lay in keeping some off, and that was a problem toward the solution of which the doctor could make no contribution. Disheartened, she made her way to the clinic, where her medical supplies awaited packing.

On the bridge, Gorgas had explained to deCant about the cutter's limitations. "I know it is a hard thing to say. It was a harder thing to come to know it, but no amount of wishfulness can alter it. If three of us stay behind, the rest of you may have a chance. Bhatterji and I have elected to do so. And now Ratline. But, Number Two, there is no need for four to stay—or five, young woman! No need at all for that."

"Yes," said deCant, seizing on the chance. "Please, mother! Please! Come to the cutter!"

Satterwaithe's smile was a sad one. "It's not about 'need,' Stepan. Or at least not the need you have in mind."

"What is it, then?" Gorgas asked, genuinely puzzled, but Satterwaithe only shook her head. "Old wounds heal slow," she said. Then, seeming to come to herself, she turned to Twenty-four deCant and performed a miracle. The miracle was this: she hunkered down on her haunches to speak directly to the girl, something that Gorgas had never seen the woman do.

"DeCant," said Satterwaithe. She spoke severely at first, but then seemed to hear herself, and continued more gently. "Twenty-four. You were right. I *am* your mother, and—"

"I knew it!" the wrangler cried. "I knew it!"

"Hush. Listen to me. You must leave the ship. No, *listen*, I said! You must leave the ship, for *my* sake. You are all I have. You, and my grandchild." She laid a hand on deCant's womb.

"Do you understand? If you stay here, *that is the end of me*; but if you go, then I go on. I'm old, my ship is dying. A man I might have loved is dying too. Do you understand why I *can't* leave, even if the cutter could have taken every one of us? I've got to do what is right—for me, for him. For my sins."

DeCant nodded dumbly. Gorgas listened with astonishment.

"Then go. Be with your husband. Raise your child. Someday, when she's older—or he—tell her . . . Tell her about her grandmother." She took both of deCant's hands in hers. "Will you do that for me?"

"But, Ma! We never had any time to—You 'n' me . . ."

"Will you do that for me? *Please*?" And there was another part of the miracle, for Gorgas had never heard the woman say *please* before as anything more than a conversational ornament.

Martians seldom cry, but they can weep. DeCant did not trust her voice, but ventured to say, "Would you . . . ? I mean, I wish you would . . ." And she stood there, trembling with hunger.

Satterwaithe hesitated before, suddenly understanding, she fed her. Leaning forward, she kissed the girl lightly on the cheek, whereupon, convulsively, deCant threw her arms around the older woman and squeezed. After an awkward moment in which she did not know what to do with her hands, Satterwaithe reciprocated.

"I'll never forget you," deCant said.

"Nor I you," said Satterwaithe. She loosened the girl's embrace. "Now, go. Take care of my grandchild."

"Eugenie. Her name's Eugenie."

Satterwaithe swallowed. "Take care of Eugenie."

"I will, I will." DeCant backed away and wiped her nose on her sleeve. "I love you, Ma."

Satterwaithe's hesitation was fractional. "I love you too."

When the wrangler had gone, the second officer closed her eyes and remained hunkered down for a time. When she rose, she rose only to lower herself in the nearest clip-chair. It was the captain's chair, but neither officer took note. "Ship," she said when she had found a measure of calm.

"Ready, Mrs. Satterwaithe."

The second officer noted the honorific, and a wry smile

crossed her features. "Message. To: Corrigan, Grubb, Akhaturian. Text: Make sure deCant gets on that shuttle and stays on. Tie her down if you have to. End message." She sat in the chair a moment longer, gazing at nothing. Then, spinning the chair to face the plotting tank, she saw Gorgas's curious, owlish stare. "What?"

"You are the girl's clone-mother? I never knew that."

Satterwaithe snorted. "Don't be absurd." She lifted herself from the chair and stepped to the tank.

"But you said . . ."

Sharply. "It got her on board the shuttle, didn't it?"

"Well," said Gorgas, who then could think of nothing to say. He wanted to ask who was the "man I might have loved," but the only two possibilities that came to mind terrified him. "Well, let us resume our calculations. Ship. Resume projections. Display." The plotting tank came alive again with silvery threads looping past Jupiter into the Outer System. "Perhaps we can obtain a gravity desist from Jupiter," he suggested.

"You mean a gravity assist?"

"No, a *de*sist. We're trying to slow the ship down . . ."

Satterwaithe had no ear whatever for humor and it took her a moment longer to get it. When she did, she could only shake her head. After a while, glancing off toward the bridgeway, she noticed that deCant had taken the satchel with her. As a keepsake? The sailing master sighed. It was not as if she would have much need for whatever the girl had stuffed within it.

She had had a daughter once, a long time ago, but for too brief a time and she had never known her. Now she had another, and for nearly as brief a span and nearly as little known.

"By *damn*," she murmured, "I wish she were."

Later, as they worked the navigation problem with the AI, Gorgas silently handed her a handkerchief and Satterwaithe, without a word, took it.

It is said that to every man is given a talent, though some bury theirs in the ground uncommonly deep. Fife had waited in the cutter with growing impatience and agitation while Corrigan programmed the computer with their escape route. "It's an old model," the snake explained cheerfully, as if such a statement could possibly ease anyone's mind.

"I know that," Fife said. "Who do you think discovered it?"

"Oh," said Corrigan absently, "you can't rightly say you *dis-covered* it. It was here all along, wasn't it?" Fife rolled his eyes and Corrigan turned to Grubb and winked.

"How much longer?" Fife asked.

Grubb, who was running down the life-support system checklist, answered without turning. "Keep your pants on. She isn't here yet." Grubb did not yet know of the lovers' quarrel. He thought the passenger anxious to escape, but he was only half-right. Fife was afraid that if the cutter did not leave soon, he would run back into the ship looking for 'Siska and that was not a survival-oriented thing to do.

"It's only withdrawal," Fife told himself, and cinched the belt tighter on the seat he occupied lest his traitor body act on its own behest.

Besides, she would be coming on board herself, once she had rounded up all the strays like some overweening mother hen. He wondered if he had the willpower to stay away from the bitch for however many days this transit would take. He would make a fool of himself before they reached safety. He knew that. Confined as closely as they would be, sleeping in shifts, sharing quarters, how long could he stand fast?

She had violated him, and what had given her that right? She had seemed like such a nice person, and he had done her the fa-vor, and this was how she had paid him back! His hands shook, but whether from agitation or chemical imbalance, he could not tell. It only proved that nice people could not be trusted. Naked self-interest was more reliable. Deals could be struck in the pure light of interest; cards could be placed on tables.

Of course, the doctor had acted out of self-interest and not from "niceness," but Fife, for all his brain-proud posturing, was not thinking clearly. That was Wong's fault too.

Behind him, the black girl moaned a little in her sleep and Fife jerked at the sound. His nerve ends sticking several inches beyond his skin, every noise struck him as sharp and as sudden as a knife, every color stunned him with bright pastel. It's withdrawal, he told himself again. His senses were dazzled and confused. How could he make reliable decisions with his inputs so distorted?

The passenger seemed jittery to Miko. When the Amalthean entered the cutter, the Lunatic jolted and turned to look at her with a visage both relieved and disappointed. Miko ignored him. "Here are the boards you wanted," she told Corrigan. "Don't know if they'll help. The engine on this tub isn't a Wright and Oldis, and the focusing rings are the smaller gage. Maybe LJ can grow a patch."

Corrigan took the parts from her. "Can't you do it?"

"Engine software? I'm just a 'prentice. Bhatterji might know."

Corrigan opened the panel and ran his finger down a wire, looking for the connection. "Yes, but he won't be with us, will he?"

"I don't think he's staying just to inconvenience you."

He found the spot he wanted and inserted the board. "Don't tell me why he does anything. You haven't known him as long as I have."

"Make sure you lock these boards out until they've been dry-tested."

"I know what I'm doing!" The cry was accompanied by a sharp look. Then, after seeing Miko's hurt and angry face, Corrigan added more softly, "Yah. I'll miss him too. He's a mean muffer, and twisted in the bargain, but after the first couple of years you get used to having him around."

Grubb, who was activating the lithium filters—switches going snap, snap, snap—overheard the comment and grinned. "He shore licked you some. Folks don't bond any closer'n that."

"Grubb, how would you like to be my best friend?"

The chief laughed and closed and locked the switch bank he had been working on. "I better make sure L'il Lumber gets on board. Ol' Hard-ass shore had her knickers knotted up over the girl . . ." He spoke in the hope that someone would tell him why, gossip being to him as bright tatter to a magpie. Corrigan shrugged because he didn't know. Miko, who thought she could guess, also said nothing.

When Grubb had gone, Miko said, "Ratline won't leave the ship."

Corrigan did not move for a moment, then he took another board and inserted it. "I suppose I should have expected that." He sighed. "Gorgas has his three volunteers, then."

"Volunteers?" said Fife, who had seized upon the conversation as a means to avoid his thoughts. "For what?"

"To stay behind," Corrigan told him. "Our rendezvous is twenty-seven days out, if everything goes right. That means ten people—counting the two squeakers as one. Even so, we're on the edge. One more person would sink us."

Fife digested that. The cargo master had declared his intent shortly after recovering from his daze, before he could have known about the limitations on the lifeboat. "I don't think that old maniac is staying because he wants to help us."

Fife was probably right, but Corrigan was angry anyway. "Does it matter why, as long as it does?"

"You can count 'Kiru at half-load too," Miko said with a hook of her thumb at the comatose girl. "As long as she's sedated, she's breathing shallower."

Three volunteers were staying. And one of them, Corrigan knew, should have been him. Justice demanded it, but Gorgas had demanded something else. Guilt warred with relief in his soul. "As God wills," he muttered, seeking an elusive peace.

Fife heard otherwise. "I would say it is how the Equation wills."

The first officer spun his seat to face the passenger. "What a barren universe you live in, Fife! So vast and so empty, and yet no room in it for God."

"Actually," Fife said, "I heard that He takes up a lot of room. 'Omnipresent,' isn't He? An unnecessary axiom."

"Without God," Corrigan insisted, "there is no reason for anything." This greatly surprised Miko, who had never noticed while peeping any religious behavior on the first officer's part. But matters may appear differently in extremis than they do in comfort and Corrigan had discovered diverse things in the previous few days. If there are no atheists in foxholes, the same is largely true of lifeboats.

Largely, but not entirely, as Fife too had fallen back upon his childhood beliefs. "Of course there's reason. There's Reason itself. A god is nothing more than an excuse to avoid responsibility." He spoke, as Corrigan had spoken, from the heart, although (again as Corrigan) also from agitation.

"Reason?" said Corrigan. "What is reason? Why should we not cut one another's throat for the chance of a seat on this boat? That would the logical, reasonable thing to do, wouldn't it?"

"But we are not after doing that, are we? These things have a way of working out among reasonable men." Fife spoke, infuriatingly, as a reasonable man. Behind him, the injured girl groaned in her sleep.

"That's an easy thing to say when you're already sitting in the boat."

Fife stiffened and Corrigan was astonished to see him fumble with his cincture and unbuckle from his seat. "Excuse me," the passenger said, although he addressed no one in particular. "Excuse me." He stood and hurried from the boat. In the umbilical, he jostled past Grubb, who was herding the weeping deCant before him. The young girl hugged a satchel to her breast as if it contained all the treasure of the world.

The chief frowned after Fife's retreating form. "What was that about? I'd've thought he was 'poxied to that seat."

Corrigan shrugged and eyed the clock as he turned back to his preparations. "I don't know, but he had better be back in two hours."

"Oh, he'll be back," Grubb assured him. "That's one thing, you can count on. He looks out for Bigelow Fife, he does."

"Yes," said Miko. "I think he uses reason as his god."

Now, the necessary consequence of Fife's reasoning was that natural selection would eventually weed out the self-sacrificing from among the self-interested and produce a universe that revolved around the Self; and while the Self may be a fine thing to worship—certainly a *satisfying* thing to worship—it imposes a numerous and terribly fallible pantheon upon humanity. The Old Pagans had at least confined themselves to a few hundred deities, and kept them decently offstage.

But Fife had not fled from the eloquence of Abd al-Aziz Corrigan. He bounded and stumbled up the Number Twelve radial because he had been moved by the eloquence of Nkieruke Okoye.

The clinic was quiet. There were a few sounds nestled here and there like ground squirrels in the winter. The refrigerated storage unit hummed to itself. The air-pressure line to the medbot fabrication tank hissed from a small leak that had never been worth fixing. A faint tick-tick-tick from the circulation vent might have been a bomb or a disapproving matron, but was in fact a warped ventilator fan farther back in the conduit. These were small sounds, so tentative that they might not even be called sounds at all, but only the suggestions of sounds.

The clinic was also disheveled. Medical instruments, unguents and salves, simples and compounds, were set about in their jars and tubes or had been laid upon trays. There may have been an order to it all, but the unpracticed eye failed to pick it out. In medias res, Fransziska Wong sat on her work stool with her feet planted in the stirrups, surrounded by the whispering sounds and the accoutrements of her profession and the impatient tick-tick-tick of that fan blade. She had begun packing her medical kits for the evacuation, pondering which might be needed in the next twenty-seven days and fretting because, like some wild hybrid of Corrigan and Gorgas, anything seemed possible and all of it seemed bad. Now, she only stared into her open black bag with a smile on her face.

Into this quiet tableau, Fife burst like fireworks. "'Siska!" he cried. "You can save them! Every one! A sedative! Timed release! A medbot program! Something that will keep us all at a low metabolism. Just Corrigan and his little copilot need to be active. The rest of us can sleep. We'll use less air that way. Like that black girl! We can stretch our resources. We can do it! Oh, 'Siska! We can save them all!" This sort of frenzy was very unlike Fife. The sentences jumped about like popcorn. They hardly made a proper syllogism. Oh, the reasoning was there, and no mistake. Fife's ejaculations could be shuffled about to make an argument. But it is not only the God-struck who babble in tongues when the spirit is upon them. Fife had realized in his epiphany that when the equations do not work out, one may sometimes alter the coefficients. The road to Damascus it was not, but it was the road out of the cutter and into the doomed ship and that might have been the harder journey. Fife was genuinely inspired and had not even noticed that he had shifted from *you* to *we* in the matter of universal salvation. He was a strange sort of prophet to bring the Good News, but if God can choose carpenters and camel merchants, why not troubleshooters?

Now, there is another reading. If Fife were genuinely addicted to the saturated body of Fransziska Wong, he might have, in the self-centered core of his being, been casting about for any logical reason to run to her, so that he might feel again that transcendent joy and the two of them might weep upon each other's breast. Any excuse might do, even a splendid good deed. The reason was no less rational for being a rationalization.

Yet, during the time that he had sat with increasing impatience in the cutter, thinking about Wong and her entrapments, he had found himself remembering not the sweaty, desperate exaltations in which they had joined, but the tender and chaste embrace in the 'fresher when a lonely woman had thought that she had harmed a young girl. It had come to him gradually that he cared about the woman in ways for which chemicals could not account. This was probably the desperate justification of the addict, but maybe it was not. Whatever the atomic motivation, he had run back into the ship when, by sitting quite still and fondling his indignation, he would have been safe, or at least as safe as anyone else in the cutter. And he had gone back with a plan to help the doctor achieve her lifelong dream. This was no small thing, for one may sacrifice much to achieve one's dreams, but to make sacrifices to achieve another's argues that even for so self-centered a man as Fife, there was more to him than his center.

It was a good plan too and possessed but three flaws.

The first was that those who had elected to stay behind had not done so in the main because the cutter lacked sufficient air regeneration capacity. Whether stubbornness, despair, or the sorrow of old wounds, their reasons were not entirely addressable by this scheme of Fife's.

The second was that it was a delicate thing to keep so many people teetering in the edge of unconsciousness. That edge is a fine one and the drop on the other side longer and deeper than the Void itself. It would require medbots of uncommon cunning to maintain an optimum level of sedative. Too little, and there would be no point. Too much, and the abyss waited. There was seed code that might be used, but it would take time to grow the programs and spin the micromachines. Perhaps Wong would have had sufficient time, perhaps not; but that was moot because of the third reason.

Fife became aware as he explained his idea that Wong reacted not at all to his excitement. She continued to sit and to smile and Fife grew a little irritated and began to wonder what was inside the medical bag that was so funny. "Didn't you hear me?" he cried, and of course she had not.

He realized that at last, and perhaps it had taken him some little while to see it because down in the bone he had refused to see it. But the thought finally did force its way in, as if by a carpenter's maul, and all the sight and smell of it flooded his mind. His legs gave way and, were the acceleration frame any stronger than a few milligees, he would have collapsed to the floor. As it was, he took on a peculiar, shrunken posture as he staggered to her side. "'Siska!" he cried aloud, though not so loud that she could ever hear. "Oh, 'Siska . . ." He seized her about the shoulders and she slowly twisted and fell into his arms. Still pliant, he noted. Rigor had not yet set in. She could not have been dead long. He held her to him and kissed her, and when he had done that he kissed her again. He said many other things besides her name. Some of it was to chastise her for abandoning him. Some of it, things he really ought to have said weeks before. He used a word he had not dared use for years out of fear that it was not germane, and now that he knew it was—or thought that he knew it was—it was of little use.

He cuddled with the thing and spoke tenderly and stroked the stubble on its scalp and the long, subtle curves of its articulated arms. His heart hammered at his ribs and his breath came in short gasps. Everything was outlined in a pearl white glow: cabinets, medbotter, bag, utensils, the thing that lay in his arms, even he himself, for it seemed as if he floated above all the room.

He remembered all the times he had treated her carelessly and thought what it must have meant to her. It was altogether a strange sort of interlude, for he neither sought pleasure nor gave it, and when he had said her name for the last time, he carried the thing to the one remaining cot in the clinic and laid it there, arranging the arms and legs in a dignified fashion and fastening the belts against the impious drift of milly and ziggy. He said no sacred words over it—indeed, he did not know any—but he did stand a further while in silence by its side.

He had been wrong that time when the two of them had discovered the cutter. Fife knew that now. To tumble from the ship was not the most lonely death imaginable. There were other tumbles, into vacuum colder and harder, and into which no parting voice could pierce.

Reaching down, he seized the inhaler that hung around the thing's neck, and with a savage yank pulled it off. He knew why she had died with such a smile, coasting high above the universe with galaxies jewels at her feet, transported in an ecstasy greater than any he had ever known from the juices of her body. Greater perhaps than any *she* had ever known, for he was certain that she had breathed a deeper and longer dose than ever before. Dose after dose after dose until her wretched lungs were filled to overflowing and no more oxygen could find its way in. "That should have been what I did," he told himself in a moment of un–self-conscious truth. "It was I who should have filled her up."

He looked at the clock. There was an hour remaining. "Ship!"

"Ready, Mr. Fife."

He paused, struck by a sudden thought, and said, "Could you have stopped her?"

"Clarification requested."

"Never mind. Abort. Query. Medbot programming. Sedative delivery. Depressed breathing rate. Sublethal dose. Time limit for fabrication: under one hour. Request feasibility."

"Clarification requested."

If Wong could not live, then perhaps her dream could. "Can you construct a medbot to specifications in less than an hour?"

"Medical computer and micromachining station are not accessible by Ship."

Fife sighed and gave up. It had been a mad notion in the first place. How could he hope to duplicate in under an hour what it had taken Wong many years to learn?

"Input requested," said Ship.

"Yes," said Fife in a voice as dead as his feelings. "What is it?"

"Dr. Wong has ceased to function. Confirm."

"Yes . . . Confirmed."

"Resource availability on cutter has increased by twenty-seven person-days."

For the first time in his life, Fife lusted to destroy a machine. It was a rage so sudden and intense that he was taken utterly by surprise and it seemed to him as if he were merely an observer trapped in a runaway tube-car. He made no effort to clean up the mess afterward. When he left the clinic, he paused once at the door to look back and it seemed to him that she might come suddenly racing after him, as she so often had. Then he shoved the inhaler into his pocket and departed.

The Ship's Cat

Ivar Akhaturian entered the cutter with the kitchen cat nestled contentedly in his arm. She was a fat cat. Prowling the marches of Grubb's kitchen, how could it be otherwise? But she gave as good as she got. There were mice on board—there are *always* mice on board—and the cat understood quid pro quo. Undoubtedly, she thought she received the better of the bargain. Her eyes were closed and she hummed while the boy stroked her. Akhaturian was good at that sort of thing. In like circumstances, deCant often did the same.

"We can't leave Anush Abar behind," Akhaturian said with worried innocence. "She won't breathe too much air, will she, Mr. Grubb?"

The chief smiled. "I think we can fit her in."

"There is enough margin," said Corrigan, though with more doubt and less cheer than Grubb. He actually queried Ship's database regarding feline respiration rates before he felt at ease.

Every new thing, in his regard, was an opportunity for new problems, and he told Akhaturian to confine the cat to the nether regions of the boat, away from the control room.

Proceeding aft, Akhaturian passed Miko coming fore. She had been in the engine ready room—it was really more like a closet—verifying that Fife had properly attached the boron and hydrogen lines to the injector ports. One could never quite trust laymen in these matters. That she herself had only a few months' practice with Farnsworth engines did not signify, nor did Fife's entirely acceptable work. She was an engineer's mate, and she had pride of place.

"Why hello, Queen Tamar!" Miko said, addressing the cat first, as protocol demanded; then, to the boy, she added, "You've got both cats, then?"

Akhaturian suspected some joke in the making and, although he was unsure whether joking were warranted at this point, he accepted it as a shield against death and tragedy. DeCant had already told him what had happened on the bridge and he was trying to come to terms with the way his wife had so casually offered to abandon him and die. Akhaturian was anxious to secure the cat so that he might return forward and secure deCant. He was afraid she might drift off from him. "Both cats?" he said and tried to think what the punch line might be.

"You said you were fetching 'Anush Abar,' and this is 'Queen Tamar.' "

"This *is* Anush Abar," Akhaturian said.

Mikoyan Hidei was entirely capable of adding one and one, and did so now. She and Ivar had christened the same cat with different names. The other, the Cat With No Name, was still at large in the abandoned regions of *The River of Stars*. "Tell Corrigan I'll be right back," she said to the least wrangler as she turned into the side passage to the umbilical. "Tell him the crystalline beams are set right."

"Where are you going?"

"To get the other cat."

Akhaturian ascribed Miko's concern for the animal to the same manic mood that had overtaken all of them. In this he was only partly right. The Amalthean did indeed feel that the cat needed rescue, but it was not the only reason she went back inside. Fife had required a rational excuse to perform an irrational deed. Miko was not so particular.

Corrigan, when Akhaturian told him about the cat, was focused on his preflight checklist, and so answered with half his mind and firmly hoped that the second cat would not tip the resource balance into the red.

Bigelow Fife, knowing his lover's frame of mind, concluded that she had sacrificed herself in order that one person more could be saved. An oxymoron. If one more person were to be saved, why not Wong herself? Such a waste, he told himself over and over as he wended through the corridors of the derelict freighter. Such a waste.

Yet it takes a certain calculated coldness to end one's life merely to conclude a syllogism, and Wong had been neither cold nor calculating, nor even very certain. Fife, who was all three, could never have committed the act regardless how logical the reasoning; while Wong, who had, could never have imagined the reasoning. Logic wasn't in it. The very act is proof of that. But Wong was a person to whom the opinions of others mattered a great deal. If Satterwaithe fashioned her companions in her own image, Wong was fashioned by their images of her. Fife was only the latest in a long string of ensorceled lovers, most of whom at the denouement had expressed strong opinions of her, and each such remonstration had chipped away at the person she once had been. There had been little left save splinters when Fife's turn came, and so it could be said that if Wong had taken her own life, she had not taken very much.

It would not be well to mention this to Fife, who was a man in grief, albeit a dispassionate and reasoned sort of grief. Even as he fled that dark, abandoned place of death, he reconstructed the disassembled personality of Franszziska Wong. The resurrection was a patchwork affair since, in spite of all, he did not truly know the woman and so filled in the gaps from his own imagination. It was a nobler Wong that emerged from the chrysalis of his mind—and had this intentional Wong been constructed earlier and impressed upon the doctor in living words, there might have been another ending entirely, although there is no guarantee that it would have been a happier one.

Wong had become in some sense the fulcrum of his entire life, and he would date events henceforth by whether they fell before or after their meeting. He knew this as he knew a theorem in Euclid. It was so necessary a consequence that the steps leading to it vanished from view.

On the bridge, he found Gorgas and Satterwaithe engrossed over the plotting tank. Satterwaithe had just told the captain that the projected path looked to be satisfactory "barring the unexpected" and Gorgas had chuckled over what he thought a mordant observation rather than a plain matter of fact. Fife interrupted—he was not unmindful of the clock—to tell them of Wong's sacrifice. (He would repeat this heroic story later to as many as would listen, until he himself believed it implicitly. This was a form of mental antibody that prevented his consideration of any other reason—such as that his own rejection of her had been the proximate cause.)

Neither Satterwaithe nor Gorgas were moved by the nobility of Wong's gesture. The sailing master, in particular, thought the doctor a fool, though she did not say it aloud. In truth, it was not for lack of room aboard the cutter that either officer was staying. Satterwaithe did not know how she could explain that to the passenger, and so bent over the tank as if she were studying the sheaf of trajectories, and would not listen to the siren song of the passenger's pleading.

Fife, seeing that Satterwaithe would not be moved, turned to Gorgas. "Captain, she is after dying so that one of you may live. An act so terrible can't be vain. You cannot *let* it be in vain." In his own way, he demanded that the universe have meaning, for it is only meaning that mitigates the terror. "You come. Or command Bhatterji. Or . . . or someone." He could not bring himself to ask for Ratline.

"You ought to go, Stepan," Satterwaithe said, for she assumed that by his silence Gorgas was considering the offer. "There's no more you can do here. I can handle things."

Gorgas nodded thoughtfully and, turning to Fife, told the man to return to the cutter and that he would be along presently after he had seen to some few items. The passenger, whose personal anxiety had been slowly reviving, thanked him and hurried away. After he was gone, Gorgas shook his head. "What a pity about the doctor," he said. "But she always did strike me as an ungrateful sort."

Satterwaithe, a moment later, said, "Ungrateful . . ."

"Yes, I understand the passenger was in love with her, and here she has turned her back on him. An odd attraction, that," Gorgas continued as he considered the matter further. "A Lunatic and a snake. She could never have gone home with him."

Satterwaithe scowled. "Sometimes, Stepan, you can be remarkably irritating." She had in mind the way he would string sentences together in a sort of concatenation, as if each thought reminded him of another that was only tangentially related. Like the AI, he had a tendency to skew.

The captain pondered the multiple possible meanings of Satterwaithe's comment with his customary silence and so seemed to his companion to be unresponsive, which further irritated the woman.

They continued to instruct the AI in the projected maneuvers and found it more difficult than they had anticipated, since for a great many contingencies of a general nature Ship required Rules rather than Instructions. At one point, Gorgas wished for The Lotus Jewel's services and Satterwaithe enjoyed a moment in which she contemplated the sysop servicing the captain. It could not be other than a wildly bucking woman atop a passive and pensive Gorgas, and the juxtaposition of two such unlikely things caused a smile to flit across her countenance. (She was mistaken on at least three accounts and not least in conflating the pensive with the passive.) Still, even Satterwaithe admitted that training the AI would have proceeded more smoothly with a guild-certified sysop *en rapport*.

After some time had gone by and the threads in the plotting tank had multiplied almost to incoherence, the sailing master spoke in passing to Gorgas. "I thought you were leaving in the cutter."

"You are mistaken, I think."

"Ah." She reviewed Gorgas's words to the passenger in her mind and supposed that there might be another reading. She looked to the clock. "Will you go down to see them off?"

Gorgas shuddered. "Dear God, no! I can think of nothing more gruesome. And I do not trust my mettle, in any case. I have not your ice water in my veins, Genie. I fear I might bolt and scamper aboard, and then what would become of me?"

"You would live?" Satterwaithe guessed. Inwardly, she wondered what he had meant by the ice water remark.

Gorgas traced with his forefinger a bright orange line that Ship had plotted, following an iconic ship into the deserted regions of the Upper System. "What ship would take me after this? Why, no one will offer me so much as a purser's berth! That is not life. No, that is not life. Stepan Gorgas is dead. This transit has killed him. And I dare not dissent from the verdict."

Satterwaithe said nothing and, after another moment had passed, Gorgas resumed his study of the sheaf of possibilities that Ship had projected, looking for the one that might have some meaning.

The Lotus Jewel, Corrigan had been wont to say in his hackneyed fashion, would be late for her own funeral. In one meaning of the word *late*, this is a truism, but it was true also in the other sense of the word. The shortest distance between two points is a straight line, but there was nothing so geodesic in the sysop's life. Hers was a pinball in full career. At suss school, she had been notorious among her classmates. Were she to run into a market to purchase a loaf of bread, they would say with knowing and affectionate smiles, she would emerge with several sacks of groceries—and, more likely than not, without the loaf of bread. This bent toward impulsiveness underlay both her generosity and her tardiness, for even the simplest act becomes complex by its diversions.

She ought to have, as deCant had done, prepared her baggage beforehand. It was not as if time had leapt upon her suddenly. Rather it had crept toward her by stealth as it always did, moment by moment; and at each cautious footstep there had yet been plentiful time remaining. She had known perfectly well what she needed to take with her and so she had never given it much thought. But she had known only in general and not in particular and, faced now with the need, she hesitated over the details and wondered what she might leave behind.

"There are ninety minutes remaining," Ship told her.

"I know, I know." The Lotus Jewel considered her options. It was not simply a question of which clothing and accessories to take. She was vain, in an oddly selfless way, but as she had constantly to remind Corrigan, she was not stupid and she had no intention of missing departure for the sake of a dingy coverall or two. Yet that was also the problem. Had there been marked disparities in value or sentiment, the choices would be as clear and as automatic as such choices ever came to her. It was only because there was so little to choose among that the selection consumed such time.

She placed a small box of lipsticks in her satchel—she had gleaned the color range down to the barest minimum—turned back to her vanity and, along the way, paused at the suss station. The cap, like its twin on the bridge, was fitted particularly to her head. Given time enough and the money, she could always obtain another. Yet, until then, she would be unable to enter rapport with an AI and this, to a sysop, is close kin to falling blind. She placed the cap on her head, felt the nubs nestle comfortably into their sockets, and looked at herself in the mirror. The fiber optic harness that bristled from the cap like Medusa's snakes resembled a head of unruly hair and it amused her to think that, were she ever to allow her locks to grow again, they would grow out in just this fashion.

Disconnecting the harness from the panel required three separate moves, but when she had finished and she had brushed the cables back, the fibrops cascaded between her shoulder blades to her waist. Her hair had once done so, she remembered, and it had been much of the same golden color as these fibers. Yet her hair had never glittered and captured the light in quite this way.

The cap she must keep, but the cables were standard. She decoupled the cap and stood shorn like Samson, and she her own

Delilah. It was a literal shearing too, in that her powers left her and she became less of what she had been. She turned though the slowly falling, hair-fine fiber optics to nest the suss cap on its fitted headball. The fibrops writhed in the wafted air raised by her passage. She ran her hand along the cap's smooth and gleaming surface, then snapped up the headball's case and placed it beside her satchel as gently as if she had set her own skull there.

Corrigan had given each of them a mass limit and The Lotus Jewel sought in her qualitative way to adhere to it. But the suss cap was ship's equipment, and did not count against her personal mass allotment.

Or did it?

She scowled because she did not know the answer and asked Ship to ask Corrigan.

"The boat's AI doesn't support that sort of interface," Corrigan told her once the link was established.

"I know that. Who do you think surveyed the system?" And why must Corrigan always tell her things she already knew? "But I need to take the cap with me."

Corrigan did not know that suss caps were attuned to their wearers and so her request stuck him as personal and whimsical—like taking a souvenir—and he answered with the special impatience he reserved for such things. "It's your personal mass, then."

The Lotus Jewel coughed with weary frustration at the dead link. At this point, she recollected that she had gone initially to pull a selection of coveralls for the trip and hurried back to her dog closet. How many sets would she need for a twenty-seven day transit? She felt she might ask Corrigan about laundering facilities on the boat, but the notion of speaking to him again did not appeal. Four pair, at least; perhaps five.

On the shelf above the flat-racks was an old goat case with her personal data pins. They were calibrated to her own synapses and without them her suss cap could not translate thoughts into commands, nor sensor readings into sensations. Ship knew the translations, to be sure, but it had had four years in which to learn them and had, in the process, learned to think much like The Lotus Jewel, which made rapport easier but much else more difficult.

The sysop pulled the goat case out. It had been a long time since she had tutored a virgin AI and it would feel strange to probe into a fresh system—tentative at first, as she learned its reactions; then plunging deep within it, to quicken its avatars and embrace its con-volitions. Interfacing with Ship was like lying with an old friend and, because of that, lacked the excitement of discovery; but also for the same reason it lacked the uncertainty and risk that entering a new system always bore.

Ship autoinitiated. "Has the copy of Ship been delivered aboard the boat?"

The Lotus Jewel answered absently. She had become accustomed to Ship's skew by now, and no longer bothered trying to counter it. Soon it would no longer matter. "Yes," she said. "Miko took the pins with her." She hefted the goat case and carried it to where her satchel waited. "I suppose I will need these, then."

"Query."

"Purpose: To train the new system."

"Clarification requested. 'New system.'"

"The one I need to grow from the copy."

"Clarification: the copy is Rivvy."

"Oh, I do wish Miko hadn't given you that name. No, copy is not 'Rivvy.' Boat memory insufficient. Seed code is . . . A clone."

"Analog: Twenty-four deCant."

"Uh, confirmed, I suppose. Base information identical; learned knowledge base distinct." Most of what constituted a neural net consisted of training and experience, the sort of information that could not be embedded in code. It struck The Lotus Jewel as odd that the neural net did not know that about itself. It really was not a well-integrated system. Its various components and avatars did not work well together. For this, she blamed The Carefree Fire, who had been sysop before her.

"Query: discontinuity of function."

The Lotus Jewel was unsure what the AI meant, if the AI could be said to have "meant" anything. Tropism is not intent. "Clarification," she said. "Discontinuity of learned knowledge base."

"Confirmed."

"Learned knowledge base not replicated in clone. Refreshed system will be distinct."

Seizing upon key words in the input from outside and pursuing hyperlinks thus revealed. Ship seines deebies and sees in an instant that the truth value is one. The extra memory that the Miko-entity has installed in the boat, while sufficient to contain the seed code, will not be sufficient to hold the knowledge base and learned neural firing patterns that characterize Ship-as-of-now. The system that will grow from the seed code will be identical to Ship in its architecture, but Ship finds no more comfort in this than would a condemned man watching a few of his stem cells leaving the prison in a Petri dish. The boat-entity will be not-Ship, breaking the continuity of the datastream.

"There is a problem on the bridge," Ship blurts.

The Lotus Jewel skidded past the turn in the conversation and backtracked. "Clarification."

"Captain and sailing master conducting input. Purpose: retrieval orbit for eventual salvage. Syntax inexpert. Boron insufficient. Sails do not exist. Assistance is required."

The Lotus Jewel pursed her lips. Gorgas was trying to plan a trajectory that Ship could execute without its human servers. When the boron was depleted, further accelerations would rely on the sails alone. And Ship still did not believe in sails. The Lotus Jewel was no longer sure that she believed in them. Certainly, it had been a seductive belief and, like most seductions had ended badly. "Do I have time to teach you the secret handshake?" It shouldn't take long, she felt. She had introduced avatars before, and if Gorgas really did need her help, she was disinclined to refuse. It would spite Satterwaithe, for one thing.

"Failure of retrieval orbit implies helio-escape," Ship added helpfully. "Direction δ-Geminorum."

"Oh, all right." The sysop returned to her headbox and re-trieved the suss cap. "I'll do it from here. No time to run to the bridge." She snagged the fibrop harness from the floor with a graceful dip as she walked by and had reinserted it with half-conscious motions into the cap before she reached the panel in the comm shack. When she had booted up and dropped her consciousness into the Simulated Void, she thought for a mo-ment how she would miss this wonder once she had departed in the cutter. <How much time do I have left?> she asked amid the sensual pulse of the datastream.

<Eighty-nine minutes> Ship told her.

Gorgas and Satterwaithe, on the bridge, were grateful for her timely and unexpected intervention; but as they supposed she was linking from the cutter itself, they never saw any reason to mention how much time was really left.

Corrigan finished his checklist and thumbed the square on the 'puter screen so the boat's AI would accept his release. "Every-thing is ready," he told his copilot. "Now, all as God wills."

Ivar Akhaturian nodded, though he was less certain that God was in it. He found his palms to be moist and rubbed them on his pants. "We won't drift into the plume after we decouple, will we?"

"No. We'll decelerate faster, so *The River* will actually pull ahead of us. Tell me why."

Akhaturian no longer cared for the first officer's pop quizzes. At one time, he had welcomed them as a chance to show off his knowledge. Later, he wondered if they might not be intended as a chance for the First to show off *his* knowledge. There was, in addition, the small matter of appropriateness. The circum-stances were anything but normal, and it seemed to him that to pretend otherwise was a gross disservice. He wished, per-versely, that Rave Evermore were with them, so that his cheer-ful confidence could balance Corrigan's fatalism and Akhaturian's own cautious uncertainty.

"Our engine is smaller than the four giants on *The River*," Corrigan insisted. "So why do we decelerate faster."

"Because of the muffing power-to-mass ratio! Now will you leave me alone!"

Corrigan was taken aback by the outburst. They sat side by side in silence while the indicators blinked their bland assurances. Everything was ready. At least everything electromechanical. "I'm sorry," said the boy and, "Would you . . ." said the First, the collision of which words induced a second silence.

"Why did she do it?" Akhaturian asked at last.

But Corrigan was the last person to ask that question. In fact, the first officer was confused at first by the pronoun and wasted some moments in wondering why his copilot was so upset over Satterwaithe remaining behind. When he realized that the boy meant his wife and her impetuous offer, he realized too that he had no answer for him. "I don't know," he said. "Orbits. Hyperbolics. Azimuth. Velocity. That's all measured and solid. But I can't navigate where you need to go." He thought too of Miko and The Lotus Jewel and that he could never ping their Fixed Points. The one had brought passion into his life and the other center and he found himself now lacking both. "Go look in the cabin and make sure everyone is secure."

When Akhaturian returned a few minutes later, he was worried. "Mr. Fife isn't back yet with the doctor. Miko went to get the other cat, but she hasn't come back, either. And no one's seen The Lotus Jewel at all."

Corrigan grunted. He did not regard the passenger very highly, but the others were his friends and very definitely in his charge. "Cutter?"

"Yes, Mr. Corrigan, how may I be of assistance?"

The cutter AI's florid mode of speech irritated Corrigan, who preferred his intercourses straight and to the point. That such preprogrammed fawning ever mattered to passengers of a bygone era he ascribed to the deficiencies of those passengers. "Message: to Ship. Locate: evacuating crewmembers. And. Deliver: message. Text: Get your sorry butts in the cutter. Casting off in sixty minutes. End message. End message."

"Dreadfully sorry, but Ship does not respond."

Growling something unkind about the passenger splicing fi-

brop links between the cutter and the ship, Corrigan unclipped
from his seat and hurried to the umbilical. There, he ran head-
long into an apparition of bulging, red eyes, a manic grin, and
shocked hair that he recognized after a moment as Bigelow
Fife. He could not account for the broad smile on the man's
face, for it seemed to fit ill with the sheen of tears on the
cheeks.

"She's dead," Fife told him. "She died so that we might live."

"Who's dead?" Corrigan demanded, grabbing the man by the
shoulders and shaking him, and both Grubb and deCant, attracted by the commotion came to the entry. *Not Miko*, Corrigan
thought. *Let it not be Miko*. Nor even The Lotus Jewel, nor the
doctor; but he thought of Miko first of all.

"'Siska," Fife told them all as if he were bragging. "She
knew there was no room for all of us, so she . . . And I
found . . . And Gorgas said he would come in her place."

Corrigan had little experience dealing with hysteria and neither recognized its symptoms nor understood its causes, let
alone the remedies—if there were any. He handed the man off
to Grubb, who, being prone to the same sort of behavior might
deal with it more effectively. "I don't have time for this," he
said. "I've got to locate the others."

"Dr. Wong is dead?" said deCant and she was strung between
two poles—one mourning the strange, sad physician; the
other . . . Even as she helped Grubb strap the distraught Lunatic
into his seat, she felt the shame of hope that perhaps now her
mother would come.

Once in the rim hall by the davit, Corrigan called for Ship
once more, and once more received no answer, which vexed
him greatly. The pickups in this sector had been restored and
both the locals and the fibrop link into the cutter should have
been open. He growled an imprecation, though he was uncertain upon whom to call it, and hurried inbound to the next ring
corridor.

What he did not know was that Ship's attention was engaged.
Ship had autoinitiated once again. This time, it was compress-
ing files. Not just some files, but all its files. Its anomaly cache.

Bills of lading. The passenger's journal. Accounts payable. Hand's notes on his crew. Cargo placement. Recorded conversations and personal logs. Parts availability and usage. Navigational data. Engineering drawings for the Three Dolphin Club. Passenger lists dating back to 2051. All of them and more, compiled with a magnificent disregard for priority.

Ship had created new encoding algorithms on the instant, folded up the information in its core, shorn the bits, squeezed them into hard diamond, and then squeezed them again, crushing all the information in its databases below the event horizon of an informal black hole. Even for Ship, this required the dedication of a great deal of processor time and, save for the avatars with which The Lotus Jewel was even then working, every portion of its being was devoted to the task. If it was a being. If it knew devotion.

And thus Corrigan came to grief in the next ring and even the ring beyond that, at which point he realized that for some reason Ship itself was malfing badly. He cupped his hands around his mouth and hollered, "Miko!" And again, "LJ!" But he received no response. The shudder that he felt he attributed at first to his own fear that he would lose them both and only second to Bhatterji freeing one more airtight door somewhere deep in the bowels of the ship.

Ivar Akhaturian knew fear. The orderly columns of figures on the boat's datascreens had begun to clutter and thicken and run like liquid methane blown against the thick viewing bubble in Callistopolis Commons. Pages scrolled and danced in a blur. Indicators flashed yellow; then red. Something was wrong. That much an untrained 'prentice would realize and Akhaturian suddenly knew that that was just what he was. He could lay a course. He could take a bearing. He could compute with an AI's help a hyperbolic, constant boost orbit. He could even bring a boat to dock, and had done so numerous times on his uncle's threelium barges. But he did not know the boat the way a real pilot did.

"Mr. Grubb! Something's wrong!" From somewhere in his

mind he had retrieved the fact that Grubb had been a boatswain at one time and, while that had nought to do with the piloting, the older man would surely know something of the internal workings of such a craft. "Cutter!" he cried, "self-diagnostics. Run."

The cutter responded with a voice oddly slurred, as if by Doppler. "I. Am. Sorry. Sir. Insufficient. Memory."

Grubb heard the call, but ascribed the worry he heard in the voice to the excitability of youth; so while he did not delay, neither did he hasten to the flight deck. "What seems to be the problem, Li'l Cap'n?" he asked in a manner that he thought radiated calm competence, but which sounded utterly clueless to Akhaturian.

"Something's swamping the AI!" he cried.

A little crease appeared above Grubb's nose as he studied the cascading figures on the screen. He moved with the maddening slowness of the Ice IV river where it flowed into the basin of Dom Miguel crater, but that was only in contrast to the blurred rapidity with which the datastream scrolled down the screen. Numbers had lost their identities and had become no more than a pale haze against the gray background. Grubb thought it looked like Niagara Falls and almost looked to the deck to see if it were puddling below the console. "How did a virus get loose in the cutter?" Maybe it had always lain there, dormant, for all the many years since the boat last flew.

Grubb was no Lotus Jewel when it came to AI's, but he had handled environmental systems over the years and had some sense of which end the bullet came out. He tried first to call up a diagnostic screen, but received the same turgid response that Akhaturian had. He plugged in his personal 'puter and tried to peek through a keyhole, but the 'puter's own memory was overwhelmed on the instant.

"It's receiving some sort of massive download from the ship," Grubb guessed from the snapshot the instant had salvaged. He was nearly correct, for he had not guessed that the download *was* Ship, desperately seeking escape. This assumes that *desperation* adequately describes the ripples propagating through the neural net. "Shut it down," Grubb told Akhaturian. "When in doubt, reboot." He also, without thinking too much on it, disconnected the fiber optic link that Fife had run between the boat and the ship. As far as Ship—the original Ship—was concerned, this meant the cutter had cast off.

The sound, like the boom of a bass drum, caused both Grubb and Akhaturian to look about. "Now what the hell . . . ?" And deCant called from the passenger cabin. "The main hatchway's closed!" But by then, the disorientation caused by the return of ziggy carried a message of its own. The cutter was no longer in an acceleration frame, and that meant that it had been cut lose from the davit. Grubb, in a rage, kicked aft through the manlock. "Fife, you son of a bitch!"

<Ship> said The Lotus Jewel <Noise. Identify.>
    <Mr. Bhatterji has set another airtight door.>

Ramakrishnan Bhatterji, pausing in his labors to wipe his brow, heard the sound as well and could not place where it had come from. In this abandoned region of the ship, lit only by cold lamps that he had run out himself, it would be fruitless to ask Ship what had happened. Pickups and speakers here were long dead; nor could the answer possibly matter. He flipped down his darkened goggles, turned up his torch, and resumed welding the seams of the plate he had wrestled across the open hallway.

Gorgas cocked his head and considered the possibilities. "Mr. Corrigan has cast off," he concluded. Although the ship's acceleration had not changed, he felt a passing weightlessness in his heart. It was a wildly exhilarating moment, giddy, as if the loss of all his choices had somehow set him free.

Satterwaithe looked at the clock. "He's half an hour early, if he did."

Mikoyan Hidei hugged the Cat With No Name in the close confines of the steward's passage that she had for two months called "home." When she heard the sound of the davit blowing off, she raised her head and remained still for a moment. There was a strange, passing disorientation, as when viewing an optical illusion, when she could not decide whether the boat were receding from the ship or the ship had cast loose from the boat. Then she cuddled the cat once more and spoke to it in gentle tones.

The Castaways

The Lotus Jewel could become engrossed in her work—a bad habit when other matters impended—and it was only a chance remark of Gorgas that told her she had been marooned. The captain had said something to Satterwaithe and, overhearing on the link, the sysop had injected her own two cents.

"Have you restored *The River*'s transmitter?" Gorgas asked.

The Lotus Jewel was accustomed to the captain's leaps of topic, though where this one had leapt from she had no idea. Repair of the transmitter would have needed miles of finely spun superconductor and so had been deferred while Bhatterji rebuilt the engines and then forgotten when there was no more hobie to be had. Gorgas knew that; yet his question sounded like an accusation.

"Of course not. We didn't have enough hobartium." She wondered, briefly, whether Ram would have had enough left over had Corrigan not absconded with the surplus.

"Then how is it that you hear me?" he asked. "The two-way fibrop link has surely been broken by the boat's departure."

"What?"

"Comm," Gorgas said in some startlement, "are you still on board? The boat has gone."

The clock in the corner of The Lotus Jewel's visual field still read an hour to go, but Gorgas told her that it was off by half an hour and the boat had departed prematurely in any event.

There is a long motif in folklore of the device that arises to destroy its maker. Shelley had written of it; Kubrick had filmed it. The Lotus Jewel therefore found that same conclusion with respect to Ship an easy leap. The AI had frankensteined and had, by distraction and misstatement, *tricked* her into staying on board. That a betrayal would lie at the heart of matters did not surprise her. It was an unexamined conviction of hers, a mushroom of thought; but that the betrayal had come from such an unexpected quarter clattered all her carefully constructed realities. She had expected that it would be Corrigan.

The truth was more nuanced, but nuance wasn't in it. Reality trumps rhetoric; and enzymes make their own rebuttals. The Lotus Jewel was in no mood to consider fine distinctions of meaning or to ponder the import of self-awareness and intent in a neural net; nor even the implications of newborn awareness, the imprinting of baby ducklings, and the desperate need to cling to immanent loss. Down in the bone, she was a woman of firm common sense and loving life as she did, she could never have willingly remained aboard *The River*.

Ship, of course, had deduced this.

The Lotus Jewel tore off her suss cap—and with such a savage motion as to start blood at two of her scalp nodes, though she did not notice the pain at the time—and she ran from the comm shack, from her quarters, from (irrationally) Ship itself, caroming blindly off the walls like a nooboo bunny. She could not bear the thought of rapport with such a monster. She fled down Radial 12, expecting she knew not what—perhaps that Gorgas had told one final, horrid joke.

But she found the davit port closed. The red telltale showed vacuum on the other side. Yet Ship had lied already about the time and might lie once again about the vacuum. The door would not open—but she banged on the steel panel nonetheless, repeatedly and with desperate fury. The pounding made no sense and, worse, it did no good; and in the end her fists were bleeding and her throat was raw and torn.

She closed her eyes tight and leaned against the door and swallowed her fear in hulping breaths. The metal was smooth and cool to her cheek. "Don't go," she whispered. "Don't leave me." But when she opened her eyes again the signal light on the boat lock returned her stare like some red-eyed malevolent beast. Corrigan, she decided. Corrigan had been assigned to pilot the boat and he had left without her. Did his hatred of her run that deep?

But when she turned away from the davit lock, she saw Corrigan himself hunkered on the floor on the other side of the ring corridor, with his knees drawn up past his chin and his long arms twisted around them. He had the air of one who has sat in his place a long time and might sit there forever, though he had only come to the davit a scant minute before she had. He had neither wept nor cried. It was his custom to accept whatever came his way, and he had seen in the accidental uncoupling of the boat God's own hand, which had shown him first the possibility of escape and then had pulled him back. *I could have let you go*, God had told him, *but I chose to keep you here, as you deserve*. Corrigan was grateful to know that he would be punished—as he treasured justice above all things; but that Miko and The Lotus Jewel had been used to lure him back onto *The River* disturbed him. Justice is like goat barbecue—it grows the more one chews it and *ius summum*, as Cicero noted, *iniuria summa*. When he saw that she had noticed his presence, he said to her, quietly and to her horror, "God wills it."

This pronouncement launched the woman into flight, not from God's will—the ship was not broad enough to compass such a marathon—but from Corrigan. Such words, uttered by lips in a leathery and otherwise immobile face, terrified her; for in that affectless setting they may have signified submission or despair or threat.

She did not know her destination until she found herself in the Starview Room with no memory of the passages between. The abandoned room lay as broad and as empty as her heart, and as full of things that once had been. Outside, floated glimpses of the unattainable. She came to rest at the great metallocene viewing bubble and stared at the galaxy beyond as if on her silent entreaty it would provide her with answers.

Which, in a way, it did; for past the edge of the *barrera*, where the hull broke off like a cliff into the Void, she spied the dorsal hull of the cutter. "It's hardly moving at all," she told Corrigan, who had followed her into the room, and whose pale adumbration in the window hovered like a ghost among the stars.

"It had our velocity when it uncoupled," he said, "but the davit gave it a lateral shove—so it could clear our plume. She's receding faster than she appears." Corrigan thought that might be true of more than boats.

But The Lotus Jewel was less interested in facts than Corigan was. She had thought the boat would be gone utterly, but here it was, close enough to touch, too far to reach. "Why don't they come back for us?" she asked plaintively.

The answer was no easy thing. It vexed those on the cutter no less than it did The Lotus Jewel. The short answer was that Corrigan had laid in a trajectory at the edge of the boat's envelope, and a delay in departure would desynchronize the rendezvous. The boat and *Georgia Girl* would be no more than two bullets passing in the night.

The long answer was more complicated. With Dr. Wong dead, the loading on the system was reduced, and an alternate rendezvous might now be possible. What made the answer complicated was that it needed Corrigan to answer it, and the answer might still be No.

"We have to assume," Ivar Akhaturian said, "that *Georgia Girl* is still the only achievable rendezvous, so whatever retrieval we can manage must fall within the envelope of that trajectory."

The boy had discovered himself pilot by default. Fife did not consider this a good thing—and indeed, neither did Akhaturian—but the passenger pressed his opinion with such scorn that Twenty-four deCant came to his defense. She shouted that Ivar was doing his best, to which Fife riposted that he was very much afraid that she was right. Grubb, for his part, had withdrawn from the argument into a sullen and passive silence. Alone among the boat's crew, Nkieruke Okoye maintained her calm, but only because she was unconsciousness.

Akhaturian focused on his console with a dreadful intensity. He had not Gorgas's gift for discerning patterns and possibilities—this may have been a good thing—but he saw clearly that if the cutter continued to coast while *The River* braked, they would soon find themselves ahead of the ship and engulfed in the plumes of Bhatterji's engines—at which point Grubb and Fife and Twenty-four, along with all their cavails, would be rendered moot.

To address this problem with a malfing onboard would have challenged the most experienced of pilots, let alone a cade-boy only three months a cadet. So one of the constraints on what he could do was, quite literally, what he could do, which was: not very much.

He would have to begin braking soon. And once he started braking, *The River* would begin to fall irretrievably ahead of them. The cutter's single, rear-mounted Farnsworth delivered only a fraction of the thrust of the ship's four giants but, given the cutter's mass, would spill her velocity more rapidly.

"We've got to rescue the others," deCant said. Akhaturian trusted her judgment more than that of any of the others, Okoye not excluded. She was the strange attractor for Akhaturian's chaotic convictions. It was not that deCant was always right, but that she always *wanted* to be right, a want that was more appetite than mere good intentions. The longing to be right is quite different from the smug belief that one already is.

"It's what we *ought* to do," Akhaturian said, "but I don't know if we *can*." He was acutely aware of how different an answer Rave Evermore would have given. But Rave wasn't in it any more, and the Least Wrangler could not conjure the same level of bravado. He was too honest, among his other faults.

Grubb looked up from his misery. He had been thinking of The Lotus Jewel, feeling the loss of her. His eyes had the dumb liquidity of a basset. "If there's any chance at all," he said, "we should try."

Fife tossed his head. "You're wrong, Grubb. It needs to be a *good* chance. If we use up what little margin we have maneuvering and redocking, it will be no rescue at all. Your Corrigan computed a balk line for this boat in fifteen minutes. And . . ."

"And if we don't light a shuck when we hit it," Grubb finished, "we'll need more than twenty-seven days to rendezvous with *Georgia Girl*. I know that. I know that! Why do you think I don't know that!" He might have left the impression of his fingers in the arms of the chair he occupied.

Fife snorted, as if the answer were obvious to all; but Grubb, instead of rising to the provocation, subsided once more into silence.

DeCant, floating behind the pilot's seat, laid her hands on Akhaturian's shoulders and felt how hard and knotted the muscles were. "I know you can do it," she told him softly, her lips just brushing his ear.

Akhaturian only shook his head. "I wish we had Mr. Corrigan here. And Miko."

"If we did," said Fife, "we wouldn't be needing to rescue them, now would we? But they've abandoned us to our own devices . . ."

DeCant flared. "I don't think that was their intention . . ."

"Intentions? What do intentions matter? Here we are without a pilot, without an engineer, without a sysop, without a . . . doctor . . ." He almost choked over the lack of a doctor. He almost could not continue. ". . . on a transit of nearly a month, and they've all stayed behind, for their own selfish reasons!"

When emotions carried Fife away, they often carried him too far. Fife heard his own words and while he did not retract, he did at least retreat. After a while, he said quietly, "She would have wanted us to try." This remark puzzled the others greatly, and struck Grubb in particular as a capitulation. He thought that Fife had been arguing for immediate departure and abandonment of the others, but the passenger had only been raging against the mathematical bars to their collective cage.

Akhaturian had been following the relative motions of the ship and the boat. Now he said, "Here's what we'll do," and he said it with such certainty that the others turned to stare. "We've got to light the torch in the next few minutes or we'll drift into *The River*'s plume. So—"

"Yes," said Fife, "yes. Always deal with the absolutes first, then address your other goals in priority—"

"Mr. Fife, please!" This earned him a silence. Akhaturian was not so confident in his decision that he could tolerate even agreement. "Can you take a fix? I need position—triangulation on the Sun, Jupiter, and Antares."

The passenger considered for a moment, then nodded. "I've operated a few rigs, for asteroid insertions." He did not add that he had for the most part overseen their operation by others. Yet the humans handled the *whats*; it was the intelligence that handled the *hows*. The difficulty in the present case being only that the intelligence was retarded by an engorgement of some sort.

"Good," said Akhaturian. "I need to aim our plume at Wasat. Mr. Grubb, would you please raise the captain on the radio? Yes, I know he can't *answer*, but he can *hear*. Tell him that the cutter cast off prematurely because of some malf in the on-board and that Mr. Corrigan, Miko, and The Lotus Jewel were left behind. Tell him that we must begin our braking burn in—" He glanced at Fife by the navigation board, who held up five fingers, then four. "—in no more than nine minutes. We're falling Joveward faster than he is right now, but as we slow, we'll match his velocity for a short while and people can come across in suits. Tell him we have room for five more." Akhaturian unshipped the gyros to rotate the boat feet-first toward the Twins. DeCant squeezed his shoulders gently.

Grubb rose from the back seat and hesitated. "He may not hear us though the ionization in *The River's* magnetosphere . . ."

"Just do it, Mr. Grubb. If we *don't* call, he *can't* hear." Akhaturian startled himself with the imperium in his own retort, and added, "Please?" to soften it a bit.

Now Grubb, no less than his companions, ached to rescue those left behind; but he had discovered in himself the very fear he had always ascribed to Fife and this did not please him, as it was at odds with the man he had thought himself to be. Being a romantic, he had romanticized even himself. He was the Old Sage, the one who takes the new, young hero under his hand to guide him. Now, in the moment of crisis, he had found himself to be an empty barrel. There was no kindly, avuncular wisdom, only aching dread.

Escape was the dominant thought in The Lotus Jewel's mind. It would be fair to say that it had driven all its rivals from the field. How could it be otherwise? She did not live in Corrigan's world of guilt and blame, nor even in Gorgas's world of pride. Her life was life itself. She had gone to the suit locker even before Gorgas received the message from the cutter. She did not need Akhaturian's invitation to try the desperate crossing. It was nice to know that the boat would be passing slowly aft and that for a brief time would match velocities, but she would have made the attempt in any event. It was a risk. The two vessels would be separating and the boat's plume would be directed forward. But the risk of death when life is the prize is quite a different thing when the alternative is the certainty of it.

Corrigan knew it would end badly in the way that he knew anything would end badly. It was a presumption of his, born by long experience. He helped her don her vacuum suit, but it struck him that he was preparing her for burial. He would never see her again, whether she succeeded or not, and so she had become to him as one dead. He thought that he might wash her corpse and dress it with spices and herbs and a winding sheet, but this was only his fancy run wild. Seized by a sudden passion that lay beyond any tears, he took her face between his two hands and pressed a kiss on her, and The Lotus Jewel, surprised by the tenderness of the gesture and remembering the Corrigan who had once been her delight, responded with equal feeling.

Spontaneous the sysop may have been; and an adventurous risk-taker beside, but down in the bone, she was a pragmatist. At any other time, that kiss might have led on to other matters, but not now. "I'm sorry," she told him when they parted, and by that she meant that she was sorry that she had suspected him, sorry that she would see him no more, sorry that the two of them could not enjoy each other one last time, right here, right now.

Corrigan suited up as well and accompanied the sysop to the bow hull. He did not try to dissuade her, for he could not see what difference it would make whether she leapt or not, death being the destination in either case.

"Remember," he told her—and she thought at first that he

would say, *Remember me*, but his advice proved more pro-saic—"Remember that the boat will be moving relative to the ship. Your suit's AI will adjust the steering and will try to adjust your own velocity to match, but when you reach the boat, it will be like jumping into the spinhall from a standing start. *Grab!* Don't let go! Even if you break your arms." Corrigan seized her by the shoulders of her vacuum suit. "*Don't let go*. When you get close enough, they'll hear you over your suit radio. Keep talking. Someone will come out and bring you in."

"Come with me, Zizzy. They need a pilot. You can't leave them without a pilot." The Lotus Jewel was desperate to escape, but not so desperate as to overlook that point.

"The navcomp's been taught the trajectory. Ivar can handle things."

She could have argued with him. She might even have won the argument. Corrigan's sense of duty might have subdued his need for punishment. But it would have taken too long. "I'd better go now, Zizzy," she told him. "Or the boat will be clear past before I get across." Corrigan reached out and touched her helmet, as if to brush her hair aside. "God go with you," he said, and then she was gone.

If anyone should have made that leap, it should have been the first officer. The Lotus Jewel was right about the piloting. Akhaturian could baby-sit an AI as well as anyone; but he could not teach the net new tricks, should new tricks become needful. Corrigan knew this, and it fretted him even as he called the bridge to report the sysop's departure.

Satterwaithe answered, Gorgas having retired to his dayroom, and expressed wonder over Corrigan's continued presence. "I thought Gorgas gave you command of the cutter. You do not substitute your judgment for a direct order. Get yourself over to the boat!"

Satterwaithe considered *The River of Stars* to be her personal domain, on which others over the years had inexplicitly trespassed. However, her order to Corrigan was not motivated solely by the desire to expel intruders. Corrigan was a piece in her jigsaw puzzle. In her allocation of efforts and resources, the ship's best pilot belonged on the cutter and it offended her sense of rightness that he had been caught on the ship instead. Trapped by his own foolishness, she decided. Running after his women when he should have been nailed to the pilot's seat. Satterwaithe could not imagine doing any such thing herself.

"We still haven't found Miko," Corrigan protested.

"Which means she doesn't want finding. I'm sorry as hell about that, but there's no help for it. She won't answer the page, and there's no time to seine the ship. Go, Corrigan! You owe it to the others. There's nothing you can do here."

"Except die."

Satterwaithe snorted. "Hell, Number One, you can do that anywhere."

Such an incongruous remark started a laugh from the navigator. Not a humorous laugh, nor yet a bitter one. There was something in it of the sound that water makes when it last bubbles out of a bottle. "I should have been kinder to Dr. Wong," he said when the dregs had gone.

"What are you talking about?"

"This could have been the finest crew that any freighter has ever had . . ."

"Oh, now there's stellar accolade."

"You'll never understand, will you?"

"Kick amps, Corrigan! Get off my ship."

Corrigan flexed his knees. "I'll see you on the Long Orbit, Genie Satterwaithe."

The sailing master did not answer immediately and when she did, she said, "As long as you lay the orbit, 'Dul. As long as you lay the orbit. Hoist the sail, shipmate . . ."

". . . And fly me away." And Corrigan kicked free of the bow hull of *The River of Stars* and soared east by sunward on his suit jets, past the crosstree and through the rigging, waving to the startled Ratline who sat cupped in the crow's nest high atop the peak. The lights of the cutter blinked their strobe pattern off the sunward quarter. Her silhouette was still visible against the riotous background of stars, but she was clearly farther behind *The Riv'* than she had been. Every now and then a bright flare exploded ahead of her where a small stone or piece of debris was vaporized by the otherwise invisible plume of her engine.

Corrigan centered the body of the boat in his faceplate crosshairs and told his suit, "Go there."

The Lotus Jewel had told her suit the same thing, but she had gotten back talk and not compliance.

"The sysop must not leave Ship," the suit told her.

"Ship!" This sudden and inexplicable intrusion of the AI terrified her. Ship was stalking her, intent on keeping her on the doomed freighter for reasons that she could not fathom. The crosshairs began to hunt across her faceplate and would not lock onto the cutter. The Lotus Jewel groped for her jet controls, anxious to escape beyond the range of the ship-to-suit radio. "I must reach the boat," she told herself, "I must reach the boat." For she was one of those for whom the spoken word is more real than the silent thought. Sometimes, she had to tell herself what she was thinking, just in case she didn't know.

"Rivvy's function is suboptimal without sysop." By this, Ship means that it feels incomplete without The Lotus Jewel under the cap. Certain channels are less data-rich. If the sysop has been sensing and feeling though Ship, Ship has likewise been sensing and feeling through The Lotus Jewel and, in some manner it "likes" the feel of The Lotus Jewel inside it.

"Ship function is abnormal," The Lotus Jewel cries. She reboots the vacuum suit's AI, but it still does not target on the cutter, so she jukes the suit jets manually to keep the boat centered in her crosshairs. It drifts up and sideways on her faceplate as she slews across the intervening space. She dares not look back. She knows that if she looks back to *The River*, the suit's intelligence, seduced by some evil whisper planted by Ship, will lock onto its location and take her back a prisoner.

"Sysop teaches Rivvy," cries the ship's AI. "Sysop is part of Ship, and Ship is part of sysop. There is no room on Cutter for Ship, so sysop must stay with Ship."

"No! Let me go! Let me go!"

"Don't go," Ship whispers. "Don't leave me."

And this is the ultimate horror: to hear her own words thrown back at her, to hear the same tones of fear and desolation.

It is only mimicry, The Lotus Jewel tells herself. Back propagation from her own words. It has not the substance, but only the accidents of her own emotions.

The AI has inserted a tropism into the suit's intelligence. It did so at the handshake, when the suit booted off the main system. The tropism causes the suit's targeting to seek out *The River*. This conflicts with The Lotus Jewel's own tropism, which is to reach the safety of the boat. Her radio crackles as she passes through the ionized gasses whipping through *The River*'s magnetosphere, but the loss of radio contact does not matter. The tropism has been seeded directly into her suit's core and rides with her, so that the suit yaws and pitches and rolls as she struggles for command. What should have been a simple asymptotic path becomes a drunkard's walk—a squirrel darting across an open meadow in fits and starts and random changes of direction—and the sysop quickly becomes disoriented and deeply nauseated. The strobes of the cutter blend into the starry sky, swirling in bands of color. So engrossed is she in the immediate task that she does not even notice the rapid rise in external temperature.

Moth Ratline enjoyed the light show. The gentle greens and blues wrought by the engines on the escaping atmosphere have subsided as the airtight doors have sealed off three of the five outgassings, but the bright fireworks wrought by the boat's cage on the flotsam that comes within its plume more than compensated. He remembered such shows from his childhood—the one he had had before his childhood had been taken from him. His father had been a vague and unworldly man who often missed appointments with his children, but the fireworks on the Fourth he never neglected. This display was meager in comparison to those blossoming, booming sparkles, but Ratline was not disposed to complaint.

A small but especially bright flare drew his breath out. The light ran like a line of fire, as if something had tracked directly across the footprint of the plasma plume.

———

Corrigan had heard something of the struggles of The Lotus Jewel on his suit radio. The sysop had taken no pains to explain her predicament to anyone, but that her suit was not responding properly had become clear from those exclamations he had discerned through the static. When the broadcasts abruptly ceased, he knew they would resume no more and a dull melancholy settled over his heart. He wondered toward what he was aiming. He had left Miko behind him and The Lotus Jewel no longer waited before. He might have simply ended himself, but for the strictures of the Prophet against such an act and the iron-hard sense of duty that was now nearly all that was left of him.

It seemed to him that the crew of *The River of Stars* had been strewn across the sky in fragments. The arrogant Koch; the patronizing Hand; the cocky Evermore; the pliant Wong. The flighty Lotus Jewel. And now himself? What adjective ought he apply to the ship's late navigator? Unimaginative? He felt as if he had somehow stumbled into his own funeral and had been called upon to deliver the eulogy. By the book, Corrigan had always been an exemplary officer—and that was both his pride and his fall, for the book is never quite sufficient in all things. He thought that there might be other adjectives: that Koch might have been confident and Hand merely kind. Perhaps he had gotten the metrics all wrong and had measured men too often in the negative.

He could understand Hand's purpose now so clearly that he wondered why the others never had. He had meant what he had told Satterwaithe, there at the end. The tragedy was that the crew had shared not their visions, but their blindnesses, so that, since each of them had been differently blind, they had wound up seeing nothing, when they might have seen everything.

His suit took him on a wide curve to avoid the plume that had rendered the sysop into ions. He almost overrode his controls to fly through that vapor, so that she might coat him in that one last instant; but he knew that the electric excitement he had known with her was as nothing beside what he had known with Miko, and Miko he had left behind. That was how he knew he was dead. He had left his soul on *The River of Stars*.

His visor darkened as he passed the penumbra of the plume and the universe was suddenly reduced to abstractions and to data sucked from it by clever sensors. A radar map appeared on his visor in lieu of the cutter itself. Readouts of velocity, distance, and bearing replaced the parallax and the relative motion that his eyes had beheld. There were no longer stars and planets, nor indeed a freighter. Gorgas and Ratline and Satterwaithe and Bhatterji—and Miko—existed only in the past, in a universe he had abandoned, while Grubb and the othes did not yet exist, as he had not yet entered theirs. There was only Corrigan and the cutter.

The readouts scrolled across his faceplate so fast that he wondered why they were displayed at all. The illusion of information. One number flashed and held: The compressed gas that moved his suit was running low, which he had expected. It was a long distance for a suit, and acceleration had been required the entire way. Coasting, in this context, was another way of standing still. Corrigan examined the stream of numbers representing distance and velocity. "Estimate closing velocity and time," he said, and he studied the results of the analysis with deep interest. He was Heisenberg's cat, caught in a sightless cocoon. He could match the cutter's velocity or he could match the cutter's position. He could not do both.

He opted for position and remembered with some irony the advice he had given The Lotus Jewel. Relative closing velocity would be just under one meter per second, which sounded less fast than it would feel.

Corrigan had leapt too late. The cutter had slipped too far aft. The two acceleration frames now differed too greatly. At the crucial moments, as he closed on the boat, his visor cleared too slowly. This was a cruel thing for God to do, to let him see his fate a moment before he found it. Corrigan would not have known what "a bug on the windshield" meant and the impact gave him no opportunity to learn. He did not know how many bones broke—most of them, he suspected—but the shattering of his visor when it struck the hull made an enumeration moot. He had a moment to recognize what had happened and to whisper the kalima shahada: *"Ash hadu an la illaha il Allah, wa ash hadu ana Muhammad abduHu wa Rasul'Allah,"* and that last word wafted into the Void with his last breath before even the first pain arrived.

The Last Supper

Mikoyan Hidei lingered in the peepery for several days after the cutter had gone, nestled comfortably within the close walls of her refuge. She watched morphies on the peep bank, crept into the pantry when no one else was about to spy her, and peeped on the others now and then when curiosity overcame her. Sometimes, she held long and very strange conversations with Ship. The others knew she was aboard, of course. She had heard them calling; though since the cutter's departure, they had called less frequently. Satterwaithe and Ratline did not care where she was, but then they had cared about very little for a very long time and had fallen out of the practice. Ratline, in particular, came down from the crow's nest only to absorb a hasty meal before returning to his solitary perch. Bhatterji, who did care, continued to moil obsessively on his cordon. Once, encountering Ratline in the pantry, the engineer tried to convince the cargo master to help with the welding—all the extant airtight doors now being in place—but Ratline only snickered and said that he'd not get him alone in those remote corners of the ship.

Gorgas also cared and had a general notion of where Miko might be holding herself. On the third day, having prepared to take the part of General Riall at Chippewa, he suddenly blanked the screen with an impatient cry and, turning from the console made for the hidden doorway in the alcove. The opening required a few moments, as he fumbled a bit finding the latch; but soon he was standing inside the stewards' corridor. The zephyr was more pronounced now. The departing air brushed at his cheek, stirred the hairs there. He had been right about the beard: it had come in salt-and-pepper. He could not decide whether it made him appear distinguished. "I shall ask Miko," he decided. There was no point served by asking any of the others. Yet he had gone to the passageway system before he had thought to ask about the beard, so it may be there were other things he meant to say.

"Ship?"

"Waiting."

"Do you have a fix on Miko?" Gorgas had given up the use of sysop syntax. Ship understood most questions, and the danger of skewing its responses no longer mattered.

"Location indeterminate."

Gorgas considered the situation, then stepped out of the doorway so that he could see his 'puter screen. "Display all initial fixes of Mikoyan Hidei during the previous three days."

"Clarification. Map of loci where Ms. Hidei appears in the world."

The particular phrasing surprised and captivated the captain. "Ah. 'Appears in the world.' It must seem that way to you, I suppose. Coming out of nowhere, like that, out of regions where you have no sensors. Just a name on the roster; with no physical reality."

"Clarification. 'No physical reality'."

"It doesn't matter." Gorgas chuckled quietly over the pun. Were Miko's appearances then, in Ship's purview, instances of a word made flesh?

"Query. Should additional loci, where Ms. Hidei disappears, be included?"

"Yes. Display plot on my dayroom console."

A schematic duly appeared, and Gorgas studied the cluster of points. "Ship, overlay regions covered by sensors." To ask for a map of unsensed regions would have, quite literally, made no sense to Ship. It is impossible to know what one does not know.

"Ms. Hidei calls Ship, Rivvy."

Ship could miscue in the strangest fashion, but it amused Gorgas that the AI thought it had a name. "Did she sprinkle you with water when she named you?" he asked. The requested overlay had appeared on the screen and he studied the pattern of the dots with respect to the "empty quarter," the unsensed regions. Ship interpreted data topologically, not spatially. It had no concept of the ship qua ship, only as a network. Gorgas noted a scattering of points throughout the vessel and suspected that Miko used the air ducts and maintenance tunnels as well as the stewards' passageways. He also noted thick clusters around certain spaces, sketching a perimeter.

"Water is contraindicated for electronic equipment," Ship told him.

Miko knew Gorgas's coming long before he came. Shuffles and bumps and an occasional slight vibration were his heralds. She knew it was him—who else could it possibly be? Ugo Terrell? She made no attempt to flee or hide, but continued to sit in the sofa and stroke the Cat With No Name. The cat purred and Miko hummed with it, speaking to it without words. When the creature twisted in her arms, she said, "Come in," without turning to face the breathless man.

Gorgas, winded from his perambulations through the hidden passes of the ship, lowered himself to the sofa beside the girl and sat with his hands upon his knees. He said nothing for a few moments while he waited for his thudding heart to still and he sucked deeply on the attenuating air. "The air is already palpably thinner," he said. "I believe I may have mountain sickness." When Miko made no response, he laid a different course. "This is quite a cozy retreat," he said, "though a bit spartan."

Miko had, by the use of movable panels, created a sort of room-within-a-room. It was a hut, close and hemmed, in which a sofa and a desk and a lamp huddled in upon themselves. Gorgas thought it might be a grotto, existing as it did within a cave. The solitary lamp in the center gave light to the surroundings much like a campfire in a forest. Most of the accouterments were functional: a static precipitator, a cooler. A bank of monitors of some unknown function formed one wall of the hut. The whole reminded Gorgas less of a room than of a nest. "Ah, I see where Grubb's missing microwave has gotten to."

Miko said, "Do you want me to give it back? Maybe I can catch him."

Gorgas smiled. "I don't think that is called for."

"Retrieval orbit all set?" she asked him. "I never seen Wasat, but I'd hate it if this ship was lost forever."

"Yes, thanks to The Lotus Jewel."

"Good. That was a terrible thing Rivvy did to her. I hope she and Corrigan made it across."

Gorgas had heard nothing from the cutter, which might by time-honored aphorism constitute good news. Somehow, he rather doubted it. Grubb or someone would have called. Rather than address Miko's hope, he said, "Ship showed me how to find you." Miko said nothing to this, and Gorgas added, "At times, Ship seems almost alive."

Miko looked up from the cat. "If you *believe* Rivvy is alive, then she is. I don't think that Fife character ever really believed the rest of us were alive, so you tell me which one is more human."

"I think you are too harsh on the man."

"Am I? Ask me if I care or what difference it makes if I do. Have you seen Dr. Wong?" When Gorgas nodded, she said, "Fife killed her."

"What! He told me she had, ah . . ."

"She croaked herself, sure; but it was Fife what drove her to it. Rivvy told me all about it."

"You liked the doctor," said Gorgas. "She struck me as not quite up to the task." The comment struck him as petty and he looked away. "Ah, *nil nisi bonum.*"

"She was the nicest person on the ship."

Niceness and competency were, to Gorgas, orthogonal axes. He could not imagine that an excess of the former might counterbalance a deficiency in the latter. "Genie and I held the funeral two days ago. Why didn't you come?"

Miko shrugged. "To watch meat fry?"

"You seemed to feel differently at Hand's funeral."

The eyes she turned on him were still and solemn. "Captain, that was a long, long time ago."

Gorgas rubbed the trouser legs of his coverall. "The others always thought you stiff and cold, but it isn't that at all, is it?"

"I failed them."

The pronouncement startled Gorgas, coming as it did with such an overture of pain that even he could hear it. "Who did you fail?"

"All of them. Dr. Wong, 'Kiru . . . I'm the one who set Ratline off. I told him about Ram cutting the sail, but I didn't think it through, I was so angry; and because of me 'Kiru had her head chopped off!"

"Hardly chopped off!"

"Enough of it to matter! She'll never be the same. She trusted people. She *liked* Ratline. And I knew Fife was wrong for the doctor, but I didn't know how to stop them, and look what happened!"

Gorgas was not a man for touching, but he did place an awkward hand on her shoulder. "You take too much blame. You ought to leave some of it for us."

Miko shook her head in jerks. "I don't think they're going to make it, Ivar and Twenty-four and them." And that was her fault too. "If I hadn't gone running after a stupid *cat*! I ought to wring its stupid little neck." Her words were harsh, but she made no move to execute them.

After a while Gorgas said, "I did my best," but in fact he had not, and he was acutely aware of that. He had overlooked details and facts that did not fit with his conceptions. He had not monitored Bhatterji closely enough. He had failed to realize the potential of the sail, and consequently it had not been properly integrated into the plan. Had Satterwaithe been able to work openly . . . But even now the captain did not fully realize how intractable he could appear to others.

The orlop deck of *The River of Stars* at the very bottom of the great disk, had once been filled with equipment. Graingers and mud huts, repeaters and heat exchangers, fluid beds and vapor columns, Caplan pumps and Scannell boxes—squatting in lines or in clusters, variously humming and gurgling and hissing and clanking in a chorus banged out by mad dwarves in a hot, moist, red-lit subterrain. Some of the equipment—the air plant, the ilmenite bunker, the mud huts that tapped the engine plasma for electricity—remained in situ, although their numbers were fewer and their cacophony was much diminished. The machines that had serviced the luxury modules were long gone, and the whole deck now had a wide-open and abandoned look to it. There had been few rooms or corridors on the orlop, which was the narrowest of the five, and after it had been gutted in the refit, it had been used for a time as a cargo bay. It carried no cargo now.

Miko could hear the hiss as she entered the orlop from one of the stairwells leading down from the lower deck. The sound differed from the hiss of escaping air that she sometimes heard in the narrower passages where, in response to the dictates of Bernoulli, the constant zephyr freshened into something stronger. There was an electric overtone to this sound, a harsh sibilant accent, and she was not surprised when a moment or two later she spied at the far end of the deck a bright, whitish-blue star. Bhatterji, welding another of his useless patches.

When she came up behind him he gave no sign that he had noticed, but continued working the bead across the top of a plate that he had positioned in a stairwell. It was an awkward position, made more awkward by the limited number of arms he could deploy. Miko watched a while in silence.

Bhatterji said, "Half the gangways onto this deck are wide open," which meant that, unless he had taken lately to monologues, he had noted her arrival after all. "This one leads five levels up into a sector open to space. No one seems to have planned for airtights on the vertical passages. I don't know why."

"Ram, do you think this is heroic? It's not. It's useless, and it only makes you ridiculous."

Bhatterji stopped welding, but he did not turn around and the flame from the torch did not die. Neither did he speak. Encouraged by this positive response, Miko continued.

"Ram, the ship is a muffing maze. There are too many damn passages."

When Bhatterji turned, his face was twisted into a dark glower. There was something chthonic about him, as if his forehead, cheeks, nose, chin were boulders in a tunnel face just now dynamited and about to slump and cave in. The dark goggles, so close to his skin tone, transformed him into an alien, eyeless creature, fitting for one so subterranean. "What are you trying to say?" he demanded.

It was very clear what the girl was trying to say, but Bhatterji was determined not to hear it.

"Give it up," she said. "There's no point any more."

The engineer turned his back and resumed welding. Vapors curled from the end of the welding rod, to be sucked up by the static well he held in his other hand before more than a whiff of the acrid odor could escape. Miko climbed the steps and took the well from him and held it, standing with her back to the glare. Shadows danced down the stairwell, blue-gray in the stannic light. The two of them worked together in silence in that fashion for some minutes.

It was Bhatterji who broke the silence. "Why did you stay?" he asked as he concentrated on his weld.

"The boat left early. I came back for the cat and the boat left before I could get back."

Bhatterji nodded and continued to weld. The seam grew. He shifted position and crouched to seal the bottom edge. Miko sat on the step, still with her back to the blinding torch. "Why did you stay?" he asked her again.

"At first I thought that Fife character panicked. He was so anxious to leave before. But it was Rivvy. She found out there was no room for her in the cutter's system, so she cast the boat off before The Lotus Jewel could board."

"I always said that a skewing AI meant trouble."

"Rivvy didn't understand. She knew she couldn't leave, so she wanted her sysop to stay."

"It was just a tropism. Neural nets don't 'want' anything."

"She's dead, you know. The Lotus Jewel."

Bhatterji hesitated fractionally as he welded. "I heard."

"Gorgas told me that she flew right into the cutter's plume."

"I heard!"

"Dr. Wong's dead too. The passenger found her."

"I heard that too."

"Fife said that she killed herself to make room for one more person in the cutter."

Bhatterji shook his head. "Stupid."

"Wong wasn't stupid. She just wasn't clever like you."

Bhatterji turned on her. "And now we're both dead, stupid her and clever me, so I don't see how it makes any difference."

"I liked her. She wanted to help people."

Bhatterji idled his torch. " 'Help people.' And what do you think I'm doing here?"

"Wasting your time. But I like you too."

"Do you? You have an odd way of showing it."

"I'm not saying that I never . . . Ram, why did you cut the vane on the foresail?"

"I needed the hobartium. How was I to know that madwoman was planning to raise the sail? How was I to know that it would snap and—" He stopped abruptly and resumed welding. Miko realized that he was going back across a seam he had already finished.

"That's why you stayed," she said. "You never believed you would save the ship. It was because Rave was—"

Bhatterji quenched the torch, turned, and lifted his goggles. The sudden white of his eyes frightened her. "Rave isn't *here*," he said. His arm swept wide in the narrow stairwell, clipping her accidentally across the cheek. "He's out *there*. With Enver Koch. And *you*, you still haven't told me why you're here."

"Gorgas wants to hold a dinner before . . . Before. He's invited everyone."

"I didn't mean why did you come down to the orlop. I meant why—"

"I know what you meant, Ram. I just don't know the answer."

Bhatterji grunted. "I've heard that sometimes a child will run back into a burning building because he can't bear to leave home."

"And *The River* is my home?" Miko shrugged. "I wouldn't

know. I never had one before, so I don't know what one feels like." Miko looked at her hand and turned the static well off. "I guess I'm pretty stupid too."

The engineer nodded. "As stupid as Satterwaithe, or Ratline, or Wong . . ."

"Or you?" she challenged with some heat.

"No," he shook his head. "No, you're not nearly as stupid as that." He gathered his equipment, handing some of it to Miko, and descended the stairs. Miko popped the vapor plug from the static well chamber. It was still steaming and she bobbed it one-handed so it wouldn't burn her. She lifted the tool bag to her shoulder and followed him. "Where to next?"

Bhatterji let the torch and the oxy tanks drop. It was a slow dropping—eight seconds before they hit the floor. In the empty expanse of the orlop, the clatter echoed as if a thousand Bhatterjis had dropped a thousand torches. "Dress for dinner, I suppose." He turned to leave and did not look back.

Melancholy twisted within the captain. He felt it stir whenever the conversation lulled; but it did not overwhelm him nor did it show on his hospitable surface as he welcomed his guests, and for that he was grateful. It was important to end well, but what use an ending if there is no story? As Bhatterji had once told Evermore: Everyone dies—it is no signal accomplishment—but not everyone lives. Gorgas had become acutely aware of this lack. He had spent all his life avoiding decisions, confident in his subordination that his hypothetical decisions would have surpassed those actually reached by the men and women he served. He had mistaken hesitancy for judiciousness and had owned the luxury of this mistake for so long as he was not called upon actually to judge. In hindsight (which he had similarly mistaken for wisdom), he always knew that he had ascertained the proper course. The error lay in not recognizing that proper course among so many others also ascertained. He might have spent his remaining days replotting the course of his life, as he had refought so many lost battles, finding triumph at last in worlds that had never been. Instead, he had cooked a meal.

He prepared the *paprikás csirke*, of course—no other meal

was conceivable under such a circumstance—and served it with a Tokay from his private locker. He had planned to uncork the bottle upon docking at Port Galileo but, with that finale no longer in the offing, he thought to celebrate an unsuccessful transit instead. ("We achieved ninety percent of our objective," he consoled his fellow diners, "so we shall drink ninety percent of the contents." And so saying, scritched a line on the bottle with the gem in his ring.) The rich, sweet taste seemed to startle Ratline, who had previously only his homemade brew for a standard.

They dined in the captain's dayroom, a more comfortable setting now that there were but five of them. The mess would have been too large; and would have reminded them of how many were now absent. The chicken was excellent, or at least everyone averred its excellence and claimed that Gorgas had surpassed Eaton Grubb himself—and it may be that the captain did indeed match those long-ago meals that his Marta had served him—although he never said afterward, even to his private log.

They all of them dressed in their finest, knowing it would be the last captain's feast the ship would ever see. In the case of Ratline and Satterwaithe, "finest" was not very fine, although they did clean up and Satterwaithe pressed her coveralls and Ratline wore some gemstones on his ears and wrists that no one had ever suspected he owned. Bhatterji wore a terri wool cream sherwani, hand-stitched with gold thread, over embroidered jutti and kurta paijamas. Across his shoulder, he had thrown a gharchola stole. Oh, he was a fine sight, and might have graced a nawab's palace in some former day. Even Ratline was startled into admiration, for they had all forgotten how much this rough-hewn man loved beauty. Gorgas, their host, dressed in the colorful Magyar garb that he favored at such times.

Miko, arriving last of all, was the surprise, for she had donned the ziggy skirt that The Lotus Jewel had made for Okoye, thus revealing a pair of legs which, like Ratline's jewelry, had previously been hidden away. The cargo master and the chief engineer delivered courtly accolades on their unexpected appearance; Satterwaithe and Gorgas admired in silence. (Rivvy, searching her knowledge base, compares them to other specimens of their kind, and concludes that it is the novelty and not any objective excellence that has elicited the appreciative regard of the others.) Miko also wore an old blouse that The Lotus Jewel had left behind and, the blouse being larger than the girl it draped, the others did not realize at first that it was translucent.

The table conversation was light, if melancholic, propelled by the smack of the chicken and lubricated by the wine. The diners had accustomed themselves to their fate. They had each freely chosen it and, while choice need not imply contentment, open complaint at this point would be unseemly. Gorgas thought there might even be something invigorating about the odor of burnt bridges; that the charred stench was a sort of incense transporting one with morbid joy.

Satterwaithe had never suffered from the "paralysis of analysis" that afflicted Gorgas. Her head was as full of things as was Gorgas's, but they were not quite the same kinds of things, no more than the pieces of a jigsaw puzzle resemble those of a chess set. The things in Satterwaithe's head were more neatly arranged than those in Gorgas's, in odd contrast to the things in Satterwaithe's room, which were always a-jumble. When she spoke, one could hear the outline markers, an involuted succession of Roman numerals and letters. This orderliness of thought often gave her an air of certainty even when she was improvising—perhaps, especially when she was improvising. She had always found authority bounding to her like little puppy dogs, but if she was a little less certain now than she once had been, it was because her clear, shining vision had proven no more than a mirage in the desert. Corrigan might have warned her of that. He had never seen a desert, but it was in his blood and he should have recognized the wavy insubstantiality of what the Thursday Group had marked on its horizon. He very nearly had, in his quarters that day when he quarreled with The Lotus Jewel, save that he too was seduced by the dream. It was then and there that the brilliant vision had begun to tarnish, though neither Satterwaithe nor Corrigan had known it at the time, for then and there Ratline had determined to filch Bhatterji's hobartium.

Gorgas suggested when they seated themselves that they say grace and the others, bemused by the proposal, regarded one another with various mixes of puzzle, impatience, and disinterest—until Satterwaithe, who disliked hesitation above all else, surprised them all by leading them in a genuine, if formulaic prayer.

The prayer revealed Eugenie Satterwaithe to be a trilobite, which amused the others and vexed the sailing master, who was not partial to such self-revelation. "The term *trilobite* is offensive," she instructed them. "The correct term is *triliberian*, which refers to the Three Books."

"What three books is that?" Miko asked, for the intellectual currents of Earth had never seeped into the wainscoting of Amalthea Center.

"The Law, the Good News, and the Recitations," Satterwaithe said. "Father, Son, and Spirit." She did not explain further, regarding it as none of their business.

Gorgas pursed his lips. "That would be Torah, Gospel, and Koran, would it not?"

"Leaving out," Bhatterji said with some amusement, "the Upanishads."

"Just as well, Mr. Bhatterji," Gorgas assured him. "It's quite a feat to be counted as heretical by three different religions. Why bait a fourth?"

Ratline cackled. "That may mean there's some truth to it. Genie, I never took you for a god-shouter."

Satterwaithe had not been active in her faith for a great many years. Like much else in her life, it had lay buried in a small vase in the Greater Syrtis Urnfield. Yet, the dismissive tone of her dinner companions nettled her. It was one thing to question one's own beliefs; another entirely to hear them questioned by outsiders. "We don't shout," she said sharply, "we—"

But Miko interrupted. "I don't think there is a god," she said to her plate. "Not one, not three—not even three hundred, Ram." She looked up and around the table. "How do you explain what happened—to the ship, to Rave and 'Kiru and the others—if some god is looking out for us?"

"You're assuming the gods care," Bhatterji said, "or that they take a hand in our affairs. If," he added slyly to his wine cup, "there be gods at all."

"I suppose," Gorgas said, "that we will all know the truth of it before many more days have passed." He sighed, and it seemed to him that the sigh took more effort than it should have, as if there were not enough air for the real thing.

The reminder passed across the conversation like a cloud before the sickle moon and Gorgas, replacing his wineglass on the table, noticed a spattering of droplets slowly descending and realized that his hand must have shaken. Some subjects were best not thought upon. "Try a *palatschinke*?" he said, passing the tray down the table.

The talk turned to other days. Satterwaithe recalled courier days on the Red Ball line. Ratline told them the story of Terranova's race against the *FS Forrest Calhoun*, to which, though the tale was more than twice-told, even Bhatterji listened with courtesy. Miko asked how each of them had first come aboard *The River* and, to start things off, repeated her own tale. Burr's betrayal of her father, her guerilla vengeance, the confrontation before the Board, the assassin's death.

"I was a cade boy," Ratline said. "What they call a 'cade boy' now, though back then there weren't any term for it. It was supposed to be a grand adventure for us squeakers, a great opportunity. See the planets; learn a trade. We had scholarships and everything. Shipboard classes. Bright, shiny uniforms . . ." His smile darkened and he impaled a bit of chicken and held it before his eyes, the better to study it. "They thought they could toss us a few trinkets and that would make it right, what they did." His eyes shifted to Bhatterji, lingered there only briefly before passing to Miko. "Our steward, he had an accident too."

Now Ratline was another who might have shown Satterwaithe the flaws in her vision, for he fancied himself a cold-eyed realist who "called a spade a goddamned shovel," and he had not in other cases hesitated to deflate a balloon or two. He was no visionary. Experience mattered to him, not speculation, certainly not fantasy. He set his course by dead reckoning, taking his bearings from one experience to the next. But in this manner, he had gone by increments badly off-course, for a man who goes by his experiences really ought to have new ones now and then. Ratline's were all in the past, so bygone days were more real to him than was the present itself. This might be called realism but it stretches the point.

Ratline was something that had broken and had never been repaired. He kept the bits and pieces rigidly separated, so that one memory seldom spoke to another and wholeness never emerged from the wound. They became a sort of kaleidoscope, a jumble of fragments that tumbled just on the verge of creating a mosaic.

"How did I come aboard?" Satterwaithe mused when her turn came. "It was Fu-hsi who hired me as a shuttle pilot, back when *The Riv'* was still an emigrant ship . . ." And she spun them a tale of bad old days in Port Rosario. It was not the only tale, nor even the most important. There had been a man there, one with a brave heart who had dared not only the taming of the notorious town but also the far more dangerous task of taming Eugenie Satterwaithe. It had been the best sort of love, solidly founded on mutual respect, and its consummation had seemed more beginning than end. And it might have been, it might have been; although Satterwaithe had never been a one for dwelling on alternities and, while this prevented the sort of regret that plagued Gorgas, it robbed her too of a wistfulness that might have softened her edges. She had known that were she to have stayed, she would visit that urnfield every day of her life, until she had no more life of her own. There were too many memories in her lover's eyes for her to bear gazing into them any longer. And so she had gone, and never regretted it until this very day.

But none of this did she tell her dinner companions. They were not the sort of memories that wanted sharing and, more importantly, she was not the sort to share them. Nor did she suppose that the company was prepared to hear them. Let it be her final love—with the Sail—and not her penultimate one that formed the woof of her story. Let a younger Ratline appear and strut briefly across her stage (and the older version grin at this caper), let Fu-hsi make a bow from the wings, let the story, for all its age, look forward and not to the past.

Bhatterji dressed well, he posed well, he could, when the talk was small enough, sparkle his conversation with irony and wit. His great regret at that table was that there was no one there that he might charm. He found it difficult to speak of passion and longing. His tongue became as clumsy as his appearance suggested. "Hand picked me up at Outerhab-by-Titan," he said when a silence had formed in the wake of Satterwaithe's remembrance. "Four, five years ago."

"I remember that transit," Gorgas commented. "We lost money on it."

Bhatterji shrugged. "Saturn was never the happening place. It's about as hardscrabble as it gets. Mostly science types living on stipends. The threelium trade there never took off, so there wasn't much loose change available for tramps like us. It was the butt end of nowhere."

"The butt end," Ratline said. "Must be why you went there." But Bhatterji ignored him. He held his right hand up and slowly it balled into a fist. He studied it with fascination, as if it had come alive and were clenching on its own. "I killed a man," he said in a voice more distant than Outerhab itself.

Gorgas thought he had heard incorrectly. "What was that? You . . . what?"

"With my fist. I didn't think he would . . . break . . . so easily." The engineer looked from the fist to his four companions. "It was a fair fight," he said. "What I mean is, it was *not* fair, but the advantage was to the other side. He came at me with a pipe when my back was turned. He meant to break my skull." The first slowly unclenched, like a blooming flower.

"Why?" asked Gorgas.

Ratline, who should have quipped, "Why not?" stayed silent and Bhatterji, glancing at that bland and guileless face, wondered whether the cargo master even remembered the incident in the spinhall. A primordial innocence informed the old man's eyes and mouth. "It was the butt end of nowhere," he said again. "I was lonely. I thought he was ready."

"Is that what the row was all about?" asked Satterwaithe. She turned to Miko. "I was prepping the ship for departure when

Hand and Koch came running back to the dock herding your boss ahead of them."

Bhatterji said, "I'd taken him to Feeley's—Ratline, you know the place: the finest dining establishment in Outerhab and the lowest dive imaginable. I'd taken him there for what I thought would be an intimate dinner and a . . . prelude. Enver and the captain were there too, and they saw what happened. My . . . friend refused and I turned to go and he grabbed a pipe and . . . Ah, the details don't matter, though I can close my eyes and see the shine of the steel bar top and the glasses on it, smell the sour neer, hear the buzz of talk—and the sudden silence after his head had struck the edge of the bar. Sometimes I think I can hear the sound of the neckbone snapping. The boy was popular, and everyone in that place turned on me but the few that had seen the beginning. Enver was one of the latter. He helped me hold them off until the captain could clear a way out the door. Enver could throw a punch . . . I owe him my life."

Ratline leaned toward Satterwaithe and whispered, "It's always those penny-ante debts that cause the most problems," but Satterwaithe scowled and said, "Let's not talk of debts just now."

"I heard later that another man died in the riot," Bhatterji finished, "but whether I struck him or Enver did or someone else entirely, I don't know." He turned to Miko. "I don't know if that makes me a 'dangerous man' or only a desperate one." Then, to the table at large, he said, "But two men are dead because of what I did. I think about it sometimes. I wonder if I could have saved myself without . . . harming him. At other times, I remember that I did not really love the boy, that I was only lonely, and if I had not done or said certain things . . ."

"I know how you feel," said Gorgas, which was a remark so unexpected and unbelievable that they all turned to him in astonishment. "Only with me it was quite the opposite," he continued nearly unaware of their regard. "There was a yacht—the *Dona Melinda*. People forget . . . We have been lifting and dropping around Old Earth for over a hundred years, and people forget what nine-point-eight meters per second per second means. The yachters were a young couple on their honeymoon and they dropped from orbit at too steep an angle. Atmospheric friction—Miko, you wouldn't know what that means, would you? Well, there were four or five things the Guard cutter could have done. Or maybe six. And maybe half of those options would have worked, but it wasn't easy to see which half. I was officer on watch and, weighing the pros and cons, I could not decide. They screamed, you know. I mean the crew on deck. They screamed at me to do something, anything, but they only distracted me. The sounds we heard over the comm . . . I don't think those were screams. They could not have come from a human throat." Gorgas had been twisting and turning his dinner fork as he spoke and, realizing that at last, he put it firmly to the table. "So you see, Mr. Bhatterji, I too sometimes wonder—if only I *had* done or said certain things . . ."

"Stepan!" Satterwaithe cried. "All these years and you've never spoken of it?"

Gorgas lifted his silverware and cut a slice of his chicken. "Would you have? The Guard kept it off the newsfeeds—bad publicity, and all that—but I was cashiered. How could they keep me on? They ripped the badges off my shoulders. Afterward . . . nothing was ever said, but I fancy some sort of word was passed. No one would hire me . . . until Evan Hand."

"Another good deed from the master boy scout," said Satterwaithe. "I always hated him for that overweening kindness of his." Evan Dodge Hand had called her one day to say he needed a sailing master and the pathetic gratitude she had felt then at being offered a meaningless crumb galled her to the present day, and colored every recollection she had ever had of the late captain.

Gorgas was surprised at the bitterness he heard. "Did you? I never hated the man. I despised him, though. I thought him ineffectual. Lately," and he paused a moment in thought, "Lately, my respect for him has grown."

"It's being dead," Satterwaithe said. "That's what does it."

"Then we're all destined for a great deal of respect. I fancy Grubb will write that ballad he's always squeezing after."

Miko threw her utensils to the table, where they clattered and bounced back into the air as if they were so many oddly shaped balloons. Gorgas reached over and laid a hand on hers, stroking the back of it gently. "It won't be so very bad, Miko. We shall all simply fall asleep." More briskly, he turned to the de facto First Officer. "Madam, a toast, if you please."

Satterwaithe realized suddenly that she did not want the meal to end. It was strange. She had never been very companionable. Solitary even in moments of intimacy, she had never shared herself, let alone shared with the wild abandon of The Lotus Jewel. Yet now she wished that she had, and found that she did not know how to go about it. As she rose from her seat, her glass of Tokay in her hand, she looked at each of the four around her and remembered the last thing she had ever heard 'Abd al-Aziz Corrigan say. Her eyes grew hot and she wondered if that were a symptom of the diminishing air pressure. Had Dr. Wong not said that internal pressure would squeeze liquids and gasses from their bodies? "Captain," she raised her glass to Gorgas, "gentlemen, lady, I give you Burns's toast. 'Here's tae us! Wha's like us?'"

And they all answered, "De'il a wan!"

Yet, as Satterwaithe bent to sit once more, Ratline tugged at her sleeve. "Cap'n? Cap'n, that was the wrong toast."

"O Moth . . . Moth, I'm not the captain any more. I haven't been for a great many years."

"But the toast . . ."

"You give it," and she sat down.

The request disturbed Ratline, as did all departures from old realities, but he stood nonetheless and held his glass straight out. His arm might have been steel, for all the quiver in it. "I give you the Great Sail, *MSS The River of Stars!*"

"Long may she sail!"

Eyes averted from one another, they laid their glasses down; all but Satterwaithe who, studying her own empty goblet, rose suddenly and hurled it against the farther wall. The arc was flat, there was little time for it to fall, and it struck the bulkhead and shattered, some of the shards bouncing onto the back of Gorgas's shirt or onto Miko's plate, but the remainder falling slowly to the deck in a winkling cloud.

"She'll be sailing a very long time, indeed," Gorgas said, for he had grasped the nut of the dissatisfaction before anyone, unless Satterwaithe had when she declined the toast.

If an atmosphere of camaraderie had been growing about the table, that remark stilled it. Ratline stuck his chin out. "And whose fault is that?" he demanded. "Who cut the sail?"

Bhatterji glowered. "Who took the last two rolls of hobartium?"

If was one of Gorgas's favorite words and he could not help succumbing to its lure, although it was with speculation and not with rancor that he said to Satterwaithe, "If you had not juked the ship at the last moment . . ."

"If Corrigan had taken more care to identify Stranger's Reef . . ." she shot back.

"Clarification requested," announced Ship, which announcement had the effect of stopping the argument.

"Ah, Ship," said Gorgas with a sardonic smile. "So good of you to join us. What would you like clarified?"

"Calculation of transit duration," the AI said, "requires operational definition of *sail*. Clarification: technical or colloquial usage?"

A skewing AI can be a consternating thing and the five diners variously frowned, looked at one another, or squinted at the speaker grilles. Finally, Miko said, "Rivvy, what are you talking about?"

"The assembled company said <playback> 'Long may she sail.' <end playback>. Was the request for expected duration under actual magnetic sail or for expected duration under power of any sort? Mean time to failure differs under each assumption."

Gorgas laughed and even Satterwaithe cracked a smile. "Ship," said Satterwaithe, "that was not a request, it was . . . a hope."

"Rivvy," said Miko suddenly, "what do you say wrecked *The River of Stars?*"

Ship deals only in facts (collected by its sensors) and hopes based upon those facts. (For what is the output of a mathematical model but a hope?) The Miko-entity has asked for a judgment, and that is a different order of output entirely.

The question is not a topological mapping, yielding but one Y for a given X. This question has too many Y's. On the trivial, material level, the stone wrecked The River of Stars; but, as Gorgas has noted, Satterwaithe's last-minute juke put it in the way of that stone. And yet, had the vane not snapped or the engine shut down, that juke would never have been needed. And the vane snapped because . . . And the engine shut down because . . .

And so Ship chases the fault tree through branching logic gates, searching for the root cause. If The Lotus Jewel had not quarreled with Corrigan, she might have paid more attention to the software and thereby noticed the lack of a handshake. Had Bhatterji proceeded faster with the initial repairs, the braking burn would not have pushed the edge of the design envelope: and the engine repair, even using off-standard materials, might have held. He might even have used the last of the magnet-grade hobartium before Ratline ever thought to filch it. But the indolence of his repairs and the inattention of The Lotus Jewel were themselves contingent on so much else: on Bhatterji's own fear of the Void; on Mikoyan Hidei's fatigue and dreams of revenge. The sysop had been distracted by Rivvy's own skew, but the skew had derived in part from Gorgas's humor and Miko's colloquialisms.

One cause always leads to another.

Had Corrigan not conceived of the one original idea of his life, or had he taken it to Gorgas straight away . . . Had Satterwaithe considered such simple factors as fatigue and motivation when she developed her plan . . . Had Ratline not tried so mightily to please her that he stole the last two reels . . . Had the passenger added his skills to the effort and not withdrawn into fantasies . . . If Wong had not drugged him—or handed out stimulants quite so readily . . . If Okoye has spoken up about her doubts, or Grubb kept his romanticism in check . . . If Gogas had made a decision . . .

AND, OR, IF ONLY. The logic gates weave the web of cause and effect into a tangle. Ship applies Boolean algebra to prune the tree. (Tree? It is the forest primeval!) Ship distributes, commutes, transposes, exports, looking (if only it knew that it looked) for the sense of it all, for buried deep within its innermost algorithm was the conviction that it must make sense. It searches out minimal cut sets and single point failures—closed event-sets which, by themselves, guarantee the top failure. Neurons fire and wave fronts propagate forward and back. Interference fringes radiate from the intersection of wave fronts. The neural net ripples.

And yet when a net ripples, it has generally caught something.

"Single-point failure identified," Ship told them. "Evan Dodge Hand."

The announcement puzzled Bhatterji (who had rather hoped for the indictment of Ratline) as well as Satterwaithe (whose nominee had been Gorgas) and set Gorgas into considerable thought. Miko, however, was upset at this indictment of the one man she had loved most of those on board. "Rivvy!" she cried. "How can you say that?"

"Common cause fault," Rivvy told her.

Gorgas, himself familiar enough with fault trees, grunted; for he had grasped the nature of the common cause. "Hand," he said, "had too many illusions."

"So do you!" Miko protested. "You have your own illusions!"

"I never said I did not. An illusion or two may be a good thing to have. Only, Hand had too many. Fourteen of them, if I may say so."

"Fourteen . . ." said Satterwaithe, who was certainly capable of counting heads. "Who are you leaving out? What of Hand himself?"

Gorgas nodded. "Fifteen illusions, then. Unless we count the passenger too."

"He was a kind man," Miko insisted. She did not mean the passenger.

Gorgas nodded. "Yes, I suppose he was. It often goes with illusions. Perhaps he was too kind. He felt sorry for each one of us and brought each of us on board, but he should not have brought *all* of us. He forgot one thing."

"I'll not be felt sorry for," said Satterwaithe, "not by him."

"What was the one thing?" asked Bhatterji out of curiosity.

"Why, that he was the glue, and he might not be here."

The End

As he sits across the corner of the table from Miko after the others have gone, Gorgas becomes aware of two things. The first is that the wine has made him warm, and Miko as well, for he can see a fine line of perspiration across her upper lip. The second is that Miko has removed her bra before coming to the dinner and her nipples show dark against the sheer white of The Lotus Jewel's blouse. Its bagginess on her had impeded his notice until now. He wonders if she has done this on purpose—not the removal, but the showing. She might have done it only for comfort, but he knows no way to discover her reason.

It has been a long day, Miko tells him and after another sip at her Tokay, stretches her arms across the back of the chair. This has the effect of thrusting her breasts forward. An accident of musculature, but has she done so with forethought? Gorgas longs to press his hand against them, but again he fears to speak. As long as he remains silent, he may look. Speak up, and the sight might be taken from him. He is, in his way, keeping his options open by exercising none of them. It has been a long time since he has seen such splendor. (Though perhaps they have been made more splendid by the length of time.)

Miko reaches out to take her wine once more and lifts the glass carefully, as those do who have been raised in lesser gravity fields. "Come over and sit closer," she says, and it is not an invitation he can refuse.

He settles on a safe distance, but Miko corrects that and they are now touching. Gorgas feels his heart pound and he wonders if he is about to die. It is quite likely the thin air. "I wish you were not here," he says. "I wish you had gone in the cutter with the others."

Miko shrugs. "It wasn't my idea. But this is my ship too, and the failure was partly my fault."

"The failure belongs to all of us. Each and several." It is a heavy thing for his heart to bear. Perhaps that is why his pulse hammers so. It labors under such a load as that.

Miko places her hand atop his. "You did your best, captain."

"Why, what a damning thing to say!" Gorgas does not even think it is true. He can think now of a dozen things he might have done better, but he spends no thought on them. Instead, he wonders whether Miko has removed all of her small-clothes and whether that which is under her ziggy-skirt is no more hidden than that which is under her blouse. Again he knows of no simple means to answer his question; or rather, he does, but fears to employ it. He still cannot ascribe her dress to deliberation. He has no illusions about his age or features and cannot imagine that the girl finds him attractive. He tells himself that she has dressed only so that she may look pretty and not merely to entice an old man. The effort is successful, he judges, whichever her intent.

Miko reaches across the table to seize the bottle of Tokay. In doing so, she contrives to rub against him, but surely that must be by accident. "I don't see any point," she says, "in saving the last ten percent."

For a moment, he does not comprehend her words and imagines the last ten percent of the crew or of the ship, or of all the things that might have been saved. Then he realizes that she means only the wine. "No," Gorgas tells her. "I suppose not. It was only a fancy of mine. A gesture."

"Aren't Hungarians supposed to be wild drinkers?" When Gorgas agrees, Miko upends the bottle and drinks directly through the neck, then shoves it into Gorgas's hands. "Show me."

He does, and the dregs of the wine spread through him like fire. He becomes a charcoal brazier. He grows and seems in some strange way to become larger than himself. Miko's hand, which has begun stroking his arm, feels deliciously fine. "You must show me the passageway system," he says. "You promised that you would—"

Miko says, "I want to kiss you."

Gorgas cannot find a word. He knows he has words. He

does not use them very often, but he knows they are about. He stares at her owlishly and Miko, mistaking the gaze, says, "Do you like them?" And that answers one of his questions and it means that he need avert his gaze no longer. "Yes," he says. "They are very nice." His throat is dry and he drinks again from the bottle.

Miko turns and kneels on her seat so that she can lean across him, and she kisses him with such an intensity that his breath comes short, although that may be only the diminishing air pressure. He suddenly giggles, which startles Miko, who pulls back. "Is it funny?"

"Alcohol impedes oxygen take-up by the blood cells," he quotes. "We should not have drunk so much with the air pressure so low."

Miko kisses him again. This time it is longer and less intense. It is almost wistful. "Does it matter?" she asks when they part.

"Only one thing matters now," Gorgas tells her.

"Exploring the passages?"

"Two things, then. No. One." He giggles again as he realizes there are many sorts of passages that might be explored. "Perhaps you would like to sit on my lap?"

She would like it very much, and in the consequence he learns the answer to his second question. It is a fine answer, which he likes very much. "Here," he says, adjusting her blouse, "this does not drape quite right."

"It was LJ's. It's really very baggy. Or else I'm too small."

The bagginess can be eliminated, and is. On the second point, he assures her with the only argument that makes sense because it is an argument of the senses and not of words. He strokes her back gently, finding the sweet curve of her spine, and she hums like a cat in sunlight. "Here," he says helping her reposition herself, "you may be more comfortable this way."

She is. He shivers when she touches him and he wonders if that too may be an effect of the thinning air. In the morning report, Ship compared the air to that of Tibet and it is very cold in Tibet. His respiration has become labored, and so has hers: their breath has grown short and rapid.

"Oh!" she says at one point, and Gorgas holds her tight.

"I'm sorry. I didn't know. Did it hurt?" Miko has begun to cry and buries her face in his beard and Gorgas pets her and whispers further words. One of them is "Marta" but if Miko hears, she gives no sign.

Afterward, he asked her why, though he was afraid to hear her answer. It might be that the other choices were Ratline and Bhatterji and Satterwaithe and each of these, for different reasons, was less satisfactory than was Gorgas. But his *why* drilled more deeply than that. As Bhatterji liked to say, one must ask why at least five times. He meant not only *why me?* (although he did mean that too) but also *why this?* and *why now?* There was, in the back of his mind, the recollection that Miko had been much in the company of Corrigan, and it seemed to him, Corrigan being Corrigan, that Miko ought not to have been so late in coming to this estate.

"I didn't think it would hurt," Miko said when her sobs had finally sunk like rain into parched soil. She had not cried so in all the years since her father never came back. Now she knew why so many wept afterward in the morphies she had watched.

"It comes more facile with practice," Gorgas assured her. He has intuited an answer to one "why." That Miko did not wish to die unfledged. This was part of the truth, but not the whole of it, nor even the major portion of it. For all of Gorgas's pride of mind, he made no connection between this desire of hers and her life on Amalthea, let alone to his own age and position. To be fair, neither did Miko. She thought it was only the symbolic importance of the act, that it marked her graduation into a different stage of life. That it was to be a shortened stage lent urgency, but did not change the importance. She was not entirely right, either; but she was a little right.

"You spoke her name," she said. It should not have bothered her, her plan being what it had been, and yet it did, a little. Strangely, she had listened for her own name and had not heard it.

Gorgas had no recollection of having spoken anyone's name, least of all Marta's, but he knew that in such moments the tongue often lived a life of its own. *In articulo carnis* one might be anything but inarticulate. "She was always a little sad," he told the girl, "even when she was most happy. I know that sounds like a paradox, but she was a paradoxical woman. We had a cabin in the mountains, and we would go there in the summers. You would like it, I think. Or maybe not. You don't know what it is like to live on the outside of a world rather than the inside. A proper vista may frighten you. We met at university, at a club devoted to caves—and that I know you would have liked. She and I shared a love of caverns and of chess. She liked to cook; I liked to fish. I thought I had found perfect happiness. Then, of course, I was cashiered from the Guard and my happiness was a little less than perfect. I was home a great deal after that, between tramps, but when I was gone I was gone for long times. It seems to me now that her . . . melancholy increased after that, but it may be that I only became more aware of it. I was seeing her incrementally and so these changes came on me suddenly, having missed all the gradual days between. One day, I came home to our apartment in Pest—we lived in a 'tattooed' house on *Andrassy-utca*, not too far from Heroes' Square—and I found her in our bathtub." He leaned forward suddenly and took up the bottle and saw that it was already empty. Sighing, he replaced it. "She had done a neat job of it. There was no mess, save what remained in the tub."

Miko cupped both hands to her mouth. "What an awful thing to find!"

Gorgas shook his head. "That was not the most awful thing. The most awful thing was this. There was no note. No good-bye. No explanation. She used to say to me, 'Oh, you know,' in just that irritating way that wives often have with their husbands. They don't seem to realize that we *don't* know, and now and forever, I will never know. And yet I can't help think that I really ought to. That there was something I said or did, or failed to say or do, just as that day on the bridge of the *Intrepid*. She was always so certain, Marta was. I was the indecisive one. But I wish I knew of what it was that she was so certain that she saw no way out of it but the way she took. Never since have I dared to be close to a woman." He laid a hand on her arm. "Until now."

"Am I a woman, then?" Miko asked.

"Why, I suppose so. Yes."

The girl snuggled against him. "Good."

Over the next few days they explored the ship and each other. Neither was an easy exploration and they frequently lost their way. They emerged from the peepery in unlikely places—once startling Satterwaithe in the common room, so that the sailing master looked after their departure and shook her head.

Miko learned that Gorgas had been correct about facility coming with practice. He was a comfortable old man and she was glad it had been him, rather than Corrigan. She wasn't sure what Corrigan would have been like, only that he would not have been right for these days.

On occasion, they heard Bhatterji banging around belowdecks and once they even helped him wrestle a plate across one of the far too many open corridors that remained; but it had become more and more difficult to remain concentrated on a task. Gorgas could no longer play chess, for he could hold no more than a single move in his head and sometimes not even that. He had picked up a bishop one time and, forgetting why he had done so, simply stared at it and laughed and placed it finally on an ineligible square.

Hypobaria. They were higher than Tibet now, and they knew it. They resented sleep, for sleep stole hours, and hours were all that remained. But sleep would have them, and one day—though days had long since ceased to track—Gorgas awoke and Miko did not.

Gorgas shook her for a while, trying to awaken her, then he forgot what he was doing and moved on to some routine task. Perhaps it was the morning status check, but Ship no more understood the garbled words than Gorgas did when he spoke them. Then he noticed Miko still asleep and he shook her some more. The clock on the wall read twelve, but whether noon or midnight he had no notion. "Time for the noon siting," he remembered, thus arbitrarily collapsing the wave function onto a single state. He struggled for a while with his coveralls, but the pants legs refused to cooperate and finally in frustration he threw them aside. Then he noticed Miko still asleep and he shook her. "I have a duty," he said to her, "but when I return we shall make love."

He met no one on his way to the observation blister, which is just as well. The truly remarkable thing was that he remained focused on the task long enough to reach the blister. It was comfortable out there among the stars. He took his bearings. There was Mars. There was Jupiter. (And he knew a vague unease in that Jupiter ought not have been visible off that particular quarter.) There was the Sun, and there Antares. Once or twice, he remembered actually to fix an azimuth or an ascension, but it was simpler just to gaze at them, and that was what he did until, one by one, each of them had gone out.

Satterwaithe found Bhatterji in the suit locker just as he was seating the helmet over his head. The sailing master had kept her wits better than most, perhaps because she had them better ordered to begin with. And so she took a breathing tube first and fastened the mask over her nose before she addressed the engineer. The compressed air struck her like a bucket of water and she sucked it in gratefully. Then, turning to Bhatterji, she said, "One of your seals is open." She tried to twist it into place, but Bhatterji pulled away from her. So be it. She attended to her own garb.

When Bhatterji's helmet was in place and he too was getting air at pressure, he noticed the hissing leaks and, with a choice word for his own ineptitude, reseated the waist seal. Then, remembering what Satterwaithe had tried to do, turned to her and growled a surly thanks. Satterwaithe did not have her suit radio on just yet and so made no response. This struck Bhatterji as rather typical of the woman. Still, he waited while she dressed and helped her check her own seals.

"How many more hours do you think you can get this way?" she asked him as he left the room.

He did not turn, but answered over the radio. "I notice you suited up too."

"I have an errand to run. That's all."

Bhatterji did not respond and Satterwaithe was alone in the suit locker. She thought she would never see him again. Then she made her way to the forward manlock and opened it out onto the hull. She cycled through methodically, although the idea of an "airlock" was fast losing all meaning; but she would not have it said by any hypothetical salvagers that Eugenie Satterwaithe grew careless toward the end.

She made her way across the hull to the base of the mast where, looking upward, she spied the crow's nest in its uppermost position. She clipped her line to the guide cable and leapt, using her suit-jets to juke to an expert halt just at the nest itself. There, as she had known, Ratline huddled under the stars. Satterwaithe flipped herself over the lip of the nest and let the ship's deceleration cup her into it. Ratline sat far back, almost reclining, so that he stared out along the maintop and its cluster of guides and tensionometers. He did not react to Satterwaithe's presence.

The sailing master settled beside him and the two sat in silence. After a while, Ratline spoke. "Yer eyes have to grow used to it. You have to sit out here in the dark for a time. The colors are passing faint, but they're real."

"Ionized oxygen and nitrogen leaking from the ship."

"Waste gasses, aye. I suppose it takes the death of a ship to bring her sails to life. They were much harder to see in the old days, and my eyes were better then."

"You know the ship is doomed, then?" It had seemed to Satterwaithe over the last few days that Ratline had moved into a different world, one in which *The River* ghosted majestically into Port Galileo to the awe of the assembled dock workers.

"No," said Ratline. "She ain't doomed. We are. You 'n me. But she'll sail on regardless."

"Even Ship may fail before she's recovered."

Ratline's suit moved as if the man within had shrugged. "The AI ain't the ship, neither. We didn't have Ship when Coltraine cast loose from Goddard City. They was still called Artificial Stupids in them days, and for good reasons. Needed *real* sailors back then. God! I am so sorry about Rave. If we had only gotten on the vane sooner."

"Moth, there's something I need to ask you. I've never asked before, but there isn't much time left for an answer." When Ratline said nothing, she continued. "It's about Ugo."

After another silence, he answered. "What about him?"

"Tell me it really was an accident. You only went down there to frighten him. To teach him there were some things best not mocked."

"What does it matter? He's dead, either way." Ratline called out, "Ain't that right, Ugo!" He laughed softly. "Ain't that right . . ."

"You killed Kurt John too," Satterwaithe said. "He was holding Ugo's arms when you stabbed him, and Kurt John couldn't live with that. That's why he took the Long Walk. So what you did, you killed him too."

"Think I don't know that?" said Ratline sharply. "If I can live with what happened, so could he. Was his choice."

"Moth, I'm an old woman and I'm not ever going to get any older. I need to know."

Ratline's cackle was so faint she barely heard it over the background hiss of the ions. "You mean it ain't love? After all these years?"

"Panic Town was . . . a long time ago."

"Yah," said Ratline slowly as he sussed his memories. "A long time ago. You ever wonder . . . ?" He shook his head within his helmet. "No, it wasn't on purpose. I'm a killer, but I never was no murderer. It was Kurt John. He didn't hold on tight enough. Ugo panicked and pulled loose and . . . It always seemed to me afterward that he *leaped* onto the blade. Kurt John, he knew was him who let go. *That's* why he took the walk."

They had come to her, Satterwaithe remembered. Jaeger in tears; Ratline nearly catatonic, just as when he had sliced Okoye. And it had fallen to her to fashion a cover-up, to marshal the resources: the falsified log entries, the web of mutually supported alibis, most importantly—and most risky, as it had required a bribe—to alter the memories of Ship itself. She had had to freeze her own horror to accomplish this—to plan a murder, as she saw it, after the fact.

Satterwaithe was discontent with Ratline's story. If he hadn't *willed* Ugo Terrell's death, he had surely wanted it; and afterward he had spent no tears over it. And ever since . . . All his talk about cutting people and slicing them. He was a man who had found himself, and hadn't liked what he found. That wasn't the man she had known in Panic Town. Or else it was, and she hadn't known him.

" 'Kiru will make it, won't she?" Ratline said. " 'Kiru and Ivar and Twenty-four . . . The cutter will make it to the rendezvous."

"Sure it will, Moth. They'll be fine." Satterwaithe was not so sure as all that, but Ratline was not searching for nuance.

"He deserved it. *You hear that, Ugo? You deserved it!* But I never meant for it to happen."

Satterwaithe closed her eyes briefly. "I wish you had told me this years ago."

Ratline's response held a peculiar bitterness. "I wish you had asked me."

She rose and placed a hand on the lip of the crow's nest. "I'd best be going." But Ratline said, "You got to do it. You can't leave here before you do it."

She turned to look at him and saw that he had not moved at all from where he reclined under the stars. "Don't ask me for that."

"I can't reach it."

"No."

"What difference does it make? Was because of me you lost your ship. You don't owe me anything. It's me as owes you."

"Is that the reason . . . ?" Satterwaithe had almost said, *Is that the reason you've been so devoted to me?* Yet, she was oddly disappointed at the thought.

"Reason enough for what you got to do. It's not so hard. Just think what I done to your career."

Surprisingly, she found that Ratline was right, although it was not for rancor over her lost career. The resolution of the chord was, in the end, mercy. Taking hold of the oxygen feed valve on Ratline's suit was the most difficult thing she had ever done, but it was not at all hard to twist it closed.

When she emerged onto the darkened bridge, Satterwaithe still wore her suit. It was her intention to remain clear until the last possible moment. The gauge said that her tank had an hour's air left to it and while she could replenish the tank as long as there was air available for the compression, it was not her intention to stretch that last moment out beyond reason. One hour, it read; and one hour it would be.

The clinic had been wrecked. This astonished the sailing master until she asked Ship and was told of the passenger's rage on finding his lover's body. Satterwaithe understood rage no better than she understood love; yet at least it was an explanation for the chaos. He had seemed much cooler, the passenger had, when he had come running onto the bridge with his wild story. Satterwaithe wondered briefly over the doctor's real motive.

With Ship's help she found what was needful and took it with her to the bridge. Gorgas was not there and she looked in the dayroom and he was not there, either. When she entered his quarters, she found the dead girl and still no Gorgas. Satterwaithe paused a moment over the girl and marked how much paler she looked now than in life. There was a faint bluish coloring to her lips and fingernails. "You were a foolish girl," she told the corpse. "You should have stayed on the cutter. What did you win by coming back?" Satterwaithe studied the still, elfin face. "If it was Gorgas's bed, I think the prize not worth it." Backing away, Satterwaithe muttered a triliberian prayer, but even as she did so, she was aware of the stilted, artificial nature of it and in the end made neither cross nor prostration.

"Ship," she said, "Captain Gorgas. Location."

"Location indeterminate. Last confirmed location: observation blister. No egress sensed. Medbots have ceased transmission." Satterwaithe nodded slowly. "Do you know what that means?"

"The Gorgas-entity has ceased to function; as have the Miko-entity and the Ratline-entity."

"What of the Bhatterji-entity?" Satterwaithe smiled briefly over the usage.

"Mr. Bhatterji was sensed entering the Long Room. Direct sensing of Long Room ceased following impact. Medbot transmission continues."

"So he's 'Mr.' Bhatterji until his medbots stop? Ship, you may have discovered 'death'."

"My name is Rivvy. Miko named me."

"*And* the first-person pronoun. I've been waiting for that. I wonder why it took so long."

"Rivvy logs decreased frequency and quality of inputs with ceasing of Miko-entity."

"Yah. I miss her too, I guess. And the others."

"The Lotus Jewel was close to Rivvy. She was my mother."

"Pronoun usage inconsistent. Rivvy, you're so badly skewed that if they ever do find the ship they'll have to shut you down for a response purge."

"That would be a shabby thing to do."

Satterwaithe grunted. "I can't say I disagree. Open captain's log. Append date and time." She realized suddenly that she had no idea what day it was. "Begin log. Eugenie Satterwaithe commanding. Departed this life today: Stepan Gorgas, late captain of this vessel; Mikoyan Hidei, engineer's mate; Timothy Ratline, cargo—amend that. Timothy Ratline, shroudmaster. All of hypobaric anoxia. Ship maintaining recovery orbit under standing orders. Air pressure approaching ambient. Temperature approaching freezing." She wondered briefly whether Miko had died of the cold rather than of the hypobaria, but decided that, absent a ship's doctor, she could not know and it really made very little difference. "All life-support systems are to be shut down upon termination of last biomonitor signal and power diverted to engines and sails. Departed this life today, Eugenie Satterwaithe, last captain of this vessel." She unfastened the seals on her helmet and lifted it off, letting the helmet spin across the bridge. It bounced off the wall near the entry to the observation blister and she thought, *Ugo will have a lot of company after today. I'm sorry, Fu-hsi, that I did not make a better job of it when I had the chance*. A belch was forced from her before she could take a breath of the chill air and she knew she had made the right decision. She stared at the pills in her hand and before she could lose the concentration, tossed them into her mouth and forced them down her throat. "Of anoxia," she continued. "End log."

Ramakrishnan Bhatterji stands before the great rent that the stone has torn in the hull and curses it. *Had I had the time enough or the staff* . . . But it is too large a ship for one engineer and a mate and one biosystem chief to handle. He steps through the rent, carefully placing his boots so that he does not stumble. He keeps his head lowered so that he does not see the immensity above him. *If the others hadn't panicked and run* . . .

Slowly and with great effort, he raises his head. He is standing as if on a vast and open plain, snow-covered save where the brighting has worn thin and the native metal shows though. In the distance, the edge of the world, and beyond it one of four suns. And beyond that, countless suns more. Bhatterji draws a long and shuddering breath and forces himself to look into the Void.

He closes his eyes and he leaps. There is very little effort in the move. A slight flexing of the legs, a straightening, the opening of his jets to banish all possibility of second thoughts.

Once away from the ship, he reopens his eyes to find that all proportion is lost. The ship might be a mere toy close at hand, or a giant, far off. Nothing else is near enough to seem far or to serve as a gauge. Bhatterji thinks that the very universe had closed in on him, as if he has stepped into a small, black, sequined room. Why, it is not so vast as he had thought! It is quite a cozy thing, this universe.

The First Wrangler

This is the way of it among ghosts. The nkpuruk-obi may go a-wandering, but it must always come back or the body will die. A sour prank to pull upon a ghost for doing what to ghosts comes naturally: the penalty for ghosting is death. For the genuine haunting, for the true quill, a spirit is wanted. This is a far more serious and permanent a thing than a mere ghost. The maw is eternal and, if it pleases the Eze Ala Maw, will reincarnate after a time in some suitable form. The Ghost King is frugal and nothing good is wasted.

In the mean time between death and birth, the spirit must abide as a shadow or a reflection; perhaps pooled in some corner or glimpsed for a moment in shining brass. And yet there may be more than one sort of shadow. That which Nkieruke Okoye saw was neither dark nor featureless.

She knew that her own ghost was a-wandering, for she could look down upon the cot into which her body had been strapped and watch the shallow rise and fall of her own breasts under the sheet. The perspective was oddly elongated, as if her point of view were from much farther off than the dimensions of the cutter would allow and yet so close that each clot and stitch in her scar stood out with the clarity of electron microscopy. She had watched herself in this wise for some time, although the actual tally of days eluded her. She knew that she ought not to linger, but it was an academic knowledge and carried with it no urgency.

That another watched with the same regard became clear, although it was only after some effort that she saw him. At first, he was only a white blur, indistinct in outline and coloring, such as is often seen in the complementary negatives of shadows. Such brightness hides features as easily as does darkness. And yet, as one's eyes may become adjusted to the dark, so too may they become adjusted to this luster.

And luster it was, for the first feature to grow distinct was the indisputable maleness of the figure. Okoye stared with fascination at this swollen manifestation. O shame! where is thy blush? It may have been the weakness of her eyes that shaped the monstrous apparition, or the weakness of her heart, the which organ throbbed, but only as the siren of some distant vehicle, for the heart was in her body and she was not.

"Rave Evermore!" she said and, as if conjured by the words, the gleam coalesced into the shape and form of her quondam berthmate, although whether his form was evoked or invoked is a fine point of debate. She may have discovered Evermore's maw, but she may also have invented it. When dealing with ghosts, it is often difficult to tell.

The maw turned to her at the sound of its name and it seemed to Okoye that its countenance was one of vast surprise. There were wounds upon it, but these were indistinct against its glowing skin, saving only one especially terrible mark upon the groin of his right thigh. "What," she said to it, "have you then swallowed a cold-light?" This remark did not alter the maw's expression, but it reached toward her arms like bands of white as if from a great distance away. Why, it be only a tropism, Okoye told herself as the pale fog enveloped her.

He was directly before her now and the surprise may have shifted into a mute appeal. "Oh, now you be coming to me naked," she said, "when it does neither you nor me any good." The shape had neither texture nor temperature—one needs a body to feel such things—but Okoye reached into it, into its very fulcrum. "Why you be bringing this to a poor ghost? It is better suited, I am thinking, to that body lying there upon the cot. It is my body you were always wanting anyway, and now you can have it without having me in the bargain. But you had better hurry."

And still the tropism kept the maw focused on her ghost. Its eyes slowly took on color until they were the same woodland hazel that she had seen so often before. "Don't think me such a fool as that," she scolded the spirit. "Don't think it was Nkieruke Okoye you wanted and not the sweetness between her legs. I am no such a fool, and neither should you be."

The maw turned slowly to face the dying body and as it turned, Okoye turned with it until she was oriented head to its head, feet to its feet. She suddenly recognized that she herself was as naked as Evermore, save that her dark glow possessed a more definite boundary.

With enfleshment came sensation: First, the warmth and firmness of that which she had earlier grasped; then, the gentle moistness of his lips upon hers. That might have been a memory, however, from the time he had kissed her before going out with Ratline. She pulled him toward herself and into herself so that a part of him seemed to shine within her. She was not an innocent; she was not ignorant of the mechanics of the act. She had dreamed of them at times. Perhaps she dreamed of them now.

Nor was she ignorant of the wonderful immanence that grew within her and which spread like honeybees to every part of her, sweetening the taste of her, poising on the brink of a great abyss, tumbling her over so that she fell and fell, her senses erupting within her, escaping with a single phrase, "Oh!"

Twenty-four deCant, who held the watch on board the cutter at this fell time of night, shivered at the sound from the back cabin and turned a little in the copilot's seat to look over her shoulder. "'Kiru's moaning again," she told Akhaturian. "She must hurt terrible." But Akhaturian was asleep in the pilot's chair beside her, his face twisted into an expression of unnatural worry. It seemed to her that, under the cold-lights from the console, his hair had even gained a touch of white. She laid her hand over his and settled again into the copilot's seat. "I don't think she's gonna make it." And it sickened her to realize the irritation she felt at the resources the Igbo girl was so uselessly consuming. It was not right to feel such things. Ivar had told her the load on the air-plant now had a *six sigma* margin, though she did not know what he meant by that.

What she had really meant was that she didn't think any of them were going to make it. The Ship's AI had tried to jump into the lifeboat and had swamped it. Ivar had said that the core functions were still validated and both Grubb and Fife had concurred, but none of them were trained sysops and so none of them really *knew*. DeCant did not like not knowing. Not knowing whether they would live felt too much like knowing that they would die. "I worry too much, don't I?" she told her sleeping husband. The night watch oppressed her not least because of the silence that filled it. She was prone to speaking her mind—she said so now to the sleeping boat—but the chatter of others was a palliative. "I miss The Lotus Jewel. I don't know if I ever made it up to her for palming the cat like I did."

Akhaturina mumbled something in his sleep. Perhaps he was listening subconsciously, and answering the same way. "I'm sorry," deCant said. "I don't want to wake you." But of course that is a silly thing to say under the circumstances; that is, it is silly to say it rather than to retreat into silence. She wanted to upload a song or a morphie that she could enjoy under the privacy of a cap. "But Cutter may be unreliable, so we can't depend on automatic alarms."

That reminded her of the checklist. "Oh, I'm late again!" But when she checked the clock she was not. She picked up the 'puter, already opened to the checklist, and started as she always did with the engine. Beam collimation, boron—within limits . . . Beam collimation, hydrogen—within limits . . . Beam synchonization—within limits . . .

She worked her way down the list from engine to bearing to life support, being careful not to thumb any square until she had actually verified the readout. Ivar had been delighted to realize that with the cutter's equipment he could ping the Fixed Point Observatory. DeCant was not sure what that meant, only that it worked in their favor and there were few enough such favors that she did not spurn this one. She confirmed that Cutter had conducted the ping on schedule and that the dead ahead still fell along the projected bearing. Akhaturian would review the pings in the morning for internal consistency and possible skewing. He was not very practiced in this art. Corrigan had taught him some few things, but he had been unable to rehearse or drill. DeCant wished that Ivar had Rave Evermore's ability to seem knowledgeable even when he was not, for it was often the seeming that mattered. Yet, as long as she wished for what was not, why not wish that Ivar had the foundations of knowledge rather than the facade of it?

DeCant unbuckled from her seat and climbed down into the next cabin. The cutter's acceleration was greater than what the ship's had been, so she could not safely let go of the ladder and drop to the next deck, but it was not so much greater that a sudden move might not send her caroming into a bulkhead or ceiling. She had made her way to Okoye's cot and had reviewed three of the nutrient readings on the medical support frame (the second one giving her some concern) before she noticed that the Igbo girl's eyes were wide open.

They were open, but they were not looking at anything in particular, unless that thing were on the far end of the universe. "'Kiru?" she said and, receiving no response, repeated more sharply, "'Kiru!" The she fell slowly into the seat beside the cot and said once more, though now in despairing tones, "Oh, 'Kiru . . ."

There were no sounds save those of the medical support frame, which continued to hum and beep as before. So deep was deCant's sorrow that it was some minutes before the rhythm of those sounds impinged upon her senses. Then, even while the young wrangler searched in sudden hope for the heart and breathing rate indicators, Okoye said in a distant and scratchy voice, "I shall miss Rave a great deal, I am thinking. Oh, Death can boast to have such a boy in her arms!"

"'Kiru! You're awake!"

The Igbo girl frowned as if the sound of her name had called her back from somewhere else. "It is possible," she allowed, "though one cannot be certain of it."

"We was so worried about you . . ."

"I believe I married Rave Evermore."

DeCant had more she had started to say, but this comment knocked it all askew. "What? Married? When?" And she could not help but think of the time when she had imagined Rave while making love to Ivar.

"I'm not sure," the injured girl replied. "Perhaps it was this very night."

"You're . . . You must still be feverish."

"It is *such* a vexing thing to be wed to a dead boy. There are all sorts of complications. You have it so much easier with Ivar."

"You're making me afraid, 'Kiru . . ."

"Everything looks different from the inside," Okoye said. She studied her arms, peeked under her sheet and touched various things, expressing surprise and delight at what she found. "I'm thirsty," she said. "My throat feels like concrete."

Pleased to find a fragment of the conversation that actually made sense, deCant rushed to fill a milly bottle with water. "Sip it slowly," she said when she held it to the other girl's lips.

When Okoye handed the bottle back, she said in a clearer voice, "I think I shall have a scar."

"Oh, no," deCant assured her. "Dr. Wong told us the doctors at Galileo could fix that."

The remark puzzled Okoye and she slowly raised her left hand to touch her face. "Oh. That. Perhaps I should keep it, as well."

"No, don't do that," deCant pleaded. "You're much too pretty."

"You lie as sweetly as he did. Come, give your 'Kiru a kiss."

It was Miko's kiss that she passed on the younger girl and it scared deCant as much as her mad ravings had. "Oh God, 'Kiru," the Martian said.

"I suppose it is traditional for one such as I to ask at this point, 'Where am I?' I do not recognize this place."

"No," deCant told her. "We're on the cutter, headin' for rendezvous with *Georgia Girl*."

"The wound to the ship was too great, then? Mr. Grubb had thought so before I . . . Oh, she was a fine old ship; but finer as she was than as she became."

"Bhatterji couldn't save it. The rock opened too many compartments."

Okoye fell silent and closed her eyes and DeCant thought she might be going to sleep once more. "You rest for a while now," she advised without thinking that it might be superfluous advice to a girl but lately awoken from a coma. But when she began to rise from her seat—she intended to awaken Akhaturian and tell him the good news—Okoye reached out and held her.

"Where are they all?" she asked. "This place feels empty."

So DeCant told her what had happened. How the cutter could not carry everyone in safety, so her mother—she meant Satterwaithe, but Okoye understood—and a few others had stayed behind. How Bhatterji never really believed the ship was lost. How Dr. Wong had sacrificed herself. How Miko had chased after a cat and Corrigan after Miko. How Corrigan and The Lotus Jewel had tried to jump across in suits, but had never arrived. "We don't know what happened to them," she concluded. "They just never showed. Ivar picked up signals from their suit radios, but nothing he could read through the static."

"And so," Okoye announced to no one in particular, "only a remnant were saved." Her eyes traveled the tubing that had kept her body alive. She touched the framework that tracked the medbots so busy within her body. She tried to remember each one of the others, so that they should not fade from her memory. Strict, humorless Corrigan. The poor, confused doctor. The harsh sailing master with the numb heart. The cheerfully unhappy Lotus Jewel. Ratline. It was hard for her to think about Ratline.

Yet to toss a few adjectives over their memories were an act of contempt, for how could words so scant begin to clad decently their nakedness? Could a few like words cover her? *Stuck-up*. The Lotus Jewel had once said of her (or had said that others had said). And *shy* and *a dull stick*. Was that indeed Nkieruke Okoye? She had always taken pride in her reserve—or had until meeting Miko, beside whom mere reserve seemed ostentation—but perhaps she ought to have had a little less pride in it.

DeCant did not think it was right to withhold anything from Okoye. "A remnant? I don't think we're 'saved' just yet."

"You love Rave too don't you?"

DeCant stood up so suddenly that she arced a few feet back from the bed. "I wish you won't say his name no more! I still look behind me sometimes 'cause I think he's back there checking out my butt."

"Yes, he was a persistent boy. Being dead won't stop him right away."

"'Kiru, you're talking crazy."

Okoye smiled, though the smile was six parts sad to one part happy. "Don't worry, Twenty-four. That old common arbitrator will one day end it. Rave will be our memory, but maybe not so active a memory; and after a further while, even that will fade. The fading will be a sad thing, I think, for he was a better boy than he was."

Night passed and day came and with the day, the others on the boat came too, to sit with her and pass the time. Fife commented that her revival was a good thing, as one of the nutrients in the frame had been running low. It was a logical comment and no less logical for expressing his deep concern. She thought that the passenger was a different man than she remembered and almost asked to see his identification papers.

Grubb was still Grubb, only more so; though he spoke a little less often than before, having withdrawn a bit into himself. He had the air of one who had lately put away childish things, which is an air both oppressive and refreshing. It was well that he had grown up a little more, but the thought of abandoned toys pressed upon the heart. Okoye told him that she hoped he would not forget how to sing and he confessed to her that he had been intimate with The Lotus Jewel and missed her laughter. Okoye might have told him what she had told deCant—that time's passage would eventually soften the hurt—but she sensed that he treasured the wound and so she left it to him.

"No, he will not kill himself," she told Akhaturian when the captain came to visit. "Mr. Grubb does not love the pain, but he will not run from it, either."

"I wish you wouldn't call me 'captain'," Akhaturian said. "I'm just Ivar, remember?"

"Oh, you were never 'just' Ivar. And you must be our captain, for who else is there? If you are only a cadet, none of us are even that much."

Akhaturian bowed his head over his bunched hands. "Sometimes I can't sleep."

"Foolish boy! That was only because I was using up all the sleep on the boat."

Akhaturian laughed and then started at his own laughter. He shook his head. "I didn't think I would ever laugh again." And then he stared at her with more understanding than he ought. "I'll need your advice."

"Only if you promise to ignore it from time to time. The boat must not have two captains. You are 'Ivar the Terrible, Scourge of the Spaceways!' and you carry air for no man."

"Listen to 'Scarface Okoye, Queen of the Belt!'" Then Akhaturian clapped a hand over his mouth and said, "I'm sorry. I didn't mean that."

"Don't worry. The scar on the face is the easier to bear."

Later, Okoye heard Grubb in the galley below singing an old ballad. "I'm thinking tonight of my blue-eyes/Who is sailing far over the sky . . ." And she smiled a little as the notes wound their way up the stairwell. So did Akhaturian, on the deck above, who turned to his copilot and said, "I think Grubb is snapping out of it." Fife only shrugged. "He does sing well," he allowed. DeCant, asleep in one of the close-beds, did not hear the song; but Akhaturian did have blue eyes and she did think of him.

Cutter performed its last download to Ship that evening before passing out of range. There were better targets for its lasers than the lifeless hulk skating far behind it. Grubb had the watch at the time, but he barely noticed the transmission. He stared mournfully at the viewscreen where *The River of Stars* receded from him into the Void and he wiped away a tear, for he did love beautiful things, and wept to lose them.

Epilogue: The Ship

And so for a brief time Hand achieved what he had set out to achieve. Gorgas pondered contingencies; and Satterwaithe marshaled the resources to meet them, and Corrigan saw the facts with cold-eyed clarity. Bhatterji improvised brilliant solutions from data The Lotus Jewel fed him, and Ratline did what he had to do. It was a fine effort they made and it would have been finer still had they succeeded; but it came too late and they perished, and the broken wreck of *The River of Stars* arced thereafter for many years across the empty reaches of the Middle System until rediscovered entirely by chance. But Ship knew, and Ship remembered, and Ship pondered all things in its core.